The Church

The Church Missionary Intelligencer, a Monthly Journal of Missionary Information

Vol. 1

SALZWASSER VERLAG

The Church Missionary Intelligencer

The Church Missionary Intelligencer, a Monthly Journal of Missionary Information

Vol. 1

Reprint of the original, first published in 1865.

1st Edition 2022 | ISBN: 978-3-75258-988-7

Verlag (Publisher): Salzwasser Verlag GmbH, Zeilweg 44, 60439 Frankfurt, Deutschland
Vertretungsberechtigt (Authorized to represent): E. Roepke, Zeilweg 44, 60439 Frankfurt, Deutschland
Druck (Print): Books on Demand GmbH, In de Tarpen 42, 22848 Norderstedt, Deutschland

THE

CHURCH MISSIONARY INTELLIGENCER,

A MONTHLY JOURNAL

OF

MISSIONARY INFORMATION.

VOL. I. NEW SERIES.

A LITTLE ONE SHALL BECOME A THOUSAND, AND A SMALL ONE
A STRONG NATION: I THE LORD WILL HASTEN IT
IN HIS TIME.—*ISAIAH* LX. 22.

LONDON

1865.

CONTENTS.

Editorial Articles.

CONTENTS.

⁎ See also Obituary of the Rev. G. F. Bühler of Yoruba in the article "Deaths in the Mission field," under the head "Miscellaneous," and "Recent Intelligence," pp. 26, 27, 156, 191, 223, 350, 351.

CONTENTS.

Mediterranean.

CONSTANTINOPLE.

EXPLORATION EAST OF THE JORDAN BY THE REV. JOHN ZELLER.

JOURNAL OF A MISSIONARY TOUR UNDERTAKEN BY THE REV. R. H. WEAKLEY AND REV. J. F. WOLTERS, APRIL 1864.

MISSIONARY PROSPECTS IN TURKEY.

ITINERATION IN ASIA MINOR.

India and Ceylon.

BHOPAL AND ITS BEGUM.

CONTENTS.

CONTENTS.

ITINERATING IN AFFGHANISTAN.

KAFIRISTAN—ITS APPEAL FOR HELP, AND THE RESPONSE.

THE AFFGHAN MISSIONARIES IN KAFIRISTAN.

THE BISHOP OF CALCUTTA ON TINNEVELLY MISSIONS.

CONTENTS.

CONTENTS.

New-Zealand.

NEW-ZEALAND AFFAIRS.

NEW ZEALAND—CHANGE OF MINISTRY AND ADOPTION OF A NEW POLICY.

THE CATASTROPHE AT OPOTIKI.

EVENTS IN NEW ZEALAND EXPLAINED AND INTERPRETED.

JOHN WILLIAMS, OF PUTIKI, WANGANUI.

CONTENTS.

North-west America.

METLAHKATLAH, BRITISH COLUMBIA.

THE INDIANS OF BRITISH COLUMBIA.

MISSIONS IN THE MACKENZIE AND THE YOUCON DISTRICTS.

THE SIOUX, OR DAKOTAHS.

Miscellaneous.

THE RECENT ANNIVERSARY MEETING OF THE CHURCH MISSIONARY SOCIETY.

DEATHS IN THE MISSION FIELD.

Recent Intelligence.

AFRICA.

INDIA.

CONTENTS.

CEYLON.

CHINA.

NEW ZEALAND.

NORTH-WEST AMERICA.

Maps.

Church Missionary Intelligencer.

THE CLAIMS OF MISSIONARY INTELLIGENCE.

Ignorance prevents sympathy. We cannot feel much interested in objects of which we know but little. There may be in a crowded town, and not far distant from us, cases of extreme destitution; and thus one may need help, and another be capable of rendering that help; but if ignorance interpose, how shall sympathy be elicited? Our Missions abroad need much help from Christian friends at home, especially in one respect—"Ye also helping together by prayer." The husbandry is going forward; the labourers are at work; they go forth, often weeping, bearing precious seed; they are broad-casting it amongst the furrows of humanity, and, in doing so, they are bearing the burden and heat of the day; but the rain is needed. We know how earnestly, in eastern lands, the rain is waited for. Should this fail, the labours of the husbandman are vain, and, instead of fields of waving corn, there are clouds of dust. So, in spiritual labours, all is dependent on the blessing which comes from God. Paul may plant, Apollos water, God giveth the increase. Nor is there unwillingness on his part. That which we need, in promise is already ours—"He shall come down like rain upon the mown grass, as showers that water the earth." But the promise must be turned into prayer, and God be honoured by humble application, on our part, for its fulfilment: then will the blessing come, largely and abundantly,

It is in this respect that Christian friends at home can yield such important aid to the Lord's work in distant lands. While the Missionary toils and prays, they can pray with him, although they cannot toil with him; and their united prayer may bring down the blessing.

Why is there not more prayer at home? Because Missionary operations are so little known. Missionary information is essential to sympathy with the Missionary work. The one is as the oil; the other as the flame which it serves to feed. Every Mission has its own touching details, its own features of interest. But these particulars are known only to a limited circle. If we would have more sympathy the circle of interest in each case must be enlarged.

One means whereby a result so desirable may be obtained is to open out the history and working of these Missions, and afford to earnestly-minded Christians the opportunity of acquiring the necessary information. This has been our object in the old series of the "Church Missionary Intelligencer," and this we purpose to prosecute, if possible, with still more energy in the new series, which this Number commences.

We shall endeavour to present the information which is needed in an interesting form; but it must be remembered that the details are essentially spiritual in their character; that they are a record of patient continuance in well-doing; and that, devoid as they usually are of exciting events, they are as dissimilar as possible to the popular literature of the day. To the mind that is without spirituality they are unattractive. This, however, is not all. It is to be feared that, even by a large circle of seriously-minded people, they are disregarded. But surely to make themselves acquainted with the progress of his truth in distant lands is a duty which they owe to their Lord; the difficulties that have been overcome, and the victories which have been achieved, these ought not to be to them matters of indifference. Where is the patriotic Englishman, who, in the time of the Crimean war, was contented to be ignorant of its eventful features, and who, wrapping himself up in a selfish isolation, declined either to mourn over the sufferings to which the armies of his country were exposed, or to rejoice in the victories which opened the way to a satisfactory and lasting peace? And shall the distant battle-fields, where the Lord's truth is in conflict with the strongholds of Satan, command no interest from those who daily plead the sin-offering of Christ before the throne of grace, and who live upon the fulness of their great High-Priest and Saviour? Is this his mind? Do they learn this indifference from Him? Can He approve of it? or can they regard it as well pleasing in his sight?

And do they not lose much by excluding from their sympathy the records of Missionary effort? Might not Ministers at home learn much from the experiences of Missionaries abroad, and be better fitted habitually to endure, and perseveringly to overcome the difficulties of their home work, when they see how their brethren in heathen lands are holding on with constant minds, amidst the greater difficulties of the foreign work?

Let this indisposition, then, to Missionary literature, which unhappily has often deprived the labourers afar off in Africa and India of that measure of sympathy and prayerful help which they so much need, be overcome. Let attention be given to Missionary details. It may be, at first, an effort, but the reluctancy will soon pass away. Minute as such operations may sometimes seem to be, they are pervaded by the mysterious actings of God's power. Like all the divine procedures, they are, in progress, slow, in effects, permanent and lasting.

It would be indeed a cause for thankfulness if, with the commencement of a new series, the circle of our readers might be enlarged. The Missions would reap the benefit. There would be more sympathy, more prayer, and more blessing.

INCREASE OF THE SOCIETY'S WORK, AND THE NEED OF AN INCREASED INCOME.

THE Church Missionary Society, in a recent appeal to its friends and supporters, directed their attention to the increase of its expenditure above the income, and that to such an extent, that, at the close of the current year, it was apprehended the income would be less than the expenditure by no less a sum than 13,617*l.*

For some years past any inequalities which have arisen between income and expenditure have been met by the Special India Fund; but this source of supply being now nearly exhausted, it becomes necessary to consider how, on its cessation, the income and expenditure of the Society shall be equalized. Shall the expenditure be reduced to the level of the income, or the income be raised to the necessities of the expenditure?

The expenditure can be lessened only by a retrograde movement in the Mission field, and an abandonment of the advanced positions which, in the prosecution of its great warfare, the Society has been successful in securing. A reduced grant to a Mission necessarily involves a contraction of the work. If, when a Corresponding Committee at Calcutta, or elsewhere, forwards to us a carefully prepared estimate, and we give them less than they have stated to be absolutely requisite for the healthful progress of the Mission, we compel them to adopt a diminished scale of expenditure and effort. In order that this may be effected, the extremes of the Mission—its latest shoots—are usually the parts of the Mission which are arrested; and as, unhappily, these are the very points in which resides the power of growth, the vital energy is thereby injured, and the whole Mission discouraged and enfeebled.

To contract, therefore, the circle of the Mission work, in order thereby to diminish the expenditure, would be indeed a disastrous alternative, which cannot for an instant be contemplated.

But how shall the income be increased? This is an important question, and requires careful consideration. Happily for this time has been given. Two legacies of large amount, unexpectedly falling in, have relieved the Society from the apprehension of any immediate deficiency, and afford opportunity for the introduction of such measures as, without any thing of forced effort, may conduce to a healthful and satisfactory enlargement of the Society's ordinary income.

This, however, cannot be accomplished unless our friends throughout the country are fully convinced that such an increase is now imperatively required, and that the necessity has arisen from no other cause than the enlargement of the Society's work.

To prove concisely, yet satisfactorily, that there has been such an enlargement, and that on a very extended scale, is the object of the present article; and that this may be effected the more readily, we shall fall back on a point in the past history of the Society, with which we shall compare our present attainments. The comparison will at once show how greatly the circle of the Society's operations has been extended.

We select for this purpose the year 1853-54, and, comparing with this the last completed year of the Society's history, 1863-64, shall point out the measure of progress which has been made during the intervening decade of years.

During the decade the stations of the Society have increased from 118 to 144; the European Missionaries from 152 to 198, the ordained natives from 21 to 61, the increase in the total of ordained labourers being from 176 to 267; the native teachers, of all classes, have increased from 1661 to 2029, the increase in the total number of labourers being from 1902 to 2336. On the whole, having regard to each item separately, and their sum total, the increase during the decade has been one-third.

To meet, then, the exigencies of this increased agency, the income ought to have expanded by one-third. But this is far from being the case, the income of 1853-54 having been 113,298*l*. If, during the decade, there had been, year by year, such an increase as that, in the tenth year, the income had been raised one-third above the income of the first year, it would have reached the sum of 151,064*l*., instead of which it rose only as high as 132,501*l*.

It is evident, therefore, even on this cursory view of the subject, that if the Missions are to be maintained in their present strength, much more if they are to continue to make healthful progress, there must be an increase of income, and that assuredly by no less a sum than 13,617*l*.

But let us examine more closely the Reports of the two years which have been selected as points of comparison. There are several of the Missions which are common to both; there are other and important Missions occupying a prominent place in the Report of 1863—64, of which in the earlier document there is no mention. We shall first enumerate the Missions which are common to both. We trust our friends will not be scared by the array of names and figures. They are our adopted Missions, and they have a claim upon us. We have done something for each of them, and these efforts are not forgotten by Him whose work this is; but there is much more to be accomplished on their behalf. Shall we regard this as a necessity which we reluctantly discharge, or a privilege to which we gladly address ourselves? Let the remembrance that it is the Lord's work decide that question. The following table will place before us the names of the Missions, and the expenditure on behalf of each during the years to which we have referred—

Missions.	Expenditure of 1853-54.	Expenditure of 1863-64.
West Africa	£9496	£7113
Yoruba	4131	5554
East Africa	941	297
Palestine	1691	2321
Smyrna	565	822
Syra	627	380

Missions.	Expenditure of 1853-54.	Expenditure of 1863-64.
Bombay and Western India	5307	8880
Calcutta and North-India	19,963	26,705
Madras and South-India	20,635	29,941
Ceylon	6226	9179
China	5163	5556
New Zealand	10,200	7347
North-west America	4002	8776

In nine of these Missions there has been an increase in the annual expenditure to the amount of 30,051*l.* In four of them—Sierra Leone, East Africa, Syra, New Zealand—there has been a decrease. The causes of this are obvious: the native church in Sierra Leone has become self-supporting; the New-Zealand Christians, before the existing war broke out, were able to do much in the same direction; the East-Africa Mission, in consequence of the unsettled state of that country, had been reduced to a single Missionary; the Syra Mission, being exclusively educational, the Society confines its help to the salary of the Missionary. The decrease on these four Missions amounts to 6127*l.* To this latter sum there is, moreover, to be added the cost of certain Missions, such as Cairo and the West Indies, which have been given up, and no longer appear on the Society's lists. These deductions being made, the actual increase of the annual expenditure on those Missions which are common to the first and last years of the decade is found to be 22,646*l.*

In the foregoing table it is at once perceptible that the great expenditure has been in connexion with the Indian Missions. In the other Missions the increase is such as might be expected to arise from the natural growth of a healthful work. But in the Indian Missions alone the increase in the annual expenditure amounts to not less than 19,621*l.*, and in this we perceive the evidences of an extraordinary effort; an effort to which the Society had pledged itself when, in their statement on the Indian crisis, the Committee declared their solemn conviction, that "by the late dispensations God had called the Christian church to new and greatly-enlarged efforts for the conversion of India." On this ground, therefore—the promised extension of the Indian Missions—they pleaded for a "Special Indian Fund," a fund which was placed at their disposal to the amount of 73,470*l.*; and that fund has been employed in redeeming the pledge of the Society, and increasing its Indian Missions to such an extent, that the cost of those Missions in a single year—1863-64—exceeded that of ten years previously by no less a sum than between nineteen and twenty thousand pounds.

Let us look into this great field of Indian Missions if so be we can discover where the enlargement has taken place. When, in one or another of the great irrigation works which are being carried forward in India, it is found, at the end of the year, that there has been a much larger outlay than usual, the engineer at the head of the department is expected to be enabled to show that the works under his superintendence have made corresponding progress. Ours is an irrigation work upon the largest scale. We are opening channels by which the waters of life may flow forth into the moral wildernesses and reclaim them. Are we following the example of the engineer when he covers the Ravee Doab with a net-work of canals, and provides for the wide distribution of those natural waters which, it is hoped, shall persuade the barren soil to fertility, and induce it to yield its harvests?

It would appear, from recent discoveries, that the conducting forth of waters for irrigation purposes is not an unmixed good; that in some tracts they develope *reh*, or the sulphate of soda, which had been lying latent in the soil; nay, not only so, but that the waters of the Jumna and the Ravee contain the principal constituents of *reh*, and bring it down with them. The effects on the productive powers of the soil are most disastrous; the crops fail, and the ryots are reduced to extreme poverty. Not only do the tainted waters cause the land to deteriorate, so as to assume the appearance of a dry swamp, but they injuriously affect human life, and arrest the increase of population. But the waters of life which issue from the sanctuary are healing: they heal wherever they flow, and give life to every thing they touch. They do not quicken into action the latent evils of the human heart; they correct those evils, and renew man's corrupt nature, so that, in this change of nature, there is foundation laid for the healthful employment of his energies. Are we, then, diligent in opening up channels by which these salubrious streams, penetrating deeper and further into the wilderness, may produce those changes which the prophet, in beautiful figurative language, predicts—"The wilderness and solitary place shall be glad, and the desert rejoice, and blossom as the rose." Let us consider.

And, first, North India. The Kishnagurh districts are supplying us with effective native catechists, and these are being planted out so as to occupy new ground: thus Pubna, Chooadanga, and Kishengunge have become branch-stations. Further to the north-west the circle of our work has been enlarged so as to include the Santhals. At Benares, a Training Institution, having special reference to the great want of our North-India Missions, a well-qualified agency, has been opened. Allahabad has been occupied. We have entered Oude, and placed our Missionaries at Lucknow and Fyzabad. Agra and Meerut, instead of being isolated stations, have become centres of operations, with their out-stations lying around them. Thus, with Agra as a centre, we have Muttra, Hatras, and Allygurh as out-stations; while in connexion with Meerut we find the Dehra-Dhoon, Kunker-Khera, Mulliana, Bulundshuhur, and Bareilly. In the Punjab the Indus has been passed; the banner of the cross has been unfurled in Peshawur; the Missionary's voice has been heard during the summer in the lovely vale of Cashmere; the Derajât has been entered; and Missionaries placed at Mooltan. Thus the stations in North India have been increased from twenty-three to thirty-one; the European Missionaries from thirty-six to fifty-five, while the native pastorate, which had no existence in 1853-54, is now represented by five ordained natives.

Moreover, the new fields of Oude and of the Punjab are of exceeding promise. Oude is like a field recently ploughed and waiting for the seed. The Missionaries, as they go forth to sow it, are welcomed, and heard, not only with patience, but with interest. The people say that "God has put his hand upon the head of the English nation, and, for this reason, there must be something good and great in the Christian religion, and the time was probably not far distant when they would embrace it too."

In the Punjab our Missionaries itinerate through the Manjha, where the Sikhs predominate, and are heartily welcomed by the people. Marvellous, indeed, is the freedom to preach the word which the Missionaries enjoy in this recently-annexed province. They go forth, no man hindering them.

Turning next to South India, we find in the Telugu Mission a marked increase. In the Masulipatam collectorate two young converts, the first-fruits of Mr. Noble's Anglo-vernacular school, have been admitted to holy orders by the Bishop of Madras; Bezwara and Ellore, as well as Masulipatam, have been occupied; while northward, on the Godavery, a new Mission, having special reference to the Koi people, has been commenced at Dumagudiem. The Madras Mission, divided into the northern and southern districts, together with an incipient Hindustance Mission at Triplicane, has received a new impulse, and is full of hope and energy. The Tinnevelly districts have increased from thirteen to fifteen; the European Missionaries in these districts from thirteen to fourteen; the ordained natives from seven to twelve, besides two who are ably helping in the Madras work. The native converts, in Tinnevelly alone, are more numerous than the aggregate of converts in the four Mission fields of Madras, Tinnevelly, Travancore, and the Telugu country ten years ago, being as 33,400 to 32,544. The Tinnevelly communicants have increased during the decade from 3357 to 4895, and exceed by ninety-five the aggregate of communicants in the four Mission fields of South India at the beginning of the decade. To God be all the praise! He giveth the increase. While, in addition to all this, the North-Tinnevelly itinerancy, with its three European Missionaries, is drawing out into energetic action the Missionary spirit of the settled churches to the south, and the evangelization of their heathen countrymen is becoming more and more to them an object of deep interest.

Nor is Travancore behind in progress. There, also, a blessing has been given. The Cambridge Nicholson Institution has been brought into action. The districts have increased from six to ten; the European Missionaries from eight to nine; the ordained natives from two to nine; the native converts from 4897 to 8000, and the native communicants from 1216 to 2102. The leaven of the Gospel is beginning to be felt in the extremes of society. Proud Brahmins have felt and submitted themselves to its power, and its penetrative mercy reaching down to the extreme degradation of the slave, has commenced amongst those poor outcasts a work of the most beneficent and hopeful character.

The Bombay Mission, also, as though its winter was past and the spring season come, has thrown out new and healthful shoots; a movement of great promise has commenced within the territories of the Nizam, where hitherto unbroken darkness has reigned, and the important department of itinerancy is being prosecuted by the Missionaries with much zealous perseverance.

So much, then, for India. Throughout that great dependency there is, in connexion with Christianity and its propagation, a life, an interest, and willingness to hear, and a disposition to inquire, which was unknown in 1854, and which did not show itself until the great crisis of 1857-58 had been decided. That crisis was like the monsoon when the swollen rivers overflow their channels, and large tracts are entirely submerged. But these floodings prepare the land for the seed. The waters, as they retire, leave behind a deposit of soft sandy mud, which is termed a *char*. Over the surface of this the seed is strewed, and the bread is cast upon the waters, in the hope that, after certain days, it shall be found in the form of a welcome harvest. It is now the sowing time in India. Let the sower go forth. "Blessed are they that sow beside all waters."

There are others of the Missions referred to in the statistical table, in connexion with which there has been a considerable increase of expenditure, and in each of these there will be found, on examination, a corresponding enlargement of the work. In Ceylon, instead of six stations, there are now eleven; and this Mission field, hitherto very slow in responding to the labour bestowed upon it, like that of Bombay, is beginning to be moved, and to cheer us with the hope that, at no distant period, the promised harvest shall come. Our stations in China have been increased by the occupation of Hong Kong and Peking; and, finally, our North-West-America Mission has extended itself northward to the Mackenzie-River district, and, crossing the Rocky Mountains, has gathered together at Metlakahtlah a Christian church from amongst the wild Indians of the Pacific coast.

So much, then, for those Missions which are common to the first and last years of the decade under review. They have very remarkably expanded, and the increase in the actual work done is more than commensurate with the increase of expenditure.

But there are other Missions which, in the Report of 1853-54, are unknown. They had no place there, for they were then unborn. But they are inscribed on the register of 1863-64, and have helped to increase the yearly expenditure of the Society. They are as follows—the Niger Mission, the Mission to Turkey, the Mauritius Mission, and the

Madagascar Mission. Each of these are Missions of primary importance. It is more especially in reference to the Niger Mission that Bishop Crowther has been raised to the Episcopate, and has been sent forth to expedite the Missionary action of the West-African churches. At Constantinople our Missionaries are contending for a great principle, and striving to prevent the closing of that door of opportunity, which, on the termination of the Crimean war, was thrown open to the Mussulmans of Turkey. At Mauritius we find that remarkable confluence of nations which constitutes it a great Missionary centre for the shores of the Indian Ocean; while to Madagascar we were summoned by reasons, the force of which approved itself to all the friends of the Society. We should not like to part with any of these new undertakings; and yet the aggregate of expenditure connected with them amounted last year to 5873*l.* Let this sum be added to the one previously indicated, 22,646, and the result is a grand total of 28,519*l.*, being the excess of the expenditure in 1863-64 above that of 1853-54.

Let it be remembered, that during the same period the income, with many fluctuations, like the ebb and flow of the tide, has increased only by 19,203*l.*—19,000*l.* of income to meet 28,500*l.* of expenditure! How can this be?

The Special India Fund has hitherto served to supply the excess of expenditure over the annual income. Thus the expenditure of 1863-64 amounted to 145,794*l.*; while the total ordinary income was only 132,501*l.*; leaving an excess of expenditure over income to the amount of 13,292*l.*, of which 12,016*l.*, as Indian expenditure, was charged to the Special India Fund.

This fund, diminished at that time to a balance of 10,750*l.*, will be exhausted with the current year. A grave crisis appeared, therefore, to await us, and that immediately—a financial year commencing with an income confessedly unequal to the expenditure; and had no unexpected help supervened, the Parent Committee would have been compelled to the painful duty of cutting down all the estimates, and contracting the sphere of the great Missionary work. For the present, however, this necessity has been averted by the seasonable advent of two legacies.

Now, then, there is opportunity afforded for the adoption of such well-considered measures as, by the blessing of God, may raise the income of the Society to a level with its expenditure, and secure that increase of 13,617*l.* which will enable the Parent Committee to meet the unovoidable increase of its expenditure.

THE TELUGU MISSION.

An able and interesting report enables us to open out the history and operations of a Mission which now, for more than twenty years, has been carried on with a holy perseverance, and which is now assuming the aspect of a field which the Lord is blessing and will continue to bless.

The field of labour.

The collectorate of Masulipatam is now known by the name of the "Krishna district." In 1841, when the present Mission of the Church Missionary Society was established, the Masulipatam district was bounded on the south by the river Krishna, on the north by Rajahmundry, on the west by the Nizam's territories, and on the east by the sea. It then contained a population of 500,000 souls, and 1600 villages, with an area of 4510 square miles. The district, under its new name, has the Nellore district for its southern limits; on the north it is bounded partly by the river Godavery, and partly by the Nizam's territories; westward it joins the Nellore and Kurnool districts, and the Nizam's territories; and on the east it is bounded by the Godavery district and the sea. It now covers an area of 8353 square miles, with a population of 1,194,421 souls, scattered over more than 2134 villages, besides three large and important towns, Masulipatam, Bezwara and Guntoor. The extent of the present district, therefore, is nearly double what it was twenty years ago.

The attention of the Church Missionary Society was first directed to the Telugu people and language by John Goldingham, Esq., then Collector of Guntoor, and now a member of the Parent Committee. A language spoken "all along the eastern coast of the peninsula, from the neighbourhood of Pulicat, where it supersedes the Tamil, to Chicacole, where it yields to the Uriya, and inland as far as the eastern boundary of the Mahratha country and the Mysore, including within its range the ceded districts and Kurnool, the greater part of the territories of the Nizam, with a portion of the Nagpore country and Gondwana," and embracing not less than 14,000,000 of people, might indeed, with justice, claim prompt and special consideration.

Yet such, at the time, were the straitened circumstances of the Society, both as to men and means, so inadequate the actual Missionary force when compared with the requirements of the Missions, and so great the difficulty of obtaining reinforcements, that at first, and with reluctance, the inviting opportunity was declined. Often has the Society been placed in such a position: the favourable opportunity, and the hearty desire to improve it,—neither of these have been wanting; but a deficiency of means has fettered its movements, and anxious, yet unable to advance, its directors have been constrained to put forth the prayer of Jabez—"Oh that thou wouldest bless me indeed, and enlarge my coast, and that thine hand might be with me!" Often, too, has that prayer been answered, and the Society been dealt with providentially, as the Apostles were dealt with miraculously, when the angel of the Lord by night opened the prison doors, and brought them forth, and said, "Go, stand and speak in the temple to the people all the words of this life."

So it happened at this time, when the commencement of a Telugu Mission was under consideration. The deficiency in funds was helped, and two gentlemen—one a clergyman and the other a candidate for holy orders—offered themselves especially for the Telugu Mission—names for ever inseparably interwoven with the history of Telugu Christianity—the Rev. Robert T. Noble, of Sidney-Sussex College, Cambridge, still spared, and still energetically labouring, and Henry Watson Fox, of Wadham College, Oxford, to whose memoir, published by the Seeleys some fourteen years back, we refer our readers, as a book which will amply repay the purchase and perusal. Very touching were the few words penned to his parents and sisters on embarking at Gravesend for India—"We do pray for you all, that the Comforter may be with you, and, supplying you with stronger faith, enable you to look, even through your tears, to the Lord, as a loving parent, who afflicts us according to his good purpose. . . . . May the blank which has been created in the daily habits of each be supplied by a more intimate communion with Jesus Christ! For ourselves, we feel we are in a very solemn and responsible situation. . . . . My chief source of anxiety is, lest we fall, by weakness of faith, by neglect of prayer, or yielding to indolence, or some other snare which Satan will lay before us to keep us from God. So long as we continue under the shelter of his wings we are safe: our temptation is to leave that."

On the arrival of our brethren at Masulipatam, the adult population claimed their first attention. How could it be otherwise, when they beheld dense masses of people wholly given to an idolatry so disgusting and demoralizing as that by which India has been defiled. In Fox's Letters, as published in his Memoirs, will be found depicted many a scene of this character, so that his heart was stirred within him. "One of our Missionaries," observes the report, "well remembers the occasion when, for the first time, the voice of the Christian Missionary was raised against idolatry in one of its most debasing forms—when a dead woman was worshipped, and ceremonies of the most revolting character performed in the presence of an admiring crowd of men and women, with immortal souls, hurrying on to an eternity of woe. Many were the villages visited by our Missionaries in those days; but it pleased the great Head of the church to suspend our dear brother Fox's usefulness, and eventually to take him to Himself. His place has never been supplied."

The necessity of schools, through which a wholesome influence might be exercised upon the rising generation, soon became apparent. The first school, Anglo-vernacular in its constitution, commenced with two Sudra boys; but the numbers rapidly increased; so that, in two and a half years, forty youths, "most pleasingly clean and neat in their dress and general appearance," presented themselves at the half-yearly examination, and were found to have made satisfactory progress in "sound, useful, and saving knowledge —sound, as based on and saturated with the word of God; useful, as calculated to qualify the native youth to discharge honourably and satisfactorily to their employers the duties of those stations which they may hereafter, in the providence of God, be called to fill; and saving, as made all to point to a crucified Saviour, who can alone deliver any man from the just wrath of God, or the dominion of his own corruptions and lusts;" and such have continued to be, ever since, the principles and characteristics of the school.

It has had to pass through its seasons of trial, as is invariably the case with these institutions in India; its time of greatest success, when the education imparted has availed to the conversion of a pupil, constituting its time of greatest danger. One of these critical periods is adverted to in Mr. Fox's Memoirs.* There our readers will find an interesting account of the conversion of a Sudra youth, Sitapâti, brought to inquiry and conviction through another young native, previously baptized, and who had found a home in Mr. Noble's schoolhouse. A momentary panic was the result. Nearly half the boys in the English school were withdrawn, the eventual loss being fifteen of the most advanced and promising; yet, notwithstanding this avowal of its character as a Missionary school, which would uncompromisingly work to persuade the students to Christianity, the vacancies were soon filled up.

It may now be interesting, by a reference to present statistics, to show how it has progressed—

At the end of 1863, there were on the rolls of the school 294 pupils, divided into thirteen classes. It has pleased God to touch the hearts of several young men in the school. As many as twelve have been received into the church of Christ by baptism. Two are preparing for holy orders.

The number of pupils has increased during the year by more than one-fourth, the average attendance being a little more than eighty per cent. of the number on the books. The total of 294 is sub-divided into the following castes—

Christians	9
Brahmins	102
Komaties	20
Sudras	113
Vaisya	2
Mohammednns	48
	294

Of this school the Missionaries in their report speak very modestly—

In drawing up a report of the state and progress of this school, there is little that can be said beyond the communication of the statistics annexed in a tabular form. And indeed it would be invidious for those who take an active part in the institution, to say more about its state as a Missionary agency, than that they trust the blessing of God continues to rest upon it, and that He is accomplishing more by its means for his own glory, than is apparent to the eye of sense. Faith can see farther, and were it not for this we should be often cast down and disheartened, if not induced to give up the work. But the thought that it is his, not our work, draws us forward, and gives us nerve to battle on. Besides, it is the faithful praying ones at home, as much, if not more than the feeble agents abroad, who really sustain the work, and are interested in it; and for their sakes,

* See "Fox's Memoirs," p. 256.

and feeling, also, that we are not merely a few skirmishers, but the front rank, so to speak, of a mighty phalanx, we desire, in the strength of their prayers, to go on humbly but firmly. This happy union renders it, however, necessary that the rest of the army should, to some extent, be kept apprised of the operations carried on at the front, and therefore, though with much diffidence, we venture to describe briefly our position.

A tree, however, is known by its fruits; and this institution is even now yielding forth fruits of such value as to render us hopeful and expectant as to its future. January 31 of last year was a memorable day in the Masulipatam Mission. On that day the Bishop of Madras admitted to holy orders two Telugu natives, Ratnam and Bushanam, Mr. Noble's two first converts. Notices of this encouraging events have been given in the "Recent Intelligence" for May last, and in the "Church Missionary Record" for October.

Since then there has been a further movement amongst the pupils in favour of Christianity. The particulars are contained in the following extracts from letters of Mr. Noble's, dated September 10th—

This morning it has pleased the Lord whom we serve to enable Oragom Sivaramakrishtamma, of our third class, openly, before all the school, to avow himself a Christian. After morning prayer, he arose and professed his faith in Christ, and then, by himself, went out to my house. The scenes of sorrow that accompany an open profession are truly most melting to all who are concerned in them. He is in his nineteenth year, though his poor father and mother, and father-in-law, are all ready to swear he is under sixteen. He has been a most exemplary student, and though we have many most excellent, he has been one of the most earnest, steady, successful Brahmins in the school.

Sept. 16—I wrote a few lines to say that it had pleased the Lord Jesus, of his infinite grace, to bring out from our third class a fine young Brahmin, nineteen years old, tomake an open avowal of faith in Christ. He was summoned before the collector and magistrate, and, after openly avowing his purpose, then, as he was leaving the office, and stepping into my bandy, he was seized by his family and friends; but the magistrate, hurrying from his seat, ran in among them, and succeeded most kindly and energetically in extricating him. Since then the police have been protecting him, as we received secret notice that they intended to carry him off. I feel we cannot be too thankful to the magistrate and police for their energetic and prompt measures to prevent further violence. The following day another young Brahmin, in his twentieth year, who has read with us two years, and who had long been very favourably disposed, came forward to embrace Christianity. There is great excitement in the town, and many of our dear boys have been withdrawn. Of these not a few will never come back.

Besides the Anglo-vernacular school, a boys' vernacular school was established in 1849, and we find in the report the following account of it—

Our vernacular school for boys was established in 1849. It was then partly a day and partly a boarding institution. In connexion with it there was an industrial branch, in which different trades were taught. This school ceased to exist in January 1863. During the fourteen years of this school's existence, God has graciously prepared fourteen of our pupils for Mission work, namely, two assistant catechists, and twelve schoolmasters, all of whom, with one exception, are usefully employed in various localities.

We desire to take this opportunity of explaining that we are indebted to the exertions of the late Miss Barber, of Brighton, and to her Coral Fund; for it was principally by means of her aid that we were enabled to establish and keep up our boarding school for so many years. Her encouraging letters, and still more encouraging pecuniary help, deserve, we think, some public recognition from the Church Missionary Society. The vernacular branch of the Telugu Mission was deeply indebted to Miss Barber, and many native agents have been trained through her instrumentality. An exception was a young man sent out by our boarding establishment, who died in Sept. 1863 of dropsy. He was associated with the Rev. T. Y. Darling, who refers to him in his report in these words—"Our godly schoolmaster, at Ragapuram, was removed from us by death in September last, leaving a testimony behind him that he feared God. I praise God for having given him to this work for a time." The poor man was dangerously ill, and had to be carried into Bunder from Ragapuram. He lingered about a week, and, after much suffering, died in peace. Some notices of him appear in the "Church Missionary Record" for 1863.* Mr. Sharkey writes—"Vinayakulu lived but a week after his arrival here. He died of water in the chest. Not a doubt crossed his mind, and he died strong in faith, rejoicing in hope. 'Jesus and his righteousness'—this was his answer, when I asked him to tell me the foundation of all his hopes. 'Rags, rags, torn, dirty rags,' was how he described his own righteousness. His father said, 'God has shut you up in a wilderness (rather, jungle).' 'Yes,' was the ready reply; 'but He has made a highway for me in it.'" Vinayakulu was educated in our boys' boarding-school, and was appointed to Ragapuram. He leaves a young widow and babe. Mr. Darling, in a note to Mr. Sharkey, writes—"I received with great grief the sad intelligence of poor Vinayakulu's death. It is a blessed thing for him to have finished his course so peacefully; but there are many to mourn his loss, and miss his humble usefulness. Associated as I have been with him in the work at Ragapuram, it is not surprising that I feel very greatly his removal, and our poor people are quite brokenhearted. But we know who has done it, and that it is a gracious God who is dealing with us. He does all things well, and his holy will be done. I pray and wait now for some one to be raised up in the place of the good man who has joined the church triumphant."

Instead of the boarding-school, a superior vernacular school has been established by the Church Missionary Society. The number of pupils that attended it at the close of 1863 was ninety-nine, including all our former boarders, of whom twenty-four are Christians, five caste boys, and the rest Pariahs.

In connexion with this school, we desire to record, with feelings of deep gratitude, the cordial interest taken in it by a Christian gentleman, Captain Faulkner, of the 42nd Madras Native Infantry. In December 1863, this gentleman was requested to attend a private examination of the school. On his return home, he wrote a kind note to Mr. Sharkey, offering of his own accord to do all in his power to enlist the sympathies of some of the residents in behalf of the poor children who attend the school. His offer was, of course, at once accepted, and he immediately circulated an appeal, which met with a liberal and altogether unexpected response. Nearly 500 rupees were collected, besides a monthly subscription of more than forty rupees. The object of this fund is to clothe the poorer lads, some of whom have not even a rag to cover their bodies; to clothe and feed a number of orphan children, rendered homeless by the closing of our boarding establishment; to enable most of the pupils to pay their tuition fee, and for their books; and to liquidate a large debt which the boarding school, when closed, had to meet. The greater part of this debt was paid by the proceeds of the sale of the roof of the cottage in which the industrial school had for so many years been conducted. But there were still Rs.259.12.11 unpaid, which Captain Faulkner's noble, disinterested Christian efforts enabled us at once to discharge. God has graciously delivered us from many fears, and signally helped us in a work which, from the beginning, had many difficulties to contend against. It is pleasing to contemplate, and must be gratifying to the Church Missionary Society's Committee, to know that the vernacular education of this Mission, such as it is, is indebted mainly to the private liberality of Christian friends in this country and in England.

One other educational institution remains to be noticed—the Girls' boarding school. The first movement in this direction was made by the late Mrs. Fox. She gathered together around her a few native girls, and the small beginning gradually acquired form and stability. "Some of the destitute girls brought their brothers with them," and the necessity of a separate institution becoming apparent, the Anglo-vernacular school rose out of that conviction. The report remarks—

In behalf of this work considerable interest was created in England by our brother Fox. That interest has never ceased, and we feel sure that the Church Missionary Society will not have us conceal the fact that the existence, the maintenance, efficiency, and happy results of our boarding establishments, are due to the cordial, persevering, prayerful efforts of private friends in England, whose labour of love is known only to One, who will in due time acknowledge even a cup of cold water given in his name, to the least of his chosen ones.

The present state of the girls' boarding school is healthful and encouraging—

It was established in June 1847. We began with six girls. At the close of 1863 there were fifty-eight pupils. Four of the girls were married during the year, two of them to village schoolmasters, one to an English writer, and the fourth to a Christian labourer. Three of the girls went up for the Government examination, and two of them succeeded in obtaining schoolmistresses certificates.

Notwithstanding the marriages in the school, of which there have been four this year, the number of girls continues about the same, for many young ones have joined. There are now in the school fifty-eight girls, and of these, thirty-one are Christians.

The value of this excellent establishment can hardly be understood by those who have not visited India, and witnessed the degraded and miserable condition of the female population of the lower classes, whose whole lives are spent in idleness and utter ignorance. The beneficial effects of education and industry are fully manifested in the cheerful, happy, and contented countenances of all the girls, which must, I think, strike every one forcibly. The children's hours are fully occupied, for when not engaged with their studies, they work for the support of the school, either in plain work supplied them by the residents, or in crotchet work, some specimens of which I have frequently sent to England, where they have been much admired. They have also their hours of recreation, when it is quite a pleasure to hear their merry voices.

Excluding from our present consideration the Koi Mission northward on the Godavery, we find in the Telugu country three points occupied by our Missionaries—Masulipatam, Bezwara, and Ellore. At these centres the work divides itself into two distinct branches, the pastoral and the evangelistic. The first of these is limited, yet important; the latter vast, and almost overwhelming. We shall be compelled, for the present, to confine our notices to the first of these, the pastoral branch, else this paper would become prolix. The evangelistic branch, as altogether distinct, may be dealt with separately.

The congregation at Masulipatam consists of 147 baptized Christians, of whom 59 are communicants. They meet three times a week for divine worship, and have a monthly administration of the holy communion. In connexion with the congregation there is a Sunday school, in attendance ranging from 88 to 120, of whom 60 to 70 are adults. Through the kind liberality of friends, rewards have been distributed to the most regular and attentive. In reference to this school, the Missionaries observe—

Though there is nothing striking about the Sunday school, yet it is perhaps not the least important branch of the Mission. In catechetical and familiar conversation the Gospel is regularly set before many, who, from want of training, are unable to follow the preacher's discourse. It is the best opportunity for instructing the women, and for making the young systematically acquainted with Scripture history. In one class the "Pilgrim's Progress," in Telugu, is read and explained to Christian servants; but, as even Paul might plant and Apollos water in vain, we beg all who see this statement earnestly to pray that the Holy Spirit may be abundantly given, both to teachers and scholars. The school was first opened in 1850. In January 1852 the number on the list was ten, and the average attendance eight.

There is a class for heathen servants, open to the servants of any of the residents. It is also satisfactory to find that church funds for various purposes are afloat, and that this congregation, from its infancy, is instructed in the duty of contributing to the maintenance of its own religious privileges.

The Masulipatam Native-Christian Widows' and Orphans' Fund amounted, at the end of 1863, to Rupees 169 . 8 . 0 (16*l.* 19*s.*), mainly contributed by the native Christians. Measures are being adopted to render this fund available for all the stations of the Church Missionary Society in the Telugu country. It was started in 1861. The increase for 1863 is Rupees 49 . 8 . 0 (4*l.* 19*s.*). One widow will have a claim on it of three rupees per month, from March next. Any donation to this fund would be most acceptable.

The Masulipatam Native-Christian Poor Fund was established in 1849. There is at present only one monthly subscriber: the rest is made up from the native offertory; and the money is devoted to the relief of poor native Christians. Two old women and one blind man are regularly supported by it. It is also liable for the funeral expenses of the poor and for the sacramental wine. At the close of 1863 the fund contained Rs. 58 . 2 . 9 (5*l.* 16*s.* 4½*d.*), Rs. 8 . 13 . 3 less than at the end of 1862.

The Masulipatam Native-Pastors' Fund was commenced in July 1862, and is entirely sustained by the contributions of the native Christians. The amount contributed up to

September 1863, by Mrs. Sharkey's school-girls, was Rs. 61.2.4 (6*l.* 2*s.* 3½*d.*). During the same time the Christian young men, who meet weekly at Di Búshanam Garu's house, have contributed about 17 rupees; and the rice, &c., of the poorer Christian families has realized Rs. 13.13.

On September 30th the sum of Rs. 87.15.2 was remitted to the Acting Secretary, with the request that an account might be opened with the Society for the fund. At the close of 1863 the total amount was Rs. 92.9.10 (9*l.* 5*s.* 2¾*d.*). But we hope that two natives may be ordained early in the new year, and the whole of the present fund would only meet their salaries, &c., for little more than one month. The need of contributions to it is at once apparent.

So far, then, as to the machinery in connexion with the Christian flock. It reminds us, in its organization, of a well-ordered parish at home—church services, Sunday and daily schools, Scripture classes, and contributions for religious purposes. But these, after all, are only means to a great end, and that end the winning of immortal souls to Christ. The conversion of the careless and uninfluenced, the growth of believers, the edification of the whole body, its increasing fitness for the work which the Lord expects from every visible church, that in its own sphere it prove to be as a central light to illuminate the darkness around,—these are results which every right-minded minister, whether at home or on the Mission field, desires to see realized. And we can thoroughly sympathize with our Missionaries when, passing on from the mere details of arrangements, they proceeed to consider the spiritual state of the Christian flock.

The dry bones which Ezekiel saw in the midst of the valley are an apt illustration of the state of our little church. How much money have you spent? how many people have you converted? are questions not unfrequently asked by people who do not know the desperate wickedness of the human heart, and the superhuman agency required to convert it to God. Such people take more interest in our educational establishments than in our congregations. An elegantly-written theme, the solution of a difficult mathematical problem, superior needlework, or sweet singing, at once elicit the admiration and satisfaction of such people. In writing of the spiritual character of our congregation, we cannot, of course, hope to convince such people that the value of a single soul, rescued from Satan's bondage, exceeds that of all the money hitherto spent upon the Mission. But God's own people will be prepared to receive and sympathize in the statement we are about to make in regard to our congregation, and we need hardly labour to assure ourselves of their prayerful interest in our work. We alluded to the dry bones seen by Ezekiel. Our people were once as near the kingdom of heaven as these bones were to life. But, like those bones, they heard the word of God; and first the sinews, then the flesh, and, lastly, the skin, enclosed the bones, and gave them form. But there was no breath in them. Such are some of our Christians: there is their open profession of faith and repentance; their baptism; their general attendance on the means of grace, and their ability to understand, admire, and assent to the truths of Christianity; but there seems to be no breath in them. There are others, again, in whom, blessed be God, this breath is in whom, as far as we are able to judge, the root of the matter is; and such are a true comfort, and no small encouragement to us, in our great and difficult, but good work.

Having concluded our notice of Masulipatam, we pass on to Bezwara, a large town, with a population of nearly 20,000, lying in a north-west direction from Masulipatam. As many as 300, if not more, Mohammedan families reside in it, most of whom are retired military officers and soldiers. Here, and at Ragapuram, in its vicinity, there is a total of 149 baptized Christians, divided into two congregations, reminding us of the Israelites, when they were like "two little flocks of kids, but the Syrians filled the country." The Bezwara congregation is already provided with the various appliances which are in operation at Masulipatam—an Anglo-vernacular school, a vernacular day school for boys, a girls' boarding-school, Sunday school, church fund, &c., while at Ragapuram we trace the commencement of like formations.

Ellore, with a population of 20,000, lies northward from Masulipatam, distant about thirty-nine miles. The congregation here is very infantile, the number of baptized persons being twenty-six. But there are encouraging circumstances which lead us to hope that "the little one shall become a thousand, and the small one a strong nation;" and amongst them this important one, that our Missionary, the Rev. F. W. Alexander, has associated with him in his work several native agents, who afford him much satisfaction and ready aid.

It is very encouraging to see our native brethren at our side. When I joined the Mission there was not a single native agent of any sort in our part of the Telugu country, and now there are six agents in the Ellore district, and many more in the other stations.

Such, then, are the points of occupation in the Telugu country, some more, others less advanced. At Masulipatam, there are four European Missionaries; at Bezwara, two; at Ellore, one. From these posts, and with such forces, we must go forth to subdue the land. Let it be done in the spirit of Jonathan—"It may be that the Lord will work for us; for there is no restraint to the Lord to save by many or by few."

IBRAHIM SAHIB.

VISIBLE churches are collective bodies of men who make a profession of scriptural Christianity. Like the tares and the wheat growing together to the harvest, they are mixed bodies, their members being neither all spiritual men nor all mere professors. There are some who have received the truth in the love of it, and there are others concerning whose state there is more or less uncertainty; but of the latter, none are removed beyond the hope of improvement. Visible churches and congregations, as things are now, cannot be ordered on any other principle; and any attempt to form a communion, which shall consist exclusively of believers, must prove a failure.

The spiritual persons are the nucleus of the church, to which, it is hoped, by the action of the word faithfully preached, the undecided elements around, in a greater or less measure, will attach themselves, so as to increase its magnitude and brightness. They are the heart of the church; the centre of its vitality; the joy and comfort of the pastors. Every individual amongst them is invested with a special interest, and regarded with an earnest affection; and this the more in heathen lands, where Christianity as yet is but as a feeble light kindled amidst surrounding darkness. These men, in forsaking all for Christ, have, almost without an exception, passed through great tribulation, and this invests them with still deeper interest. One exemplification of this has been forwarded to us by the Masulipatam Missionaries. The history of this man shows how gradual oftentimes is the transit of the soul from darkness unto light, and how severe are the trials of first converts. It has always been so. In every nation they have had to pass through a fiery ordeal, heated to a greater or less degree of intensity. But it is one that is overruled for good. That amongst the first converts there should be a large proportion of genuine and spiritual men is of primary importance. They lie at the foundation: what if, when the superstructure has made some progress, they should all prove unreliable, and give way? But this initiative trial is a testing process, and the profession which is hypocritical and deceptive is, to a great extent, detected, and sifted out: "when tribulation or persecution ariseth because of the word, immediately they are offended." The Telugu Missionaries write—

For some months a Mohammedan, a convert to Christianity, attached himself to our congregation. His history, with which our Missionaries are, to some extent, connected, is full of interest, and may be of use to our fellow-labourers in other fields, situated in similar circumstances. It is this—

Ibrahim Sahib Talib-ul-din is a native commissioned-officer of Her Majesty's 11th Madras Native Infantry. According to his own account of himself, he was at one time a most bigoted Mussulman, and regarded Christians and their cause with the utmost contempt and hatred. One day the thought occurred to him that the best weapon against Christianity was the Bible itself. With this view he obtained of the Rev. W. Dawson, a London Missionary, a copy of the Hindustanee Bible, and set about reading it daily, until he actually finished the entire volume. But the Bible was not the only book he studied: some of Dr. Pfander's works attracted his attention, and he read them also. There was also another link in the chain of events that prepared his mind for the reception of the truths which he wished to refute. An intelligent, but careless young officer in his regiment, who was indifferent to his own spiritual welfare, endeavoured, in his official intercourse with Ibrahim Sahib, to impress the latter with views depreciatory of the Bible and Christianity. Soon after, sickness compelled this young man to proceed to Europe, where his soul experienced a change, which made him bitterly regret the part he had taken to keep his fellow-Mohammedan soldier from the faith. On his return, however, to his regiment, one of the first duties he discharged was to retract, in Ibrahim Sahib's presence, the anti-Christian statements which he had before made. Many and long were the discussions which this young officer had with Ibrahim Sahib; and so powerful were his appeals to his conscience, that Ibrahim Sahib often felt unable to return any satisfactory replies to the questions put to him. Ibrahim Sahib ascribes his first impressions of the truth of Christianity to this young officer. Time rolled on. His regiment was removed from station to station, and at last it was ordered off to Burmah on foreign service.

The Bible was Ibrahim's constant companion, and he read it, not only for himself, but also to his wife, to whom he explained the truths of Christianity. A great change was working in him. He was no longer an enemy to the Christians, and he even esteemed the Bible the best book he had ever read. The time for embarking had arrived. He communicated his views on Christianity, and his resolution to receive baptism after his arrival in Burmah, to his wife, who was prepared for the announcement, and was not therefore disposed to oppose it. He left India, and his wife went to live with her father, a pensioned subadar, residing at Ellore, near Masulipatam.

Ibrahim Sahib was not without Christian instruction in Burmah. This time it was not an officer that was appointed of God to teach him; his spiritual guide was a lady, the wife of one of the senior officers of his regiment. She was a devout and humble follower of the Lord Jesus. Her words of encouragement, of instruction, of reproof, and Christian love, often expressed in notes written in Hindustanee by herself, were a great means of grace to Ibrahim Sahib, whose boldness for Christ was gradually manifesting itself. At last, not, however, without much mental conflict, some sinful hesitation, and many painful trials, he offered himself for baptism to the Baptist Missionaries in Burmah. The baptism over, Ibrahim Sahib was called to endure even personal violence at the hands of his former co-religionists.

It is a satisfactory sign when a convert, in speaking of his baptism, attaches to each of the parts of that ordinance its proper value, in accordance with the teaching of both Scripture and history. Ibrahim Sahib was a remarkable instance of "being born again, not of corruptible seed, but of incorruptible, by the word of God, which liveth and abideth for ever." The human instrumentality which was so blessed to him he found in his own regiment. Once possessed of the one thing needful, he cared little about the outward mode of baptism. In all his intercourse with our Missionaries, his mind invariably dwelt on the thing signified by baptism, and he never once expressed a desire to study the unhappy differences of Christians on this subject.

The intelligence of his baptism soon reached Ellore: he communicated it himself. It was received with apparent satisfaction, and, strange to say, instead of expressions of resentment, and threats of expulsion, his friends forwarded to him, in more than one letter, words of sympathy and kindness, advice and welcome. There was, however, one individual—the Kázi—who was not disposed to be quiet. Paid by our Government for watching over the religious interests of the Mohammedan population at Ellore, and filled with the characteristic bigotry of his countrymen, he sought, in various ways, to induce Ibrahim Sahib's wife to decline the pecuniary support she was receiving from her husband, and to remarry. Her father was threatened with expulsion from caste if he protected his daughter, placards of the most insulting character were pasted on the walls and doors of his dwelling.

After an absence of three years, Ibrahim's regiment returned to India, and, without loss of time, he repaired to Ellore. At first he was allowed frequent and long interviews with his wife. She more than once expressed her willingness to join him, but she was afraid of her people. Ibrahim Sahib endeavoured to conciliate his wife's parents; but the Kázi's influence was all-powerful, and they could not safely restore their daughter to her husband. Ibrahim's difficulties began to thicken, and, finally, he was ordered not to approach the house in which his wife lived, or to have any intercourse with her. Once more the wife was privately counselled by the Kázi to bring an action against her husband—to charge him (falsely of course) before witnesses, whom he (the Kázi) would duly instruct, with having forcibly entered her father's dwelling-house, and threatened her life with a drawn sword. But the wife remained true to the interests of her husband, and at once rejected the diabolical proposition. She was now narrowly watched, and even her relatives went so far as to hint that adultery, under her circumstances, was no crime. She steadily resisted the temptation planned for her fall, and her husband's disgrace, and continued to meet her husband secretly, in the presence of a mutual trustworthy friend, and communicated to him all the difficulties that surrounded her, and the utter hopelessness of her case. The trial was indeed a sore one to the husband. Twice he visited Masulipatam, and sought the advice and aid of the Missionaries there. The case was an important one, in which we felt deeply interested. A similar case had been tried in a distant Zillah court, and the wife was delivered to her husband. The advantages of a similar decision in our district also were great. There were also converts whose wives were prevented, by parents and friends, from joining their husbands. We felt that we owed it as a duty to the Telugu church, to lend all our aid to Ibrahim Sahib, for the recovery of his wife, and we were much assisted in our proceedings by the case alluded to above.

In 1862 a Hindu in Cuttack embraced Christianity. Influenced by his brother, the convert's wife refused to live with her husband, who applied to the magistrate for protection. The magistrate referred the case to his deputy, a native, who decreed that the convert was "at liberty to take possession of his property, but, as the wife was unwilling, he could not compel her to live with her husband, and that, in regard to his property and the guardianship of his children, the police should be directed to see that the petitioner was not opposed in the exercise of his lawful rights." The convert was not, of course, satisfied with this strange decision. He appealed to the magistrate, who referred him to the Civil Court. The Civil judge reversed the decision of the deputy magistrate; admitted that the father was still the proper guardian of the children, of whom there were five, of ages varying from three to eleven years, and who were, therefore, minors; recognised the principle that the husband was justly entitled to his wife's society, be her religion what it may, provided only that they were married according to the religion they both professed at the time of the celebration of the ceremony, and that the husband had not forfeited his right by cruelty or adultery; and decreed that the wife and children be made over to the convert. The judge, however, feeling that he had no certain law to guide him in such cases, referred his decision to the High Court of Bengal for its opinion. The High Court declined to give any opinion on the question of the magistrate's jurisdiction in the case submitted by the judge of Cuttack, and declared its incompetency to issue any general rules for the future guidance of judges in similar cases. Upon this the Civil judge of Cuttack ordered his judgment to be carried into effect. Such was the happy termination of the case at Cuttack, which was no small help to us in advising Ibrahim Sahib what to do. In his case we were told by our legal adviser that the Mohammedan law legalizes the marriage of a Mussulman with a Christian; that, according to Macpherson's "Treatise on the Civil Procedure," page 26, "a claim to the personal custody of a woman, on the ground that she is the wife of the complainant, is cognizable by the Civil Court." That the same author says, in another place (page 140), that a suit instituted by a husband against his wife, who refuses to cohabit with him, may be laid in the very court in whose jurisdiction the refusal takes place; that a suit for the recovery of a wife is one for specific performance; that all the Civil Courts, including the District Munsiff's Court, are empowered by the new Civil Procedure Court (Act viii. of 1859) to entertain suits for specific performance (192); and that if the wife, of her own accord, refuse to join her husband, the husband may use all means, short of violence, to take her, or to insist upon her rejoining him. Although the Civil judge at Cuttack ruled that a magistrate had no jurisdiction in matters of this kind, we were advised to apply to the magistrate of Coconada before appearing in a Civil Court. Ibrahim Sahib accordingly petitioned that magistrate to order his wife's parents to restore her to him. The magistrate summoned the parties before him, and personally examined the petitioner's wife, who, after a long conversation with her husband, deliberately chose to remain under her father's protection. The magistrate suffered her to do so, remarking that the petitioner, if he still wished to prosecute the case, should bring an action into the Civil Court. This was a sore trial to Ibrahim Sahib, but he knew full well the various influences which were brought to bear on his wife by her relatives; how they were constantly by her side, the promises they held out, the threats they employed, and how narrowly they watched every avenue of access to her. Even before the magistrate certain expressions dropped from her lips, which left no doubt upon Ibrahim Sahib's mind as to her intentions; and if she refused to join her husband, she only yielded to a pressing necessity. The tears of an aged father, the sorrow of her mother, the cries of her sister, the persuasion of her friends, and the threats of the Kázi, were more than she could well endure; and it was evident, from her subsequent conduct, that she was only waiting for a suitable opportunity to join her husband, without danger to herself or injury to her parents, whom she dearly loved. The husband had now no alternative but to institute a suit in the Munsiff's Court at Ellore. Thither he proceeded, accompanied by one of our Missionaries, to advise him in the prosecution of his suit. After some delay, and some reluctance on the part of one native pleader to conduct the case, a complaint was drawn up and filed in the Munsiff's Court at Ellore.

Every thing was progressing when Ibrahim received a secret message from his wife. She intimated her wish to join him at once; that this could only be effected during the night; and that she would be ready at a certain spot to accompany him home. The time and place having been arranged, Ibrahim Sahib was true to his appointment. But her escape that night could not be effected; and it was deferred to another night, but with no better success. At last a third message arrived, and this time more than ordinary preparation was made by us to escort the wife in safety to her husband's temporary abode. But Ibrahim Sahib's courage failed him. He returned without his wife, declaring, that as she had not made her appearance at the appointed time, he would not go again. The night was dark and cloudy, the rain was falling fast, the clayey ground was dangerous to tread on, a few people were still walking in the street, and Ibrahim Sahib was frequently accosted by strange voices. He positively refused to go back to the appointed place for his wife.

We were much disconcerted; but, ere long, a message was brought that the wife was out, seeking her husband. We immediately ran out, but it was too late. The woman was missed by her friends, and lights were seen in every direction. The women of the house were conducting a strict search. We, however, succeeded in getting to the wife, whose hand, at our prompting, was immediately seized by her husband, and she slowly walked side by side with him. But this was not to last long. Some half a dozen women, with shrill cries, made a dash at her, seized her left hand, and pulled with all their might in an opposite direction to that taken by her husband. The noise and excitement increased, and the wife clearly saw that she could not, at that time, accompany her husband. She asked him to allow her to return home, and he did so. We returned to our tent much mortified and distressed. Ibrahim Sahib now blamed himself that he had not waited for his wife, as he might then have escaped with her before she was missed. The next day Ibrahim Sahib received, to his great surprise and joy, a message from his father-in-law to come and escort his wife home. The night's proceedings proved, beyond contradiction, that the daughter preferred her husband's home to that of her father's, and the latter was apprehensive lest this fact should be employed by us as a ground for a fresh complaint against him, that he was detaining his daughter against her will. No time was to be lost now. A conveyance was procured, and Ibrahim Sahib went himself with it for his wife. No more trouble was given. The wife, all her property, and her child, were made over to the husband. We instantly made arrangements for having the party conveyed to Rajahmundry, and one of us accompanied them. Every attention was shown to us by Captain Taylor, a Christian gentleman of that place. We then proceeded to the coast, and there secured for the party a native vessel, through the kind aid of Mr. Dennison, a gentleman connected with the Upper Godavery. Ibrahim Sahib and his wife reached their destination in safety; and we have since heard that they are living together in peace and happiness. To God be all the glory!

With reference to similar cases to that of Ibrahim Sahib, it is clear that there is no well-defined law to guide our Indian judges in the formation of their judgment. There are, indeed, certain broad principles which cannot be forgotten in arriving at a correct view concerning cases in which the happiness of a convert to Christianity is involved. But sometimes even principles are lost sight of by judges, and the law of God made to yield to the pleasure—the whims of man. Who has not heard of Hemnath Bose? Sir M. Wells ordered the lad to be given up to his father, and yet Sir W. Burton, in 1846, and Sir Edward Gambier, in 1847, allowed the converts, one of whom was a minor, and the other a girl only twelve years old, to return to the Mission house. Sir Lawrence Peel, in 1856, decreed "that a youth under sixteen might, if he chose, return to the Mission house. (See "Church Missionary Intelligencer" October 1863). "Cease ye from man, whose breath is in his nostrils, for wherein is he to be accounted of." "It is better to trust in the Lord than to put confidence in man."

METLAHKATLAH, BRITISH COLUMBIA.

"BEFORE 1857 no Protestant Missionary had ever traversed the wilds of British Columbia, nor had attempts been made to instruct the Indians;" and yet they consisted, not of a few wanderers dispersed over an immense extent of territory, but of many thousands; so that it might have been supposed that their numbers alone would have secured some small measure of attention, during the long term of English sovereignty over Vancouver's Island and the adjoining mainland, known in the records of the Hudson's Bay-Company as New Caledonia. They are divided into two classes, the coast or fishing Indians, and the inland tribes. Involved in all the misery of heathenism, exposed to the ills inseparable from human life, and yet "without hope and without God in the world," they claimed, and still do claim, from those who are living in the enjoyment of the full light and privileges of Christianity, the deepest commiseration. They have to pass through the same sad scenes of domestic sorrow and bereavement which occur in Christian lands. Sickness comes, and native customs aggravate the sufferings of the patient. The native rattle is whirled about his head; nay, more; "incisions are made where pain is felt, or fire applied by means of burning tinder, made of dried wild flax." At length death supervenes, and then, as the remains are borne to the grave, there is the bitter wailing of those who sorrow without hope. At home we find, that when the winter of affliction comes, we need all the strength which Christianity can impart to support us, and that we have to borrow by faith from the bright promise of the future, to lighten the sombreness of the present. But to the heathen mind the future is a dark uncertainty, from which he shrinks. In whatever direction he looks, all is obscured. The past is no more: it has perished from his grasp; the present is clouded with the gloomy mists of sorrow; and the future is as the dark black night. There is a mystery in his existence, and he cannot understand it. If he asks, Whence these sorrows? why this death? no voice of revelation breaks the silence. Groping after God, and unable to find Him, he regards Him as a sublime abstraction, who has committed the government of the world to demi-gods and sub-creations. These are supposed to be of every possible hue, malignant and benign: they fill the air, the earth, the water. Amidst this chaos, the evil spirits are the most regarded, because from them the Indian fears injury, and to such the chief offerings are made. These malignant spirits seem to him to exist on every hand, and he is in constant fear of them. The animal tribes typify them, and thus birds and beasts are to him full of omens: "he hears them talk in the tempests, he sees them in dark clouds, they beset him in every possible angry sound which the jarring elements can make, and they crawl in the very insects of curious shape that creep out of the earth." Where is he to find protection from the terrorism by which he is surrounded? He yields himself to the influence of the medicine-man, and becomes entangled in a subtle system of pretended sorcery and divination. The medicine-man, in the opinion of his tribe, excels in the knowledge of, and power of influencing, the spirit-world. His great object is to sustain this reputation, and he has recourse to a system of subtle tricks and concealments. He withdraws into the woods, and there secretes himself that he may hold converse with the supernatural. He comes forth in a religious frenzy, and, like the waters of a lake when yielding to the influence of a strong wind, the tribe becomes excited, and is moved by him to acts of cruelty, which, in more quiet moments, would be regarded with aversion and disgust.

Moulded under such influences, we cannot wonder at the dark traits of the Indian character, and the opposition which Christian Missionaries, on first coming amongst this people, are sure to encounter from the native priesthood.

We shall now proceed to state the circumstances in which originated the first Missionary effort on behalf of the long-neglected tribes of British Columbia.

In the spring of 1856 the Editorial Secretary of the Society attended as deputation the Anniversary Meeting of the Tunbridge-Wells Church Missionary Association. There he met Captain Prevost, R.N., who had just returned from Vancouver's Island, and who, witnessing the degraded condition of the Indians, felt solicitous that a Mission should be commenced amongst them. So we continually find it to be. The heart of some Christian man is moved to compassionate a portion of our race, lying in the degradation of heathenism. This is of the Lord. It is the Saviour on his throne who is moved with compassion towards the multitudes, because they are scattered abroad as sheep having no shepherd; and acting on the hearts of those who live near to Him, and are in sympathy with Him, He prompts them to make an effort for the extension of his Gospel, and the salvation of immortal souls. It was thus that Samuel Marsden was the instrument of commencing the New-Zealand Mission.

Captain Prevost, availing himself of the opportunity, entered into conversation with the Editorial Secretary on the subject of the Vancouver-Island Indians, and earnestly inquired whether some effort could not be made on their behalf. He was invited to draw up an article on the subject. This he did, and it was published in the "Church Missionary Intelligencer" for July 1856.

This brief notice produced its results. In the list of contributions published in the "Church Missionary Record" for March 1857 appears the following item—"Two friends, for 'Vancouver's Island,' 500*l*. Captain Prevost's notice of Vancouver's Island, and the aboriginal tribes there and on the mainland, drew forth that contribution.

Just about this time Captain Prevost was appointed to the Pacific station, in command of H.M.S. "Satellite;" and, with the sanction of the first Lord of the Admiralty, offered a free passage, and every assistance in his power, to any Missionary whom the Committee might be willing to send with him. Mr. Duncan was at the time one of the Society's students in the Highbury Training College. It was judged that he was one to whom might be entrusted the responsibilities connected with this new sphere of action, and it was proposed to him that he should go forth. The time was short: only ten days remained before the sailing of the "Satellite;" but he was ready, and, trusting in Him who has said, "Lo, I am with you alway," he went forth, the first Missionary to the Indians of the British territories on the Pacific.

As might be expected on entering so rude a field, he has had much to endure in the way of difficulty and danger. He first performed divine service on October 11, 1857, and on the 13th opened his school with five half-breed boys. His proceedings were carefully observed, the chiefs and others coming to visit his school, and, when he and his pupils knelt in prayer, regarding them with serious looks, and expressing their approval by the invariable "Ahm, Ahm." But still, however, without any diminution, the old heathen scenes of murder continued to be perpetrated. With the new year he commenced his labours amongst the Indians without the Fort, and, in the hope of winning their confidence and esteem, decided on visiting them from house to house. "I confess," he says, "that cluster after cluster of these half-naked and painted savages was, to my unaccustomed eyes, very alarming; but the reception I met with was trul wonderful and encouraging. Some would not be content until I took the chief place at the fire. My inquiries after the sick were always followed by anxious glances and deep sighs; a kind of solemn awe would spread itself at once."

After two years his work began to tell. He was enabled to address them in their own tongue, and his school was filled with children and adults; and now opposition commenced. The medicine-men resolved that the school should be closed while their rites lasted. They tried to intimidate the Missionary, but in vain. "The Lord," says

Mr. Duncan, "enabled me to stand calm, and without the slightest fear to address them in their own tongue with far more fluency than I could have imagined possible." In vain the head chief, who was the leader of the medicine-men, raised his voice, stamped on the floor, and stormed furiously: he did not succeed. In these struggles the Missionary's life was imperilled, a ferocious savage, called Legaie, attempting to kill him. The people around watched to see whether he would be intimidated, and shrink from the work. He became more bold. "I have been," he observes, "for some time desiring to speak to the cannibal chief. To-day the opportunity was afforded me, and I had some talk with him. This man heads the most degrading superstition this people have got; but he is a young man, and has a noble look. It will be a hard struggle if he ever sets himself to escape from the meshes of that horrid custom which he has taken upon himself to perpetuate; but I hope and pray God may give him light and strength for the conflict, and bring him, clothed and in his right mind, to the feet of Jesus. He met my proposals very kindly, and promised to come under my instruction when he returned from a journey on which he is now going."

And now came the first expression, on the part of a native, of faith in Jesus as a Saviour. It was the case of a young man dying of consumption. Beside him sat one of Mr. Duncan's pupils, a young woman, very intelligent, and able to read portions of the Bible. She interpreted, with tears in her eyes, entreating the dying man to call on God. Then the Missionary knelt down: all was hushed, and he prayed that mercy might be vouchsafed, for the sake of Jesus. The sufferer knew of Jesus: he had learned the leading truths of the Gospel, nor, during his long illness, would he ever permit the medicine-men to approach him with their rites. He died assuring the people of his safety.

The first baptisms took place on July 26, 1861, when fourteen men and five women openly professed Christ before their countrymen. This drew out more strongly the spirit of persecution, and the converts were severely tried and tempted.

It was now decided to form a Christian college at a place called Metlahkatlah, the old home of these Tsimshean Indians, which they had left to live near Fort Simpson, that they might have trading facilities. Such a step was rendered necessary, not only from the anxiety of the Christians to escape from the sights and thraldom of heathenism, but from the rush of miners in search of gold, many of whom made Fort Simpson their winter-quarters, bringing with them serious evils. The old villages are not too distant: they are situated about fifteen miles from Fort Simpson, in a lovely channel, always smooth, and abounding with salmon and shell-fish, with plenty of beach room, and plots of ground suitable for gardens.

Here they were visited by the Bishop of Columbia in April 1863. The little band of fifty who had first moved to Metlahkatlah had increased to 600 from different tribes, and a village had been formed, consisting of well-built cottages, in which, under the influence of Christianity, men dwelt side by side as neighbours who had been in mortal feud all their lives. The bishop, in the fifth report of Missionary proceedings within his diocese, thus describes the work which was prepared for him at the Church Missionary station—

It was my office to examine a number of these Indians for baptism. I was several days engaged in the work. One day I was engaged from eight in the morning till one o'clock the next morning. It was the last day I had, and they pressed on continually to be examined. Night and darkness came. The Indians usually go to bed with the sun, but now they turned night into day, in order that they might be "fixed in God's ways," they said. "Any more Indians?" I kept saying, as eight o'clock, nine o'clock, ten o'clock, twelve o'clock, and one o'clock came: and there were always more Indians wishing to be "fixed" on God's side. I shall never forget the scene. The little oil lamp was not enough to dispel the gloom or darkness of the room, but its light was sufficient to cast a reflection on the countenance of each Indian as he or she sat before me. The Indian countenance is usually inexpressive of emotion; but now, when they spoke of prayer and trust in God, there was the uplifted eye, and evident fervour; and when they spoke of their sins, there was a downcast look, the flush came and went on their cheeks, and the big tear frequently coursed from their manly eyes. Their whole hearts seemed to speak out in their countenances.

The bishop introduces the answers made by the candidates on examination, and some notices of the most remarkable amongst them. In the group we find the name Legaic, the chief who had attempted Mr. Duncan's life, notorious as having been a most savage and desperate man, stained with every crime. In his answers he thus expressed himself—"I want to take hold on God. I believe in God the Father, who made all things, and in Jesus Christ. I constantly cry for my sins when I remember them. I pray to God to wipe out my sins. I am anxious to walk in God's ways all my life. If I turn back it will be more bitter than before."

This man, the principal chief, has made greater sacrifices than any other. He has left his tribe and all his greatness. Although largely bribed to return, he has stood fast. Once ferocious in his temper, he now bears patiently the ridicule of his friends, and returns kindness.

Another, Neeash Lakah Noosh, called the Lime chief, a fine old man, blind of an eye, when asked if he wished to become a Christian, replied—

For that object I came here with my people. I have put away all lying ways, which I had long followed. I have trusted in God. We want the Spirit of God. Jesus came to save us. He compensated for our sins. Our Father made us, and loved us because we are his work. He wishes to see us with Him, because He loves us. When asked about the judgment, he said, the blood of Jesus will free those who believe from condemnation.

This man is most consistent, trying to do simply what is right.

Among the female candidates, also, the answers of Wahthi, the wife of Legaic, are very touching, exhibiting the experience of one who, deeply troubled because of sin, and earnestly looking for peace through the blood of Christ, had not yet found it.

I wish to put away evil and have a clean heart. I feel the pain of the remembrance of sin so bad I would sometimes like to die. I want to see God's face, but feel little hope; still I determine to persevere, though miserable. Loss of relatives, and finding no peace and rest, and feeling myself in darkness, led me to look to God. I know that God sent his Son Jesus to die for our sins.

In November 1863, Metlahkatlah was visited by the Rev. R. J. Dundas, and some brief extracts from his journals will bring the good Missionary and his work very vividly before our readers.

We went to Mr. Duncan's house. It is solidly built of large square timbers. We next went into his school-chapel, an immense circular building, some sixty feet in diameter, capable of holding some 700. Like English children, the young Indians, I dare say, prefer play to work. We stood at the door and watched them on the shingle below playing prisoners' base. At the sound of a gong they all hurried up to the school—of all ages and sizes, from fourteen downwards. They ranged themselves in order, boys on one side, girls on the other, and, led by Mr. Duncan, sang most beautifully. They sang several catches in three parts. Some had beautiful voices, and certainly their performance was quite equal to thoroughly good national schools at home. Afterwards we went through the village, entering several houses. Almost everywhere the same neatness and order were perceptible, the exception being generally new comers, still heathen; for, as I told you, any Indian is received as a resident who conforms to the laws laid down by Mr. Duncan, and renounces all heathen practices.

Oct. 25: Lord's-day—It was a pretty sight to see the whole population, old and young, at the sound of the bell, thronging to worship God. No need to lock doors, for there is no one to enter the empty houses. Every soul is assembled in the one place, and for one purpose. As they entered, the men took the right and the women the left hand of the great circular hall. I was surprised to learn from Mr. Duncan afterwards that he had never bidden them to do this: they seemed to have adopted the arrangement instinctively. Service began with a hymn in Tsimshean. He led with his concertina. The air was very plaintive and beautiful—sung by some 200 voices, men, women, and children: it thrilled through me. Then followed prayers in Tsimshean, at the close of which all joined in the Lord's Prayer in English. Then followed a chant—one of the Psalms he had translated and taught them—to a fine old Gregorian. His address, or sermon, of nearly an hour, was upon the story of Martha and Mary. His manner and gesticulation were animated and striking, very much after their own style. Their attention never seemed to flag throughout. He asked me to address them, which I did, shortly, upon their present light as compared with their past darkness, and the difficulties they must expect in their new course of Christian discipleship. Mr. Duncan interpreted for me. Before separating, they sang again in Tsimshean a sort of sacred air, which seemed familiar to me, and was exquisitely beautiful. I found afterwards it was the anthem, "I will arise and go to my Father," somewhat altered, and made more Indian in its character. It suited their voices admirably. I closed with a short prayer in English, and pronounced the Benediction.

The service was most striking. It was hard to realize that three years ago these all had been sunk in the deepest heathenism, with all its horrible practices. What hours, what whole nights of wrestling in prayer, have been spent by this single-minded faithful servant of God, in humble supplication that he might "see of the travail of his soul!" and how has he been answered! There is nothing too hard for the Lord.

On the Tuesday the examination of the candidates for baptism took place.

I went on shore in the afternoon, to take up my quarters with Mr. Duncan. About four o'clock the bell was rung, and the whole village assembled at the schoolhouse, when Mr. Duncan told them that on the following Sunday, those who desired it, and also, on examination, approved themselves, would be admitted to holy baptism. Candidates were to assemble that evening at seven, to give in their names. In his address to them he was very pointed and stringent—fencing in, as he afterwards told me, the door of admission—so anxious was he that only the really converted should offer themselves. He told them the strict uncompromising requirements in those who thus sought to join themselves to Christ and his service. Better that they should postpone so solemn and awful a step than come to it unprepared. At the hour appointed the candidates were assembled. Fifty-five gave in their names. Several were absent who would have come forward had they been there; but, as my coming was never anticipated, at least 150 to 200 were away for their last hunting and fishing excursion before the winter, and would not be back for some weeks. Out of fifty-five who offered I accepted thirty-eight—twenty-one males and seventeen females. I was strongly impressed with the real earnestness and devotion of those who came forward, and with their acquaintance with the simple saving truths of the Gospel message. Some cases were indeed most touching.

One said, "Mr. Duncan came and told us of our evil ways. *I was deep in the ground then;* but when he told us how God loved us, I wanted to be free and love God: that was the first time I thought of Him." Another said—

I pray every day to Him. I say to Him, "Oh, my great Father, pity me! I am poor and weak, help me; wipe my sins out of thy great book." Another said, "Jesus is now an Intercessor. He stands between us and God. He died for our sins. His blood is strong to take our sins away. We must take hold of the hand of Jesus."

These are some answers of an elderly woman—"I want to take hold of the hand of God. He is willing to pity me: our sins killed Jesus; but his blood saves us. I must leave all my sins, for Jesus suffered for them. We shall stand before God; we must see God's righteousness. He will give his hand to the good, but He will put the wicked away from Him." This woman, who cannot be less than fifty, has had no instruction from Mr. Duncan, save what she has heard in church. It has come chiefly from her own daughter of fifteen, who is one of the Mission-house inmates, and has been with Mr. Duncan for four years, his best and most promising young convert. She has been baptized by the Bishop, and has now been the instructress of her parents, both of whom will be baptized by me to-morrow.

From two or three elderly men I got, of course, answers less full. It is hard for them to remember truths so as to give definite answers in words. They feel and know more than they can explain. In a few cases Mr. Duncan said, if I would allow him, he would not put any questions to them formally, but would leave them to tell, in their own way, why they sought for baptism. And very touching it was even to listen to them, though I could not understand them. One, with tears streaming down, said he was very old, and must soon die; but he wanted to be at peace with God. He knew his ways had been bad all his life; but he had no light; and now he wanted to belong to Jesus, for he knew Jesus loved him and died for him. Of course I could not hesitate in such a case, and gladly accepted him.

On the next Sunday, November 1, the fifty-two candidates were baptized—

At the proper point in the service, one by one, the candidates stepped forward in front of the assembled congregation. Mr. Duncan called up each by his heathen name. In answer to my request, "name this person," he gave the new Christian name, and by it I baptized him "in the name of the Father, and of the Son, and of the Holy Ghost." As I held the hand of each while receiving him or her into the church of Christ, and signing him with the sign of the cross, I could often feel that they trembled with deep emotion, and on returning one by one to their places each knelt down in silent prayer.

Here then, in these distant wilds, amidst the degraded and superstitious Indians of the Pacific, the Gospel of Christ is accomplishing marvellous things. The agent is humble; the power is of God. Our readers will now be prepared for more recent intelligence from this green spot in the desert, contained in the following letter from Mr. Duncan, dated July 25, 1864—

I see my last letter was dated as far back as January, and deeply do I regret this very unsatisfactory state of my correspondence, for I know that many events have passed me unrecorded which would have been interesting to you. However, I still hope for better things in this respect. I still look forward to a change when I shall get through some of the engagements which at present crowd upon me. Often when I would take up my pen, my jaded mind and almost constant interruption deny me; and thus I pass on from day to day—events crowding on each other, so that an attempt at full and consecutive records is out of the question. I must therefore be content to gather up a few of the most prominent matters, and place them before you.

While I say this is very unsatisfactory, and distresses me, yet I have much to comfort me when I do collect my thoughts for correspondence. *I can indeed say my cup runneth over.* The Lord is with us of a truth. Through hosts of trials and over mountain difficulties, his hand is still carrying us. God's Holy Spirit is indeed at work in the midst of us, for many whom I have seen mad in sin, are now sitting clothed and in their right mind. Many who used to despise, mock, and hate me as well as the message I brought, are now changed to loving and obedient children, and are earnestly inquiring the way to Zion. To God be all the praise and glory!

A little while after writing you my last letter I made a visit to Fort Simpson. I will give you the entry in my journal—

Feb. 6, 1864—I have just returned from a visit to Fort Simpson. I went to proclaim the Gospel once more to the poor unfeeling heathen there. I started on Thursday, preached twice on Friday, and returned today.

There is evidently a shaking of the dry bones there; but this I could see plainly, that the Indians are by no means ripe as a whole to remove to us yet. Some talk of coming soon, and spoke well. I laid the Gospel again distinctly before them, and they seemed much affected. The most pleasing circumstance of all, and which I was not prepared to expect, was, that Paul Legaie and Clat (the one in times past a formidable enemy and opposer, and the other one among the first to hear and greet the Gospel) sat by me, one on either side. After I had finished my address on each occasion they got up and spoke, and spoke well. Legaie completely ashamed and confounded an old man, who, in replying to my address, had said that I had come too late to do him and other old people good; that had I come when the first white traders came, the Tsimsheans had long since been good. But they had been allowed to grow up in sin; they had seen nothing among the first whites who came amongst them to unsettle them in their old habits, but these had rather added to them fresh sins, and now their sins were deep laid, they (he and the other old people) could not change.

Legaie interrupted him, and said, "I am a chief, a Tsimshean chief. You know I have been bad, very bad, as bad as any one here. I have grown up and grown old in sin, but God has changed my heart, and He can change yours. Think not to excuse yourselves in your sins by saying you are too old and too bad to mend. Nothing is impossible with God. Come to God: try his way: He can save you." He then exhorted all to *taste* God's way, to give their hearts to Him, to leave all their sins; and then endeavoured to show them what they had to expect if they did so—*not* temporal good, not health, long life, or ease, or wealth, but God's favour here and happiness with God after death.

Clat also spoke at great length. He said, from his youth he hated heathenism, and could never be prevailed upon, not even by threats, to join them in their follies. But he did not know of any better way; but by the time he became a man God sent his word to the Tsimsheans. He soon saw that he and his people were in the dark, and that God's word was a light, a great light shining in the darkness. He kept his eye fixed upon it, and started off towards it; he persevered till he grasped it; and now he found it to be good and sweet, a great light to his heart. He said many more things I cannot now recall.

What a glorious change was this since my first going round the camp to preach the Gospel in fear and trembling. Now I had two important men gathered out and on my side, speaking more distinctly than I could these glorious and saving truths, and trying to enforce them.

After they had finished I got up and pointed to those two as witnesses of the truth I had declared the years I had been here. The Indian audience seemed much affected.

Late in April last I made a visit to the Nishkat Indians of the Naas River. I was anxious to go for two reasons; first, because the Romish priests had lately been there trying to disaffect the minds of the Indians towards me; and the second reason was, I felt desirous to communicate the good news that Rev. R. R. A. Doolan* was coming to help us, and that now we should be in a position to take up the Naas Mission in earnest.

I met crowds of Indians, all glad to see me. I spent two nights and a whole day with them, busy all the time conversing, visiting their sick, and preaching, and the response I met with was truly encouraging. The universal cry was, Come, come and help us.

All the evil the priests had done did not amount to much. I quickly put to shame their malicious statements, and had some happy opportunities of contrasting the truth as it is in Jesus, and the effect the truth had produced at Metlahkatlah, with the priests' mummeries, and the effect they had produced upon the Indians south, who had tried them for fifteen years.

The difference is no less than the difference between life and death, and this even these poor heathen could discern. While speaking of Naas, I am led at once to announce the arrival of our dear brother Doolan. We welcomed him here in the Mission schooner with Mr. Cunningham*, the second of the month, and he and Mr. Cunningham started five days ago for this new field of labour.

During Mr. Doolan's short stay here, he saw something of the working of this Mission, baptized one adult and four infants, married one of the girls adopted by Mrs. Tugwell while here, a truly Christian girl, to the young man, S. Marsden, whom I hope soon to have as a help in the school. He also copied a good many of my papers on the Tsimsheans, and somewhat matured his plans in concert with Mr. Cunningham relative to the work before them.

They are gone, and I trust the Lord has gone with them to keep them faithful, and to establish and maintain his own work in another dark part of the earth.

I put the matter before Mr. Doolan, relative to the Mission and who was to go, thus—1st. That the Mission must be taken up; 2ndly, From past connexion with these Indians, and also from my knowing the language, prejudices, and difficulties so well, I ought to go; but as I am placed here, it is quite impossible for me to go, as nobody yet can take my place; hence Mr. Cunningham must go: and Mr. Doolan saw at once and embraced the call as from God, to accompany Mr. Cunningham, and struggle together with him, and pray together over the first difficulties of this new and interesting Mission field. I also think it will be better for themselves to go at once and deal with the heathen mind in its darkness and strongholds of iniquity. They will have their sympathies awakened, and their energy aroused, and they will feel more need for constant intercourse with God in prayer, than if they remained here, where there is scarcely a vestige of heathenism left.

Robert Dundas, a young Tsimshean, accompanies them, who we hope will prove of much service in assisting them with the language, and helping in school.

Other young men with me are promising well to become very useful in the Mission work around when the doors open for them.

Our plan is, as soon as possible to have an Indian schoolmaster placed at the head of each of the two great rivers near us; the Naas river, which is a little north, and the Skeener river, which is a little to the south.

I am happy to tell you that a trading party, with Legaic at its head, started up the

* Appointed by the Church Missionary Society to the Tsimshean Mission.

* Sent out by the Church Missionary Society.

Skeener river a few days ago, carrying with them a Christian Indian, David Hall, who is to be stationed about 200 miles up the river, to trade with the interior Indians. He will make his light shine, I have no doubt; and I must, as soon as possible, have a schoolmaster alongside of him, and the two might, with God's blessing, do great good.

While Mr. Doolan was here, upwards of thirty adults came forward to beg for baptism, in addition to about ten who had applied some time ago; but as most of them would be leaving me almost immediately for the salmon fishery, to be away for six or seven weeks, I thought it prudent to postpone the ceremony till they return, when they will have all the winter before them for instruction.

About October Mr. Doolan intends paying us a visit, when he will most likely baptize over forty adults. There will be some very interesting cases. These are the stout-hearted sinners who have long refused to take the yoke, though convinced of the truth of the Gospel.

After the Indians returned from the Spring fishery, I commenced school for the adults, and so had school three times each day—about 120 children, morning and afternoon, and about eighty adults in the evening. I have had no assistance as yet in the school, but I propose soon to employ S. Marsden to help me with the children.

I am thankful to be able to tell you that thus far I have been able to restrain all here from visiting Victoria, excepting, of course, those who go in the Mission schooner. It has been a very great struggle and test for some, but they have submitted rather than go against my will in the matter.

I must here acknowledge as very encouraging the implicit obedience the Indians render: some instances I might record would, I am sure, greatly interest you.

I am also happy to be able to report that the constables, as a body, are very true and faithful.*

Last winter they were severely tested. One of their own body, and a very influential one too, having gone wrong, was brought before us, and that by his very bosom friend; and we had to sit over his case till after midnight to reclaim him. I punished him by fining him five blankets, and should have kept him in custody unless he had confessed his error and begged pardon. If you had heard the kind and powerfully melting language which, one after another, his brother constables poured upon him to convince and subdue him, you would have rejoiced, I am sure. It was really wonderful. They triumphed, and with tears the prodigal returned. But part of the sentence was, that he was to leave the settlement for a short time, as I could not allow him to be seen in our midst. The day after, a deputation of constables waited upon me to beg for this part of the sentence to be cancelled. They came direct from a meeting to which he had been called, and after hearing his sorrowful words and good resolutions, they promised to use their influence to obtain permission to remain at the settlement, but not to go from his own house for some time, or until I gave him leave. Having pleaded so well and so earnestly for him, I consented to their proposal.

About three weeks after this he came to me, in company with his accuser—his bosom friend—saying that he wished to see my face, and speak before all the Christians that night. So after the adult school was over, I ordered all to leave the room who were not Christians. This was done, and the penitent then came in, and made a very affecting speech indeed. It was very wonderful to see and hear him, a naturally proud and a very influential man, from his eloquence and general character. He bitterly deplored his sin, praised God for his mercy, thanked me and all his friends for the trouble we had taken with him, expressed his sorrow and shame that he had given us pain, and disgraced the name of Christian, and resolved, in God's strength, to lead a new life, and be more watchful. He then warned all present against sin, begged them to watch and pray, confessed he had found the hiding of God's face more bitter than death; and again and again besought them to avoid all manner of sin, and the first approach of it.

The Christians then shook hands with him, and some, I have no doubt, were in tears. Thus the wanderer was restored.

As I have neglected to keep record of many events which would have interested you, I will just take what comes to hand. A note has been given me by a young woman, to send down in the schooner to her sister, who is leading a wicked life at Victoria. She has succeeded in reclaiming one of her sisters, and hence she wrote again to this one. [N.B. These women did not leave this settlement for Victoria; they were from Fort Simpson.]

"*Metlahkahtlah.*

"My dear Sister—I send this little news to you. I very much wish to see you, my sister. I tell you sometimes I very much cry because I remember your way not right. I

* *Vide* "Recent Intelligence," Church Missionary Intelligencer, July 1864.

want you to hear what I speak to you. Come now, my sister, I hope you will return and live in your own place. Do not you persevere to follow bad ways. You must try to forsake your way; repent from your heart. You hear our Saviour Jesus Christ. Cast all your bad ways on Jesus. He know to save us when we die. I very happy because I see my brother and sister come again. I thank God because He hear always cry about you.

"I am, your crying Sister,

"ELIZA PALEY."

I am happy to tell you our secular affairs are still having God's blessing upon them, and are prospering. Ten of our young men are now away trading with the surrounding tribes, and others are going.

I have also five employed in the schooner, and I am about putting the vessel entirely into the hands of the Indians.

I have ordered the agents at Victoria to have Samuel Pelham registered as master, and I have made John Tait supercargo. I know it is a great risk, and I may be blamed; but I take the step in God's name, and do so without fear or misgiving.

All our gardens, about 140 in number, are all looking well.

Our village work and building are progressing steadily, and I trust I shall soon have the Mission buildings complete, and without having to put down any of the cost to your account.

Recent Intelligence.

BISHOP CROWTHER AT LAGOS, &c.

ON a previous occasion we referred to the gratifying reception which Bishop Crowther met with at Sierra Leone. Additional information respecting his proceedings will be found in extracts from letters, which we now publish.

The Rev. James White, our native minister at Otta, in the Egba province of Yoruba, between Lagos and Abbeokuta, in a communication recently received from him, thus refers to the Bishop's arrival at Lagos—

Aug. 22, 1864—Anticipating the arrival of Bishop Crowther by the mail from England, I left for Lagos this morning for the purpose of welcoming him.

Aug. 23—This day the Rev. W. Morgan, Mr. Pearse, and myself, met at the Rev. T. B. Macaulay's, purposing to go in a body to receive the Bishop on shore, but we were soon informed that he had landed, and was at the Government house. We proceeded, therefore, to meet him, when we espied him coming, together with Mr. Mackenzie, accompanied by the Rev. J. A. Lamb. On our meeting we bade him a hearty welcome, and expressed our joy at seeing him again. He received us most warmly. Mr. Lamb returned home, and we accompanied him, first to his son's, and then to his own residence, where we spent much time with him. He had scarcely a moment's respite, for visitors came from all parts of the town to see him. The Bishop signified to us his intention of holding a special ordination on the morrow for the Rev. Mr. Mackenzie, acting chaplain at Cape Coast, who proceeded, with the Bishop, to this place, for the purpose of receiving priests' orders.

Aug. 24: *St. Bartholomew's-day* — Divine service was held at Mr. Lamb's church, Okofaji. The Rev. L. Nicholson read the prayers, and Mr. Lamb preached the ordination sermon, from Matt. v. 16. The sermon being over, the ordination service commenced, in which the Bishop was assisted by Messrs. Lamb and Nicholson. The ceremony being over, the sacrament of the Lord's Supper was administered to as many as were disposed to receive it.

This being the first ordination held at Lagos, and the first performed by a black bishop, there are few occasions more grand, more solemn, more novel, and exciting greater interest and curiosity than this, and every right-minded man, who is an eye-witness of the solemnity, cannot but leave the place deeply impressed, and constrained to say, "What has God wrought!" In Bishop Crowther we behold the top-stone of the spiritual temple of Jehovah, that was in building in Africa by the Church Missionary Society above half a century ago, put on; and we cannot but congratulate that Society for the success which has crowned all their efforts in West Africa. It is an event which calls forth the gratitude and praise of every individual interested in Africa and its cause, for enabling the Society to bring their work to this present finished state. The Lord hath indeed done great things for us, whereof we are glad.

The "Anglo-African," of Oct. 29th, briefly refers to the Bishop's further proceedings—

H.M.S. "Investigator" left Lagos on the 27th of August, having on board Bishop Crowther and his two sons, and Mr. Robins, artist, for a passage np the Niger. She was towed down to the mouth of the Nun by H.M.S. "Rattlesnake." On arrival there she was joined by Dr. Eales, Lieutenant Sandys, first lieutenant of the "Rattlesnake," as second in command, and Lieutenant Bourchier, R.M.L.I., to remain at Lukoja instead of Dr. Baikie, who was to proceed to England. The bar of the Nun being crossed in safety, the "Investigator" proceeded up the river on the 31st. She was very heavily laden with luggage and stores. No signs of hostility were shown by any of the villages: on the contrary, they seemed anxious to communicate, and pointed to palm-oil puncheons, several of which were seen in the villages passed the first three or four days. At the Mission stations of Onitsha and Gbebe all were well. At the latter place Bishop Crowther and his two sons left the ship. At Lukoja they met Dr. Baikie, whose little settlement was in a thriving condition. Dr. Baikie accompanied the expedition to Bida, and a very satisfactory visit was paid to Masaba, the powerful Mohammedan King of Nupe. The "Investigator" this year passed up a very narrow, winding creek, to within eight miles of Bida. This creek has never been navigated before, and great difficulty was experienced in ascending and descending it. All the men and officers enjoyed excellent health, and all were pleased and interested with their trip. The general opinion on board is that the Niger is a magnificent river, and that trade, in the most valuable products of Africa, would be abundant, and most lucrative to us, if factories were established at different stations on the river, and a steamer provided to carry the produce collected down to the mouth. On descending, Lieutenant Bourchier left at Lukoja, and Mr. Robins remained with him, with the consent of the commander of the "Investigator." Dr. Baikie and Bishop Crowther returned to the mouth of the Nun, and will come to Lagos by the mail, the former to proceed to England. The two Messrs. Crowther, jun., remained at Gbebe.

At the mouth of the Nun they found the West-African Company's Factory had been erected by Captain Derecourt, of the schooner "Manchester." Trade in palm-oil there was abundant: powder and muskets in great demand. Land was granted by the chief of Ida, a fine town above Onitsha, for a Mission settlement. The "Investigator" was fifty-seven days in the river. The following presents were sent down by Masaba, viz. for Her Majesty the Queen, a large four-horned ram from Bornou, a valuable mat, and country cloth of native manufacture. For the Governor of Lagos, a horse; and many other presents were given to the officers.

King Masaba also wished them to take, as presents for the Queen, two fine camels and an ostrich, but it was found impossible to bring them in the ship.

HURRICANES IN INDIA.

On Oct. 5th, the first day of the Doorga Poojah, Calcutta was visited by a dread calamity. The previous day the barometer was nearly at its usual height; but early on the morning of the 5th it commenced to fall rapidly. Then came the cyclone, travelling from S. S. E. in a north-westerly direction, the centre, or vortex of the wind passing, at its shortest distance from Calcutta, between two and three in the afternoon, some fifty miles to the south-west.

It then appears to have described a curved track, taking a north-easterly course, passing between Calcutta and Burdwan, and crossing the eastern districts towards Kishnagurh and Kooshtea. The rate at which the vortex travelled was slow, not more than ten to fifteen miles an hour.

Beginning at north-east, the gale veered "gradually to east, then very rapidly shifted to south-east, then round to south, and finally to south-west, when it abated. The most critical point was the sudden shift to south-east, when the squalls were heaviest; and, it was at this time that ships parted from their moorings in greatest numbers, the mooring tackles, or their cables, snapping with the sudden jerk in a new direction."

Most of the shipping in port lie along the eastern or Calcutta side of the Hooghly, with their heads up stream in a northerly direction, in tiers of from two to five abreast, in one continuous line, extending, with few breaks, for about three miles from Armenian Ghat to below Kidderpore. They are moored by heavy tackles secured to anchors laid down at regular intervals, each ship having in general two cables out to the two buoys ahead from opposite hawse pipes: astern they are moored in a similar manner. Each buoy, or rather mooring, has therefore in general four cables attached, tending to pull it in as many different directions. The buoys in most cases having four ships moored to them, and seldom less than two, there is little room left for them to play beyond the rise and fall of the tide. The cables are drawn pretty tight, and the successive tiers thus form a nearly unyielding whole—a floating, but too rigid a structure, as the event proved. The wind from the eastward driving broadside on to these comparatively immovable masses caused a tremendous strain on the mooring tackles, and took them on their weakest point, the force they are chiefly intended to resist being that of the tide on stem or stern in a direction fore and aft.

When this sudden pressure from the east came upon the shipping, the stern moorings gave away, and the first tier, forging ahead, disappeared to leeward through the mist. They were soon followed by others, and, scattered helplessly about, they drifted along "in great numbers, in indescribable confusion, smashing and fouling each other with masts, and spars, and sails, in every variety of wreck, some mere hulks, dismasted and swept, others in perfect trim."

The river was now an awful sight. The wind had by this time shifted to the southward, and blew, if possible, with greater fury directly up the stream, and soon set up a short irregular surge, sometimes blown flat, sometimes forming a misty union with the air. The gusts tore the water along in great strips and masses of spray, and with the rain it was so thick at times that hardly any thing could be made out.

Thus, hour after hour, the appalling strife continued. Huge trees were tossed about as if they were wisps of straw; the crash and din were incessant.

The natives were paralyzed, and could do nothing. The storm beat and roared like successive discharges of artillery: it tore down verandahs as if they had been of tinder; and after all this had lasted several hours it was seen, as when the universe is at unrest it is always seen, that man could do nothing but hope and wait. In the midst of the disaster there was one circumstance to be grateful for—the catastrophe had happened by daylight. Its horrors would have been vastly aggravated if it had fallen upon us in the darkness of night. But the desolation of that day will never be forgotten. It lies upon us all now like a heavy personal trouble. We have been in one of those situations when the strongest among us is as a little child, and when mankind look on awe-stricken at the manifestation of God's power, and dread some nameless evil. We behold what a few hours of a mere strong wind can destroy, and realize that it is even thus that all the works of men's hands must pass away, and all their thoughts perish; that we can labour at our puny purposes only while the Eternal wills it; that all our triumphant deeds are foolishness to Him who "maketh the earth empty, and maketh it waste, and turneth it upside down, and scattereth abroad the inhabitants thereof."

For a hundred miles round Calcutta gloom and desolation have been spread. The loss of life has been great, the misery inflicted extreme. Would that the heathen might be led to recognise in this the power of God, and listen the more readily to the still small voice of Gospel truth, speaking peace by Jesus Christ!

But, we regret to say, it is not Calcutta alone that has been stricken. We have, in another part of this Number, introduced a review of our Mission work in the Telugu country, with Masulipatam as its centre. It is here, on this part of the coast, that another tremendous cyclone fell with a devastating stroke on Nov. 1st, causing great destruction; nor has our Mission escaped. Our European brethren are, we trust, all safe; but there has been, we fear, loss of life, as regards the Christian natives, and great wreck of Missionary property. The following letter from our Missionary, the Rev. J. Sharp, to his parents, contains, as yet, all the information which has reached us—

Nov. 7—When you receive this you must give humble thanks to our Heavenly Father, through Jesus Christ, that I am alive to write it. Last Tuesday (November 1) was windy, more or less, all day, and rainy. Between four and five P.M. it became very much so. I got home from school soon after five, and we had some dinner under great difficulties. Afterwards the servants all went to their homes, and we fastened up. But the wind kept becoming more violent, and blew from all quarters; the rain streamed in torrents into the house, and the noise of the elements was deafening. I ran about, fastening doors and windows as well as I could, moving the furniture away from the stream of rain, and baling out the water, my wife helping me most energetically. But the doors and windows began to come off their hinges, and break their fastenings. We blocked them up with all the heavy furniture we could get, but all in vain. At last, between eleven and twelve, we found water rushing into the house, and rising most rapidly. Every thing began to float. The house floor is raised a yard or more above the compound, yet the water inside was above our knees, and we knew not how much higher it might get, for it was from the sea, two miles off. Mrs. Sharp was bent on going out to the back of the house, and trying to cross to the nearest house, but I knew how deep and muddy it must be, and would not hear of it. We then tried to go outside, and climb the staircase, which goes from the verandah to the house-top. Twice Mrs. Sharp was perfectly unable to advance, from the water, wind, and rain, which struck us like hailstones. The third time we succeeded in reaching the staircase, and climbed it on hands and knees. Mrs. Sharp was all but blown over. We crawled along the top into one of the elevations of the roof, and just managed to get inside among the rafters. The wind and rain beat upon us, and we had little on but night-clothes. We had to keep one another warm by constant rubbing, and felt at times overpoweringly sleepy. A light, which we left below, shone through the chinks of the ceiling, and was a great comfort to us, as it showed that the water had not risen high enough to extinguish it. We prayed often, and little expected to see the dawn, for the walls shook with the wind and waves, and, I thought, would certainly fall. But we were heard, and preserved till the dawn came —an unspeakable relief. The staircase was all but gone, but we were able to descend it when the storm abated. The desolation around is indescribable: all our out-houses flat, our furniture carried away for hundreds of yards, trees down, many houses fallen, and hundreds of corpses. The Sharkeys lost thirty-three girls. Other native Christians and East Indians are gone. The Europeans are almost all alive. We have had great difficulty to get food. One day I got, very thankfully, some horse-grain. Mrs. Sharp's horse is gone; mine lamed. Every thing around is ruined, but we are alive. Let us be thankful.

Just as we were going to press, we received the following letters from our Secretary at Madras, the Rev. W. Gray—

Nov. 12—I will postpone all other matters to let you know, by the mail just come in, of the sad calamity to Masulipatam. Enclosed is an extract respecting it from one of the daily papers. Though the cyclone swept over Masulipatam on the night of the 1st inst., I have not had a word direct from any of our beloved friends there yet, and all I have heard is from Brother Darling, in a letter just come to hand. He gives a most appalling account, but I have every hope that, as he heard it from a native, it may not be accurate. He says (writing from Bezwara, on November 7th)—"You will be concerned to hear that we have not yet had any direct communication with our dear friends in Masulipatam since the night of the storm, and there has been no *tappal*. Mr. Wilson, the head assistant collector, has received expresses, from which we learn that nearly the whole of Masulipatam and its suburbs have been submerged by the sea, which rolled in for several miles. All European lives have been saved, bnt many East Indians and thousands of natives have perished. He has also been asked to send supplies of grain from this place, and coolies to help to bury the dead. A pestilence is feared. He has learned no more particulars, but we hear dreadful accounts of the distress from natives who have escaped, and come over to Bezwara. I do not know what to say about the rumours which reach us, or whether we can credit all that we hear, but the suffering is doubtless very awful. I give you the worst, as I have received it. I saw a respectable Brahmin this morning, who declared that what he stated is true. He said that all our Missionaries are safe, but that Mr. Noble had a narrow escape, having been found nearly dead. Many of the converts had perished. All the girls of Mrs. Sharkey's boarding-school were killed, also Mallazza and his wife; Bushanam's wife and Ratnam's wife and children, but Bushanam and Ratnam had escaped. Mr. Sharkey's boarding-school boys had also escaped. The Mission house, as well as many other European houses, had been washed away. Oh that I could contradict any part of this sad intelligence! I shall write again as soon as we hear any thing authentic."

It was only a few days before that I had heard from Mr. Darling of the great damage done to Bezwara also by the cyclone. His own house had been in part blown down, but no injury of person had been sustained.

P.S.—*Nov.* 13—I have just received another letter from Mr. Darling, enclosing a short line from Mr. Sharp.

Mr. Sharp says—"My dear Darling, Colonel Anderson told us yesterday that you and the Ellingtons had suffered much by the cyclone, so one line of sympathy and joy that you are all alive. So are we, by God's great mercy. The sea came into our house about a yard deep, with awful violence: we, with the greatest risk and difficulty, got to the top of the house. I can't tell the story now. Every thing is ruined, and hardly a habitable room in the station. Thirty-three of the Sharkeys' girls, Adiamma and Prakasham (Bushanam's wife and little son), Mallazza and Fanny, Mamazza and his family, with hundreds upon hundreds drowned. . . . The whole place one mass of desolation and corpses. . . ."

Mr. Darling adds—"Mr. Noble and all his house, including servants, are safe."

Extract from a Madras Daily Newspaper, dated November 12, 1864.

The Madras Government have forwarded to us the subjoined extract from a letter in which the collector in the Kistna District describes the fearful effects of the hurricane which has just passed over Masulipatam. The letter will best tell its own sad tale. It requires no comment, and we are sure that the first feeling of all who read it will be, that energetic measures should be taken without a moment's delay to relieve the wide-spread misery occasioned by this terrible disaster. It comes home to us with far greater force than even the Calcutta tragedy, for it has happened in our own Presidency, and the sufferers are allied to us by ties which it is our first duty as citizens to respect. The public will be rejoiced to learn that the Madras Government have lost no time in furnishing "medicines, stores, and such essentials." But still, private assistance should be, as soon as possible, forthcoming. We earnestly trust that the Government will lose no time in convening a public meeting to devise measures for organizing a relief fund. We venture to promise, on behalf of the community, that such a step will meet with universal and most cordial support. We would also suggest that the fund should be extended to the relief of the sufferers at Cuddalore.

"*Masulipatam, November* 3.

"MY DEAR ——,

"I have to report the most fearful calamity to this place. On the night of the 1st November a cyclone commenced at 7 P.M., and continued to increase in force until twelve, from whence it gradually decreased until daylight. At nine or ten P.M. the sea rose and swept over the whole place, inundating the entire town, and washing away whole streets. It rose a foot or so in my house, and more; three or four feet in some others. Every house in the cantonment is gutted, and I should imagine four-fifths of the town are totally destroyed. Not a single house has escaped serious injury. Most providentially there have been no deaths amongst the Europeans. Amongst the East-Indian community, Mrs. Jameson, and Mr. and Mrs. Scott of the Engineer's Department, and Mr. Carr, have been killed. The native dead may be counted, I fear, by thousands.

"The typhoon extended certainly twenty miles inland, I do not know how much further. The treasury has been blown down, but the boxes are there—the records all destroyed. I fear the store of medicine in the dispensary will have been spoiled; also in the regimental hospital.

"There is rice in the bazaar now, and I do not anticipate scarcity of food. Thousands, however, are houseless, and must perish if not assisted. I wish you could get me sanction to spend what is necessary in that way, and in clearing ruins, and burying the dead. The latter work I am doing as fast as possible. I want sanction for 30,000 rupees, to be spent, if necessary. I trust it may not be necessary to spend so much. I have been out the last five hours, and am dead beat."

CHINA.—FUH-CHAU.

FUH-CHAU FU (*i.e.* "Happy city"), or Hokchui, as it is called by the inhabitants, the capital of the province of Fuh-kien (*i.e.* "Happily established"), is situated in latitude 26° 5′ north, and longitude 119° 20′ east, on the northern side of the river Min, and about thirty-four miles from its mouth. It lies in a plain, surrounded by hills, and watered by the Min, and which is thus alike beautiful and fertile. Suburbs extend from the city to the river, which is three miles distant, and stretch along its banks. A small islet in the middle of the river has been rendered available for the construction of a singular stone bridge, 420 paces long, which connects the banks. North of the island it reposes on forty, and south of the island on nine solid stone piers.

The city itself is surrounded by a wall thirty feet high and twelve feet wide at the top. It is divided into wards and neighbourhoods, each of which is under its own police and headmen, who are responsible for the peace of the district entrusted to their care. The walls, which are eight miles in circumference, enclose several hills; one to the south-east, covered with dwellings, and another to the north, surmounted by a watch-tower. To the south are the Wu-shih-shan, or Black-stone hills, a beatifully wooded spot, about 250 feet above the plain, where many temples and pavilions have been built. Here is the British consulate, and, on the same hill, the Mission houses of the Church Missionaries.

The surrounding country is divided by serpentine canals into plats of greater or less extent, and is dotted with hamlets and cottages, or, where the ground is higher, with graves and tombstones.

The province contains 57,000 square miles and 15,000,000 of people, the population of the city being about 1,000,000. They speak a dialect peculiarly their own, and possess decidedly marked characteristics, which distinguish them as amongst the most enterprising, hardy, and industrions portion of a great industrious nation.

And what is the spiritual state of these many millions? The hills outside the city are reserved for burying-places, and there the dead lie in vast numbers. These dead are the sombre type of the existing generation, from whose living masses these cemeteries are being continually recruited, for these mouldering bones and ashes are not more destitute of natural life than the busy millions around are of the life of God.

The Rev. Stephen Johnson, of the American Board of Missions, was the first Protestant Missionary who occupied Fuh-chau, landing there Jan. 2nd, 1846. Four years subsequently the Church Missionary Society sent thither the Rev. Messrs. Welton and Jackson as its first Missionaries. Since then we have lost by death Mr. Welton, who died in England in 1858, his constitution having been utterly broken down by six years' Missionary effort in China; the Rev. F. M'Caw and Mrs. M'Caw, of whom the latter died soon after her arrival in the country, in a short time being followed by her husband: more recently we have lost our valued brother, the Rev. George Smith.

Our Missionaries at this city, at the present time, are the Rev. Messrs. Wolfe and Cribb; and we now introduce some recent communications from Mr. Wolfe, which, after this brief sketch, will, we think, be more interesting to our readers. They are dated Sept. 17th—

I am sure you and the Committee will be glad to hear of an addition to the number of disciples here, however small; so that I wish to inform you, that on Sunday, the 4th inst. I admitted into the visible church of Christ, by baptism, two very interesting young Chinamen. The addition of only two may seem a small matter or cause of rejoicing to some who know not the value of souls, nor the difficulties that are to be overcome in the conversion of a heathen to Christianity; but I am sure, to us who labour among the Chinese, and witness the cold indifference with which they listen to the message of redeeming love, and the contempt and scorn which have to be endured by those who abandon the superstitions and follies of their countrymen for the religion of Christ, the fact that two have been added to our little body is a matter which fills us with joy and thankfulness. These two young men have been under instruction for some time, and have thus made such rapid progress in the knowledge of divine things, that, when they earnestly asked for baptism, I felt I could not refuse it to them. My good and faithful catechist, Kin Taik ("Seeker of souls"), was the means of their conversion. This good man is worth gold. On the occasion of the baptism the doors of the chapel were left open, and the heathen, who wished to witness the ceremony, were allowed to do so. I am thankful to say not one of them abused the privilege, and every one was as quiet as possible. After the first lesson, which was read by one of the catechists, the two candidates were led up to the communion-rails by two of the native brethren, Kin Taik and Knong Me, and then, before God and the church, and before a number of heathen, they pledged themselves to be the disciples of Jesus, and willing to follow Him through evil and good report. They publicly renounced all their former superstitions. They were then baptized, and received in the beautiful words of our service, "into the congregation of Christ's church." The heathen appeared much interested. I observed among them one of our bitterest opponents, a Confucianist, who, although he cast many a bitter and contemptuous glance at the catechumens, did not attempt to interrupt us. The address was delivered by the catechist, Kin Taik, from Colossians ii. 12. He showed the nature of baptism, and the duty of all those who have put on Christ. It was a very excellent discourse, and showed that the preacher himself experienced that spiritual life of which the apostle speaks—that he had risen with Christ to a life of righteousness from a life of spiritual death. It is cheering to be able to speak thus of any of our converts, and I do not remember the day when I was so much cheered as while listening to this good man addressing his Christian countrymen, and exhorting the newly-baptized, his own spiritual children, to live worthy of their profession, and of the name by which they were called. The two young men are respectable scholars, according to the scholarship of the country; and though they are not entitled to be ranked among the literary class, they are tolerably well acquainted with the Chinese classic characters. One of them speaks the court dialect as fluently as his native patois. This circumstance may be of use to the Mission in some future time, as there are in the city upwards of 12,000 persons of the same class with himself, and using the same dialect, who never yet had the Gospel preached to them. At present the young man is foreman in a commercial establishment in the city; but I fear that already the storm is rising, and that he will be compelled to resign his situation, as he will not work on the Sabbath, nor any longer be a party to the deceit and fraud inseparably connected with a Chinese mercantile house.

In perusing these accounts of one and another brought out from the darkness of heathenism to the acknowledgment of the one true God, and Jesus Christ whom He has sent, our readers will bear in mind the great difficulties which the early converts, in a large heathen community, have to contend with. They are, as Mr. Wolfe observes, hated and despised, and it is no easy matter to give up all for Christ. Yet this every Chinaman does when he embraces sincerely the religion of Jesus; a fiery trial, which, however, has been endured by many of them.

May the lives of our Missionaries be prolonged; may great grace and good health be given them; and may they be spared to see a congregation of numerous and earnest converts raised up, which, in the city of Fuh-chau, shall be as a light in a dark place.

HOW GOD PREPARES HIS PEOPLE FOR ENLARGED SERVICE.

THE Lord has a great work to be accomplished upon earth. Men have been taught to pray, "Thy kingdom come; thy will be done on earth, as it is in heaven;" and that prayer shall have its full accomplishment. It is not His purpose that the world should remain in its present state of disaffection to his high authority. "I have sworn by myself, and the word is gone out of my mouth in righteousness, and shall not return, that unto me every knee shall bow, every tongue shall swear." He who spake these words claims the earth as his rightful conquest, as the spoil which He has wrested from the enemy. The god of this world had offered to instal Him into the possession of the kingdoms of the world and the glory of them, if only, abandoning the interests of his Father, he would become his vassal, and recognise his supremacy by an act of worship. The Captain of our salvation, rejecting all compromise, wrestled with him in mortal conflict, and prevailed. And now, at the Father's hands He has received the world as his dominion, and as the reward of his work. "Ask of me, and I shall give thee the heathen for thine inheritance, and the uttermost parts of the earth for thy possession." They are his by divine purpose and appointment; they shall be his also in fruition, and by a universal acknowledgment of his authority: "all kings shall fall down before Him, all nations serve Him."

Meanwhile, it is the time of warfare. Between the house of David and the house of Saul there was long war; but "David waxed stronger and stronger." Weapons have been provided by which this warfare may be carried on, until the grand consummation be attained, and great voices in heaven shall announce, "The kingdoms of this world are become the kingdoms of our Lord and of his Christ; and He shall reign for ever and ever." These weapons are not carnal, for carnal weapons would avail little in a conflict such as this. They are weapons of offence which, in the world's estimation, are utterly contemptible, as much so as the means adopted by the Israelites were to the men of Jericho, when instead of the battle array there was the peaceable procession, and instead of the sword and spear there were the priests blowing the rams' horns before the ark of the Lord. Yet before these despised and apparently unsuitable means, the wall of the city fell down flat, because God's power wrought mightily: and thus, although the weapons of our warfare be not carnal, yet are they "mighty through God to the pulling down of strongholds."

So noble is the warfare, so sure the victory. But where are the soldiers to use the weapons? for angels cannot wield them. If, by an experimental acquaintance with the Gospel, they were qualified to use these weapons, they would, without an exception, offer themselves for the work. A human agency is needed—man's co-operation. How is it that the men who willingly offer themselves for the Lord's work are comparatively few? It seems to be now as in the days of Deborah and Barak. Noble tribes there were who responded willingly to the call of Barak. They rendered each what aid they could. "Out of Ephraim was there a root of them against Amalek; after thee Benjamin among thy people; out of Machir came down governors; and out of Zebulun they that handle the pen of the writer. And the princes of Issachar were with Deborah. Zebulun and Naphtali were a people that jeoparded their lives unto the death in the high places of the field." But there were others that skulked and kept away. "For the divisions of Reuben there were great searchings of heart. Gilead abode beyond Jordan; and why did he remain in ships? Asher continued on the sea-shore, and abode in his breaches." And how is it there are so many at the present time making a profession of godliness, but yet keeping aloof on the outskirts of the battle, and rendering no effectual assistance? How is it that they who go forward to the front are so ill supported, that, when they call for help, there are few to come? How is it that, as they fall at their posts, there is such reluctance to be baptized for the dead, and to take up the sword which has fallen from their grasp? Are the Lord's professing people up to their work? Are they, in spiritual tone and vigour, equal to the demands of the time in which they live? Is there but a little love, and a feeble service, when there ought to be much love and devoted service? And how shall this be corrected? How shall devotedness of service to the promotion of the Gospel, in all ranks and amidst all nations, be increased?

Information of a valuable character appears to be afforded in the sixth chapter of Isaiah. That chapter does not refer to the prophet's conversion. He had been already for some time in the discharge of the prophetical office (see Isaiah i. 1); and was so acquainted with the details of the long reign of Uzziah, that he became their historian (2 Chron. xxvi. 22). Moreover, the prophecies which have place in the previous chapters bear upon them the stamp of a gracious man, who knew the evil of sin, and the need of being cleansed from its defilement. What, then, does it refer to? A deepening of the work of grace already wrought in his heart.

An illustration will explain what is meant, one taken from the process of wood-engraving.

A block is prepared of the size and thickness required. It is then, on one side, made exquisitely plain and smooth, so as to receive a drawing. On this the design to be engraved is drawn in blacklead; and, when the drawing is finished, it looks very pleasing; but it is superficial, liable to be rubbed off, and unable to impress itself on other objects.

This, therefore, is only the beginning of the work. The strokes of the pencil mark so much of the block as is to be spared or left standing: all the rest is to be cut away. This the engraver proceeds to do with the points of very sharp knives, or with chisels and gravers. The design is now no longer on the surface, but in the wood—wrought into it—and now it cannot be rubbed off. You may break the block, but you cannot remove the impress it bears. And now it is able to re-produce itself in impressions. The printing-ink is then applied, and the process is managed in the same way as letter-printing.

Now the drawing of the design on the smooth block is like the work of parents in Christian education. With much care they pencil out the lines of divine truth on the young minds they have to train for God; but the Spirit of God must sink the teaching into the heart, and make it inwrought into the character, else it will have no permanency; and thus, sometimes, it is unhappily rubbed off.

In this work the Spirit uses the word which is quick and powerful, and sharper than any two-edged sword, &c. In carrying it out he humiliates nature, lowers the man in his opinion of himself; as he does so, convincing him of the value of divine truth, and giving Him, who is the great object of that truth, increasing prominence in the character. He lowers self, and lifts Christ up. (2 Cor. iii. 3; v. 5.) Thus the transfer of the image of Christ to the heart is fixed, and then it becomes re-productive. The man works off impressions, and on the acts and services in which he is engaged puts the stamp of Christ. (Col. iii. 17.)

Now it is possible that a design might be cut into the wood, but not with sufficient depth. Enough of the natural block might not be cut away, and thus the lines and features of the design might not stand out with sufficient prominence. In this case the impressions worked off from such an engraving would be feeble and indistinct; and so with Christian truth in the character: it may have been received and dealt with experimentally; and yet, in order that the Christian character may be distinct in feature as well as strong and vigorous in action, it may require in all its tracery to be deepened.

And that was precisely the prophet's case. He was designed for an arduous work. It was needful that the features of his gracious character should stand out in bold relief. The Spirit of God, therefore, wrought upon the old lines, upon the old experiences, and deepened them.

This is what is wanted, we believe, at the present day. There is a great work to be done. There are many opposers and gainsayers. It is a time for the Lord's people to be more bold, vigorous, active; to be more decided themselves, and more earnest in stamping their impress upon others. In this respect the work of grace in the heart needs to be deepened.

It was this Peter experienced—"When thou art converted, strengthen thy brethren." Not that he had not been converted before, but that the work was now deepened. He knew more of himself, more of his Saviour; he trusted himself less, and his Lord more. And so, when in this sense converted, he was anxious that the same reduplicative process should be wrought in them, whom he had been instrumental in bringing to the faith of Christ. (1 Peter vi. 10.)

Let it be observed that this important work is wrought by the Spirit of God on the heart, not by means of novelties, not by excitement, but by the same old truths operating on the old experiences. The sense of sin was deepened; and the renovating action of the Gospel rendered more decided and powerful. The prophet brought into the presence of the Triune God was abased under a sense of his defilement, and as he cried, "Woe is me! for I am undone; because I am a man of unclean lips, and I dwell in the midst of a people of unclean lips, for mine eyes have seen the King, the Lord of Hosts," the angel flew, having the live coal taken from off the altar, and laid it upon his lips, saying, "Lo, this hath touched thy lips: and thine iniquity is taken away, and thy sin purged." A beautiful emblem of the application of Christ's sorrow to the sorrow of the heart, so as to give beauty for ashes, the oil of joy for mourning, the garments of praise for the spirit of heaviness.

The mercy of God coming in with such vivid action on the keen sense of sin, bringing with it healing influences, changing the midnight of the soul into a clear day, without a cloud in the firmament, or a doubt to interfere with the full enjoyment of the sense of reconciliation, filled the man with gratitude and thankfulness. Love, the grand motive power, occupied his soul, like the glory of the Lord when it entered into and filled the temple; and when that Triune God, who had dealt so graciously with him, was pleased to indicate his need of human agency, with an unhesitating surrender of himself to the service of the Lord, the prophet answered, "Here am I; send me."

Is there not now the same appeal, on the Lord's part, to those who profess to be his people? Does it not come from heathendom, from Christendom, from home, from abroad? Does not the boldness of scepticism rebuke our coldness, and the ingenuity of the promoters of evil summon to a like ingenuity for good those who would promote the Lord's cause? Tidings reach us from distant lands of great disasters, sanguinary wars; of tribulations, in which our fellow-men are involved, their earthly prospects all obscured, while, alas! in the direction of eternity, all is dark too. Are the Lord's people doing all they can? Could they not do more, pray more, give more, labour more? Yes, if they loved more. Let, then, those who are charged with the ministration of the word aim at the deepening of the work of grace in the heart; and may the Spirit of God crown the effort!

Come, Holy Ghost, eternal God,
  Proceeding from above,
Both from the Father and the Son,
  The God of grace and love;
Visit our minds, into our hearts
  Thy heavenly grace inspire;
That truth and godliness we may
  Pursue with full desire.

Thou art the very Comforter
  In grief and all distress:
The heav'nly gift of God most high,
  No tongue can it express;
The fountain and the living spring
  Of joy celestial;
The fire so bright, the love so sweet,
  The unction spiritual.

Thou in thy gifts art manifold,
  By them Christ's church doth stand;
In faithful hearts thou writ'st thy law,
  The finger of God's hand.
According to thy promise, Lord,
  Thou givest speech with grace;
That through thy help God's praises may
  Resound in every place.

O Holy Ghost, into our minds
  Send down thy heav'nly light;
Kindle our hearts with fervent zeal,
  To serve God day and night.

THE DURBAR AT LAHORE.

In whatever light the Punjab be regarded, whether in a military point of view, commercially, or as regards the energetic character of its population, it must be admitted that there is no part of India of more value to Great Britain.

Its military importance was demonstrated at the time of the great mutiny. Instead of being paralyzed by its isolation from Calcutta, it became a new centre, and from thence were those measures put forth which arrested the temerity of the mutineers, and by the fall of Delhi, broke the right arm of the great conspiracy. How much more is not its importance enhanced now, when the Sindh railway from Kurrachee to Hydrabad, the Indus flotilla between Hydrabad and Mooltan, and the near completion of the railway from Mooltan to Lahore and Umritsur, have brought the land of the five rivers so much nearer to England, and increased the facilities for the conveyance of troops and heavy stores.

And as it commands the North-west Provinces, so is the Punjab equally valuable as a defensive position against any danger which might threaten from the north-west. The passes of the Suleiman range, the Khyber, Bolan, and others of less note, these gates of entrance into the plains of India from the north-west, are in British hands, and can be closed or opened as they who approach from the uplands of Asia come with peaceful or hostile intentions.

Commercially, the position of the Punjab is such as becomes a great emporium, while its attractiveness as a rendezvous for merchants is increased by its own natural resources and the characteristic energy of its people, advantages which, as its inhabitants come increasingly under the power of those grand civilizing influences which England is engaged in imparting to them, will become more and more developed. "There is, perhaps," observes Sir Alexander Burnes, "no inland country of the globe which possesses greater facilities for commerce than the Punjab, and there are few more rich in the productions of the mineral, vegetable, and animal kingdoms. Intersected by fine navigable streams, it is bounded on the west by one of the largest rivers in the world. To the north it has the fertile and the fruitful vale of Cashmere to limit its sceptre: so placed, that it can export, without trouble, its costly fabrics to the neighbouring kingdoms of Persia and Tartary, China and India. Situated between Hindustan and the celebrated *entrepots* of Central Asia, it shares the advantage of their traffic, while it is itself blessed with an exuberance of every production of the soil that is useful and nutritious to man. The productions of the Punjab relieve it from any great dependence on external resources. Its courtiers and chiefs may robe themselves in the shawls of Cashmere and the strong and beautiful silken fabrics of Mooltan. Its citizens and husbandmen may wear the cheap textures of the native cotton. Every animal may be fed on the grains indigenous to the country; and a range of mountains, entirely composed of salt, furnishes the necessary ingredient of food, while the upland parts yield condiments and fruits to season the daily bread."

This productive county, by the channel of the Indus, and the free port of Kurrachee, is now in direct communication with the western world. On the conquest of Sindh, in 1843, Lord Ellenborough's proclamation nominally opened the Indus to commerce; yet was it virtually sealed up until the beginning of 1853, when river dues were abolished. And now, as the communication between the Punjab and Kurrachee is being improved and facilitated, the raw produce will find its way, continuously and uninterruptedly, by the line of the Indus, in exchange for the manufactures of Europe. Even when in isolation from the sea, Umritsur was the grand *entrepot* for the trade with central Asia. The caravans which came down with spices and dried fruits, dyes and drugs, skins and carpets, chintzes and leather, through Peshawur, Dehra Ismael

Khan, and the Bolan Pass, deposited their loads at Umritsur. Wools and borax from Thibet, shawls and carpets from Cashmere, sugar and grain from the Doabs, all passed through this bonded warehouse of northern India. But now that its direct communication with Europe is becoming so established as to command confidence, its commercial importance will be indefinitely increased.

In these territories, favoured with so great natural advantages, on the development of which are now being brought to bear the statesmanship and scientific power of Great Britain, is located a population of nineteen millions and a half, of which nearly thirteen millions are found in the British portions of the Punjab, including the cis-Sutlej states, and the remainder in its political dependencies.

It is not, however, to be supposed that the population is equally distributed over the face of the territory. Nothing can be more remarkable than its sudden alternations of sparsity and density. Two contiguous districts often exhibit in this respect an extreme diversity. But this is easily intelligible, the population clustering where the means of irrigation are most available, and the cultivation of the soil facilitated. The submontane portion of the Punjab, about one-third, is generally fertile; the remainder being a wild tract, with exceptional strips of civilization. Towards the north, and near the Sutlej and Jumna, the cis-Sutlej states are fertile, but degenerate into sand towards the south. The trans-Sutlej states are in their upper half hilly, and even mountainous, while the portion below the hills is a rich plain. The next three Doabs, the Baree, the Rechna, and Chuch, are fertile towards the north and along the margin of the river, while towards the centre and the south the land is elevated, and covered with brushwood. In some former era, however, the waste was occupied, and in the magnificent works of the Ravee-Doab canal system of irrigation Government is preparing the way for the re-peopleing of the waste. The fourth and last Doab, the Sindh Sagur, is rugged above the salt range, and below it sandy.

The population rises in density according to the productive capabilities of the soil. In the cis-Sutlej states, the rich district of Umballa presents a population of 426 persons per square mile, while Ferozepore, with its large sandy tracts, sinks to 186 persons per square mile. In the trans-Sutlej states, Jullundur, the richest district in the Punjab, rises so high as 513; while in the Lahore division, where the rich environs of the capital melt away into a central waste, there are not more than 210 persons to a square mile. The Umritsur, Goordespoor, and Sealkote districts, although inferior in the numbers of their population to Jullundur, are far above the proportion of Lahore, presenting respectively averages of 436, 470, and 475 persons per square mile. It is in these districts which include Umritsur, the religious capital of Sikhism, and their original and peculiar territory, the Manjha, that the Sikhs, to the amount of 200,000, are chiefly congregated. Returning to the distribution of the population in the Mooltan division, the averages are low, viz. 44 and 74 persons per square mile, the country around being one vast wooded wild, and, except round Mooltan and its canals, having but little cultivation. In Dehra Ghazee Khan, and Dera Ishmael Khan districts, with their wild trans-Indus frontier, 59 and 87 persons per square mile are the proportions. Lastly, Peshawur, with one fertile valley, has 193, while the mountainous district of Kohat has only 35.

These investigations are appropriate to a Missionary periodical, for it is with population that our Missionaries have to do; and when they are confessedly few in number, the more populous districts, unless there be contravening reasons, will be selected for their location. Thus our Missionaries occupy Umritsur as a centre, itinerating from thence throughout the Manjha. Peshawur is another centre of action. They are found also at Mooltan and Dehra Ismael Khan; but although the population at these points is comparatively thin, they are nevertheless important points, and it was needful they should be occupied. Indeed, all these cities, Umritsur, with a population of 123,000; Peshawur, 54,000; Mooltan, 25,000; and Dehra Ismael Khan, 16,000, possess, from their situation, elements of increase, especially Mooltan, which promises to become a great *entrepot*, and one of the first cities in North India.

Over these dominions the sceptre of British supremacy is extended, and merciful is the influence which it exercises. What changes have taken place within twenty and six years! The Maharajah Runjeet Singh was then the lion of the Punjab; and then was enacted the *champ de drap d'or* of Ferozepore, where the Governor-General, Lord Auckland, appearing with the imposing magnificence of an Indian potentate, passed with his suite through the superb display of the Maharajah's body-guard, one troop dressed in yellow satin, with gold scarfs and shawls; another in cloth of gold, scarlet, purple, or yellow, their long beards protected from the dust by draperies of silver or gold tissue, which enveloped their heads. That grand spectacle passed away, and in a few months was succeeded by a scene of a very different character. The old lion, worn out at last by his own excesses, was laid on his death-bed. His treasure-chests in his famous fort of Govind Ghur, at Umritsur, filled with twelve millions in gold, could not buy off the dreaded enemy. The vain effort to obtain a respite was indeed made by him. His celebrated string of pearls,—300 in number, and literally the size of small marbles, all picked pearls, round and perfect in shape and colour—he gave to one temple; his favourite horses, with all their jewelled trappings, worth 300,000*l*., to another. Nay, fear dealt with him as he had dealt with Shah Soojah, extorting from him the koh-i-noor, "the mountain of light;" for although the order was not executed, he had commanded it to be sent to a third temple, in the hope of propitiating the gods. But his time was come. He died, and on the funeral pile his remains were consumed to ashes, his four very handsome wives, and five Cashmerian slave-girls burning themselves with his body, the principal wife setting fire to the pile with her own hands.

With his death the key-stone of the imperial arch he had erected fell to the ground; the concentrative power of the Sikhs was broken. On the border of the Sutlej they struck for all or nothing—to win India or vacate the throne of the Punjab. They fought and lost, and the dynasty, like the ashes of the old ruler, was scattered to the winds.

And now there is another ruler installed, and other scenes of imperial grandeur are being enacted.

On the 14th of October last the princes and chieftains of the Punjab territories assembled to welcome, on his arrival at the railway station at Lahore, the Governor-General of India. He was no stranger to them. As Sir John Lawrence, Chief Commissioner of the Punjab, they were well acquainted with him. They had known the strong hand of the Christian administrator—strong to encourage the loyal, to repress the disaffected, to correct evils and abuses, and to provide means for the amelioration of a long-oppressed and degraded population. They came to do him honour as the representative of their sovereign, and as one whom they personally honoured. There was the young Rajah of Puttiala, blazing in diamonds, whose father had so signalized himself by the important services rendered by him in the time of the mutiny.

He came ready to receive the kindly greeting almost affectionately bestowed in memory of the gallant monarch to whom the youth succeeded; and close by stood the gallant and frank successor to the indomitable old Rajah of Jheend. Then came Kupurthala, Star of India elect. Out of the same carriage which held the old friends, Lawrence, Montgomery, and Macleod, stepped also the last almost of the Sur-dar-wallah of that aspiring family who once hoped to grasp the sceptre in Lahore citadel.

These nobles introduced the Governor-General into a city which it was difficult for him to call to his remembrance, so improved had Lahore become during the few years which had elapsed since his departure from the Punjab.

The Lawrence Hall was the centre of attraction, as close to it were pitched the vast encampments of the Maharajah of Cashmere and Jummoo, and those of Puttiala and Jheend. Certainly the Asiatic is never seen to better advantage than when enthroned in tents. The grand sweep of the golden houdah of elephants, the tramp of variegated horsemen, the glitter and sheen of the dresses and accoutrements, all made up a brilliant picture. The railway station itself was a wonderful piece of successful grouping. So admirably were the police arrangements devised that not a single accident, or even inconvenient pressure, occurred. Yet almost the whole of the invited durbarees had assembled in exquisitely varied habiliments—martial, civic, ambassadorial, and even priestly. Outside, Lahore seemed to have emptied itself bodily on to every prominent mound and earthwork to catch a glimpse of the Viceroy. Frontier chieftains wagged their grim old heads, and stroked their beards, at hearing the familiar "Shabash" issue out of the former Chief Commissioner's mouth, while a pat on the back to one or two old recognised friends—and who was there that Sir John did not know, may be asked?—sent them home with delight: they had not been called to the meeting unrewarded; they had seen and shaken hands with the great ruler once more; the well-known voice had been heard, with an effect more than equivalent to that of the best orations translated through an interpreter. There, in the heart of the Punjab, was a populace of probably not less than 250,000, grouped on a plain flanked with the tents of powerful nobles and monarchs, attended by a combined retinue of perhaps altogether 80,000 men. The whole British force, European and native, if mustered, would hardly amount to one-twentieth of the above formidable armament, yet no interruption occurred. Wondrous was the scene around the Lieutenant-Governor's residence. Men of all degrees of rank, of all nations, creeds, languages, and colours, waiting patiently and contentedly in equipages of every conceivable kind, grouped under such shady spots as could be found, simply to have a word or two with "John Lawrence." Nor were they disappointed. Each had his small say, and what he heard in reply was brief paternal advice, given with frank, earnest simplicity.

On October 18th was held a public Durbar, where assembled the princes and chiefs of the Punjab. There were present two Maharajahs, one of Cashmere, attended by fourteen relatives and principal Sirdars; and the Maharajah of Puttiala, attended by twelve of his Sirdars; seven Rajahs, some by name known to us here in England, others whose titles as yet sound strange to us—Puttiala, Jheend, Kupurthala, Mundee, Maleir Kotta, Furreedkote, Chumba, Sookeit—each with attendants more or less numerous, according to their rank. Besides these princes, each of whom was honoured on his arrival and departure by the firing of a salute, there were Sirdars and Nawabs, the principal native gentlemen of the Punjab and its dependencies, and the leading chiefs on the Peshawur and Derajât frontier. The Governor-General took his seat in a Durbar under a royal salute, and then, surrounded by the civil and military officers at Lahore, addressed, in Hindustanee, the assembled chiefs to the following effect—

Maharajahs, Rajahs, and Chiefs—Listen to my words. I have come among you after an absence of nearly six years, and thank you for the kindly welcome you have given me. It is with pleasure that I meet so many of my old friends, while I mourn the loss of those who have passed away.

Princes and Chiefs—It is with great satisfaction that I find nearly 600 of you assembled around me in this Durbar. I see before me the faces of many friends. I recognise the sons of my old allies, the Maharajahs of Cashmere and Puttiala, the Sikh chiefs of Malwa and the Manjha, the Rajpoot chiefs of the hills, the Mohammedan Mulicks of Peshawur and Kohat, the Sirdars of the Derajât, of Hazara, and Delhi. All have gathered together to do honour to their old ruler.

My Friends—Let me tell you of the great interest which the illustrious Queen of England takes in all matters connected with the welfare, and comfort, and contentment, of the people of India. Let me inform you how, when I returned to my native country, and had the honour of standing in the presence of Her Majesty, how kindly she asked after the welfare of her subjects in the East. Let me tell you when that great Queen appointed me her Viceroy of India, how warmly she enjoined on me the duty of caring for your interests. Prince Albert, the consort of Her Majesty, the fame of whose greatness and goodness has spread through the whole world, was well acquainted with all connected with this country, and always evinced an ardent desire to see its people happy and flourishing.

My Friends—It is now more than eighteen years since I first saw Lahore. For thirteen years I lived in the Punjab. For many years my brother, Sir Henry Lawrence, and I, governed this vast country. You all knew him well, and his memory will ever dwell in your hearts as a ruler who was a real friend of its people. I may truly say that, from the day we exercised authority in the land, we spared neither our time, nor our labour, nor our health, in endeavouring to accomplish the work which we had undertaken. We studied to make ourselves acquainted with the usages, the feelings, and the wants of every class and race, and we endeavoured to improve the condition of all. There are few parts of this province which I have not visited, and which I hope that I did not leave in some degree the better for my visit. Since British rule was introduced, taxation of all kinds has been lightened, canals and roads have been constructed, and schools of learning have been established. From the highest to the lowest, the people have become contented, and have proved loyal. When the great military revolt of 1857 occurred, they aided their rulers most effectively in putting it down. The chiefs mustered their contingents, which served faithfully, and thousands of Punjabee soldiers flocked to our standards, and shared with the British troops the glories, as well as the hardships, of that great struggle.

Princes and Gentlemen—If it be wise for the rulers of a country to understand the language and appreciate the feelings of its people, it is as important that they should have a similar knowledge of their rulers. It is only by such means that the two classes can live happily together. To this end I urge you to instruct your sons, and even your daughters.

Among the solid advantages which you have gained from English rule, I will now only advert to one more. It has given the country many excellent administrators. Some of the ablest and kindest of my countrymen have been employed in the Punjab. Every man, from the highest to the lowest, can appreciate a good ruler. You have such men as Sir Robert Montgomery, Mr. Donald McLeod, Mr. Roberts, Sir Herbert Edwardes, Colonel Lake, and Colonel John Beecher—officers who have devoted themselves to your service.

I will now only add that I pray the great God, who is the God of all the races and all the people of this world, that He may guard and protect you, and teach you all to love justice and hate oppression, and enable you, each in his several way, to do all the good in his power. May He give you all that is for your real benefit! So long as I live, I shall never forget the years that I have passed in the Punjab, and the friends that I have acquired throughout the province.

Thereafter the chiefs and gentlemen were separately introduced to the Viceroy and Governor-General. Nuzzers were presented and Khilluts conferred.

Who is there to whom the truths of Christianity are precious, and who has enthroned the Saviour as King within his own heart, that does not in such a scene feel himself reminded of events far more glorious; as yet, future indeed, but certain to be realized, when "the kings of Tarshish and of the isles shall bring presents; the kings of Sheba and Seba offer gifts. Yea, all kings shall fall down before Him, all nations shall serve Him." Blessed shall that moment be, when, recognised as universal King, Jesus shall reign in righteousness, and execute judgment and justice on the earth; when the nations, contented under his rule, shall no longer be like the waves of the ocean, agitated by fierce winds, and tossing themselves to and fro, but when, soothed into serenity, they shall, mirror-like, reflect the goodness of the Lord.

Amongst the assembled chiefs there was one on whom especial honour was conferred. On the day before the great Durbar, the Rajah of Kupurthala was invested with the insignia of the most exalted order of the Star of India, the great princes, and, amongst others, the Maharajah of Cashmere being present at the ceremony. He was addressed by His Excellency in words to the following effect—

"Rajah Rundheer Singh, Rajah of Kupurthala—It is with much satisfaction that I find myself empowered by Her Most Gracious Majesty the Queen of England to confer on you so great a mark of her royal favour as that of the Star of British India. This honour has only been granted to those princes and chiefs who unite high rank with great personal merit. It rejoices me to instal you among the chosen number.

Your grandfather, Sirdar Futteh Singh, was a chief of considerable renown. He was the well-known leader of the Aloowalia confederacy, and the companion-in-arms of the great Maharajah Runjeet Singh. Your father, Rajah Nihal Singh, was an old friend of mine when you were yet a youth. When he passed away, your highness succeeded to his duties and his responsibilities, and have worthily discharged them. When the mutiny of 1857 broke out, you were one of the foremost chiefs of this country to do your duty, and range yourself on the side of the British Government. After the fall of Delhi, your highness headed your troops, conducted them to Oudh, and there assisted in recovering that province. For these services you received at the time much praise and liberal rewards; and now, to crown all, you are about to obtain a most signal mark of honour from Her Majesty the Queen of England and India. In the name, then, of the Queen, and by Her Majesty's commands, I now invest you with the honourable insignia of the Star of India, of which most exalted order Her Majesty has been graciously pleased to appoint you to be a Knight.

"I have addressed you in Hindustanee, in order that the princes and chiefs now present may the more readily participate in this ceremony, and that your relatives and friends may be more highly gratified; otherwise I should have spoken in English, for I know that you thoroughly understand my language. This circumstance, no doubt, has operated as a bond of union between your highness and my countrymen."

At the conclusion of the address, His Excellency placed the ribbon and the collar of the order round the Rajah's neck, and delivered to him the Star. The Viceroy, the Maharajah of Cashmere and Jummoo, and the principal Government officials present at the ceremony, then shook hands with the Rajah, and congratulated him.

We confess there is something remarkable in this. Two other chieftains there had been, who, if their lives had been prolonged, would have received the same honour—the Maharajah of Puttiala, and the Rajah of Jheend. Both, however, had passed away, and their sons and successors occupied their place. But the Rajah of Kupurthala remained; and he, whose services have been thus openly recognised and rewarded, is the only one of those assembled chieftains who as yet has openly avowed his sympathies with Christianity. He and his brother, Sirdar Bekrama Singh, were present at the Punjab Missionary Conference, held at Lahore in December and January 1862-63, the Rajah himself taking part in the discussion on the important subject of female education. Having expressed his sense of the importance of such a movement to India, he observed, that "the education of females was not forbidden by the religion of the people; but it was disrelished by the men. In many high families, especially in the Punjab, women do read—chiefly religious books. They are forbidden to learn to write, particularly among the Rajpoots, because the jealousy of their husbands makes them afraid of the power this would give them to correspond with others.

"The great difficulty was to know how to get at the females of this country. They were shut up so closely, that it was almost impossible to have access to them. This must be done through the men. He would advise that efforts be made to enlighten the men as to the advantages to be derived by their wives from education. Christian gentlemen should associate more intimately with natives of the country, and their wives would then have access to the zenanas."

That he should have thus openly identified himself with the proceedings of this Conference is precisely what we might have expected from a prince who, in his town of Kupurthala, with his family and brother, attends, on the Lord's-day, divine service in a church built at his own expense — "a noble monument of the first Indian prince, who has raised, instead of temples to Shiv and Kali, a sanctuary for the living God."

On that occasion the Conference passed the following resolution—

That the Conference desire to express their hearty sympathy with His Highness the Rajah of Kupurthala, in his desire to impart the saving truths of the Gospel to his subjects.

They believe that, in doing so, he is disinterestedly seeking the highest welfare of the people God has committed to his charge. They thankfully acknowledge the power and grace of Almighty God, which has enabled him to manifest so much liberality and zeal in the cause of Missions; thus setting an example to others, having like authority and influence, worthy of all imitation. The Conference earnestly prays that his own soul may be sanctified wholly by the same truths, and that, with many of his grateful subjects, he may wear an everlasting crown of glory with our Saviour Jesus, in the kingdom of our common God and Father.

This, moved by T. D. Forsyth, Esq., C.B., was seconded by D. F. M'Leod, Esq., C.B., in the following words—

As I believe that, with the exception, perhaps, of our respected brother Goloknath, I have had an earlier cognizance of His Highness the Rajah of Kupurthala's leanings towards the Christian faith than any one else now present, I beg cordially to support the resolution which has been proposed; and I need hardly say that, in common with all who love the Lord, I have watched the Rajah's progress with exceeding interest. When he visited me, with his brother Kunwar Suchet Singh, some years ago, at Dhurmsala, brother Goloknath being then one of the party, they refused to march on Sundays, or to make offerings at the Hindu shrines; and even then he desired to attend divine service, though deterred for the time by his followers insisting on accompanying him. He has not, as yet, formally avowed himself to be one of us, but he has set up an altar of family devotion in his own household, at which I, and others here present, have been privileged to kneel with him. And while the power of the Holy Spirit alone can complete the good work which we may hope he has begun, it is for us to pray, that the blessing from on high may be poured out upon him and his.

This tribute of Christian sympathy was as gratefully bestowed by the conference as the Star of India by the hands of the Governor-General. The investiture of the latter recognised him as a loyal feudatory of the British Crown; the former recognised him as a native prince who, convinced himself of the truth of Christianity, avowed his convictions in the presence of heathen India, and invited the other chiefs and princes to follow his example.

Would they might be induced to do so! At least, if unconvinced themselves, we trust they will refrain from opposition. There was one present on that occasion to whom we would respectfully tender that advice. It is dangerous to obstruct the course of Christianity. The people of Oude, who, during their late uprising against British power, passed through the furnace of tribulation, dare not oppose. They say—"It is evident that God has put his hand upon the head of the English nation, and for this reason there must be something good and great in the Christian religion, and the time is probably not far distant when we will embrace it."

And it would seem, also, as though God put his hand upon the head of those native princes who, by publicly identifying themselves with Christianity, lend their influence to dispel the prejudices which obstruct its progress; but let others, who oppose and repel Missionaries from their dominions, beware lest God place his foot upon their neck.

THE CYCLONE AT MASULIPATAM.

The details of the desolation wrought at this city by the influx of the sea, forced by the hurricane beyond its wonted bounds, are now reaching us, and they are so numerous, that to particularize them seems nearly impossible. The sorrows of years appear to be accumulated within the brief space of a single night. Such a night of horrors as that of November 1st, at Masulipatam, has not often occurred in the mournful annals of the human race.

Masulipatam, on the western shore of the Bay of Bengal, and on the south side of a branch of the river Kistnah, is situated on an extensive plain, stretching westward to the Ghâts. In the midst of this swamp, which is overflowed by the sea at spring-tides, stands the fort. About a mile and a half north-west of the fort there is a slightly elevated ridge, and where it falls so as to be little raised above the level of the swamp, stands the pettah, or native town, the population of which has been variously estimated at from 60,000 to 90,000.

At three o'clock on the afternoon of Tuesday, November 1st, the wind was a little high, and the boys of Mr. Noble's school were laughing as it snapped the boughs off the trees. At a quarter before six the schoolhouse was shut up, the doors being well closed, and all made tight. By this time several large trees were down, and heavy rain had set in. The wind now shifted rapidly from west to north and east, and about eight it blew a furious hurricane, the rain falling in torrents.

In Mr. Noble's house they were soon obliged to open umbrellas within doors, else they would have been forthwith wet through, for the rain did not fall in drops but in streams. Soon the water stood on the floors one or two inches deep. Some of the young people were now kept busily occupied in fastening up the bolts of the east doors and windows, which continually drew with the force of the wind. The bolts, however, broke, and the cry was heard, "The sea-water is come in." As the house-basement is nearly four feet high, this at first seemed incredible, but soon it was beyond doubt. At last there came an awful roar: away went bars, bolts, and panels; the doors flew open, and in rushed the sea. A terrace, which might be reached by a western window, was first thought of as a place of retreat; but the water had risen within an inch or two of the window, and escape in that direction was cut off. There was a ladder in the verandah, which it was thought might be had, and thus enable the endangered family to climb upon the wooden ceiling. Accompanied by his maty, Mr. Noble attempted to reach the front verandah through the hall; but scarcely had he opened the inner door into the hall, when, in the pitchy darkness, a sea struck him, rising about three feet. It was a moment of imminent danger; but he was enabled to rush back, and, as he says, "The Lord saved my life." They now hastened into the inner room, mounting on cots and drawers, and, bidding a final farewell to each other, betook themselves to prayer, expecting to be either drowned or buried in the ruins of the house. In this state of suspense, calling on Him who was their only hope, they waited. In about an hour and a half the wind changed to the E.S.E. and S.; and although the waves still dashed against the walls, and the wind and rain continued violent, the waters began to abate. Their hope revived, and, changing their wet clothes as far as it could be done, about two o'clock, being quite worn out, they fell asleep, sitting on the cots and drawers.

Thus in Mr. Noble's house there was no loss of life. Amidst extreme danger, all had been mercifully preserved. But soon they came to know that it was not so with others of their friends and fellow-labourers. Just as it was light, a cry of distress was heard, and the horse-boy, who had climbed a tree, and thus been saved, was seen wading through the deep waters. "More are coming," some one soon exclaimed, and then appeared struggling on, with their servants, Ratnam and Bushanam, the two young Brahmin converts, whose admission to holy orders by the Bishop of Madras was mentioned in our last Number. They had tried to escape in the dark, and, in the effort, some of the little party had been swept away. Bushanam had lost his wife and child, and sad were the wailings of the bereaved husband and father. Ratnam's wife had nearly shared the same fate, having been drawn back out of the flood by Bushanam's uncle. As the light increased, and they were enabled to look about, nothing could exceed the wreck and desolation; stables, cow-houses, godowns, all flat; the eastern end of the house broken down, the great doors wide open, the hall full of prickly pear-bushes, broken tables and chairs; sea-water, mud, and books, being strewed over the floor. On a closer examination it was found that the eastern foundations of the house were sapped, and that if the flood had continued much longer the hall must have fallen. But now anxiety was drawn to another point: the house of Malayya, the school-teacher, was flat, and no one knew what had become of him. His body, and that of his wife, were subsequently found, the former at the jail, the latter close by. He was, by universal testimony, a true Christian: he was, besides, a very valuable teacher, and had been married only four months. What is earthly has perished; what is spiritual survives. "All flesh is as grass, and all the glory of man as the flower of grass. The grass withereth, and the flower thereof falleth away; but the word of the Lord endureth for ever;" and in the enduring nature of that word, which, when made known to him, he, through grace, received, Malayya now participates.

But sad as these events were, the loss of life at Mr. Sharkey's was far greater. It will be remembered, that, in our recent review of the Telugu Mission, we referred to the girls' boarding-school, a deeply-interesting department of labour, which had borne much fruit during the fifteen years of its existence, and promised more. About two years ago an examination of this school was held, at which most of the ladies and officers residing at the station attended, and "unanimously expressed themselves greatly delighted with the creditable manner in which the girls acquitted themselves.

"Several of the girls," observe the Missionaries in their report, "had lately undergone a strict examination in the various branches of education, in order that they might act as teachers. There are many who have been trained in this excellent school now acting in that capacity; others have married native-Christian catechists, who are all, we hope, testifying, by their precept and example, that the untiring energies, and the ever watchful care and affection bestowed upon them in their youth, both as regards their spiritual and moral welfare, has not been in vain.

"Some very elegant articles of crotchet work were exhibited as done by the children. By the sale of work more than 238 rupees have been realized during the year. The instruction previously given is chiefly by means of the vernacular, and the way in which the children answered the questions put to them in scripture, spelling, geography, and arithmetic, quite satisfied all those who were able to understand them. Some of the replies were interpreted by Mr. Sharkey; but when the finger pointed to Quebec on the map, or traced the courses of the Missouri and Mississippi, their knowledge commended itself to all present. The first class repeated several of the Articles of the Church of England. Not the least attractive part was the singing, in which all were amazed to find three parts correctly sustained—alto, treble, and tenor. Thus Jackson's Te Deum was given throughout, besides one or two pieces of a lighter character."

On this interesting school the deluge broke with destructive power, no less than thirty-three of the poor girls having been swept away. Mr. Sharkey, in a letter dated November 15, thus describes what happened—

God has showed us great troubles and adversities, and yet turned and refreshed us. He has brought us from the deep of the earth again. The first of November can never be forgotten. The day was a wet one. The wind blew with more than ordinary violence, and we all felt that a storm was at hand. But we went through our day's work, attended school both morning and evening, paid the Mission agents, and I returned home as usual. The wind increased, and at ten o'clock P.M. there was a terrific hurricane. We made all our preparations by way of guarding our doors and windows. We had scarcely done this, when a cry of "The sea, the sea," was heard. It came from some of our servants who had previously taken refuge in our kitchen, and who, with great difficulty, contrived to reach the room in which fifteen girls and ourselves had taken refuge. A minute after we had admitted them in, the sea rushed into the house, and I had just time to put the children on our large cot, and take my position at the only door which we all had to guard. But the bolts gave way. Door after door was carried off, and we were completely at the mercy of the wind and waves. Our children behaved nobly, and we were enabled to pray together with great calmness, and commit ourselves to Him who once said, "Peace, be still." The water rapidly increased in depth. I was waist deep in it, when the rising water suddenly stopped, and receded as fast as it came. We then removed the children to another room, and *wished for the day.* The rain was pouring into the room in torrents, and the wind was still violent. The night was dark, and we had no light after three A.M. There were two things I cannot adequately describe —the feeling of gratitude when the water began to recede, and the sense of joy with which we hailed the first gleam of morning light. "O Lord, thou hast brought up my soul from the grave: thou hast kept me alive." God has been to us a strong rock—a house of defence to save us.

During the night we had often thought of the children in the bungalow adjoining our house. *We were not able to render them any assistance;* and though the bungalow was a strong building, we had many fears. The next morning told us what had been done. My heart breaks to write it. No less than thirty-three children were either drowned in or swept away by the flood! The building stood, but every door in it was carried off, and the wave knocked down every thing before it. The hospital, in which there were several children, and which adjoined the bungalow, came down. Every article of furniture was washed away, and only twenty-five of our dear children were spared to tell us of the dying shrieks of their fellows, and their own miraculous escape. They were nearly naked, and we were little better ourselves. My valuable library, all my Telugu manuscripts, and materials for new works, collected during the last twenty years, and a large quantity of our furniture, have either disappeared or are irreparably damaged. Our girls' school-room is down: our house is scarcely habitable, and we are now staying in two small rooms in the Commissary's office. Bunder is no longer what it was some months ago. It is difficult to recognise it.

To my utter astonishment, the Buttayyapet house is still standing, but it has received much injury. The walls surrounding it have, some of them, fallen down, and from what I hear, many of my day-scholars have perished. The boarders have been spared. Both our schools have been closed, for a time only, I trust. Exclusive of our girls, we have lost nineteen members of our congregations. No two persons seem to have suffered alike: each has his own tale of woe to tell.

I am now sitting alone in a corner of my former house, with the ruins of our property scattered all around, and the compound filled with dead and dying trees, prickly-pear bushes, mud, and rubbish of every kind. With reference to my own loss, I feel comparatively little, although I am almost a beggar; but the thought of our dead children is too much for us. Still God has done all things well, and in wrath remembered mercy. He has not dealt with us after our sins. Our prayer is, that the visitation we have just had may be abundantly blessed to us; that it may humble us to the dust; make us more devoted to his cause; teach us not to make nests for ourselves, and live in needless luxury and ease; fill us with a deep sense of our vileness, and a precious sense of his love to us; and keep us ever ready for his coming. It is remarkable that some of our heathen servants, in that dark and terrible night, prayed to Jesus for help. I am not able to tell you a fraction of all our troubles. Pray for us.

Amongst other girls who were lost, mention is made of Lakshmi, or Lakshmamah, on the point of being married to one of the teachers. This young believer, for such she was, is safe folded in her Saviour's arms, far above the ills and sorrows of earthly life. Her brother, Ramchandradu, a Brahmin convert, thus touchingly refers to her death—

Through the mercy of our Lord Jesus Christ, I and my brother Venkataramayya escaped this general destruction which happened on the 1st of this month. I must proceed to relate the mournful story of my dear mother and sister Lakshmamah. My mother and my sister were both staying in the same room. The flood began to come at about half-past ten in the night, and, to escape which, they tried to get to Mr. Sharkey's large bungalow, and while they were attempting to escape they were swept away by the sea. In the morning we found my sister's body in Mr. Sharp's compound, but my mother's body had entirely disappeared. Some say she was found, but I do not know the truth. I must not stop here, but I must relate some particulars concerning them. I feel great comfort in thinking of my dear sister, that she is enjoying her rest with her Redeemer. Mr. Sharkey bears testimony to her good conduct, and there was evidently a great change in her latterly: without the least doubt, I believe that she was a true believer in the Lord Jesus Christ, and she is resting now from all the troubles and cares of this present evil world. I feel grieved only through my weakness because I wished, though not the wish of

God, to enjoy her company a little longer, as it is natural; but it is far better for her to depart and to be with Christ, as saith St. Paul.

I do not know what you will think when I say that more than 20,000 if not 30,000 souls were lost in that single night. I know, in many families, one out of a family consisting of eight or nine persons surviving. This is a dreadful visitation, yet the surviving people seem to go on just in the same way after the catastrophe as before it. The loss of property is so great that I cannot tell you.

In our last Number we introduced a brief letter from the Rev. J. Sharp. We have now received from him the following fuller communication, which vividly describes the morning of desolation following that night of horrors, and the pitiable state of destitution to which the survivors were reduced—

The whole day (November 1) was more or less windy. . . . . About four P.M., whilst at school, I saw a palmyra-tree blown down upon a house opposite. Before five it was too dark to see to continue the lessons, and in pouring rains, flooded streets, and in violent gusts, we prepared ourselves, as best we could, to get to our homes. The last person to whom I bade farewell in the little bungalow was Malayya, to see him no more on earth.

After I reached home the violence of the wind was so great that we had to go round securing the windows and doors, one after another, more and more. The wind gradually went round from south-west to north-east, but gusts came from all directions at once. The rain coming through the ceiling became so great that it baffled all my efforts to keep it under by baling. Mean time the doors broke from fastenings and hinges. . . . . The noise was so deafening, we had to shout at the top of our voices when close to each other. The skylight windows fell in fragments, and we began to fear for the roof.

About eleven P.M. we found water floating into the house and rising most rapidly. . . . . We went and looked out, and all was black water around us, rising and surging, and then we found that it was the salt sea. The floor of the house is raised a yard or more above the compound, yet the water rose two feet or more inside. In our back bath-room, which was lower, I find the mark stands as high as my face. We managed, by continually relighting all the lights within our reach, to keep a few burning. . . . . We went forth as we were into the storm, the rain and spray pelting us like hailstones, and the water above our knees, with a powerful current. Thinking the current would have less effect on the walls if it had an exit, before deserting the house I got the large doors at the back opened to give it an outlet. Three times we tried to pass to the outside steps, and were driven back twice: the third time, on hands and knees, we crept up, but Mrs. Sharp was all but blown over the side. We crept along the terrace on the top, holding on as well as we could. We got inside a little doorway among the rafters, but durst not go far in for fear the large beams should fall upon us. A light, which we left in the room below, shone through a chink for a time, and cheered us much, as it showed that the water had not risen high enough to extinguish it. Our thin garments were no shelter against the rain: we were numbed and sleepy from cold and fatigue, but kept one another awake and warm by constant rubbing. Many times we thought of our relatives and friends in Masulipatam, and committed them and ourselves to the keeping of the Lord Jesus. . . . As soon as we durst we crept a little out to see whether the steps by which we had ascended were standing. We found them still so, but much of their foundation and props gone. The scene of desolation around us was indescribable; the country all around under water, except a spot here and there; hedges washed away, trees uprooted and broken by hundreds, with many a corpse in view, and here and there a wail or shout. When the wind and rain permitted we descended, feeling bruised all over. All the large book-cases were fallen, most of the furniture washed out, the rooms filled with a *debris* of broken furniture, prickly-pear hedges, bricks, books, aloe-trees, &c. We were very hungry, and found a bottle of oatmeal, some jam, a little brandy, and a little tapioca, of which we partook, and then waded through the water to the commissariat house to the north of ours, as it stood a little higher. Many were seeking the same refuge. After a little time we tried to wade to my wife's sister's house, to see whether she and her four children were alive, but the water was too deep. I found them afterwards all alive, though much of their house had fallen. They lost their carriage and three horses. I got a bottle of tapioca, and returned to my wife, the water in some places being breast high. Each was asking any one he met that he knew, who was alive and who was dead. Everywhere were corpses and dead animals; even the crows had disappeared. . . . . On my return I found Mr. Sharkey come in search of food, and almost distracted, as thirty-three of his school girls had been drowned. I gave him a bottle of oatmeal, a pot of jam, and a pint bottle of beer. Then came an embassy from Mr. Noble for food. Bushanam had lost his wife and only child. I had but the tapioca and a pot of marmalade to give. Mrs. Sharkey and forty girls came over to the commissariat office, and many natives in the afternoon. Of course every thing was salt, and not a drop of fresh water was procurable. However, I got a fire, and cooked some of the oatmeal with the salt water as porridge for the girls. I also found in my house some port wine. Next day it was very hard to find food. We got some oranges, plantains, &c. Every one was very thirsty, but not till late in the day was a well of sweet water discovered on the inland side of the town. I picked up a few potatoes in our compound, and we did the best we could, but the distress in every direction was terrible. The run on the fresh water was so great, that it became necessary to refuse access to many. . . . . Many died from want, salt water, and exhaustion. Some of the gentry have not suffered near so much as those whose houses were near the sea, and they kindly sent round what provisions they had. Some of the natives, too, brought us a little good rice, fruits, &c. For several days the obtaining of food was very difficult, though the collector and others exerted themselves exceedingly. Then the corpses were decaying, and the smell was terrible. The salt water seems to have gone ten or twelve miles inland. I cannot attempt to tell any of the sad things we have heard and seen. The dead can hardly be less than 20,000 here and in the neighbourhood. Most of the native houses are fallen and the mud ones washed away.

This hurricane, and the inroad of the sea by which it was accompanied, appear indeed to have been of unprecedented severity. At the fort the waters were thirteen feet deep: at Mr. Noble's house they stood six feet deep, surging, rolling, and splashing ten or twelve feet high in the large hall. Even as far as Bezwara, thirty miles distant, there has been some loss of life and great destruction of property. The half of the Rev. T. Y. Darling's house there has been blown down. He says—

Fearful would have been the consequences if the storm had lasted another half hour longer than it did at its height. We cried to the Lord in our trouble to graciously hear us. When the outer walls of the house began to fall, and the glass doors and windows dashed in, we took refuge in one of the old bathrooms, which was the most sheltered part of the house; but even there the walls shook. We had fears that we should be driven out without any shelter; but God had mercy upon us, and delivered us. . . . Our boys' schoolroom, which was being enlarged, and the work half finished, has been fearfully injured: the whole of the new part was levelled to the ground. The godowns in the school compound, and our catechist's house, are in total ruins.

The distress all about is very great, for every one suffers: not a single house escaped. We have not yet received any account from any of our out-villages. The country is quite flooded, and all the crops blown flat to the ground. This will produce great scarcity by and bye, I fear.

The telegraph communication in every direction has been stopped.

Mr. Noble adds—

Perhaps 30,000 is not the whole of those who perished. Cattle innumerable. The storm raged inland, as far as we yet know, sixty-eight miles; the inundation, three miles along the coast from Piddapatnam to Nizampatam, a space of about sixty miles. It is three weeks since it occurred, yet I hear a thousand corpses lie unburied to the south, and bodies of cattle without number.

Besides the lamentable loss of life, the destruction of property has been enormous. Mr. Noble has lost books, the largest and most valuable of them on the lowest shelves being sadly damaged, many hopelessly so, and much besides of private property within and without doors. So great was the need in this household, that supplies of any kind would have been welcome. The two native ministers are utterly destitute: all that they had is gone. Mr. Sharkey's house and out-offices require repairs to a great extent: the girls' school-house is in ruins. "Our school furniture." he observes, "maps, books, &c., all have perished. Our poor Christians are houseless and without clothes."

So, just as we review this Mission, that from an infantile condition has been springing up with so much promise, suddenly it is sorely bereaved, and crushed for the moment under the weight of a great calamity. But shall not the Judge of all the earth do right? It is like Job's case, when wave on wave of tribulation fell upon him, and "there came a great wind from the wilderness, and smote the four corners, and it fell upon the young men," so that they died. But all was overruled for good. The work of grace was deepened in Job's heart, and, after a time, his losses were repaired, and he was reinstated in more than his former prosperity. Let us believe it will be so. The Mission will rise up out of its ruins stronger and brighter than it was before, and more fitted to bring the Lord's word to bear on the heathen around, many of whom, we trust, under the effects of the losses they have sustained, will be found more ready to receive the Lord's message.

THE EDUCATED CLASSES OF INDIA.

AN able pamphlet has been recently published by the Rev. J. Barton, M.A. It is the substance of an address delivered by him at Cambridge to the members of the University Church Missionary Association, on a subject, in the presence of such hearers, specially appropriate, and to all persons who are interested in the welfare of India, and who are observant of the changes which are in progress there, of commanding interest, "the Educated Classes of Calcutta."

During his residence in India, Mr. Barton's attention has been very much directed to this important class, the first educated natives of India; and the Committee of the Church Missionary Society has just placed in his hands an important trust. They have selected him as the Principal of the Church Missionary College about to be opened in Calcutta, for the special benefit of those young natives who are aspirants after knowledge, and who left to themselves, are so apt to gather the knowledge of evil and disregard the knowledge of good. The subject, therefore, on which he writes, is not only one with which he is well acquainted, but on which he feels the deepest interest.

We wish it were possible to transfer the whole pamphlet into our pages; but this is not practicable. Mr. Barton, therefore, at our suggestion, has condensed its contents, and brought the salient points of this large subject within a brief compass. This we now give to our readers, not only with the view of affording to them information on one of the most remarkable movements which India has yet witnessed, but in the hope that, on his departure from England for India, Mr. Barton will leave behind him remembrances which will elicit in his behalf much prayer and sympathy.

Amongst all the past varying phases of the progress of Christianity, there perhaps never was a state of society so remarkable, or one so fitted to arrest the attention of every thoughtful Christian, as that which now presents itself in the two chief cities of modern India, Calcutta and Bombay. For in India, as has been well remarked by Dr. Mullens, Christianity has assumed a position which it never occupied before, not even in the days of pagan Rome, viz. one of antagonism to a religious system which, in the number of its votaries, the antiquity of its origin, and the strength of its priesthood, stands unrivalled and alone. The paganism of Rome, as well as of Corinth and Athens, had but a slight hold upon the great body of the people; it had no compact priest hood, no elaborate system of caste interwoven with all its social customs; so that, no sooner did Christianity once come fairly to the front, than the hoary giant at once fell prostrate, and never reared its head again. On the other hand, the efforts of Christian Missionaries in modern days have been chiefly directed to small tribes or sections of nations, never numbering more than two or three millions at the most, with a religious faith generally of the rudest description. Such have been the Red Indians of North-West America; the Maoris of New Zealand; the liberated slaves of West Africa; the Malagassies; the Hottentots; and the scattered islanders of the Pacific; all of which, fruitful as they have been as Mission fields, form but limited communities, and neither by their numbers, by the antiquity of their religious systems, or by the strength of their civilization, have given Christianity an opportunity to put forth all its powers, and show itself equal to meet the highest national demands.

And even in India itself, those Missions which have hitherto borne most fruit have been directed to small tribes or isolated communities, such as the Shanars of Tinnevelly, and the Kols of Chota Nagpore; the former of which have been but very partially under the influence of Hinduism, while the latter, though geographically belonging to India, are yet as politically, socially, and religiously distinct from the great bulk of its inhabitants as if they lived in Madagascar, or the islands of the South Sea.

It is a matter of peculiar interest to every thoughtful Christian to watch the progress of Christianity amongst such a people as the Hindus, who, in numbers, comprise one-eighth of the inhabited globe; whose religious system is the growth of thirty centuries, and so bound up by the iron fetters of caste with all their social customs, that it seems almost impossible to separate the one from the other; and whose civilization, though inferior indeed to ours now, was far superior to any thing which mediæval Europe could boast of, and reaches far back to the days when Britain was unknown, when Rome was not built, and when even Greece was only just beginning to have a history.

What, then, has been the effect on the Hindu mind of the past forty years' contact, not only with Protestant Missionary effort, but also with the indirectly Christianizing influences of English literature, English political and commercial activity, and, above all, of a Government which, whatever may be its shortcomings, has always been conducted, so far at least as regards its internal policy, with the most scrupulous integrity, and a real and conscientious desire to promote the welfare of its subjects? It is not too much to say that the changes which have passed over the whole upper stratum of Hindu society during this period have been far greater, and far more momentous in their results, than those which the railroad progress of scientific discovery has effected within the last century in England.

Decay of Hinduism as a religious system.

The days of Hinduism are undoubtedly numbered. The testimony of Hindus and Christians alike is unanimous upon this point. There are, it is true, a considerable number left of the old class of orthodox Pundits, who still try bravely, though in vain, to stem the advancing torrent, and seek to maintain that gross and corrupt mythology which they feel to be, not merely morally, but also intellectually, untenable: yet even they acknowledge but too sadly that they and their system must, ere long, be swept away by the advancing tide of intellectual and religious inquiry. Listen to one such professor of the old school at Bombay—"Hinduism is sick unto death," are his memorable words: "I am fully persuaded that it must fall. Nevertheless, while life lasts, let us minister to it as we best can."

The state of society, both in Calcutta and Bombay, has been thus well described by Dr. Mullens.* "All the educated young men stand in the position of antagonism to the old system. They would be heartily glad to slip their necks out of its yoke: they cheer vociferously all attacks made by their countrymen upon its errors, and never attempt to say a single word in its defence. Yet still they belong to it, yield to it, get on with it as they best can; for they all fear the social penalties consequent upon quitting it for ever, and all are waiting till every one else shall quit it, that these penalties may be rendered harmless. Hence it is that this large and very influential class, numbering now from 15,000 to 20,000, accept a position of compromise, within the system they professedly condemn, and outside the Christianity which offers them all they need."

The Brahmo Somaj.

Out of the educated class a considerable number have formed themselves into an organized religious Society, under the name of the Brahmo Somaj. These men stand very much in the same relation to the old Pundits on the one side, and the more radical section of the reformers on the other, that Socrates and his followers stood to Aristophanes and the conservative party on the one side, and young Athens on the other, in his day. In a lecture on the "Clouds" of Aristophanes, recently delivered to the Bethune Society of Calcutta—a literary and debating club, formed by the educated natives among themselves, with a small admixture of Europeans—the Bishop of Calcutta ably worked out this comparison, and sought to teach these would-be reformers, that if Socrates, who never had any thing better than the light of reason and conscience to guide him, so compeletely failed in his aim, how much more would they, if they trusted to unaided reason alone, and persisted in rejecting that only safe and sure guide of revealed truth, which Christianity offered them.

The object of the Brahmo Somaj, like the Socratic school of old, is to restrain liberty from degenerating into license; to cast off the false and retain the true; and this they endeavour to do by retaining the current mythology as a system of symbols and allegories,

* See "Christian Work" for November and December—"The Brahmin Reformers of Bengal."

under which they shadow forth the principles of pure Theism. For aggressive purposes this Society has now a house or temple for weekly worship; they have a subscription fund for sending out preaching agents and the establishing of propagandist schools; they have classes of disciples and inquirers, a large body of full members, numbering from 3000 to 4000, gathered from the higher and wealthier classes; and their influence is at once pervasive and powerful. Their religious creed is a compound of the old Vedantic philosophy with modern Deism, borrowed from the works of Theodore Parker and Francis Newman, which are widely read and studied.

Religious aspect of the movement.

But what, it will be asked, is the attitude assumed by the members of the Brahmo Somaj, and the whole body of the educated Hindus generally, towards Christianity? and how far is this intellectual movement likely to affect the progress of the Gospel amongst them? It is undoubtedly the fact that the position they have hitherto assumed is one of entire antagonism to the fundamental truths of Christianity. And yet those best acquainted with them, and who have watched their many varying phases of opinion during the last thirty years, are disposed to look upon this movement hopefully, as indicative of a change for the better. It must not be forgotten, that for a Hindu to become a Deist is a very different thing from a Christian making shipwreck of the faith in which he has been brought up, and becoming a Deist. What is retrogression —sad retrogression—in the one, is really progress in the other. The Bishop of Calcutta speaks thus of the movement in his recently published charge—

"The worship of the Brahmo Somaj is an evidence that man cannot live without some religion to satisfy his spiritual aspirations. Yet these aspirations cannot derive any permanent support from the mere guess-work of a system of intuition; nor can a religious sect long continue to draw its whole ethical system from the Gospel without discovering, that in order to practice Christian morality man's heart must be animated by Christian faith; nor is it conceivable, that those who are looking forward to death, and 'something after death,' should be content to rest on conjectures and baseless hopes, when they have before them the sure promises of Him who has opened the kingdom of heaven to all believers. *We can therefore only regard the religion which this sect professes as a temporary substitute for the truth of the Gospel.*"

And so, too, Dr. Duff,—who has watched them narrowly for thirty years, and seen them constantly shift their gronnd, first from Atheism to Vedantism, from that to Neo-Vedantism, or natural Monotheism, and from this again to the present system of Intuitionalism, expresses his strong hope that they will end at last in positive belief, such as they can only find in the revealed truths of Christianity.

In a published letter to the General Assembly of his church on this subject,* he mentions a remarkable admission made by one of the leaders of the Brahmo Somaj some years ago. After pressing him hard, in the presence of about a dozen of his followers, as to the practical uselessness of his system, always fluctuating and changeable, in contrast to the glorious truths of Christianity, which, like their Divine Author, are the same yesterday, and to-day, and for ever, he replied—

"Well, it is true what you say. We have no certainty, no fixity. We are here to-day, and may be elsewhere to-morrow. We are now following *reason*, and we know not whither it may lead us. We know where we are now; we know not where we may be hereafter. The plain fact is, that when we gave up the inspiration and the divine authority of the Vedas we cut our cables, got loose from our old moorings, and have since been drifting about wherever wind and tide may lead us."

A candid confession certainly, but still not an unhopeful one for the future. The whole religious system of this sect cannot indeed be regarded but as a marked tacit avowal of the truth and superior excellence of Christianity. It is the merest makeshift with which hundreds of its professed adherents are seeking to stifle their convictions and satisfy those spiritual longings and religious needs of which they are so deeply conscious.

They are like mariners who have set sail upon the pathless ocean in search of some imaginary *terra beata*, and, after being tossed about for years by the ever-varying winds of human philosophies and conflicting opinions, they have sighted at last the long-looked-for land; but they fear to cross that bar of angry surf which lies between them and the haven where they would be. It requires more moral courage, more child-like trust in God, than they have at present, to attempt the passage: still they show no symptoms of wishing to turn their backs to the land, and put out to sea again. On the contrary, when any of their number, more courageous than the rest, set forth, calling humbly, yet believingly, on their crucified Saviour to help them through, they watch their

* Report of the Conference on Foreign Missions, with letter from Dr. Duff, Nov. 1861.

course with almost breathless interest, and not seldom give outward expression to the wish that they had only courage to follow.

Thus the baptism of three brothers of the name of Dutt, with their wives and children, —members of highly respectable families, and one of them occupying a high official position, —which took place in Calcutta about three years ago, was commented upon by a leading Hindu newspaper in the following remarkable terms—

"This event is one of those signs of the times which unmistakeably point to a better future. The event is ominous of a great change in the state of Hindu society. We are not Christians ourselves, *neither are we anti-Christians*, and we entertain a very great and most sincere respect for all true followers of Christ."

Another Bengalee of this same class wrote thus a few months ago to the "Friend of India"—"A spirit of religious inquiry is at present awake among the Bengalees; *and it is my certain belief that the transition from Polytheism to Deism, now being effected among us, will ultimately end in Christianity displacing the various religions which prevail in India.*"

It is moreover a remarkable and encouraging fact, that it is not from our Missionary schools and colleges that the ranks of the Brahmo Somaj are supplied, but from the colleges and schools maintained by Government, from which all distinct religious teaching is excluded. Three years ago Dr. Duff ascertained, that out of 1632 members then on the roll of the Somaj, there were but very few, probably not more than a dozen, who were ex-students of his own institution.

Those educated in our Missionary institutions, even though not baptized, still know thoroughly what Christianity is, and cherish a sincere respect for it and its teachers, so that they have not much sympathy with the intuitional pretensions of the modern Brahmist school.

Is it not then our duty, as Christians, to throw ourselves heartily into this turbid stream of intellectual and religious excitement, and seek to guide some of these frail barks that are being borne down by its headlong current, safely to the shore? Shall we not man the life-boat, and go out to rescue some of the poor, faint-hearted, wavering ones, who still linger at the very edge of the surf, longing, yet fearing to come over? If we refuse to hold out to them a helping hand, perchance a storm may come and blow them far away from the coast, now so near to them, and the opportunity of rescuing them may be gone for ever.

The means to be employed. — Educational agencies the most successful ones.

The means to be employed must be adapted to the peculiar state of thought and feeling which characterizes the present movement. It is both intellectual and religious. As Max Muller has truly said—and the thought has been endorsed by the Bengalees themselves—"The Hindus have ever been a nation of philosophers. Their struggles have been the struggles of thought; their past—the problem of creation; their future—the problem of existence. The present alone, which is the real and living solution of the problems of the past and the future, seems never to have attracted their thoughts, or to have called out their energies;" and, in spite of more materializing influences which their contact with the practical, sturdy, money-getting spirit of our Anglo-Saxon race has brought to bear upon them, the Hindu still remains essentially the same that he ever was. He is still "the most religious being in existence;" and the sphere in which his mind still finds most room to act, is that of religion and philosophy. Hence, probably, it has arisen that the only Missionary agencies which have been brought to bear *successfully* on this class, have been those which may be strictly termed educational.

The illustrious Missionary, who has always led the van in all attempts to bring the Gospel to bear on this class of Hindu society, and to whose influence all that is hopeful in the present movement, in a Christian point of view, is mainly owing,—Dr. Duff, was profoundly conscious of this, and the result has amply proved his wisdom and foresight.

Proposed Church Missionary College in Calcutta.

Among other means suggested for accomplishing this end, the Bishop of Calcutta expresses a hope that a college may be established in Calcutta, in connexion with our own church. He says, "I should rejoice to see in Calcutta an institution, under the general control of one of the two Missionary Societies of our church, in which undergraduates of the University may be educated up to the B.A. standard, under purely Christian influences."

The existing institutions insufficient to meet the present need.

At present there are only two colleges in which native students can receive such higher education, after a previous preparation up to the matriculation (or entrance) standard, at one of the numerous schools in which Calcutta now abounds. These are the Presidency

College, under the immediate control of Government, and the Free-Church Institution, which Dr. Duff founded, and so long presided over. The first necessarily excludes all direct religious instruction, though not a few of its students have been attracted to Christianity, and, in some cases, brought actually within the pale of Christ's church by the Christian influence and Christian teaching of one of its most distinguished Professors. The latter is, of course, directly and distinctively Christian, and great has been its usefulness. Its converts are to be found throughout the length and breadth of North India: as native pastors, as schoolmasters, as catechists, as well as in secular capacities, they have been centres of light wherever they have gone. But excellent as this institution has been, and *is*, it is wholly inadequate to supply the daily increasing demand for higher education, which the rapid expansion of the Calcutta University has called forth.*

Two other Missionary institutions, viz. those of the London Missionary Society, and the Established Church of Scotland, have indeed recently receded from the position which they formerly occupied, and are now simply preparatory schools, educating up to the matriculation standard; as also Bishop's College, which, however, has always been mainly theological in its character, and therefore adapted for *Christian* students alone. The Church Missionary Society has hitherto abstained from employing high-class education as a branch of Missionary effort in Calcutta; partly through unwillingness to enter on a field already occupied by other Missionary bodies, and partly from their funds and interests being attracted to other fields of labour. The state of the case being now, however, materially altered, the Committee has carefully reconsidered the subject, and resolved to adopt the Bishop of Calcutta's suggestion, and establish such a college as he has proposed forthwith.

The educational staff of the college will consist of two or more Missionaries, who have received a European University education, and one or two native professors, graduates of the University of Calcutta.

Appeal for Funds in aid of the College.

The current working expenses of the college will be wholly met by the income arising from the Cathedral Mission endowment, made over to the Church Missionary Society by the late Bishop Wilson, supplemented by the fees of the students, and a Government grant-in-aid. Thus the college will not be any additional burden on the general fund of the Society subscribed in England. Funds are, however, required for two special objects, both closely affecting the prosperity and influence of the college: 1st, for the establishment of a library; and 2nd, for the endowment of special theological scholarships to encourage more directly the study of the Bible. At least 500*l*. will be required to carry out these two objects, and to place the college upon an efficient footing. There is at present a grand opportunity for infusing a Christian element into the present movement, but it must be seized at once. Some of the most influential native gentlemen are already endeavouring to establish cheap *Hindu* colleges, and otherwise pre-occupy the ground, and it is most desirable to present at once a bold front, and assume the lead; for if we linger, or take half-measures, the ground may be wholly pre-occupied, and the opportunity for ever lost.

* The number of candidates at the entrance examination has increased regularly year by year, from 240 in 1857, to 1500 in 1864. The number of candidates for the B.A. degree was, in 1858, 13; in 1859, 30; and in 1864, 66; and there is every prospect of as great a progressive increase for some years to come.

PRIMARY VISITATION OF BISHOP CROWTHER.

No time has been lost by Bishop Crowther. Leaving Liverpool on July 24th he reached Lagos on August 22nd, in time to get a passage on board the "Investigator," just about to leave for the Confluence. At Gbebe he held a confirmation. At Idda he succeeded in obtaining an interview with the king, and securing his consent to the immediate commencement of a Mission; at Onitsha he admitted to deacons' orders the native catechist, Mr. Coomber, designed to occupy Gbebe, and then returned to the Nun on October 16th, on his way to Lagos and Sierra Leone.

The points of vitality in these lands, where Christianity has come into action, are far apart. Yet are they respectively of great importance. Each little movement is the centre of hope to the surrounding dark heathen country. Small as it may be now, yet in reality it is capable of unlimited development; but in order to this it requires to be watched and tended. Some intercommunication is needed between the different stations, to cheer the hearts of the isolated labourers, and yield to them active help. This the Episcopate, if filled by a truly spiritual man, whose heart is in the work, and to whom God has given a right judgment in all things, is capable of doing. The Bishop can set in order the things that are wanting: he can ordain, confirm, build together the materials which have been gathered in; give them form and stability. But it must be an itinerant Episcopate; rapid in its action; quick to supply what is wanting, and to improve opportunities; and to this the European Episcopate has been found unequal. Devoted men have found themselves placed in painful situations, with a perception of what is needed to be done and an anxiety to do it, and yet at the same time disabled by the influence of the African climate on their health. In this conflict several of them have laid down their lives. In the admission of a native to the Episcopate, the office has been set free from such hindrances, and the animating effect of this is felt all along the banks of the Niger. "Can this be real?" asks Bishop Crowther, when engaged in the first ordination on the banks of the Niger: "is this the way Christianity spread to remote countries in the first centuries of its promulgation? . . . . If so, let the church of Christ buckle on her harness, for this is the time of her action." We believe it to be so. We believe that this important step will, under God, accelerate the Mission work abroad, and encourage the friends of Missions at home; and we thank God that on the Church Missionary Society has been bestowed the honour of introducing the first native clergyman to the office of a Bishop.

Aug. 24: *St. Bartholomew's-day*—Held an ordination at Lagos, when the Rev. Lambert McKenzie, deacon, was admitted to priests' orders: Revs. J. A. Lamb and L. Nicholson assisted.

Sept. 15—Held a confirmation at Gbebe, when twenty-one candidates were confirmed; viz. five Sierra-Leone settlers and sixteen native converts. This being the first time this rite was performed in this Mission, and the first since my appointment, the ceremony was peculiarly solemn: the candidates for baptism, and other heathen, were present to witness the proceeding.

Sept. 12—17 were spent in examining Mr. Coomber, preparatory to his being admitted to deacons' orders, and also the candidates for baptism for that rite.

Sept. 18: *Lord's-day*—Wet morning: the service was interrupted. Had a Sunday school at half-past eleven A.M., at the close of which I addressed the attendants, and dismissed them. Had the evening service, and preached to an attentive audience.

Sept. 19—To-day was the time I had fixed upon to go to Idda, with the intention of seeing the Ata, and to arrange about establishing a Mission station in that town, about which repeated promises had been made, but could not be accomplished hitherto. The unsettled state of the town of Idda since the last five years had become much worse since the last two years, a great many of Aboko's family having deserted the town on account of their quarrel with the king; but, however, I think a quiet and friendly visit to both parties alone, in the absence of the steamer higher up the river, will not be without some good results, although I may not be able to accomplish all my wishes at one visit. To do this with greater effect, I applied to the three managing chiefs here at Gbebe, to find me a canoe to take me to Idda on a visit to the king. They tried to shun the task, as they very much feared the Ata, and might incur his displeasure, in consequence of his taking offence at their proceedings. I therefore urged the necessity of my going to Idda upon grounds which they could not object to, and by a little present to keep down their fears and doubts about my reception, assuring them that they had but done their duty to their king by assisting my getting to Idda, and were to leave the consequences with me, I persuaded them to provide me with a canoe manned with their own boys. Six A.M. was the time fixed upon for starting, at which time myself and Mr. Coomber had made ourselves ready; but we were to go through the ordeal of disappointment, always attending strangers depending upon the native mode of doing business. Abraham Ayikuta, a native convert, who was appointed as headman of the canoe boys, went down early to the river side to prepare the canoe, but on his arrival there it was not to be found: some woodcutter was said to have taken it up the river to cut wood, and a messenger was sent to hasten it back. By eight o'clock no intelligence had arrived about the canoe: by nine o'clock one of the subordinate chiefs came to tell me that the canoe intended to convey us to Idda was at his disposal, but that the head chiefs had not given him a share of the presents I had made them, and yet his canoe was to be made use of: that if I would do something for him the canoe would forthwith be produced. I saw at once that they intended to make as much of me as possible by this intended trip to Idda, so I determined to listen to no such story. I told the man I had done what I considered right, and that I would not give him any thing extra; he must apply to the head chiefs for his share of the present. In short, no canoe was obtained till six P.M., after the whole day had been spent in constant expectation of the return of the canoe, and also in doubt whether I was not deceived. I was glad to get a canoe and start, however late in the evening it might be. Amadako, the head chief, behaved himself very satisfactorily. He came down to the water-side to hasten the canoe being made ready, took off his sandals, and waded to the canoe, to arrange the baggage properly; and I was not sorry when we at last pushed off from the landing-place, at about half-past six P.M., towards Idda. About three hours from Gbebe we halted at a place called Itsena, where we had our supper, and waited till the atmosphere was lighted up by the moonlight, and then dropped down to Shuter Island on the 20th, at five P.M., where Abaje, one of Aboko's family, has newly erected a village, and collected his people together since the quarrel with the Ata. Here we landed, and paid a visit to Abaje, who received us very kindly. I told him the object of my going to Idda, and also gave him a word of advice of the necessity of their being reconciled to the king, and returning to their home at Idda. From this place we dropped down to Akaya's village, another of Aboko's family. Spoke also with him as I did to Abaje. The reply of both to my friendly advice was very hopeful of an inclination on their part to submit to the king. From Akaja's village we dropped down to Idda, at one P.M. We proceeded direct to Aboko's house, who was very glad to see me return according to my promise when the steamer halted here a fortnight ago to communicate with the shore. He believed me to be a true person, because, when he communicated my promise to the king, neither of them would believe that I meant to do what I had said, but merely to raise expectations, and to disappoint them, and that if I did nothing else, the fulfilment of my promise was satisfactory to him. After a long conversation on different subjects, we were shown our lodging at Akaya's house, in care of a keeper during his absence from Idda with his party.

Sept. 21—Gave Aboko his presents, consisting of a fancy border white sheet, a cushion case of damask patchwork, and a smart velvet smoking cap, which pleased him very much. I showed him the presents intended for the king, consisting of a large white calico sheet, tastefully worked upon with many devices, cut from printed calico, of flowers, birds, ferns, &c., and tastefully arranged on the white ground sheet, which was very much admired. These fancy worked sheets came from the Ladies' Working Association, through the Rev. H. W. Sheppard, at Emsworth. I had kept these nice and suitable cloths with a view to make a proper use of them at Idda, a place of great importance, to which we had an eye these many years, but hitherto no opportunity had presented itself of taking a permanent step. The remainder of the presents, consisting of a patchwork silk scarf, lined with red taffety, beautifully fringed with borders; two rich velvet bags, a velvet cap, and a patchwork cushion case, all these from the Reading Ladies' Working Association. These articles being select, suitable to a king, and being ladies' handiwork, I purposed to make the best use of them, to convince the people and king how superior civilized nations are through knowledge and the reception of Christianity, and how low and inferior is the condition of those who are without them, and what they, both male and female may also be, if they receive the Gospel.

The next, and most difficult part of my work, was to get an interview with the king. Messages were sent three times to-day to the Ata, to give us an interview, but without success. The presents were proposed to be sent first to the king, in order to induce a hasty interview when he sees them. I refused to do so unless I took them myself. Another message was sent to urge an interview: this was accompanied by another messenger from two persons of influence from the king's quarters, who wanted some presents in the shape of kola nuts, to move them to induce the king to give an audience. As these were but small things, I gave a yard and a half of cloth to each, in compliance with their request. After this a promise was made that I should see the Ata, but the time was not fixed. I took it patiently, although it would derange my plan of being back to Gbebe on Saturday to administer the Lord's Supper to the communicants, and to baptize the candidates for baptism; but to see the Ata is of very great importance, because when once this great difficulty is gone through, the way will be opened for our future operations at Idda.

During my detention at Aboko's house, while the messengers went to the Ata, in the course of conversation some superstitious belief was let out by Aboko. It is believed that when the great men, such as the king, chiefs, and other persons of note in this country die, they go to the white man's country, and become such as I am, travelling with the white men, having adopted their habits; hence they regard us as their countrymen who have died, and taken our next state in the white man's country, and are therefore feared. Aboko wanted to know whether the white man's country was not in the neighbourhood of God's residence (Paradise), and consequently much nearer to God than the black man; and whether, by looking into the book, we could not see and know when any one is about to die, that is, how much longer that person has to live in this world.

It is also believed that when we see any person of note, such as the Ata, we take him in a book to the white man's country. The magic of photography, which they saw Samuel take at Gbebe, confirms their idea of this notion. I was glad that I did not take him with me to Idda with his photographic machine, which would in all probability have so frightened the Ata, and kept him shut up in his place, that there would have been no possibility of seeing him at all during my stay at Idda, lest he should be photographed, and taken to the white man's country, which would have been construed into hastening his death, that he might be removed to that country.

These are some of the Ata's fears, which no doubt must work very powerfully on him. Besides these, there are lucky and unlucky days to the Ata. From one market-day to another there are three intervening days as follows—

Eke, a market-day, unlucky for the Ata to see strangers.
Ede, an intervening day, lucky or good day.
Afo „ „ unlucky or bad day.
Uko „ „ lucky or good day.
Eke, repetition of the first, a market-day, unlucky for the Ata to see strangers.

From Eke to Uko. Four days; four days is their cycle of reckoning, the fifth day being a repetition of the first, so their every alternate day is unlucky for the Ata to see strangers. This mode of reckoning their market-days at the interval of four days is common from Yoruba to Igara and Ibo country. What remains to be ascertained is, what is the origin of this reckoning, and which is the beginning of these days. Whether the Jaguta of Yoruba corresponds with the Eke of the Igara and Ibo is yet to be ascertained. Besides these lucky and unlucky days, the Mohammedans have made the people to believe that Friday, their Aljima, is an unlucky day to undertake any work of importance, and the Ata did not hesitate to add this to his stock of unpropitious days; so if a stranger happens to arrive at Idda, on a visit to the king, on a Thursday, which may be an unlucky day, then Friday, which would be lucky to see the king, will interfere with the visitor, because though, according to the market regulation day, it is lucky, yet this Mohammedan superstition is regarded by the king, so that he would not be seen; then Saturday will be an unlucky day: the visitor must wait till Sunday before he can see the Ata. I had to go through all these before I could see the king on Sunday. This statement will throw some light on the difficulty of seeing the Ata, who is hemmed in by heathen and Mohammedan superstition. I did not know so much before, till I had to learn it by my quiet visit to Idda.

While detained here I gleaned some information about the countries on the back of Idda. One might travel from Idda to Onitsha by land through the Igara country, if it had not been rendered unsafe by a tribe of the Ibo, called Igbo, who are hostile to travellers by plundering their loads, kidnapping their persons, and selling them away into slavery; and if there happens to be a horse among the passengers it is killed, and eaten up. Through this tribe Igbo, European goods find their way by land to Idda, such as gunpowder, brass rods, and other trade goods. When Idda is once secured, the Igbo can be worked through from it and Onitsha.

The influence of the Ata extends to the inhabitants of the mountains called Apoto, taking all the triangle piece from the Confluence following the course of the Tshadda up to the border of the Mitshi country. This last people are hostile, because they are kidnapped by the people of Idda, and sold away into slavery. We found them in this disposition opposite Ojogo, on the Tshadda, in 1854. They are justly hostile to their oppressors. The people opposite Idda, on the Niger, are called Kukuruku, from their peculiar practice of calling at one another in such an unintelligible crowing sound, as if a cock was crowing. Masaba's soldiers continue to be a great annoyance to this people, by kidnapping and selling them into slavery.

Sept. 22—To-day being an unlucky day to see the Ata, I made up my mind to wait till Friday, which was lucky, not knowing that the Ata has also borrowed the Aljima of the Mohammedans, and added it to his unpropitious days. Being ignorant of this, I vainly hoped to accomplish the object of my visit, and to start for Gbebe soon after, so as to be there by Saturday evening. Several of the eunuchs paid me a visit, some of whom expressed a wish to see the presents intended for the Ata, which I showed them: they were much admired. They left with a promise that a messenger would be sent to Aboko, to announce when the Ata was ready to see me.

Sept. 23—In the course of the day Aboko paid me a visit. He met one of the eunuchs with me, and stopped a long while, when the time was passed in general conversation. As he made no mention of the time to see the Ata, the day being a lucky one, when he was about to leave I asked him when I was to see the king. He replied that he had received no message as yet. I then told him that as I had been here now four days, and had not seen the king, and to-morrow being to him an unlucky day, when I was not likely to see him, I had made up my mind to return to Gbebe, as I could not understand this delay in seeing the Ata, otherwise than that he did not wish to see me, and I did not wish to force myself to be seen. Aboko felt annoyed and ashamed at the king's delay, and he quite approved of my intention to return, though he was very sorry I could not see the king. No sooner was my intention to leave on Saturday morning heard by some persons about the king, than they hastened to apprise him of it, and to urge his giving me an early interview.

Sept. 24—Having partly arranged on Friday evening for an early start to-day, before I got up from my mat, about half-past five A.M., two messengers were waiting for me, one from the king and another from Aboko, begging me to have patience; that he, Aboko, was going to see the king, and arrange about the interview; but if I was determined to go away without seeing the king, that would not interfere with the friendship between me and him. The king's messenger gave me a reason of the delay; that his head eunuch, called Ogbe, one of the king's guardians, was sent to a neighbouring village to get something to entertain me with, but he had not returned in time. I told him that this was a very weak excuse, inasmuch as the king had not yet seen me, nor heard from me what I had to say, whether good or bad, before he was so anxious to look for presents for me; that his seeing me, and hearing what I had to say, was of greater importance to me than all the presents he could give. He assured me that I should see the king to-morrow, if that would not desecrate our Sabbath. I told him that was the best day for me to see the king, and talk about the introduction of Christianity into his country, because the blessing of God rests upon such an object upon that holy day. Considering that I could not get to Gbebe on Saturday, and being unwilling to work the canoe boys on Sunday, as there is no favourable halting-place for us on the banks at this time of high water, after having received the favourable messages of this morning, and the Aboko's and the king's messengers' assurance that I should see the king to-morrow, I made up my mind to stay.

Abraham, our faithful convert, has made himself very useful to me, though he was suffering acutely from boils about his knee-joint, which were very sore and painful. Mr. Coomber and myself applied ourselves to dressing him, for which he was very thankful.

In the course of the day two eunuchs paid me a visit from the king, to thank me for my patience, saying that I was a true lemamu (chief priest), for no one else would have stayed so patiently, and that I should surely see the king to-morrow. These new messengers, having seen the presents, returned home. They gave another reason for my detention as follows: that a child of the king was sick, so Ogbe was sent to see how it was, and he had just returned with the news that it was getting better; that from the anxiety of the child's sickness, and Ogbe's absence, the king could not have seen me with comfort at an earlier date. This was another version.

Abraham told me that there are many mischievous persons, who go about to frighten the king: that if he should see an Oibo, he would surely take him (by photograph), and carry him to the white man's country. These simple statements will show how childish even the great men in heathen countries prove to be under superstitious impressions which they cannot easily get rid of.

Sept. 25: *Lord's-day*—I got an early breakfast: soon after which Mr. Coomber accompanied me to pay a visit to Aboko, to hear if there was any sign of his preparing to move the visit to the Ata. He was absent from his usual seat in the verandah, but ordered a mat to be spread to seat us. Not long after, an eunuch made his appearance, to summon us to the palace. Aboko also soon made his appearance, ready dressed for the occasion, and told me we should soon go to see the Ata. I asked for a few minutes to return to our lodging, to get ready, and was soon back, when we started for the palace, the eunuch taking the lead. We had first to halt at a lady's, holding a higher position over Aboko: her title is Onupata, which I cannot now explain. After we were introduced to her, and the customary routine of salutation passed through, she dismissed us to Ogbe, a eunuch of great influence, said to be one of the guardians of the king. Here, also, we were seated, with much respect, next to the eunuch, while Aboko took his seat at a very great distance. As he was our host and leader, I hesitated taking the first seat till he had preceded me, but he declined. Ogbe entertained us with kola nuts and palm wine, after which he accompanied us to the palace. We had to wait for about half an hour outside, under a tree, till due preparations were made within, when we were summoned to the presence of the Ata. He was the same person whom I saw in 1859, and I saw him in the same room, and he was dressed in the same tobe. I recognised him at once on entering in. He saluted us heartily, when we were seated on a mat spread for us. After a pause, I commenced relating the object of my visit to Idda on this special occasion. Abraham, who was especially asked for by the king to accompany me to the palace, was my interpreter. I spoke in Nupe, and he interpreted in Igara to the king, although I have not the slightest doubt that the king himself knew as much Nupe as Abraham, it being a commercial language on this part of the river.

I told him the objects of my coming were simply three. First, that I was come to fulfil the promise I had made some years ago of establishing a place of worship and school at Idda, for which land was promised me, but I was not in a position to take it up then; but that now I am quite ready to commence operations as soon as I have the sanction of the king.

Secondly, That this is the third time the ship, the "Investigator," had gone past Idda without the captain seeing the Ata, which did not tell well in his favour, because the white men always visit other kings down and up the river, and keep up friendship with them; but with the Ata they had not that facility. I wished to know what difficulties were in the way, that we might come to an understanding, and arrange to remove them, that the friendship between the Ata and the white man may be as familiar as it was at the time of the old Aboko.

Thirdly, That as we intend establishing ourselves at Idda, I should be glad if the Ata would take the ruinous state of a large portion of his town into consideration, and act as a king ought to do, by calling together the elders of his country, and consulting to put an end to the quarrel between him and the Aboko's family, recalling them to rebuild their houses, in consideration of the good services to his country of their grandfather, who was a worthy friend to the white men; for our sake, who now interpose; but, above all, for God's sake, who might never forgive us if He were to keep his anger for ever. These three objects were of great importance. The king, no doubt, had heard of them before, because I repeated them before many persons during my stay while waiting to see the king; but to hear it direct from me gave it a greater weight. The little court-yard was filled with spectators, who listened and gazed without noise, or stir, waiting to hear the Ata's reply.

To my first proposition the Ata said they could not refuse to give us a place to build and establish ourselves at Idda; but though he is the Ata, he should have to inform others (his councillors) of it first, before he gave a final answer.

Secondly, as regards the European visitors, he did not refuse to see them; but the shortness of their notice was the cause. His practice was like that of Masaba, or any other king, but he hoped to arrange to see them on their return.

The third head of my proposition needed a deep consideration, so I did not press for an immediate answer. After this I delivered the Ata's presents, exhibiting them one by one to advantage, calling his attention to the needlework as the doings of English ladies, who took great delight in making these special articles for him at my request, and adding that the little girls in his town would be taught to do the like when we are once established here. That the Ata was much pleased with these things, as already described under the date of the 21st, I need not say. He presented me with twenty kola-nuts, twenty very large yams (about 2 cwt.), four pots of palm wine, and one goat and one sheep. I was thankful the Lord had so far given us success as to enable us to see and gain the confidence of the Ata and his people. But the king had been told that I had the sun (*i.e.* the watch) about me, which he should like to see. I got up and opened the watch, which I held to his ears, that he might hear it tick plainly. I then opened the case, that he might see the working of the spring. The Ata had also been told of my glass lantern, and he would be very glad if I would order one like it for him; also a pair of long boots, with a pair of spurs, and a large umbrella. I wanted to see the size of his foot, and he immediately took off his sandal, which articles I promised to order for him. Ogbe and Aboko also ordered a few articles, but inferior to the king's. Both Ogbe and Aboko have promised that, when I am ready to build, I have only to give each one his share of labour, and it will be immediately executed.

In the course of conversation, Abraham, who had picked up a little English, spoke to me in English, in which I replied. The Ata, who took notice of this, said in the Igara language, "Ayikuta understands the English perfectly," which was confirmed by all the courtiers. With this state of feeling towards us, I took leave of the Ata. Close by the king's palace was an elderly woman of rank, whose title is Omada Ogbe, who expressed a wish that we should call at her house. We did so, and she received us very kindly, and presented us with kola-nuts and a kid. On our return home Ogbe presented us with a kid and sixteen yams, and promised that he would do his share of work in building at our intended establishment at Idda. Aboko made the same promise; but these promises must be received with moderation. We retired to rest at the close of the day with thankful hearts for the tokens of God's favour shown to us on our visit to this place.

Sept. 26—Preparations were made for an early start for Gbebe, and by eight o'clock A.M. we were down at the water-side; but our canoe was not there. The keeper was told last night that we should be going early this morning, and he was to get the canoe ready, and this morning a messenger was despatched to tell him that we were ready to go down with our packages. He told him all was right; that he was just going to the opposite island to fetch it. We had to wait two full hours: neither the keeper nor the canoe was to be seen. I sent to Aboko to find me another canoe, as the one I brought from Gbebe must have been sent somewhere else by his canoe-keeper. He came down, and appeared much annoyed at the conduct of his man. As there was no alternative, he gave us his old canoe, the only one available at the time, to take us to the opposite island, where a market was held with the Abo people, telling us if we should find our's there, to take it from the keeper, and leave the old one to him, or else go with this as far as Akaya's village, where he was almost sure the keeper must have gone. It was not till half-past eleven o'clock that we pushed off from Idda, having wasted three hours and a half this morning for want of our canoe. It was in vain that we looked around the market on the island; neither the canoe nor the keeper were there, so we had to make towards Akaya's village with this old and unwieldy canoe, by far too large for the hands provided for our little canoe from Gbebe; but Abraham exerted himself to encourage the boys, and it was midnight before we got to the village, having to contend at times with very strong currents. This incident will show what little dependence must be placed on natives, with whom time is no object, in managing important business at a given time.

Sept. 27—I applied to Akaya to provide me with a better canoe to take me up, which he promised to do when he had spoken to his brother chiefs. They being busy with the Abo traders, had very little time to attend to my request till the market was over, so I prepared to lose another day here. In the mean time Abraham got information from a boy, who saw our canoe in the neighbourhood of Gbebe, and that if a look-out was kept, the canoe might be seen going down the river in the course of the next day. So they did. About eleven o'clock the canoe was seen coming down laden with merchandize for Idda. The boys shouted at the sight of it, and immediately paddled towards it, and seized it. There was a regular row between Abraham and the man in possession of it. I had to send them to Akaya to settle the matter, and I was very thankful to get the canoe again, not only for our own convenience, but for the sake of the chiefs who borrowed it last week at Gbebe for our use to Idda. Here it was found out that the keeper had hired it out on his own speculation during our detention at Idda. The canoe had been away five days, and it was an abominable lie the keeper had told us, saying it was just taken to the opposite island, and his pretending to go for it was to get out of our way.

On our arrival at Akaya's village we found Ogbe's messenger on a friendly message to Akaya and his friends, which indicated that my friendly advice to the quarrelling parties had taken some good effect.

Sept. 28—Akaya having presented us with a goat and eleven yams, and supplying us with an additional hand to pull against the current, we started from the village early this morning, and halted a short time at Abaje's village on Shuter Island, for a visit to the chief. We put up for the night at a village a little below Beaufort Island. Next morning we started, and arrived at Gbebe about three o'clock P.M., and were glad to be back again, after an absence of ten days.

Our canoe boys, superintended by Abraham, behaved remarkably well, for they worked hard to the latest hour of the evening. Next morning they for the first time received the wages of free labour, for which they were very thankful, and readily promised to go with me again when I want them.

Oct 2: *Lord's-day*—After the morning service I administered the sacrament of the Lord's Supper to our little body of twenty-five persons; and at the afternoon service I baptized ten adults and seven children, all children of our converts. When I was preparing the converts on Saturday, two of the mothers presented their children, and asked why they should be left out, when they who would have devoted them to idols have given themselves to the Lord. I referred to one of the fathers, also a candidate, but not yet ready to be baptized, and asked if he would not like to make an idol for the child. The mothers said no; it was in their power to do so; their husbands have nothing to do with it. This application brought to my mind the text, "They brought young children to Christ, that He should touch them;" "Jesus said, Suffer the little children to come unto me, and forbid them not, for of such is the kingdom of heaven." At the commencement of our establishment here, the Nupe settlers were the most forward and promising, but they, being under Mohammedan influence, are frightened back; and now the Igbiras and Bunus, who are entire pagans, are giving us much encouragement. Those mothers who were baptized with their children are Igbiras, the real inhabitants of this town.

Oct. 3—Went up to Lokoja, on a visit to the "Investigator," after her return from Bida, and also to settle some accounts with Dr. Baikie, and to fix the boundary of the land intended for a Mission house and place of worship. Returned to Gbebe late in the evening.

Oct. 14—All preparations having been made, and wood taken in from our station at Gbebe, the "Investigator" weighed for Idda, a little before noon, with Dr. Baikie on board. Having halted for an hour or so, to communicate with Abaji, chief of the village on Shuter Island, we arrived at Idda just about sunset. According to arrangements, I took Mr. Coomber with me, and landed to stop overnight on shore, so as to be near, and push on the arrangements to see the Ata as early as possible next morning. My last visit here from Gbebe had the desired effect: it prepared the people to expect my return with the certainty of seeing the Ata at the right time. On my seeing Aboko, he immediately despatched messengers to the principal persons to announce the arrival of the ship. Soon after, he himself started out to see those in authority. Having ascertained the time to see the Ata, I wrote a note to the "Investigator," to acquaint the gentlemen of the arrangements, and when they were to leave the ship on the visit to the Ata. Although the accomplishment of the visit was certain, yet it was another and more difficult thing to hasten or move the people to do it at a given time. Ten o'clock was fixed upon, so as to get through every thing by twelve, and weigh for Onitsha, where we calculated to arrive on Saturday evening, and to spend a quiet Sunday; but it was not till after twelve o'clock that we could start Aboko from his house, to lead us on to the king's quarters. We had to go through the same routine of visiting the lady Onupata, who had very little or nothing to say beyond endless salutations. She was presented with a scarf from the Commander, after which she sent us on to Ogbe, one of the head eunuchs and the king's guardian. Here we were again entertained, as usual, with kola-nuts and palm-wine. Ogbe was quite alive to the importance of the visit, and he sent messengers to the Ata to hasten the interview, as he was about starting with us to the palace. Soon after, he took the lead to the palace, so called because the Ata resides thereabouts; but, properly speaking, a mass of ruins and rubbish, overgrown with bushes of every description, instead of well laid-out gardens, in which vegetables, fruit-trees, and flowers of every variety might have been grown to perfection in the rich soil, at the elevation of about 150 feet from the level of the river; but so this place has been since I first entered it in 1854, and so it will be, if the king and his subjects are left to themselves, without the light of the glorious Gospel of our Lord and Saviour Jesus Christ. The uncultivated state of the country, and the irregular and confused masses of walls, built without plans, and which afford no comfort to the inmates, are outward pictures of the state of their minds as regards spiritual things. Their dark minds need spiritual light, as their outward confused circumstances need the regulating hand of civilization. But to return to the subject of our visit. We were detained about half an hour when preparations were completed within, and we were summoned by a eunuch to appear before the Ata, who was seated on his throne, a high stool in an open, narrow courtyard, where a mat was spread for our seat right before him. The ceremony of passing the kola-nuts round was no sooner over than the object of the visit was entered into. As the commissioned-officers will fully report this, I need only say the visit was a most successful one. I never saw any of the Atas so open, free, and familiar with foreign visitors as on this occasion: he met all the proposals of the commissioners without hesitation. He could not deviate from all that his predecessors had agreed upon in the former treaty with Her Majesty's Government. His presents were then delivered, with which he was much pleased. Having presented six coverings of white satin to introduce the subject of my Mission establishment here, before the king and his courtiers, I put the question pointedly to him, viz. that I wanted to know at once whether the king would grant the piece of land selected or not, that I might know what preparations I should have to make at my return next season. The Ata conferred with his courtiers, and then asked whether what I had brought was all I intended to give. I told him no; that was to open the matter before the court, according to their suggestion, and I should wait to hear what they would require of me. The Ata said it was not their practice to charge for land to build upon, but he desired me to do for them the same as I had done at the Nun, at Onitsha, and Gbebe, all of which they had heard of. My last question was, "Does the Ata grant me the land or not?" adding, that as regards what I should do for them, they must leave that to myself. The Ata replied, "The land is granted you." This closed our interview most satisfactorily. The Ata had an order to make for England. Ogbe and other councillors called me and the gentlemen aside to show us something, which they kept very private, covered with cloth. On withdrawing into a corner of the court-yard, and concealed from the gaze of the assembly, the Ata's crown, studded with cowries, was shown, with the velvet cap I presented him a fortnight ago. The Ata's request was, that a crown, according to the pattern of his cowry-studded one, should be ordered for him; but instead of being decorated with cowries, it should be covered over with gilt tassels, like the cap I presented him.

As Dr. Baikie was going to England he took the pattern, and undertook to execute the Ata's orders. I had already had some orders from him, and was very glad to be relieved of this by Dr. Baikie.

After this the Ata made his presents of goats and yams, so we left the court with the best feelings of the Ata and his courtiers. I am thankful for the leading of God's providence in the steps I had taken to visit Idda quietly and alone, as I had done in the absence of the steamer, to prepare the way for a better understanding between us. To know the people in this country you must be amongst them, mingle with them, study their mode of doing things, and yield to them according to their idea for the time being. When once you have gained a footing, you may then, and with success, gradually correct their ideas, and get them to fall in with you in civilized ideas and modes of doing business.

After leaving the court, I did not forget to propose paying our respects to the old lady, Amada Ogbe, who had been useful in moving the king to give an early interview. A present of two scarfs was prepared for her, according to my request. She received us kindly, and presented us with a kid. Thus terminated our visit to Idda this day, and perhaps the most successful I had witnessed for a long time, when taking into account a public consent of the Ata to the establishment of a Christian Mission station in his capital city of Idda. Got on board about four P.M. Abraham Ayikuta, who had come down again with me in the steamer as an interpreter, having been paid off for his services, and having got into his canoe, the "Investigator" weighed immediately, to give as much time as possible to get towards Onitsha before dark.

Oct. 16: *Lord's-day*—Before noon we anchored off Onitsha. I lost no time in landing and proceeding towards the Mission station with Mr. Coomber, who was this day to be admitted to deacons' orders, the first in this Mission on the banks of the Niger. While at Gbebe every preparation was made for the occasion: an assisting clergyman was only needed to accomplish the object.

We met the congregation at service, so the people were detained when the ordination service was performed, and Mr. Coomber was admitted to deacons' orders. The native converts did not fully understand what it was, but our Mission party entered into it with heart and soul. There was nothing grand in it, but a peculiar solemnity pervaded the whole service. The place of ordination, the congregation among whom it took place, the candidate for ordination, the assisting priest, and the officiating bishop, presented such a novel scene, as if a new thing was taking place in Africa. Can this be real? Is this the way Christianity spread to remote countries in the first centuries of its promulgation? Is the nineteenth century the time when "many shall run to and fro, and knowledge shall be increased"—when "the wilderness and the solitary place shall be glad for them, and the desert shall rejoice and blossom as the rose?" If so, let the Church of Christ buckle on her harness: for this is the time of her action. "Enlarge the place of thy tent, and let them stretch forth the curtains of thine habitations: spare not: lengthen thy cords and strengthen thy stakes. For thou shalt break forth on the right hand and on the left; and thy seed shall inherit the Gentiles, and make the desolate cities to be inhabited." Her efforts are becoming more permanent in Missions among the heathen; her zealous Missionaries, who had been training up a Timothy or Titus for the work of the ministry, may have long entered into rest, or been beaten back to retire, through broken health, from the Missionary fields of labour in heathen lands, yet their fruits remain: those of the labours of early Missionaries in the West Africa Mission are becoming reproductive on the banks of the Niger. If the Lord give the word, great shall be the company of the preachers. Let us, then, watch the leadings of His providence, and be on the alert when He beckons us to move forward. I will refer to the journals for full information of Onitsha station. The Lord seems working with his servants in bringing souls to Himself. I deferred confirmation at Onitsha on account of the shortness of time. The "Investigator" was ready to leave the next morning, and the candidates were not fully prepared. My plan was to land at Onitsha, and wait for the West-African Company's new steamer, according to former arrangements, which would have given me some weeks' stay at this station, and then to return to the coast in her; and if she did not come, I proposed to return to Lagos overland: but hearing of the unsettled state of affairs still between the war parties in Ijebu, in which case I might be shut up in the country, and thus lose twelve months, which would entirely derange my plan of visiting Bonny, returning to Lagos, and then to Sierra Leone on business connected with the Mission, I changed my plan thus to return to the coast in the "Investigator:" determining, should I meet the new steamer on the way to or at the Nun, to join her, if she was going up to Onitsha, and return with her to the coast. On my arrival here I found that she is not coming out till after Christmas. I am thankful for what the Lord has enabled me to do. Since I left Liverpool, on the 24th of July, I have been on the move till now. My arrival at Lagos, on the 22nd of August, was very opportune. I came just in time to join the "Investigator," which was going up the Niger, where I had seven full weeks to visit the stations, and successfully accomplished many objects preparatory to future extension. Had I waited for the West-African steamer, this year would have been lost to me for visiting the Niger Mission.

S. A. CROWTHER, Bishop.

Recent Intelligence.

THE MISSION ON THE GODAVERY.

THIS new Mission work, now deprived of a resident European Missionary, is nevertheless sustained in action by the native catechist, Razu, with the valuable help and Christian counsel of Captain Haig. The God of Missions has decided that the native shall be forced forward into the front rank of service. We would have kept him in the rear; but the matter is taken out of our hands. Under the disabling effects of climate the European dies, or is compelled to return home, and the native presses forward to sustain the work, which otherwise would fall to the ground, and the Lord does not fail to sustain him. We are constrained to admit his effectiveness, and to use him. Our wisdom it will be to furnish these men with every needful appliance which Christian instruction is capable of affording, and using them with confidence for important posts. This Mission was visited by our Madras Secretary, the Rev. W. Gray, in July last. The result of his observations will be found embodied in the following notes—

July 21—On my return from Dumagudiem, I take the first available opportunity of writing to you, for the information of the Corresponding Committee, some account of what I have seen with regard to the infant Mission there.

I left Madras by the "Barham" on Saturday evening, the 2nd inst., and reached Coconada on the following Monday morning. I left Coconada on Tuesday afternoon by canal boat, and reached Dowlaisheram on Wednesday evening at five, and found, immediately on arriving, that the up-river steamer 'Prince' was leaving early next morning. I accordingly took my passage in her, and we started on Thursday morning at eight. We made a very favourable passage up against the rapid stream, and cast anchor at Gollagudiem (twenty miles south of Dumagudiem) at half-past three P.M. on Saturday. From thence I made a very jolting journey, all the way through thick jungle, to Dumagudiem, which I reached at eleven on Saturday night, having accomplished the journey, with considerable ease and comfort, in exactly one week.

I will now endeavour to give you some account of what is actually being done, as regards our Mission work in Dumagudiem. It consists of two parts, viz. (1) that amongst the large body of natives (coolies, &c.) employed on the river works in Dumagudiem itself; and (2) that amongst the Kois in the outlying villages.

The cantonment of Dumagudiem (the head-quarters of the Godavery Navigation Department) lies on the left (or British) side of the Godavery. Farthest to the north of the river lies the Mission house, situated on a slight elevation above the other houses, and in, perhaps, the most healthy part of the cantonment. Then between it and the river come the houses of Captain Haig, Major Stevens, the executive engineer, and those of some of the subordinate engineers. Almost on the banks of the river (perhaps a mile from the Mission house) lies the principal native settlement, composed of people drawn from many different homes for the works. In this settlement lives Razu, in a neat tiled house, and next door to him is the temporary church of his own building; and around him live the members of the little native church which is being gradually drawn out from amongst the heathen. Near to this are the hospital, a long thatched building, and Dr. Houston's house. All the houses in the place are mere temporary buildings. Their walls are wattle and daub, their inside is unplastered or unfinished, and they are thatched with jungle straw. But they are nevertheless very comfortable. All around is an endless jungle, and tigers are said to wander at pleasure in it.

In addition to the native settlement of which I have spoken, there are at least three others along the river bank. A very large one has been formed on the Lunkah, an elevated island on the river, conveniently situated for the works. But the one in which Razu is living is the only one in which we have Mission interests. There are at present 2000 people congregated at this barrier, and there are often very many more.

Our native congregation in Dumagudiem seems to me, from what I have seen of it, to be fairly promising, though in its nature only a fluctuating and temporary one. There seem to be always three distinct elements recognised in it. First, there are those who have come over to Christianity in the place itself. Since the beginning of 1862 the baptismal register shows that there have been twelve adult baptisms. Of these, four have been peons in Government employ; one, a cultivator (Razu's brother-in-law, a man of fifty years of age); two, gentlemen's servants; one, a Gomastha; one, the younger brother of a peon; one, a Cooly; and two women. Secondly, there is a small Baptist party, who came up to the works a few years ago. There are not more than eight of them. They had been in Rangoon, connected with the officers' mess, and had been baptized by the American Missionaries there. Sir A. Cotton found them disengaged in Madras, and sent them to the works. Thirdly, there are a few Christians who have come from other places, such as Ellore, Bezwara, &c. Bellary has furnished the settlement with a native-Christian baker.

All the above are collected into one congregation; and Razu, in the absence of a regular pastor or catechist, ministers to them. He has regular services on Sunday, and once during the week, and there is a school in the church at four o'clock every Sunday. I was greatly gratified with seeing this Sunday school on one of the Sundays of my stay there. There were forty learners, and the teachers were Captain Haig, Mr. Rhynd, a young European on the works, Razu (who had a woman's class), and two others. Almost the whole church is thus brought under regular systematic Christian instruction, and the effect cannot but be, under God's blessing, good. I should have mentioned that there is a day school for boys of the settlement, held also in the church, with about forty boys in daily attendance.

But while Razu thus faithfully, according to his ability, ministers to this native congregation, it is easy to perceive that his heart is set on the conversion of the Kois. Perhaps, as so much has been said and written on this interesting convert's antecedents, it will be sufficient for me to mention here the impression I formed of him myself.

I confess, when I saw him first, I was very much struck with the man's appearance; and all that I saw of him afterwards impressed me with the idea of his being a man of much humbleness of mind, while possessing great unconscious influence on all about him. His whole life, so far as I have heard it, seems to have been that of a man anxious to do what his conscience approved as right; and I could not help thinking, in connexion with him, of that Centurion, who was "a devout man, and one that feared God, with all his house." I could not tell how many stories I have heard in illustration of that honesty of purpose which has made him so respected and so influential amongst all. The following little incident from my journal will show the kind of influence he possesses, and the way in which he uses it—

"*July* 14—As we (Razu and myself) returned home (from a Koi village) we fell in with a large encampment of Brinjarries, and I proposed that we should go and tell them about salvation. Razu most gladly assented, and he immediately approached the encampment, and called the men to come out. This was in a large open glade, with dense jungle on every side. Here and there were the tall, gipsy-like Brinjarry women, with their curious picturesque dress, and their large jingling ornaments. Droves of cattle were everywhere about; and inside the low tents, formed partly of coarse, dark-coloured cloth, and partly of boughs of trees, men, women, and children were lying lazily on the ground. When Razu called them, about ten wild-looking men and as many boys came lazily out, and Razu, taking a piece of coarse sackcloth which he found, stretched it on the ground, and, with exquisite politeness, requested them to be seated on it. They did so, with the air of men who felt that they were invited by one who had a right to command them, and sat down, and Razu told them of the one Saviour, Jesus Christ."

And now with regard to the Kois, whom it is the especial object of our Mission to reach. They lie very sparsely scattered over a large area, and it would, I believe, be impossible to do any thing more than conjecture the actual number of them. I was told in Dumagudiem that they are to be found from twenty or twenty-five miles inland on both sides of the river, all along downwards from about forty miles above Siroircha to about twenty-five miles above Rajahmundry; that is, in fact, that they are to be found all through the civil Godavery district of the Central Provinces on the left bank, and through an equal strip of territory on the right (or Nizam's) bank of the river. They lie within an area of perhaps 120 by 40 miles.

Already, I am glad to say, four villages have been in a manner taken possession of, by the establishment of schools in them. Their names are Nuddagudi, Nallapilly, Dhubanuthuloo, and Singaram; and they lie around Dumagudiem, the farthest being about six miles from it. In the first of them there is a really good school under a master (Gungiah) sent up by Mr. Sharkey. When I visited it I found twenty-seven Koi boys in it, and I confess I was astonished at the progress the boys had made during the nine months of the establishment of the school. The first class answered fairly in the history of our Lord, read well, did notation and multiplication very fairly, and wrote Telugu from dictation very well. Considering that nine months ago these poor boys had perhaps never even seen a book, their progress is, I think, really good, and shows decided intelligence.

In the second village above mentioned there has also been a school commenced. On the evening of my visit to it I found the schoolmaster teaching his boys under a shady tamarind-tree, the schoolroom (which the Kois are helping to build) being not yet completed. There were thirteen pupils, the two first in the class being actually men who had imbibed a strong desire for learning, and, with this view, had been let off from work by their relatives. They were all learning to read. They repeated the Lord's Prayer and the ten commandments in Telugu, and wrote words very nicely in the sand. This school has been in existence for only a few months. After the examination was over, Razu made an address to the Kois, of whom about twenty-five had come together. Some of them were handsome, well-looking men, and all of them had the appearance of being well off. Though many of them have a very marked peculiarity in physiognomy, it did not appear to me that ordinarily they are distinguishable from the same class of Hindus. The boys in the schools, I thought, had a very marked peculiarity of expression, but I did not notice it so much in the men.

The other two schools do not need any particular mention. They have been but recently established, and have not as many boys as either of the two first mentioned.

The Committee, should, I think, look upon their Missionary at Dumagudiem *as the Missionary of the Kois and the Kois alone*, wherever found, and to direct his efforts to seeking after them.

Our work should be, I think, to search out this neglected people little by little, village by village; to do this jungle work as much as possible by natives accustomed to the climate; and to make the Kois gradually, as God will permit, their own teachers.

For such a work as this, for searching out a people scattered over immense jungles, it seems a matter for consideration, whether it would be even necessary for the Missionary of the Kois to reside at Dumagudiem at all. It will be borne in mind that, in two years hence, works, workmen, engineers, and all, will probably be removed to a point higher up on the river.

In conclusion, I will only say that I think that this Mission presents a large and most interesting field to the Society; but only in so far as it is regarded as a Mission in quest of that scattered people; and so far we have every encouragement to go on. Providential circumstances have marked the history of the Mission, so far as it has gone. It has enjoyed the frequent prayers of the pious men who have commended it so strongly to the Society's notice. A pioneer has been raised up for the way, the very man we should have chosen for it, if we had ourselves the choosing of him. Let us hope in God that we shall be able to go on, working and praying, until another aboriginal tribe shall have been raised up in Central India to show forth the praises of Jehovah.

TALAMPITIYA.

In a recent Number of this periodical we placed before our readers the particulars of an interesting movement which has taken place in favour of Christianity at this point in the Kandian country. It may be the beginning of a new era in the Ceylon Mission, if fanned by the breath of prayer. This we desire on its behalf, and to quicken this we publish some new and interesting particulars respecting the little Christian flock, communicated by our Missionary, the Rev. J. I. Jones. These little movements are the stirrings of the dry bones in the dark valley of heathenism. Is the church prepared to take them on her heart, and invoke the breath of the Spirit of God, that they may be deep, lasting, and reproductive? Missionary results claim from us this sympathy and help. Whatever else has been done by us is incomplete unless this be superadded.

Nov. 26—I am thankful to be able to report the admission to the church by baptism of fourteen adults from Talampitiya and Hewadiwela, making, in all, twenty-seven within the last twelve months.

I visited that part of my district in October, and examined the candidates. I found that nine men and five women had acquired a good knowledge of the doctrines of Christianity, and as they professed faith in Christ Jesus as their only Saviour, and expressed in decided terms their entire rejection of Buddhism, I felt no hesitation in baptizing them. Several of them had been under instruction for a long time, and had given very satisfactory proofs of stedfastness and faith. Four of the women were wives of men who were baptized last December, and the fifth was now baptized with her husband. She is a very intelligent woman, and is, I believe, doing all in her power to teach her female neighbours.

Inquiry seems to be spreading in the villages, and though there is much opposition on the part of some, I hope that this year will witness nearly as many baptisms as last.

I was obliged to leave the district immediately after the baptism, but after a fortnight's absence I returned to it, and spent a week, visiting and preaching in the villages which belong to Talampitiya, having large and, generally speaking, attentive gatherings.

Talampitiya, though called a village, is really a district, as large as an extensive English country parish, and including no less than fourteen smaller villages. Our converts are gathered out of about ten of these, so that they are scattered over a large area; and as most, if not all of them, seem zealous in making known the truth to others, we may hope that, under God, the leaven will soon work throughout the whole of Talampitiya. The Christians confidently hope for and expect this.

A most important movement, suggested by Hunapola, has commenced among the converts. Each, according to his ability, is setting apart a portion of his land, making it over to the Society, towards the maintenance of a teacher among themselves. The land already promised is worth at least 50*l.*, and I have no doubt others will in time give sufficient for the support of a native pastor. May God hasten the day, if it be his will, when we shall see a holy, devoted man ordained to take charge of these people, who, by their liberality, bear witness both to what the Holy Ghost has wrought in them, and to their desire to have spiritual ministrations provided for them.

In addition to their gift of land, the Christians are subscribing for the purpose of building a small church in their village. Almost all are giving 10*s.* each, and those who are too poor to give money will give their quota in work. One man has given a valuable piece of land as a site for a church and little bungalow, which is to be erected close by as a residence for the catechist and pastor, and for me when I am in the village.

Another circumstance I regard as even more important and encouraging. Two of the men baptized in December 1863, Abraham and Paul, asked me to sanction their going out together to preach in the villages around. I replied, I should be most thankful if they would do so, and that I doubted not God would give them souls for their hire. I said, further, that though I could not give them any salary, I would willingly give them a small sum to meet expenses in travelling. All such help was declined. They said they needed nothing, they only wished to go, with my permission, devoting to the work of preaching the Gospel to others the time they would redeem from the cultivation of their fields.

"CAST THY BREAD UPON THE WATERS; FOR THOU SHALT FIND IT AFTER MANY DAYS."

"The Koheleth"—the son of David, and king in Jerusalem—"the assembler," who gathered the people together, that he might teach them knowledge, and instruct them with the wisdom which cometh from above, sought out and set in order many proverbs; and amongst his "acceptable words" are these, in which there is alike encouragement for the evangelist who, in distant lands, is sowing the seed of future harvests; and an incentive to those at home who, with ample means to help in so great a work as that of Christian Missions, have as yet done but little.

To the Missionary in the field of labour there is encouragement in these words. "Cast thy bread"—the bread corn, the seed of future harvests—cast it upon the waters: useless as such a proceeding may seem to be, it is only apparently so: "thou shalt find it after certain days." The seed-sowing in Bengal known as chittânee, or scattering, illustrates this. Situated on the basins of the Ganges and the Brahmapootra, Bengal comprises the entire of the great delta formed by the joint waters of these two rivers, the whole country towards the sea being an extraordinary reticulation of water-courses. During the periodical rains, all the lower parts of Bengal contiguous to the great rivers are overflowed, and form an inundation of more than one hundred miles in width, which commences in July, and continues probably for three months. On receding, the waters leave behind a deposit of soft sandy mud, varying in thickness, according to circumstances, from four inches to as much as three or four feet. This is termed a *chur*. On this, before it can bear the weight of a man, the seed is scattered, and the bread is cast upon the waters, in the hope that, in the form of an harvest, it will return after many days. In thus scattering his seed, the husbandman risks much. The chittânee sowing must take place at once, else the chur would dry up so rapidly as to become hard on the surface. And yet the very expedition which is needed invests the process with uncertainty, for it can scarcely be known whether the floods have ceased. They may return, and the seed be lost. And yet the ryot sows. "He that observeth the wind shall not sow; and he that regardeth the clouds shall not reap." Although an ignorant heathen, he disregards what is discouraging, and uses the present opportunity.

Let the sowers of the Gospel seed, at home and abroad, imitate his example. Difficulties, discouragements there will be, and unbelief will at times suggest the hopelessness of the undertaking; yet because of these, let them not withhold their hand. "In the morning sow thy seed, and in the evening withhold not thy hand; for thou knowest not whether shall prosper, either this or that, or whether they shall be alike good." In their case there is no uncertainty: "My word" . . . "shall not return unto me void but it shall accomplish that which I please, and it shall prosper in the thing whereto I send it." A harvest there shall be, although it may be after so many days, that the hand which sows shall not be the same as that which reaps; yet "both he that soweth and he that reapeth shall rejoice together."

Bengalee agriculture affords yet another illustration. The inundations, as already stated, occur about July. Seed sown in April, May, much less June, would not have reached maturity in time to be cut before the inundations of July commence. This, of course, matters not as to seed which can be sown in uplands, and beyond the reach of the floods. But there is one kind of seed which cannot be so dealt with—the *Amun Dhan*, or water-rice. This, requiring a well-watered soil, must be sown in the very lands which are liable to be inundated; nay, not only in the places, but at such a time as unavoidably leaves it exposed to the action of the flood; for it is sown in May or June, to be reaped in November. This would seem to be labour in vain, a throwing away of precious seed. And so the Missionary knows that upon his work will surely come floods of tribulation. He is tolerated so long as his efforts seem vain; but so soon as results appear, persecution of some kind is sure to commence. Thus, at Constantinople—the instant the Turks began to be moved, and Mohammedan inquirers sought instruction, the authorities interfered, exiling the converts, and restricting the action of the Missionaries. If the floods are sure to come, of what use to sow the seed? And yet the sowing of the Amun Dhan may well encourage the evangelist to sow his seed, even upon the spot where the flood is sure to come, and so to cast his bread upon the waters. Although inundated, the plant is not lost: it lives through the inundation, and yields its harvest; for it possesses a remarkable and happy property of rising in growth during the floods, so that, the stem elongating as they increase, the ear is always kept above them. If only the waters flow in upon it with any thing like moderate rapidity, the plant in its growth keeps pace with their increase; so that, instead of three feet, its usual height when there is no flood, it rises to seven or eight feet; nay, in the Backergunge district, where the Amun Dhan is much cultivated, it has been known to attain to twenty feet. Thus, although the stalk requires to be longer than the depth of the water, because of the inclination given to it by the force of the stream, yet still is the ear kept above the flood, and lives on, eventually to ripen.

God will take care of his own work, and so sustain it that the most apparently adverse circumstances shall be made to work for the furtherance of the Gospel. How remarkably the nature of the Amun Dhan illustrates the growth of the divine seed in Madagascar. The seed was sown there by the first Missionaries, and having sprung, the new plant had gained some height and promise, when the floods came—oh, how heavily!—and Christianity, in its young but tender growth, was left alone in the midst of the waters. To human judgment it seemed as though it must needs perish. But God kept it; gave to faith an unexpected power, so that it grew with the emergency, and the infant church, raising its head above the waters, was enabled to say, "Why art thou cast down, O my soul? and why art thou disquieted in me? Hope thou in God; for I shall yet praise Him for the help of his countenance."

Let us look in other directions, and see whether new thoughts may not be supplied to us.

Rice may with truth be termed an aquatic crop. Even the mountain grain cultivated in Cochin China and amongst the Himalaya chain, and by some called dry rice, is not raised without the aid of heavy periodic rains. In the more hilly parts of Madagascar, "small streams are intercepted as near as possible to the tops of the hills, on the sides of which the rice-grounds are formed in long narrow terraces, which are supplied with water from the streams already mentioned. These terraces vary in size and number, being frequently not more than three or four feet wide, and often rising one above another on the sides of the hill, to the amount of twenty or thirty in number. When covered with water, preparatory to sowing or planting, they present a remarkably singular appearance, resembling an immense aqueous causeway, or flight of steps, from the level ground towards the top of the hills."

In Madagascar, when rice is about to be sown, the ground is carefully prepared. Softened by the action of water let into the field, the clods are broken and reduced to a very fine earth. "The field is then made as level as possible by a thin sheet of water being conducted over its surface. It is now deemed ready for the seed, which, in sowing, is literally cast upon the waters." When the plant has reached the height of five or six inches it is transplanted into other fields: "each field is divided from the rest by a small bank about six or nine inches wide, the top of which being generally raised six inches above the field, forms a smooth foot-path, affording great convenience to the labourer employed in the field. By the side of these paths little rills are led over the entire plain, so that every field may be watered when necessary. These rills are supplied from canals, which, in the neighbourhood of the capital, convey water to the remote parts of the plain, extending from the Ikiopa, a large and winding river, which flows around great part of the capital, adorning the landscape, and clothing the valleys with fruitfulness and verdure. Every field is perfectly level, it being necessary at times to cover it with water several inches deep."

Yet the bread cast thus upon the waters, is found "after many days." The rice-fields in the vicinity of Tananarivo, the capital of Madagascar, are pleasant to look upon in the months of January and February. Conceive "an immense plain, of many square miles in extent, unbroken, except by here and there a tree or cottage, divided into several thousand fields, varying in size from half an acre to six or seven acres, all covered with luxuriant growing, or healthful yellow and ripening grain, the large bearded ears of which shine and rustle as they wave beneath the passing breeze, and bend, from the weight of the grain, sometimes half way to the ground, while the cluster of the stalks produced by a single seed is often so large that the reaper cannot with one grasp gather it into his hand."

In China the process of cultivation is very similar. Rice-grounds consist of neatly enclosed spaces, the clay-banks surrounding them seldom exceeding two feet in height. "The primary operation of tillage, ploughing, is performed with a very primitive implement, consisting of a beam-handle and coulter, but no mould-board, as laying over the 'sidelong glebe' is beyond the rural knowledge of the Chinaman. The buffalo, or water ox, is then called in to draw the three-barred harrow with wooden teeth over the surface, after which the earth is deemed sufficiently pulverized to receive the seed. Having been steeped in a liquid preparation, to accelerate germination and to avert the attacks of insects, the seed is sown very thickly, and almost immediately after a thin sheet of water is induced over the enclosure." After transplanting, the irrigation process is still needful, for the rice will not thrive without it. Sometimes a natural brook furnishes a sufficient supply. Chain-pumps, with their line of buckets, worked by a foot-mill of proportionate dimensions, are in common use; or the bamboo water-wheel is preferred. These may frequently be seen at work on the banks of the rivers, turned by the force of the stream, and with the utmost regularity conveying water up to reservoirs in the heights above for the purpose of irrigation. Some of these wheels measure forty feet in diameter. Each rice-field being partitioned into minor enclosures, the waters without difficulty are conducted, as circumstances require, from one plantation to another. Thus aided, the rice grows rapidly, until, as the crop approaches maturity, the sluices are closed, and the ripening grain promises the sower a rich reward of his labour. Strange process this; destructive to any other plant; healthful to the rice-plant. Without the water the hot sun would prove too powerful for the plant, but sun and water unite in forming the warm humidity which is so grateful to it.

So in the case of God's people: their growth is under peculiar circumstances. They have the divine presence and favour, but lest this should be more than they can bear, it is tempered with tribulation in the world. These waters are seldom absent: they are never permitted to be too deep; but they are let in anew from time to time, as the great Husbandman deems it necessary, and in the midst of these the growth is carried on. It is so with individual Christians: "through much tribulation we must enter into the kingdom of God." But where sufferings abound consolation also aboundeth by Christ. The presence of the suffering renders possible the abounding of the consolation: the sun can afford to be more powerful, because the waters are around the growing plants. Under suffering the mind is in a subdued state, and bears without elation special manifestations of the divine favour. Divine comforts tempering present sorrow combine to form the circumstances which are most favourable to the growth of the Christian: "tribulation worketh patience; and patience, experience; and experience, hope," &c.

And so it is with our Mission churches: their growth progresses amidst many trials. Often the work is so tried by humbling dispensations, that it barely overtops the waters; and the world despises it, and is incredulous as to the possibility of its ever coming to a harvest. Nevertheless it has lived on, and in many instances yielding the full corn in the ear, has become productive of new Missions. The labourers who in these distant fields of divine husbandry have prosecuted the work of evangelization have done so, and still continue to do so, amidst many difficulties; but "they that sow in tears shall reap in joy. He that goeth forth and weepeth, bearing precious seed, shall doubtless come again with rejoicing, bringing his sheaves with him." Then shall be the "luxuriant-growing, the healthful, yellow, and ripening grain," the "large-bearded ears, shining and rustling as they wave beneath the passing breeze, and bending from the weight of the grain sometimes half-way to the ground," and the cluster of stalks, the produce of a single seed, so large, that the reaper shall not be able, with one grasp, to gather it into his hand." "There shall be a handful of corn in the earth upon the top of the mountains"—this is all that is available at the beginning of the great enterprise—"a handful of corn," and that in the most unfavourable situation; but the *fruit* thereof shall shake like Lebanon:" "neither wave nor shake conveys the full force of the Hebrew verb, which suggests the additional idea of a rushing noise like that of the wind among the cedars of Lebanon."

What a glorious undertaking this to be permitted to take part in—this, for which there is marked out such a glorious consummation—to sow the precious seed, and thus prepare the way for that predicted time, the true golden age of our world, when

> The swart Sabeans and Panchaia's King,
> Shall cassia, myrrh, and sacred incense bring;
> All kings shall homage to the King afford,
> All nations shall receive Him for their Lord.

What help is needed? Much in every way. Hearts and hands are needed; gold and silver are needed. The men are few: they are so few, that they go forth weeping, overborne in mind and body by the magnitude of the work. The means are spare. It is said, that "to Him shall be given of the gold of Sheba." As yet, however, but little of it has been presented to Him. If the value which men attach to the Gospel truths and opportunities with which they are favoured was to be estimated by what they give to promote their extension throughout the world, the result would be too painful to be stated.

But let the rich in this world attend to the admonition of the Koheleth—

"Cast thy bread"—"send thy bread"—"upon the waters." The image is borrowed from seafaring and commercial enterprises. A man freights a ship: perhaps both ship and cargo are his own property. He invests a large sum in the undertaking. The risk was much greater in those days, when there were no insurance offices; and the figure, in order that it may carry with it its full force, must be regarded as borrowed from those earlier times, when, if a man ventured on commercial undertakings, he had to do so at his own risk, that risk being considerable. All this might have been avoided by retaining his money at home in his coffers; but then, as now, he preferred to send it forth in the hope that eventually, although it might not be until after a long delay, it would bring him back a large return. King Solomon engaged in such enterprises, and therefore from experience he could encourage others to do the same. He had at sea a navy of Tharshish with the navy of Hiram. The navigation was a lengthened one, for it was only once in three years that the navy returned; but the result was a successful one, for the ships brought back "gold and silver, ivory, and apes, and peacocks;" and so "king Solomon exceeded all the kings of the earth for riches and for wisdom."

There are many at the present day who imitate the wisdom of Solomon. They send forth their bread upon the waters. British commerce is co-extensive with the world. Far off, to the east and west, the long extent of the American coast, the shores of China and Japan, are to be found in busy action the merchants and sailors of Great Britain. Stormy seas, unhealthy climates, deter them not, and although every year there is loss, both of ships and life, yet these are only the exceptions, and by the great majority of those who go forth the enterprise is accomplished in safety, and with gainful results. If this were all that the wise man recommended when he said, "Send thy bread upon the waters," it is already fully appreciated and zealously carried out.

But the traffic which he recommends is one of a different character, and one far from being so generally acceptable. Let gold be used for the promotion of God's glory and the salvation of souls, and men send forth their "bread"—their substance—on the waters, that in distant lands the cause of true Christianity may be promoted, and nations raised from ignorance and degradation. He who spends his substance on selfish purposes keeps his riches at home: he who employs them in the service of God, in the propagation of Gospel truth, and the promotion of man's highest interests, sends forth his bread upon the waters. They who do so shall find it after certain days: it may be many days, but it shall come back to them. Money so dealt with is transmuted into good works. He who is ready to distribute, willing to communicate, large-hearted towards his fellow-men, because Christ Jesus the Lord has dealt bountifully with him, becomes rich in good works. He is engaged in the most lucrative commerce, and changes the perishable riches into that which is imperishable. He is not losing, but laying up in store. When the great shipwreck of the body takes place, and by faith in Jesus Christ laying hold on eternal life, he emerges from the flood, and stands in safety on the shore of the better country, his wealth, his substance, sublimed into evidences of his faith and love, shall be found to have preceded him. "I was an hungered, and ye gave me meat; I was thirsty, and ye gave me drink; I was a stranger, and ye took me in; naked, and ye clothed me; I was sick, and ye visited me; I was in prison, and ye came unto me."

"Cast thy bread upon the waters; for thou shalt find it after certain days."

KAFIRISTAN—ITS APPEAL FOR HELP, AND THE RESPONSE.

In another article we shall refer to Peshawur, and others of our trans-Indus stations, as frontier Missions of great importance. West, and south-west, beyond the Khyber and Kohat passes, which Peshawur commands, lies the Affghan territory, with the large towns of Cabul, Ghizni, Kandahar, &c.; in the same direction the northern provinces of Persia; in a north-westerly direction the extensive countries of Turkistan and Bokhara, with the large central towns of Balkh, Khiva, and Bokhara. These countries affect the productions of India and the manufactures of Europe, and export the yield of their own soil and climate, that they may obtain them in exchange. The Lohanis are the great carriers. Before the mountain passes between Ghizni and the Indus are blocked up by snow, they come down in vast caravans of several thousands, the whole tribe moving bodily, men, women, children, and cattle, their goods being placed on camels and ponies. They arrive at Mooltan in October and November, bringing raw silk, goats' wool, camels' hair, goods, furs, &c. Some of the caravans proceed in advance to Delhi and the Gangetic provinces; but others remain at Mooltan, and dispose of their goods to native agents, who forward them to Hindustan. The Affghan traders make up their investments at Mooltan during the cold season, and the return caravans arrive from Hindustan in April, when they all return to Affghanistan. Of the wealth of these Lohanis some idea may be formed from the following fact, stated by Sir B. Frere, when Commissioner of Sindh—"I have heard of the wife of an eminent merchant of this tribe, whose husband had been detained at Delhi longer than he expected, offering the Kaffila-bashee (head of the caravan) demurrage at the rate of 10,000 rupees a-day to defer the upward march of the caravan, and enable her husband to rejoin, as she knew, if left behind, he would be unable to follow them through the passes, except at great risk to his life, and the property he might have with him."

Thus at all these Punjab stations the Missionaries meet with men of various races, and they are thus preparing for future Missionary efforts in countries which are not yet accessible. It would be a rash attempt if our Missionaries were as yet to enter Cabul with the intention of doing the work of evangelists; but although they cannot enter the country of the Affghans, the Affghans come to them. This is the case especially at Peshawur, and there several of them have been converted to Christianity. They are men of resolute character, true to their convictions, whatever they may be, and fearless in confessing them. In addition to this, the Pushtoo language is being firmly grasped, and rendered available, both by the press and by *vivâ voce* use, for the extension of the Redeemer's kingdom.

And now another and more distant nation has come forth from the deep recesses of Asia, and, by its representatives at Peshawur, appealed for help. The Rev. W. Handcock, one of our Missionaries at that station, has forwarded to us the following intelligence—

April 11, 1864—The importance of Peshawur as a Mission station appears not merely in the city itself being a centre of Mohammedan learning and influence, but also in its being a frontier city, and close to the Khyber Pass, the great channel of communication with Central Asia.

Now and then this frontier Mission is brought to bear upon countries in advance, where evangelistic efforts have not yet penetrated. Last month I had to record the deeply-interesting interviews with the prime minister of the Ameer of Cabul, and his acceptance for himself and the Ameer of copies of the sacred Scriptures. This day I have to mention visits received from four inquirers from Kafiristan, a country lying beyond the mountains north of Cabul. The name Kafiristan, "land of infidelity," has been given to their country by the neighbouring Mussulmans in consequence of the rejection of Mohammedanism by its inhabitants. They are, however, not ashamed of their name, for when speaking of themselves they use the term "Kafir." It is remarkable that, though their territory is surrounded by powerful enemies, it is not known ever to have been conquered. Historians even say that Tamerlane, who subdued the empires between the Hellespont and Central India, retired baffled in his attempt to overcome the people of this kingdom. Though the language of the Kafirs is quite distinct from those spoken at Peshawur, yet one of the four visitors has been some little time in the country, and, having mixed with the Affghans, is able to make himself understood in Pushtoo; and it is through the medium of this man, named Gara, that we are able to hold intercourse. He is about thirty years of age, and is a man possessed of much intelligence. His appearance is rather striking. He is of middle stature, firmly, but not clumsily built, with blue eyes, and a complexion as fair as a European. He says that the people in his country, who dress in the skins of goats, live by cultivating the soil. They worship the stone image of a god named Addrakpanow. Before this idol they offer goats in sacrifice, throwing the blood on the image. Beyond this they seem to have few religious ceremonies; and, possessing no written language, they have not an elaborate system of worship like that of the Hindu.

The Kafir who gives this information and his companions show every desire to hear the Gospel of the Lord Jesus Christ. They manifest their wish to receive instruction in Christianity by proposing to remain a few days in Peshawur, and to embrace every opportunity of gaining information respecting those things which belong to their eternal peace.

April 16—The day has arrived for the departure of the Kafirs. During the time that they have been with us they have displayed great eagerness to hear of Christ. And one result, by the blessing of God upon his word, has been, that their confidence has been shaken in their own idolatry. They have, moreover, invited us to commence a Mission amongst their countrymen, assuring us that a messenger with such glad tidings would be well received. They themselves are returning home, resolved that henceforth they will not bow the knee to Addrakpanow, but that they will serve Him "who has put away sin by the sacrifice of Himself."

We hope and pray that they may reach their country in safety. If they are detected as Kafirs when passing through Mohammedan Cabul, they will either be put to death, or, after being most barbarously treated, they will be doomed to perpetual slavery. In consequence of these dangers two of them will travel, in disguise, as fakeers, and the other two will travel by night and hide during the day.

It is gratifying at this time to see the Missionary zeal of our own native Christians. Two of them, Jonah Messeeh and Fazl-i Hukk, have offered, in the face of so many dangers, to accompany the Kafirs and share their lot.

May God hasten the day when Kafiristan, though hitherto, as is supposed, unconquered by man, shall be brought into subjection to the Gospel of Christ!

Our readers will expect from us some information respecting this people, and the country from whence they come. In cases of this kind the "Church Missionary Intelligencer" may legitimately become somewhat geographical. In the present instance there is a necessity laid upon it, for Kafiristan is one of those countries of the great Asiatic continent, respecting which little comparatively is known; nor did it appear at first where recent and reliable information might be obtained respecting it. However, in the "Journal of the Asiatic Society of Bengal," No. 4, 1859, we have found a paper, "Notes on Kafiristan," by Captain H. G. Raverty, 3rd Regiment Bombay Native Infantry, and from this we have compiled the following information.

We shall, then, request our readers to look to that portion of the map of Asia which lies between the 34th and 37th degrees of north latitude, and the 69th and 74th of east longitude, for there are to be found the culminating ridges and slopes of the Hindu Koosh, divided into a number of independent states, all lying to the north of and between the Cabul river. and the Indus. Of these, Kafiristan—a word derived from the Arabic *Ka-fir*, "unbeliever," and the Persian participle, *istan*, "a place or station," is one. On its north boundary lie the Usbek states of Kunduz and Badakhshan; to the south it is separated from the Cabul river by certain districts of Affghanistan; to the east lie Chitral and Kashgar; and on the west it is bounded by mountains and the Panjshar river, which separates it from the Kohistan, or highlands of Cabul. It is a country of ridges and steep spurs of the Hindu Koosh, enclosing "narrow and fertile valleys, descending in terraces towards the Cabul river and the Indus, in a north-east and south-west direction."

"The valleys are watered by numerous streams, somewhat like the ramifications and reticulations of a leaf, which, running east and west, fall into the five considerable rivers which intersect the country." The largest of these rivers, and the most easterly, separates the upper part of Kafiristan from Chitral, or Kashgar, another of these obscure countries, of which perhaps less is known than even of Kafiristan. It joins the Cabul river ten miles below Jelalabad, where it bears the name of the Kamah: higher up it is known as the Kunar; and higher up still, towards its sources, as the Kashgar, or Chitral river. West of the Kamah two other rivers, having their courses in the southermost slopes of the Hindu Koosh, unite their parallel and not very distant cources, and, under the name of Alingár, flows into the Cabul river some miles west of Jelalabad; while, still more to the west, a third river, the Tagat, or Tagao, after receiving the contributions of various streams from the valleys of Kohistan, falls into the Cabul river forty miles east of the city of Cabul.

The fifth river, rising in the northern part of Kafiristan, and on the northern slopes of the Hindoo Koosh, flows almost due north, until, uniting with the Wardoj river, it falls into the Panj, or upper branch of the Oxus.

Numerous small streams, running from the transverse valleys, and fed by the snows which generally cover the ridges and lofty mountains on either hand, increase the volume of the larger rivers, so that, in the time of the melting of snows, they can "be crossed only by rafts, formed by tying together the inflated skins of beasts, and laying straw on the top of them." Almost every valley has a river flowing through it, "on each side of which is deposited the rich alluvium washed from the mountains by the heavy rains of the winter and spring months."

There is much diversity of temperature and variability of climate, caused by the occasional great difference of elevation, some parts of the country being considerably depressed. In the more elevated tracts the summer heat is never oppressive, and in the winter months the snow lies on the ground for many weeks together. The more depressed valleys again are well-sheltered from the cutting blasts of winter; and although surrounded on all sides by beetling mountains capped with eternal snows, the heat in the months of June, July, and August, is considerable. In some of the most secluded places it is rather oppressive, and is sufficient to bring to perfection great quantities of excellent grapes, and other fruits, constituting a large portion of the people's food. From the grapes a good deal of excellent wine is made, for which indeed the Kafirs and their country are somewhat notorious in this part of Asia.

During the spring months, and towards the end of August and September, copious showers fall, but not for any lengthened period. "In the winter violent snow storms are of frequent occurrence, which block up the passes between the hills, and cut off all communication between the different valleys, often for weeks together."

The roads or footpaths are narrow and difficult in the extreme, and, every here and there, intersected by frightful ravines, yawning chasms, and foaming torrents. These the Kafirs cross by means of rope bridges—now leading along the brink of tremendous precipices and frowning cliffs — now winding through deep and narrow hollows, dark almost at mid-day. Travellers also incur not a little danger from fragments of rock and stones, that—either loosened by the rain or wind, or disturbed by wild animals and the numerous flocks of goats that crop the herbage on the higher hills and beetling crags, at the base of which they tread their way—every now and then come rolling down with a fearful crash reverberated on all sides.

If the road should be a frequented one, these primitive bridges are made by connecting together four or five stout and strong ropes, made of goats'-hair, by slighter ones at about six or eight inches distance from each other, laid transversely just like the shrouds of a ship's masts with the ratlines across. These are fastened to the trunks of trees on either side, and stretched as tight as possible. Should there be no trees sufficiently near the spot, the ropes are either attached to strong stakes driven into the ground, or made fast to the rocks. On each side of this suspension bridge there is another rope by which a person crossing may steady himself. Some people crawl on their hands and knees, and others, less timorous, walk across: still the depth of the yawning abyss beneath, accompanied at times by the deafening sound of the foaming torrent that seems to shake the very rocks, renders this mode of crossing, even to those accustomed to it, fearful in the extreme.

Other bridges, when the narrowness of the chasms will permit, and trees of sufficient length are available, are formed by placing three, four, or more logs side by side. The Kafirs cross the smaller chasms and mountain-torrents of no great breadth by means of leaping poles. In the use of these they are exceedingly expert, and, being a particularly active race, can climb the steepest hills.

Horses, mules, asses, and camels, being unknown in Kafiristan, burdens are carried by bullocks, or on men's backs, chiefly by a tribe of people called Baris. These people are the Pariahs of the country. They carry on all the mechanical trades, such as blacksmiths, weavers, carpenters, cutlers, the Kafirs considering arms and agriculture as the only occupations which are worthy of their attention.

Such, then, is a brief sketch of the mountain home of the Si'ah-posh Kafirs, or Black-clad unbelievers, so called from the black goat-skin garments which they wear. It has been a mountain fastness to them where they have been enabled to preserve their independence in a marvellous way. Often has their subjugation been attempted by the great conquerors which have played their part from time to time in the history of Asia, but failure has universally ensued. Timor tried to reduce them; the emperor Baber made forays into their valleys; the Mohammedan chiefs of the mountain principalities on their borders confederated against them. On all these occasions the Kafirs suffered more or less severely, yet still survived as an independent nation. All around Mohammedanism prevails. Kashgar, Kunduz, Affghanistan, the petty states north-west of Peshawur, all have been Mohammedanized; while Kafiristan stands forth like an island amidst the surrounding deluge. Experience proves how much more severe an obstacle Mohammedanism presents to the progress of Christianity than heathenism. The various systems of heathen error were formed in ignorance of Christianity: Mohammedanism, on the contrary, in the contemptuous rejection of it. It claims to have superseded the Christian dispensation; assumes superiority over it; and fills the minds of its followers with prejudices against it. Hence into Mohammedan kingdoms, where "the faith" holds the political power in subserviency, and uses it for its own purposes, Christian Missionaries usually obtain no entrance until a period of decadence ensues, and the empire becomes enfeebled. Thus Turkey, preserved from dissolution by the aid of Christian powers, has been compelled to tolerate the Christian Missionary; but it is with reluctance that she does so, and so soon as she can venture on such a step, delays not to cripple his action; while beyond the frontiers of Turkey the Mohammedan kingdoms of Asia are closed against the Christian Missionary. But Kafiristan is available. Retaining its ancient heathenism, it has refused submission to the arrogance of the Moslem. What a position, then, for Christianity to occupy! Entrenched there amidst those rocky eminences, it might from thence act with converting power on the outlying portions of the Mohammedan kingdoms around, and kindle a light in the very heart of Mohammedan Asia. There is surely no enthusiasm in supposing that this isolated country has been conserved from the domination of Mohammedanism for some special purpose.

But let us learn something about its people. The Kafirs, by their own account, are divided into eighteen tribes, of which ten retain their ancient faith, and observe their former customs. Of the remaining eight, one whole tribe has been proselyted to a lax Mohammedanism; four more have been, for the most part, so, but not entirely; while, of the remaining four, only a few have changed their faith. Fourteen of the tribes may now be regarded as constituting the whole of the real Kafir race. "Those who have abandoned the religious observances of their forefathers, and who dwell in the hills and valleys bordering on the Affghan territories to the south and west, are called by that people 'Nímchahs,' a Persian derivative from *ním*, 'half,' or the 'middle,' and *chah*, a particle added to nouns to form diminutives, and to express somewhat of contempt."

The so-called Nímchahs continue to intermarry with the Kafirs and Affghans indiscriminately. They also act as guides on either side, when the Kafirs attack the Mohammedans, or when the latter make forays into the country of the former, and sometimes even join in these expeditions. They are excessively ignorant of the Mohammedan creed, and most of them even appear ignorant of the necessary forms of prayer. They all drink a strong undistilled wine, which they keep a long time before broaching, another proof of their connexion with the Si'ah-posh tribes.

Of four of the Si'ah-posh tribes the dress is precisely alike—

The dress of the Kamuz, Kampar, Kattar, and Wae-kal tribes consists of a shirt, drawers, neither very tight nor very loose, and a *lungi* or scarf, all of coarse cotton, besides a black dress similar to that worn by the fakeers, or devotees at Cabul, consisting of a wide *chokah*, or cloak, with short wide sleeves, made of a peculiar sort of wool. This they put on over the under-dress; and over all are worn the goat-skin garments.

The remaining tribes wear a dress called a *chakman*, which is sometimes brought to Cabul for sale, and is manufactured from wool of various colours; drawers, called *buzo*, also made of wool; and a shirt of coarse cotton cloth, as worn by the other tribes.

In the winter season, on account of the snow which lies on the ground for several months, in the more elevated districts, they are in the habit of wearing shoes of black goats'-hair, woven strongly together; but in the summer they substitute the *charuk*—a sort of half-boot made of goat-skin with the hair outwards, to lace up in front, and similar to the boots worn by the mountaineers of Panjsher, who are, by all accounts, converted Kafirs, and the shoes of skin with the hair on, worn by the Scottish highlanders.

Few of the Kafirs cover the head; and, when they do so, it is with a narrow band of fillet made of goats'-hair of three different colours—red, black, and white—about a yard or a yard and a half in length, wound round the head.

The females dress in a similar style to the women of the Kohistan or highlands of Cabul, viz. loose drawers tight at the ancle; a long shirt or chemise; a *chadar* or veil; and a small scull-cap, under which the hair is plaited.

Their ornaments or trinkets consist of flat bracelets on the wrists, necklaces, and ear-rings, and rings on the fingers. Those of the rich are mostly of silver, and rarely of gold; whilst the ornaments of the poorer classes are generally of brass and copper. The men wear rings in the ears and on the fingers only.

Those females whose fathers or husbands may have slain one or more Mussulmans have the peculiar privilege of ornamenting their caps and locks with *kauri* shells. Young virgins, instead of the scull-caps, fasten a narrow fillet of red cloth round their heads, which they adorn with shells, if entitled to the privilege. . . .

The Kafir towns and villages, several of which contain 300 and 400 houses, are almost invariably built on the steep acclivities of the mountains, on account of the general irregular nature of the country they inhabit, and also, as being better in a defensive point of view, in case of invasion. Some few are situated in the valleys and on the table-lands, towards the northern parts of the country. They never dwell in tents, but some are said to dwell in caves.

Their houses are generally built of stone, in frames of wood, with flat roofs, and of one storey in height. Some dwellings contain, according to the means of the owner, several rooms, furnished with wooden benches or tables, stools made of wood, and sometimes of wicker-work covered with goat-skin, for the Kafirs cannot squat down in the oriental fashion; and in this point, in particular, they bear a striking resemblance to Europeans in being unable to sit crossed-legged with any comfort. Their beds are made of wood, and similar in form to the Indian *charpae*—a simple frame with short legs, over which they lace bands of leather.

The Si'ah-posh tribes are rich in herds of oxen or cows, and flocks of sheep and goats, the latter of a very superior breed. They also rear immense numbers of fowls. They eat beef, but the flesh of sheep and goats, particularly the latter, is more commonly consumed, as also the game they capture in the chase, such as deer, antelope, ibex—the antlers of which they set up in their places of worship—and the *kuchar* or mountain sheep, and other smaller animals.

Their other articles of food consist of unleavened bread, milk, curds, butter, honey, a few herbs, vegetables, and fruit, which latter their country produces in great quantities, and of excellent flavour.

All classes of people drink a great deal of wine, as do most of the inhabitants of the neighbouring countries professing the Mohammedan religion—the Chitralis or Kashkaris, who are considered to be of the same stock as the Kafirs—the people of Gilgitt, and Gunjut, belonging to Yasan—the Badakhshanis and the Nímchahs, who are either converted Kafirs, or descendants of those who have intermarried with their Mohammedan neighbours. On public occasions the Kafirs are very liberal with it, and it is put into vessels and placed in convenient places, where all who come may help themselves. There are stringent regulations regarding picking the grapes before a certain day, and great care is taken in their cultivation.

Once in the year a grand and ancient festival is held, which continues from twenty to forty days. Its details would not bear exposure to the daylight; yet such appears to be all the religion which they have—"The people sat down to eat and drink, and rose up to play." The great wonder is, that, without any thing of religious truth in the midst of them, consigned to ignorance and isolation, they have been enabled to retain their independence, and are so superior, in point of intrepidity and their mode of warfare, to the surrounding Mohammedans, "that hitherto none of their enemies—save for a very short period, and then only in far superior numbers—have been able to oppose them with success."

On the day following the conclusion of the great annual festival, bands are organized, with the object of making raids into the Mohammedan territories. The kowál, or bard, stimulates the assembly by reciting the deeds of their ancestors, chiefs who have distinguished themselves utter their impassioned harangues, and the warriors set forth.

"A few years ago the Si'ah-posh had no firearms whatever amongst them; but at present they are much better provided with flint-lock pieces than the people of the Kohistan of Cabul." It is doubtful whence these are obtained, whether they are of Russian manufacture, or find their way from the Punjab or Cashmir by way of Gilgitt and Chitral.

The original weapons of offence used by the Kafirs are bows and arrows, the former about four feet in length, the latter nearly two; and a long and broad knife of a peculiar curved shape, and about two feet in length. They also use a smaller knife, about twelve or fifteen inches in length, for cutting their food with. Some few possess swords, the spoils of their enemies.

It must be observed that these forays are simply reprisals for wrongs which they have suffered from the Mohammedans, who continually make inroads into their territory, for the purpose of carrying off slaves and cattle. The Kafirs lose no opportunity of avenging themselves, and are constant in their endeavours to destroy them, as enjoined by their religion and ancient custom. In fact, the young warrior who has not on some occasion ennobled himself by killing a follower of Islam is not allowed to sit in the assembly of his tribe, or to share in any public diversions. And "yet when a Mussulman throws himself on the generosity, and places faith on the word, of a Kafir, he is treated by him in the most hospitable manner. If one of the former people falls by chance into the hands of the Kafirs, when not on their yearly crusade, and says that he is a friend or acquaintance of a certain Kafir of a certain tribe, they release him; and even if such person happens to be accompanied by a second party, he has merely to say, 'This man is my friend, and I am the friend of such and such a Kafir (mentioning his name) of a certain village,' in order to obtain his companion's release also."

In religious matters the Si'ah-posh tribes appear to be exceedingly ignorant, and their few forms and ceremonies are idolatrous. They consist chiefly of sacrifices of cows and goats to their deities, whom they call Shuruyah, Lamani, and Pandu, which latter the name would lead us to suppose to be one and the same with the deity of the Hindu pantheon known under the name of Yudhishthira.

They have hereditary priests who assist at the different feasts and ceremonies, and who are supported by voluntary contributions, and a double share of victuals and wines at festivals. Their influence is very slight, and the elders and chief men of tribes appear to hold all authority.

Each village contains a temple or place of worship, differing but little from the dwellings of the people themselves, and in which the wooden representations of the three deities before mentioned are placed. The walls are generally ornamented with the antlers of deer.

Fire appears to be necessary in most of their religious ceremonies; and a Kafir has an antipathy to extinguish it by water, or even to blow out a flame with the breath; yet they do not keep up the sacred fire like the followers of Zartusht, and do not even seem to know any thing concerning it. At the same time, a number of their usages bear great resemblance to those of the Gabrs, of whom they are probably an offshoot, but whose characteristics have gradually declined during the many centuries they have been separated from the parent stock. The Badakhshanis and others, inhabiting the surrounding countries, are probably descended from the same race.

The Magian religion was not exclusively confined to Media, but extended to the east to Bakhtra (in which the royal residence was first situated), and as far as the stupendous mountains of the Indian Caucasus and the valley of the Oxus, the whole of which extensive tracts of country—where numerous ruins attributed to the Gabrs still exist—were included in the mighty empire of the Medes. It is also evident, from the Zendavesta, that it was in these regions the religion of Sapetman Zoroaster "first took root and flourished, and thus it became the parent land of the civil institutions of the Medes."

"The Si'ah-posh claim to be the brothers of the Farangi, and, according to the traditions preserved among them, they affirm, that, coeval with the spread of Islamism, they occupied the countries to the south of their present location, and have been subsequently compelled to seek for liberty and for safety, among the mountains and valleys of the Hindu Koosh, from the insupportable tyranny of their Mohammedan neighbours, whom they designate 'Awdál.' They appear, therefore, unquestionably to be the remnant of the aboriginal inhabitants of the country to the south of the Cabul river and Central Affghanistan, as at present constituted. This is confirmed by the traditions of the Affghans also; from the existing histories in the Pushtu, or Affghan language; and from the writings of other Mohammedan historians.

"The safest mode of entering the Kafir country is to get one of them beforehand to become security, after which a person may go from one end of it to the other without the slightest danger.

"When foreigners enter the territory of the Si'ah-posh tribes they are treated with great kindness and hospitality; but they try by every means to induce strangers to remain. Their boasting that the Farangi are their brothers would appear a sufficient guarantee for the safety and kind treatment of any European who may penetrate into their secluded valleys.

"The Kafirs have European features, and a highly intellectual cast of countenance. They have both blue and dark eyes, arched eyebrows, long eyelashes, and broad, open foreheads. Their hair varies in colour from black to lightish brown; and both males and females are tall and well made, and of handsome figure. Some of the females are said to be particularly beautiful. They all go about unveiled."

Captain Raverty concludes his notices with the following paragraphs—

In summing up the character of this unsophisticated and highly interesting race, I may remark that they appear by all accounts, and even from the descriptions of their enemies, to be of a merry and sociable disposition, and, though quick to anger, are as easily appeased. Hospitable to a fault, they treat their guests more kindly than brothers. Even their enemies allow that they are as sincere in their friendship as in their enmity; are faithful to their agreements; and hold boasting, lying, and duplicity in sovereign contempt.

Lieutenant Wood, in the interesting work, "A Journey to the Oxus," remarks concerning them (in which I most cordially agree) that "they resemble Europeans in being possessed of great intelligence, and from all I have seen and heard of them, I consider they offer a fairer field for Missionary exertion than is to be found anywhere else on the continent of Asia. They pride themselves on being, to use their own words, brothers of the Farangis; and this opinion of itself may hereafter smooth the road for the zealous pioneers of the Gospel."

Fortunate indeed will be that man who has the opportunity of first exploring these regions; and still more so he who is destined to disperse the dark clouds of idolatry which now hang over them, by the bright light of Christianity.

It is deeply interesting, therefore, to find, not only that some of this race have been in communication with our Missionaries at Peshawur, but that they have shown great eagerness to hear of Christ, declaring their determination, on their return to their own country, to put away their false gods, and bow the knee only to Him whom the Father hath highly exalted. So impressed have they been with the truth and value of the Gospel, that they have invited us to commence a Mission amongst them.

And now we have something more of deep interest to state. Difficult and perilous as the enterprise is, yet some have been found willing to go on a Christian mission to Kafiristan. Our Missionary at Peshawur, Mr. Handcock, under date of October 10, informs us—

Two converted Affghans, not counting their lives dear unto themselves, have responded to a pressing invitation from the people of Kafiristan to preach the Gospel in that part of Central Asia. They left us on their perilous enterprise about a month ago, marching by way of Cabul. Their commission is, at the present time, to act more as pioneers than as permanent residents. In a few months, therefore, God vouchsafing to spare them, we hope to see them again, and to report concerning their undertaking.

Let it be remembered that the Si'ah-posh regard the Affghans as their most relentless foes. They sometimes enter into a truce of friendship with the people of Badakshan and Chitral, when they exchange weapons, and, until these are returned, they remain at peace; but with the more cruel and bigoted Affghans this is rarely done. Yet here are two Affghans—men who, had they remained Mohammedans, might have headed a predatory party into Kafiristan—at the peril of their lives venturing thither on a mission of mercy, desiring, after the example of their great Master, not to destroy men's lives, but to save them. What a wondrous influence true Christianity exercises! How great its reconciling power! How true it is that in reconciling the sinner to God, it reconciles man to his fellow! The feet of these Affghans had once been swift to shed blood, but now how beautiful upon the mountains of Kafiristan will be the feet of them "that bring good tidings, that publish peace!"

Surely friends at home will not fail to help forward this deeply-interesting movement by their prayers.

NEW ZEALAND AFFAIRS.

In April 1864 an address was presented to Sir George Grey, the Governor of New Zealand, signed by a very large number of British noblemen and gentlemen. It had reference to the unhappy war in New Zealand. After expressing their deep regret at the failure of his efforts to establish a system of self-government in the native districts, and their disappointment at the renewal of hostilities, they proceeded to express their earnest hope that "His Excellency would avail himself of the first favourable opportunity to terminate the war by negotiations, and that any overtures of peace made by any of the natives would be at once listened to." Especially they deprecated the confiscation of native lands, as a policy which would close the door upon any possible settlement of the existing difficulty except by the sword, and thus lead to the extermination of the native race. They prayed him, therefore, in the hour of victory, "to temper justice with mercy, and give to the world another bright example of magnanimity and forbearance."

The Governor, in his reply, assured them, that, "in his readiness to receive any overtures made by the natives in arms, his own feelings were in entire consonance with theirs." On the land-confiscation policy he expressed his conviction that the future safety of the colonists required the alienation of a considerable portion of land from the natives who had risen in arms, and its occupation by European settlers; but at the same time assured the memorialists that a sufficiency should be reserved for themselves and their descendants, and guaranteed by a secure tenure.

The Governor's responsible advisers also drew up a memorandum in answer to the address. This document is very different from the Governor's. There are assertions made in it which are not sustained by facts. Thompson, designated as the leader of the rebel party, is accused of having, announced in writing under his own hand, his determination to carry on the war to the utmost extremity. Thompson, when the horizon first became clouded, and there were symptoms of an approaching storm, wished to mediate between the extreme parties on both sides to promote peace. He came to Auckland for this purpose in 1857. He could obtain no access to the Governor, and was not only coolly but rudely treated. Finding his people without law, the old heathen customs broken down by their abandonment of heathenism for a profession of Christianity, and nothing set up in their place, he then favoured the King-movement. Yet, in 1861 this same Thompson, or Tamehana, went down as a peacemaker to Taranaki, where the war was raging, and, withdrawing the Waikato tribes, for a time stayed that conflict.

Again, when, unhappily, Tataraimaka was taken possession of by the Queen's troops, before Waitara was surrendered, and the war was renewed, Thompson restrained the Ngatimaniapoto, who were urgent for an attack upon the English villages within the Auckland district, and even upon the town of Auckland itself. His interference saved Auckland, which at that time lay comparatively defenceless. He went further. Descending the river, he placed himself in communication with the Queen's principal magistrate, proposing that a great effort should be made for the preservation of peace. "But no encouragement was given him, nor were any negotiations entered into."

Both sides had now reached a position of mutual distrust. The colonists feared an onslaught on Auckland; the natives felt persuaded that the British meditated an invasion of their territory, and that the effort was about to be made to dispossess them of their lands. The Maoris did not attack Auckland; but the British took the initiative, by the expulsion of the natives from their villages near Auckland, thus sending them adrift in the midst of the Maori winter, although a large proportion of them were sick and infirm. They then crossed the Maungatawhiri into the Waikato territory. From that moment Thompson hesitated not, but, on the defensive, and in that which he considered a righteous cause, joined the natives in arms.

The responsible ministry, in their memorandum, further stated their conviction, that as Waikato was the head of the rebellion, it was necessary "its neck should be broken;" that its tribes should be subjugated; and sufficient material guarantees be taken in order to secure the peace of the frontier. As yet, in the opinion of the responsible ministry, this material guarantee had not been secured. Although Ngaruawahia, the capital of the Waikato, had been wrested from the Maoris, and with it the plain of the Waikato, it was yet necessary, according to their view, that the Thames' valley, with its opening into the Gulf of Hauraki, and the sea-port of Tauranga should be added to the spoils, in order to facilitate the settlement of the new colonial possessions, and provide them with commercial outlets, Raglan, on the west coast, being severed from the Waikato plain by limestone ranges of a very rugged character.

No sufficient material guarantee having been, in the opinion of the ministry, secured, it was necessary that the war should proceed, and that the more, because, as they asserted, the Maoris, "as a body, had not shown the smallest symptom of any desire to terminate the war, nor had they made any overtures of peace." The Blue Books inform us why they had not done so. So long back as May of last year, Sir George Grey, in a despatch to the Duke of Newcastle, states, that "Rewi, the redoubtable chief of the Ngatimaniapoto, had declared his own anxiety, and that of his people, to make peace, and live quietly by the side of the white man; but that they were deterred from laying down their arms by the severity of the terms which had been proposed to them; and they declared this to be the reason why they did not accept the terms offered them by General Cameron after the fight at Orakau, because they felt convinced that they would all be sent to Auckland, as the prisoners were from Rangiriri, and never perhaps be liberated.

Finally, as to the confiscation of native lands, the responsible ministry declared alike their conviction of its necessity, and their determination to effect it. It was, in their opinion, according to Maori custom, and involved in it nothing "abhorrent to the moral sense, or previous habits of thought of the Maori race." They asserted that the natives would not consider themselves conquered unless their lands were taken. Moreover, the more insolent of the Maoris, when the war commenced, had threatened to do the same by the Europeans. They would "come to the settler's house and say, 'Oh, that house will suit me very well; that room will do for my wife; that shall be my bed: wait a little; by and by you will see;'" and because the worst of the Maoris had threatened to act wrongfully by the Europeans, the responsible ministry felt themselves free to retaliate like wrongs on the Maoris.

Thus, for various reasons, the confiscation of Maori lands was, in their view, imperative. The Maoris were no longer to be regarded as an independent people possessed of rights, but as a subjugated people, dependent entirely on the clemency of the responsible ministry, who, convinced that nothing would be more injurious to the native race than the possession of large territories under tribal tenures, were prepared, not indeed to amend the title, but to take away the lands, "making of course ample provision for the future." In referring to the severity of the terms likely to be imposed upon them, the insurgents had especially in view the treatment awarded to the chiefs who had surrendered at Rangiriri and who had ever since been retained in captivity. The detention of these men had, no doubt, produced the worst effect on the warring tribes, and prevented them sueing for peace. They felt sure, that so soon as the war was ended, these men would either be transported to some island, or imprisoned, and eventually hanged. So convinced was the Governor of the injurious effect produced by their detention, that he remonstrated with the ministry on the subject. The correspondence will be found in the Blue Books.*

The Governor pressed for a decision in their case: he thought it sufficient if some of them were brought to trial, and others released on conditions. Ministers, on the contrary, were of opinion that such would be an unwise and dangerous experiment: they preferred that they should be all brought to trial before a military commission. On this point there arose a serious difference of opinion, the Governor declaring that the punishment which his responsible ministers advised should be inflicted upon all the native prisoners *exceeded in severity that which Great Britain has ever before inflicted upon any people under such circumstances*, and that he could not take upon himself the responsibility of giving effect to their advice.

In the correspondence which ensued, which is well worthy the consideration of those who wish to have a clear understanding of New-Zealand affairs, it comes out that this question respecting the prisoners was not the only one on which the Governor and his responsible ministry differed. We have referred in previous papers to the unhappy instructions issued to the officer in command of the troops sent to Tauranga, to the effect that he was to destroy the crops and cattle of the natives on both sides of the harbour, although on the west side there had been no disaffection; and our readers are aware of the panic which was thus caused; of the remonstrance of our Missionary addressed to the Government; of the delay which supervened before an answer was received; of the flight of the friendly natives into the woods; and of the desperation to which the insurgent natives were driven, resulting in our disastrous discomfiture at Tauranga. It appears now that this delay arose from a difference of opinion between the Governor and the ministers. In a memorandum, dated April 29, 1864, the former observes—"When the expedition was sent to Tauranga, his present responsible advisers advised him to issue orders that the crops and cattle and other property of the natives on the west side of the harbour should be taken possession of, and he then declined to issue such orders: even in the case of the hostile natives at Tauranga he would only sanction their supplies of food and their cattle being taken possession of."

In New Zealand, so long as the Governor and the responsible ministry are agreed, the administration can be carried on. But when differences of opinion arise on impor-

* July 15, 1864.

tant questions, then it becomes difficult to see what course is to be pursued. Who is to rule the decision, the Governor or the ministry? Mr. Cardwell, in a despatch, dated July 26, 1864, has decided this point. He observes—"In my despatch of May 26th, I had stated to you plainly 'that an army of 10,000 English troops had been placed at your disposal for objects of great imperial concern, and not for the attainment of any local object; that your responsibility to the Crown is paramount; and that you will not continue the expenditure of blood and treasure longer than is absolutely necessary for the establishment of a fast and enduring peace;' and also in my despatch of June 27th, when I had received intimation of this unfortunate difference between yourself and your advisers, but without the full particulars which have reached me by this present mail, I again stated, that while I fully recognised the general right and duty of the Colonial Government to deal with matters of native policy, properly so called, I considered, that while active operations are being carried on under the conduct of Her Majesty's officers, and in the main by Her Majesty's military and naval forces, it was for the Governor personally, as representative of the Imperial Government, to decide upon the fate of persons who were taken prisoners in the course of these military operations."

"The question of responsible government in a colony, where in ordinary times the civil and internal policy is directed by the ministers, but where, in cases of emergency, the safety of the inhabitants is secured, and peace and order are restored, by the aid of the naval and military forces of Her Majesty, is not a question to be discussed or argued at a moment like the present. Whatever may be the precise limits of the authority vested in the ministers, and of the power and responsibility of the Governor as the servant of the Crown of England, an army like that now operating in New Zealand has not been sent to the colony, and will not be maintained there, subject to any other authority than that of the Crown, and you appear rightly to interpret your position."

We cannot be surprised that this decision has led to the resignation of the ministry; and we now look anxiously for the next mail from New Zealand.

Meanwhile we place before our readers the following papers—letters from Maori chiefs residing near the river Thames to those noblemen and gentlemen whose signatures had been annexed to the Memorial addressed by the Aborigines' Protection Society to the Governor. They have been forwarded to the nobleman whose name appears at the head of the signatures, the Earl of Chichester, by a gentleman of the name of Graham, residing at Auckland, who, in doing so, assures his lordship that the Memorial had been read by every tribe, and had done much good by showing the Maoris that "the Christian people of England, as well as many of the European colonists in New Zealand, feel for them, and desire to live at peace."

The letters of the Maori chiefs will be read, we doubt not, with deep interest, and excite much sympathy in their behalf.

The first letter is from the Ngatapukenga tribe of the Thames district, one which, with its allies, had not been in arms against the British.

(Translation).

Hurwaki, New Zealand, Sept. 27, 1865.

O friends, the loving chiefs of the benevolent council [*i.e.* the Aborigines' Protection Society], who are uniting in one the nations created by God, for, though their languages are diverse, God made them, and, though their skins differ in colour, God made them.

Greeting. We have heard of your affectionate regard for the Maoris, published in the newspapers [*i.e.* the Address of the Aborigines' Protection Society, published in the New-Zealand newspapers]. And now we are persuaded that God Himself influenced you to send this love hither [*i.e.* the Address presented to Sir George Grey], as we sit musing over the many, many evils to which this island has been subjected. The love of our European friends residing here, those who eat with us out of the same dish, is not like this manifested by you.

O, council of gentlemen, or chiefs, bishops, ministers, Christian men, children of God, yonder, in that great land of England, we affectionately greet you from this far-distant land; for the heart [of the Maoris] now speaks to you thus—"Though our bodily presence is far off, our spirit is with you."

And now, as your thoughts for the preservation of the Maoris have taken root, be strong; for you are fulfilling the words of Christ, which are—"Thou shalt love thy neighbour as thyself." Be strong; will you? Yes.

There are two points, in your Address to the Europeans residing in this island [*i.e.* the Address presented to the Governor of New Zealand], which are good, namely, that the war in this country should be at once terminated; and, secondly, that the land of the Maoris should not be taken from them.

Hearken. The observance of these two points will be the salvation of the Maoris stretching away from north to south. All the Maoris are agreed on these two points, for the blood of the European is shed on his money, but as to the blood of the Maori, it is shed on his own land.

(Signed) TE KINOREHUA,
TAWHIHURITANGAKI,
TE TIKI TE WHATARAU,
TE POTAHI,
TE REIITI,
TE RONGOTOA,
And all the rest of the tribe.

Auckland, Nov. 7, 1864.

(Translation.)

Horotun, Place in New Zealand,
October 29, 1864.

O friends, the assembly of English gentlemen [*i.e.* the Aborigines' Protection Society] who wrote to Governor Grey not to take the land of the Maoris, or allow it to be taken by Pakehas, or colonists, and not to allow the Maoris to be killed, which sentiments were published in the newspapers of this island—We native chiefs rejoice on account of [these sentiments of yours]: from the rising of the sun to the setting thereof [*i.e.* from one end of New Zealand to the other] these your sentiments will be admired by us. We admire or esteem these words, for by them we are saved [*i.e.* if these principles are adhered to, the war will be at an end, as the Maoris are simply fighting for their lands]. Because of this [*i.e.* the kindly feelings of the Aborigines' Protection Society towards the Maoris] the chiefs of New Zealand say, Let the chiefs of England come to New Zealand [*i.e.* a deputation or an agent of the Aborigines' Protection Society] to put an end to this foolish war. Do you hearken all of you: the excellent sentiments expressed in the Address you sent hither [*i.e.* the Address of the Aborigines' Protection Society to Sir George Grey], do you cause them to be enforced in England, where are the houses of treasure and the houses of Maire (Mira salicifolia) [*i.e.* in England, where all that is grand and beautiful in art and sublime in sentiment meet the eye and the mind]. You cause the points mooted by you to be settled yonder [*i.e.* in England]; then we shall be saved here [*i.e.* in New Zealand]: or if you plead our cause in England, and prevail, we Maoris shall be saved from the horrors of war, &c. Let your mission [of mercy] be hastily executed, so that we may speedily be saved from the works of the Europeans [*i.e.* saved from war]. We are waiting to be saved [*i.e.* friendly intervention], and wondering from what quarter mediators will come.

If you are clear about the matter, or if you approve, send a member of your council hither to us to inquire into the wrongs or errors of this island, for the good things of this island, as well as the bad things, are unknown to you. Let our affairs be seen with your own eyes, and do not suffer intelligence to be carried on to you by the winds, lest there should be any doubts in your minds, and you should conclude that the Pakeha side is right or wrong, or the Maori side right or wrong. This is the reason why we send you this message. We have heard of your large brotherly love to the Maoris. It was the European race who brought the Gospel to this barbarous island; also the sword to kill those they [*i.e.* the Missionaries] had instructed. And now they [the Maoris] have no wish to lift up the sword which kills the body, but they wish to have "the sword of the Spirit, which is the word of God."

O friends, the chiefs of the council [*i.e.* the Aborigines' Protection Society], be all of you powerful to raise us up, so that we may stand on our feet, or stand erect and come back to Christianity [*i.e.* war has driven Christianity far from us], for death, that is to say, war, is the work of Satan, but peace is from God.

(Signed)
TE OHA TAOTAO, and all his tribe.
From KATAKATE, and all his tribe.
From TE KORO, and all his tribe.

There is one affecting incident mentioned by Mr. Graham which we must introduce. When Colonel Booth lay dangerously wounded, a native chief (Davis) left the Gate Pah to fetch the dying soldier some water. While thus engaged he was struck by a fatal shot. The colonel and the Maori died the following day.

ARRIVAL OF OUR MISSIONARIES AT AMBOANIO, IN THE PROVINCE OF VOHEMARE, MADAGASCAR.

OUR two Missionaries having commenced their labours in Madagascar, we resume our notices of that island. We have been silent on this subject for many months. Nor is this surprising. The disappointment connected with King Radama made us dumb: we could only lay our hand upon our mouth and wait. Few there have been on the page of history who promised so well, who so rapidly deteriorated, and whose life, and short reign, commenced amidst the enthusiasm of a delighted people, terminated in so dread a catastrophe. We remember Mr. Ellis's interesting notices of him and his visits to Madagascar, especially where in his preface he says—"The accounts comprised in the following pages of my intercourse with the people, especially with the young prince, the queen's son, and heir to the throne, for the preservation of whose valuable life the affectionate anxieties of the people are at times intensely excited, will, I most sincerely trust, increase the interest felt in the people of Madagascar, and particularly in the young prince personally, by the English generally, and more especially by the religious portions of the community." Assuredly the notices of that intercourse which occur in the pages of that book were well calculated to excite such an interest. To one passage we shall refer. The prince's life was in much danger from the ultraists of the idolatrous party, at whose instigation the Christians had been so bitterly persecuted, and who well knew that the commencement of Radama's reign would terminate this cruelty. The prince was therefore remonstrated with, "for going about with so few attendants." "But," he added, "I put my trust in God. If it be his will that I shall live He will protect me." He had experienced this protection. Some short time previously "one of the idol-keepers was said to have concealed himself, with some of his adherents, in a part of the way along which the prince was expected to pass. The assassin had raised his spear as the prince approached; and, if not actually making the thrust, it was so near his person, that the prince either seized or dashed aside the weapon with his hand. The attendants of the prince secured, and would have despatched the man at once, and the chief officer, it is said, gave orders for him to be put to death that night; but the prince interposed, and said, "God is the sovereign of life. He has preserved my life, and it is not necessary for its continued preservation that I should destroy the life of this man. Let him live, but be sent to a distant part of the island, and then so secured as to prevent further mischief to me or to others."

Yet, while introducing these and many other favourable notices of the prince, Mr. Ellis made us aware that there were elements in his character which, if not controlled, might lead him into excesses. "The temperament of the prince is ardent and impulsive. Hence his conduct may at times be hasty; and this tendency has not been restrained by the discipline of a sound education. His disposition prompts him to rely on others: hence his greatest danger is from false or pretended friends, and his greatest want is wise and faithful counsellers. Still there is much to excite admiration, if not surprise, in the amount of his intelligence, and the soundness of his judgment."

Happy indeed had it been for him if he had submitted himself unreservedly to the hallowing influence of Christianity. But this was wanting. We have no doubt of his conviction that it was the true religion, but he did not personally embrace it. He sympathized with the native Christians who had suffered so severely; he befriended the Missionaries, who, so soon as the island was re-opened, hastened to resume the long-suspended work; but he made no profession of faith himself. There were habits to which he was addicted, incompatible with his doing so. "If thy right eye offend thee pluck it out and cast it from thee." This he was not prepared to do; and these indulgences laying waste all that was hopeful in his character prepared him for destruction.

At the same time we cannot help thinking that we do not yet know all the particulars connected with Radama's death. Additional light may yet be cast upon this tragedy, which may show that other influences were at work than those connected with his own personal misconduct; although no doubt his own delinquencies rendered him vulnerable, and easy to be overthrown.

As regards the present state of things, it must be remembered that "the Queen and her Government are patrons of heathenism, although honourably upholding the rights and privileges of the native Christians." It is not, however, to be supposed that "the privileges of civil and religious liberty are fully understood by the Government or enjoyed by the Christians in their largest extent."

We have now the gratification of stating the arrival of our two Missionaries, the Rev. Messrs. Campbell and Maundrell, at Madagascar. The province, into which they have entered, is the most northern of the island, and is called Vohemare. Ellis, in his history of Madagascar, describes it as mountainous and thinly populated. Of its mountainous and, we trust, healthy character, there is no doubt; and as to its population and resources we shall soon be in a position to place before our readers further information. There is no town or village called Vohemare: this is the name of the district or county, its chief town, where our Missionaries are, being Amboanio.

We have received letters from both our Missionaries: they are in a journal form, and we think it better to give the extracts as we find them, as the various points of information will thus come out more naturally. The first extracts are from the letters of the Rev. H. Maundrell.

Nov. 8, 1864—Mr. Campbell and I left Mauritius on Wednesday last, November 3, and to-day we have sighted once more the heights of Madagascar. The sun set this evening over the hills and mountains to the west of our position, and made our view of Madagascar a pleasing one.

Our voyage from Mauritius, owing to the extreme kindness and attention of Captain Rosalie, the quiet weather, and the certain hope that I was enabled to enjoy of reaching our destination, has been the most pleasant of any I remember.

Nov. 9—The weather was rather rough and squally during last night, and I began to fear that we should again fail in reaching Vohemare. My fears were increased when I found, on going on deck this morning, that Captain Rosalie was uncertain of his position, not knowing whether he was to the southward or northward of his port. He continued to sail to the northward, and about ten o'clock A.M., to our great satisfaction, he sighted Vohemare. In less than two hours the "King Radama" was lying quietly at anchor in Vohemare harbour. The entrance to this harbour is narrow, but not near so narrow and difficult as persons represent it. With the wind to the south or south-east, vessels of any tonnage might enter the bay without risk. Steamers might enter at any time. A short time after our arrival a kind of pratique officer, with a few guards, came aboard, and demanded the objects of the captain's visit, to report the same to the Governor, who lives at Amboanio, a town about eight miles distant from Vohemare, and much larger, being the Hova settlement of this part of Madagascar.

After tiffin, Mr. Campbell, Captain Rosalie, and I, went ashore to visit the town. The people, both Hovas, Betsimasarakas, and Sakalavas, were exceedingly pleased to see us. They were not a little astonished to hear Mr. Campbell and me speak their language, and concluded that we had been at Antananarivo. At one time I had about ten children running by my side, who were telling me the different names of shrubs and plants. Poor boys! may the time not be far distant when they shall know the efficacy of one name, of which they are yet ignorant!

From what I have heard of Tamatave and its vicinity, the physical difference between that place and Vohemare appears to be this: the extent of flat country is much greater at Tamatave; here the mountains, in many places, rise up almost close to the sea-shore. In being viewed from the ocean, they appear to have something of the character of those between Tamatave and Antananarivo, in rising tier above tier towards the interior of the island; but the regularity of this is altogether broken. They present a striking contrast to those of Johanna. The latter are densely covered to their summits with every description of rank vegetation, while the former, in many parts, exhibit the bare rock, or the red sandy soil. They have certainly a mineral appearance, and seem to me to resemble the Berkshire and Wiltshire Downs, except that they are not chalky, but are rather of quartz.

The Bay of Vohemare is a fine sheet of water, four miles long from south to north, and two and a half from east to west. The waves of the Indian Ocean are shut out of this bay by a long reef of coral which runs from north-west to south-east, and through which is the entrance to the harbour, about ten or twelve yards from Vohemare Point, to the south-east. To the north-west and south-west, the opposite side of the bay to that of the villages, are the mountains of Vohemare, which I have described, and which make, with the waters of the bay, a pleasing, picturesque, and magnificent view. On the remaining level country to the south are scattered the comfortable houses of the small village of Vohemare.

Of the people I must not say much at present. They are a mixture of Hovas, Betsimasarakas, Sakalavas, and Antakaras. The Hovas appear by far the most intelligent and civilized, as well as the most favourable to Christianity. They are found in large numbers at Amboanio, Angovey to the south, and at Automboka to the north. The two latter places can be reached in five days from the former. It was in the dialect of the Hovas that Mr. Campbell and I were instructed by dear old Simeon at Mauritius, and it is to them we are most intelligible in conversation. Their's, too, is the court, and the only written language of Madagascar, as well as being very similar, in many respects, to the Betsimasaraka and Sakalava languages. Consequently, we are more or less understood by all. Here I may say that I cannot be too thankful for the time I spent in Mauritius in the study of the chief language of the whole island of Madagascar.

The Hovas hold a position with respect to the Missionary, and to the other tribes of Madagascar, similar to that which the Jewish converts did in the time of the Apostle Paul. Many of them having received the Christian faith at Antananarivo may be found professing that faith in the remotest parts of their country. For instance, the Governor of Vohemare, we have heard, is a Christian, and has built a small house of prayer and praise for himself, his wife, and a few others, at Amboanio. It is, therefore, by this people—the Hovas—that the Missionary must work upon the other tribes. A great work, I believe, lies before Mr. Campbell and me. We are by no means perfect, yea, we are only babies in the Hova language. We must endeavour to become perfect in that, and give all diligence to acquire the Betsimasaraka and Sakalava dialects, and then, by God's blessing, a most extensive field of usefulness, in preaching the blessed Gospel of Christ, will be opened before us. Oh, may the Spirit of God be with us, to bless our feeble efforts!

Nov. 10—I have spent the whole day on shore, so also has Mr. Campbell. The people are "ravoravo" (delighted) to see us, and apparently have great love for us. The Aide-de-camp of the Governor greeted me in a manner I was never greeted before. Another man pressed me to himself too closely for my comfort. The Governor is expected to-morrow.

Nov. 11—On shore again the whole day. Heard that the Governor would arrive to-morrow. During the day his officers read to the captain, Mr. Campbell, and myself, a letter which had come from him corroborating this, and conveying his vetomas to all the white people on board the "King Radama." Many people continue to arrive at Amboanio from the country with rice and poultry. Vohemare will be quite full to-morrow. Two Frenchmen are living here. One is the last representative of the Lambert Company. He has been at Vohemare two years. The other is a man of considerable intelligence, and speaks very fluently in Malagasy. He has spent, at different places, seventeen years in the Island of Madagascar, and has at last settled at Vohemare, where he is trying to cultivate cotton.

Nov. 12—The captain, Mr. Campbell, and I went on shore directly after breakfast this morning, to await the arrival of His Excellency the Governor of Vohemare. The white Malagasy flag was hoisted at eleven o'clock to announce his arrival at the end of the village. Then he stopped at the house of one of his captains to dress. After the lapse of two hours, during which all persons were kept in anxious expectation, the Governor's stately procession to his habary commenced. First of all was heard the noise of drums; then appeared a number of women walking, and dressed in white and differently-coloured lambas; then came the wife and child of the Governor, carried in a palanquin, and followed by more female attendants; next came the "ampivavaka" (sorcerer); and afterwards appeared the Governor himself, borne in a palanquin, dressed very much as an English gentleman, (white trousers, black satin waistcoat, black cloth coat, white collar, black tie, and high hat), preceded by a small band playing with drums and violins, and followed by his soldiers and officers, bearing muskets, swords, and spears. When this procession reached the house of habary, the Governor's officers and soldiers formed into a circle in front of it. Here various military and state performances took place, a short address was delivered by His Excellency, and pieces of music occasionally played by the band; amongst the rest "God save the Queen." This preliminary being finished, the Governor retired to the house and dined. Soon afterwards he sent for Captain Rosalie, Mr. Campbell, and myself. He met us at the door, and we were introduced to him by Mr. Guinette. Captain Rosalie finished his business first, and then retired with the French gentleman. Mr. Campbell then gave the Governor our two letters of introduction from Mr. Lemein, the Malagasy Consul at Mauritius, and the Bishop of Mauritius. Mr. Campbell and I had translated the bishop's into Malagasy. With the help, therefore, of Charles le Bon, all things were made plain to the Governor. He appeared very glad to see us; so also did his wife, who was sitting at his side from first to last. He said that he had heard from Tamatave, and from the capital, of our coming, and had awaited our arrival month after month. He and his wife, with two or three more, are the only baptized Christians here. Oh, what a mercy to have them! In alluding to the work of the Missionaries in Madagascar, the Governor said, that as the sun dispels the darkness, and sheds light and comfort upon the earth, so the light of Christianity was beginning to shine amidst the darkness of his own country. He alluded also to the times of persecution, showed us a Bible which he had buried beneath the sand in those times, and repeated the passage of Scripture that gave him and his fellow-Christians comfort when forsaken by all his friends, viz. Matt. xii. 49, 50, "Behold my mother and my brethren! For whosoever shall do the will of my Father which is in heaven, the same is my brother, and sister, and mother."

"*Nov.* 13: *Lord's-day*—Our first Sunday in Madagascar has strikingly shown us the necessity of the knowledge of God's word amongst the people. The whole day has been spent by them in buying and selling. Trade has been increased by the debarkation of goods from the "King Radama," and the small village of Vohemare, at other times quiet, has resembled to-day the smaller market-towns of England, or in a measure the bazaar of Port Louis, Mauritius. While going in and out amongst the people, I told them of the manner in which the Lord's-day is observed in England and other Christian countries, and in every case they confessed that it is wrong to work and trade on this day. But I will turn to a more pleasing subject. Mr. Campbell and I had scarcely finished breakfast this morning, on board the vessel, when the Governor's private secretary (a Christian) came on board, with a message from him to this effect—"The Governor says, the Lord's-day has now come, and he wishes you two white men to come and join with him in singing and prayer. We at once accompanied the messenger to the Governor's house. He was reading the Bible when we arrived, and his wife seated at his side. After a little general conversation, he alluded to the meetings for prayer, &c., which he used to enjoy in Mr. Freeman's time, and expressed a wish that all of us should now join in like manner in singing the praises of the Lord. The order of our meeting was as follows:—Many hymns were sung, some to English and some to Malagasy tunes. (I believe this singing lasted quite two hours—I was completely fatigued.) Then I read the first chapter of the Acts of the Apostles, Mr. Campbell the Litany, and Charles le Bon concluded with an extempore prayer. Afterwards we had some more singing, and an explanation given of the morning, evening, and other services of the prayer book. There were present, besides ourselves, the Governor and his wife, his secretary, two other officers, two females, and the players on the violin. The Governor seems exceedingly fond of music and singing, and was really delighted to find that I had an harmonium on board. How I wish I was a better performer upon it. I think that no person should leave England as a Missionary to Madagascar without some knowledge of either singing or music.

In the course of the evening I met the Governor again, walking with his officers and soldiers. He again asked if there were many Bibles on board, and then, in the course of conversation, he took me aside, and said, "Have you yet had fever?" Upon my saying yes, he assured me of what I had often heard, that there is very little fever at Vohemare and Amboanio. I need scarcely say that the nature of the country (its elevation and the prevalence of a good strong south-east trade wind during the greater part of the year) accounts for this fact.

Nov. 15—On board the "King Radama" in the morning writing letters. The Governor's wife and child came off to tiffin. Some of the officers objected to the Governor's coming. He was compelled to sit on the shore watching us.

Mr. Campbell and I accompanied our guests back to the village. As the Governor was anxious to see the harmonium, I took it from its case in his own house, and began to play.

Crowds of people soon gathered together to listen. There were as many discords as concords in what I played, and Mr. Campbell, who cannot play a single tune, performed as if he had been a professor of music. The Governor, his wife, the officers, and all the people appeared as much delighted as they possibly could be. Handel himself could scarcely have pleased them better. After the excitement of the occasion had subsided a little, the Governor chose two hymns, which were sung to the tunes Irish and Martyrdom.

The following extracts are from the letter of the Rev. T. Campbell—

Nov. 8—Sighted Madagascar this evening at five o'clock. That part which we saw I seemed to recognise as an old friend. I believe I saw it all four months ago, when I passed it by with a sorrowful heart. We had a very extensive view of the country, its plains and its mountains, and gazed upon it till sunset, and long after that. The length of coast which we saw this evening could not be less than forty or fifty miles. The captain has just now turned the ship's head, and we are destined to "beat about" all night.

Nov. 9—Got up early, as usual, and had a fine view of Madagascar, as the sun rose and shone upon it. In consequence of the strength of the current here the captain did not know whether we were to the leeward or to windward of Vohemare. He had not been there for twenty years, and did not remember the physical geography of the places past which we were sailing. We went down to breakfast, leaving the captain on deck, and, as soon as we had finished, we came on deck again, and were met by the welcome news that we were within a mile or two of our destination. There was a strip of land stretching out into the sea, and Vohemare Bay lay behind it. The shore here looked charming: we were no more than half a mile from it, if so much. The rich green vegetation reminded me of the coast of Praslin, or, what comes nearer the mark, like the green trees of old Erin.

The ship now suddenly turned the corner of this point, and in five minutes we were anchored in Vohemare Bay. Here was a sight which is not easily forgotten by any one who sees it. The nice little town, with a considerable number of neat cottages, built in regular order, and surrounded with large green mangoe and palm-trees, which seem to be weighed down by the weight and number of their fruits. The bay is a most beautiful sheet of water, about three miles long by about five broad, bordered by large green trees, and in the greater part there is anchorage for ships of the largest size. Altogether it is quite a picture. The entrance to the bay is not so narrow as I was led to expect. I believe the "Duke of Wellington" or the "Great Eastern" might be brought in here with perfect safety. The bay is almost encircled by three tiers of mountains, one rising behind the other, not exactly in regular order, but you see the peaks of the second and third range here and there. Those nearest the bay are not wooded, but covered with grass, which makes rich pasture land for the thousands of cattle which are here bred by the natives. The mountains in the distance appear to be partially wooded. I have often seen in Ireland and England hills and mountains as like them as possible.

When we had anchored but a short time a canoe pushed off from the shore, full of men—the officer of Customs and his train, consisting in all of about eight persons. Two of them carried naked swords, and most of them had almost naked bodies. Their hair was long, like a woman's, and curled in that neat manner which may be seen on the Malagasy women who come to Mauritius. They soon introduced themselves to us by the *Akory hianao?* "How are you?" and we had a long chat with them as they sat in the cabin, while the chief man wrote down the ship's cargo, &c. He asked the name of the ship, the captain's name, the number of bales of cloth on board, and the number of barrels of rum. When he heard that there were only fourteen barrels of rum on board, he and two or three others said, *Tsy ampy*, "It is not enough!"

As soon as they had learned that we were English, their faces brightened up in a most extraordinary manner, and one of them said that "The Governor likes Englishmen." This statement was music in my ears. We told them that we wished to see the Governor at once, and were informed that we should not be able to see him for two or three days. This was not very encouraging; however, all we could do was to submit. The Governor lives several miles from this, in the Hova town of Amboanio, which contains, I hear, about five or six hundred inhabitants. The town opposite to our anchorage is called Hiarana, and contains about three hundred people—Hovas, Sakalavas, and Betsimasarakas. The natives here have no idea whatever about numbers. If you ask them how many people there are here or there, all the satisfaction you can get is that there are *ritsy*, "few," or, *maro*, "many," as the case may be.

After tiffin, the captain, Mr. Maundrell, and I, went ashore, and paid several visits to the houses of the people, who received us with the greatest kindness, and conversed with us with much affability and apparent pleasure. They seemed delighted at the thought of our remaining with them, and teaching them the Gospel of Jesus Christ, about which they knew nothing whatever.

We returned to our ship, where we must remain till we have seen the Governor, and obtained a house, and were much pleased with our visit, both with the character of the people and the appearance of the country. The interior of the houses is clean and neat; the walls are covered with matting, as are also the floors.

There is also a Romish catechist here, a Malagasy, from Nossibe, who told me that there were no Christians here at all. He meant Romanists, and I was very much pleased to hear this statement. He intends, to leave this the first opportunity. While he remains I hope to instruct him a little in the Christian faith, and send him home wiser than when he left it.

Nov. 10—Had a beautiful view this morning from the ship of all the country around the Bay of Vohemare as the sun arose and lit up each hill and valley. The hills nearest the bay remind one of English downs. The mountains here are not as high as some of those past which we sailed a few days ago; and the earth, where it is broken on the sides of the hills, is as red as that of Devonshire. The breeze in the morning was strong, cool, and bracing, and I have been told that it is the same during eight months of the year.

We went on shore again to-day with the captain; and while there a messenger arrived from the Governor, telling us that it was his intention to come in three days. As soon as the messenger fully understood who and what we were, and that it was our intention to remain here, he took all the Hovas into a house, and there held a kabary, which resulted in their sending a letter to the Governor, requesting him to come to-morrow, as we want a house to live in, and a place in which we can stow our baggage.

The Secretary of the Governor, who is a young man about eighteen years of age, was delighted when I spoke to him in his own language, and expressed his pleasure when I told him that I would teach him to read, and also to write better than he can do at present. I wished him to have a walk with me; and in his company I visited about a dozen houses, and spoke to the people, who appear to be very ignorant.

Nov. 11—Visited the people this morning again, in company with Andriamifidy, the Secretary. I read portions of the word of God to them. They listened attentively; but it appeared quite evident to me that they must undergo a great amount of simple instruction before they can relish the Gospel. We must begin at the beginning, and take it for granted that they are ignorant little children, and treat them accordingly. It will be a work of time; but the Christian Missionary must write *nil desperandum* on his banner, and remember, at the same time, that it is God alone who can give the victory.

If any of our friends at home imagine that Madagascar is christianized, they are labouring under a fatal delusion. The people here are sunk in the grossest sin and ignorance, and morality is a thing totally unknown among them. I tried to preach to the people thrice to-day, and am happy to say they listened very attentively; and I heard some of them repeating the name Jesus Christ several times, as if they wished to remember it.

Nov. 12—The long-expected Governor came to town to-day, with all his train, consisting of about fifty women and twenty or thirty soldiers, and almost as many officers. The women were clothed in lambas of every hue, white predominating. They led the van, and followed each other in a line; behind them came the wife of the Governor and her little child, sitting on a filauzana, or palanquin; behind her came about a dozen men, carrying swords. They were dressed in all sorts of European dresses. One had hussar's red trowsers and a black coat; another, a bright green coat and a straw hat; another was completely equipped in the suit of a French naval officer; and some appeared to be Kroomen on board an English man-of-war. Altogether they were a motley group. Next came a man upon a filauzana, clothed with scarlet, and having a curiously-shaped hat upon his head, not unlike a bishop's mitre. I was told that he was a kind of soothsayer. A number of half-naked soldiers followed him, carrying a gun and bayonet over one shoulder, and a long spear over the other. The band, consisting of drums and fiddles, preceded the Governor, who brought up the rear. All the women of the place followed him up closely, singing and clapping their hands. As soon as they came opposite to his house they held a kabary, and the intervals were enlivened by several tunes from the band, but the fiddles were completely drowned by the noise of the drums. After the kabary the Governor sent for us. We told him our business, and produced our credentials. Charles Le Bon placed our wishes before him in most eloquent terms; and he expressed his delight at our coming among them. His name is Rainikotomavo. He is about forty years of age, and not at all unlike the Rev. Charles Kushalle, who was lately ordained by the Bishop of Mauritius. He has not yet settled about a house for us, as he is obliged to hold another kabary with the officers upon this subject.

In the evening he sent for us again, and requested us to sing with him, which we did for about an hour. He seems to me to be a thoroughly good Christian man. He showed us his Bible, which he had buried in the earth during the reign of Ranavalona. He told us that he knew our old Malagasy teacher, Simeon Adrianomanana.

Nov. 13: *Lord's-day*—The Governor sent for us this morning at about eleven o'clock, and requested us to sing with him, which we were not slow to do. After singing for a long time, Mr. Maundrell read the first chapter of the Acts of the Apostles. I then asked His Excellency if we might pray, and told him I should use the Litany. I led the service, and Mr. Maundrell and Charlie responded. The Governor expressed himself much pleased with the Prayer-book. After remaining in his company for about two hours and a half we left, and had a walk through the town. It was not unlike a fair-day in a country-town at home, as all the people were busily engaged in selling their eggs, poultry, &c. One man offered to sell me tobacco; and I took this opportunity of telling him, and all around me, that I was a Christian, and that Christians did not buy or sell on the Lord's-day. They seemed perfectly satisfied at this, and talked about it among themselves. Afterwards I tried to preach on the Commandments, and was listened to with great attention by a considerable number of people. They expressed themselves much pleased with them, shaking their heads, and saying, "Very good, very good." May the Lord breathe upon these dry bones, that they may live!

Nov. 14—I had several conversations with the Governor to-day, and find him to be really a man of God. I only wish that he had more power than he has. A Governor in Madagascar is absolutely nothing. Before he can do any thing he must consult all his officers, and if *one* of them objects, the Governor's proposition comes to nought.

Nov. 15—Came on shore early this morning in order to arrange our house a little, while Mr. Maundrell remained on board to write his letters. I put our house in order for the time being, as we do not know at present whether we shall settle in the Hova town of Amboanio or here at Hiarana. There is no town or village called Vohemare. This is the name of the district, or county, as we would call it at home; and Amboanio would be the county, or assize town.

While I was arranging the house the Governor and his wife paid me a visit, and were much pleased with the appearance of every thing. He is always attended by an officer and about six soldiers. These men guarded the doors while His Excellency was in the house.

In the afternoon the Governor's wife and child visited the "King Radama," and had tiffin with us on board. She is a very nice person, modest and lady-like in her way, and, as far as I can judge, she is a good Christian woman.

During the day a good number of people came into our house to look about them, and I took the opportunity of reading to them the first three chapters of Genesis, and tried to explain them. I was greatly helped in my explanations by the shrewd remarks of some of the people.

In the evening Mr. Maundrell opened his harmonium, which is at present in the Governor's house, and played several tunes, while I sang. The music soon drew together a houseful of people; and although the instrument was out of tune, and Mr. Maundrell only a tyro, yet his music had almost the same effect upon them as the lute of Orpheus had on the inanimate creation.

The latest intelligence we have received respecting our Madagascar Mission, is contained in the following paragraph from a letter of the Rev. P. S. Royston, dated Mauritius, Jan. 7, 1865—

I received letters and journals last evening from Messrs. Campbell and Maundrell, which I must postpone to next mail, as I have not yet had time to read them. They were both well and hopeful, living in their "own hired house," a few miles inland from Vohemare, in a cooler, healthier, and more important place—the usual residence of the Governor of Vohemare. He is most kind to them, and they consider him a pious Christian. The "Queen's-messenger," a most important officer, had just left for the capital, to obtain, if possible, the royal permission for them to reside in Madagascar. He was kindly disposed to them.

Recent Intelligence.

METLAHKATLAH.

FROM the sketch given of this Mission in a previous Number, it will be seen how large a blessing has rested on the teaching of Christ crucified. By what other means could such changes in so short a time have been effected? What would have so subdued the savage nature of these Indians, and made them willing to come under the yoke of social order and restraint? The change accomplished here must be ascribed to the power of God; and that transforming power has wrought, through the preaching of Christ crucified, "to the Jews a stumbling-block and to the Greeks foolishness; but to us who are saved, both Jews and Greeks, Christ the power of God, and the wisdom of God." Such evidences that the Gospel of Christ, when faithfully dealt with, has, in our own day, lost nothing of its efficacy, are peculiarly grateful and seasonable; and that because there is abroad a philosophy and vain deceit which would eliminate the atonement from the personal work of the Lord Jesus Christ, and, reducing his death from a great sin-offering and sacrifice to an example only, change that message of mercy to sinners, which tells of pardon full and free, purchased by Christ's death, and ready to be conferred at once and without delay on all who earnestly apply for it, into a modified Socinianism, a cold system which carries with it no light, no warmth, no power to renovate man from a death of sin to a life of righteousness. May the Lord multiply such testimonies, at home and everywhere throughout the wide Mission field, wherever Christ is preached, for nowhere else can such results be looked for. If men, conceiving themselves wiser than God, decline to adopt his mode of action, and employ instead thereof certain devices of their own, they must expect to meet with disappointment.

The following paragraph is an independent testimony to the progress of the work at Metlahkatlah, extracted from one of the colonial newspapers—

PROSPECTING TOUR ON THE NORTH-WEST COAST OF BRITISH COLUMBIA.

Skeena river.

Mr. McKenzie and his party left Fort Simpson on the 10th of March 1864, and soon got to Skeena river, which they ascended for a distance of 150 miles. At this place they commenced prospecting, and found gold. Only five days after they had commenced washing the river rose, and they were obliged to suspend their operations. Whilst they were waiting for the water to subside, the Indians came and told them that they must go away, as they had frightened all the salmon from the river by discolouring the water with the dirt from the sluices. The salmon fishing being a failure, the Indians attributed the cause to the miners, so they became incensed, and ordered the parties off forthwith, otherwise they would return again and shoot them. The prospecting party being shrewd calculating Scotchmen, considered discretion the better part of valour, and, the inducements to remain not being great, abandoned the field rather than accept the alternative. The country through which the Skeena river flows is very similar to that described as watered by the Naas river. Game abounds in all directions, and can easily be procured. The mountain sheep are met in large flocks. The only kind of mineral, other than gold, found by the party, was lead, some specimens of which were brought into camp by one of the prospectors. The party returned to Skeena river in August, to Metlahkatlah settlement, where they remained a few days.

Metlahkatlah settlement.

On reaching this place on the coast, about seventeen miles from Fort Simpson, the party were astonished to witness all the external and internal evidences of civilization. There are about 600 natives residing in the settlement, and they live in comfortable wooden houses, built in modern style, and with glass windows. The interior of each dwelling is divided into separate apartments, and what little furniture they contain is kept in good order, and clean. There is a garden attached to each house, which the owner cultivates, and in them all Mr. McKenzie saw excellent growing crops of potatoes and turnips. The people, both male and female, are all comfortably clad, the result of their own industry and provident habits. The village contains a church, part of which is used as a school during the week. Mr. McKenzie attended divine service on Sunday, and was amazed at the sight of the large congregation of native converts assembled. Their deportment and solemnity during the service he declares could not be excelled by any Christian congregation which he had ever previously united with in worship. Mr. Duncan read the Church Service, and afterwards preached in the Indian language. It was evident to Mr. McKenzie and his companions that the natives took a deep and intelligent interest in the services from beginning to end. The apathy and listlessness which is observable in the countenance of an untutored Indian has entirely departed from the Metlahkatlahs. Most of their faces are remarkable for an animated appearance and intelligent expression. Mr. Duncan teaches school during the week, and instructs the natives how to use the appliances of modern civilization in cultivating their gardens, building their houses, and sawing timber, as well as many other useful arts. He also superintends the village store, acts as magistrate, settles all disputes that may arise, and, in fact, has his hands full in performing the arduous labours which devolve upon him, and which have resulted in such complete success as scarcely to be believed, unless, as Mr. McKenzie states, it has been witnessed. The contrast between the Fort-Simpson Indians, among whom Mr. McKenzie resided last winter, and the inhabitants of Metlahkatlah, is like that between darkness and light: at Fort Simpson all is gross ignorance, barbarism, degradation, filth, and evil; whilst at Metlahkatlah, civilization, progress, enlightenment, cleanliness, and Christianity, are everywhere observable. The Indians belonging to the settlement live by fishing, hunting, and trading. The Mission store, which Mr. Duncan superintends, supplies all their wants, and at rates much cheaper than similar goods can be procured from the traders who infest the coast. The profits arising out of the store, Mr. McKenzie is satisfied, goes to the benefit of the Mission fund, Mr. Duncan having no personal interest in it whatever. He is anxious, so far as Mr. McKenzie could ascertain, to give up the management of the business the moment some of the Indians are sufficiently instructed to take it off his hands; and when that time arrives, which may not be long, he will be glad to be released from all connexion with it. Natives have now the exclusive management of the Missionary schooner "Carolena," and the other small vessels built at the settlement. Several of the Indians act as constables, and have performed their duty with much intelligence and strict integrity. So much confidence has Mr. Duncan in them, that he would have no hesitation in sending them to arrest their own near relatives. Mr. Duncan has lately built a house for himself, or whoever may take his place hereafter as resident Missionary. He intends erecting ere long a sawmill, soap-factory, bakery, smithy, and having the Indians trained to perform all the work connected with those branches of manufacturing industry. Mr. McKenzie bears willing testimony to the amazing amount of substantial good done by Mr. Duncan. The beneficial influence which he exerts over the natives is not confined to those under his charge alone. The improvement, which he has been the zealous instrument of bringing about has become extensively known among the wandering Arabs who inhabit the British possessions of the Pacific, and the tribes are now desirous of being instructed by Missionaries. Mr. McKenzie, in his travels up Naas and Skeena rivers, has heard the Indians express the most fervent wishes to have "good men" labouring among them. Mr. McKenzie in his narrative has only spoken of what he witnessed himself, and he is not a bad witness to facts coming under his own observation. He is an intelligent Scotchman, who has travelled a good deal, and, like most of his countrymen, is not easily deceived, being of "an inquiring turn of mind." He has given valuable testimony about the change that can be wrought among the natives, and it should stimulate both the Government and the people of these colonies to put forth all their energies for the elevation of the thousands of Indians who are their fellow subjects, living in the same colonies.

To this we have to add additional information from Mr. Duncan, received since the publication of our February Number—

Oct. 31, 1864—My last letter to you was dated about three months ago, and was a brief review of the Mission work and progress.

About the middle of August last I received an official letter, as magistrate for the district, from the chief officer at Fort Simpson, giving me information against a smuggling sloop lately arrived there, and from which the Indians were obtaining intoxicating drink.

It being contrary to the law of this colony

to sell liquors to Indians, I immediately despatched a warrant to arrest the master of the vessel; and the sad result of it was, that the five Indians serving the warrant were fired upon by the three white men on board the sloop, one being killed on the spot, and other three severely wounded. The sloop got away, and it was not till the following day that the Indian unhurt returned to the settlement, bringing his three wounded companions in a canoe.

Unfortunately at the time I had very few people left in the village, so that we were unable to follow the murderers while within a reasonable distance of us.

After I had done all, and the best I could for the wounded men, I determined to run down to Victoria, it being unsafe, from the unsettled state of the coast, to send the Indians alone.

On the 25th August I started for Victoria in a small boat, and on the 5th September, by seven A.M., I was in Nanaimi, the nearest white settlement, having been brought, by a gracious God, safely through many perils on the sea, and perils by the heathen.

I need scarcely say that as soon as possible I communicated the shocking tidings to the Governor of each colony, to Admiral Denman, and to all our friends. All deeply sympathized with us; and Governor Seymour, of British Columbia, lost not a moment of time till all the needful despatches were written, and forwarded to the two neighbouring Governments, Russian and American, and to the Admiral of the station, calling upon all to do their utmost to seize the murderers, and hand them over to justice. The Governor also engaged a doctor to visit the wounded men, and Admiral Denman sent up H.M.S. "Grappler," with the doctor and myself on board, to the settlement.

I cannot express to you the anxiety I felt while away, and how restless I was to return to the sick men. But God was better to me than my fears. We arrived on the 4th instant at Metlahkatlah, and, to my great relief, I found the wounded men doing well, and all the settlement going on prosperously. I called a meeting of the village on the evening of our arrival, to return thanks to Almighty God that He had remembered us in our affliction.

In my addresses, both before going to Victoria and since my return, I have been greatly helped in opening to the Indians the passages and truths from the Scripture, which this late dispensation of providence illustrated; and I have been shown by unmistakeable signs that this severe chastisement, with which it has pleased God to visit us, will be productive of great good to us.

It would take me too long to detail to you the series of Indian laws of revenge and compensation which this sad occurrence and its sequences have revived, met, defeated, and dispersed for ever; and how the Christian laws on these matters have been put forward in strong contrast—approved, magnified, and made to triumph; and how, for the first time, a calamity, which would have called forth only savage fire and relentless fury in the Indian, as heathen, has only called forth patient endurance and lawful retaliation in the Indian as Christian.

To God be all the praise, who can even make the fury of man to yield him glory.

To the foregoing communications we add some extracts from the letters of the Rev. R. R. A. Doolan. They relate to the commencement of a new station on the Naas river.

Oct. 26—Permit me, before proceeding to write on more serious matters, to thank the Committee for their kind letter of the 21st of June. I trust that my last letter of July 8 has duly been received. In it I mentioned that I and a companion were on the point of leaving for the Naas river.* On the 20th of July we left this place, and, on our arrival at Naas, took up our residence in the house of one of the chiefs. The Indians seemed very much pleased that we had come, and helped us, as far as they could, in setting up our tent in the house, and in bringing us food in the shape of salmon. Our first step was to look out for a suitable site for a house, hoping before winter we might have a small house erected; and as the Indians are divided into three villages, separated from one another by narrow channels of the river, it was a difficult matter to pitch on a spot which should be equally advantageous for all. The Indians, seeing us busy in preparing the ground for the house, then believed we intended remaining during the winter. They could scarcely credit it, as the cold is so intense. Our difficulty with regard to a schoolhouse is for the present removed, by renting for a year, from one of the chiefs, an old deserted Indian house, built in the most populous of the three villages. To put this in order before the winter was our next step. The chiefs, and some of the other men came forward very readily, and lent us bark and plank for roofing and flooring the schoolhouse, telling us they did not intend treating us as the Tsim-

* *Vide* "Church Missionary Intelligencer" for January last.

sheans had treated Mr. Duncan. As the time of the year when we arrived was midsummer, most of the Indians were away making food, but from the very first a small band of young men stuck to us, and these, with others, we employed in cutting wood for the house. To show the anxiety manifested by some among them to learn "the book," as they call the Bible, I will give you one instance. Two young men came down from their own village, a distance of thirty miles, and remained with us over two weeks, till forced to return by want of food. Their sole motive for coming was to learn. Another lad, the son of a chief, has from the first remained with us. He has been sorely tempted more than once to leave. Four times in one afternoon men came to him, as he was working for us, trying to induce him to accompany them to a whisky feast. He refused to go, telling them if he did we should be ashamed of him. I trust he will soon learn to resist temptation from higher motives than these. His father and mother are very angry with him, and have cast him off, because he keeps with us. He tells us he constantly prays to God. At present he is here; and, at Mr. Duncan's suggestion, he is going to remain with him, under instruction, during the winter. I trust the Spirit is leading him to inquire after the Saviour, and that in the spring, should it be the will of God, he may be ready for baptism, the first-fruits from Naas. We trust, also, that another Naas lad may be induced to spend the winter here, under instruction. The manners and customs of the Naas Indians are so similar to the Tsimsheans, that to describe them would be giving but a repetition of what Mr. Duncan has already written. We have some difficulties to contend with, which he did not find among the Tsimsheans: one will arise from the different circumstances through which a man becomes a chief amongst them. With the Tsimsheans, the chieftainship is hereditary; but at Naas, if a man accumulates, either by industry (and they are, without exception, the most industrious of the Northern-Coast Indians) or by marriage, a certain amount of property, he becomes a sort of chief amongst them. Polygamy is very prevalent among them: one chief has no less than five wives. In becoming a Christian, he loses this precedence among his fellow-men, and one of the most difficult questions that will arise is this—How to maintain a chief's social position on his embracing Christianity? Mr. Duncan, who has thought much on the matter, has felt this, and hopes eventually to meet the difficulty. A few extracts from my journal may be interesting—

"*July* 24: *Lord's-day*—A large whisky feast going on. Went to the second village, and collected, in Kadsonaha's house, ten men and fourteen children. A short address was given. They all promise us their children to do what we like with, but the grown-up people say they are too old to turn. Went to the third village, where we got together fifteen men and ten children.

"*July* 25—Engaged all the morning looking out for a site for our house and school. One of our hostesses, as our host has three wives, was busy painting herself before the fire with pitch and a decoction of berries. Above the fire, hung on horizontal sticks, are salmon and salmon spawn drying, as our host went out on Saturday night, and brought home as many as thirty large salmon, some weighing thirty pounds. In the chair of state sits the lord of the house. Two little children, one with nothing but a short shirt on, run about the house. Boxes of grease line the sides, and nets hang up here and there. Two old women, wrapt in dirty blankets, squat round the fire. In another corner is our tent and boxes, and near us are three young men learning to read.

"*July* 31: *Lord's-day*—Mr. Cunningham and myself went to every house in the three villages, inviting the people to attend service. Began service about ten A.M., and had fifty-eight at our first meeting. Charles Ryan, a Christian man from Metlahkatlah, who happened to be then at Naas, gave a very nice address. The heads of his discourse were—1st. We had come for no profit for ourselves, but to teach the laws of God. 2. As they were good, they were worth striving for. Bad people, like chaff, driven about. 3. His own experience at Fort Simpson, that he at first mocked at what Mr. Duncan told them. 4. Now he considers he was then mad, and concluded by asking them to try and learn to be good. Visited the second village: attendance less: two canoes followed us, thirty-six in all. On proceeding to the third village, a sloop hove in sight, which, I have no doubt, kept some from attending.

"We hear a medicine woman rattling over a sick woman near the house. She is a very wicked woman. She pretends she has been dead for eight days, that she can tell what the crows say, what the children when they cry say, and many other fooleries. A fine instance of bravery I heard of Charles Ryan. When at the fisheries, an old medicine man and his wife came rattling over a poor sick woman. He saw she was too weak to bear it, and ordered them off, telling them they were great deceivers. As they were great medicine people, the Indians advised him to leave off, but he told them he would give them ten dollars if they killed him by the morning. The Indians looked at him in the morning, half afraid that he would be dead, but when the medicine man saw he was quite well he made off.

"*Aug.* 4—Heard this morning that the Indians are having a whisky feast at Lakunkidah. Watched them most of the day. I did not think it expedient to go over. Saw the party go from one house to another, and at last they stopped at the house of a young man, for whom they were yesterday working. Saw an instance of temptation. An old man, led on by Kingzardu, a chief, who is doing all in his power to undermine our work, who had his arm round the man's neck, seemed to be going very reluctantly: when he got within a hundred yards of the house, down he sat. Kingzardu was now joined by another man, and between the two the old man was led step by step into the house. I thought of the devil and his agents, and how impossible to resist him, but for the grace of God. The drunken feast was carried on far into the night, as at ten o'clock I still heard the drums (or, what they use for substitution, simply boxes) beating.

"*Aug.* 25—A strange picture. In a large house, dimly lighted by a wood fire, are eight men, sitting round the fire. One, an Englishman, a Missionary, sitting in a chair: another, a Tsimshean lad, his companion, one, he trusts, of God's dear children, sitting on another chair, and the other six wild up-country Indians, returning from a visit down south. One, suffering from rheumatism, is quite naked, and exposing his body to the warmth of the fire. A strange picture, as the light gleams on one and then on another of their dirty, wet, and rather forbidding countenances."

May the Lord guard this infant Mission, in which is wrapped up the hope of national preservation and improvement to the numerous Indians inhabiting the British territories on the North Pacific. Satan has long exercised over them his malignant sway, and reduced them to great misery; and no doubt this spot, which has been wrested from him, and where there have been so rapidly thrown up defensive works of so great strength, will be an object of especial malice, so that the most subtle devices will be used to injure it. Let us Christians at home entreat the Lord on its behalf, and in earnest prayer commend it to his safe keeping, that it may be in his sight as the "vineyard of red wine," of which He is pleased to say, "I, the Lord, do keep it; I will water every moment: lest any hurt it, I will keep it night and day."

DISCRETIONARY AGE OF YOUTHFUL CONVERTS IN INDIA.

We had to notice, some time back, the unfavourable judgment delivered last year by Sir M. Wells, in the case of Hema Nath Bose, a Hindu youth, who, being convinced of the truth of Christianity, desired freedom to profess it, but was compelled, by the finding of the court, to return to his parents.

Since then two decisions have been ruled directly contravening the judgment of Sir M. Wells; one at Bombay in May last, and the other in August last at Umritsur.

The first of these cases is thus narrated in the "Times" of India—

Mr. John Connon, on behalf of the Rev. Alex. Forbes, of the Church of Scotland's Mission, appeared yesterday (May 9?) in chambers, before Sir Joseph Arnould, Kt., to show cause why a writ of *habeas corpus* should not be issued against him to produce Wittu, a Kamattee, son of Dhummu Mullu. Dhummu. The complainant, alleged that his son, in reference to whom he made the application, was between fourteen and fifteen years of age; that he had, on Saturday the 7th of May, repaired to the Church of Scotland's Mission to receive baptism as a convert to Christianity; and that he declined to return with him to his house. He therefore claimed the assistance of the court to procure the custody of his son, in order that he might exercise over him the parental authority to which he was entitled.

Mr. Marriot and Mr. Green appeared as complainant's counsel, instructed by Mr. Venayek Hurrychand. Mr. Forbes and the youth Wittu were present in court.

Mr. Forbes being called, stated that the young man Wittu had been a pupil in the Church of Scotland's Institution for nearly three years; that he had privately received special instruction in Christian truth during the greater part of the last six months; that he had sought admission to the Mission house of his own accord, and had given as his reason for quitting his father's house, that he was there compelled to practise idolatry, which was contrary to his convictions of duty; and that he desired to learn more of Christianity, and to receive baptism. Mr. Forbes added that Wittu's parents, and other relatives, had had free access to him, and every opportunity of persuading him to return to his home; that he did not employ any restraint, or claim to exercise any authority over Wittu, but merely received him as a guest.

Subsequently a large number of witnesses were examined on behalf of the complainant, with the view of proving that the youth was, as alleged, between fourteen and fifteen years of age. The evidence was of the most contradictory and indefinite character; but the result at last elicited was, that Wittu had been born in October 1848, and that therefore his age was then about fifteen years and seven months.

This conclusion did not seem to be questioned by the counsel on either side; and it therefore remained for the judge to determine whether the circumstance that Wittu had not completed his sixteenth year (the age of majority in Hindu law) entitled his father to claim his custody, and to request the court to make an order for him to be given into his charge by force, if necessary. Against a finding to that effect, Mr. Connon, on behalf of the youth, made an eloquent and impressive appeal to his lordship.

Sir Joseph Arnould, in giving judgment, remarked, that in the first place his decision was to be regarded as delivered upon a writ of *habeas corpus;* that though such a writ had not actually been issued, yet this arose solely from the extraordinary haste which was required by the complainant's attorney, who was unwilling to delay until the writ could be issued in due form. He observed, secondly, that the evidence afforded sufficient proof that the youth who had been brought before the Court was of the age of fifteen years and seven months; that consequently the only question to be decided was, whether there was in Hindu law an age of discretion distinct from an age of majority; that Sir Mordaunt Wells had last year, in the High Court of Calcutta, given a judgment that there was no such distinction, and had affirmed, that before a youth could choose his domicile he must have completed his sixteenth year: but from this opinion of the Calcutta judge he entirely dissented; that, according to English law, the age of majority was fixed at twenty-one, and the age of discretion at fourteen, which was also the age of responsibility for criminal acts; that in India the age of majority was sixteen, and that at which responsibilty for crime commenced was twelve, the law thus recognising the greater precocity of Indian youths; that, according to strict analogy, the age of discretion ought also to be fixed at twelve, but that he was not inclined to go so far, but was certainly of opinion that the period of life at which discretionary rights commenced should not be fixed at a more advanced age than that in England, and should therefore be regarded as at least fully attained after the completion of the fourteenth year. Applying these principles to the present case, he should order that Wittu Dhummu be allowed to choose the place of his domicile. Sir Joseph Arnould thus put to the youth in court the question, "Do you desire to reside with the Rev. Mr. Forbes, or with your father?" when he distinctly expressed a desire to stay with Mr. Forbes. Although the question was not necessary for a decision, the learned judge said he would, for his own satisfaction, ask why Wittu did not choose to go with his father. It was then answered by Wittu, that he desired to learn more of Christianity, and that his parents would not allow him to become a Christian.

The order of the court was then explained to the large crowd of Kamattees who had gathered about the court-house, and under the warning that any attempt at a breach of the peace would be punished severely, they soon dispersed peaceably. Mr. Forbes afterwards left with the boy in his charge.

The more recent case is taken from the "Lahore Chronicle" of Sept. 3rd—

A CONVERT CASE.

COURT OF ASSISTANT COMMISSIONER, LAHORE.

CIVIL SIDE.

Gobind Sahai, v. the Rev. C. W. Forman, American Presbyterian Mission, Lahore. In re Brij Lall.

Judgment was delivered in this case in the vernacular on the 5th August 1864.

The plaintiff sues the Rev. Mr. Forman, of the American Presbyterian Mission, Lahore, for the custody of his son, Brij Lall, Brij Lall himself unwilling to go with his father.

The Court has to decide—

1st. Whether any age has been fixed by law to which the guardianship of nurture or parental control over the person of a child extends.

2nd. If the law has fixed such an age, is Brij Lall within it or not?

3rd. If the law has not fixed such an age,

is Brij Lall of an age and understanding to form his own opinions, and judge for himself in important matters?

1st. The last published decision of the High Court of Judicature, Calcutta, in a case of this kind, was that of Mr. Justice Wells *in re* Hem Nath Bose. The Judge said he was of opinion that plaintiff's counsel had correctly stated the Hindu law; and the law of the High Court entitled him to the custody of his child up to the age of sixteen years.

One of the principal cases prior to this is Regina *v.* Ogilvy, in which Sir Lawrence Peel ruled—"When an infant, supposed to be improperly in custody, is brought up on a *habeas corpus*, the court will (if the infant appear to be capable of exercising a sound judgment and discretion) allow him to depart wherever he lists; minority simply will not entitle a father to the custody of his child: and, again, the court will take into consideration the question whether the child does, or does not, possess sufficient intelligence to enable him to judge for himself." The infant was, in this case, under sixteen years of age.

The opinion of Sir Mordaunt Wells, indeed, seems not to have been altogether without precedent (Queen *v.* Clarke *in re* Alicia Race); but a perusal of judicial opinions on analogous causes leads to the conclusion, that there is a leaning to the feeling, that the law of the case has yet to be definitely established; and that we must look much to the understanding of the minor in each particular case.

It may not be irrelevant here to observe that the age up to which kidnapping of a male child is punishable under the Indian Penal Code is fixed at fourteen years. (Sec. 361.)

Minority is fixed by the Benares school of law at sixteen years, though Government has, for certain purpose (*e.g.* minority under Court of Wards), fixed the age at eighteen years.

"But the Punjab Civil Code, the substantial law of this court, sets the matter at rest, and also establishes the position, that freedom from the parental control in such a matter as that before the court will depend, not upon the age of the minor, but on his understanding.

2nd. The court is thus not bound to enter upon the second issue; that is, as to whether or not Brij Lall is within the age of pupilage or not, if it is satisfied that he is of mature and competent understanding, and a free moral agent.

3rd. The Court, then, has only to decide on the issue of fact, whether Brij Lall is of mature and competent understanding, and a free moral agent.

The court, on the appearance of Brij Lall, recorded its opinion that his appearance betokened an age about seventeen (17) years. His father, the plaintiff, alleges that his age is thirteen (13) years and eight (8) months, and attempts to corroborate his assertion by an alleged copy of his *janm pattrah*, or Brahminical record of birth. This document sets forth that Brij Lall was born in Katik 1907. As the original should have been produced, the document is worthless; but, in the opinion of the court, it underrates the age of Brij Lall, who, were he sixteen (16), would be a well-developed youth for his years.

Brij Lall was himself examined in open court. He has been studying English for three years and a half at the Mission school, Jhelum; was second in his class, and a monitor; got a prize at the Educational Durbar at Goojerat. With regard to his change of religion, he says—"Mr. Taussaint (Missionary at Jhelum) did not persuade me to be a Christian, only 'persuaded me.' When I saw the Korân (part of it), and Shaster (verses of it), and the Bible, I perceived that Christianity is good. I came to Lahore to convert my religion. When I came, I went to Mr. Forman, but he did not persuade me at all. I have seen my father twice at the Mission premises, once in the bazaar, when they took me by force, and once at their house."

The whole of the above, and much more, Brij Lall stated in distinct English. The court is fully satisfied that, so far as a youth of the age of sixteen (the extreme age contended for by the Calcutta courts) can have mature and competent understanding, so far this young man has it; that he is an exceedingly intelligent lad; and that he is a fully responsible moral agent. This opinion of the Court is confirmed by the facts of the case. Brij Lall set out from his father's house at Jhelum to come to Lahore to prosecute his inquiries after Christianity, or, as he said, his studies. This was a bold step for a lad, and showed earnestness of purpose and character. He came, entirely with his father's consent (who supposed that he was going to study at Lahore, and had probably no idea of his intention of changing his faith), which goes to show that his father placed confidence in his conduct. In conclusion, the court would add that nothing like force appears to have been used on the part of the Missionaries, that is to say, Brij Lall was not prevented from holding intercouse with his parents: he saw them repeatedly after they came to Lahore, at the Mission premises, and at their house in the city, and elsewhere.

The Court finds that it cannot uphold plaintiff's claim to the custody of his child, Brij Lall, dismisses it accordingly, and allows Brij Lall to go where he pleases.

Lahore, 5th August 1864.

THE BISHOP OF CALCUTTA'S VISITATION IN THE PUNJAB.

AT Simla the Bishop preached five times, two of his sermons being followed by collections, the one for the Kangra and Umritsur Missions, and the other for the endowment of the Simla school.

Kangra was reached on Friday, October 7th, where the Bishop and Mr. Cowie were the guests of Mr. Merk. There are two new churches at Kangra. The one, built by Government in the Fort, was consecrated on the following day. The church was quite filled by an attentive congregation of soldiers.

The other church is still unfinished, and is due to the exertions of Mr. Merk. It is beautifully situated on the same plateau as his house, commands two glorious views, and exactly overhangs the celebrated golden temple of Durga. It is intended for the use of the native Christians, but it is hoped that, as at Umritsur, many of the heathen will attend its services. In the course of the day the Bishop examined Mr. Merk's Mission schools for boys and girls, and was much pleased with both. In the evening he went up to Dharamsala, and on Friday evening, October 14th, entered Dalhousie. . . . . .

On October 20th, the Bishop reached Sealkote. On Friday and Saturday the Bishop visited the hospitals and the schools of the 20th Hussars and the Artillery. On Sunday, the 23rd, he preached twice in the Cantonment church.

On Tuesday Mr. Baly took the Bishop to see the American Presbyterian Missionaries in the city of Sealkote, and went over their industrial school.

In the afternoon a confirmation was held in the cantonment church. Thirty-four were confirmed, mostly soldiers. Some of them (belonging to the band of the 93rd Highlanders) had travelled all night, to be in time for the service, having been away with a wing of the regiment at Lahore, where it formed the Viceroy's guard of honour at the great Durbar.

Thursday, October 27th, was chiefly devoted to seeing the great improvements which have been made at Lahore since the Bishop's visit in 1860, especially the pretty native gardens which encircle the walls, and have taken the place of a zone of sand, filth, and ruins which formerly polluted the whole neighbourhood. On Saturday, October 29th, Messrs. Keene and Fitzpatrick came over from Umritsur to spend Sunday with the Bishop, and they were accompanied by Mr. Stuart, who was visiting some of the Punjab Missions of the Church Missionary Society. The American Presbyterian Missionaries, Messrs. Forman and Newton, were also invited. On Sunday, October 30th, he preached thrice.

On Tuesday, November 1st, the Lieutenant-Governor and the Bishop went to the American Mission building in the city, and were greatly struck by the sight of 900 boys in their many-coloured turbans and shawls, gathered together in one large hall, from the network of branch schools which the indefatigable and devoted Missionary, Mr. Forman, has spread over Lahore, and from which, if many actual conversions have not yet resulted, yet the good fruits of increased intelligence and morality, and a really friendly feeling to Christianity and Christians are sufficiently apparent. On that evening, at nine o'clock, the Bishop left Lahore for Ferozepore, which he reached early on November 2nd. The chief interest of the visit centred in the native confirmation. The 32nd Regiment Native Infantry (Muzbee Sikhs) are now quartered at Ferozepore, and Dr. Smyth, rightly regarding the Christians among them as his parishioners, has instituted a service for them every Sunday in the vernacular, and prepared sixteen of them for confirmation. These were confirmed in the station church on Thursday, November 3rd: the service and an address, were in Urdu. The event excited so much interest in the regiment, that all the men (heathen and Christian alike) requested permission to come and see it, and accordingly the nave of the church presented the unusual sight of an attentive congregation of Sikh soldiers.

On Monday afternoon, November 14th, the journey was continued. Rajpore was reached at sunrise, and Mussoorie at midday. Here the travellers were the guests of the Rev. R. N. Maddock. A special service, with a sermon from the Bishop, was held in Landour church on November 16th, and on November 17th fifty-one young persons from both stations were confirmed in Mussoorie church. In the evening of the same day a large addition to the cemetery at Mussoorie was consecrated, the effect of the ceremony being increased by the excellent style in which Mr. Maddock's pupils sang (unaccompanied) the metrical version of Psalm xc. As the party stood on the mountain side, surrounded by Himalayas, it was impossible not to feel the solemnity and beauty of the verse—

Before the hills in order stood,
Or earth received its frame,
From everlasting Thou art God,
To endless years the same.

Calcutta Christian Observer.

WATERS IN THE DESERT.

"WHEN the poor and needy seek water and there is none, and their tongue faileth for thirst, I the Lord will hear them, I the God of Israel will not forsake them. I will open rivers in high places, and fountains in the midst of valleys."

Thus the Lord has promised. Of his merciful interference in the case of deep temporal distress, when, in the literal sense, water was so needed, that the tongue failed for thirst, affecting instances are on record. Hagar was in this extremity, when, in the wilderness of Beersheba, the water was spent in the bottle, and, casting the child under one of the shrubs, she went and sat her down over against him a good way off, that she might not see his death, and lifted up her voice and wept. Then God heard; and the angel of God, coming on a mission of mercy, opened a well in the wilderness, and opened her eyes to see it, that the child might live.

But there is a deeper thirst than this—the soul's sense of need; a need so great, that, unless relief be vouchsafed, it must die. In the vast wilderness of heathenism are there none to be found who have this thirst upon them?

One or two instances we can give. They may be regarded as the specimens of a large class, and may thus stimulate the efforts of the church at home to supply the wants of these poor wanderers.

Two hundred and forty miles north of Rangoon, two hundred miles south of Ava, one hundred miles west of Siam, and eighty east of Prome, is situated the city of Tounghoo, the capital of a province of about 8000 square miles. This old city, surrounded by a wall some twenty feet high, and thick enough, with an inner embankment, for a carriage-drive, has its broad streets shaded with palms, its temples, pagodas, and palace. The modern city lies chiefly without the walls, extending some three miles along the river Sitang; and here are the bungalows of the English residents, for Tounghoo is no longer shut up in the hands of the Burmese. Since 1853 it has become a British possession, and an important centre of Missionary effort.

The population consists of some 50,000, of whom 20,000 are Burmese and Talaings; the rest are Karens, once the occupants of these plains, but driven back by the Burmese, and obliged to seek shelter in those mountain ranges which are seen close at hand. On the east, rising pile on pile in glorious sublimity, the mountains approach within a few miles of the river. There are the highland homes of these races, the real Karen land. This mountainous country extends over an area of 2000 square miles. On its north lies Burmah; on its east, the independent Red Karens. Over these mountains, rising 5000 feet above the sea, are scattered 50,000 Karens, of six different tribes. Up to the time of British annexation, these tribes were in a state of constant feud, inflicting on one another grievous injuries; but, since then, Christian Missionaries have been at work amongst them, and a great change has been wrought in their character and habits.

They are described as of very interesting appearance, fairer and larger than the more southern Karens, the young people often showing both red and white, in strong contrast, in their countenances. The men wear tunics, after the manner of Scotch plaids, striped according to their tribe. The women's dress consists of two garments, the robe and the jacket. The robe is striped according to the tribe, and girt around the waist. The jacket is white or blue, embroidered with brilliant silk floss, sometimes representing a sunrise, or the evening, with stars coming out on the deep blue sky.

Here, in these mountain districts of Tounghoo, there were, in Dec. 1863, 6000 baptized Christians, with 150 native preachers, and 134 village schools, with upwards of 2000 pupils.

It will be interesting to trace the beginning of this work. Some three years before the last Burmese war, a Karen, named Dumoo, was in trouble at the loss of a daughter, who had married, and gone southward with her husband he knew not where. He resolved to go in search of her, and joined, for this purpose, a company of Burmese who were going south. On entering the British frontier they were suspected of being dacoits, and were for a time detained. During this trouble Dumoo attached himself to one of the Burmese, a native of Tavoy. On their liberation, without any particular reason he determined to accompany this man to his native city, which had been for many years a Missionary station. Thus led, by a way he knew not, he wandered on two hundred miles further from his friends and among strangers. At the time of his arrival, the small-pox was raging at Tavoy. Dumoo was struck down, and, during his illness, was sheltered in a Burmese kyoung, or monastery. There, as he lay fluctuating between life and death, strange thoughts came upon him—thoughts about his soul, its nature, what was to become of him when he died—thoughts he could not answer, and which he could not put away, for they had taken strong hold upon him. The sense of spiritual need, the deep thirst, had come upon him ; and water to quench it, this he craved, although where to find it he knew not. There were Christian Missionaries in Tavoy who could have told him, but they were white men, and he did not wish to see them. He left the city, and wandered forth into the jungles amongst the heathen Karens, who knew nothing, and could not help him; but the sense of need was as strong as ever upon him, and as the tradition of his forefathers had taught him that the Karens once had books which, because of God's displeasure, they had lost, the idea of a book rose in his mind as that which could solve his doubts. He then heard of a Karen who had invented a method of writing the Karen language, and who professed to have superior wisdom ; and forthwith Dumoo set out on another long journey across the frontier of Tavoy to the borders of Siam, to find this man. But when he had searched him out, it was only to be disappointed : he was a pretender, a well without water. His long journey seemed to be in vain, and he was more perplexed than ever. Turning back, he scarcely knew whither, he providentially fell in with two young men from the Karen theological school in Tavoy, who were spending their vacation in the jungle as Scripture readers. These men had a book—a book which spoke by letters; and as they read and he listened to its utterances, they were to his soul wonderful: they told him what he wanted. So exactly did they meet the deep cravings of his spirit, that from his inmost soul he exclaimed, "I have found what I want." The well was opened for him in the wilderness, and his eyes were opened that he might see where to slake his thirst. In his intense desire he gave these young men no rest until he had learned from them the wonderful magic of the alphabet.

When the young men returned to Tavoy, Dumoo repaired to a Christian village, and attached himself to the native pastor. His earnestness and docility astonished every one. He laboured that he might read: his heart was opened to take in more and more of Christian truth, and he could not be silent. What he knew he communicated to those around him, telling them of the Saviour he had found. In him the Saviour's words found an exemplification—"If any man thirst, let him come unto me and drink. He that believeth on me as the Scripture hath said, out of his belly shall flow rivers of living water." Having slaked his own thirst, he became himself a well of water in the wilderness. At length came the white man, the Missionary, to visit his people in the jungle. Amongst the first to greet him was Dumoo. He had never seen a white man before, but he had no fear. He met him, not with the cringing of a slave, but with the frankness of a free man. Of such a man the Missionary might well say, "Can any man forbid water that these should not be baptized, which have received the Holy Ghost as well as we?" He was baptized, and his efforts and entreaties to win men to Christ were unceasing. He thought of the native hills, the mountain villages, and the friends he had left there. He thought of the darkness, the thick darkness which had brooded over them for generations, and he longed that they should have that light which had made glad his own sad heart. He longed to go back that he might tell them of Jesus; but he was inexperienced, and felt how desirable it was that he should have a colleague. He fixed upon Sau Quala, whose paternal home was the first house, in which Ko-thah-lbyu, the first Karen convert, made known God's mercy in Christ; who, when he first heard it, said within himself, "Is not this the very thing we have been waiting for?" and who, since his baptism in 1830, had been unremittingly engaged in evangelizing his countrymen. Hitherto the labours of this good man had been confined to the provinces of Tavoy and Merguin; but now Dumoo pleaded with him for the "regions beyond," and urged him to commence the work of evangelization among the numerous Karen tribes that stretch away towards the north-east from Tounghoo, that his feet might be beautiful on the mountains as he proclaimed glad tidings of good things, and published peace. He felt sure that they would hearken; that there would be a great ingathering of souls; that churches would be raised up; that they would support their own teachers. It was a hard struggle, for the churches of Tavoy would not let Sau Quala go. Moreover, the American Missionary did not think that new ground should be broken up until that which had been gained had been made more sure. Dumoo meanwhile had been received into the theological school at Tavoy. There he learned to write, and acquired a considerable knowledge of the Scriptures; but nothing caused his stedfast gaze to be turned aside from the one great object he had in view—to go back and preach the Gospel to his countrymen, and persuade others to go with him. At last Sau Quala could no longer resist. He resolved to go, and once his resolution had been formed, the prayers and entreaties of the churches could no longer detain him. In vain, in a joint memorial, they remonstrated. A meeting was convened, and the subject brought under consideration. "What could we do," was the answer of the Missionaries: "for more than a year this man has desired to visit a distant region, never yet visited by a minister of the Gospel, there to plant the standard of the cross. We looked at the subject carefully; we spoke, we wept, we prayed; and all—the very men who had signed the adverse memorial—arose, and with tears approved his going." The moment was opportune: the war with Burmah had just ended, and Tounghoo was among the ceded districts. Sau Quala and Dumoo, accompanied by two others, set out for their destination, Sau Quala making Tounghoo his centre, and Dumoo entering the Shwaygyeen district to commence the work there—a work which has been very largely blessed of God; and there, according to the Report of July 1864, he is still labouring, his name appearing at the head of the native preachers.

A little before Sau Quala and Dumoo left for Tounghoo, a native brother had fallen asleep in Jesus, whose experience very much resembled that of Dumoo. He was not a Karen, but a Buddhist, and of respectable position, his brother being Governor of Shwaygyeen under the Burmese Government, and he himself being collector of taxes among the Karens in the same district.

Being a thoughtful educated man, he had searched deeply into the claims of Buddhism, and was convinced that it was not of God. There is no doubt that his intercourse with the Karens had been profitable to him. In contrast with the atheistical principles of the Buddhist system, they had made him acquainted with their traditions of an eternal God, the creator of the world, who undergoes no change, is subject to no decay, and thus there was awakened in his mind a strong desire to know the truth. Laboriously did he seek for it, and it was not till after long delay that he found it. First he met with a Brahmin ascetic, and, mistaking his austerities for holiness, became his disciple for two or three years, until he discovered that he was a deception. But, although disappointed, he did not abandon in discouragement his search after truth. In fact, he could not do so, for his soul was athirst, and he wanted water.

The Mohammedans next attracted him. He entered into their mosque, and listened.

He found that they agreed with the Karens in believing that there was one eternal God, the creator of all things. But how was he to approach Him? how obtain his favour? This he hoped to have learned from the Korán, but in vain: it opens no door of access to God; and he left, convinced that the secret of life was not among the Mohammedans. Then the Romanists attracted him, and from them he heard for the first time of Christ as the Saviour of men. But when he was told to pray to the Virgin, and to seek the intercession of the saints, his soul revolted, for he said, "If human beings are to be worshipped, I would rather worship Gaudama as a man than this woman." So he left the Romanists. In doing so it seemed as if the last hope of of relief was extinguished, and then followed a long period of distress and darkness. In this state he came with his family to Maulmein, at a time when Dr. Judson was there, and took up his abode not far from the zayat where Dr. Judson was accustomed to preach. Thither he soon found his way, and attentively did he listen. He had long been seeking rest, and could not find it. There was a deep want in his soul, and he had long and vainly sought to quench this thirst. But there was One who had observed him, and was now about to fulfil his own promise—"When the poor and needy seek water, and there is none, I the Lord will hear them, I the God of Israel will not forsake them. I will open rivers in dry places, and fountains in the midst of valleys." Dr. Judson read out the words of Jesus—"If any man thirst, let him come unto me and drink." He preached Christ as the Saviour of sinners, to whom all in need might come, and drink as from an overflowing fountain. Myat Kyau came and drank, and was refreshed.

He had found that which he sought, and now he also found, that if he would have this treasure as his own he must part with all else, for his family opposed him, and his brother persecuted him, and he discovered how true it is—"A man's foes shall be they of his own household." It was no doubt a hard struggle. It is fearful to part with all one loves on earth, wife, children, friends; but to part with Christ, even for the sake of these, that he could not do. He left them, and yet prayed for them, for his heart yearned towards them; nor were his prayers without result, for his wife and two sons not only rejoined him, but became themselves followers of Jesus. From that time, for many years, with unremitting energy he taught the truth to his countrymen, and "many were the fruits of his labour, not only among the Burmese and Talaings, but also among the Karens. His labours were not confined to Maulmein, but almost every village and hamlet in the province heard the Gospel from his lips. He knew the Karens well: having been officially employed amongst them, he was acquainted with their character and language. "The Karens," he said, "are not like the Buddhists: they have no idols, no priests, and if the teachers would go amongst them, great numbers would listen and believe the Gospel." So continually did he revert to the subject, that the Missionary, Wade, was induced to visit a Karen village, Dongyan, about twenty miles north of Maulmein. At first the poor people fled: they had never seen a white face before, and thought they were Government officers. But when assured they were teachers, they gathered round them, and said, "If you are come to tell us of God, we are happy: we will listen. Our fathers say the Karens had once God's book, written on leather (parchment), and they carelessly allowed it to be destroyed. Since then, as a punishment, we have been without books, and without a written language. But our prophets say the white foreigners have this book, and will, in future time, restore it to us. Behold, the white foreigners have come. Have you brought God's book? Our fathers have told us that when the white foreigners bring us the lost book, and teach us the true religion, we must listen and obey; then prosperity will return to us: but if we do not listen and obey, we shall perish without remedy." In this village there is now a flourishing church.

Myat Kyau laboured until he lost his sight. He then had a child to lead him about;

and when his increasing infirmities disabled him from active effort, he would sit in his verandah, speaking to all who would listen of the love of Jesus. When he "fell asleep" a large concourse of all classes of Christians and heathen attended his funeral. The memory of the just is blessed. But in Myat Kyau we again see how useful these earnest, anxious souls become when brought to the knowledge of Christ's salvation. Such men, when found and gathered in, become true Missionaries.

We shall now introduce another of these deeply-interesting cases from a portion of the Mission field, with which we are ourselves connected.

In the Telugu country a small group of people were seen, a few months back, approaching the house of one of our Missionaries at Bezwara. They were low-caste people, Malahs, very like the Pariahs of the countries more south. The servant, thinking they had come to beg, sent them away, when, happily, the Missionary saw them, and called them back. They had come for Christian instruction. No Missionary agent had first visited them, and convinced them: they had come of themselves; and they had been led to do so in this way. One of them, named Venkiah, began to doubt about the goddesses whom they worshipped. It came into his mind that there must be above and beyond them some great being, who was worthy of being known and worshipped. This idea fastened upon his mind, and he was wont to wander about by himself, thinking over it. And then he used to break out, and say, 'Why do you remain hidden from us: why do you not make yourself known to us?' This ignorant heathen had begun to feel a thirst to which many are strangers who have been brought up in the midst of Christian privileges. He felt there was a want, a need in his soul, which earthly things could not quench; that he wanted God, and he knew not how or where to find Him. This, it may be repeated, is a want which many have never felt who bear the Christian name. If only they have the comforts and conveniences of life, they think that they can dispense with the necessity of knowing God, and, in fact, they do live without Him. They have never felt the intensity of that strong thirst. It would be well for them if, in this respect, they had got as far as this heathen man.

Well, while in this state he had a dream. It is difficult to say what means God may be pleased to use with a soul which, like this, is shut out from all opportunities. He dreamt that he saw before him a man of singular beauty, who looked kindly upon him, and told him he was his friend. This dream had a great effect upon him. He talked much about it to his friends, and seemed full of hope that, in some way or other, he would be helped to the knowledge he wanted.

While things were in this state, some of Venkiah's people went into the neighbourhood of Bezwara, to attend a fair, and there they heard one of our Missionaries preaching. As they listened, it seemed to them as though what he said very much resembled the things which they had so often heard Venkiah speaking about; and on their return they told him. This was good news to the seeking soul. It was like the star when it reappeared to the wise men as they sought after Him who had been born King of the Jews, and came and stood over where the young child was. Venkiah, with some of his friends, sought out the Missionary, and from his lips he heard for the first time of Him who is the one living and true God, and of what He has done for man. The Lord had heard him. He opened rivers in high places, and fountains in the midst of valleys. The means of Christian instruction were unexpectedly afforded, and by these people are thankfully received, for they know what it is to thirst, and are glad to slake it.

Venkiah is now a baptized Christian, and, like Dumoo, as the teacher of his own people, is earnestly engaged in leading them to the wells of salvation, from whence he drew the water that refreshed his own soul. The work amongst the Malahs is going on prosperously. Recently four principal families among them, in placing themselves under

Christian instruction, broke their idols before the whole community as an evidence of their sincerity. Since then they have had to endure much trouble, but, although beaten, they have been enabled to endure. May this prove to be the beginning of a work as large as that which has graced the hilltops of Burmah.

These are only a few specimens of a large and deeply-interesting class of people dispersed abroad in heathen lands. Shall we not help them? Let us only, in those thirsty wildernesses, open a few wells, and they will soon be multiplied into many. But if, when we have the opportunity, we refuse to take the initiative, what likeness is there between Christ and us? These men, when they had drunk themselves, thought of others, and hastened to relieve them. If we have no such compassion, and will engage in so such efforts, it is simply because we have never known what it is to be thirsty, and have never experienced the joy of drawing water out of the wells of salvation.

SIR R. MONTGOMERY'S FAREWELL DURBAR AT LAHORE.

ON the 7th of January last Sir R. Montgomery terminated an able and successful administration of the Punjab, by a farewell Durbar at Lahore.

Sir R. Montgomery, the second son of an Irish clergyman, the Rev. J. L. Montgomery, of Moville, County Donegal, was educated, until fourteen years of age, at a school in Londonderry. Amongst his schoolmates were four brothers, Alexander, George, Henry, and John Lawrence. Assuredly Ireland is not altogether an incumbrance to England: she has not failed to yield to her distinguished men, who, in times of special responsibility and danger, have proved to be precisely the men which were wanted. A long list of such names might without difficulty be drawn up.

Accepting a direct appointment to the Civil Service, he reached India in 1828, and was appointed assistant to Mr. Thomason, at that time magistrate and collector of Azimgurh. Here we find him imbibing the spirit and following the example of his chief, whose attention had been drawn to the fearful practice of female infanticide extensively prevailing throughout that district. Of this, one exemplification may be introduced. Amongst the Baees Rajpoots of Kooha, on the borders of Oude, numbering 10,000, not a single daughter was forthcoming. Mr. Thomason, therefore, was actively engaged in the adoption of such measures as might lead to the abandonment of so unnatural a crime, and in his efforts he was ably assisted by Mr. Montgomery.

In 1839 he was appointed to the magistracy of Allahabad, carrying with him into this new sphere of action the zeal on the subject of infanticide which he had first imbibed from Mr. Thomason. He soon discovered that the crime was perpetrated to a fearful extent among the Rajpoot tribes on the borders of the Rewah territory. Having first tried persuasion without effect, he resolved on more vigorous measures. These soon began to tell. At the end of two months, of four female infants born, three were living, the fourth having been killed by the administration of Mudar juice. The number of the rescued ones increased, although slowly, and under the pressure of unremitting vigilance, until, in 1842, Mr. Montgomery was enabled to express his hope that, so many girls being now alive, the people were beginning to get reconciled to the custom of sparing them.

The Cawnpore district was Mr. Montgomery's next charge, and he was so employed when the second Sutlej campaign brought the Punjab under British sway. At that important juncture Lord Dalhousie placed the illustrious brothers, Sir Henry and Sir John Lawrence, at the head of the new administration, and Mr. Thomason, the Lieutenant Governor of the North-west Provinces, being called upon to select some of his best officers to be Commissioners of districts in the new province, named, with others, Mr. Montgomery and Mr. Donald McLeod, the present Lieutenant-Governor of the Punjab. To Mr. Montgomery was assigned the head-quarters division, that of Lahore.

Attention was drawn to the existence of infanticide throughout these territories. The Bedees, lineal descendants of the Sikh prophet, having their nucleus at Dera Baba Nanuk, were specially referred to in the official report addressed by Major D. Lake to Mr. Montgomery, "as fearfully addicted to this crime, so much so, indeed, that a thousand families of them for the last 400 years had destroyed all their female offspring. Preliminary information having been obtained from various quarters, Mr. Montgomery, in 1853, condensed the whole into an able and interesting report. As the excess of marriage expenses was one of the sources of the crime, he suggested that the great principle of their voluntary reduction should be adopted, and that, with a view to the accomplishment of a result so desirable, a meeting of the heads and most influential men of the tribes known to practice infanticide within 200 miles of Umritsur should be held at that city at the next Dewallee festival. These suggestions were fully approved of, and recommended by Sir J. Lawrence to the adoption of the Supreme Government. The Governor-General's minute is worth recording—"The Governor-General in Council has read these papers with deep interest and gratification. He can conceive no purer or higher source of pride for the public officers of a state than such a record as this of the wide and rapid success of their exertions on behalf of the honour of our rule in the rescue of suffering humanity; exertions which are eminently calculated to reflect honour on the British name, and to add largely to the material happiness of the people whom Providence has lately confided to our care," &c.

A proclamation was issued; the meeting announced; and at Umritsur, in the end of October 1853, there was a vast gathering of the leading natives from the surrounding districts, Rajahs and tributary Jagheerdars, high Rajpoots from the hills and plains, wealthy Bedees, Brahmins, Khutrees, and Mohammedans. In the absence of the Chief Commissioner, it was presided over by Mr. Montgomery, as Judicial Commissioner, and Mr. Edmonstone, Financial Commissioner, supported by Mr. McLeod, and Mr. G. C. Barnes, Commissioners of the Jullundur and cis-Sutlej divisions. After three days' deliberation, a great durbar was held, that all with one heart and voice might declare publicly their intention of suppressing the crime. Pavilion tents were pitched capable of accommodating 3000 people, the upper end being appropriated to the English functionaries and native chiefs, with their personal attendants, seats for about sixty of them being arranged in a semicircle. A form of agreement had been drawn up, which declared infanticide to be a crime "hateful to God, and execrable in the eyes of Government, and of all pious and good men." Numerous copies of it were handed about. The Rajpoots and other chiefs affixed their signatures, binding themselves thus to the suppression of the crime, and the abandonment of that pernicious system of excessive marriage expenditure which was one of its chief causes.

In the discharge of his office as Judicial Commissioner, Mr. Montgomery perceived the necessity of introducing into the courts a simple procedure, which might secure the administration of prompt, cheap, and substantial justice; and accordingly the Punjab Civil Code was drawn up by Mr. Temple, under his immediate superintendence.

And now came the cyclone of 1857, that stormy season which burst with so sudden a force on the English power in India. On the 11th of May an obscure telegram reached Lahore, having reference to some disaster which had occurred; on the 12th the outbreak at Meerut became known. The situation at the moment was this—at Meean Meer, the military cantonment, six miles from Lahore, were stationed three native regiments of infantry, one of cavalry, the Queen's 81st Foot, two troops of horse artillery, and four reserve companies of foot artillery. Within the city walls, at the north-west angle, stands the fort, or citadel, containing extensive magazines and manufactories of warlike stores. This was occupied by a native infantry regiment, a company of Europeans, and a company of foot-artillery. The native force in the Punjab was fully cognisant of the Poorbeah conspiracy, and a plot had been arranged. On a particular day, when one wing of the native regiment at the fort was to be exchanged for another, and about 1100 sepoys were thus brought together, they were to rise, murder their officers, seize the gates, take possession of the citadel, magazine, and treasury, overpowering the small European force. A bonfire was to acquaint the troops at Meean Meer with what had been done. All the troops were then to rise, and the jails having been broken up, and 2000 prisoners liberated, the Europeans, military and civilians, were to be murdered indiscriminately.

At this tremendous crisis, the Chief Commissioner was absent at Rawul Pindee; but his zealous and able colleagues were not left without that wisdom and decision which were so urgently required. Mr. Montgomery rose to the emergency, and, on his own responsibility, counselled the perilous measure of disarming the Lahore garrison. On parade, on the morning of the 13th, after some manœuvering, the whole of the native regiments found themselves confronted by the guns and by five companies of the Queen's 81st. At a given signal they were ordered, the sepoys to pile arms, the sowars to unbuckle sabres: they hesitated; but grape-shot and port-fires were ready: they knew it; they yielded. The troops in the fort were similarly disarmed. Lahore was saved, the Punjab preserved from dread confusion, and, in the preservation of its tranquillity, provision made for the overthrow of the rebellion in the North-west Provinces, and the restoration of British rule throughout India.

When Sir John Lawrence felt it necessary, for the restoration of his health, to return to England, his mantle fell on Sir R. Montgomery, who was transferred from the Chief Commissionership of Oude to the Lieutenant-Governorship of the Punjab. With the exception of the Umballa campaign, his administration of six years has been a period of unbroken peace, during which the resources of the province have been remarkably developed. The great railway from Umritsur to Mooltan is completed. The splendid Baree Doab canal already pays 46,500*l.* from the increased value of the land and the general irrigation rates. The general revenues have augmented by nearly half a million. The expenditure on public works has risen from 45,320*l.* in 1859 to 636,228*l.* in 1863. Trade has proportionably expanded, and wages have risen one-fifth. The tea plantations in the Kangra valley are surpassing the most sanguine expectations of those men who embarked their capital in this enterprise; while the silk operations at Umritsur, the establishments of the Indigo Company at Mooltan, and of the Belfast Corporation in connexion with flax, are full of promise. In the educational department the schools have increased from 565, with 2773 scholars, in 1856, to 6177, with 80,292 scholars, at the present time. Amidst these evidences of progress, the advancement of the great cause of female education has been conspicuous. It was especially becoming that the same high officer who had taken so active a part in rescuing from an infantile death so many native girls, should move the national mind to the adoption of measures which might fit them for the life thus unexpectedly prolonged to them, and initiate a grand educational movement, which will not stop until it has brought in Christianity to its aid.

Now let us pause a moment. It is not to laud man that these notices have been put together, but for the enforcement of a great principle. Does personal Christianity unfit a man for a career of high and honourable usefulness? Young men going out to India sometimes entertain misapprehensions of this kind. They speak as if they thought that to become religious is to become eccentric, and that personal devotedness invests a man with recluse and disagreeable habits. Thus they persuade themselves that to entertain serious religion is to subject oneself to a disadvantage, and embarrass oneself with an inconvenience in the race of life. Is this founded on fact, or is it a delusion? Let the career of such men as Sir Henry Lawrence, Sir John Lawrence, Sir R. Montgomery, Sir Herbert Edwardes, Mr. McLeod, and many other God-fearing men, whose names are connected with the affairs of the Punjab, answer that question. Undoubtedly, then, it is a delusion, but an unhappy one, because it strengthens the indisposedness of the natural mind to religion, and supplies the young man with an excuse for his rejection of those claims which Christianity urges on his conscience. No; influential Christianity does not hinder. It does not withdraw a man from the various paths of useful employment which open to him in the affairs of life, and consign him to an inactive existence, the monotony of which is diversified only by mystic speculations. This were indeed to "go out of the world," an issue which He never intended who said, "I pray not that thou shouldest take them out of the world, but that thou shouldest keep them from the evil."

Influential Christianity does not hinder; nay, but is this all? This were indeed cold. Surely it does more than this—it helps. Does it not do so in every path of life? Is it not the great sustaining principle? Enterprising, persevering men, indeed, we have known, who have worked on without bringing in Christianity to their aid. But there are, nevertheless, moments of deep trial, of heavy discouragements and unexpected danger, to which natural determination of character is found unequal. Such experiences are always liable to supervene, especially in the various branches of official duty connected with India, in the great future of which there is so much uncertainty. At such times the value and sustaining power of influential Christianity is tested and proved.

Let a scene be recalled: it is at the Lucknow Residency, when straitly shut up. On a bed in the north verandah of Dr. Fayrer's house lies a wounded man. Evidently he is no ordinary person, for around him are grouped the staff and principal persons of the garrison; and, besides, he is loved, for there is not a dry eye: it is Sir Henry Lawrence. He has been dangerously, mortally wounded, and life is fast ebbing. It was then, at that moment, that Christianity proved its power. Earthly honours and distinctions were at end. What then, if, in the discharge of his duties, to acquire such—a few fading wreaths—had been his object. But no; he had been actuated by a higher motive. "Ye are not your own, but bought with a price; wherefore glorify God in your bodies and spirits, which are God's;" and he had only gathered earthly honours, incidentally as it were, and by the way, but for himself he had learned to look forward to something better worth, an inheritance incorruptible. He could therefore afford to part with them, and, in doing so, to leave with his brothers-in-arms a lesson not to be forgotten. Having nominated his successor, he earnestly pointed out the worthlessness of all human distinctions, recommending all to fix their thoughts upon a better world. He referred to his own success in life, and asked what it was worth then. But the hope which the Gospel gave him, what, then, was that worth?

Yes, Christianity, when received and honoured as it ought to be, helps. It is not only when life is failing that it helps, but when energies are unbroken and the man is in full activity. How many a man of ability has failed when least expected. Great expectations had been formed of him. At length the great testing moment of his life has come. He does not rise to the emergency: he disappoints. How many a man, just as he is urging his course forward with every prospect of success, has fallen into some gross inconsistency, or has become the victim of some chronic weakness, some infirmity of temper, which removes him from the class of reliable men? Influential Christianity, duly cultivated, would have preserved him from such reverses. It would have taught him conscientiously to watch over himself. It would have enabled him to detect the latent weaknesses of his character, the parts which needed to be especially guarded against. It would have convinced him of his own inability to accomplish this except by faith in Christ, and brought him in prayer to the throne of grace for needed help; and thus his path would have beenas the path of the just, "shining more and more unto the perfect day."

But there is another question, and another subject of inquiry. Is it necessary, in order that a high functionary may duly and beneficently administer the affairs of a vast territory, inhabited by millions of heathen and Mohammedans, that he should ignore his Christianity; that he should conceal his regard for it within the privacy of his own family, or the secrecy of his own breast, and in public demean himself as though it were to him a matter of indifference? Is it necessary that he should do violence to his convictions, and put to shame his own sense of uprightness by patronizing the idolatrous temple, and frowning upon the Christian Missionary, and this in order to cajole the heathen? The result to be obtained is not worth the sacrifice. But these high Punjab officials never adopted such a course. They have never hesitated to avow their respect and love for Christianity, and their conviction of its truth. They have never discouraged Missionary action; nay, they have encouraged its advance, if only in its proceedings it were wise and discreet. When, on February 9th, 1851, a local Church Missionary Association was formed at Lahore, the names of its officers included those of Sir H. Lawrence, as President, R. Montgomery, Esq., John Lawrence, Esq. Again, in December 1853 a public meeting was held at Peshawur, with a view to Missionary efforts among the Affghans, the Commissioner of Peshawur, Sir Herbert Edwardes, being in the chair. Did the Punjab, because of this, suffer more from the convulsions of the mutiny than other parts of India? Were the people more disaffected, or rebellion more rife? Let well-known facts answer that question. And when the survivors of this noble band were raised to higher functions, the same wise and frank procedure marked their course. The Derajât had become a portion of our Trans-Indus possessions, and after long trouble with the border tribes, they had been quieted. It seemed the mature time for the introduction of Christian Missions, and the opening of wells of life in this parched land. But the initiative was not with the Church Missionary Society: it was taken by the high officials of the Punjab. Colonel Reynell Taylor and Sir Herbert Edwardes moved the Committee on the subject. In doing so they had the sanction of their chief. In a letter to Colonel Taylor, dated August 1861, Sir R. Montgomery writes—"It is not the duty of Government, or of their servants, to proselyte: this is left to those who have devoted their lives to the work. But I rejoice to see Missions spreading, and Dera is a fitting place for the establishment of one. But one will not suffice. Dera, as a centre, should be taken up first, and then Bunnoo, and Dera Ghazee Khan. The whole frontier, from Peshawur to the Sindh frontier, will then be lined with Missions. It is my earnest prayer that the knowledge of the true God will, from these points, cover the vast Suleiman range, and enter into the homes and hearts of the myriads of Asia. . . . As an earnest that I desire to see the Missions established, I will give 1000 rupees to each, as taken up."

Well, therefore, might the Missionaries of all denominations in the Punjab, at the close of the farewell Durbar, present to Sir R. Montgomery, the following address—

SIR,—In view of your approaching departure from India, we come, on behalf of the Missionaries resident in the Punjab, to bid you farewell.

Permit us to assure you of the high esteem and the affectionate interest with which, as a Christian Governor, you are regarded by their entire body.

It has pleased God to use your instrumentality in many ways, for promoting the material, the social, and the moral welfare of the people of this province. At this we, whose lives are devoted to their highest interests for time and eternity, cannot but rejoice; for this we cannot but be grateful to the Father of all mercies.

In the various philanthropic measures which have marked your administration, no class of the people seems to have escaped your notice. This is shown by your various schemes for developing the material resources of the country; by your efforts to secure a speedy and impartial administration of justice; by the encouragement you have given to education, including that of the female sex; by your earnest endeavours to effect the complete abolition of infanticide; by your strict adherence to the principle of religious neutrality—an adherence which has restored to native Christians rights too long ignored by Christian rulers; by the aid you have extended to small European communities in the erection of churches; and, finally, by your kindness, courtesy, and affability to all classes and conditions of the people.

To such things, under God, we may surely attribute in no small measure the high character borne by the Punjab Government; the prosperity and plenty with which the country is blessed; the peace, quietness, and sense of security which reign everywhere; and the feeling of satisfaction with the English rule, which we believe to be on the increase.

Your name being thus associated with so much in the history of the Punjab that demands our admiration and gratitude, it is with the sincerest regret that we see you about to retire from the midst of us. Yet we venture to hope, that, after your return to England, the Lord may still give you opportunities of serving his cause in India. We cannot doubt that He has purposes of great mercy to the people of this country; and we believe that, for the furtherance of any measure tending to this end, which his providence may bring within your reach, you will never be found wanting.

Our prayer is that the richest of God's blessings may rest upon yourself, upon Lady Montgomery, and upon all the members of your family.

And now, in testimony of the respect and Christian affection cherished for you, by ourselves and those we represent, we beg your acceptance of this Bible and timepiece.

JOHN NEWTON,
ROBERT CLARK, } *Committee.*

Lahore, Jan. 7, 1865.

The reply is as follows—

REVEREND SIRS,—I thank you for your address. I value it most highly, as coming from a body of earnest and faithful men, unconnected in any way with the Government service, who have devoted their lives to the highest interests of the people, and of whose unwearied and self-denying labours I have been a witness.

I value it all the more, because, as a ruler over this province, I have endeavoured, whilst giving to your body the fullest and freest scope, to preserve that religious neutrality which all the subjects of this great empire, with their varying creeds, have a right to expect from Her Majesty's Government.

I rejoice at the prosperity of this province, on which a blessing has indeed rested, and at the progress of the noble race it contains. I thank God that I have been privileged in some measure to aid in their advancement; and my highest aspirations will ever be for the welfare of the people amongst whom I have so long dwelt, and for whom I entertain the strongest attachment.

But to you, Reverend Sirs, belongs the credit of having been the pioneer of education in this, as in other parts of India; and, at the present time, some of the most flourishing educational institutions in the province are conducted by members of your body.

I most highly value your prayers for myself, for Lady Montgomery, and for my children. I accept with the sincerest thanks the testimony of your friendship.* The Bible you have given me will ever be prized by me, and whilst perusing the blessed words it contains, my thoughts and prayers will often revert to you all, and to your work.

But was Sir Robert, a less able administrator, because he was a Christian, not in name, but in reality? What, because he feared Him, who says, "By me kings reign, and princes decree justice. By me princes rule, and nobles, even all the judges of the earth. I love them that love me, and those that seek me early shall find me." Or still further, was he less popular among the natives because he avowed his Christianity? were they less attached to him? Let the proceedings of the last Durbar reply.

As his last administrative act, he was anxious it should be so ordered as to leave behind good and lasting impressions, so that, convinced how strongly he felt upon these points, the native chiefs and gentlemen, after his departure, might continue to persevere

* A handsome clock and Bible, with a suitable inscription.

in their efforts to encourage education generally among the people, and female education in particular. It was intended, therefore, that it should be marked by the distribution of titles of honour to such of the native nobility and gentry as had been most zealous in the promotion of these important objects. It was held on January 7, 1865—

At twelve P.M., the hour fixed for the Durbar, all the gentlemen invited to attend had taken their seats. First, on the right of the Lieutenant-Governor sat the Rajah of Kapurthala, wearing the Star of India, with his brothers, Sirdars Bekrama Singh and Suchet Singh, immediately behind him. Next to him sat the Rajah of Faridkot, a chief, whose possessions lie on the south side of the Sutlej; and below him Sirdar Shamsher Singh, head of the Sikh aristocracy. Next in order was Rajah Harbans Singh, adopted son of the late Rajah Tej Singh; and beside him Narandar Singh, a child born to Rajah Tej Singh in 1859.

Precisely at twelve o'clock Sir Robert Montgomery entered the Durbar tent with his staff, the whole assembly rising to receive him. He then addressed the chiefs in a short speech. He spoke of the sorrow he felt at leaving them, and the province in which he had laboured so long. He praised their efforts in the cause of female education, and announced that His Excellency the Viceroy had been pleased to sanction the bestowal of titles of honour upon such of the honorary magistrates of Lahore and Umritsur as had distinguished themselves by labouring for the improvement and embellishment of their respective cities.

Of the Lahore magistrates, the first called was Ali Raza Khan, an old man, upwards of seventy years of age, who received the title of Nawab. This gentleman is of the Kizibash tribe, and his family was, in 1738, brought from Persia, by Nadir Shah, and located in Cabul. His services to the British Government have been very great. When the British army first entered Cabul he was placed at the head of the Commissariat department, and throughout the succeeding troubles he did his best to keep the British army well supplied. It was chiefly through his aid and by his money that the English officers and ladies whom Muhammad Akbar Khan was transporting to Turkistan were enabled to make their escape, and he ransomed and saved from slavery a large number of native soldiers of the British army.

As the services he had rendered to the English in Cabul made his life there no longer safe, he, with his family and many of his tribe, accompanied the British army back to Hindustan, and received from Government a pension of 9600 rupees per annum.

During the two Sikh wars, he, with his sons and dependants, fought on our side; and in 1857 he raised a troop of horse for service before Delhi, which behaved with the greatest gallantry. One of his brothers, by name Takki Khan, was killed in action with the rebels, as were several of his nephews. At the close of the disturbances he received a grant of a talukdaree of 147 villages in Oude. Upon Abdul Majid Khan was the title of Nawab also conferred. He is the eldest representative of the old ruling family of Mooltan. His grandfather, Nawab Muzaffar Khan, his father, Shahnawaz Khan, and four of his uncles, were killed in the gallant defence of the city against Maharajah Runjeet Singh in 1818. He has been active as an honorary magistrate, and is well deserving of the honour of Nawabship now conferred upon him.

Ajodhia Pershad, an old, white-bearded man, was then called forward, and received the title of Dewan, which will be continued to his son Baijnath, Extra Assistant Commissioner of Lahore.

After these gentlemen had received the suunuds of the Supreme Government conferring their titles of honour, many of the chiefs who had been most active in promoting education received from His Honour the Lieutenant-Governor letters of commendation, with khilats, shawls, and other presents. The most noticeable among them was Baba Khem Singh, high priest of the Sikh faith. This liberal-minded man has used his great influence well and wisely. He has exhorted the Sikhs to educate their daughters, and has himself founded numerous girls' schools in the districts of Jhelam and Guzerat. To him the Lieutenant-Governor presented two double-barrelled guns, for he is a keen sportsman.

The Rajah of Kapurthala, who is always found on the side of enlightenment and progress, then rose, and, addressing the Lieutenant-Governor, stated his intention of giving 200 rupees a month for the endowment of certain schools. The representatives of the chiefs and people of the two cities of Lahore and Umritsur then came forward, and presented to His Honour an address in Persian, in a handsome case of gold and ivory. The following is a close translation—

"To SIR ROBERT MONTGOMERY, K.C.B., *Lieutenant-Governor of the Punjab.*

"*From the* CHIEFS *and* GENTLEMEN *of the Cities of Lahore and Umritsur, representatives of the people of the whole Punjab.*

"Your Honour is about to leave us, with

all honour, for England, your native country, and our grief for your departure will never be effaced, and your liberality and benevolence will never be forgotten. Your departure for Europe is honourable and propitious, and you leave a glorious name behind you.

"It is impossible for us to express our thanks for all your kindness. Our children and our children's children, throughout time, will be mindful of your good deeds.

"Your Honour came to this province at the time of the annexation; and you were first appointed Commissioner of Lahore: it was the commencement of a new rule, and of a new order of things; but through your kindness, and impartiality, and justice, all, both nobles and peasants, rich and poor, were contented and grateful, and the business of the State was well performed. The country was happily settled; encamping grounds and roads were made; trees and gardens were planted; and rest-houses and granaries for the use and comfort of travellers were built. By your energy and good management, thuggee, dacoity, and highway robbery were stopped, the people were secure, and the country became populated; and these crimes have been so completely extirpated, that their names are now all but forgotten.

"Schools were established in towns and villages, and a Government college and medical hall were formed, in which thousands may obtain a good education and means of livelihood; and our nobles have acquired the unfading riches of science and wisdom.

"When our good fortune appointed your Honour Judicial Commissioner, the practice of female infanticide, common in some tribes, was stopped. The people of this country were preserved from a great crime, and the lives of their infant daughters are now for ever secure. The extravagant expenditure at betrothals and marriages, which was in some measure the cause of the murder of our girls, has been, by you, regulated; and betrothals and marriages are now easy of accomplishment.

"What can we say of the Criminal and Civil Administration? The offices are full of the records of your good government: you had compiled a Civil Code, which is a clear exponent of Mohammedan and Hindu law and the local customs of the people.

"In 1857, it was much owing to the energy of your Honour that the province was preserved in peace. What you did at the disarming of the mutinous Sepoys at Meean Meer, in guarding the jails, and in extinguishing the flame of sedition which threatened the destruction of the whole province, are matters of history. The preservation of the capital was the preservation of the entire province.

"It is owing to you that we now possess a conviction that the Government appreciates our loyalty, and knows that we will not betray its confidence: our prosperity and our loss is now one with that of the State.

"You were selected to be Chief Commissioner in Oude, and when that province was restored to tranquillity, at length our good fortune brought you again to us as Lieutenant-Governor, and your benevolence and good deeds in this office are beyond our praise. From a wilderness the country has become like a garden in spring. Upon the deserving amongst us you bestowed ranks, titles, and estates; to the great chiefs the right of adoption was secured; scattered estates have been consolidated. Punjabees have been encouraged to enter the armies of the State, and portions of our jageers have been upheld in perpetuity; our honour has been increased, and we feel that we are acknowledged as well-wishers of the Government. From the establishment of Municipal Committees the people have received much benefit, and the introduction of the new police has caused the diminution of crime, and has given confidence to the public.

"Your Honour has well commenced the education of those very girls whose lives were preserved by your labours, and whose betrothal and marriage you had rendered easy. These, and many other good deeds, will ever preserve your memory fresh amongst us.

"At the commencement of 1864 you inaugurated an Industrial Exhibition, collecting all the products of the Punjab in a stately and matchless building, which you had caused to be erected at the capital. You gave rewards and certificates to mechanics and workmen, and encouraged them to improve the manufactures of the province. The gardens and canals you have made around the city of Lahore, are proofs of your kindness and liberality. All have received benefit: what comfort and convenience have all derived from railways and telegraphs. The increase of commerce and of wealth and prosperity we have no need to mention.

"Our one regret is that you must so soon leave us. May the merciful God convey you home with all peace and safety; may He speedily restore you to us again with increased honour; and may He ever preserve a kindly memory of us in your heart!"

On the conclusion and the address, His Honour rose and replied in Urdu to the following effect.

"Sirdars and Native Gentlemen,—I thank you with all my heart for your address.

"I have not done all you attribute to me,

but I have done my utmost to further your interests, welfare, and happiness.

"When I came among you, fifteen years ago, your country was indeed a wilderness, its highways unsafe, its revenues wasted, the anarchy and war, following upon the death of Maharajah Runjeet Singh, had brought ruin on the country, and misery on the people.

"I thank God I have lived to see the desolation of those days changed for prosperity and contentedness.

"But I cannot claim to be the sole author of this great change: it was commenced by my illustrious predecessors, Sir Henry and Sir John Lawrence. I have endeavoured to carry on—with the assistance of other able officers—what they had successfully begun. In so doing we have all been animated with the same feeling, an earnest desire to promote your interests and well-being, and thus to carry out the wishes of our most gracious Queen.

"The appointment of honorary magistrates from among the chiefs and gentlemen of the province—to which you allude as one of the measures of my administration—has, I rejoice to say, been attended with great success and satisfaction to all. The election of Municipal Committees for the government of your cities has been equally so. These measures have been dictated by a policy which I have ever advocated of associating, as far as possible, the people with the Government in the business of administration.

"By these means honourable employment has been afforded to a large body of native gentlemen, and their knowledge and influence have been secured for the benefit of the people and the State.

"But this success is not only attributable to the exertions of your rulers, but to the satisfactory way in which you yourselves have responded to my call.

"The striking improvements in the capitals of Lahore, Umritsur, and other cities, the wonderful progress of female education during the last two years, bear testimony to these results at once gratifying to me, and honourable to yourselves.

"It has been my endeavour to open out your resources, by encouraging the construction of roads and the promotion of works of public utility, and to facilitate by these means an increase in your exports, and the general improvement in the trade and wealth of the province.

"I now bid you farewell, with my best wishes for your future happiness, in the assurance that your country will continue to advance in its career of prosperity, and that you yourselves will continue to prove, as you have done already, loyal and faithful subjects of Her Majesty.

"Your future ruler is one who, like myself, has long lived among you, and your interests could not be left in better hands."

Sir Robert Montgomery then left the tent, and the Durbar broke up.

It was attended by almost all the officers and gentlemen resident at Lahore, and by many who had come in from the neighbouring stations of Umritsur, Gujranwala, and Ferozepore.

We doubt not that Sir Robert Montgomery will long be remembered in the Punjab as a wise and beneficent ruler; and at home we may well concede to him, on his arrival, that hearty welcome which is due to one who, by the frank avowal of his Christianity, and the good works whereby he was enabled to adorn his profession, best commended it to the attention of the natives.

THE INDIANS OF BRITISH COLUMBIA.

"Where the white man settles, the red man disappears." That it has been so in numberless instances is indisputable. Nations, once numerous, have dwindled away, until a feeble residuum is all that is left, sparsely scattered over numerous tracts of country. Their decadence is symbolized in the mountain streams of their native land, which, in the time of the melting snow, are swollen and impetuous, but, with the advancing year, when the floods are over, and the sun has become intense, if not entirely dried up, are reduced to a feeble streamlet, which with difficulty finds its way among the rocks once buried beneath the turbid waters. How is this to be accounted for? Is it a law of Providence, or has the white man, proving unfaithful to his mission, come to the homes of the red man, not as the benefactor, but as the destroyer of his species? Had he been true to his Christianity, and brought it with him, his goings forth would have been full of blessing to the nations of the earth. But they have been few who have done so. Usually, when going forth to emigrate, and find for himself in the far West a new home, the white man has disembarrassed himself of his Christian obligations as inconvenient, and has gone forth determined to recognise no law but the strength of his right arm. Hence there have been wrongs and reprisals. The Indian suffered: he found himself defrauded in trade, or his lands were encroached upon. Taking up the hatchet, he used it indiscriminately, and the innocent suffered for the guilty. Then the white man rose to arms, and there was war between the settlers and the Indians. In these conflicts the native races were invariably worsted, and fell back before the conquerors, leaving behind them the seashore and its supplies. Becoming more and more enfeebled, they ceased to resist, and submitted themselves to the domination of the stranger. Thus they learned his vices, and became abject and degraded; and the enfeebled remnants of the tribes which once claimed as their homes the area of the United States, are now to be found in the lands assigned them eastward of the Mississippi, where the tide of civilization, so called, is rapidly pursuing them, and where, unless, under the influence of Christianity, they begin to till the ground, they must find their graves.

Shall the same sad history be reproduced in the British territories which extend along the shores of the Pacific? In those wintry regions known as North-west America, the native population, the Loucheux Indians on the Youcon excepted, is in the same sparse and fragmentary state. Although no emigrant population has established itself there and risen into states, yet, from various causes, the Indians have dwindled down to a remnant. But in British Columbia and Vancouver's Island they are yet numerous. In the latter government the male aboriginal population is computed to be from 12,000 to 17,000.

On the mainland, between the parallels of 49° and 54° 40′ north latitude, are three nations of Indians, speaking different languages, each numbering 10,000 souls. The first of these is to be found at Victoria and on the Frazer river; the second at Fort Rupert and the north end of Vancouver's Island; the third at Fort Simpson, Nass river, and Skeena river: the Queen Charlotte Island Indians constitute a fourth group of about 10,000.

From contact with the white man these tribes were remarkaby secluded, until gold was discovered in British Columbia, and adventurers began to flock thither. It is but a brief period since the solitude of this portion of the American continent was invaded, yet the Indians are already and disastrously suffering; not, indeed, from the violence of the white man, for as yet they are able to protect themselves, and there is, besides, British law and government in the land, but from his vices.

Predisposed to imitate the bad example of the various adventurers who throng these coasts, the Indian soon becomes infected with vices more rapidly destructive than those which of old he had been familiar with. The plague has commenced. How shall it be arrested? The Gospel message—this has power. Like Aaron's censer interposed between the dead and the living, it can stay the pestilence. But there is not a moment to be lost. It is, with the Indians of these coasts, now or never. That which is to be done must be done quickly; and they who would engage in this mission of mercy must do as Aaron did: he "took, as Moses commanded, and ran into the midst of the congregation." It is no experiment. God has already manifested on these coasts the conservative power of the Gospel. No one can read the details of Mission work at Metlahkatlah without being convinced that, by the same means as those which have been pursued there, the Indian may be preserved from the destruction that threatens to engulf him.

Let our readers peruse the following letter, written by our new Missionary, the Rev. R. A. Doolan, on reaching Metlahkatlah in July last. The change accomplished by the simplicity yet power of Christian teaching; the contrast between the heathen and converted Indian; the opportunities for immediate and extensive effort; the urgent need that they should be speedily improved,—all this powerfully impressed him. May the same effect be produced upon the church at home, that we may arise and do the Lord's work!

On landing, I was met by most of the Christian people of the village, anxious to shake hands, and show their pleasure at my coming amongst them. Mr. Duncan tells me that this was quite spontaneous on their part, as he had never hinted at such a proceeding. The village is very suitably situated, both as regards health and beauty. It comprises about fifty double and single houses, similar to labourers' cottages at home; a large Mission house, now in course of erection, the work for the most part of Indians; a large octagonal building, used during the week for a school-room, and for service on Sundays; a store, and a sawpit. Mr. Duncan is going to erect another store, as the present one is too small for the trade that is springing up between the Tsimshean Indians and those of other tribes. The two streets form, as it were, two sides of a right-angled triangle, the Mission premises being at the apex, and fronting the sea. Before the houses are small gardens, and the road is being made before them, also fronting the sea. A few of the Indians talk very good English, and many understand it, though they do not speak it. The contrast between the Indians stationed here, and those of other tribes, is very striking. It is especially noticeable when they meet together for trade. A few days ago, two large canoes of Queen Charlotte islanders came across to trade blankets for fish-grease: on the one side the Christian Indian, dressed in suitable decent clothes; on the other, his heathen brother, with nothing but a blanket to cover his nakedness. The Indians told us, that in former years, when the Queen Charlotte islanders came to trade, each party brought forward their property, the Tsimshean his grease, the others their blankets, and that all the guns were loaded ready for a fight, and very seldom did they part without bloodshed. What a change Christianity has wrought! My ignorance of the language has prevented me speaking on spiritual matters, but nothing could exceed the attention paid to Mr. Duncan whilst preaching on Sunday. It has been thought advisable that I should go to the Nass river, sixty miles north-east of this, where the people have long expressed a desire for teachers. This place is a centre of heathenism, and I trust the Society will approve of the step we are about to take. The tribe called the Tsimsheans is a most important one, and their desire for teachers, from whatever motive it may arise, is exceedingly gratifying. A door seems opened for preaching to them the Gospel. The priests have already paid them a visit, and, should the field not be occupied, they will, no doubt, next spring return. I felt some little hesitation at first in leaving Mr. Duncan, but he proposes to engage an Indian, Samuel Marsden, as teacher of the school, which will lighten his work. We also consulted on the advisability of sending a catechist to the head of the Nass river, to open a school, and had found a man very willing to go, but his wife so strongly objected that the matter is at present in abeyance. I pray and hope God will raise up some among themselves to go forth, and tell their heathen brethren the truths they themselves have learnt.

The occupation of this spot has long been desired by Mr. Duncan. It was visited by him in 1860, and the welcome which he received from the Indians on that occasion is so interesting that we shall retrace it. On entering the Nass river, which opens into Observatory Inlet, a scene of exceeding beauty presented itself. For ten miles straight before them opened up the river, with a channel two miles in width, and chains of towering mountains rising parallel to it on either side. Soon they met a very large body of Indians, not less than 2000, strangers from different quarters, who had come, some of them over 150 miles, to fish. On reaching the lower villages of the Nishkah Indians Mr. Duncan was welcomed by the friendly chief, Kahdoonahah, who had invited him thither, and who danced for joy at his arrival. The rights of hospitality having been duly discharged, arrangements were made for a meeting on the morrow, when there met together a large number of Indians. After the native ceremonial of singing and dancing had been performed, Mr. Duncan began to address them. Every countenance was fixed upon him, the Indians unanimously responding at the termination of every clause, and that with especial solemnity whenever the name of Jesus was introduced. At once every tongue uttered Jesus, and for some time kept repeating that blessed name. So soon as he had concluded, an universal cry arose of "Good is your speech; good, good, good news! We greatly desire to learn the book: we wish our children to learn."

In September 1860, Mr. Duncan again proceeded to the Nass river, with the intention of ascending it to a higher point than he had yet done, and reaching a village of the Nishkah Indians called Kitwillukshehth, a chief named Kinsahdah accompanying him from the lower villages. His narrative of this journey is so touching, and brings before us so vividly the eagerness of these poor people to be taught, that we print it *in extenso*—

Sept. 17, 1860—The river averaged 100 yards wide so far as we have gone. The banks are thickly wooded. Mosquitos, though comparatively few now to what they are in summer, I found very troublesome.

In the morning we passed a canoe with two Indians in it, fishing. They gave me two large fresh salmon. We also met the chief, Akshahtahn, floating down the stream in a small canoe, all alone. He gave me a warm greeting, and presented me with a beaver-skin, and a pole to push us up the river.

Leaving Akshahtahn, we soon came to a temporary village of a tribe we had passed.

The chief, Nagahhon, invited me into his house, and gave me a large black-bear skin. He sat down beside me, and said he remembered me. His heart told him I was from heaven (not, of course, meaning this literally). I explained to him the object of my pushing up the river, and that, on my return, I would like to speak to him and his people of God's message to us. He reiterated "ahm, ahm" ("good, good").

Finding that we should not be able to reach the Kitwillukshehth before dark, I thought it best to halt about six P.M. We pitched ourselves on an island in the river. On landing, we picked up a beautiful salmon, which had recently jumped out of the stream. The ravens had picked out its eyes, and we enjoyed the remainder of it.

After supper I had a lonely but delightful stroll. The little island on which we were encamped seemed but a small patch in the centre of a stupendous amphitheatre. The mountains and glaciers all around looked awful and majestic.

When I returned I mustered my little crew for evening devotions. The chief seemed willing to join us, and I spoke to them from the first Psalm, where God's people are compared to trees growing by the river-side. When we had sung our evening hymn we knelt in prayer.

Sept. 8—Awoke early this morning, and found every thing about us very wet with the dew. After breakfast we proceeded on our way, and arrived at the village before noon, having encountered several difficult places in the river.

Before we reached the village Kinsahdah pointed out to me a mountain on our left, and in it a peculiar perpendicular rock. The rock, he remarked, is a great *nok nok;* and then he commenced relating the tradition they hold about the river and surrounding country being on fire. "The children of the Kitwillukshehth village were one day amusing themselves by catching salmon, and tormenting them in this way—They cut a slit under the fin on the back of each, deposited a small stone in the wound, and then cast them back into the river. At the sight of the fishes plunging about in great agony, the young people and children laughed and danced, showing how much they enjoyed their cruel sport. But a huge mountain, some distance beyond the village, and a great nok nok, looked on their proceedings, and felt greatly ashamed. That night issued from its bosom a tremendous fire, which made its destructive way towards the Indian village. Soon the bed of the river and the immediate adjoining country boiled and burned. The Indians fled to a distance, but the fire roared on. What could have caused the mountain to be angry? They knew of nothing but the wicked play of the children. What was to be done? They agreed to burn all the dogs in sacrifice to the mountain. This was done, but it failed to abate the fire. They then concluded it would be necessary to burn the children that had committed the sin. Some of the parents refused to give up their terrified children, and so the fire went on. At last all were led to yield: all the guilty suffered, and the fire ceased to spread further, and gradually cooled down. They marked the spot in the bed of the river where the fire stopped, and this being opposite to the peculiar-looking rock in the mountain which Kinsahdah pointed out to me, they gave it the honour of having stopped the fire, and called it a great nok nok."

Before Kinsahdah finished his story, he took care to convince me that there really had been a fire, by showing me stones that had been fused by its power; and on arriving at the village I could see stretching before us an immense lava plain, rent in every direction by deep fissures.

When we were about two miles from the village we came to a temporary house, and the only persons I could see were a young man and an elderly woman. Without saying a word to me, the young man set off as fast as he could run to the village, to tell them of my coming.

A chief, named Agweelakkah, and one of his men, both dressed in their best, and the chief with an umbrella over his head, as a sign of his greatness, met me about a quarter of a mile from the village. I soon found that but few Indians were at home, and that these few were very busy smoking salmon, for which purpose they had erected temporary dwellings some little distance from this village.

Agweelakkah expressed his sorrow that I had found them so unprepared, he not being able to invite me to lodge with him, but asked me, as a favour, to go and sit down a little time in his rude house.

I had my little tent pitched on the stony bank, a huge fire built, and the boys cooking fresh salmon, which had been brought in by the Indians.

After we had eaten, the chief came, and said that he was preparing his house in the village for my reception, and that shortly he would send to invite me in the usual way, in order to perform the *ahlied* before me in honour of my coming. I told him that I did not wish to see them play. I had a solemn message to deliver, and their exhibiting their old customs before me would not be agreeable. He then assured me that what he was about to do was only their way of showing how welcome I was, and that I should not be shocked with what he would do. Kinsahdah seconded his remarks by saying that the beating of their drums and performance which followed was to them what the book was to us. I think he meant by this, that as we assemble to hear the book, so they assemble to hear the nok nok, or spirit, speak through their chief; or else he meant, that as we give a paper to those whom we honour and wish to remember, and be remembered by, so they exhibit their wonders to those whom they desire to honour.

As I had no desire in the least to offend them I thought I had better go, though I felt great trouble and anxiety of mind about complying.

When they saw me approaching the house they began beating the drum. I found my seat prepared on the right side of the house. A man was standing by it when I entered, and, on seeing me, he stamped his foot, made a motion with his hand to the seat, and cried at the top of his voice, "Keah shimauket keah."

Though seated with such marks of honour, I felt very uncomfortable, and looked round the house with rather a displeased countenance I am afraid. At the head of the house, and fronting the fire and the door, was suspended a canoe's sail, acting as a curtain to hide the actors which were about to appear. Several men were pacing about in front of the curtain, while opposite me on the other side of the fire sat a group of women. All eyes were fixed on me, and many kind glances given me, but I could not return them, as I wished to show them that I sat there against my will.

Presently an elderly man came from behind the curtain, holding a long rod in his hand. He solemnly paced the floor in front of the curtain for a little time, and then said, in a strain of inquiry, "Heaven is about to put away the heart (the way) of the ancient people, is it?" A voice replied that it was even so. He then said something about the book and myself, which I could not catch, as these Indians have a dialect of their own, which differs in some respects from the Tsimshean. This sounded so strange that I began to feel interested.

Presently the chief, Agweelakkah, appeared from behind the curtain. He was dressed in his robes, and held a rattle of a peculiar shape in his hand. He had a thick rope round his neck of red dyed and undyed bark, twisted together and tied into a rose, which rested on his chest. His dress was pretty and becoming. He first turned towards me, and said something which I cannot recall; and then, putting himself into a beautiful attitude, with one hand stretched out and his eyes directed towards heaven, in a solemn voice he thus addressed God—"Pity us, great Father in heaven, pity us. Give us thy good book to do us good and clear away our sins. This chief (pointing to me) has come to tell us about thee. It is good, great Father. We want to hear. Who ever came to tell our forefathers thy will? No, no. But this chief has pitied us and come. He has thy book. We will hear. We will receive thy word. We will obey." As he uttered one of the last sentences a voice said, "Your speech is good."

As I gazed and listened, I felt as I can

scarcely describe how, for I was by no means expecting to witness what I had.

The people sat very solemn and attentive during the chief's prayer, but when he had done they commenced singing some of their chants, the leader composing the words and intoning them over verse by verse, when they are taken up and sung with great force, accompanied by clapping of hands and beating a drum. As the composer went on I tried to catch what they were singing about, but failed. On inquiring afterwards I could get nothing more from them than they were singing about us, and what their own hearts said. When the singing was over, the chief then turned to me, and made a speech to the following effect. They wanted me amongst them. They wanted God's book. They wanted to cast away their bad ways and be good. He said he had heard some of the news from God's book in a conversation with me in my house at Fort Simpson a long time ago, and he had told what he heard to his people on his return home. They pronounced it good. They loved me, and wanted me amongst them. After the speech he presented me with two beavers'-skins, to show his good heart towards me.

I then spoke a few words to them, and invited all before my tent in the evening, when I would address them from God's word.

On leaving, several pressed me to step into their house. All seemed glad to see me. Many had put on their best clothes. I saw a great many children running about dressed. Many sauntered about me: a general holiday seemed to prevail.

Before I returned to my tent three men came formally to invite me to another chief's house. They stood at the door of the house in which I was sitting, and shouted out their message. Again I heard the drum; again I was seated; and I saw we were to have a repetition of what I had just witnessed in Agweelakkah's house. The chief (whose name is Peecap) acted, and he said a great many things like what I have just written. They welcomed me. A great epoch had come in their history. God was sending them good news, &c. He gave me two bear-skins.

Soon after the Indians began to assemble around my tent, and in a very few minutes I had nearly every man, woman, and child in the camp around me, in all about eighty souls, all that were left at home, the others being away gathering food. I judged the village to number about 400 souls. Among my congregation was an old blind chief—Thkahteen—from a village further up the river.

After seeking God's help, I began my address. The Lord enabled me to be solemn and earnest. I set Jesus before them clearly, and I think it was one of the most affecting meetings I have ever held. The old blind chief kept on responding to all I said. He was most earnest and zealous in exhorting the people to listen and obey the word of God. He continued uttering the name of Jesus for some time. "We are not to call upon stones and stars now," said he, "but Jesus. Jesus will hear. Jesus is our Saviour. Jesus! Jesus! Jesus Christ! Good news! Good news! Listen all. Put away your sins. God has sent his word. Jesus is our Saviour. Take away my sins, Jesus. Make me good, Jesus." This and much more he said in a like strain. It was delightful to hear him. The people sat very attentively, and many, like the old chief, often reiterated the name of Jesus. It was growing dark before I dismissed them.

I had not long been seated after the meeting before Kinsahdah came, and said the old blind chief and several people wanted to come to our evening devotions. As Kinsahdah expressed it, the old man wanted to hear me sing, and then he would die; meaning, I suppose, he wanted to hear me sing before he died. We made at once a bright fire. The wind was rather too high, and blew the sparks and smoke about too much. The blind chief soon came, and we assembled, about thirty altogether, round the fire. I sang several hymns in English, and the chant in the Tsimshean tongue. After which I asked them all to kneel down and I would pray to God. They all readily obeyed, and I trust the Lord heard my prayer, and will answer it to the glory of his own name, and for the benefit and salvation of these poor long-lost people.

Sept. 9: *Lord's-day*—This morning I met again about eighty souls, in a house which they had cleared up for our use.

I addressed them on the life and religion of Abraham, and how he showed his faith in a coming Saviour. I then set Christ before them. They were very attentive to my address, and soon made remarks on what I said.

I then taught them to sing the little hymn, "Jesus is my Saviour," which I think some of them learnt; after which I requested them to stand up in a solemn attitude while I prayed to God. They did so. I found this better than getting them to kneel, as that often occasions so much confusion when there are children, the attitude being a novelty to all.

We finished, and I felt grateful to God for the two meetings He had permitted me to have with these people. I truly hope that the blessed name of Jesus, which they have all learnt, and some for the first time, may prove precious to many.

I was kept very busy most of the remaining part of the day, conversing with several around my tent, and writing out papers for the children, and also for some adults.

Sept. 10—About noon I arrived again at the temporary village, which I promised on my way up to preach at when I returned. The chief again came out to meet me, when I requested him to sit down on the bank, and his people, and hear what God's word said. I had about eighty souls here too. After my address, &c., there was a general stir to gather me some food as presents. A number of women and children seized their baskets, and set off to their potato-gardens.

The chief wished me to accompany him and the party, in order to show me the site of their forefathers' village. They led me some half mile through mud and bushes, having only a very narrow trail for our road. When we arrived at the spot—which was a large flat of land, about one-third of which I found occupied by the potato plant — the chief and his party turned round and said, "This is the place where our forefathers lived, and they told us something we want to tell you. The story is as follows—" One night a child of the chief class awoke and cried for water. Its cries were very affecting—'Mother, give me to drink,' but the mother heeded not. The moon was affected, and came down, entered the house, and approached the child, saying, 'Here is water from heaven: drink.' The child anxiously laid hold of the pot and drank the draught, and was enticed to go away with the moon, its benefactor. They took an underground passage till they quite got clear of the village, and then ascended to heaven. And," said the chief, "our forefathers tell us that the figure we now see in the moon is that very child; and also the little round basket which it had in its hand when it went to sleep appears there. Now, we ask you, is this true or not? We want you to tell us."

So I commenced, and, by a familiar illustration, and appealing to their common sense, I soon succeeded in shaking their faith in this ancient tale; for they turned to one another after I had done, and exclaimed, "Certainly! certainly! and how greatly the ancients lied. Did they not?"

Before I got away, my canoe was laden with potatoes, presents from the children.

In an hour or two we arrived at the principal lower village.

I assembled the few, about fifty or sixty souls, on the beach. Before I began to address them I sent my boys to cut me some sticks. On their returning, with the required number, I stuck nine in one row and five in another in the sand. I then told them that the nine sticks represented nine large villages of Indians, who stood on a river far south from here a few years ago, but rum, and disease from immoral practices, had cast them down and destroyed them. They were warned before the evil day came, but they heeded not: now they are fallen and gone. Here I knocked down the nine sticks which I had set up.

Afterwards I said, these five sticks are to represent your five large villages on this beautiful river, standing now. I also come to warn you. Listen to my voice. If you follow the course you have begun, yet a little while and you will fall too. Here I dashed the sticks down. Soon you will be lost and miserable.

They seemed greatly affected at this simple illustration, and immediately a great talk ensued.

I then went on to say—Now I have told you of your enemies, I will tell you about God, your Maker, for I have his word, and if you will follow it, you will yet become a happy people.

I then set some of the most prominent truths of the Bible before them, and especially about the Lord Jesus dying to reconcile us to God, whom we have offended with our sins.

They seemed to drink in the word, and the responses many of them made when I finished were very encouraging. May the Lord open their hearts to receive his blessed truth!

I then went to the next lower village, about half a mile further down the river, but there seemed to be nobody at home. We could only muster fifteen souls.

I then told them the same that I had preached to the other villages, and begged of them not to forget to tell their relatives what I had said, when they returned from their fishing-stations.

We then moved away homewards. It was near night, so we soon put into a little creek, lit a fire, and partook of a hearty meal. I was very tired, but happy. After our usual evening devotions we retired to rest.

However anxious Mr. Duncan might be to help this people it was impossible for him to do so, as he was alone; and matters remained in this state until the beginning of 1864, when the Nass Indians again claimed his attention. The Metlahkatlah Indians are, many of them, earnest Christians. On the Sunday evening, after the usual services have been concluded, they have a meeting of their own, attended by upwards of a hundred. After singing and prayer, one or two of them exhort the meeting, the sermons preached by Mr. Duncan during the day forming the basis of their addresses.

Nor is it only within the settlement that they are thus earnest. Wherever they go they carry their religion with them, always assembling on the Sunday for worship, and getting as many as possible of the heathen to join them.

An Indian of Fort Simpson, who, although not a resident of Metlahkatlah, had yet received much instruction from Mr. Duncan, had been up the Nass river to some of the most remote villages, a distance of a hundred miles from the station. While residing there as a fur-trader, he diligently used his talent for God, setting forth the Gospel where it had never been preached before, and meeting with so much encouragement, that seven young men came down with him to Metlahkatlah, that they might hear from the Missionary's mouth the things of which he had spoken. They had intended returning the next day; but when Mr. Duncan pressed earnestly on their minds and hearts the great truths of the Gospel, they decided to remain until after Sunday, that they might receive further instruction, and carry it back with them to their waiting and thirsty tribe.

"They were anxious," says Mr. Duncan, "to carry in their hands a portion of God's word, so I wrote out for each, on a piece of paper, 'This is a faithful saying, and worthy of all acceptation, that Christ Jesus came into the world to save sinners.' I also gave the Indian trader and teacher some further instruction, and pointed him out portions of Scripture suited to him and his flock.

"Before he arrived here, he wrote me a very encouraging letter (for I have taught him to read and write), a copy of which I would like to have forwarded to you, but I must forbear."

So inviting was this opportunity for good—and there was the more reason that it should be at once occupied, for the Romish priests are busy, like astute traders, trying to palm upon the Indians their miserable counterfeit of Christianity, and to prejudice them against the Christian Missionary. The anxiety which he exhibits to secure spiritual results is at once dispensed with, and they proceed to an indiscriminate administration of baptism. Then, provided they shut the door upon the Protestant Missionary, the proselytes are at liberty to retain their medicine work and old customs; for with the priests of Rome the conversion of the heathen is a superficial process, and if the old material of heathenism will only take their gilding, and assume the new face they put upon it, this is all they care for.

We are now happy to inform our readers that Mr. Doolan has reached Nass river. In October last he arrived amongst these anxious people, and commenced erecting a house, to their great astonishment, for they could scarcely believe that he was going to pass the long and dreary winter amongst them. He has rented from one of the chiefs an old deserted house, which he was fitting up as a school-house. The Lord bless the work, and crown it with a large and speedy ingathering of souls!

Let one remark close this article. The Lord is manifestly, and in a remarkable manner, disposing the hearts of this people to hear and to receive the truth. He knows their danger; that the time is short, and the crisis urgent. He therefore gives to them the craving after Christian instruction, and to us the opportunity and high privilege of imparting it. This alone can rescue them from the peril by which they are surrounded. Shall we fail at such a moment? That would be an indelible disgrace. Men and money are wanting: who will help?

MISSIONS IN THE MACKENZIE AND THE YOUCON DISTRICTS.

We wish to speak in this article of two distant Missions, so distant and far removed from those scientific appliances which, in more favoured lands, facilitate communication, that, ere despatches can reach us from them, a period of between seven and eight months is required. The more distant they are, the more needful it is that they be remembered. If, of the children of a family, some are at home, others in far-off India or New Zealand, does true affection remember the distant ones less? Are they not, because far away, more the objects of anxiety, so that many prayers are offered on their behalf? And so with respect to these far-off stations: they are the children of the Society, and claim from us an affectionate solicitude.

One of these stations is Fort Simpson, on the Mackenzie River. The Fort stands on an island at the junction of the River of the Mountains (Rivière aux Liards) with the Mackenzie, in latitude 61° 51′ 25″ N., and longitude 121° 51′ 15″ W. This large tributary originates in the recesses of the Rocky Mountains, its feeders lying to the westward of the highest peaks. By one of these affluents, Dease's River, boats pass through the mountains, and, after much trying and perilous navigation, reach a Company's post called Pelly Banks, at the junction of the Pelly and Lewes, the distance from Fort Halkett on the River of the Mountains to this point by the winter route, which is usually as direct as the nature of the country will admit, being 540 miles. From Llynn canal to the north of the island of Sitka, on the western coast, not far north of British Columbia, native traders travel twice in the year to Pelly Banks. We are thus enabled to discern the faint traces of new lines of communication with the Missions on the Youcon, whereby they may be reached with more facility from British Columbia than by the old and tedious route of North-West American lakes and rivers.

On the Pacific coast we have pushed our Missions up the Nass river, which flows into Observatory Inlet, at the mouth of which Fort Simpson (British Columbia) is situated. This river is described by our Missionaries as opening up in a magnificent channel a mile in width. Its course is not laid down in any map in our possession, but it comes from the north-east, and probably approaches the Liard River, which, as already stated, falls into the Mackenzie at Fort Simpson (North-West America). In fact, if the Missions which we are now opening up to our readers be extended over those parts of British America which lie immediately east of the Russian boundary, and in the direction of those tributaries of the Youcon which flow in from the south, they will come into communication with our Missions in British Columbia; and thus that country, as it becomes settled, will constitute an important basis of evangelizing operations. The native-Christian community, which Mr. Duncan is raising up at Metlahkatlah, will then be placed in a position, to render important services, by influencing the tribes immediately contiguous to it, and moving them to act on the tribes immediately beyond them. Thus a series of efforts may be generated, the pulsations of which will be felt as far as the Arctic Sea.

We shall briefly state the circumstances in which these Missions originated. Stanley, English-River district, on the boundary line of the Crees and Chipewyans, was occupied by us in 1849. The Romish Missionaries pushed further north, having established a Mission at Isle-à-la-Crosse in 1846: from thence they advanced to Slave Lake.

It is not necessary to explain to our readers the teaching of the priests of Rome. They are already aware of its character. One extract from their own publications will suffice to show how grievously they have adulterated the bread of life. Monsignor Vital Grandin, Bishop of Satala, and coadjutor of the Bishop of St. Boniface, writing to the directors of the Propagation of the Faith from the Mission of St. John the Baptist, La Crosse Island, December 3, 1861, gives the following account of a death in an Indian family, that of the second son. The father was absent, and the mother, seeing he was near death, wished to prepare him a little. "My child," said she to him, "you are God's child: Jesus is your Father, and Mary is your mother. You are going to see them." And then, her heart failing, she burst into tears. The dying boy raised his eyes for the last time to his disconsolate mother, and said to her, "Why do you weep, since I am going to see Mary, my Mother? Tell my father not to weep either, because Jesus also is my Father, and I am going to see Him." Thus the true objects of religious dependence are removed to a distance from the sinner by the intrusion of an idolatrous object.

In 1857 it appeared that the priests were intending to enter the Mackenzie-River district, and, by pre-occupying the minds of the Indians, indispose them to the Gospel message. It was resolved to anticipate them. Accordingly, Archdeacon Hunter left Red River in January 1858. At Great Slave Lake he was met by the priest Grollier, who openly declared his intention of opposing the establishment of a Protestant Mission at Fort Simpson, and doing all in his power to prejudice the Indians against our Missionaries. In pursuance of this intention he proceeded in the same brigade of boats with Archdeacon Hunter to Fort Simpson, a destination which was reached August 16th. In Archdeacon Hunter's diary of the next day we find the following entry—"Rose, and commended myself and this special work afresh in prayer to God, seeking divine wisdom and grace to direct and aid each day that I continue in the district, that I may be privileged to sow the seed faithfully, and that it may spring up to the praise and glory of God. Here, in the far north-west, the Gospel finds, at the first time of its publication, representatives from two opposite and diametrically opposed churches, Protestantism and Popery, the true and false Gospel coming in contact at their extreme out-posts, like two waves rolling from opposite directions of the ocean, which here meet and dash against each other." Assisted by the half-caste French servants and their wives, the priests laboured strenuously, and as they were told that all Protestants go to everlasting misery, the Indians were at first indisposed to hear our Missionary. The truth was permitted, however, to achieve a triumph in the conversion from Romanism of one of the officers of the Company, a French Canadian. Here, for the first time, Archdeacon Hunter was visited by some of the Loucheux Indians from Peel's River, a tributary of the Mackenzie near its mouth. Archdeacon Hunter remained in this remote field until June 1859. On leaving Fort Simpson he was enabled to look back on the results of his labours there with much thankfulness. "Surely the time to favour these poor benighted Indians is come. Surely these smiling faces I see around me will no longer be left in darkness, no man caring for their souls. They look all energy and intelligence, and listen gladly to the message of redeeming love."

He was succeeded by the Rev. W. W. Kirkby, who reached Fort Simpson in the summer of 1859, having met Archdeacon Hunter on his return. The church of Rome, alarmed at the entrance of one faithful Missionary into the field of her anticipated triumphs, threw in a strong body of priests. Mr. Kirkby therefore found himself face to face with these men. Under date of May 22, 1860, he writes—"The Romanists are endeavouring to concentrate their efforts for the conversion of the Indians of this district. When I came they were just establishing their first Mission in it: now they have Fort Resolution, Fort Rae, Fort Good Hope, and, I fear, will have Fort Liard also. There are now four priests and brothers here; and in the fall the newly-appointed Bishop of Isle-à-la-Crosse is to visit Fort Simpson, and will bring two or three more priests with him. . . . . They are really heart and soul in their work, and would verily compass sea and land to make one proselyte. The worst is their zeal so completely overleaps all sense of truth and justice that the most unscrupulous means are used to accomplish their purposes. The most extravagant falsehoods and frauds are freely laid under tribute. The priests all belong to the order of 'Oblates,' and therefore little else is to be heard but the praises of Mary."

In 1861 Mr. Kirkby visited Fort Liard, 200 miles from Fort Simpson and 2450 miles from Red River, Fort Norman, and Fort Good Hope, the furthest point reached by Archdeacon Hunter in 1859. On his way down the Mackenzie he met several parties of Esquimaux, who appeared disposed to be troublesome, if not dangerous. Ascending Peel's River there were found at that Fort a large number of Loucheux Indians, who received him most kindly, and listened attentively to his message. "The Indians, to a man, expressed the greatest delight in what they had heard, and thanked me over and over again for coming down to see them. Pictures, crucifixes, medals, that the priest at Good Hope had circulated among them, were all brought and cast at my feet, so that I had dozens of them. Some of the pictures were well executed; others are mere daubs; but all, of course, were illustrative of Romanism. A large one of the Virgin Mary bears the following title—'Veritable portrait de la très Vierge Marie, mère de nôtre Seigneur Jesus Christ, d'aprés le portrait peint par St. Luc Evangeliste. Des graces sans nombre sont attachées à cette image.' Then follows the picture, after which are enumerated her appearance, dress, virtues, &c., with a command to pray to her."

Mr. Kirkby now made arrangements to pass from Peel's Fort into the Youcon district. A range of mountains has to be crossed in order to reach La Pierre's House, a post on the Rat River, which falls into the Porcupine River. This latter stream, flowing in a south-westerly direction, is descended to its junction with the Youcon, where Fort Youcon stands. The Youcon is there three miles wide, flowing on in a westerly direction until it enters Behring's Sea, its embouchure being, as some think, in Norton's Sound, or, according to others, between Cape Stephens and Cape Romanzoff, where it is known by the Russians as the Kwichpack.

On reaching the summit of the ridge "a magnificent view presented itself both ways, but especially in the direction we were going. A large valley lay stretched out before us of many miles in extent, with a lovely little river playfully winding its circuitous way through the midst, the whole scene recalling the sensations I had experienced when I stood upon Portage la Loche, the highest point of land between Hudson's Bay and the Arctic Sea, and now the basin of the mighty Mackenzie is crossed. In a few days I hope to see the waters running to the Pacific. I knelt down and prayed that the entrance of Gospel light into these new regions might be abundantly blessed of God."

La Pierre's House is situated in a valley surrounded on all sides by mountain peaks. Carrying with him the good wishes of all the Indians at this place, whom he had diligently instructed during the few days of his sojourn, he embarked to descend the Rat River; at first, as it threads its way through the mountains, very narrow and crooked, until the large tributary, the Porcupine, is reached. Descending this, he entered the Youcon, a magnificent river, three miles wide, but studded with islands, the current of which they had to mount for two miles, in order to reach the Fort, where Mr. Kirkby was greeted, on his arrival, by 500 Indians, all of whom were filled with astonishment and delight on seeing him. Day by day he addressed himself to the work of instruction, and eagerly was he listened to. The hearts of these men, so notorious for turbulence of character, were powerfully moved by the love of the Gospel message. Their most renowned medicine-man arose, and, in the presence of all, renounced his curious arts. How evil and degraded they had been, they themselves confessed. Eight of them, with expressions of the deepest sorrow, and earnest purposes, God helping them, never to be such again, declared openly that they had been guilty of murder; thirteen women confessed that they had slain their infant girls; many were polygamists; but from that day they resolved that the practice should cease. When bidding them farewell, after a sojourn of a week, they were all deeply moved, and earnestly begged him to come again next year, nor would they be satisfied until they had obtained a promise from him. A chief from the Russian territory near Behring's Straits said that to him it all seemed like a dream; that he did not know whether he could carry much of what he had heard to his people, but that next year, if alive, he would bring a number with him, that they might hear for themselves.

The next year Mr. Kirkby fulfilled his promise. On May 26th, 1862, he left his home and family at Fort Simpson. We have his journal before us: it is deeply interesting, but too long to introduce here. On reaching Fort Good Hope he learned that the priest, Mons. Seguin, had started a month previously, on the ice, in the hope of reaching the Youcon before him, and prejudicing the Indians against the truth, so that, on his arrival, he should find the door closed.

On arriving at Peel's Fort he found the priest there. He had already, at this place, done much injury. The Indians avowed themselves perplexed, and knew not what to think. Mr. Kirkby proposed an appeal to the Bible, and sought out the priest for that purpose, but he declined all disputation. With the Esquimaux, of whom several were at the Fort, Mr. Kirkby was more successful than with the Indians. Some of these were from the coast westward of the Mackenzie. He was much struck to find that one of them wore a powder-horn, with this inscription—

"H.M.S. Enterprise, Camden Bay, July 2nd, 1854."

The priest, having decided to accompany the Missionary to La Pierre's House, and perhaps to the Youcon, Mr. Kirkby treated him with all courtesy, and they set out together, our friend with four Indians and the priest with two. Up the steep hills they clambered, reaching the "top of the mountain" by five o'clock in the evening. The prospect was lovely. Sitting down on a stone, Mr. Kirkby sang the noble Missionary hymn of Williams—

"O'er the gloomy hills of darkness,"

"with comfort, and with hope that the prayer it breathes might ere long be answered if only the Lord would open the eyes of the Indians to see, and their hearts to feel

"That divine and glorious conquest
Once obtained on Calvary."

Mr. Kirkby adds—"How great and blessed would be the change produced, as great and as beautiful as nature has produced upon the mountains around me. A few short months ago winter reigned throughout; all was cold and dreary, uncheered and unenlivened by a single ray of the sun. But when he regained his strength, light, heat, and beauty were restored, and a hundred little bubbling streams, which are running down the mountain sides, tell forth their joy and gladness. So will it be with the minds of the poor Indians, when the Sun of Righteousness shall rise upon them with healing in his wings."

The way onward was difficult; the mountain rivers swollen, the sun in mid-day intensely hot. They fell in with an Indian tent, and two families, who knew Mr. Kirkby, welcomed him. They gave him a good supply of fresh meat, "the half of which I gave to the priest. He was thankful for it, as I was myself, not having had any for a week or more."

On reaching the last ridge they looked into the valley of the Rat River. "It is one of the most beautiful and picturesque views I have had the good fortune to see. It is beyond comparison superior to the very extensive and beautiful one seen from the coxcomb at Port la Loche. The extended valley, with its winding stream, looking in the distance like a silvery thread, the snow-capped mountain peaks all around, with dark pines growing down their sides, form something like what I imagine rich Alpine scenery to be."

At La Pierre's House there was found a considerable body of Indians. They gathered round the Gospel Missionary, and waited perseveringly on him for instruction. The priest was unsuccessful. But for the two Indians who had come with him, he would have been alone. For these he had full mass at his tent door. All, however, was in vain. He resolved, therefore, to accompany Mr. Kirkby no further, and to retrace his steps to Peel's River.

At Fort Youcon were found gathered many Indians, and they were soon increased.

June 27—In the middle of the day the Indians about the Fort espied a long dark stripe across the river, at a great distance up the stream. At once the report was raised, More Indians coming. My European eyes could not yet detect them, but after awhile, by the aid of their paddles and the assistance of a rapid current, they were in full view—eighteen canoes—and very pretty and picturesque they looked gliding along. They were the whole tribe of Hun Kutchin. It is the only time in the year they can visit the Fort. All were in the native dress, profusely decorated with beads and hyaqua shells. They started up a song when within hearing, the air of which was very sweet and plaintive. The Kutchin are certainly the most musical of any Indians in the country. Indeed they are the only ones, so far as I know, that possess really native airs. Mr. Lockhart has succeeded in transferring eight or ten of them to paper, which he has kindly given me permission to copy any time I please. The strangers were all present at evening service. A few of them were here last year: the others heard for the first time to-night the glad tidings of a Saviour's love, except what they may have learned from their friends during the winter. May their visit prove a blessed one!

The next day—Lord's-day—was a really Missionary day, 400 or 500 heathen being assembled to listen; and thus, from day to day, his time was occupied, until the Indians began to break up for their hunting-grounds, and it was time for Mr. Kirkby to return homeward. "The chiefs want to know why I do not remain altogether, and send a letter for my family to come down in the fall, forgetting all about the mountain, and the difficulty of transport, &c. If ever we can have a resident Missionary here, he must be a young man requiring little, and prepared to rough it, just as the Company's officers do; and really there is no reason why we should not, for if these gentlemen will do it for furs, we may surely be content to do it for souls."

At Peel's Fort, on his return, Mr. Kirkby found the priest, who, disconcerted at his ill-success, rudely repulsed Mr. Kirkby's courtesies, breaking forth into a long tirade, which he concluded by predicting that England would yet become thoroughly Romanized.

The Youcon has now its resident Missionary, and such a one, we trust, as Mr. Kirkby wished for. The Rev. R. M'Donald (county born) reached Fort Simpson from the Red River in August 1862, and, immediately on Mr. Kirkby's return home, started for the Youcon, which he reached the middle of October. The journey across the mountain ridges was not of a summer character. Snow ankle-deep, rivulets to be crossed, the waters of which were half up to the knees and more, falling snow, no shelter, little wood to make a fire with. Notwithstanding all these, our young Missionary says—"There was no portion of the whole journey from Red River that I enjoyed more: it was, in fact, quite a recreation, after the boat travelling of more than a thousand miles." At Peel's Fort, La Pierre's House, the Youcon, the Indians joyfully welcomed him. From one of the chiefs of Peel-River Fort he had a strong speech, representing the want they felt for the knowledge of God, and earnestly pleading that he should remain with them; the chief contending that he and his band of Indians stood as much in need of a Missionary to lead them as the Youcon or any other Indians. At the Youcon he found the priest: he had not been able to effect any thing, the preference of the Indians being for pure Christianity.

Our last communication from Mr. M'Donald is dated June 1st, 1863. He had found the Loucheux language very difficult to pronounce, many of the words being guttural and dental, but he was overcoming it, and had begun to translate. He had been on several expeditions, visiting the Indians in their camps. One was eighty miles down the Youcon; another to the Gens du Large Indians, residing among the mountains, 200 miles northward from the Fort. He found these people encamped in a deep valley between two mountains, some of the peaks of which towered up to the height of about 1500 feet or more. They were greatly rejoiced to see him, and with them he spent nearly forty days.

In another month or so we shall be expecting to have fresh tidings from Mr. Kirkby and Mr. M'Donald, and more especially as to the proceedings of last summer, when many Indians, of various tribes, were expected at the Youcon.

In one of the last journals received from Mr. M'Donald, dated La Pierre's House, June 24th, 1863, he says—"The priest, Père Sequin, who passed the winter at the Youcon, is here, on his way to Fort Good Hope. He has not effected any thing among the Indians. They all appear determined to remain firm on the side of the Gospel."*

Now, then, we have prepared our readers for the following paragraph from the "Annals of the Propagation of the Faith," vol. xxv., September 1864, No. 152—

The Rev. Father Grollier had scarcely landed on the Mission of St. Joseph, when, confiding it to the care of Divine Providence, he started off for Fort Simpson (63° of latitude), where the Protestant minister had directed his steps. The Father was immediately welcomed with enthusiasm by the savages, and he at once paralyzed the deleterious influences of heresy. Presents of all kinds were lavished on the Indians by the minister, but his generosity could gain neither their esteem nor their affection. They said to him, "Your presents are good, but you are bad yourself, at least your religion is bad. You are only a man like one of ourselves; you are not a priest. We will not listen to your words." The Rev. Father Grollier returned soon after to the Mission of St. Joseph, in order to make preparations for the approaching campaign. The following summer, being anxious to anticipate the approach of error, he had resolved to carry the standard of the Catholic religion as far as the Fort Good Hope, and to establish there the Mission of our Lady of Good Hope, in the 67° of latitude.

In the mean time the Rev. Father Gascon set off for Fort Liard in pursuit of the wolf who had entered the fold there, while the Rev. Father Eynard established the Mission of St. Michael the Archangel at the extreme end of the great Slave Lake. Towards the end of the following winter, Father Gascon arrived at the same post, that he might help to consolidate his work. Their efforts were crowned with complete success. Father Grollier ascended the river, and visited Fort Norman during the summer of 1860, following the track of the Christian enemy as far as Peel's River. His apostolic zeal and his sufferings, so generously endured for the glory of God, were crowned by the blessing of a complete victory. In the same manner, and with like success, the minister was tracked everywhere. In the following summer Monsignor Grandin arrived with a new reinforcement: his presence fortified and encouraged the new-born faith of the savages. In 1862 a new Protestant minister had the audacity to traverse all our Missions, and erect his tent in Youcon, on the Russian territory. He was followed by Father Seguin, who paralyzed his attempts; and at length, in 1863, the Rev. Father Gascon established a Mission in the midst of the Esquimaux, in 69° of latitude. Thus it was that one success followed the other, until the work of the Missions has been extended to the extremity of the Polar Circle, thanks to the alms of the Propagation of the Faith, which supported the Oblate Fathers while they devoted themselves to the charge confided to them of evangelizing these immense regions. The first foundations are now laid, and there is every prospect of success, provided the assistance be continuous which will enable the Missioners to remain there.

Neither in the measures which they pursue on the Mission field, nor in the accounts which they send home, do the Oblate Fathers appear to be very scrupulous.

* Mr. M'Donald's journals are printed *in extenso* in the "Church Missionary Record" for the present month.

Recent Intelligence.

OUR readers will be prepared to find this portion of our Number more fragmentary than the previous pages, into which are introduced articles on various subjects, intended to be, however they may fall short of this, of an integral character.

We have received despatches from Jubbulpore, Peshawur, and the Mission stations in China, extracts from which will be found to contain various points of interest.

INDIA.

Jubbulpore.

Jubbulpore is on the route from Allahabad to Nagpore, 222 miles south-west of the former, and 156 north-east of the latter. It is our only Missionary station in the Central Provinces. At Nagpore there is a station of the Free Church of Scotland, and then, across a vast stretch of territory, as far as Dumagudem, in the Lower Godavery, we find no Missionary station whatever. As the stations are so few, it is the more necessary that they should be hopeful, and exhibit symptoms of spiritual vitality. If the wells in the desert be few, there is the more reason that they should gush up with water. We are thankful that our Missionary at Jubbulpore, the Rev. E. Champion, is enabled, in the following extracts, to mention facts which show that God is blessing the work. The first extracts are dated December 28th of last year.

"It is with much pleasure and thankfulness to God that I write to inform the Committee of the baptism, on Christmas-day, of Moulwee Safdar Ali and another young Mohammedan. Some of the notices of the Moulwee have appeared in my journal from time to time, and you probably heard at Benares that Pundit Nehemiah had come here to confer with him and his friends, at their request. The result is as above stated.

"If I were not deeply sensible that this is all God's work I should hesitate to speak of the Moulwee in the terms I must speak of him, if I speak at all, lest I should seem to glory in man. He has, however, been so clearly a subject of the sacred influences of God's Spirit, that, in speaking as I do, I feel I am but exalting God's grace in him.

"He appears for many years to have been of a thoughtful disposition, and anxious as regards his soul. In this state his mind was directed to the consideration of Christianity, and he read, only to find fault at first, Dr. Pfander's works. Still truth seems to have gained upon him; and when Nehemiah was here about three years ago they became acquainted, and he has often told me that one-half of the difficulties which possessed his mind were cleared away by their intercourse. Up to this time he had not seen our Bible, and, at Nehemiah's suggestion, he came to me, and procured this and other books. In this way our intercourse began. He was a most thoughtful and indefatigable reader, and often visited me, and propounded difficulties, and asked for explanations, which showed he read with great care, and possessed great powers of mind. I answered his difficulties to the best of my ability, and always found what I said was received with impartiality and serious attention. He soon confessed himself much struck with the morality of the Bible, which he said surpassed any thing he had ever met with, and at length declared that Christianity was far better than either Hinduism or Mohammedanism: still some doubts remained regarding the inspiration and authenticity of the Bible. Nor was this exercise of mind a mere intellectual one. He plainly said it was peace to a troubled mind which he sought. As he came to me from week to week I wondered at the great change I saw going on within him, and could entertain no doubt as to the final results. His last request to me, as I was going to the Benares Conference, was, that I would ask the Missionaries to pray for him.

In this, and other events, the Christianity which had already imbued his mind displayed itself. He had given up attendance on the Mohammedan prayers long since, and was so open in the expression of his predilection for Christianity, that the Mohammedans declared he was an Isai, and his relatives threatened to take away his wife. This was the state of things when Nehemiah came, whose kind and sympathetic instructions cleared away his remaining doubts, and decided him to be baptized at once. On my return journey, when forty miles from Jubbulpore, I received this delightful information; and on the very evening of my arrival he called, requesting, as his mind was quite made up, there might be no delay. He is the Deputy Inspector of Schools in this district, and receives a salary of some 150 rupees per month. Thus his motives were beyond doubt. He is a man, too, of sound education and irreproachable character, highly respected by his superiors and all who know him.

"The younger man is at present a Government village schoolmaster, and is the fruit of Safdar Ali's inquiries. He was formerly his servant, and, when in that capacity, began to read the New Testament with him. Two days ago, when reading part of the 11th of Hebrews to him, and explaining how we (and he especially) have to give up much here, but only, like Moses, in hope of a much greater reward hereafter, he said, 'A thousand, thousand thanks to God for his mercy. I was only worthy of eternal fire.' This seems to indicate a right sense of the sinfulness of sin and of the exceeding greatness of God's grace in Christ. The determined way in which he stepped into the water after the Moulwee (they were baptized by immersion, at their own request) was very remarkable.

"It only remains that I should ask your prayers for them during this trying time, when they have to see the sorrow of those they most love, and to endure their anger."

The movement has not stopped here. In a subsequent letter, dated January 16, 1865, a third case of conversion is referred to.

"I have again the pleasure of informing you of another addition to our church here. Yesterday I baptized Moulwee Kazim Bakhsh, a friend of Moulwee Safdar Ali, and indeed the fruit of his inquiries and earnestness. He is a man, too, I have every reason to believe, of the same stamp, a man really taught of God, a real inquirer after salvation. From the time when he first decided to become a Christian he has shown great stedfastness of purpose and moral courage. He was away when Safdar Ali and Kazim Khan were baptized, and I feared the treatment they received might deter him from coming forward; but of his own accord he came in from Sepora, where he is schoolmaster, and asked to be baptized at once. In a day or two he leaves for his village, there, all alone, to take up the cross of his Lord. We pray God to be with him and keep him.

"The former two baptisms created a great sensation among the Mohammedans of Jubbulpore, and Safdar Ali has often been called on to give a reason for the hope that is in him. At a meeting of about seventeen respectable Mussulmans, some of them declared, that, after what he had done, it behoved them also to inquire whether these things were so. This is a great deal for a bigoted Mohammedan to say, and therefore it is no wonder that the greater number wish to suppress all inquiry, and pass the affair over as quietly as possible,

"A number of tales have been circulated in the city, such as that, at their baptism, we made them eat swines' flesh, and so on; but one story is, I think, remarkable. They say that now Moulwee Safdar Ali's pay from Government is reduced from 120 rupees to 60 rupees per month, and that, when he goes to see any European gentleman, whereas formerly he was accommodated with a chair, now he not only does not get a chair, but not even a stool."

These first-fruits in a station, which has been hitherto so bare of results, call upon us for thanksgiving, and for earnest prayer that He who has done so much will do more, and light up a beacon-fire in the dark interior of Central India.

Peshawur.

In the autumn of 1862 this frontier station was occupied by several valuable Missionaries, who appeared to be in all respects well fitted for the work. All these men have been removed by death and sickness. The Rev. T. Tuting and the Rev. Roger E. Clark died at Peshawur, and their graves mark the spot where they laboured. The Rev. J. McCarthy and the Rev. Robert Clark have been compelled, from ill-health, to leave, the one for England, the other for Umritsur, and the station has been left in charge of two very young Missionaries, the Rev. T. R. Wade and the Rev. W. Handcock. Yet the Lord has been with them, and the work has not been without fruit. Some extracts from their despatches, more especially in the present enfeebled state of the Mission, will be read with interest. The following is from Mr. Handcock's letters—

Preaching to the heathen.

Jan. 1865—The glad news of salvation by Christ has been proclaimed in different parts of Peshawur. But in no place has it been more frequently set forth than from the steps of the chapel under the great peepul tree. In front of this chapel, which was built by Colonel Martin, sometimes in one assembly you would recognise among the Affghans people from Cabul, Persia, Bokhara, and Cashmere. Crowds of listeners can always be obtained, though they are not, as a rule, so orderly as one could wish, for the Affghan Mohammedans are so bigoted, that no sooner do they hear a doubt thrown out as to the truth of the Korán, than they become excited, cry down the preacher, and break up the assembly. Notwithstanding all this, however, three out of the seven who have this year been admitted to the church of Christ by baptism were more or less listeners to the preaching in the bazaars before they became inquirers. Indeed, the very opposition made by the Mohammedans seems to have been the turning-point in leading one of the number to inquire into the truth of Christianity. This man is a Syud, and somewhat advanced in years, and is likely to prove of great use to the Mission, seeing that he is well read in Arabic and Persian. The circumstance, however, which seems more particularly to have arrested this man's attention, was the harsh treatment which a Mussulman friend of his received. This friend went one day within the porch of our chapel, the weather being inclement, and knelt down to pray, according to the Mohammedan custom. The Mussulmans who were passing at the time, on seeing this, came up, and abused him for praying in what they considered to be a polluted place. On the Syud hearing of the treatment which his friend had received, he rightly conceived it an evidence of bigotry. From that time he wished to know more about Christianity. He therefore read the New Testament and the Mizan-ul-Haqq. It pleased God to enlighten him, and he became a Christian. Thus the Psalmist's words were fulfilled, "The wrath of man shall praise thee."

Two journeys have been made with the object of making known the name of Christ among the Affghan tribes. One was in the month of September last. The civil magistrate, Lieutenant Sandeman, was extremely kind in entertaining the Missionary, and in affording some protection during his itinerancy amongst the wild and fanatical tribes of Euzufzaie. In looking back upon the journey we cannot but see evidences in many places of a desire to hear the word of God. No doubt we often had to contend with those who were unwilling to hear the Gospel, with pride and bigotry and angry look; but generally we were kindly received and willingly listened to; and on no occasion did any one refuse to accept a tract or a copy of the Gospels. This latter forms a very promising feature in this Mission field, for if the word of God is only read amongst them, by the help of the Holy Spirit, important results will follow. And whatever dark points the Affghans may have in their character, as a thievish and bloodthirsty people, there is much even in their present state to recommend them. Indeed, no one could go amongst this energetic, brave, and hospitable people without pitying their delusion by the false prophet, and without breathing a prayer for their conversion.

Mr. Wade confirms the expressions conveyed by the reports of his colleague—

This has not been a year full only of sorrows and trials. Many a bright bow has shone forth amidst the dark clouds to comfort and cheer us. We have been visited by a number of Pathans from the district, and some of them have been willing to pay money in order to obtain the Scriptures in their own language; whilst to others, who were poor, we have given a Gospel, or other small book, free.

In March last, when Mohammed Rafek

Khan was here on political business as Vakeel from Cabul, he visited us twice, and received very readily a copy of the Scriptures—the Old Testament in Persian and the New Testament in Pushtoo—to take back to Amir Shere Ali Khan, his master. He also himself, together with the doctor who accompanied him, received the New Testament in Pushtoo, and promised to read it carefully.

Our little native congregation, too, has been gradually increasing. During the past year there have been seven adults baptized, and just half of them have been Pathans, so that now there are in connexion with this Mission, including women and children, nearly fifty native Christians.

Last summer two of our Pathan Christians expressed a wish to go on a Missionary journey to Kafiristan. The late Mr. Lowenthal, when consulted about it, said that the risk of life was so great that they ought not to be allowed to go. However, after consulting other friends, permission was granted. They left Peshawur on the 7th September, and were absent little more than three months. Had they been recognised in Cabul as Affghan Christians, they would probably have been slain; and even when in Kafiristan they were not altogether free from danger, for on one occasion they saw twenty-eight Mohammedans butchered in cold blood, after being invited to a friendly feast. A few days ago two Kafiristans paid us a visit at Peshawur. One of them knew nothing but the Kafiristan language, but the other, who also knew Pushtoo, acted as the interpreter. They are a very degraded but interesting people, and we trust God will soon open a way for the introduction of Christianity and civilization into their country.

CHINA.

Intelligence from the Missionary Stations of this empire are doubly interesting at the present moment, when hopes have been entertained that, the Taeping rebellion having been crushed, peace would be restored to this distracted land. We fear, however, that insurrection is now chronic in China. It is manifest that the Tartar dynasty has lost control over the outlying provinces, and that the utmost it will be able to effect is to hold in allegiance the northern provinces. Sooner or later, in some form or another, the southern provinces will become independent.

Fuh-chau.

Our Missionary at this important city, the Rev. J. Wolfe, communicates to us, under date of January last, the following intelligence respecting the progress of his work—

Jan. 11, 1865—It will cheer you to learn, that since my last communication to you we have had four persons added to our church, two adults and two children. One of the children is the son of our old faithful chapel-keeper; the other is the daughter of one of the adults admitted to baptism at the same time. The baptism of one of the adults, a very clever young man, took place towards the end of October; the other, with the two children, took place on Christmas-day. It was very pleasing and cheering to see the latter bring his little daughter to the font in his arms, and there consecrate her and himself to God by holy baptism. We were all very much interested in this man, as he was formerly one of our most bitter opponents. He used to come to our chapel for the sole purpose of abusing the catechist, and interrupting our service, and troubled us very much. On one occasion we had to remove him from the premises. After this he did not make his appearance for some months, during which time we lost sight of him altogether. One Sunday, however, he came again, and took a seat at the lower end of the building. When service was over, I went to talk with him. I did not at first recognise him. He said, "Sing Sang, don't you know me?" I said, "No, I do not." "You ought," said he, "to know me." After this I had some very interesting conversation with him, and I found that the Spirit of God had been at work in his mind (for I cannot ascribe the change which took place in him to any thing else). He had given up idolatry, and had very correct views of God. He said he wished to become a Christian, and to worship Jesus; that he clearly saw we had the truth. I told him we should rejoice to receive him into our little company, but he should wait, and place himself under instruction, and show signs that his desires were sincere. After this, he attended all our meetings for prayer and instruction, and rapidly grew in knowledge and in faith. He gained more knowledge of the

Scriptures for the few months he was under instruction than some of our members have gained during the whole time they have been with us. The result was his baptism on Christmas-day. At first he was unwilling that his baptism should take place on that day, "for," said he, "I am not worthy to be baptized on the day that my Saviour came down into this world." I explained that it was most appropriate that the day on which Jesus was born into the world to save sinners and establish a church should witness a soul admitted into his church. With this explanation he was satisfied. He is now very zealous, and already has brought some of his friends to inquire about the Saviour. Before he became a Christian he carried on a very lucrative business in connexion with the idolatrous temples, &c., but he could not continue his business. He not only had to give up this business, but had to suffer a great deal of persecution from his former acquaintances. He has frequently been seen in the streets, surrounded by a crowd of people abusing him, and blaspheming that holy name by which he is now called. He was not ashamed of Jesus, but bore a simple and clear testimony before his abusers. Under these circumstances, I felt perfectly justified to help him to get a new business, in which I believe he will do well as a Christian man.

Ningpo.

Our Missionary, the Rev. A. E. Moule, in a letter dated December 31, communicates to us several points of interest, the most important of which is the occupation by his brother, the Rev. G. E. Moule of Hangchow, recently freed from the Taepings.

Ningpo, Dec. 31, 1864—One sign of life, though it be but infant life at present, is the renting and furnishing a house for divine service on the shores of the eastern lakes, *at the expense of the Ningpo and Tsong-gyiao churches.* A native is Secretary and Treasurer, and a native Committee consult together, referring matters of difficulty to my brother for advice. Our dear old brother Bao, alas! has not yet fully rejoined us. We cannot but hope, however, that God will have mercy upon him and upon us. He attended morning service regularly.

My brother's breaking ground in Hang-chow will, I am sure, call forth the prayers of the Home Committee. He feels very deeply the feebleness of the effort, so far as human power is concerned, for he himself is not strong, and the only native catechist who can be spared to accompany him has but indifferent health; but we felt that, in a certain sense, the effort must be made now or not at all; now, before the people of Hang-chow, just escaped from a fierce fire of trouble, grow cold and proud as before. God grant that we may at least hold the ground till reinforcements from home enable us to occupy that vast city in force.

Hang-chow is some one hundred miles distant from Ningpo, and we have sometimes felt reluctant to move forward and inward so far, when districts lying within sight from our house-top are so seldom, so imperfectly evangelized. I have been making an attempt to follow, at a very great distance, the plan adopted in the Tinnevelly itinerancy. The districts around Tsong-gyiao are very thickly populated, and I am hoping to visit each place once every two months, if possible. I am, however, at present imperfectly acquainted with the number of places, and I am but feeling my way, having no good map. The district I am hoping to work extends some ten miles on each side of Tsong-gyiao, except on the south-east, where flows the river, within one mile of our chapel, and in the north-west direction, where the plain is bounded by the San-poh hills, distant some four miles from Tsong-gyiao. Z-kyi, a city, is the western limit. This city, before the Taeping invasion, was a beautiful, rich, and proud city, with some 30,000 inhabitants. It is now slowly rising from dust and ruin, and may contain half that number.

There are besides, in this district, five towns of from 8000 to 10,000 each, four of from 2000 to 4000 each, seven of from 1000 to 1800 each, besides a large number of places varying in population from 600 to 60 each. I visited in all, during the months of March, May, October, November, and December, seventy-one places, large and small. One of these I visited five times, four of them four times, six of them three times, twenty-one on two occasions, and the remainder but once. I trust, with God's help, to go through them all in order this year.

One precious fruit has, I trust, resulted from this work—the old woman baptized on December 18. She heard the Gospel in a neighbouring village last May.

JOHN IV. 35.

"SAY NOT YE, THERE ARE YET FOUR MONTHS, AND THEN COMETH HARVEST? BEHOLD, I SAY UNTO YOU, LIFT UP YOUR EYES, AND LOOK ON THE FIELDS; FOR THEY ARE WHITE ALREADY TO HARVEST."

THE Saviour, for the encouragement of his disciples, draws here a contrast between the natural and the spiritual harvest. When men are sowing the seed of the natural harvest, they encourage themselves by the reflection that their labour shall not be lost; that they shall have a harvest, but that it will not come at once; that they shall have to wait for it at least four months (v. 35). But in spiritual husbandry it is not necessarily so. There, indeed, the seed must be sown, and we must take care that it be right seed, taken from the granaries of truth (Lev. xix. 19; Deut. xxii. 9, 10); and as the spring-time, in which men sow the seed of the natural harvest, is a bleak and laborious time, so men, in going out to sow the seed of the kingdom, must prepare themselves for inconveniences. It will not answer if men will sow only when the weather is fine, and they can do so without discomfort. It will not do to speak the truth only when it is popular, and to garble it when to speak plainly would expose us to unpopularity. We must sow when the wind is in our teeth. Men, moreover, must be prepared to endure personal toil and hardship. They who would sow this seed must, like John the Baptist, gird up their loins and go to work. They must be, by the grace of God, men of resolute character, and of abstemious habits (Matt. xi. 8). What an example our Lord presents in this particular. He sowed the seed of the kingdom, yet in what a cold and adverse season; in what poverty, amidst what opposition! Behold Him on this occasion; see Him: He had made a long journey on foot, He was wearied, and He sat thus on the well. He did the best He could under the circumstances: He made use of the rough stones, and was glad to sit upon them; and He was there alone. He was thirsty: He would gladly have had of the water in the well, but He had nothing to draw with, and the well was deep. He had almighty power, and He drew largely and unsparingly from those stores for the benefit of others. He fed the thousands in the wilderness, but for Himself He drew nothing. Then let not his servants, his labourers, be surprised if, in doing his work, they have something of hardness to endure. Let them look to their Master, and be still, and go on with their work, enduring hardness.

But for the encouragement of such He brings out a special point in this passage. He comforts the sowers of the seed of the kingdom with an assurance that they shall have an harvest, and that it need not necessarily be a deferred harvest. Sometimes it is so. Sometimes the harvest is so long deferred that the labourer who sowed it is gone to his rest before it comes, and other hands are brought in to reap it. But it is not always so. The spiritual labourer has not always to say, as he sows the seed, "it is yet four months to the harvest." It this present case of Samaria it was not so. What took place there presented a pleasing contrast to the general character of his labours. His labours were usually a deferred harvest, especially as regarded the Jews. Of these He might say, "I have laboured in vain. I have spent my strength for nought, and in vain,"—"and indeed that harvest is even yet a deferred harvest." But here He had sown a little seed, and a harvest was already being yielded. He had spoken to one woman: He had not gone to seek her: it was incidentally that she came to Him; and this woman was by no means of a good character; and, moreover, she was very bigoted and prejudiced in her Samaritan notions. Yet He did not disregard it, because it was a little opportunity. Light, in its communicative action, does not despise the smallest crevice, but makes its way in where it can; and so true love for souls will not disregard the least opportunity. Neither did He decline to speak to her because she was depraved, and say "It is no use; she is irreclaimable, and it is not becoming that I should address myself to her." He did not turn away his heart, and leave her to perish in her sins without an effort. He did not despair of her because she was so bigoted and narrow-minded. He spoke to her, and how kindly! He told her of her need, and where she might find help (v. 10). He bore with her dulness, and the difficulty she felt in taking in any thing of a spiritual nature. He stooped to explain to her that He did not mean the water in the well; He meant water for the soul. He pressed the matter home upon her by a reference to her own private character, and the guilty secrets of her own life, and reminded her what need she had of the salvation of God. He had just time to tell her all (verses 25, 26) before he was interrupted by the coming of the disciples. But it was enough. The woman's heart was touched. He had gained his first Samaritan convert; and she became an active agent in communicating to others her own convictions. She had learned a great secret; a great good had come to hand. She had found at the well what she never expected. She had in her own mind no doubt. He had told her all the secrets of her life, and yet, while He had told all, He had dealt so gently with her. Her heart was overflowing with the wondrous news. She leaves her water-vessel behind her. She dealt with the water as Jesus dealt with the bread. If to his disciples he said, "I have meat to eat that ye know not of," so to any of her people who asked her, Where is the water you went for? and what have you done with the vessel? she could say, "I have water to drink of which ye knew not of." But she wished that they should drink of it, that their hearts might be glad as her's was. Her heart was brimful of the good news, and it flowed over so soon as she got back into the town. "Come," she said, "come, see a man that told me all things that ever I did: is not this the Christ?" And her words carried weight with them. Perhaps the contrast with her previous life made them the more extraordinary. That one of her character should take an interest in such subjects was indeed remarkable. It seemed to them a sort of miracle. The curiosity of the people of Samaria was awakened, their interest excited. There was a great stir and movement in the dull town. "They went out of the city, and came unto Him."

Jesus saw them coming. How soon the seed He had sown had yielded its results. "Say not ye, There are yet four months, and then cometh harvest?" And now it was not four months; only a few moments; and He was about to gather in his sheaves. "Behold, I say unto you, Lift up your eyes, and look on the fields; for they are already white to harvest."

Let us, in doing the Lord's work, remember that the harvest may be deferred, but that it also may be quick and immediate. Let us desire the one, and fall back on the other. The one will stimulate zeal; the other prevent disappointment.

Let us never despise a small opportunity. The greatest results have often originated in the most unlikely beginnings. Take the first opportunity you have presented to you. Lay hold on the first persons, no matter what they have been previously. The worse they are the more they need Christ. If they have been depraved, it is because they have not known Him. But He can, and often has, transformed the worst. In the conversion of one you may be raising up a host. Let the following brief reference to the apostle of the Karens, by an aged member of the Mission, suffice for an example—

The American Missionaries, in the earlier period of their Missionary labours in Pegu, had schools and a few converts at Moulmein. The Karens, at that time, were only known as tribes, more or less savage, inhabiting the mountains and valleys of Burmah. The few Burmese converts had heard their Missionary teachers express a wish to become acquainted with them, and, finding one who was a debtor slave to a Burman, one of them paid the small debt, and took him into his family. His excessive rudeness and passionate temper rendered him any thing but an acquisition to a Christian household; and although he gave some attention to the new religion, it was found necessary to put him away. This was the embryo Karen apostle. Dr. Judson paid the debt that was due on him; and, in order to give him one more opportunity, took him into the Missionary compound. It soon became perceptible that Christianity was beginning to exercise upon him its healthful power. Gradually light dawned on his dark soul. He seemed deeply penitent, confessed his sins, and sought earnestly, by prayer, the pardon of his offences, and reconciliation with God through Jesus Christ. After baptism he gave himself heart and soul to the acquirement of Christian knowledge, and then went forth to awaken and instruct his countrymen. He loved much, for much had been forgiven him; and, having received mercy, he fainted not. The preaching of Christ crucified was, in his estimation, the work of paramount importance. He had experienced the power of the great sacrifice for sin, and felt an unquenchable desire to proclaim it to his people. His efforts were blessed. The Karens from the mountain villages of Tavoy flocked in from the distant jungle, for Ko-thah-byu had found them out, and they came in to see and hear the white teacher of whom he told them. So great was his usefulness, that he has been called the apostle of the Karens, and his labours are perpetuated in Sau Quala, for one of the first houses which he entered to make known Christ was that of Sau Quala's father, and his simple words so touched the heart of the youth, that he received and welcomed the message as the great boon which the Karen people had been waiting for.

Only let us be in earnest. Let us go fresh from Christ, and full of Christ. Let us go and be alone with Him, and then go back to our kith and kin. Then there will be a life, a freshness about us; and there will be that about us which will carry conviction to the minds of others.

And then we may be of use, however obscure we be. See, this was but a woman, one of the lower orders; yet, because she was genuine, what a stir she made! And so with those who are poor and despised. They may carry such a genuine Christianity with them into their low estate, that they may be the instruments of great good. You may make a great stir in your town—a great stir for Christ. Why should you doubt the possibility of it, with this woman before you? A woman—how great her influence for evil when so used! but, on the other hand, how great her influence for good when, as a genuine and loving Christian, she uses it for Christ!

THE BISHOP OF CALCUTTA ON THE TINNEVELLY MISSIONS.

The following article was contributed to the "Calcutta Review" by the Bishop of Calcutta, after his visit to Tinnevelly as Metropolitan, and is now reprinted by the Church Missionary Society with his consent.*

Dr. Caldwell informs us, in a note to his most instructive and interesting lectures, that on arriving at a certain rectory in England to attend a Missionary meeting, he found the clergyman and his wife engaged in a hot dispute as to the position of Tinnevelly, the lady maintaining that it is in India, the gentleman that it is in South Africa. We do not suppose that any of our readers are in need of such elementary information as was required to terminate this controversy, but we are inclined to fear, from many recent indications, that some of them have very little conception of the work which is going on there, and of the progress which Christianity has made in certain parts of India. Partly no doubt from the fact that Missionaries often fail to write

* As our readers will perceive, the article is long, yet to have divided it would have destroyed its interest. We therefore introduce it as we have received it, and we think our readers, forgetting its length in the interest which attaches to it, will approve of our decision.—Ed.

their reports in an attractive style, but still more from a painful lack of interest in the subject, it seems the fashion to pass by even carefully-prepared statistics as "unsatisfactory and vague." Indeed, we observe with regret that some English writers take a pleasure in undervaluing what has been done, in blackening the character of their native fellow-Christians, in representing Missionaries as merely commonplace clergymen, who live in comfortable houses, and go through a certain amount of routine work, not differing very much from that of an English school or parish, and in proclaiming that the only true gospel for India is the gospel of railroads and telegraphs. We can indeed understand why Cardinal Wiseman should have asserted that Bishop Heber had "greatly exaggerated the number of Protestants in his time," though, in fact, trustworthy returns showed that he had underrated it. But it is less easy to perceive why persons who pride themselves on their Protestantism should misrepresent the reality through mere carelessness and imperfect inquiry. One writer, for example, has lately asserted that the native Christians in the whole of North India only amount to about 8000, because he finds that number given as the sum of the converts of one Society of the Church of England.* The sympathy and liberality shown towards the Mission cause are not so extensive that we can allow them to be weakened by a statement that the result is less than one-third of that actually reached. The elaborate statistics of Dr. Mullens, carefully prepared from correspondence with the Missionaries of all denominations, show that the number of native Protestants in North India, *i. e.* the Presidency of Bengal, excluding Burmah and the Straits, is 26,075. This result is obtained by adding to the converts of the Church Missionary Society, who alone amount to the abovementioned 8000, those of the Propagation Society, the Established Church of Scotland, and the various nonconformist bodies.

We think, then, that, having met with many instances of this strange indifference to the facts of the case, we may do some good if we lay before our readers a sketch of one of the most successful Missions in India, that in Tinnevelly. What we shall say is gathered partly from reading, partly from our own observation. And at least we can assure them of this, that having ventured to remonstrate with those who depreciate the work of Missionaries in this country without investigation, we shall take pains not to exaggerate its results, even in that province where they are most conspicuous. We shall record nothing but what we either saw ourselves, or believe on trustworthy authority.

It is hard for any one who has not visited Tinnevelly to form an adequate conception of the peculiar character of its scenery. If the traveller ascends one of the church towers which are now happily scattered over the district, he sees before him an undulating plain, of the colour of fire, studded with straight, stiff palmyra-trees, and diversified at rare intervals by belts of bright rich green. These barren regions are called *téries*. A *téri* may be described as a gently sloping hill, consisting entirely of red sand, and supporting no vegetation but the palmyra. Towards the lower part of this hill the water lies very near the surface, and thus the peasant is here enabled to cultivate a luxuriant garden of plantains, which relieves the otherwise desolate appearance of the country. This description, however, applies not to all the province, but to its southern portion only; for it is divided into two sections by the Tamravarni, or "copper-coloured" river, which, rising in the ghâts, passes between the towns of Tinnevelly and Palamcotta, (the former the native city, with its huge temple of Siva, the latter the English station and fort,) and at last enters the Bay of Bengal a little south of Tuticorin. From the position of its sources it is swollen by the rain of both our monsoons, and hence interposes between the southern and northern portions of the province of Tinnevelly a rich tract, which produces annually two abundant crops of rice. When we pass to the north of this fertilizing stream, we lose the peculiar features which have been just described, and find ourselves in a blistered black soil, from which, at present, a large number of bales of cotton are constantly travelling to Tuticorin, and are there shipped to supply our Lancashire brethren with work and subsistence.

But the scene of the tale now to be told is confined to the sandy region south of Tamravarni. In Northern Tinnevelly the number of Christians is comparatively few, and the organization of the church incomplete. Those who think it wrong that Missionaries should have roofs to cover them, and complain that they "follow in the steps of a train of predecessors, and make no new experiment," will hardly be prepared to hear that in this part of the country a Mission was organized in 1854, which altogether confines itself to itineration. The Missionaries have literally no fixed home. They "move their tents from place to place throughout the district (1200 square miles), and thus, in 1862, the Gospel had already been preached to as many as

* Macmillan's Magazine, Vol. X. p. 484.

300,000 souls in 1400 villages. Four bodies of converts had then been baptized, and numerous inquirers were constantly presenting themselves."* Xavier himself did not show a brighter example of self-sacrifice than Ragland, the devoted founder of this itineration, who, after four years' ceaseless labour, laid down his life in carrying out a work for which he had abandoned the academic fame which gathers round a fourth wrangler, and the substantial comforts of a fellowship and tutorship. One peculiar feature of interest in this Mission is, that it is largely aided by the church in South Tinnevelly, a regular monthly succession of catechists being supplied from the settled Christian districts, to work under the English itinerating evangelists, and supported from the funds of a native Missionary Society.

And this recalls us to these settled Christian districts, which are to furnish the main subject of the present article. They are, as we have said, situated to the south of the Tamravarni, and they are, from a variety of causes, almost co-extensive with the cultivation of the palmyra, so that, as Dr. Caldwell says, "where the palmyra abounds, there Christian congregations and schools abound also, and where the palmyra disappears, there the signs of Christian progress are rarely seen." For the palmyra is cultivated by men of the Shanar caste, to that caste Christianity was first preached in Tinnevelly, and in the same caste its growth has been most rapid and extensive. These Shanars, or palmyra-climbers, who have scarcely spread beyond the limits of Tinnevelly and South Travancore, are probably not of Aryan origin, but belong to the non-Brahminical or aboriginal people of India, and therefore are Scythians by race, and cousins to the Mongols, Turks, and Finns. Their language is the Tamil, the most classical and polished, and also the most widely spread of the Dravidian tongues. When the Brahmins arrived in South India, they introduced among the inhabitants the elements of civilization, and also separated them into a number of castes, which may be roughly classified under two well-defined divisions. The higher of them consists of various castes falling under the general name of *Sudra*, the middle class of the South, the merchants, manufacturers, and artificers, who form the most important section of the population. Of the second division, which mainly consists of agriculturists, the Shanars are unquestionably the first. Below them come various other grades, including Pariahs and prædial slaves, and ending with wandering gipsy tribes. Though the conversions have occurred chiefly among the Shanars, yet Christianity has also spread downwards among the Pariahs and still lower castes, while its influence has now begun to be felt both among Sudras and Brahmins, of whom a small number have joined the church. Still it will be sufficient for our present purpose to confine our attention to the Shanars, as infinitely the largest and most important section of Tinnevelly Christians. They are all engaged in cultivating, and the majority in climbing, the palmyra, the richer members of the caste being owners of trees, and the poorer working for them, while between them are some who are at once proprietors and labourers. The palmyra, most useful of palms, but not beautiful in the eyes of those who have seen the taliputs and kitools of Kandy, is straight as a ship's mast, from sixty to ninety feet in height, and crowned with a plume of fanshaped leaves. Its wood is used for beams and rafters, its young root is edible, and its fruit, when unripe, contains a refreshing and wholesome jelly. Its leaves, in their old age, thatch the Tinnevelly houses; in their infancy they are turned into stationery, on which the natives write with iron pens. Mats, too, and baskets, are made from them, and a single leaf is large enough and firm enough to be used as a bucket. But the most precious product of the palmyra is its saccharine juice, which supplies the whole country with food. Fresh from the tree, it forms the family breakfast; boiled into a hard black mass, called *jaggery*, it is eaten at mid-day; and by its sale is procured the curry and rice, which is the universal dinner. Refined into white sugar, it is readily purchased in the European market; and crystallized into sugar-candy, it is often seen distending the greedy jaws both of native and European children. If left to ferment, it is changed into the toddy, which is commonly used as yeast, and too often, by the lower castes (though never by the strictly temperate Shanars), as an intoxicating drink. In order to procure this sap it is necessary to ascend the tree, for it flows only from the flower-stalks immediately under the leaves. Every day the Shanar labourer arms himself with a staff, surmounted by a small horizontal piece of wood projecting on each side a pail made of a palmyra leaf, some tools, and small earthen pots, in a bag attached to his waist; and then, having placed his staff against the tree, stands on the top of it, fastens his feet together, and, clasping the trunk alternately with his hands and bound feet, climbs speedily to the top, where he bruises each flower-stalk, attaches it to one of his earthen pots, or empties into the pail the

* Church Missionary Atlas, 1862, p. 39.

sap which has been collected since his last ascent. Each tree must be climbed at least twice, and sometimes three times a-day, for the purpose of either trimming the flower-stalks, or emptying the sap into the pail, for if it is left too long in the little pot it infallibly ferments. The life is a sufficiently active one, for most of the Shanars perform these operations on fifty trees day after day for eight months in the year. Their extraordinary agility may be admired every evening by the visitor to Tinnevelly as he takes his sunset walk in the village or palmyra forest; and the remembrance of the scene remains behind as one of the most vivid impressions of his tour.

The religion of the Shanars, before Christian preachers came among them, was devil-worship. This is a proof of their pre-Brahminical origin, for their superstitions are identical with the Shamanism of the ancient Mongol and Tartar tribes, and may still be seen, not only in India, but among the Ostiaks and other heathens of Siberia. It prevails also in Ceylon, where it is mixed up in strange and impure conjunction with the nobler creed of Buddha; for neither Brahmins nor Buddhist priests were ever intolerant of other religions, provided they could bend them to their peculiar policy, which is merely the establishment of their own paramount influence. If this point is conceded, then the foreign superstition becomes a *religio licita*, or rather, to quote Dr. Caldwell's expressive metaphor, it is united with the Hindu or Buddhist system in a "cunningly devised mosaic." Demonolatry is purely a religion of fear: bloody sacrifices are offered to avert the wrath of certain malignant spirits, who take delight in blasting the crops, withholding rain, spreading murrain among cattle, and visiting men with sunstroke and epilepsy. They have no temples, but are honoured by the erection of whitewashed pyramids, generally of mud, or of thatched sheds, open in front, and decorated with hideous figures of bull-headed monsters, or hags devouring children. Such a structure is called *pei kovil*, or, "devil's house;" and round one of them the demonolaters may be seen, from time to time, gathering for a devil-dance, the most important and essential feature, says Dr. Caldwell, of their worship.

"The officiating priest, or devil-dancer, who wishes to represent the demon, sings and dances himself into a state of wild frenzy, and leads the people to suppose that the demon they are worshipping has taken possession of him; after which he communicates to those who consult him the information he has received. The fanatical excitement which the devil-dance awakens constitutes the chief strength and charm of the system, and is peculiarly attractive to the dull perceptions of illiterate and half-civilized tribes. The votaries of this system are the most sincerely superstitious people in India. There is much ceremony, but little sincerity, in the more plausible religion of the higher classes; but the demonolaters literally 'believe and tremble.' In times of sickness, especially during the prevalence of cholera, it is astonishing with what eagerness, earnestness, and anxiety, the lower classes worship their demons."

These demons, it should be observed, are supposed to be the spirits of dead persons, who, in life, were conspicuous either for their crimes or their misfortunes. It is well known that in one place the spirit of an English officer, who had been the terror of the district, was supposed to be the presiding fiend,* and was propitiated at a *pei kovil* with offerings of cigars and ardent spirits. The story is sufficiently revolting, but is important, as an illustration of the horrible superstition against which Christianity has to struggle, and of the hindrances which are too often opposed to its progress by those who profess to be its disciples.

We must now shortly sketch the course of events by which this simple race has, to a great extent, been turned from the worship of devils and spectres to the worship of the Lord Jesus Christ. The fathers of Protestant Christianity in India are the two Danish Missionaries, Bartholomew Ziegenbalg and Henry Plutscho, who were sent out to Tranquebar in 1705, by King Frederic IV., *great-great-great*-grandfather of our Princess of Wales. The work which they began, after many difficulties patiently borne or valiantly overcome, at last excited some sympathy and interest in England, and was recognised and aided by the Society for the Promotion of Christian Knowledge, which, however, for a long time, only employed Lutheran Missionaries from Denmark and Germany, a striking proof, we fear, of the stupor in which the English clergy were sunk during the last century.

In 1756, when the first jubilee of the Mission was celebrated, it was found that 3000 Hindus had been brought over to the Christian faith,† and that the work had been extended from Tranquebar to Madras, Cuddalore, Negapatam, Seringham, Trichinopoly, and Tanjore. The last place was the special scene of the labours of Christian Frederic

* Eastwick's "Handbook for India," part I. p. 142.

† Kaye's "Christianity in India," ch. III.

Schwartz, who arrived in India on July 17, 1750, and may be considered the founder of the Tinnevelly Mission; for this great evangelist did not confine his labours to the province with which his name is indissolubly connected. His journeys were frequent; and in the course of them he came to Palamcotta. The first notice of the place and its inhabitants in his diary has a special interest now that the grain of seed which he planted has become a goodly tree.

"At Palamcotta, a fort, and one of the chief towns of Tinnevelly, about 200 miles from Trichinopoly, there resides a Christian of our congregation, Schavrimuttu, who, having been instructed, reads the word of God to the resident Romish and heathen; and an English sergeant, whose wife is a member of our congregation, has, in a manner, taken up the cause. A young heathen accountant had heard the truth with satisfaction. He was at Trichinopoly, listened to all that was represented from the word of God in silence, and promised to place himself under further instruction. The sergeant made him learn the five principal articles of the catechism, and then baptized him. It grieved us that he should have baptized the young man before he had attained a distinct knowledge of Christianity. Besides, such an inconsiderate step might prove injurious both to the heathen and Roman Catholics. May God mercifully avert all evil!"*

The date of this extract is 1771. Altogether Schwartz paid three visits to Tinnevelly, and succeeded in forming a small congregation in the fort, which he placed under the charge of Jänicke, another Missionary of the Christian-Knowledge Society, and a native catechist, named Satyanáden, whom he ordained after the Lutheran manner. Satyanáden made many converts among the Shanars, and these formed themselves for mutual protection into a distinct community in the heart of the palmyra forest, and built a village, which they called *Mudal-úr*, or, "First Town," a name intended to express their hope of many other Christian towns yet to come. It still remains as a station of the Propagation Society, with its parsônage and church, the latter spacious and convenient, but of a primitive ugliness, which contrasts with the excellent taste shown in some of the later ecclesiastical buildings of the province. Satyanáden, however, was recalled to Tanjore, and the Mission was for a long time entirely neglected, till, in 1815, it was visited by Mr. Hough, the excellent chaplain of Palamcotta, who wrote to the Christian-Knowledge Society a most encouraging account of the Christian order and stedfastness which he observed among the converts in Mudal-úr and its neighbourhood. Nevertheless, small heed was paid to his statement by the authorities at home, for that was an age when Tory churchmanship was still represented by Bishop Pretyman, and Whig churchmanship by Bishop Watson. So the work must have fallen out of the hands of the Church of England altogether, had not the Church Missionary Society, from which a new life and energy was proceeding and gradually diffusing itself through ecclesiastical circles, stepped into the gap, and selected Rhenius, whom Dr. Caldwell describes as "one of the ablest, most clear-sighted, and practical and zealous Missionaries that India has ever seen," to carry on the work which Schwartz had begun. Although this Society has the credit of sending to India the first Missionary ordained in the English church, in the person of the Rev. W. Greenwood, who was appointed to Chunar in 1815, yet Rhenius, according to the precedent set by the Christian - Knowledge Society, was chosen from the Lutheran ranks. Hence it happened that, after sixteen years of labour, his connexion with his English employers was unhappily closed, in consequence of his independent action on certain questions of ecclesiastical order and government, but not till he had, by himself or his agents, added to the flock of Christ above 10,000 souls. We fully believe that the points on which he claimed free action were such as could not be yielded without violating the distinctive principles of the Anglican communion as an organized Society; but yet it should always be remembered that the result of his pastoral superintendence was to infuse a real church life into the Mission, and to establish practices which are specially valued by truehearted members of the Church of England. By him female education was vigorously promoted, associations were established among the native Christians for religious and benevolent purposes, and the people of every Christian village were assembled morning and evening for united prayer in church. Moreover, in one vital point, his method was superior even to that of Schwartz: he was the first Missionary labouring under the English church by whom caste was systematically repressed. His body rests in the graveyard at Palamcotta; and however much we may regret the peculiar line of action which marred his thorough usefulness and loyal allegiance to the English church, yet there is hardly any Missionary whose memory we should regard with heartier gratitude, since he was the true originator of the chief evangelistic triumph

* Pearson's "Life of Schwartz," ch. XIV.

which has been won in India. His son did not share his scruples, but was ordained by Bishop Blomfield, and is now a Government chaplain in the diocese of Madras.

But our estimate of Rhenius's labours must not be limited to their immediate result. Indirectly they were of immense service in rousing from its slumbers the Society for the Propagation of the Gospel, which had inherited the responsibility of that for Promoting Christian Knowledge, by taking over its Indian Missions. In 1835 a Missionary was sent to superintend "the sheep that had been left to their fate in the wilderness;" and we have a strong testimony to the reality of Shanar Christianity, a forcible answer to the suspicion that, if Tippoo were again to rule in India, all the native converts would apostatize, in the memorable fact that he found more than 3000 persons who had stedfastly adhered to the worship of God in Christ, although neglected for a whole generation by their English brethren in the faith, persecuted by their heathen neighbours, and visited by a pestilence which swept away one-sixth of the population in South Tinnevelly. Since that day of renewed energy in England the work has steadily and continually advanced; so that, in 1857, Dr. Caldwell, who has himself taken a conspicuous part in carrying it forward, bore the following testimony to the progress which it had made in twenty-two years—

"Missionary labourers followed from year to year, for the church at home had awoke, the Propagation Society had awoke; the Madras Diocesan Committee of that Society had awoke; and when I now look around in Tinnevelly, instead of the two districts which existed when I arrived (Mudal-úr and Nazareth), I am rejoiced to see seven, in addition to a new Mission in the Ramnad country, each of which is provided not only with practical superintendence, but also, in a greater or less degree, with the means of extension and advancement. The Church Missionary Society also has been continually lengthening its cords and strengthening its stakes, so that it has now thirteen or fourteen Missionary districts, where it had only six when I arrived, and has established besides an organized system of Missionary itineration in the northern and less christianized portion of the province."

It is another source of satisfaction to the visitor of Tinnevelly, that whereas he may have brought out from the heated theological atmosphere of England a notion that the Propagation Society is high-church, and its sister Society low-church, and may have seen some cautious canon or rector shake his head at the one for neglecting church principles, or heard perhaps a fervid rhetorician denounce the other for ignorance of the Gospel, he finds the Missionaries of both working together in perfect harmony, with no rivalry except the rivalry of good works, helping each other by counsel, by interchange of experience, by Christian sympathy, by intercessory prayer, and feeling that, in the midst of pagodas and devil-dances, both church principles and Gospel principles are best promoted by a hearty union of labour in preaching Christ crucified, and training those who trust in Him in the sober piety of the English liturgy.

So the work proceeded, languidly and with many interruptions, for about sixty years, vigorously and with a hearty will, for nearly thirty. Altogether almost a century has passed since Schwartz recorded his hopes and fears for the one doubtful convert in the fort of Palamcotta; and now we find in Dr. Mullens' statistics a tale of 45,361 native Christians in Tinnevelly, from whom the word of life has spread westward over the ghâts into the independent kingdom of Travancore, where the Congregationalist Mission in the south numbers 22,788 Christians, still chiefly Shanars, and the Church Mission in the north (where this impressible caste is no longer found), 7919.* The Tinnevelly congregations are under the spiritual care of twenty-four European Missionaries and fourteen ordained natives, besides a large number of catechists and schoolmasters. To this record of constant advances there has been one exception. As our Lord predicted that offences would come, as St. Paul said that heresies must test the constancy of those who are approved, as St. John lamented that many false prophets had gone out into the world, so the infant church of Tinnevelly has been distracted by a schism. Into the events which led to that schism we decline to enter, for we should be involved in a painful and profitless criticism on the judgment of those who had to deal with a most embarrassing dispute. Suffice it to say, that, mainly in consequence of certain questions connected with caste prejudices, which too often

* Altogether, taking Tinnevelly and the provinces immediately adjacent, the number of native Protestants is as follows—

Tinnevelly (Church Missionary and Propagation Societies)	45,361
South Travancore (London Missionary Society)	22,788
North Travancore (Church Missionary Society)	7,919
Ramnad (Propagation Society)	4,997
Madura (American Board of Missions)...	6,372
	87,437

retain a great influence over the Shanars, even after their conversion to that faith in which "all are one in Christ Jesus," a number of native Christians, amounting, as we believe, to more than a thousand, in the districts of Nazareth and Mengnanapuram, seceded from the church, and formed themselves into a community, in which caste rules were restored. They have fallen, we hear, into various extravagancies, and especially they have conceived a fanatical hatred for every thing European; so that they have even restored the Jewish Sabbath, keeping Saturday holy instead of Sunday, under the strange belief that Europeans introduced the observance of the first rather than the seventh day of the week. Still, even this melancholy perversion has furnished a testimony to the reality of their Christian belief; for amidst many aberrations from the doctrines which they were taught by their fathers in the faith, they have never shown the slightest tendency to return to heathenism. Indeed, we lately heard that about half of them were already dissatisfied with their separatist position; and it was hoped that the influence of Mr. Thomas, the valued Missionary of Mengnanapuram, who has recently come back from England to the scene of his labours, would induce them again to join the church. We earnestly trust that this expectation has been, or soon will be, realized.

Our readers may now perhaps, if they have had patience to follow us thus far, be desirous to know what a traveller actually sees in Tinnevelly, and what is the aspect presented by daily life in a Christian village. Many things at once remind him of a flourishing and well-organized English parish. There is a church, which sometimes, as at Mengnanapuram, is a gothic building of considerable architectural pretensions; there is the Missionary's bungalow, a neat unpretending parsonage, standing in a pretty garden, and almost invariably provided with a capital swimming-bath; there are schools for boys and girls, generally with simple, but airy and comfortable accommodation for boarders; and there are the native cottages, often laid out in regular streets, with a large tree in the centre of the village, under which the headmen administer justice, for the Tinnevelly Christians have not lost the national love of municipal organization. This system, perhaps the most striking feature of Indian social life, has afforded peculiar facilities for the consolidation of Christianity in the south. When a village becomes Christian it forms itself at once into a Christian municipality, in which Church and State are united together by bands which Arnold himself would hardly have riveted more tightly. The catechist is received as the counsellor and director of the headmen; and the Missionary, resident at the central station of the district, is recognised as the superintendent of all the communities scattered through it. The complete acquiescence of the people in his rule was illustrated in an amusing way by an answer given to the Government Inspector, who was examining an aided Christian school in political knowledge. "Who," he asked, "has the chief authority in this country?" "The Queen," said the children, as duly taught in the catechism. "But she is 10,000 miles away: who carries on the Government in the country itself?" "The Queen sends her orders to the Missionaries." "To the Missionaries!" exclaimed the affrighted Inspector: "is there not a great man who lives at Madras, and rules over this part of India?" "Yes, Sir," replied the children, "the Bishop." The headmen employ themselves not only in settling civil and social disputes in their village, but in enforcing obedience to Christian rules and church discipline, in securing the regular attendance of the children at school, and of all the congregation at church, and in collecting money for religious and charitable objects. They are elected by the people, and confirmed in their appointment by the Missionary; but the office is almost hereditary, though it would not be conferred on an unworthy representative of a respected family. When any thing goes wrong in a village the Missionary appeals to the headmen to set it right; and, sometimes by personal visits from house to house, sometimes by assembling the people under the great tree, and haranguing them, they do their best to effect their object. Those who are discontented with their decision are apt to appeal to the Missionary; but in some places, as in Dr. Caldwell's district of Edeyenkoody, a central *punchayet*, or court of appeal (called in Tamil *nirjáya sabei*), has been instituted, to free the Missionary from the need of serving tables, and enable him to devote his time to the word of God. Though this national habit of municipal organization certainly helps to consolidate a newly-formed Christian church, yet it is not always favourable to the extension of the Gospel; for when the divine message is first brought to a heathen village, the headmen often make strenuous efforts to oppose it. Hence, too, it happens, that when a portion of a village becomes Christian, it forms itself into a separate municipality, which generally remains independent of the other, and sometimes happily absorbs it.

The catechist, as we have seen, is an official who stands by the side of the headman, a kind of Mikado to the Tycoon of a Tinnevelly village. It must be remembered that the ordained Missionary is concerned with an entire district, comprising many villages, Christian and heathen. Thus Dr. Caldwell has the care of twenty-four Christian congregations, and Mr. Schaffter, of Suviseshapuram (*Gospel Town*) superintends nearly forty, and seems perfectly familiar with the general spiritual condition of each, able to say which is "lukewarm," which "has a little strength and keeps Christ's word," which has "left its first love," and which abounds in "charity and service, and faith, and patience, and works," so as to administer to each the necessary counsel, or exhortation, or reproof. Residing himself at the central village, where are the church and boarding-schools, the Missionary is represented in each out-station by the catechist, who has sometimes been resident there from the time when a few of its inhabitants were first persuaded to abandon their idols and place themselves under Christian instruction. When the Gospel is first preached in such a village, there is of course no school there, and none of the population can read. Accordingly a native teacher, carefully trained for the work in one of the two seminaries which have been established for this purpose, is sent to live among them, to give them daily lessons in the facts and doctrines of Christianity, to guide them in Christian habits, to prepare them for baptism, to assemble them for daily prayer, and to spread the Gospel among their heathen neighbours. At first the duty of teaching their children also falls upon him; but when the number of Christians increases, this part of his work is taken off his hands by the appointment of a schoolmaster to the village. These out-stations are of course visited at regular intervals by the Missionary, and it is hoped that in time an increasing number of the catechists will be ordained and become native pastors, supported mainly by their own flocks. We have seen that the foundation of an indigenous ministry has been laid; but in spite of the impatience of some friendly and some captious critics in England, it would be very wrong to hurry its progress by presenting any native candidate for orders, till his character and qualifications have been thoroughly tested for "an inefficient or inconsistent clergyman is an evil scarcely to be endured even in a long-settled church, and, in one just struggling to maturity, would be absolutely fatal to its growth in grace and the extension of its borders."

But the chief interest of a visit to Tinnevelly, or, at all events, of a Sunday in Tinnevelly, centres in one of the principal stations where the Missionary resides, and where the congregation is most numerous and most completely organized. We have said that a short service, consisting of a selection from the liturgy, followed by an exposition or catechetical lecture, is held in each church twice a day, the morning worship being chiefly attended by women, as most of the husbands are then climbing the palmyras, and the evening by men, whose wives are preparing the family dinner. But on Sunday all attend, and the sight is most impressive and encouraging. Take Mengnanapuram as an example, where is the finest church. On the floor are seated 1400 dusky natives, the catechists and schoolmasters in full suits of white, the poorer men only with waist-cloths, the women often in gay but not gaudy colours, the schoolchildren massed together in two squares, all profoundly attentive to the service, kneeling reverentially during the prayers, joining heartily in the responses, and listening eagerly to the sermon, which is often broken up into a catechetical form. "Can you finish that text for me?" inquires the teacher, or "What did I say would be the second head of my sermon?" and an answer is given in full chorus from the part of the church to which he addresses his question. Moreover, the more intelligent of the congregation keep up their attention by writing notes of the preacher's words with their own styles on slips of palmyra leaf, and any catechist from an out-station who happens to be present often uses these notes as a foundation for his own sermon when he is next among his people. When to this we add that the singing is admirable, soft, melodious, reverential, and accompanied by an excellent harmonium, we shall convince our readers that a service at Mengnanapuram impresses a visitor, even though ignorant of Tamil, with a sense of freshness, reality, and earnest Christian life, which is often wanting when he sees a fashionable English congregation lolling in their seats during the Confession and Lord's Prayer, without a single audible response, or drowsily listening to a wearisome harangue which has been chosen almost at haphazard from some well-worn stock of sermons, and is now repeated for the twentieth time.

But the Missionary's Sunday work is by no means limited to his two services. In the course of the day he generally holds an adult school, and in his instructions he is actually assisted (at least at Edeyenkoody, and probably elsewhere) by the children and grandchildren of the pupils. For it often happens that the young alone have received a regular education: the generations now in middle life were won from heathenism when their school-days were over, and of these only a portion have been taught to read, the rest receiving *vivâ voce* instruction, and learning by rote portions of the catechism, or Scripture texts, or summaries of history and doctrine.

"It is wonderful," says Dr. Caldwell, "to see how patiently and good-humouredly the older people submit to be taught by their juvenile teachers. Though they look to the teacher for the words of the lesson, and repeat them patiently again and again till they know them by heart, it sometimes happens that they have a clearer insight than their teacher into the meaning of the lesson. The teacher depends, perhaps exclusively, upon his lesson notes, while the pupil has had the lesson written on his heart by the great Teacher himself. . . . I was once examining a very old man, who wished to be baptized, and, according to custom, I asked him, amongst other things, if he could repeat the Belief, which I knew he had been taught. He made the attempt, but, after a few incoherent sentences, gave it up in despair. At length he raised his hand and said—'I'll tell you, Sir, the meaning of it. We are all sinners, and the Lord Christ undertook for us all, and if we believe in Him we shall be saved. I know that, and that is all I know.'"

There are also many special services and classes for Christian instruction during the week; often the Litany and a short sermon on Wednesday at noon, when work ceases in the Hindu villages; and Friday is not unfrequently devoted to the instruction of the catechists, who come into the chief station, and are systematically trained by the Missionary, both in the theory and practical use of theology;—in the theory, by the study of Scripture, and perhaps of Butler and Pearson; in the practice, by the preparation of sermons, and their actual delivery in his presence. In fact, the teaching and training, church-going and school-going, are so constant, and the exercise of discipline so peremptory, that a Tinnevelly village feels the influence of its pastor to an extent which would be considered intolerable in an English parish; and there seems to be some danger lest the bow should be a little overstrained, and lest difficulties should arise when Christianity has spread more widely, and education made more progress among the wealthier classes. At present, however, there is no doubt that the people heartily enter into this rigid discipline, and regard it as perfectly natural. And the problem of adapting the system to a state of things more nearly resembling the long established Christianity of a European country is one which the Missionaries of our generation will perhaps hardly be required to solve; though we should be glad to be assured that their attention was turned to it, and that they were preparing for its solution. Especially we would have them careful about too much interference with harmless national customs, and imposing upon their converts a yoke of merely English habits, as distinguished from Christian feelings and practices.

Besides this watchful care of the older population, the Missionaries have organized an efficient system of education for both sexes. In some of the more important Christian villages the proportion of the population at school amounts to twenty-five per cent., and the general average in the part of the country occupied by the two Societies reaches sixteen per cent. According to the statistical tables of Dr. Mullens, there are in the Christian schools of the province 12,044 children, in which total are included a considerable number of heathen. Most of the schools are vernacular day-schools, and the instruction includes, besides the indispensable three Rs, Scripture, catechism, geography, and a little Tamil poetry. It is fortunate that the Tamil language possesses a respectable literature, which is constantly receiving accessions from the labour of the Missionaries in translating English books, so that its students are provided with a tolerable supply of intellectual food. There are, as we have seen, some superior boarding-schools, among which that for girls at Edeyenkoody is distinguished for the beauty of the lace made by its pupils from European patterns, and for the very efficient manner in which it is worked, partly as a training school for mistresses, and still more as a seminary in which "the more promising daughters of the native Christians are brought up to be specimens and patterns to the rest of the community of what Christian women ought to be, so that by their influence the character of the whole community may be raised." To this end they are taken into the school at a very early age, and are brought under the eye of the Missionary and his family, by whom they are "instructed, not only in useful knowledge, but in the habits and proprieties of the Christian life."

But at the head of the education of the district are five institutions, four established at Palamcotta by the Church Missionary Society, and one (which is, in fact, a combination of two) at a small village twelve miles from Tuticorin, and bearing the singular name of Sawyerpuram (Mr. Sawyer's town), by the Society for the Propagation of the Gospel. The four institutions at Palamcotta are, a flourishing English school, attended by more heathen than Christian boys, a training school for catechists, another for schoolmasters, and the "Sarah-Tucker Institution" for mistresses. The English school, which is, strange to say, efficiently conducted by a blind master, has been an instrument for bringing to Christianity several of the heathen among the wealthier classes; but in its general aspect and course of study it does not differ from the kindred institutions with which we are familiar in Bengal. The seminary at Sawyerpuram, a large training school both for catechists and masters, under the care of Mr. French, a zealous and intelligent layman, is remarkable, among other merits, for the proficiency of its pupils in music. We listened with real pleasure to the performance by them of a selection of English anthems and glees, including such pieces as "Sleepers, awake," "Lord, for Thy tender mercies' sake," "Forgive, blest shade," "Come unto these yellow sands;" and it was impossible to deny that art, as well as Christianity, has a powerful effect in bringing nations together, and effacing distinctions of race and colour, when we heard these swarthy Tamil boys singing melodies with which we had been familiar of old in English cathedrals and concert rooms. On the other hand, the chief special characteristic of the training school for masters at Palamcotta is the ardour with which the pupils devote themselves to athletic sports. Not even Professor Kingsley, nay, not Tom Brown himself, could be dissatisfied with such a development of muscular Christianity. as they would witness in the play-ground. Rather, we doubt whether either of those heroes would be eager to join the embryo schoolmasters of Tinnevelly in leaping and pole-climbing, under the full blaze of the midday sun in N. lat. 9°, and with the thermometer at 85° in the shade. Some persons who have hitherto regarded a Missionary institution as a kind of Trappist convent, only conducted on puritanical principles, will imbibe (as Coleridge said when he first read "Undine") an "absolutely new idea" from the following "Programme of athletic sports," for which prizes were given by the vivacious master of the Palamcotta Training College, and contended for last Christmas by his pupils in the presence of all the Europeans in the station, civil and military, young and old, male and female. We will only premise, in explanation of No. 8 on the second day's list, that the words *across the bath* mean *through the bath*, and that the bath is a swimming bath of considerable depth and width.

PROGRAMME OF CHRISTMAS GAMES.

PALAMCOTTA VERNACULAR TRAINING INSTITUTION,

(Rev. T. Spratt's.)

On the 28th and 29th December 1863, at three P.M.

FIRST DAY,

FOR ALL BOYS UNDER 14.

1. Flat Race.
2. Running jump—distance.
3. Ditto—height.
4. Standing jump—distance.
5. Ditto—height.
6. Throwing cricket ball.
7. Pulling match.
8. Best performers on parallel bars.
9. Ditto on horizontal bar.
10. Ditto on swinging ropes.
11. Ditto on ladder.
12. Ditto on horse.
13. Hopping race.

OPEN TO ALL.

14. Throwing cricket ball.
15. Pulling match.
16. Best performers on parallel bars.
17. Ditto on horizontal bar.
18. Ditto on swinging ropes.
19. Ditto on ladder.
20. Ditto on horse.
21. Hopping race.

SECOND DAY.

OPEN TO ALL.

1. Flat race.
2. Running jump—distance.
3. Ditto—height.
4. Standing jump—distance.
5. Ditto—height.
6. Hurdle race.
7. High cockolorum jig, jig, jig.
8. Steeple chase (round the compound across the bath).
9. Pickback race.
10. Sack race.
11. Camel tournament.
12. Scramble for squibs, &c.
13. Putting.
14. Chatty race.
15. Jumping high with long pole.
16. Hop, step, and jump.
17. Climbing the greasy pole.
18. Long race.

(*There will be a display of fireworks in the evening of the second day.*

There are some, perhaps, who may think that a list of high jumps and flat races is an incongruous element in so holy and sublime a work as the conversion of a nation to God. There are others to whom it will recall happy and healthful memories of their school-boy days, and who will not grudge to their Hindu fellow Christians the recreations which they once so heartily and, on the whole, innocently enjoyed. And all, we trust, will call to mind the Apostle's prayer, that 'spirit, soul, and *body* may be preserved blameless,' and so come to the conclusion that the good Missionary, who thus tries to train his boys in manliness and hardihood, as well as in Christian knowledge and mental culture, does well in regarding all three parts of human nature as alike objects of God's fatherly care, and designed for his service.

There is one difference between the educational policy of our two great Missionary Societies in Tinnevelly which deserves a short notice, as it involves an important principle. The master of the Sawyerpuram College trains his pupils in English, which is not admitted into the *curriculum* of the catechists' and schoolmasters' institutions at Palamcotta. The reasons for this exclusion are not far to seek, but, with one exception, unsatisfactory. It is said that a knowledge of English tends to make a young native convert conceited, gives him European and anti-national tastes, produces in him indifference to his countrymen, and unfits him for the simple and humble employment of a village catechist or schoolmaster. But this is only arguing against the use of a privilege from its abuse. If the knowledge of English confers substantial intellectual benefits on its recipient, we may trust that God's grace will deliver him from any temptations which may follow; and undoubtedly the more truly Christian a student becomes, the less likely he is to be arrogant and unpatriotic. An illness is often made the means of sobering a reckless profligate, and weak health escapes some moral dangers to which strong health is exposed; but we do not therefore cease to take precautions against disease, or voluntarily diminish our bodily vigour. Just so we have no right to deprive our native students of the chief means of cultivating their mental powers which we are able to give them. Without English they cannot obtain that knowledge of theology which a religious teacher ought to possess. It is true that some works of our standard English divines are translated into Tamil, but translations are but broken reeds for a student to depend upon; and some of these so-called translations of theological books are mere epitomes and abstracts of the originals, like the cram-books and abridgments by which the inferior tutors at Oxford and Cambridge push their pupils through the littlego or greatgo, with the minimum of trouble to the crammers, and of profit to the crammed. Moreover, the study of English is spreading more and more widely among the heathen. We must not allow the Christians to be inferior to them in knowledge, and in the power of taking a proper social position. It is true that "to the poor the Gospel is preached," and we welcome a Shanar or Pariah convert with no less thankfulness than a Brahmin. But the goodly tree must push forth its branches upwards, the higher castes as well as the lower must be brought to the knowledge of Christ, and therefore the influence of native Christians should be such as gradually to leaven all society. Indeed, there is among them an increasing desire to learn English, and any hindrance to this legitimate aspiration chafes them with a sense of injustice and unkindness, as was sufficiently shown at the recent conference of Missionaries in the Punjab.* There is, however, one argument against teaching English to those who are to be masters of village schools, which undoubtedly requires attention. It is said that, as they are to teach in the vernacular, they must be trained in it, since otherwise they will never become familiar with the technical terms used in geography, arithmetic, geometry, and the other branches of knowledge which they are to impart to their pupils. Above all, they should be thoroughly acquainted with the vernacular text of Scripture, which they must quote in giving religious instruction, just as an English clergyman in preaching cites the authorized version in his sermons instead of his own translations (possibly more accurate) of the Greek and Hebrew. But these evil consequences will be entirely averted by adopting a suggestion of Mr. Spratt, the same thoughtful Missionary who so wisely encourages the Palamcotta gymnastics. He proposes that the ordinary lessons should be given through the medium of the vernacular, but that English should be taught for two hours a day as a foreign language; so that it would occupy the same place in the Training College which Latin and Greek take in a public school at home. Such a plan would, we think, be an improvement on that adopted at Sawyerpuram, where the boys receive all their instructions in English, and so incur the risk of an insufficient acquaintance with their own language. Still more marked is its superiority to the system in which English is omitted altogether.

And now our readers will be asking, What

* Report of the Punjab Missionary Conference, p. 159 ff.

are the results of this revolution? for to such a name the change which has been described is surely entitled. Are these southern Christians clearly and decidedly superior in morality to their heathen neighbours? In abandoning heathenism, have they shown signs of an inward change, a conversion of the heart to God; or have they merely adopted a new creed and profession? To this momentous subject, and another of scarcely inferior interest, the consideration of the causes which have led to so great a result, we shall address ourselves during the remainder of this article.

Now first as to results, it is almost sufficient to say that these Shanars, and other converts of the south, were demonolaters, but are now Protestant Christians; that they did worship at *pei kovils*, but do worship in churches; and that they were left in absolute ignorance of things human and divine alike, till the Missionaries came with their schools, and sermons, and Bible classes. So vast an outward change necessarily involves something of an inward change: they could not have been persuaded to prefer the peaceful simplicity of the Christian hymn to the frantic orgies of the devil-dance without a thorough alteration of their tastes and feelings; and, in truth, the visible and tangible results of the change are any thing but insignificant. The civilizing influence of Christianity is shown in the neatness and order which marks the Christian villages, in the cleanliness of the Christian compared with the dirt and untidiness of the heathen Shanars, in the social elevation of women, the happiness and purity of domestic life, the open and intelligent countenances of the children in the Mission schools. It is not shown in any diminution of drunkenness, for happily that hindrance to Christian work does not exist among the Shanars; and it is a remarkable fact, that though their palmyras furnish them with an unfailing supply of intoxicating drink, they have never formed any taste for it. But it is shown very remarkably in the liberality of the converts. The sums which they contribute to religious and benevolent objects, and the interest which they take in them, may well put to shame the nominal Christianity of too many among our own countrymen. These poor agricultural labourers have their Church-building Societies, Missionary Societies, Societies for the relief of Christians in distress, Tract, Book, and Bible Societies. Their charitable funds are managed at a *Dharmmasangam*—a public meeting duly convened for the purpose of voting grants for good objects; and Dr. Caldwell relates, as an illustration of the interest taken in such works of benevolence, that on one occasion, when he asked why no women from a certain village were present at a *sangam*, he was told that the river was swollen, so that the women had turned back, but the men had swum. He adds that the village was eleven miles off, so that, for a purely disinterested purpose, they took a walk of twenty-two miles in one day, and twice encountered "perils of waters" in swimming a swollen Indian river. Dr. Mullens tells us that the whole contributions of the Tinnevelly Christians to religious purposes, in 1861, amounted to 19,326 rupees, a sum which will appear very considerable when we also read that the wages of a good labourer are about eight annas a-week, and that there is not a single native Christian in the Edeyenkoody district whose weekly income averages more than two rupees and a half. Another tolerably fair test of the depth and earnestness of Christian conviction may generally be obtained from the attendance at the Lord's Supper. Now the proportion throughout Tinnevelly of communicants to baptized persons is stated to be one in six; in some villages one in five: if it is anywhere less than one in eight, the religious condition of that village is regarded as deplorably low. Compare this with the state of any English regiment in India. Ask any earnest chaplain what would be his feelings of joy and thankfulness, if, in a military congregation of 1000 persons, including officers, soldiers, and their wives, 200 were regular communicants; and what an index such a proportion would furnish of the moral and spiritual condition of his flock. And yet the comparison is not a fair one, for in an English military station there is of course nothing like the number of children which we find in a Tinnevelly village.

But though, in general, the aspect of the church in the south of India is not encouraging, yet it would be irrational to expect that all the faults of the Hindu character should have been eradicated in the first or second generation of Christians. The civil authorities of the province complain that the converts are not free from a litigious spirit, and that when a Christian appears in a court of justice, it would not be safe to assume that his evidence is necessarily trustworthy; and the same fault is found with the Kól converts in Chota Nagpore. We think it right to mention this, the one blemish alleged against Shanar Christianity by the English, who observe it impartially, and admitted by the Missionaries and the more thoughtful among the converts. But we do not think that too much stress should be laid upon it, or that it should diminish our sympathy with our native brethren, and our belief that God has worked among them a real and vital change. The most important part of the accusation, that of untruthfulness, results partly from the national timidity, partly from the lying and roguery which are so often paramount in our courts of justice, from the influence of native *mooktears* and other rapacious animals, and through which an English Judge has to wind his weary way with infinite labour and disgust. It must also be remembered, that only the inferior section of our native Christians come into the courts: the more advanced and spiritually-minded among them never appear there at all. But even if we overlook all these extenuations, and view the sin in its worst aspect, we Englishmen must not censure too severely this hereditary taint in our Hindu fellow-Christians, when we remember, with shame, how drunkenness pollutes the poor, and selfish worldliness the rich, among our own countrymen. In comparing the Christianity of Tinnevelly with that of Europe, or the English communities of India, there is one important distinction which has been well pointed out by Dr. Caldwell, and which we must not forget—

"In an old Christian country, especially in our crowded cities, many of those who call themselves Christians never enter a place of Christian worship, never bow the knee to God in prayer, never open God's word, know nothing of God except as a name to swear by. Such persons have no right even to the name of Christians; and when they are called by that name it can only mean that they are not Mohammedans or Buddhists. In Tinnevelly such persons would not be called Christians at all: their names would be erased from our church lists, and Christianity would be discredited by the supposition that they are hers. When we speak of nominal Christianity in Tinnevelly, we speak of something which has a certain right to the Christian name. *Our* nominal Christians come to church, they send their children to school, they contribute to the funds of our various Societies, they submit to discipline in a remarkably docile manner; in short, a very considerable number of our 'nominal Christians' would be reckoned very good Christians, and very good church people too, in some parishes in England; and if we call them 'nominal' Christians merely, it is because we have not seen in them what we have longed to see, 'the power of godliness,' the new life of real spiritual Christianity, and find it necessary to distinguish them from that much smaller, but much more interesting class of native Christians, who show that they are animated by the Spirit of Christ."

But this extract reminds us that we originally put the question in a graver form than that in which we have answered it, for we asked whether, in abandoning heathenism, the Christians of Tinnevelly had been truly converted to God, whereas we have only recounted certain outward signs of morality and civilization. Yet perhaps the question was, in truth, too solemn either to ask or to answer, for it is not ours to judge of a true inward conversion: "the things of God knoweth no man, save the Spirit of God." We can only say that the Missionaries, who certainly are not impulsive enthusiasts, painting every thing around them with rose-coloured tints, but inclined perhaps to take too low rather than too high an estimate of their disciples, fully believe, amidst many disappointments and anxieties, such as St. Paul encountered among his converts, that in each congregation God has raised up a seed to serve Him, a little flock of Christians, who show the genuineness of their Christianity by their eager interest in all means of improvement, their zeal in good works, the largeness of their alms-giving, the quiet consistency of their lives, the piety which sanctifies their homes, their conquest over caste prejudices and national faults, and their devout confidence in God's love. More than this it is not given to man to say; but we have in these signs a sufficient foundation for the belief that Christianity has not only brought to the people of Tinnevelly the blessings of knowledge and civilization and outward morality, but that, in the divine book of remembrance will be recorded, the names of many among them who have "feared the Lord and thought upon his name."

We have spoken with entire confidence as to the results of the Gospel in Tinnevelly: we find it harder to add a few final words as to the human means and agencies by which they have been produced.

In comparing the rapidly successful and constantly progressive work of the Missionaries in South India with the nearly stagnant conditions of too many Missions in the Presidency of Bengal, we cannot sufficiently account for the difference by any marked peculiarities either in the method pursued or the character of those who have been brought under the influence of Christianity. The Karens of Burmah, indeed, appear to be a people specially fitted for the reception of the Gospel; and the Kóls, of Ranchi, were at least free from the prejudices of Hinduism. The Tinnevelly peasants so far resemble them that they belong, as we have seen, to the aboriginal races of India, and not to the Aryan conquerors. The worship of devils is, on the whole, more revolting, and therefore more easily renounced than even that of Durga and Krishna, in which certain truths of religion are obscurely hinted, and with which at least great national traditions are connected; whereas the ceremonial of the *pei kovil* is the simple result of terror, and must vanish before a comparatively faint ray of enlightenment, or the simplest appreciation of the truth that God's essential character is love.

Still the Shanars have certain prejudices which might well have prevented them from embracing a religion which involves the principle of spiritual equality and brotherhood. We have seen that they are naturally tenacious of their caste; and latterly there has been current among them a strange notion (actively propagated, we believe, by the schismatics of the Nazareth district), that they are a princely race like the Rajpoots, and that their progenitors were palmyra-climbing kings. Some Venetian sequins are occasionally dug up in Tinnevelly, relics of a time when Tuticorin was a great trading port; and these coins, like others of the republic, are stamped with a bishop's mitre and pastoral staff. Some of the Shanars believe these emblems to represent the tool-bag and climbing-stick used in mounting their beloved trees, to which they undoubtedly bear a considerable resemblance. Hence they conclude the sequins to be the coinage, not of the ancient spouse of the Adriatic, but of their own royal ancestors, cultivators of the palmyra like themselves. Fancies like these, intensified by the bitterness of caste feeling, are doubtless serious hindrances to the power of the Gospel, and may be set against the facilities afforded to its extension by the fortunate exclusion of the Hindu pantheon from the Shanar religion. And thus we must regard the success with which God has blessed the Missionaries rather as the reward of their own self-denying exertions than of the "honest and good heart" of the people among whom they have sown the heavenly seed. One difference between the system which they have followed and that which prevails in Northern India is this—they have laboured, not in large cities, but in the heart of the country, and in the very midst of the peasantry. Now in towns the personal influence of the ablest and most devoted Missionary is as nothing when compared with that of the Brahmins and the power of caste. We believe that frightful persecutions have often been set on foot to prevent conversions to the faith of Christ in a large town or thickly populated district of India; but in Tinnevelly the Missionary has had a fairer field: he has taken up his abode among the peasantry, made himself acquainted with their wants and feelings, and so gradually taught them to respect his character, to place confidence in his friendship, to value his advice, to regard him as a teacher sent from God. Personal influence, important in the prosecution of any good work, is, among the Hindus, all-powerful; and in Tinnevelly the influence of the Missionary and his family has happily soon been followed by that of the small congregation, by the sight of Christian worship, the boons offered through the Christian school, the growing intelligence, comfort, and respectability of those who follow the new way. The Missionaries say that just at present our Lord's warning, that a man's foes shall be they of his own household, seems hardly applicable, in its full meaning, to Tinnevelly, so frequent are the cases in which a family is brought to Christ by the influence of a single member of it, or a whole village, through the electric flash communicated by a Christian household established in the midst of heathenism.

There is, however, one policy which the southern Missionaries have not adopted, and on which we are desirous to dwell for a few moments, because of late there has been a tendency to revive the notion that it furnishes the true hope of converting India, and the starting-point from which men should proceed towards that noble object, which, of all others, is most worthy of the great name of Christian England. They have not thought it necessary to wander over the country imitating the native jogis, and casting off the amenities of European civilization. They do not feel called upon to sacrifice those very moderate comforts, such as a punkah or a glass of wine, which, though they might appear luxurious in a cold climate, are, in many cases, necessary for life and health in this. They do not think it wrong to "bathe and change their linen twice in twenty-four hours;"* on the contrary, we have commented on the wide expanse of their swimming-baths; and he who has had any experience of bazaar preaching, at the close of a hot Indian day, will hardly grudge the preacher the satisfaction of a clean shirt when he sits down to his evening meal. This same complaint, that the Missionaries cannot hope to christianize the people till they renounce their accustomed mode of life was made some years ago in an article of this Review,† and

* Macmillan's Magazine, vol. X., p. 488.

† "If the Missionaries are to have any success at all, they should be a sort of Christian Nanuks in the land, English Gooroo Govinds, lighting up the entire country into a blaze of awakened enthusiasm by the contagious spectacle of their own downright, fiery, and eccentric earnestness. We should have Christian fakeers, wild, rough, fervent, not the sober and decorous,

we may be allowed to cite the answer to it given in a charge which was then addressed to the clergy of one of our Indian dioceses—

"So far as I have observed, the charge that Missionaries lead luxurious lives is absolutely groundless. In this city, indeed, considering the expense of living, and the extremely moderate scale of your allowances, I fear that it is difficult always to procure even all those comforts which are necessary for health and efficient work in India; and in no Missionary's house in the Mofussil have I seen any thing inconsistent with the position of a man devoted to the task of building up Christ's kingdom among unbelievers, and therefore clearly bound to lead a simple and self-denying life. But when you are advised to turn yourselves into Christian fakeers, you may answer that asceticism is no part of the Gospel system; that whatever you may attempt in that line can never rival the deeds of the Mussulman fakeer and the Hindu jogi; that the attempt to simulate native practices has already been made by Robert de Nobili and the Jesuit Missionaries of the seventeenth century; and that the result was not such as to encourage a fresh experiment. In a higher and truer sense than theirs, though not certainly with more self-abnegation, which would be impossible, you will try to impress the people with the reality of your mission and the divine beauty of Christian morality, by your kindness, your devotion to your work, your earnest efforts to understand their wants and feelings, your readiness to meet their difficulties, and the entire consistency of your lives with the doctrines which you teach. In Cyprian's time the preachers of Christianity did not spread the Gospel in Carthage by any attempt to rival the devotees of Astarte, but by devoting themselves, in spite of a bloody persecution, to the work of nursing the sick and burying the dead during a time of pestilence, 'knowing that it became Christians, by well-doing, to heap the burning coals of shame on the heads of their enemies.'"*

clockwork gentleman of the white-neckcloth school." — *Calcutta Review*, vol. XXX., p. 388. There is much to the same effect throughout the article, including the monstrous assertion (put into the mouth of a native), that "the Missionaries ride in proud vehicles, indulge in costly and refined observances, their doors are besieged by pampered menials, at noon there is worshipful company being received, at eventide the *huzoor* and his *mem* are proceeding forth to take the air." This same style of objection is reproduced in the recent article in Macmillan's Magazine, only in a much kinder and less unreasonable spirit.

* Primary Charge of the Bishop of Calcutta, 1859, p. 52.

We believe that the attempt to christianize the Hindus by a mimicry of the ascetic practices of their own jogis, if the Missionaries who ventured upon it escaped from it alive, could only result in a religion resembling that form of Romanism which prevails in some of the darkest corners of India, and of which it has been truly said, that "no element of heathendom is wanting in it: there are huge idols, which the native congregations appear to appreciate, under the titles of St. Christopher and St. Lawrence, as readily as if they had been called by the more familiar names of their own mythology; and except that the incense is somewhat better, and the priests somewhat cleaner, one might fancy oneself in the Black Town during the Durga Poojah."* This was not the ideal which the Missionaries of the English Church in Tinnevelly set before them: they aimed at building up a church of intelligent and devoted Christians, capable of offering to God a reasonable service, and of knowing that, when they turned to Christ, they were not following cunningly-devised fables. No doubt, in all real Christianity, self-sacrifice is an essential feature, and it has not been neglected by the Missionaries of the south. Among them are men who are quite competent to take their place in the ranks of scholars and divines, and of enjoying keenly all the pleasures of refined and intellectual society. Yet they prefer remaining in the wild palmyra forest, that they may seek out "the sheep of Christ who are scattered abroad in this naughty world;" they do not shrink, if need be, from the duty of "sleeping in native huts, living on native food, going afoot from village to village through the sun of June, and the exhalations of September, talking of Jesus to the ryots in the field and to the women at the well;"† but they believe that they are also preaching Christ practically if they exhibit, in a half-converted village, the pattern of a Christian home, and the parsonage of a Christian pastor, such as is the spring of comfort and blessing to many a poor parish in England. One advantage, indeed, they have enjoyed, which we are loth to mention, but which, we suspect, has told far more in favour of their cause than any assumption of the character of fakeers would have done. There is scarcely any part of India which is more removed from contact with Europeans than Tinnevelly. Dr. Caldwell says, that in

* Macmillan's Magazine, vol. X. p. 487. It is strange that the author of the article, seeing that this has been the result of the experiment made by the Romish Missionaries, should wish it repeated by their Protestant successors.

† Macmillan, *u. s.*

many of its secluded districts the peasants have never seen the face of an English layman. Now it is quite true that no healthier influence can be exercised over a Hindu village than that of a brave, manly, and energetic English magistrate or settler, especially if his home is graced and purified by the presence of a good wife, not uninterested in the people around her. We thankfully acknowledge that such examples of the Christian life are becoming more and more frequent; but still we must confess with shame that too often the conduct of the English in India has been quite the reverse of this, and that their lives have often furnished the most formidable arguments against the religion which they profess. We are painfully convinced that the grievous inconsistency of European nominal Christians, and not any want of self-sacrifice in the Missionaries, has been hitherto one principal reason why the progress of Christianity in India has been so slow and disappointing. Such a hindrance, however, has but rarely opposed the truth in Tinnevelly: the people have seen the Christian life exhibited to them only in its very best and purest form, and it is not wonderful that they have been attracted by it. But whatever be the cause of the success of Missionaries in this remote province, the fact cannot be gainsaid: their labour has received the seal of God's approbation, and they have their abundant and constant reward in the gradual ingathering of the harvest; for in Tinnevelly, unlike the rest of India, the same men who sow the seed are permitted also to reap the crop. Their work, as we have seen, is spreading in various directions; every year fresh bands of earnest converts are admitted into the ranks of Christ's army; and wherever the holy church throughout all the world acknowledges its Lord, its members may thank Him for the genuine Christian piety which his Spirit, through the agency of these devoted pastors, has implanted in the hearts of many thousands of simple peasants in Tinnevelly and Travancore.

NEW ZEALAND—
CHANGE OF MINISTRY, AND ADOPTION OF A NEW POLICY.

ON the 25th of October 1864 the Governor of New Zealand issued the following proclamation—

The Governor having been authorised to extend, upon certain conditions, Her Majesty's clemency to those tribes who have engaged in the present unhappy rebellion: Now, therefore, I, Sir George Grey, the Governor of the colony of New Zealand, do hereby notify and proclaim that I will, in Her Majesty's name, and on her behalf, grant a pardon to all such persons implicated in the rebellion as may come in on or before the 10th day of December next, take the oath of allegiance, and make the cession of such territory as may in each instance be fixed by the Governor and the Lieutenant-General commanding Her Majesty's forces in New Zealand.

All those persons who have been engaged in the rebellion who may desire to return within any part of the ceded territory, or within the limits of any European settlement, will be required to deliver up any arms or ammunition in their possession.*

Mr. Cardwell, in a despatch dated January 26th, 1865, thus refers to this measure—

I approve the step you have taken in issuing a proclamation stating to the rebel natives the terms on which Her Majesty's clemency will be extended to them. In my last despatch I expressed my great regret that some sufficient steps had not long ago been taken with this view. I cannot but think that at some former periods, as, for instance, immediately after your success at Rangiriri and the occupation of Ngaruawahia by the Queen's troops, or again after the success of Colonel Greer at Tauranga, the opportunity might have been seized with great advantage of making known the terms on which those who had been in arms might return to their allegiance. It may be doubted now whether, after the unfortunate escape of the prisoners and their establishment in a fortified position in the hitherto undisturbed district north of Auckland, the same prospect of success attends the measure. Nevertheless, I do not hesitate to approve it.

It appears, then, that in the judgment of the British minister opportunities had occurred during the progress of the war, which, had they been duly improved, would in all probability have led to the submission of the insurgents, and the termination of

* All the extracts in this article are taken from the official Blue Books.

hostilities. Two such favourable junctures are specified, "after the success at Rangiriri and the occupation of Ngaruawahia," and again "after the success at Tauranga."

The first of these was specially referred to in our Number for August 1864. After their defeat at Rangiriri on November 20th, 1863, the insurgent chiefs made overtures for peace in a letter addressed to the Governor. It was replied to by the Colonial Minister, requiring, before any negotiations were opened, that they should surrender their arms. Dissatisfied with this reply, they again wrote to the Governor—"O Friend, O Governor, Salutation. We are awaiting the reply of our letter. Can it have reached you or not? These are the words of that letter. Restore the Waikato men (the chiefs taken prisoners at Rangiriri). Suffice for you the dead. Enough." The Governor then communicated to them his resolution—"The General must go uninterrupted to Ngaruawahia. The flag of the Queen must be hoisted there. Then I will talk to you."

To this the natives agreed. In an interview with the friendly chief, Wi Te Whero, they declared that they were afraid to give up their arms, lest they should be made prisoners of, as those had been who had given themselves up at Rangiriri; but that they would surrender Ngaruawahia without opposition, leaving the King's flagstaff, the first which had been raised in New Zealand, standing, in order that the Queen's flag might be hoisted on it. This promise they fulfilled. No resistance was offered, and Ngaruawahia was occupied by the troops on December 8th, 1863. Now, then, an opportunity had arrived. The Governor had promised the insurgent chiefs, that, on the occupation of Ngaruawahia by the troops, he would talk with them, but he never came. Instead of this, the troops continued to advance, to the great disappointment of the Maoris, and of Tamehana in particular, who was most anxious for peace. He retired to Maungatautari, a stronghold of his, higher up towards the sources of the Waikato. There he was again visited by Wiremu Nero, a loyal chief, and to him he declared his intention of ceding to the British rule all the land from which he had been driven as far as Ngaruawahia; but that if more were required, he would then resist. "The gift," he said, "to your father and younger brothers is this—Meremere has been given up, and Rangiriri, and Paetai, and Rauwhitu, and Ngaruawahia, and this flowing stream. They are my gift to your fathers and brothers: as for me, I shall remain here. If the Governor follow me here, I shall fight. If not, I shall remain quiet."

The other chiefs also were resolved on defending themselves, if, not contented with the large cession of territory which they were willing to make, the British authorities aimed at further conquests, and pushed the troops further up the river. Hence the sanguinary contests which occurred at Te Rore, Rangiohia, and at Orakau, where 300 natives, attacked in an earthwork by 1500 British, bravely defended themselves, the survivors breaking through the cordon of troops, and many of them escaping, although so hotly pursued that many native women were shot down.

The survivors having fled in the direction of Rewi's country, a friendly native was sent forward by the General to communicate with them. Rewi, on that occasion, declared that he and his people were very anxious to make peace, and to live quietly by the side of the white people, but that they were afraid of being dealt with as the natives captured at Rangiriri had been. These men had thought that they would be permitted to go free, and live within the lines of the troops. Instead of this, they had been detained as prisoners, with an uncertainty as to whether their lives would be eventually spared.

Thus anxious for peace, yet distrustful of the intentions of the Pakehas, and afraid to surrender their arms, the natives kept aloof, and the war continued, until, on April 29th, the conflict at the Gate Pa, Tauranga, took place, in which so many brave men, officers and soldiers, fell. In the portfolio of one of the officers was found a sketch of the native fortification, taken on the morning of the day of battle. He sketched the place where he was to fall, a gallant officer, and, better still, a godly man.

How was it that the opportunity of terminating this distressing war, which occurred on the occupation of Ngaruawahia, was not improved? Where was the Governor, that he did not come and talk with the chiefs as he had promised? Tamehana, in a letter to Bishop Pompallier, speaks very decidedly on this subject—

Matamata, Aug. 9, 1864.

Greeting to you. O Sir, I received your letter of the 21st of March 1864. You desired me to reflect well on that letter, the bearing of which was to put an end to the war. O friend, the war is over; and if it had been stopped at Rangiriri we should have been since that time without war and in perfect peace, for those of us who became prisoners there, and asked for peace, had our consent; and we went in consequence to Ngaruawahia. But when I observed that the soldiers still arrived at Taupiri, then I said to the chiefs of Waikato, let us get up and go to Maungatautari, leaving, for peace sake, the land where we are at present. When we were at that place (at Maungatautari) some of the native prisoners sent to us went there, and in the mean time the soldiers arrived there also. Hence I said again to the same chiefs (of Waikato), let us go to Pateteri. Finally, here I remained, quite disappointed (in my hopes of peace). Don't suppose, then, that I am a man wishing for war. No, I am not, and even now I remain quiet. When the above prisoners came to me, saying, "Give up Waikato," I have fully complied with their proposal. Here ends my answer to you.

Your child,
(Signed) TE WAHAROA TAMEHANA.

The responsible ministry of the day, in a memorandum dated October 10, 1864, cast the blame upon the Governor, in the following paragraph—

If, however, it be true that there was an opening for peace after the battle of Rangiriri, the Colonial Secretary can only regret the more that the advice which ministers, a few weeks later, so strongly pressed upon His Excellency, that he should open communications with the rebel natives at Ngaruawahia by visiting that place in company with his ministers, was not carried into execution. The Colonial Secretary believes, that whether Thompson's present statement be correct or not, an opportunity was lost on that occasion, and the natives have too much reason to complain that faith was not kept with them by His Excellency, who had promised to talk with them after General Cameron should have arrived at Ngaruawahia.

The Governor, in answer, declares—

The course which I followed in this case was adopted by me on the advice of my late responsible advisers, against my own strong wishes and convictions, with an evident desire of avoiding a rupture with them: they were therefore responsible for what I did, and it was their duty to have defended my proceedings, instead of objecting to them.

From the papers and memorandums referred to by the Governor in proof of this, it appears that General Cameron, on the occupation of Ngaruawahia, had suggested to the Governor the desirableness of his coming to head-quarters, and affording to the insurgent chiefs an opportunity of communicating with him, inasmuch as a refusal to entertain their proposals would probably be the means of "driving them to desperation." With this suggestion the Governor was anxious to comply, but his responsible advisers did not approve of his going alone, and thought it necessary that he should be accompanied by some members of the Government, an arrangement to which the Governor had a strong objection. The result was, that neither went. Instead of this, the expectant chiefs were informed, that if they wished to know the intention of the Governor, they must send a deputation to Auckland; a step which, with the remembrance of the native prisoners in the hulk "Marion," at Auckland, they would never venture upon.

It is not without reason, therefore, that Mr. Cardwell, in his despatch of January 26th, 1865, observes—"I cannot but think that immediately after your success at Rangiriri the opportunity might have been seized with great advantage, of making known the terms on which those who had been in arms might return to their allegiance."

We now turn to the other favourable juncture indicated in Mr. Cardwell's despatch—"After the success of Colonel Greer at Tauranga." As the result of that victory (June 21, 1864), 133 natives, including several chiefs of high rank, came in, and laid down their arms; and on that occasion the Governor, in a despatch home, expressed his "every hope that the war in that part of New Zealand is virtually at an end."

The responsible ministry also felt the importance of the crisis, and were anxious that it should be followed up, not in the direction of peace, but of war. They proposed, therefore, to the Governor, that as soon as possible an expedition should be sent "from Waikato to William Thompson's settlements at Matamata and Peria, where it was reported the natives had stores of supplies, and were planting crops," while "another effective blow should be struck at Taranaki and Wanganui." They proceeded, moreover, to avow more openly their land-confiscation policy, by proposing the establishment of a frontier line from Raglan or Kawhia on the west coast, to Tauranga on the east.

The commander of the forces, however, found himself unable to keep pace with the eager desire of the responsible ministry for more war and vast appropriations of land. The winter rains had set in, and active military operations, even where practicable, could not be carried on without heavy loss in transport of animals and material, as well as serious injury to the health of the troops.

On the subject of the land to be confiscated, and the establishment of the proposed barrier line, General Cameron thus expresses himself in a memorandum to the Governor—

I have next to consider the memorandum of ministers relative to the occupation of rebel land.

It is proposed to confiscate and permanently occupy the following tracts of country—

1. The Waikato country, as far as a line across the island from Raglan or Kawhia to Tauranga, excepting certain portions to be reserved for such natives as may return to their allegiance.

2. A portion of the country of the Ngatimaniapoto tribe.

3. Land on both sides of the town of New Plymouth, to an extent not defined.

4. Land north of the Waitotara River to a point ten or twenty miles north of the Patea River, including Waimata, which place is, I believe, sixty miles from Wanganui.

I need hardly inform your Excellency that it would be impossible to carry the whole of so extensive a plan into effect, "in a speedy and satisfactory manner," with the force at my disposal. The establishment of the proposed frontier line between Kawhia and Tauranga, that is to say, the formation of a complete chain of posts nearly 100 miles in length, and passing for a considerable distance through dense forest and mountainous country, would alone employ nearly all the troops in the province, including Tauranga, leaving no reserve for an emergency in other parts of the island; for, in addition to the garrisons of the posts on the frontier, and of those which might still be required between that line and Auckland, it would be necessary to have the power of concentrating at the shortest notice, at any point of the line, a force sufficient to repel any attack that might be made. The supply, moreover, of so many troops, distributed over so great an extent of country, without roads, would necessitate the addition of a very large number of men to the transport service.

To ensure, therefore, the rapid execution of the whole plan of occupation proposed by Ministers, which involves the conquest of part of the difficult country of the Ngatimaniapoto tribe, large reinforcements would be necessary, the exact amount of which it is impossible to estimate, without more definite information as to the extent of land to be occupied, and a better knowledge of the country than I find it possible to obtain. The number of troops required would, however, be greater than the Imperial Government would probably be induced to send, especially for the purpose of occupying territory, the defence of which might involve their detention in the country for many years, until a sufficient number of military settlers could be found to supply their place.

I do not wish it to be inferred, from the preceding observations, that I object to the frontier line between Tauranga and Kawhia or Raglan (which I consider a good one), or that I offer any opinion on the expediency of occupying the tracts of country described in the memorandum of ministers; but I wished to point out that the whole of the plan proposed by them could not be carried out rapidly (the particular point on which your Excellency has asked my opinion) with the force at present in the colony, nor the whole frontier line above referred to taken up at once, without employing more troops than can be spared for the purpose in the present state of affairs.

Whatever plan for the confiscation and occupation of native lands may be decided upon, I think it should not be based upon the expectation that further reinforcements will be sent from England, but rather upon the probability that a reduction of the present force will be ordered before long by the Imperial Government.

The Governor, in a despatch to Mr. Cardwell, dated July 29, 1864, expresses also his views on the measures suggested by the responsible ministry. He states his unwillingness to the immediate prosecution of active warfare, not only for the reasons urged by the general, but also because he considered it "more advisable by a short delay to give the ignorant misguided natives time to reflect, and return to their allegiance, rather than by hurried proceedings to drive them to despair, and to give them no opportunity of making terms, for they are exceedingly ill-informed as to our intentions, and the steps they should take."

On the other point he adds—

My own views on the subject of the proposed extensive confiscations of native land, not according with those of my advisers, I delayed taking any steps in reference to this subject until I might ascertain my own position in relation to it, and whether or not any powers were to be left in my hands. The receipt of your despatches, No. 43, of the 26th of April, and No. 65, of the 26th of May last, having clearly defined the powers that are, in this respect, to be entrusted to me, I will now discuss the subject with my responsible advisers, and endeavour to arrive at some joint decision of a satisfactory nature, taking care to obey the instructions which Her Majesty's Government have recently issued to me.

In the despatches here referred to by the Governor, Mr. Cardwell had stated, that while recognising the general right and duty of the Colonial Government to deal with matters of native policy properly so called, he considered, that while active operations are being carried on under the conduct of Her Majesty's officers, and, in the main, by Her Majesty's military and naval forces, the direction of affairs must be considered as entrusted to the Governor, and that, as the representative of Her Majesty, he must be held responsible by the Home Government for the employment of those forces, and the measures in which they might be emyloyed. This decision called forth, as might be expected, a lively protest from the responsible ministry, and in forwarding this document to the Home Government (August 26, 1864), the Governor took occasion to draw a graphic sketch of the anomalous position in which he found himself placed.

The colonial ministers at present possess and exercise here, upon all ordinary subjects, all the powers usually held and exercised by ministers in those countries where the system of reponsible government prevails. In addition, they now, as I understand them, protest against not being allowed to exercise, absolutely, powers which would virtually give them a very large control over the naval and military forces and the naval and military expenditure of Great Britain.

I think that in deciding upon the protest now transmitted the following points should be considered—The colonial ministers are responsible to the General Assembly for colonial matters; but, as I will presently show, the General Assembly does not, even in such matters, exercise such an active supervision or control over their acts and proceedings as the Parliament of Great Britain exercises over those of the British ministry. And when it is remembered that the General Assembly is in no way responsible for the mode in which Her Majesty's naval and military forces are employed, or for the naval and military expenditure of Great Britain, I think that that body would exercise little or no control over the colonial ministers in reference to those matters.

The members of the General Assembly are collected from great distances, are drawn away from their own private avocations, to which they are anxious to return as speedily as possible. The settlements from which they come are also removed by long distances from the capital, and have frequently interests of a totally different character from those of the population inhabiting districts where there are many natives. From their remoteness from the seat of Government, the information the inhabitants of such settlements possess regarding public affairs is limited. It is frequently only such as the Ministry of the day think proper to suffer to transpire. Hence less interest is taken in what may be termed general public affairs, as distinguished from provincial public affairs, than would be imagined; and public opinion, regarding general public affairs, is, in the settlements remote from the capital, formed upon limited, often erroneous, information. When, therefore, the General Assembly meets, some time elapses before the members can thoroughly acquaint themselves with what has passed since their last meeting; and ere they have fully mastered this, the time for their separation has almost arrived. Sometimes, also, papers upon important subjects are only called for after the Assembly has met for some time. I believe, in some cases, the printing of these papers has been hardly completed when the Assembly has separated. The sessions of the General Assembly are also not only short, but by far too infrequent to enable them to exercise such a control over public affairs as is exercised by the Parliament of Great Britain.

For instance, the General Assembly met at its last session on the 19th of October 1863, and was prorogued on the 14th of December of the same year, after a session of only fifty-six days, and it may probably not meet again until the month of March 1865; that is, not until after an interval of fifteen months.

Whilst the General Assembly exercises so feeble a control over public affairs, what is termed the Cabinet bears but a faint resemblance to the strong and powerful ministry which can be formed in Great Britain. Since September 1861 there have been three ministries in New Zealand. The present Cabinet consists of five members, one of whom has been absent in England during the greater part of the time of the existence of the present ministry. Two other members of the ministry have been frequently absent from the capital, so that the direction of affairs involving largely the interests of Great Britain in the employment of her military and naval forces, and the expenditure of their funds, has rested at such times in the hands of the remaining two members of the ministry, who are the two partners who compose one of the leading legal firms in the town of Auckland. And it was on advice thus tendered to him that the Governor was frequently expected to act in the most important affairs of imperial concern. The protest I now enclose is made by this Cabinet, and not by the General Assembly, and it is made before your last despatch is known in the colony, and before public opinion has been in any way formed or expressed on the subject. . . . . .

It should also be remembered, in reference to the two distinct populations in this country, that the native population, who are the largest landed proprietors in the northern island, are unrepresented in the General Assembly. The other population, the European one, is the governing body. Necessarily, in a civil war, the feeling of race exercises some influence. Men's passions more or less lead them to adopt extreme views, and to hasty and often ill-considered acts, in which they are sustained by a public opinion to which there is little or no counterpoise; so that, surrounded by such influences, it would be very difficult for a minister, endued with the very calmest mind, to arrive at a correct conclusion. And this difficulty is greatly increased when he has to please a constituency in which almost universal suffrage prevails, and which is often composed of one race engaged in a civil war with a race which it is to govern, and which is to be subdued by an army supplied by the mother-country.

To the settlement of the land-confiscation question the Governor had now to address himself. It was necessary that the quantity to be forfeited by the natives should be decided upon, and that the more so, because the Home Government, in a despatch dated April 26th, had instructed the Governor to put forth a proclamation, granting, in Her Majesty's name and on her behalf, a free and absolute pardon to all parties (murderers excepted) who, before a certain day, should take the oath of allegiance, and cede such territory as might in each instance be required. The principles, therefore, which were to regulate the confiscation, needed to be defined. The responsible ministry wished to avoid pledging themselves to any limit, and desired that the quantity should eventually be regulated by whatever might be required to defray the expenses of the war, &c. The Governor declined to adopt this suggestion.

The views of the Governor and his responsible advisers differ also on the subject of cession of territory. They, in their memorandum, look only to the acquisition of territory as a means of aiding, by its sale, in defraying the expenses of the war, or for the purpose of being devoted to military settlements, and they ask the Governor to give an assurance that the cessions taken shall be to the extent required for these purposes. The Governor views the cession of territory as a punishment inflicted to deter other natives from engaging in rebellion, and as a punishment which is, as far as possible, to be in each instance apportioned to the degree of guilt in which the several tribes have been involved. The whole of the territory thus taken will of course be available for the objects mentioned by ministers, but he cannot take a man's land to a greater extent than the limits of justice warrant because it may be wished to get it to plant settlements on. He cannot, therefore, give the vague assurance asked for.

The Governor then persisted in a specification being made to him, as to the number of acres which would be required for emigrants and settlers, and also the number required for sale.

Thus urged, the responsible ministry hesitated no longer. They proceeded to state, that, in the province of Auckland, they would require one million of acres, and in Taranaki and near Wanganui 600,000 more; making a total of 1,600,000 acres of land.

On this requisition being laid before him, the Governor, in a despatch to Mr. Cardwell, October 8, 1864, observed—

In the memorandum of the 3rd inst. I for the first time received a statement of the quantities of land to be taken, in cessions or otherwise, which they would now deem sufficient, viz. 1,600,000 acres, although it appears that this quantity falls very far short of what was proposed in the General Assembly, and that they only made this modification for the purpose of avoiding any imputation even of prolonging the war for the acquisition of territory. Out of this quantity they required 600,000 acres to be taken at Taranaki and Wanganui; that is, more than 900 square miles. As I thought that hardly 100 miles length of territory between these places still remained in the hands of the natives, and that that country was probably, on the whole, of no immediate value for settlement for an average distance of nine miles inland, it appeared, if I was right in thus thinking, that the result would be that I should have to take the entire native territory of friendly natives and all others in that district. I therefore asked my responsible advisers to furnish me with tracings which would show approximately the boundaries of the territory it would be necessary for me to confiscate in the Waikato country and in the province of Taranaki and near Wanganui.

You will find, from the memorandum of the 4th inst., that they stated that they were, even at that date, unable to supply tracings which would show even approximately the boundaries of the territory that they proposed to confiscate, and that they had not sufficient information to determine even the precise localities.

It was impossible to act on such vague statements. It seemed wrong that Her Majesty's forces should be sent to conquer land anywhere, with no direct and certain object aimed at. It seemed due equally to the European inhabitants of this country and the natives that the aim and scope of the war should be determined, and that it should be known what we required, and the acquisition of what territory would bring the war to a close.

These tracings, when at last furnished, showed how wide a difference existed between the Governor and the responsible ministry on the confiscation question. The Governor proposed to take as the frontier line the river Waikato as far as the southern bend, a chain of military posts being extended eastward from that point to the Hauraki gulf. From the Auckland isthmus thus enclosed he proposed the ejection of all hostile natives, the lands which had belonged to them being confiscated for colonial purposes. From the southern bend of the river a line of fortified posts was to be thrown forward as far as Paetai and Ngaruawahia, places which were to remain in the permanent possession of the colonists, their connexion with the Auckland district being maintained by armed steamers on the river.

The boundary line traced by the responsible ministry was, however, far to the south of this. It commenced on the west coast, not at Raglan, but at a point still further south, Kawhia. As it went inland it dipped still further south, so as to include the

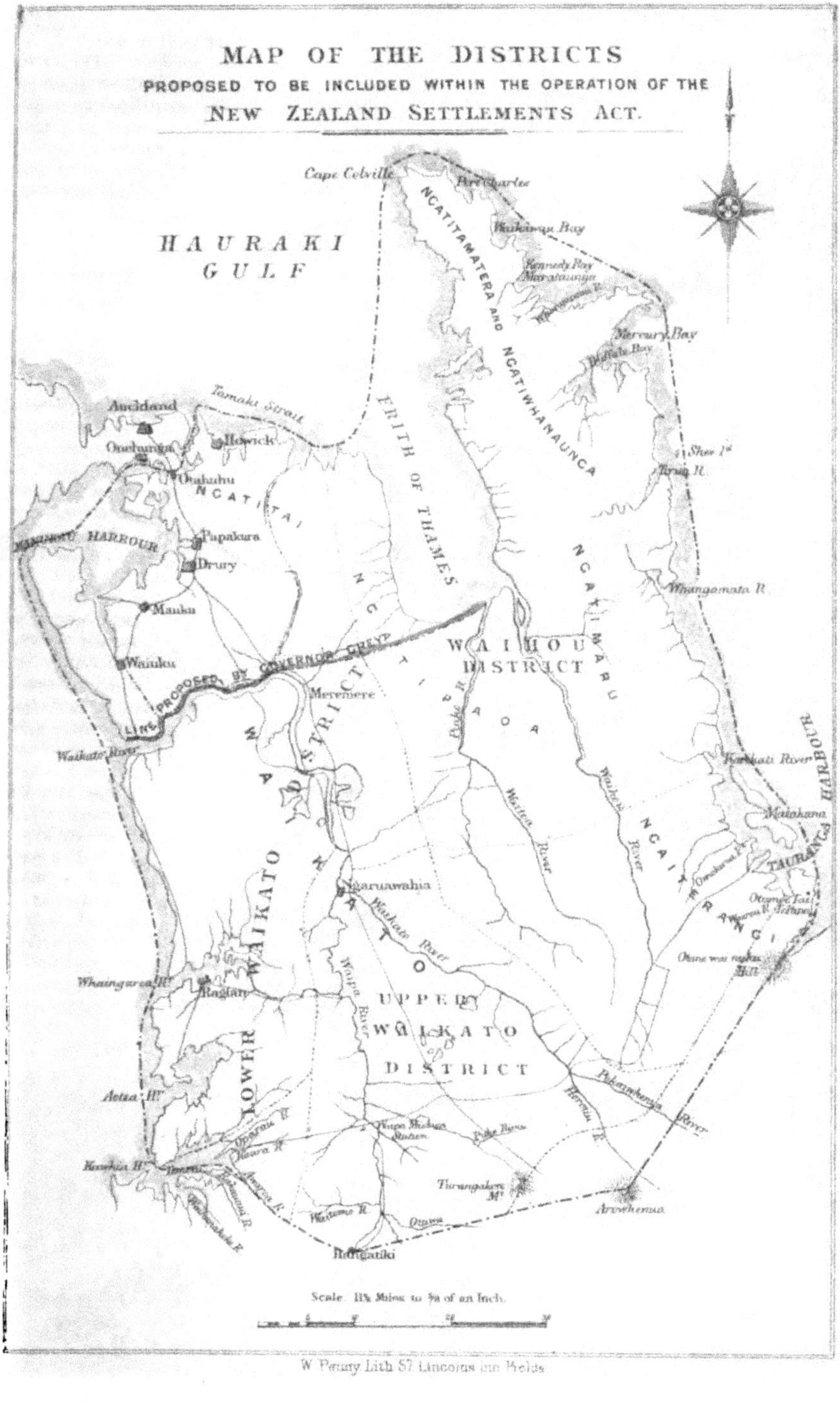

MAP OF THE DISTRICTS PROPOSED TO BE INCLUDED WITHIN THE OPERATION OF THE NEW ZEALAND SETTLEMENTS ACT.

W. Penny Lith 57 Lincolns Inn Fields

head-waters of the Waipa and Waikato Rivers, and then turned north-east, until it came out at Tauranga harbour on the east coast. This frontier line then embraced the whole of the Upper and Lower Waikato and Thames districts, or a tract of country larger than that included within the Governor's boundary line by no less an amount than 1,172,160 acres.

On this disputed point the Home Government was called upon to adjudicate, and nothing could be more clear than the decision to which it came. In a despatch dated August 20, 1864, Mr. Cardwell says—

> I have read with great regret the continuation, which has reached me by this mail, of the correspondence between yourself and your responsible advisers on the subject of terms of peace proposed, or to be proposed, to the natives, and of the extent to which the principle of confiscation ought to be carried. It is quite true, as stated in one of these minutes, that the principle of confiscation had been sanctioned by you, and that your sanction of it had been approved by the Duke of Newcastle; but the application of that principle is a question of degree, and in my despatch of the 26th of April I conveyed to you, as fully as I could, the views which, after the most deliberate consideration of a subject so important, Her Majesty's Government desired you to adopt. Referring to that despatch, which had then been printed by order of Parliament, I stated to Mr. Reader Wood that his acceptance of my proposal for a guaranteed loan would be regarded by Her Majesty's Government as an assurance, on his own part and that of his colleagues, of their desire cordially to co-operate with you in that just and temperate policy towards the native race; and his reply, which was also subsequently laid before Parliament, was perfectly satisfactory and complete in this respect. I feel, therefore, that you are, on every ground, fully entitled to expect, and I trust you will have received, from your Ministers, all possible assistance and support in carrying your instructions into effect. Nothing could be more calculated to excite a strong feeling of disappointment and even of indignation in this country, than any well-founded belief that the war was unnecessarily protracted in consequence of any indisposition in New Zealand to give full effect to a just and generous policy towards the native race. I know that it is your own desire to carry such a policy into effect; and I have nothing now to add, either to the instructions in which I have conveyed to you the views of Her Majesty's Government, or to the assurances I have given you, that in using every legitimate means to give effect to those instructions you may count upon my cordial support.

By these instructions the Governor resolved to abide, and the ministry, finding it impossible to give effect to their extensive confiscation plans, tendered their resignations on September 30th.

Mr. Weld undertook to form a new ministry on the following principles—

1. The withdrawal of the British troops from the colony in order to put an end to the evil of a double Government, it being understood, when this has been accomplished, that the Governor is to be guided entirely by the recommendation of his constitutional advisers, except in such matters as directly concern imperial interests and the prerogatives of the country.

2. The appropriation of so much land, being *a part* of the territory belonging to the insurgents, and now in military occupation, as may suffice for the use of a large number of military settlers, with whom engagements have been entered into.

3. The adoption of suitable measures for the restoration of order and tranquillity in the western districts—Taranaki and Wanganui.

4. The transfer of the seat of Government to Wellington.

This policy, being the same which had been indicated by Mr. Cardwell, was substantially accepted by the New-Zealand House of Representatives in December last.

In the policy attempted to be carried out by the ex-ministry there were several injurious elements which obstructed the pacification of New Zealand. One was, that however desirous the insurgents might be to return to their allegiance, no communication would be opened with them until they had first laid down their arms. By the harsh treatment to which the Rangiriri prisoners were subjected, the natives were made apprehensive that if they laid down their arms they would be similarly dealt with; and then they were told that unless they did so there could be no peace. Thus they were literally driven to desperation, and the most sanguinary conflicts arose from the resistance of hopeless and desperate men. This is now rectified, Mr. Weld's ministry having agreed not to demand from such natives as may desire to return to their allegiance a surrender of their arms as a preliminary condition.

The other injurious element was the wholesale confiscation of native lands contemplated by the ministry. Even the 1,600,000 acres demanded by them from the Governor was but a modification of the vast expectations at first entertained, and made known by the Colonial Treasurer to the House of Representatives on the second reading of the Loan Bill in the following words—

> If we take the whole area of land in the rebel districts, it will be found that it amounts to eight and a half million acres, and we have obtained information from persons well acquainted with the districts and the quality of the land, that one-half of it will be available for settlement; therefore we have for settlement 4,250,000 acres. If we deduct from that the quantity required for the location of European settlers and natives, there will be a balance of 3,000,000 for sale, reserves, and for the preservation of the territory of those loyal natives who may not be desirous of disposing of their lands. I said there was a balance of 3,000,000 of acres, and supposing we set apart 500,000 acres for roads and reserves, and 1,000,000 for land that may be retained by loyal natives, it will still leave 1,500,000 acres for sale. Of course it would not be desirable, if it were even possible, to dispose of this land at once; but by bringing it into the market judiciously, it appears to us that 1,500,000 acres, economically dealt with and properly sold, will realize at the very least 2*l.* per acre, and 3,000,000*l.* will be obtained at the time these arrangements are completed.

Now, while there is to be required from the insurgent natives a forfeiture of lands, yet this cession, or confiscation, is not to be carried further than may be consistent with the permanent pacification of the island, and the honour of the English name.

Meanwhile, in pursuance of the new policy, instructions have been given to General Cameron to arrange for sending home five regiments. We do sincerely trust that, in connexion with the Taranaki district, unquestionably a subject of anxiety, no new complications will arise to prevent this being done.

BHOPAL AND ITS BEGUM.

In our Number for December 1864 we introduced some brief notices of this native state, and the loyalty which its princes have ever shown towards the British Government, and more particularly during the fiery ordeal of 1857-58, when the Begum, by her staunch and undeviating adherence to the old alliance, and refusal in any way to compromise herself with the mutineers, rendered very important services to the British Raj, and afforded a refuge and means of escape to many fugitive Englishmen and their families. The Begum's visit to Bombay, on her way to Mecca, led to the article respecting Bhopal, to which we have referred, in which we expressed our deep regret, that within the limits of that native state no Missionary effort had ever been attempted. We are not aware that this appeal has drawn out any expression of sympathy towards a state which is deserving of so much good at our hands, but from which we have hitherto withheld the only good which could suffice to repay the debt of obligation which we owe. But the following passages from the communications of our Missionary at Bombay, the Rev. J. G. Deimler, will show that, encouraged by the intercourse which he had with the Begum's attendants while she remained at Bombay, he has been led to contemplate a Missionary journey to Bhopal.

May 23, 1864—I am much obliged to you for the thought you suggested of urging upon the Moslems the fact of our Saviour's resurrection from the dead. I dwelt upon it on a former occasion, but I am very glad to have my observation especially directed to that grand fact, which proves, indeed, the Godhead of Jesus, and which carries with it an indisputable testimony to a thoughtful Mohammedan. It is remarkable that the Mussulmans believe that Elias, Jesus, John, Chiyar, and—the Sheahs add—the Imam Mahdi, have not died, but are alive, whilst "the seal of the prophets, the Lord of all the prophets," Mohammed, is dead, and buried at Medina.

As it is not unlikely that the Begum of Bhopal, having accomplished her pilgrimage to Mecca, will proceed to England, it will be of interest to you if I tell you that I found, during nearly two months, at the end of the last and the commencement of the new year, a very interesting field of labour amongst her followers. You will find an interesting account of the state of Bhopal in the "Indian Gazetteer." The Begum of Bhopal, with her suite, and some hundreds of followers, was staying here, near my residence, on her way to Mecca. The Begum has thrown off her seclusion, and administers herself, with energy and wisdom, the affairs of the state. She is a staunch ally of the Government, and is, as a Mussulman, free from bigotry, and has some regard for Christians. The majority of her followers were, like her, Mohammedans, some Hindus, a few Roman Catholics, and a couple of Armenians. A man of note amongst the Roman Catholics was Meseeh Sahib, of French extraction, whose grandfather came from the Isle of Bourbon, whose father was a kind of Wazeer, and whose widowed mother is a Jagirdar, and lady of honour to the Begum. I found my way amongst these interesting people by distributing tracts, books, and Scriptures, which were eagerly sought for by the Christians, Mohammedans, and Hindus, the majority perhaps of whom could read. On the first of my visits to the large compound in which they were residing, I presented Dr. Pfander's works to the Nawab, a near relative of the Begum, who very courteously and thankfully accepted them. Afterwards I met him several times, when he always very politely received me. I was told that he had the Tariq-ul-hayat read to him. With the Christians I held much intercourse, in which I endeavoured to bring home to them the great truths of Christianity, and a conduct consistent with the Christian faith. They were intelligent, unprejudiced, always happy to see me, and to gather around the padre. They were especially eager to get Bibles in Hindustanee, of which I could give them only a few copies of the Old Testament, these being out of print; but I gave them a large supply of the New Testament, a friend of mine supplying me with many copies. They also asked for copies of Dr. Pfander's works, to be better enabled to refute the Mohammedans. The Christians, as well as the Mohammedans and Hindus, called very frequently on me. The first, on my invitation, promised to come to my house on Christmas-day, for divine service, but afterwards, changing their minds, they went to the Roman-Catholic church. The Mussulmans gladly received, and asked for, the Mizan-ul-haqq, and were less prejudiced and more polite than any Mussulmans I ever saw in Western India or East Africa. One of them, an engineer, who spoke English, requested me to bring for him Sale's Korân, that he might be able to compare, with greater facility, the Mohammedan with the Christian religion. To him, and to another Mussulman, at their own request, I gave my address, that they might be able to write to me. These two men invited me to come to Bhopal. They said that they would be my friends: the Mussulmans there would more willingly hear my message than those at Bombay, whom they considered bad people. Also Meseeh Sahib, with the Christians, said that it would give him great pleasure if I would come to Bhopal, and stay in his house. They also said that there is a (Roman-Catholic) padre at Bhopal—I believe an Italian—who has been there about a year, who always says mass, but does not yet know the Hindustanee language. Some of the Hindus asked for the New Testament in Hindee. I went freely in and out amongst the people as the padre, and they were happy to show me their respect, and perhaps some little service. In fact, I never met any natives who were so polite, so easy of access, and to whom I could minister with such acceptance and pleasure, as these. I am sorry that Mrs. Deimler was not here: she might have called on the Begum; but I trust some book will find its way to her, and do good to her soul.

What a difference between these people and those of the Guicowar of Baroda, whose camp, with 5000 followers, I once visited during his residence at Bombay. I found nowhere a hearing. Close to the Rajah's pavilion there was an old Mussulman fakeer, occupying his own little tent, and pluming himself in his fine shawl, a very holy man, not deigning to give me an answer, and sneering at having a tract shown to him. And there was a potilwan (zero, wrestler), who, bidding me sit down, unloosened his shawl, to exhibit proudly before me his fatness and strength, and, looking at a tract, returned it as a thing useless to him. With a sad heart I returned from that camp.

Reverting to the people of Bhopal, and calling to mind their friendly intercourse and their invitation, do you not think that this may be a Macedonian voice bidding me to make a call there? I may be enabled to do so when the railway from Bombay, in the direction of Bhopal, is finished, and to see whether the everlasting Gospel will have access there, and Christ be glorified. I am anxious to have your opinion and advice on the subject. I also ask your prayers for a blessing on the books and tracts that have been carried to Bhopal. . . . .

The Begum has returned to Bombay from her pilgrimage, and stayed during a part of the rainy season at Poona, where she was duly honoured by the Governor. I should consider it a high privilege to see a way open by which I could carry the Gospel of Christ to the native state of Bhopal.

Recent Intelligence.

MAURITIUS.

The following instance of earnest effort put forth to bring a wretched criminal, under sentence of death, to repentance, has been communicated to us by the native minister, the Rev. C Kooshalle—

An Indian, named Jarain, was recently condemned to be hung for murder. Being informed of this unfortunate man, I went to see him at the civil prison. At first, when he saw me, he was terribly frightened, and begged me to ask for pardon from the authorities, by holding both his hands up in a piteous manner. Not being able to obtain pardon, or rather, being assured that pardon for him was impossible, I explained to him that it was useless to ask for pardon from the earthly judges, after committing such a horrible crime; that it would be better to ask pardon from the heavenly Judge before whom he stands in worse crimes, for which he will be condemned to greater punishments than that of being hung. The criminal very attentively heard my explanations about the soul he has to look after, and where and how he can obtain pardon.

When he was fully convinced of my statements, though not easily, he said, that if he had known it before he would never have committed such an act; and that, "since Jesus Christ died for *his* sins, and there is time yet to ask for pardon and to obtain it, he would not ask pardon from his earthly condemnation, but submit to it with fortitude;" and he asked me what he should do to obtain this pardon. I told him that he must believe on the Lord Jesus Christ, and be baptized in his name. Since that time he always asked to be baptized whenever he met me, but I always put it off, to know the depth of his belief in Christianity.

It appears, in my absence one of the Romish priests went to him, and, explaining about Christianity, asked him to be baptized, showing him the crucifix. The man replied that he understood nothing of what was said to him; that he had another priest (meaning me) who spoke in his (the criminal's) own language; and that, if he had any thing to learn, his former priest would teach him. So saying, he turned his back towards the Romish priest, who, finding that the crucifix and his French language were useless, went away without success.

When I went again to see the man, he related the above circumstances to me, and urged me to baptize him at once. When I asked on what proofs I could baptize him, he said that he fully believed in Jesus Christ, who died for his sins, and could pardon him for all his miserable sins, and give him everlasting life.

I never saw or heard of an Indian with such a memory as this man. He astonished me by repeating, in his own words, every circumstance I related to him from the Scriptures, and repeated the Lord's Prayer, to the great astonishment of the jailers, after only hearing it three times.

On the eve of his execution I baptized him, being fully convinced that he had embraced Christianity, not only by his outward appearance, but also by his words, repeating every sentence he heard from the Scriptures through me. Late in the evening I went to spend the night with him, together with a catechist and a schoolmaster. When the schoolmaster spoke to the condemned to testify his belief, he repeated the history of Lazarus, which he had heard from me a few days before, and said, though he was a sinner he was sure that he would be borne on Abraham's bosom, as was Lazarus. He also repeated the parable of the prodigal son, and said that the prodigal not only took away half of the father's fortune, but also went away from him to spend it in riotous living, and added he believed he should be received back to his Father's bosom, as was the lost son. And from time to time he asked us to leave his room, that he might pray alone, which he did every time we went out.

On the morning of his execution he said he could not walk, being weak. After telling him that he should not be frightened, but courageous, he consented to walk, and walked faster than I and the catechist. The catechist, pointing to the gallows when we came in view, asked him if he knew what it was, and if he was afraid, to which he replied, "Why should I be afraid? I know the messengers are waiting there to carry me to Jesus Christ."

Arriving at the scaffold, I prayed that he might be pardoned for his sins, and be received into heaven as a penitent sinner. Immediately after, he prayed a prayer, which I translate literally, as near as the language can admit—"O Jesus Christ, I am a great sinner. I have sinned so many times that I cannot count them. I have been punished in the prison for my crimes. My sins are greater than these mountains here. The stars of heaven may be counted, but my sins are uncountable. The sands of the sea-shore may be numbered, but my wickednesses are innumerable. By sin my soul is as black as coal. As the coal is made white (into ashes) by fire, so, O Christ, wash my soul by thy precious and holy blood, which thou hast shed on the cross. Amen."

A few moments after, the penitent man was no more. His immortal soul left his condemned body. May the Lord have received him by his angels into his glorious kingdom, there to praise his glory for ever and ever!

CEYLON.

THE following fact, communicated by our Missionary at Baddagama, the Rev. G. Parsons, encourages the hope that the apathy on religious subjects, which has so seriously retarded the progress of Gospel truth among the Singhalese, is giving way—

Feb. 16, 1865—You will be glad to hear of an important controversy which has just taken place at Baddagama between ourselves and the Buddhists. For some time past the common people have felt that Christianity and Buddhism cannot both be true. But to decide which is true they regard as the work of their teachers. They have found their own inability to answer the arguments put forth on the Christian side, and have long wished to see the question referred to a controversy between their own priests and the teachers of the Christian religion. These feelings have, no doubt, tended to promote the present controversy, but the more immediate cause was a conversation held between my preparandi and the priests of the neighbourhood, which resulted in a challenge to the priests to come to a formal discussion. This challenge was accepted, and the 21st of November fixed for the discussion. On that day we met. The Christians numbered about 100, and the Buddhists about 500, with sixteen priests at their head. Having no controversial leader, they put forth an abusive man as their spokesman, and his endeavour was to avoid a controversy, and the day was spent, therefore, in discussing preliminaries and arranging for a future day. Finally, the 8th of February was fixed for the controversy to commence. Great preparations were made by them, and our people thought it right to be well prepared also. They accordingly wrote to me, as I was attending the Missionary Conference in Kandy, authorising me to invite to the controversy some special controversialists, and promising themselves to pay his travelling expenses. I was pleased at this, and requested the Rev. D. de Silva, of the Wesleyan Mission, an able controversialist, well versed in Pali, and skilled in bringing forth from their own Pali books weighty arguments against Buddhism, to attend. Mr. de Silva most kindly undertook to come down, bringing with him such Pali books as he thought necessary.

The controversy commenced on the 8th and lasted till the 13th. We met every day (except Sunday) from one o'clock until six. Our side numbered about 150 Christians, including some of our Wesleyan neighbours, who gladly joined us. On their side were over fifty priests, and more than 1000 Buddhists. In this vast assembly were the fathers and brothers of many of our dear Christian people. Among their priests they had the great controversialists, one of whom had been brought from Colombo. Our expectations, therefore, were fully realized, and the controversy became a general struggle between Christianity and Buddhism, in which the whole of the Singhalese race must feel interested, although it was confined merely to the Baddagama district. It was arranged that five papers should be read by each party, each paper containing a number of questions or charges against the religion of its opponents. We allowed them to bring forward the first paper. This contained charges of inconsistency in the statements of the Bible with reference to the attributes of Jehovah. This was answered; and a similar attack made by us on Buddhism. They answered this in a very unsatisfactory way, and the battle was from that time in our favour.

In their second charge they brought forward a large number of quotations from the Bible, endeavouring to prove that its statements are inconsistent and undeserving of credit. These were all answered, and the answers worked up by Mr. de Silva in a noble defence of the truth, the effect of which was withering to the Buddhist side. Our defence was read out on Saturday evening, and when we met on Monday they instantly proposed to carry on the controversy on a new plan, their aim being, without doubt, to stop the controversy. The whole day was spent in resisting their endeavour, and in attesting the copies of our defence. The headman of our district, fearing a breach of the peace from the excited state the Buddhists had been in since the reading of our second defence, had officially informed the Government. On Monday evening, therefore, our public controversy was abruptly ended by the appearance of two Government officials, who required us to cease forthwith from publicly meeting together. Arrangements were therefore made for continuing the controversy by correspondence, and next day I drafted and sent to the chairman of the Buddhists a copy of proposed rules, and am waiting his reply. On the same day we held a thanksgiving service in the church, and Mr. de Silva, before leaving us, delivered a heart-stirring appeal on the whole subject. I have great reason to be thankful to God for the whole. Much prayer has been offered up by our Christian people, and many plain indications of God's presence seen and acknowledged. Our people have stood firm to a man, and are greatly encouraged. They took a deep interest in the whole. In some cases I feared they would overtax their strength.

NEW ZEALAND.

A REMARK was made recently by a friend in which there is much force. He said the question, as regards the Maoris, was not whether they had gone to war, because that, however to be regretted, did not disprove their Christianity, and that the more so, as, whether justly or not, they considered themselves engaged in a defensive war; but whether, in the carrying on of the war, there has been such a marked contrast between the way in which they prosecuted war when in their heathen state, and their present conduct, as to prove that Christianity has exercised a powerful and improving influence on the national character.

Upon this point there is no doubt. Let the noble act of the chief be remembered, who exposed his life that he might bring water to Colonel Booth, of the 43rd, when lying mortally wounded at the Gate Pah, and received in doing so his own death wound.

We shall keep this point in view, and, at some future time, deal with it more fully. Meanwhile, let the two following extracts be read. The Rev. C. S. Volkner writes—

I shall allude to a few instances which may illustrate how Christianity has shown its fruits in the Maoris of my district during this disturbance. While they were encamped near Opotiki, I went to have service with them. Some of the Ngatiporou were rude, and said I should not have service with them, because they hated the white skin. Immediately after prayers nearly all the people expressed their indignation against the men who had insulted their minister. They demanded that they should make an apology, and attend my services every time whilst I was there, and if they refused to do so, they should be expelled. The offenders apologized, and attended service regularly and willingly whilst I was in camp. Whilst the natives were at Otatuarahau, some military and civil officers from Maketu passed without observing a picket that lay concealed. It was a strong detachment, with their guns loaded. They knew them to be officers, but as they had not come then to fight, the chief forbade his people to fire. When the officers passed them again, on their way home, the chief stepped out, and told them in what danger they had been, and kindly warned them not to come this way again. Whilst at Maketu, they got possession of some of the commissariat cattle. The teachers considered them to be stolen property, and advised the people to drive them back. They did so, although they were so short of food at the time, that for several days they had only two potatoes each as a day's allowance.

Three days after their defeat at Io Matata, whilst they were still lamenting over those slain there, and especially over the chief who was murdered by the natives at Maketu, four men of that tribe arrived at Opotiki, in running across the country from Turanga. They were ignorant of what had lately happened. Their arrival caused great consternation amongst the better-disposed people. According to their old usage, these men must be killed as payment for the murdered chief. The widow of this chief, and also the widows of those slain in the late engagement, already cried for payment. The men were detained, and much fear was entertained for their lives. Committees were held for two days and a night. The better feeling prevailed. It was decided by the Committee—"In the dark time of ignorance and barbarism these men would have been killed as payment for the chief who had been murdered by their tribe. But those times have passed away, and we can see in the light of the Gospel that these men are not guilty of the blood of our chief, and we will not soil our hands with innocent blood." The men were informed of the decision of the Committee, treated kindly during their stay, and, when they started on their journey, were safely conducted beyond the boundary.

At any other time this would show how Christianity has prevailed over barbarism; but at the time it occurred, and under all the circumstances connected with it, I relate it as a great triumph of the Gospel over heathenism.

The second extract is taken from the letters of the Rev. R. Taylor, our Missionary at Wanganui, dated Jan. 11, 1865. It refers to a ministerial visit paid by him to some loyal natives, up the river, who had engaged and driven back a body of insurgent natives, on their way to destroy the British settlement at Wanganui.

On the 6th of January I went up the river to Ranana, which I reached the following afternoon. I found there the natives from Hiruharuna assembled for the sacrament, so that I had a full church in the evening. I held my usual service with the communicants. Their chief anxiety was to know whether they could safely approach the Lord's table after they had been fighting and shedding human blood. I told them that this cause, being a just one, having fought against those who came with the avowed intention of killing and eating them, and of destroying the European settlement, and likewise of putting an end to the Christian faith, they were perfectly justified in taking up arms in their own defence. Still, they said, their hands were defiled with blood: was it right they should partake of the Lord's Supper? I told them that I thought they might; moreover, that the Bishop of Wellington had said the same. They said that another thing humbled them, viz. the way their foes were treated when slain: although they had carefully avoided plundering the dead, yet their Popish allies were not so scrupulous: they not only took their green-stone *meri*, but took their ear ornaments and other things; therefore they ought to make an atonement-offering to God: for although they knew that the ancient offerings of bulls and goats were only typical of Christ, still they should give some token of their sorrow, and they proposed to rebuild their church, both as a memorial to Hemi, their late teacher and chief, who had first built it, and as a token of their sorrow to God. Hakopa, the present teacher, said he thought it wrong for teachers to fight: their business was to pray; that Moses did not fight, but continued in prayer all the day, so that Aaron and Hur had to hold up his weary arms; that, though they had pressed him to fight, he had refused, but remained at home in prayer.

Jan. 8—I had the first service by six. It was well attended. Several communicants presented themselves who were not present at the former meeting, although they had no reason for being absent. I declined receiving them on that account. At ten I had a very full and attentive congregation. I was quite surprised at the collection: 17*l*. 16*s*. were placed in the plate. This large sum was to be devoted to the rebuilding their church. Eighty-eight received the sacrament. Hakopa gave 1*l*., and, having about ten shillings, he gave them to those who had no money to put in the plate. I had a very long conversation in the church after the service was over, and I felt quite comforted with the clear scriptural views he had of the way of life through Christ. This was very gratifying to me, for, as I went to church, I passed the Popish natives repeating their litany to Mary,

Peter, and all the saints, to pray for them. If God's word had been in their hearts, as in Hakopa's, they would not have said it. I had another good congregation in the evening. I baptized seven children. I had another long talk in the evening on the same subject as in the morning, and was pleased to see their tenderness on blood-guiltiness. It is a singular feature in this war, that they are fighting against their head chief, who is a heathen.

CHINA—NINGPO.

THE city of Ningpo, in 30° north latitude, is situated at the confluence of two large rivers, one of which runs from the north-west, and the other from the south-west, leaving the city surrounded on two sides by rivers, and in the centre of a beautiful plain, twenty-five or thirty miles in diameter, dotted over with villages and farm-houses, and bounded by a circuit of hills, broken only for the flow of the rivers, which a few miles below the city find an outlet in Hang-chow bay. The rice-fields of the plain during the summer encourage to some extent intermittents and diarrhœa, but the winters are cold.

During the hot, and, to Europeans, dangerous season at Ningpo, our Missionaries have been at the little sanatorium which they have obtained amongst the hills, visiting the city, so as to be present at the Lord's-day services, except when prevented by illness. That this should be necessary would appear to be, at the first view, of it one of those unavoidable hindrances which occur in the prosecution of Missionary work. Yet the contrarieties are not by any means as much so as we should be inclined to think. Often they are made, very unexpectedly, to work for the furtherance of the Mission. And so it has proved to be in the present instance.

The Rev. A. E. Moule, in a letter from Ningpo, dated October 3, observes—"The daily preaching to the heathen in one or other of our city chapels was continued regularly by our city catechist, with the voluntary and unpaid assistance, for six or eight weeks, of an umbrella maker outside the west gate, who has been a Christian for some three years. Their labours were, we trust, not without fruit, for in August they reported two applicants for baptism from amongst the hearers.

"We cannot but hope that this time, during which we were obliged in a measure to be absent from the church, has been a time of some slight development of the native agency towards an healthy independence."

Meanwhile, at some distance from Ningpo signs of vitality are becoming apparent.

"A little place has been hired on the shores of the Eastern lakes, some twelve miles from Ningpo, at the expense of the church funds of Ningpo and Tsong-gyiao. An old Christian lives there in charge of the chapel, and to make the two ends meet—for his salary, paid also by the native Christians, is but 1000 copper cash, some five shillings a month—he keeps a tobacco shop, a most honourable occupation in China, tobacco here being a very far less deleterious drug than at home.

"There are resident in this town, Dao-kong-soen, which I have often mentioned in former letters, two baptized brothers; their mother and uncle, and the betrothed wife of the younger brother being also baptized. The second brother also desired baptism, and his wife seems to be in a very hopeful state of mind. I have just returned from a short visit to the lakes. May God's blessing rest upon this tender plant, and cause it to take root and bear much fruit."

The importance of China as a Mission-field is as great as its populousness and the character of its people, which, when brought under the influence of Christianity, will yield valuable fruit.

THE RECENT ANNIVERSARY MEETING OF THE CHURCH MISSIONARY SOCIETY.

THE Sixty-sixth Anniversary Meeting of the Church Missionary Society was held in Exeter Hall on Tuesday, May 2. The hall was well filled, although we think there have been anniversary meetings at which we have seen it more crowded. The Report of the Society's proceedings during the year which had just ended was listened to with much interest. The healthful growth and consolidation of the native churches, their advancement in all the important elements of self-ministration, self-support, and reproductive action, afford satisfactory proofs that they are no exotics, artificially reared, and liable, whenever exposed to the vicissitudes of the weather, to fade and perish, but healthful plants which have taken root in the land, and which will not fail to increase and spread.

These results of past labours constitute an important basis for new operations, and, backed up by the native churches, the Society is called upon to prosecute vigorously the aggressive movement, and to press onward into the "regions beyond," in the full belief that as we do so we shall be permitted to see the Gospel of Christ accomplishing still greater victories. Every thing, indeed, is favourable for such a movement: the Missionaries are anxious to break up new ground, and doors of opportunity are open in various directions; but there is one difficulty, and because of this the Society, at so interesting a crisis, is compelled to pause—the increase in the income of the Society by no means keeps pace with the increase in its expenditure. Year after year a deficiency has occurred which has been met by payments from the Special India Fund; but that fund is now exhausted, and the Society enters upon a new year of labour without any thing to fall back against, in case the current year, after the example of its predecessors, should yield an insufficient income. The Society, then, is compelled to arrest its steps. The opportunities are inviting, but, if entered upon, expenses will accrue, and there are no means of meeting them. This is the anxious point in the present position of the Society. She is like a vessel that, in entering a bay, has grounded on a shoal. Will the tide so rise as to liberate her? All on board are earnestly watching whether indeed it will be so. Have the contributions of English Christians to this great work reached their maximum? We cannot think so. We look for a spring tide, which, coming in with freshness and power from the great ocean of Christian love, will lift the Society over its difficulties, and enable it to go on.

The addresses delivered on the occasion were well calculated to stir the hearts of Christian friends, and move them to fresh effort. It would be impossible to introduce them into the pages of our periodical, as they would necessarily exclude all other matter, and leave the friends of the Society without that monthy supply of Missionary information which is as necessary to the maintenance of the Missionary spirit as the oil is to the light which the lamp emits. His Grace the Archbishop of Canterbury moved the first Resolution, and, in doing so, bore his testimony, so weighty and influential from one in his position, to the value of the Society—

It is a very great satisfaction to me to have the opportunity of once again in this hall publicly testifying my great admiration and my deep sense of the invaluable services to the church which this Society has rendered, and of assuring you of my most cordial sympathy in the work in which it is engaged. It is now very nearly fifty years since, in the earliest days of my ministry, I became associated with this Society, and I used then to listen to the ardent advocacy of the cause by those holy and devoted men who founded the Society, and who have now gone to their rest. And unquestionably in those days the Society, though conducted upon the same principles which it now advocates, was one which was in no respect received with that favour by the great body of the Church with which, I am thankful to say, it is now accepted. It was a sort of slight and reproach to a person to be associated with it, in some quarters at any rate; and thanks be to God for the great change which He has permitted to take place. Among those who were the original founders, or, at any rate, the original supporters of this Society, I should imagine there is scarcely one who still survives; and I believe that, during the past year, we have lost one who was associated with that noble and devoted band—I refer to the venerable Dr. Marsh. I well recollect him in years past, and I can figure him to myself standing here as the advocate of the London Society for the Conversion of the Jews, and addressing the children of Hebrew converts in words of wisdom and love, his countenance beaming with benevolence. It was my privilege to be present when, for the last time in public, he addressed his parishioners and neighbours, charging them to adhere to the faith delivered to the saints, to love the word of God, the Bible, which he held to be the word of our Lord Jesus Christ, and alone able to save the soul. It was a scene and a spectacle which assuredly I shall never forget. With regard to this Report, it is undoubtedly, in some degree, of a chequered character; but there is much to encourage and cheer us in the great and glorious work in which we are engaged. If I am allowed to fix on the one feature which strikes me as especially encouraging, it is that of the increased efficacy of the native agency. Why, what an answer is that to the sneers and scoffs of those who assert that there have been no results, or next to none, from Missionary exertions. Take the case of the Niger district, and the fact of a Native Bishop having been there appointed for the first time. What an answer that again is to those who pretend to say that the African is incapable of being converted to true Christianity; that he is only capable of a religion like Mohammedanism. It is not merely that we have so many native deacons and native priests, but among them one has been found perfectly competent to superintend the interests of the church of Christ in that quarter—one who undoubtedly, from the short intercourse I have had with him, convinced me that he does possess, in an eminent degree, those qualities which specially fit him for that office. I have seen in him a calm wisdom, a humility, a firmness, and a full comprehension of the sacred and important nature of his office; and, in short, I am satisfied that he really does possess most, if not all, of the qualities which specially characterize the office he holds. Now, it is not only in the chief pastor of the church of the Niger district, beyond the limits of the colony. that we have an answer to the scoffs of the sceptic; but let us take the condition of the church of Sierra Leone itself. There you have proofs enough of their zeal in extending their own church without calling upon the aid of this Society. You have also proof that they are willing to follow the apostolic rule of weekly collections, according as it has pleased God to prosper them; an example, I think, that might perhaps be followed elsewhere. You have proof, also, in a colony of only 40,000 natives, of 9000 persons being under instruction—children, and perhaps some adults. What proofs these are of real Christian zeal. Then, again, if we pass to New Zealand, although there, unquestionably, we have less encouragement, yet allow me to say that I have some means of knowing the condition of the church there, and also the circumstances attending some of the different tribes. There is a wide distinction to be drawn between the tribes of the north-east and of the south-west. It appears that many of the tribes of the south-west are of a disposition much less humane, and (whether converted to Christianity or not I cannot say) they have committed atrocities of a dreadful character. But, as regards the Maoris of the north-east, I can bear testimony to their condition; and I may mention an anecdote besides that which has just been read of the Christian who administered water to the dying soldier. I believe it is true that they abstained from all spoliation of those whose bodies remained with them during that night; and, in that camp or pa, when entered afterwards, were found some beautiful forms of prayer, used previous to the engagement. We thus see that a spirit of true Christian love prevailed even among those warriors, and that they were warriors civilized by Christianity. Another anecdote I may relate to prove their excellent spirit. Some of our young officers, from the camp in the neighbourhood of Tauranga, were in the habit of making excursions for amusement and sport, when the chief in a camp two miles off sent a message to the commander, desiring him to warn them not thus to expose themselves, as it was likely they might be cut off by some rifleman, and then the tribe would be accused of murder. Now I think that that was a most friendly act. Then, again, there was a chief who became a prisoner in our hands, and so grateful was he for the treatment which he met with that he sent this message to his friends in the opposite camp—"Mind you treat your prisoners well, for I have been treated kindly." I delight to tell these anecdotes, because it proves the influence of Christianity over the mind of these people, and is again and again an answer to the calumnies which state that our Missionaries do nothing. With regard to the native organization, it is so important, that I think we should encourage it to the utmost of our power. You see that it is utterly impossible, considering the millions, not only in India, but in so many other quarters, who are still without the Gospel of our Lord Jesus Christ, for the inhabitants of this small island to send out English Missionaries to meet all their wants. You must perceive the absolute necessity, therefore, of the work being carried out, to a great extent, by a native agency. We, of course, will still send out our Missionaries to plant the seed there. That seed will spring up and bear fruit, but that seed, we hope, will be planted in a field beyond, and that the native soil will produce additional native fruit. I do not know that there are any other parts of the Report on which it is necessary that I should specially dwell, excepting the somewhat discouraging fact of the great deficiency in our funds. I am sure there is wealth enough, and more than wealth enough, in England, among those truly devoted to the service of their Saviour, to supply that deficiency, if we really set our hearts to the work; and I earnestly hope and sincerely pray that at our next meeting we may testify that the appeal made to us has not been without its effect, but that we have all been impressed with the duty we owe to our blessed Lord and Saviour, to those souls which He came to redeem, and which are still without his saving knowledge. Let there be more labourers sent into the harvest, and a more abundant supply of the means of supporting them. At any rate, I am sure you will all join most fervently in the prayer that the Lord of the harvest may again come, that his kingdom may come; that He may soon take the heathen for his inheritance, and the uttermost parts of the earth for his possession; that his saving health may be known to all nations; that He who is Lord of glory may speedily come to rescue his church from her trials, and to lead the church to that kingdom the gates of which He has opened to all believers.

BRIEF SKETCH OF THE MISSIONARY LABOURS OF THE LATE REV. C. W. ISENBERG.

Mr. Isenberg's first sphere of Missionary labour was Abyssinia. The circumstances which led to the commencement of a Mission in Abyssinia are so remarkable that they ought not to be forgotten. M. Asselin de Cherville, French Consul at Cairo, having conceived the idea of translating some well-known European book into one of the Oriental languages, in the hope that it would attract the attention of the literary world, selected for this purpose the Bible, and, for the language, the Amharic. Amhara is the western part of Abyssinia, its capital being Gondar. Although the province is small, its dialect is spoken throughout at least half Abyssinia. In carrying out his object, M. Asselin employed a learned Orientalist named Abraham. For forty years he had been a traveller, having accompanied Bruce in his explorations, and afterwards having resided in India, where for three years he had studied under some Englishman of learning. Born in Abyssinia, he was not only master of his native tongue, but of Persian, Italian, Greek, and other languages. For ten successive years the work was prosecuted, and at length it reached its termination. Two Abyssinians were employed as copyists, and the following portions of the work were distributed—Genesis, in quarto, to the Prince Regent; Exodus to the Rev. M. Renouard; Leviticus and Numbers to the Pope; Deuteronomy to the French Institute; Joshua and Judges to the King of France; and the Book of Genesis, in small quarto, to the Rev. William Jowett, for the British and Foreign Bible Society. Eventually the work was purchased by that Society. Abyssinia was thus brought before the attention of British Christians. The Rev. W. Jowett, moreover, in his work, "Christian Researches in the Mediterranean," introduced a chapter, entitled "Thoughts on a Mission to Abyssinia;" and this no doubt led to the commencement of a Mission to that country by the Church Missionary Society.

On August 15, 1825, the two first Missionaries to Abyssinia received the instructions of the Committee. It was a remarkable day that: we wish we might be privileged to see like ones in our time. No less than twenty-four Missionary agents were on that day dismissed to their respective spheres of labour—seven English clergymen, five Lutheran clergymen, three laymen, and nine females—some for India, others to West Africa, Jamaica, and the Mediterranean. Gobat and Kugler were the two Missionaries for Abyssinia; and in the former of these we recognise the venerable Anglican Bishop of Jerusalem. They entered Abyssinia December 28, 1829. One year after, Kugler was removed from his earthly labours. When aware that he was going to die, he said, "I could have wished to live longer, that I might proclaim the salvation which is in Jesus to these poor people; but the will of the Lord be done." After that he repeated several times, in the Tigré dialect, "I do not at all fear: weep not for me. It is far better for me to die than to remain here." He then began to pray in Tigré—"Lord Jesus, bless me! Show mercy on me! Receive me to thyself! Thou, O God, art my Saviour—my Father! I have no Father but thee! I come to thee! Receive my spirit! Prepare a place near thyself!" He then began to pray in German, saying the same words. He added, "I give thanks to thee, O Lord, for all the mercy which thou hast manifested towards me! Thou hast been favourable to me to this very hour!" When his voice began to fail he said to his brother Missionary, "I can speak no more. Tell these people (there were many standing by) that Jesus is my portion; and that they must on no account weep for me, as they are accustomed to do. Perform no Tescar"—a sort of gathering of priests and people to pray for the soul of the departed. Soon after, he fell asleep in Jesus.

After his death, the country being in distraction from civil war, and the chief, Sebagadis, who had befriended him, having been slain, Mr. Gobat was compelled to seek shelter in the monastery of Debra Damot. At length, after much sickness and many dangers, he left Abyssinia, where he had been for three years, reaching Cairo in February 1833, and proceeding thence to London and Germany.

Meanwhile the Committee at home had provided a successor for Kugler. Mr. C. W. Isenberg, a native of Prussia, entered the Church Missionary College, Islington, in 1830. He was admitted to deacons' orders by the Bishop of London in June 1831, and, a year subsequently, to priests' orders. Having been appointed to the Abyssinian Mission, he left immediately afterwards for Cairo. There, in August 1834, he was joined by Mr. Gobat, and, setting out from thence, they reached Massowah December 20, 1834.

The translation of the Scriptures into the dialect of Tigré first occupied the attention of the Missionaries, and towards the end of 1836 the work was fast approaching completion. Mr. Isenberg also commenced the translation into Amharic of the Book of Common Prayer; and, in August 1836, was enabled to report it nearly finished. Portions of the Ethiopic and Amharic Scriptures were distributed, and earnestly did the Missionaries impress on friends in London the desirableness of having the whole of the Amharic Scriptures printed, and that speedily. Painful evidences were indeed presented to them of the great spiritual destitution of the people. The cholera entered Abyssinia for the first time, and pitiable was it to hear the crowds, as they went in procession through the streets, imploring—"For Christ's sake, have mercy upon us, O Lord! For Mary's sake, have mercy upon us, O Lord! For Christ's sake, have mercy upon us, O Mary!" In the autumn of 1836 the Rev. S. Gobat was compelled, from ill-health, to leave Abyssinia; and the Rev. C. H. Blumhardt, having been appointed by the Parent Committee to the Abyssinian Mission, reached Adowah May 18, 1837.

In the beginning of 1838 the emissaries of the Church of Rome succeeded in prejudicing the minds of the Abyssinian ecclesiastics against the Missionaries, and exciting against them so formidable an opposition, that Oobeah, the chief who had hitherto protected them, finding himself no longer able to do so, desired them to leave the country, eight days being granted them to make the necessary arrangements, during which their enemies were prohibited from coming near them. "Thus," as Mr. Isenberg observes, "we were turned out of the country into which we had considered ourselves happy to have been called to proclaim the Gospel in the midst of a fallen church, and concerning which we thought we had several indications implying that the time of its salvation was near."

At Cairo, in September 1838, they were joined by Dr. Krapf, who, having been attacked with fever while collecting information at Mocha, on the Red Sea, with a view to attempt an entrance to Shoa, the southern province of Abyssinia, had been obliged to return to Cairo.

Having resolved on endeavouring to reach Shoa from a point south of the Straits of Bab-el-Mandeb, Messrs. Isenberg and Krapf proceeded to Tadjurra, which they used as their starting-point into the interior, and, after many difficulties, succeeded in reaching the frontier of Shoa. By the king they were favourably received, remaining there for five months, during which they were diligently occupied in conversational preaching and discussion, and in obtaining a great variety of information. Mr. Isenberg having made considerable progress in the translational department, revisited Europe, with the object of printing the works he had prepared, reaching London on April 20, 1840. Various Amharic works, and others in the Galla language prepared by Dr. Krapf, were thus carried through the press.

Mr. Isenberg left London on his return to Abyssinia in the spring of 1842, the Rev. J. Muhlheisen being associated with him, in consequence of Mr. Blumhardt, his former associate in Tigré, having been transferred to the North-India Mission. At Cairo they met Dr. Krapf, and the three Missionaries, with Mrs. Krapf, sailed for Tadjurra, with the view of re-entering Abyssinia. But the door was closed. A series of obstacles presented themselves, which they found to be insurmountable. Dr. Krapf proceeded to Aden, in the hope of reaching the Galla tribes of South-eastern Africa from the Indian Ocean, an attempt which issued in the present East-Africa Mission amongst the Wanika. Messrs. Isenberg and Muhlheisen, landing at Massowah, penetrated into Northern Abyssinia, distributing copies of the Scriptures to the number of 2000. At Adowah their steps were arrested. The Abuna, to whom they addressed a letter, vouchsafed no encouragement. Oobeah, the ruler of Tigré, refused to see them, and commanded them to quit the country. Accordingly they retraced their steps to Massowah, and, falling back on Cairo, awaited there the further instructions of the Committee.

Just at this time the Bombay Mission had been visited by sickness. The Rev. H. Mellon, bereaved of his wife just at the moment when he was himself prostrated by sickness, had been placed by his brother Missionary, the Rev. G. M. Valentine, on board the mail steamer for England. The steamer, after buffeting tempestuous weather for five days, was obliged to put back to Bombay, disabled. On landing, Mr. Mellon found that Mr. Valentine was dead, having been carried off by cholera two days after his departure. A prompt reinforcement, to sustain the Mission work, was necessary, and Messrs. Isenberg and Muhlheisen were at once transferred to Bombay.

Into the details of labour presented by his new sphere Mr. Isenberg heartily entered, but without losing his sympathies for East Africa. Slaves liberated from Arab vessels in the Persian Gulf were brought into Bombay from time to time, all from the coast of East Africa. On behalf of these poor strangers Mr. Isenberg addressed himself to the Committee, praying that he might be permitted to devote a considerable portion of his time to them. He had with him at the time of his first application five boys and twenty-three women from the Galla country, thirteen women from Gurague, some from the Suaheli coast, and one boy from the kingdom of Zindjero, south of Gurague. The projected arrangements were cordially sanctioned by the Committee, and friends on the spot were anxious to improve to the uttermost such an opportunity for good to Africa; but the Government refused their concurrence, preferring to place the boys, some in the Mechanics' Institution, others in the Indian navy, while the females were distributed indiscriminately among Christians, Mohammedans, and other families in the island.

Still, however, Mr. Isenberg had opportunity for giving Christian instruction in the Amharic as well as in the Mahrathi language. God blessed him in both. Waifs and strays from Abyssinia drifted to Bombay, and he watched for them, and became their friend.

In 1852 Mr. Isenberg was compelled, by ill-health, to visit his native land, remaining there until October 1853, when he returned to Bombay. Immediately after his arrival he was called upon to take part in the baptism of thirteen Africans, liberated from slavery, who had been under instruction for nearly two years.

Some of the most important papers connected with the Bombay Mission work were furnished by Mr. Isenberg, for, energetically identifying himself with every branch of it, the Money school, the native congregation, the itinerancy, the translation department, he knew it all. We would particularly refer to the "Church Missionary Record" for 1857, in which will be found large extracts from his journals. We refer the more specially to these papers, because some of the places which stand out with most point and freshness in the Bombay Mission at the present time are there adverted to. Yeolah is described by him as an important place, with a population of 10,000, with much traffic and industry. "It was," he observes, "a place of peculiar interest to all of us, and, when arriving there, I prayed with fervent supplications that the Lord would be pleased to make our short visit instrumental for the spread of his Gospel and the salvation of many souls." This town is now among the recognised stations of the Society, a native minister, the Rev. Appaji Bapuji, being located there. Jalna and Aurungabad are also mentioned. Speaking of the latter place, he says—"I offered tracts for gratuitous distribution. I had with me in my cart three bundles, one of which contained Hindustanee and Persian, a second Mahrathi, and a third Guzeratee tracts and books. I went into the cart to distribute them, directing Appaji to stand behind me, to assist me. No sooner had we commenced distributing, than a complete rush was made by the people on the cart, one being more anxious to get tracts than another, and in less than five minutes the whole of the three bundles were distributed. A number of applicants remained unsupplied, whom I requested to come to the bungalow, where I would give them whatever tracts I had to spare. The people raised a loud shout when we left the place, and we lifted up our hearts to God for a rich blessing on the seed sown."

And may not this be the seed which is now springing up? Our Missionaries inform us of a spirit of inquiry which has sprung up amongst the Mang population of Aurungabad and the surrounding districts, not universal, but confined to a few families and relationships; and thus we read of ten individuals baptized at Aurungabad, the first-fruits to Christianity from amongst the population of that part of India.

That these itinerancies and the instructions given are not altogether lost is not unfrequently shown by incidental circumstances. The Rev. E. Rogers was itinerating in 1858, accompanied by Appaji. They came to a place called Jalgaum, where Mr. Isenberg and Appaji had been on the occasion of the tour to which we have already referred. On entering the town, Appaji was immediately remembered, and a little girl, about eight years of age, evidently sent by one of her own sex older than herself, came and asked him if there would be preaching, and, when evening came, she was seen among the hearers.

In 1861, during the absence in England of the Rev. W. S. Price, Mr. Isenberg took charge of the Christian village of Sharanpur, near Nasik, and here, amongst other branches of work to be superintended, he found an African asylum, commenced in 1860, in which were twenty-nine boys, belonging to different nations. Most of these boys and youths retained a certain amount of the knowledge of their own tongues, conversing in them among themselves, especially in Galla, Kihiao, and the Zanzibar languages. They were apprenticed to different trades, blacksmiths, carpenters, weavers. Mr. Isenberg was enabled to report favourably of them. They conducted themselves well, some of them giving very good hopes of future usefulness: of two or three he entertained the hope that a work of grace had begun in their hearts. "Is it," he asks, "too much to hope that they may in future materially assist in the spread of the Gospel in their native country?"

In the "Church Missionary Record" for 1863 will be found some very interesting accounts by Mr. Isenberg of baptisms at Sharanpur. Among them were five East Africans—two youths and three girls. During the year 1862 no less than thirteen East-African boys and four girls had been baptized.

Some of these Africans—four youths and three girls, the most reliable, and who have been considered best fitted to be useful—sailed from Bombay some months back, to join Mr. Rebmann at Kisuludini.* They left Bombay about the time of Mr. Isenberg's death. He had reached Stuttgart, Germany, on the 5th September 1864, and died there October 10th, aged fifty-eight. For results such as these he had earnestly prayed and laboured. Although transferred to Bombay, he had never lost his deep sympathy for the East-Africa Mission; and although compelled to leave Bombay before the departure of these youths, he knew of all the arrangements, for he had himself prepared them. He succeeded in implanting in the Bombay Mission a deep solicitude for Africa, a sympathy which, now that Bombay has sent back to Africa some of her own sons, whom she had received and instructed in the Gospel of Christ, until they were fitted to go back and help in the evangelization of their countrymen, will, we doubt not, deepen and strengthen; and that the more so, as the Rev. J. G. Deimler, one of the Bombay Missionaries, was originally intended for East Africa, and, like Mr. Isenberg, feels himself prompted to do all he can to hasten the time when "Ethiopia shall stretch out her hands unto God."

Thus faithful men, having done their work here, the measure of work which their Lord meted out to them, are transferred to their rest. "Blessed are the dead which die in the Lord from henceforth; yea, saith the Spirit, that they may rest from their labours, and their works do follow them."

MISSIONARY ITINERATION IN THE PUNJAB.

In our Number for February we availed ourselves of the Governor General's Durbar at Lahore to place before our readers the land of the five rivers, now awaiting a conquest far different from any which it has yet experienced. Many are the vicissitudes to which this

* Their arrival at Kisulidini is thus referred to in the following extract from a letter written by the late lamented Missionary, the Rev. J. Taylor, a short time before his death—"I have to mention the return to this land of six Africans, originally slaves, but liberated and trained at Bombay. They are, two married couples, and two girls for two of the Christian young men. It is a sad fact that we have only one female convert here, and she is the wife of Mr. Rebmann's housekeeper at Mombas. These Africans who have come have done so with a simple desire to benefit their countrymen. The late lamented Mr. Isenberg had the choosing of them, and he wished to send only those in whose hearts he thought the work of grace had at least commenced. With God's blessing they will be a real blessing to the station. One is a smith, the other a carpenter, and a mason is shortly to follow. Mr. Rebmann is greatly rejoiced to receive them. He feels that this of itself is an ample reward for all their labours. The Mohammedans of Mombas are astonished. They have before said that the poor Wanika converts were becoming better (*i.e.* superior) than themselves. Now they meet Africans who speak English and Hindustanee, in addition to their own language."

country has been subjected. Wave after wave of invaders, compelled, from various causes, to leave their old ancestral homes on the uplands of Asia, have forced their way through the passes of the Suleiman range, and swept like a deluge over the Punjab, on their way to the Gangetic plains and the rich tropical lands of India. Alexander the Great, resolved on universal empire, crossed the Indus more than 2000 years ago, and, overthrowing the native princes who attempted to withstand him, was at length arrested, not by hostile armies, but by his own soldiers, who, appalled at the prospect of deserts, and marshalled hosts which awaited them, refused to follow him any further. Towards the commencement of our era the Getes, or Jats, a Scythian race, bearing down the resistance of the Indian kings, established in the Punjab successive dynasties.

In due time followed the wild scourge of Mohammedanism under various forms—Arabs, Turks, Mongols. By these successive strokes the power of the Hindu dynasties was completely broken. In 1526, Baber, a prince of a nominally Mongol house, became possessed of Cabul, and from Cabul, invading India, laid the foundation of the Mongol empire.

In the beginning of the sixteenth century the Sikh religion rose like a misty exhalation from the turbid flood of heathenism and Mohammedanism which prevailed around, and by the Hindu Jats the new faith was eagerly embraced.

"The Jats are seated along the Jumna from Agra to the Himalayas, to the west of that river and throughout the Punjab." From the Jumna to the Ravee they constitute the great mass of the population, and, in smaller numbers, extend much further. Towards and along the Indus they had been, in common with other agricultural tribes, converted to Mohammedanism; but in the country between the Jumna and the Sutlej, called the Malwa, and again in the country between the Sutlej and the Ravee, called the Manjha, they had remained lax Hindus, and were rapidly absorbed by the new religion. In the beginning of the seventeenth century the execution of their high-priest by the Mohammedan governor, who ruled the country as a dependency of Delhi, changed the Sikhs from an inoffensive sect of religionists into a band of fanatical warriors. Under Guru Govind they assumed a military organization, and engaged in frequent and sanguinary contests with the armies of Delhi. Rising up as a local power between the Affghans on the one side and the Mongols at Delhi on the other, while these races were contending for the mastery of the Punjab they increased in strength, and, as the Delhi empire declined, and the Affghans, wearied out by the pertinacity of the Sikhs, retired within their own boundaries, the followers of Nanuk were left undisputed masters of the Punjab. In the beginning of the present century Runjeet Singh appeared upon the field, and, under his rule, the Sikh power reached its zenith, only to be crushed upon the banks of the Sutlej by the strong arm of Britain. On March 24th, 1849, the Punjab was annexed, and the last fifteen years have constituted an era such as that territory has never known before. There has been rest throughout the land, so far as it is possible for a nation still in heathenism to be at rest. But an equitable and firm administration has done all that has been possible to give security to life and property, to improve the character of the people, and develop the resources of the country.

And now a new element has been introduced into the Punjab, one which, amidst the alternations of former times, was altogether unknown, and, in the days of Runjeet Singh, had no permission to cross the Sutlej. Yet is it the true remedy for nations, without which there may be indeed outward glory, but no internal peace, no true, no lasting prosperity. The American Missionaries had been in the Cis-Sutlej territories since 1834; but, with the termination of the first Sikh war, they crossed the Sutlej to Jullundur, and, so soon as the Sikh armies were defeated, occupied Lahore. But England had annexed the Punjab, and the British soldiers who had wrestled for the victory felt that the Punjab must have English Missionaries. They desired to present a thank-offering to God, and to erect a memorial of a great national crisis and deliverance, and they decided that both could best be done by the establishment of a Christian Mission. They subscribed largely; they memorialized the Church Missionary Society on the subject; and our first two Missionaries reached Umritsur in 1852.

What has been done during the thirteen years which have passed away since then? Not much numerically. We see that Dr. Mullens, in his "Ten Years' Missionary Labour in India," sets down the native Christians in the Punjab at so high a number as 1579, of whom 416 are communicants.* Admitting such to be the case, let us compare it with the population, viz. 19,500,000! and how infinitesimal it seems. Notwithstanding, however, this disproportion, a great foundation work has been accomplished: the language, the Punjabee, has been acquired; the Missionaries are no longer strangers; the people, in the vicinity of the Missionary stations, have become familiarized with their presence and labours; they purchase books, they listen to their addresses, delivered at the bazaars, at the melas, in their villages; they begin to know the distinctive truths of Christianity, and to converse about them; there is but little opposition, the instances being rare in which the Missionary is not kindly received. Little flocks of Christian natives have been raised up here and there. They are very small, yet, small as they are, they have yielded to the Missionaries several valuable and persevering helpers, one of whom is in holy orders, and acts as pastor to the native flock at Umritsur, while others help in schools or itinerate with the Missionary. In short, the leaven has been introduced into the lump, small indeed in bulk, but genuine in quality, and, by the blessing of God, it will work.

Our most central station for the upper portion of the Punjab is Umritsur; for the lower portion of the province, where the rivers converge to the Punjnad, Mooltan. Peshawur and Dehra Ismael Khan are frontier stations, both commanding the passes which, through the Pathan and Belooch tribes, open into Affghanistan.

Umritsur constitutes a most important centre for Missionary action. It is situated in that division of the Punjab which, with the exception of Jullundur, is the most densely populated. There are five districts in the Lahore division—Lahore, Umritsur, Goondaspoor, Sealkote, Goojranwalla. Of these, Sealkote has a population, according to the last census, of 475 to the square mile; Goondaspoor, 470; Umritsur, 436. In this division, moreover, is to be found an unusually large proportion of that section of the population to which our attention ought to be specially directed—the Sikhs—there being within its limit not less than 200,000 Sikhs. It must be remembered that the Sikhs, notwithstanding the supremacy which they have exercised, and the prestige which has attached to them, constitute, after all, but a fraction of the Punjab population, the calculation being that the total of Sikhs is not more than 500,000. They require attention; first, because of their manliness of character, so that they frankly avow their convictions, and, if brought under the influence of Christianity, appear well adapted to supply a valuable native agency; and, secondly, because Sikhism is dying out. The British conquest broke the power, not only of the Sikh rule, but of the Sikh creed. Other religious systems are still vigorous enough to proselyte, and aware that the Sikh religion is dead, they come like vultures to feed upon the carcase. It is astonishing how many native itinerators are at work in the Manjha, diligently endeavouring to gain Sikhs over to some of the various forms of Hinduism. The old Sikhs are dying out; the new Sikhs initiated are but few; the children of Sikhs become Hindus. Thus they lapse back to their original root; for Sikhism rose out of Hinduism, and to this it is disposed to return. Precisely at such a juncture Christianity, in its Missionary action, is providentially introduced into the land, in order to prevent such an

* See "Mullens' Ten Years in India," p. 93.

issue. As yet, however, little has been done. Two years ago, the Rev. W. Keene expressed, at the Punjab Missionary Conference, his conviction that at that time not more than sixty Sikhs had been baptized. The character of Sikh converts is thus stated by him—"They are docile, easily attached, out-spoken, and warm-hearted. They are not generally so quick and intelligent as the Mohammedan and Hindu converts, but they are pains-taking and anxious to learn." We must, then, awake to the importance of the crisis. It is an opportunity which will soon have passed away, requiring a strong Mission and energetic effort to use it while it lasts. The Sikhs present a glorious field of operation, and it is indeed surprising that from among the Christian men of England there are not more volunteers for this service.

Our staff of Missionaries at Umritsur is at present reduced to three, who, with such native help as they can obtain, are thus placed in the midst of a division comprising a population of 3,458,694, the city population *per se* being not less than 122,184. Within its limits, besides Umritsur and Lahore, there are 6 towns, containing more than 10,000 and less than 50,000 inhabitants; 11 containing more than 5000, and less than 10,000; 436 with more than 1000, and less than 5000; and besides these, 4273, containing less than 1000.

Besides Umritsur, another centre of operation amongst the Manjha Sikhs has been formed at Narowal, some few miles distant from the capital. Here, residing in their own homes, there is a little flock of Christians, of some position among their countrymen. A native catechist, Paulus, is at present in charge, but a Missionary bungalow has been erected, and we hope soon to hear of its being occupied by a European Missionary.

For so extensive a sphere of labour, and with so few Missionaries, but one mode of operation is available—that of itineration; and perhaps it is well that we are forced away from centralization, and constrained to adopt this, for it is the most effectual. Mr. Keene and Mr. Brown have both been employed in this way, and we have their journals and reports before us, from which we would select some few extracts calculated to inform our readers as to the nature of the work, and thus draw forth interest and sympathy on behalf of those who, in these far-off lands, are bearing the heat and burden of the day. Perhaps, too, there might be some who, as they read, will feel it to be a personal reproach that there are so few in a field where so much may be done, and who will find it impossible to get rid of this feeling of self-reproach in any other way than by offering themselves for the work. We find Mr. Keene, shortly after the Lahore Conference, starting in itineration from Attari, a railway station mid-way between Lahore and Umritsur. This tour lasted forty-nine days. "Nine times," observes Mr. Keene, "I struck my tents, while my native brethren and myself visited 105 villages, sometimes on foot, generally on horseback, in the time specified." In the heart of the Manjha, surrounded by the villages of the Sikh Jats, he found himself welcomed by the various classes. Such was the preponderance of Sikhs, that, during the whole tour, only two Mohammedan villages were visited. At a village, Gidari Bhagyari, he found in a dharmsala an old fakir, whom he had met on a former occasion, and to whom he had given a copy of Barth's "Bible Stories" in Gurmukhee. This the old man had read through several times, and now he received a Gospel.

In the Punjab Conference, held two years ago, D. F. McLeod, Esq., C.B., suggested that attention should be particularly directed to the devotees and separatists that are to be met with throughout India. He referred to the fact that one of the members of the Conference had himself met with a sect which acknowledged and used the Bible as their book of devotion, and he expressed his conviction that there are scattered throughout Hindustan many such sects of separatists similarly disposed. He then proceeded to observe—"I have often been inclined to think that these sects, scattered through the plains, and the aboriginal races, scattered through the hills, may be intended by the

Almighty as nuclei, round which it will be for us to build up a really indigenous evangelization; and, until very lately, I believe neither of these classes have received the attention which both seem to me to deserve at our hands." . . . . "I know of no class in India that seems to me so likely to afford men suitable for future pastors as the various tribes of religious devotees and separatists, who abound on all sides, especially those that have abandoned idolatry. Amongst these devotees, Mohammedan as well as Hindu, I believe two very different descriptions of votaries will be found; one, those who adopt the mendicant's garb, as a cloak for idleness and profligacy of every description; the other, men weary of the world, or disgusted with the priesthood and the absurdities of a false religion, and searching for something which shall give peace to their souls. To this last section belonged Nanak, Kabir, and other founders of sects professing various forms of Deism; and to the same appears to me to belong the Ramaya, now settled at Chakkia, under the auspices of the Sigra Missionaries."

Referring to the report of the Rev. J. M. Brown, we find that on one occasion, being unable, from the press of other engagements, to go out himself, he sent out two of his Christians on itineration.

Edward and Sadiq, two Christians, went out in December, returning in February. Unable to go myself on account of station duties, I sent out the two Christians I had then in my care. They returned with a good report, and I trust their work has not been unproductive of good, sent forth as it has been in faith with prayer. They preached freely, no man hindering, and were heard gladly; going more than fifty miles distance from Umritsur, and returning by Narowal in time to attend the large yearly mela held there, having sold some rupees' worth of the Holy Scriptures and other religious books.

We find Mr. Brown on one occasion at Dehra Nanak, where the descendants of Nanak reside. Of his reception in this place he says—

Feb. 13, 1865: Dehra Nanak—People in my tent all day. During my stay I gave new books to all who could show any which they had received before. One showed me a large portion of the Bible in Gurmukhi, given by Colonel —— many years ago. Some of the people are anxious for an English school The place is about thirty miles from Umritsur, in a straight line. Visitors crowding the catechist's tent all day. When here with Mr. Bruce, in the spring of 1861, the people could not be persuaded to buy a single book scarcely.

The Gurdaspore district had particularly attracted Mr. Brown's attention, and he was anxious to traverse it with itinerations. From Narowal, therefore, he advanced into the Shikargarh portion of it, accompanied by three native brethren, Elias, Sadiq, the second son of Paulus, the aged catechist at Narowal, and John.

The mode of proceeding is thus stated—

While it continued hot in the middle of the day I generally went to two or three villages in the morning, and two or three in the evening, and sent John and Sadiq together to two villages morning and evening. Returning to my camp this evening I found it all illuminated, it being the time of the Dewali mela—the favourite season for the Sikhs to make a pilgrimage to Umritsur. The Diwali is the festival of lamps. The pilgrimage to Umritsur this year threatened to be something more than common, if the reports which got about are to be relied on. Ram Singh, the leader of the movement, was prevented from paying his respects to the Sikh temple, by being officially detained on the other side the river Bias, and several of his followers were well taken care of by the police till the festival was over. An incarnation from the east is expected to bring deliverance to the Sikhs, and the man alluded to above, according to the report of the Loodiana Mission, probably thought, since he bore the name of Ram Singh, that he must be the expected avatar.

The numbers who gathered round him at the different addresses may be collected from the following paragraph—

Dec. 5—Marched to Nyna Kot. The Gospel has frequently been preached at this place. It lies on the high road from Sealkote to the hills close to Trimmee Ghât, the spot where Nicholson, with his column, marching from Umritsur to Gurdaspore (forty-four miles) in one night, cut a large body of rebels to pieces. Round about this town there are villages in numbers. The people listened attentively in the bazaar. The village audiences now begin to be very large. Seldom less than sixty or a hundred come together, the chief part of their field work being over.

Dec. 8—Marched to Iklaspur. This was our first halting-place last year, when commencing this village to village itineration. In the evening, at one of the villages, I had a very large congregation of full 150 men, women, and children, owing to a wedding-feast that was going on. I told them the parable of the prodigal son. Amongst the villages preached in the next day was Buqa. I recollect failing to reach it last year. About 200 people came together and heard what I had to say.

Mr. Brown then refers to some of the native itinerators, who, taking advantage of the relaxed state of the Sikh system, and the little hold it has upon its followers, are perambulating the country to make disciples—

Dec. 31—One of my native brethren met the Rattar Chattar Maulavi yesterday. He is well known round about, and has a very great name amongst the people. They were flocking in bands to pay their respects to him. His name is Imam ali Shah, and he lives near Baba naull ka Dehra, keeping open house, when at home, for all who like to come. To-day I met Bhagwan Das, of the Ram Das Math, or college, like Imam ali Shah, going from the village to visit, receiving the homage of his disciples, and their gifts; and two days afterwards another great man, whose name I have not noted, from Ramnagar, on the Chenab, who appeared very intelligent, taking my side against a Mussulman disputant. I have alluded to these to show that we are not the only aggressors, the only itinerators, even in this district, during the cold season. I have already alluded to Ram Singh and his new sect of followers.

We shall now run on with such extracts as we think embody points of interest—

Jan. 6, 1864: Gamraula—I have got back into the Shikargarh pergunnah to-day. At one of the villages a Lambardaress showed me no small politeness. I found afterwards that the Lambardar, her husband, was dead, and, in the absence of her son, she undertook to officiate, a more pleasant work than most widows in this country perform, and will continue to do so till the elevating and saving power of Christianity has rent the land in twain, severing living humanity from the shackles of a dark superstition and a living death. It was a new sight to see a woman holding my horse—a new sound to hear a woman arguing the question of salvation through the Saviour, acknowledging her guilt as a sinner, but also maintaining her confidence in Mohammed as a vicarious absolver.

Jan. 9—Marched to Fugwal. At one of the villages which I preached in to-day I had just mounted my horse, when a man came after me, and asked for a Gurmukhi book which contained any thing about Jesus. I replied, "How do you know that there are Gurmukhi books which speak about Jesus?" He answered, "At a certain village (Dynot) a man has got some." On reaching the village of Fugwal—a very small place, which I should not have gone to in preference to any other, only I went to it last year, and it breaks the march better—I was at once beset with visitors. One man stayed with me several hours, showing me some Gurmukhi books he had got last year, and evincing a knowledge of their contents, well borne out by their worn appearance. He also brought his two brothers. These people turn out to be of the same caste as the man who asked for the Gurmukhi book. Their chief man's name is F——. He is of the weaver caste, and a Kabir Panthi. He and his brothers eat my bread. I have asked him to come with me and learn all about Christ, and afterwards to return and tell his disciples. His disciples are scattered over a great number of villages.

Jan. 11—In the direction of some of the villages where F——'s disciples live. At one of these a man seemed to listen very attentively. I asked him what he thought of Christ. The crowd said, "Take him with you;" and to him, "Go and be a Christian." He followed me about two miles to Dynot, where I found G——, the man with the Gurmukhi books, very ill. He showed me what he had, and said he had got them from one of the Sealkote brethren. This man believes in the Lord Jesus Christ as the Saviour. I would fain hope, from what I have seen, that there is a movement going on amongst the weaver Kabir Panthis round about, and amongst the Chamars.

Jan. 13 : Tera—Met another Kabir Panthi. He came from a distant village for books. I told him the Lord's Prayer, and made him repeat it after me.

The Kabir Panthi's history Professor Wilson has given, in his work on the Hindus. Kabir was a weaver, said to have been found, when a child, floating on a lotus in a pond near Benares, by the wife of a weaver named Nima. He flourished about the beginning of the fifteenth century, and succeeded to the estates and doctrine of Ramanaud. Kabir's successor was Nana Shah. Hindus and Mussulmans alike claim him for a teacher, and vie in honouring the resting spot of his remains. It is no part of the religion of the followers (Kabir Panthi) of Kabir to worship any deity, or to observe any rights or ceremonials. They render their homage chiefly in chanting hymns, exclusively to the invisible Kabir. They admit but one God, the creator of the world; and, in opposition to the Vedanta notions of the absence of every quality and form, they assert that he has a body formed of the five elements of matter, and that he has a mind endowed with the three gunas, or qualities of being. Of course, of infallible purity and irresistible power, he is free from the defects of human nature, and can assume what particular shape he will: in all other respects he does not differ from man, and the pure man, the Sadh of the Kabir sect, is his living resemblance. The essence of all religion is to know Kabir in his real form.

The Kabir Panthis, whom I have met, seem very simple and well-disposed. I could have wished to leave a Christian amongst them, but have none to spare.

Jan. 18—Marched to Bambiyal in the Pathankot Tihsil. In leaving the Shikargarh pergunnah I find that, through the good providence of God, we have been able to reach 491 villages in that thickly-populated district. My map exhibits sixty-one which we did not reach. We have missed some we preached in last year, while others missed then have been reached now. This gives 552 villages in all. I am told, however, that there are 739 in the district. I cannot help thinking there is an error in the calculation. I know almost every foot of ground contained in its 500 square miles of surface, and am able to see from the map each village we preached in. Our reception has, on the whole, been very favourable, and we may hope, under the divine blessing, for good and blessed results.

Jan. 19—The pergunnah we are passing through is not a large one. Being situated near the foot of the hill, and on lower ground than Shikargarh, it is full of rivers and nullahs, and the people lie in scattered, thinly (apparently so) populated hamlets, and are eminently stupid, even when making every allowance for my own inaptitude at speaking and understanding their tongue.

Jan. 20—Marched to Ragubili towards Umritsur, working down the hither side of the Ravee to several small villages in the morning, and to others in the evening. At one of these latter ones (Ghila Chuh) I found myself able to speak very fluently, and not at all tired or weary in proclaiming the word of my blessed Lord and Master to-day. The people in this last village were extremely attentive (chiefly Sikhs), one of whom was almost persuaded to return with me.

Jan. 23—Marched yesterday and to-day. Encamped at Dostpur. Spent Sunday at Dostpur: went to three villages in the afternoon, all within a mile of my tent; and as it will give an illustration of my plan of working, I will here relate what occured. At the first I sent my salaam, as usual, to the Lambardar, or headman, and having found out the dharmsala where the people collect, asked for a charpoy, or bedstead, and sat down under the shade of the village pepul-tree. In about ten minutes I had got a good congregation—between twenty and thirty persons—one of them evincing, as is generally the case, more intelligence than the rest, and evidently appearing more anxious too. I had spoken for about half an hour, and arose to go. The people, however, requested me to stay longer. The man alluded to said the people were very hard of understanding, and that I had better stay a week or so, and then some impression might be made on them. In about another half hour I got up to go again. They still wished me to remain: this I said I could not do, as an east wind had begun to blow, and I should get ill. They then assisted me to the village hut close by, and we all went in, and sat down there for a long time. The native brethren with me mark a very friendly feeling in the villages (Gurdaspore Pergunnah) we are now visiting. I asked the man in the first village to-day if he would come and be my guest, and learn about Jesus, in order to be able to tell the village people, since I could not well stay so long as ten days at his village. Dostpur is about forty miles from Umritsur.

Feb. 10—We are now itinerating in the Gurdaspore Pergunnah, and marching along a line parallel almost to the route we followed when leaving the Shikargarh district for Umritsur. This time towards the hills again, and we are in the very heart of Sikh hamlets.

Feb. 18—Marched to Lakhowal. At one of the villages to-day I met a respectable man, who said he had several books, obtained some years before at Gurdaspore. He came to my tent in the evening, bringing some of them. I gave him others.

Feb. 29—At Gunja, a village on my way, the good people requested me to remain longer, which I did, and they gave me a rupee: this, having touched it as usual, I requested the Lambardar to remove; but he said, "No, you are a padre, and it is right that padres should be cared for by us." And, after a long talk, finding I could not refuse their gift, I took the rupee, saying that I would distribute it in alms. At a village in the afternoon I met two respectable Sikhs, who were shortly joined by a Nanak padre on an itinerating tour. He had come from Umritsur, and knew about the Saviour, having often heard the word preached in the bazaars, naming Mr. Keene as the Missionary he knew, and mentioning a favourite preaching spot and resort of his. He endeavoured to maintain some long and foolish arguments, and afterwards followed me to another village, when I got him to tell the people what I had already said to him. I afterwards invited him to come and live with me, and be a padre of Jesus Christ. "We are both padres: live in my tent, and eat my salt, and ride my horse, and go with me every day to tell the people about the Lord Jesus Christ." Of course he promised to do so. Not yet, however, not yet: it is too soon to expect to have a half-naked mendicant, with a great coronet of plaited hair, riding side by side with one, and preaching Jesus. Still fakirs have the real Missionary element within them, and I am only happy to bow to the long experience and sage council of our beloved Financial Commissioner, in his Essay on a Native Pastorate, read at the Lahore Conference in 1862-63, when pointing them out as the class from which we may hope and long for our evangelists and pastors. For we must not be led away by the view that they are all of them most wicked and depraved. Doubtless it is the case with a great majority, but there are many really in earnest after the one and the true, the real and the unseen, and the heavenly and undefiled. Oh that they might find the Lord Jesus Christ to be the way, the truth, and the life! I have omitted to mention, in its proper place, that an inquirer from Suhba Singh ka Qila, one march from Narowal, joined me at the beginning of the month. He appears very anxious to learn, and very willing to do any work that I may have. He has left his mother at Umritsur, and is himself a shawlmaker by trade, a Mussulman by religion, and a partial Cashmeree in tongue.

March 10 — To Undouri, a large Hindu town in the Kangra district, which I visited two years ago. The people remembered my visit, and one brought me a book I had given him. Another told me I had given him a book about Jesus, which was very good, and it also told him the right way to live. The people did not flock so much to my preaching, but the boys were very attentive. It being a holiday at the school, I got into a portion of a temple, and made them all sit round about while I spoke. In the evening to Mirthal bazar. One man did his best to stop my preaching, and partially succeeded. He turned out to be the school moulwee.* We have now left the Pathantot Pergunnah. It extends over a surface of 167 square miles. We have preached in nearly every village. I am now marching down the Gurdaspore district, which lies between the Bias and the high road. Spent Sunday at Sirkia, going in the morning to a village where there was a math. I called on the Mohant, but he was away. His followers showed me no small kindness, and offered to put me up when I came that way again. I preached to them in the court-yard of the math, and gave them some books.

March 14—Hitherto the native brethren have worked heartily, readily, and willingly: in truth they are getting strong on the whole, and seem to take a real and lively interest in it. Paulus, who is always ailing at Narowal, confesses that his bodily strength has been wonderfully renewed, and finds no difficulty in preaching in four villages daily, which generally includes seven or eight miles riding; and sometimes, when I go off in an evening on foot he comes after me.

March 16—Reached Kanowar. Sent Edward and Sadiq off in a slightly different direction. They were absent four days. This is my third visit here. I found the Brahmin, Hai Dyal, to whom I had lent a Hindu Testament last year. He had been reading it, and knew a great deal of its contents. He said that he understood the Gospel, and believed that Jesus Christ was the Son of God, the Saviour of the world. He had been making inquiries for me whenever he met any Sahib. I had a large congregation in the bazaar. Hai Dyal offered to accompany me, having influence with the people, and to show me how willingly they received the truth of the book which I had given him. One evening he took me in his pant, on a

---

* This class of men are the chief disputants and principal opposers of the Missionary.—(ED.)

jhil close by, and we conversed together about the Redeemer. He is one of those who seem not far from the kingdom of God. I promised to send him a Satmat Nirapan, which I have since done. In connexion with my visit to Kanowar two years ago, I may mention that, while at Sakia, a bricklayer came to me for some Punjabee books. He said I had given him the Psalms in Punjabee at that time, and he and his family read a portion of them daily.

March 23—On my road to Sugovindpur two villages were inhabited by Sikhs. At the first of these (Kathan) one of the men went some way with me, conversing as we went, and said, "I believe, as you say, that Jesus is the Son of God, and that I must believe in Him, and seek to have repentance for my sins." I made him repeat the Lord's Prayer, and promise to worship the Saviour. At a second village the Lambardar offered to accompany me to a third, whose headman was very sick. It is a mark of these people that they are always ready to let you know when any one is sick. I found the sick Lambardar under the treatment of a native doctor. A fine lot of Sikhs came together. I told them, as I had often told others, that my own impression, from reading the life of Nanak, is, that if he had lived now, and heard as much as they did of the Lord Jesus Christ, he would at once believe, and therefore it was their duty to do so too. Arrived at Sugovindpur about eleven o'clock, having started at sunrise. Ganga Rawi, the old Brahmin alluded to in the last report, is still alive. He called on me in the course of the day. Other people from this city tell me that he wishes to receive the Saviour. He stayed with me continually till we left. I pray the Lord Jesus to draw him unto Himself. If spared to lie down and die quietly on his bed, I should not be at all surprised by his sending to be baptized. Many called to see me—old acquaintances — expressing their joy. I would fain hope and earnestly pray the Lord would begin a work in this place, the people are so evidently well disposed to hear the word.

May 4—In bringing these journal extracts to a conclusion, I am further conscious how little they contain of an exciting nature: no wonderful deliverances, no providential escapes, and no extraordinary exploits, nothing of the romance of Missionary labours; and many will say, on perusing them, very little to encourage. They contain enough, however, of material which, if worked by a better hand, might be interesting to those who love so much to hear what Missionary labourers are doing in various parts of the Mission field. As a simple record of an attempt to carry out the late lamented and beloved Ragland's plan of working, they may not, to some extent as least, be of an unattractive nature.

And, 1. I would notice, that with all the trouble and labour of continual marches, my native brethren, Paulus, Edward, (catechists), and Sadiq, Daniel, John, Nazrat, Allah (readers), have striven to work willingly as unto the Lord. What with striking our tents in the early cold morning, then preaching, and often arriving after all before our baggage, and getting no food till late in the day, they have never complained to me.

As often as possible they went two and two, which is much the best plan, as one helps the other.

Every morning and evening we had service: and while my tent was open at all times for them to come and read, or ask questions, yet my teaching was chiefly at the morning and evening services. In the mornings we have gone through the Psalms, with Mr. Owen's, of Allahabad, Commentary. They have lasted the whole journey. In the evenings I have taken them through St. Matthew's Gospel. I am in hopes that each of them can give a satisfactory answer to any Mussulman respecting it. This Gospel sufficed for our evening expositions. On Sundays I have taken St. John's Gospel, and we have got to the end of the eleventh chapter. It has thus been my object to keep up a sort of Scripture class in camp; and though it has required preparation and study, it has been of equal benefit to myself.

2. For the first two months I had a Christian colporteur with me. I am sorry not to have kept an account of the number of books parted with, but the total sum received has been about ten rupees. Of course a large number was distributed gratis, and to all who could show any which they had received on any former occasion.

3. When time allowed it I made a point of sending for or going to the village school, and, after a short examination, to give them books.

4. My plan, when reaching any village, has been to send a salaam to the Lambardar, or headman, or to find out his house, and then adjourn with him to the village dharmsala, or gati, a pepul-tree, or musjid, and then wait for the people to collect. My seat has more frequently been the root of a tree or straw matting, unless the villagers brought a charpoy (bedstead). The people seemed always glad to welcome me, though an utter stranger, in the majority of cases.

5. The avidity with which the people receive and read our books is remarkable. A large number were sold or otherwise disposed of. We realized ten rupees during the itineration from this source. I really think that they value the books. Our thanks are indeed due to the Loodiana Mission.

Such is a specimen of the itineration which is going forward in the Punjab. It is as yet but the sowing time; but how important this, for the divine seed is incorruptible, and, if the sowing precede, the harvest in God's time will surely follow. But how marvellous is it not that the vast territory of the Punjab should thus be open to the labours of Christian Missionaries, and that they can itinerate amongst its population, not only with safety, but with a welcome. And how many are there not that appear to be thoughtful, inquiring, buying Christian books, reading them in private, and able to produce them on the next visit to the Missionary, whole, but well used. We see why England has been permitted so extensive an empire. Where English rule prevails, there is room for the entrance of the Gospel. To our Missionaries in the Punjab we would apply the words of the prophet— Blessed are ye that sow beside all waters, that send forth thither the feet of the ox and the ass!"

OUR MISSION IN VOHIMARE, MADAGASCAR.

WHEN British Columbia was discovered to be a gold-producing country it began forthwith to be diligently explored, and journeys were made into the interior with much difficulty, and no slight amount of danger, in order to ascertain its capabilities, and the places where the industry of the miner was most likely to be repaid.

Many of these explorations have been published, and, no doubt, have been perused with much attention by those who were interested in that particular matter on which they were intended to throw light.

We enter new Mission fields in search of that which is more precious than gold. We seek to rescue immortal souls from the degradation of sin, in which they have been lying, and to present them to the Lord, that in them He may be glorified. But, like the miner, we must explore, in order that we may understand how we may set to work with most prospect of success. We have to acquaint ourselves with the people, their character, superstitions, prejudices, habits. We must ascertain how the gold lies, whether imbedded in the quartz, or deposited on the bars of the rivers; whether the return will be eventually rich, although requiring the expenditure of much previous labour, or whether it be only surface gold, easily obtained, but likely to be soon exhausted. With some races the Missionary process is slow, with others there is more rapid developement. Thus we must also have our explorations and prospectings.

Such we conceive to be the position of our two Missionaries on the north-east coast of Madagascar. They are, so to speak, prospecting—examining the country and its people, and endeavouring to ascertain where and how they may, with most prospect of success, settle down to Missionary work. In this initiative state of things their journals surely will be as interesting to us as reports of exploring parties to gold speculators; and therefore we publish them as they arrive. We shall thus best excite interest on behalf of Madasgascar and its people, and obtain for our Missionaries that support of earnest prayer which is a felt thing with them in a distant land. The annexed journal is by Mr. Campbell—

Nov. 17, 1864—In the evening I attended the Governor's dinner, which was served up at half-past six o'clock. Covers were laid for twenty persons, and that number sat down. There were sixteen men and four women—the Governor's wife, and three others. The plates were nicely arranged, with a glass, knife and fork, and spoon, beside each. There were several bottles of beer, claret, and rum arranged along the middle of the table, and four candlesticks. There were two long bottles, which were placed upon plates to prevent the grease from spoiling the table-cloth. The first dish was soup, then beefsteak; afterwards roast beef; next, curry and rice; then stewed fowls; and, lastly, cutlets. As I was pretty hungry I enjoyed a little of each of these dishes. Before dinner and after it there was a toast drunk to the Queen of Madagascar. It was drunk with the greatest solemnity, while the troops outside presented arms at the word of command from one of the officers, who bawled out to them from the dinner table. The other toasts drunk were, "The Governor and his wife," "Captain Rosalie, of the 'King Radama,'" and "The two Missionaries." The toast-drinking was not such an extensive business as it is at home, as one small bottle of beer was quite enough for eight or ten persons, and the same might be said of the claret. The Governor is a very abstemious person, and drinks scarcely any thing but water. Mr. Maundrell and I were placed by the Governor at his right hand, while the captain of the "King Radama" and a French gentleman were placed at his left. During the whole time we were sitting at dinner the band strummed away outside, and I felt it to be the greatest relief imaginable when the fiddlers stopped for a moment to rosin their bows. At nine o'clock the Governor suggested that it was time to retire, which we did, after spending a very pleasant evening.

Nov. 18—Engaged in writing letters, and making preparations for living as comfortably as possible in our new home, as the "King Radama" leaves in the morning, and we shall be obliged to look after ourselves when she goes.

Nov. 19—The Governor sent for us this morning in order to bid us good bye. He also visited us as he passed our house, the soldiers drawing up before the door. He goes to prepare a house for us at Amboanio, and will send for us and our baggage in three or four days. In the evening I visited a number of houses, reading to the people the word of God, and striving to explain it: they listened with great attention, and thanked me greatly for my visit. I paid a visit to the Romish catechist, and found him reading the Malagasy Testament which I gave him the other day. He seems to love it, and used one of the strongest words in the language to express his delight at having it. He promised to come to our service to-morrow. May the reading of the word of God lead him out of the mazes of Romanism into the freedom of the religion of Jesus Christ!

Nov. 20: *Lord's-day*—Our first Sunday, I may say, in Madagascar, for although we were here last Sunday, yet we had no house, and were living on board ship. At eleven A.M. I sent my servant round to inform the people that there would be a service in our house at twelve o'clock noon. At that hour about twenty-four women, six men, and a number of children, came, and seated themselves very quietly upon the floor. We had a regular Church-of-England service in Malagasy. Mr. Maundrell read a portion of the morning service and the Litany in his surplice, while I preached in my gown. We began with a hymn: Charles Le Bon and I responded, as the people had no Prayer-books, nor could they have read them if they had had them. I lent the Romish catechist a Prayer-book, and set him beside Charles: he joined in the service, and expressed himself much pleased. He told me that he should like some instruction from me, which I promised to give him daily. Who knows whether this man may not do a great work among his countrymen when he returns to Nossibé. As I did not feel competent to preach a regular sermon in Malagasy, and as I did not wish to be stumbling and stuttering, I thought that the best thing I could do would be to give them Christ's Sermon on the Mount, which was listened to with as much attention as if they had been used to such things. I interspersed a few remarks in the course of my reading, and tried to illustrate the sayings of Christ by something which was familiar to them. We have reason to be thankful to God for this beginning of his work.

In the afternoon I sat down in our verandah, and seeing two men sitting at the door of a house opposite, I called them, and read Revelation xxi., about the new Jerusalem. Before I had finished, half a dozen persons were round me. I spoke to them for about half an hour, and then retired, leaving them to think about what I had said to them. In the evening I visited several houses, and read and spoke to the people. In one house I found half a dozen young men, and read to them Matthew ii., concerning the birth of Christ. One of them, who sat by me, repeated and explained to his fellows every word that I said. They were pleased when I told them that I had left home, friends, and country, for the sole purpose of preaching Jesus to the people of Madagascar. It is my firm belief that this people will yet be brought to a knowledge of Christ. May the Lord hasten that glorious time!

After dinner Mr. Maundrell and I sang some Missionary hymns, which reminded us of our Sunday evenings at dear old Islington.

As we sang my favourite, "O'er the gloomy hills of darkness," I thought of poor Madagascar.

Nov. 21—Rose early this morning, and about the first thing that I saw was the Romish catechist sitting at his door reading his Malagasy Testament. This seems to be almost his constant occupation since he received it. He came to me for instruction, and I spoke to him for an hour and a half on the commandments, drawing his particular attention to the second, which I showed him was omitted in his catechism. I explained to him the reason of this, which appeared to satisfy him. I also spoke to him on saint-worship and Mariolatry, and caused him to read to me Revelation xxii. 8, 9, at which he was quite astonished. I told him that the priest at Nossibé would burn his Testament, as the Romish Church does not like it, because it exposes her own departure from its doctrines. He replied "that he would guard it jealously, and keep it safely in his box; and that he would read it night and morning to his wife and friends."

In the afternoon and evening I visited, as usual, a number of houses. The people always listen most attentively, and I hardly ever fail to find one person at least who repeats and explains every thing that I say.

In my walk I met with two Sakalava fishermen, who were arranging their canoe, in order that it might be ready to start early in the morning. I saw one of them mixing something, and asked him what it was. He replied, *fanafody*, "medicine." Having asked him what it was made of, he said, "sand," and showed me how he made it. He had a small piece of sandstone, which he scraped with a piece of iron, mixing the scrapings with a little water, until he had made it into a paste on the stone. Then, taking his forefinger, he dipped into the paste, putting some on the forehead, temples, and neck of his companion; then, holding forth the stone, the man whom he had anointed licked off some of the paste, and swallowed it. The remainder he put upon the bows of his canoe and on his spears. I asked him why he did it, and he told me that it was to enable him to catch many fish. He showed me other things about his canoe which he called medicine—little pieces of wood, bones, and beads strung together, not very unlike the old rags and rotten bones which the Church of Rome calls relics. I told the man that his boat did not require these things, as it could not be sick like a man. He laughed at this, and took all my remarks in good part.

May this people soon be led from their vain superstitions by the light of the Gospel of Jesus Christ!

Nov. 22—This morning I gave a Sakalava who is able to read, a New Testament, on condition that he would give me a Romish book he has in exchange for it. I told him that the book which he had contained many falsehoods, but that the contents of the Bible were written by God, and that, therefore, every word of it was true. I have been studying the language the greater part of the morning, and visiting in the evening. The people are always pleased to see me, except perhaps the little children, some of whom cry tremendously, and run away, hiding their faces in their mother's lambas. If I happen to touch one of these fearful ones, they yell, as if my hand were a red-hot poker.

Some time ago, the Sakalavas stole about forty bullocks from some of the people who live here, about thirty of which, I have been told, belonged to the woman from whom we have rented our house. Her bullocks were found yesterday in the forest, and brought home to her. She is now living in a house opposite to ours. This evening about forty or fifty women came before her door, and began singing lustily and clapping their hands, the noise of their hands keeping time with their voices. They stood in this way for about an hour, and then sat down, when rum was served out to them by the mistress of the house. They seemed to relish this after their singing, and sang for about half an hour longer; then, rising up, they went to the enclosure where the bullocks are kept, and sang there for a short time; after which they dispersed. They came, according to the custom of the country, to rejoice with their neighbour, who had found that which she had lost. It reminded me forcibly of the parables of the lost sheep and the lost piece of money.

I gave the Romish catechist, whose name is Jean Louis, a lesson on Christian doctrine today. He is not the only gainer by these lessons, as he is well up in Sakalava and the other Malagasy dialects, and I get him to give me the Sakalava equivalents for Hova words. The Sakalava dialect is as different from the Hova as is that of the *patois* of Yorkshire from the language of the best society in London. Jean Louis tells me that he is afraid that his superior, the Père of Nossibé, will be displeased with him, because he has made no converts since he came here. If he should be displeased with him he says that he will return here again, as his mother is in this place. He also told us that he never saw the whole New Testament until I gave him one, and the French priests only gave the people little bits of it, and kept back the best part.

Nov. 23—Studying the language during the

earlier part of the day, and in the afternoon had a long conversation with Jean Louis. I gave him a good deal of instruction in doctrine, and marked with a pencil in his Malagasy Testament a great number of texts, which strike at the very roots of the Romish system. I got him to read them to me; after which I read and explained them fully, showing him how antagonistic to the word of God were the doctrines and practices of Romanism. Though a comparatively young man, he has seen a good deal of the world. He has been at each of the Comoro islands, at Seychelles and Mozambique, as well as at St. Mary's and other places about Madagascar. We have just heard that we are to start for Amboanio in the morning. "Lord, make our way plain before our faces!"

Nov. 24—Began very early this morning to make preparations for our departure for Amboanio. At six A.M. a number of men came to carry our luggage; and, as it had not been packed, we had to begin at once and pack up what we really wanted, leaving the heaviest of our things behind us, and a servant to look after them. Twenty men carried what we wanted, besides eight more for our filanzanas. We started, without breakfast, at nine A.M., and were jogged along for about an hour, when our bearers rested under a tree, where we ate a biscuit and a piece of cold meat, which we had brought with us. We were then carried along till we came to a Frenchman's, called Guinet, which we reached at eleven A.M. As he had heard that we were coming, he had a good breakfast spread out for us on a mat, under the shade of a tree. As we were hungry, we did justice to his oysters and his curry. When we had finished we rested in his hut till nearly two P.M., when we pushed on to our destination. We had to cross a broad and, apparently, deep river, called Mauambery, and there we found a canoe, which brought us all over in a very short time. We went on for about half an hour after crossing the river; and when we reached the brow of a high hill, Amboanio burst on our view. It is built upon the top of a little hill, and is not unlike pictures of Antananarivo which I have seen, only on a very small scale. When we got near the town four officers met us, and bade us welcome, after which we pushed on, and were carried to the door of our house. It is a fine house of the kind, built entirely of raffia. It has only one room, about thirty feet long by about eighteen broad, with one door, and three small windows, *i.e.* holes in the sides of the house, with shutters to fill them up. It pleases us very much, and will do for us well until we can get a better one. The Governor's wife and several others came to bid us welcome, and also to tell us that His Excellency would be with us shortly. In about an hour he appeared, accompanied by about twenty soldiers, and as many officers, preceded by a fiddle and drum band. The soldiers presented arms, while the band struck up "God save the Queen," at which the Governor and officers took off their hats. When I heard our own national anthem played in this distant land my heart almost danced with joy. I of course took off my hat; but it was our own Victoria—whom may God preserve!—that I was thinking about all the time. After the usual salutations the Governor and all his officers came into our house, and sat and talked with us for about two hours, during which time the band played *sans cesse*. When the officers left, the Governor, his wife, and the other Christians, remained behind. They had provided dinner for us, which was soon served up. Eight soldiers guarded the house while the Governor was in it—two at the door and two at each window—with guns and bayonets crossed. This is always done when the Governor enters a house. For so far we are well pleased; but we do not yet know whether we shall be permitted to remain here, as the Hovas must hear from Antananarivo before they can permit it.

The country through which we passed this morning was really beautiful. For about three miles the whole of the country to our left was a forest of large trees, while that to the right was hill and dale, covered with grass, upon which immense herds of cattle were grazing. It still reminded me of home scenery: it was altogether English. I saw nothing to make me think that I was not in England, except the black backs and curly hair of my bearers. There are none of those unhealthy swamps here which are no numerous on the coast in the southern part of the island. We only saw one lake of any consequence, which our bearers told us was *Rano Zanahary*, "Water of God," and that it was a kind of medicine. As soon as we had passed the trees on our left, the sea appeared, and we went almost parallel with it for about four miles. From this to Manambery, a distance of about three miles, the country was almost devoid of trees, but still beautiful. When we got up to the top of a hill, and looked back, the hills, mountains, valleys, and sea looked charming: my pen is quite unable to describe it. After crossing the river we had to ascend a pretty steep hill, after which we had a comparatively level road till we got to Amboanio.

It was my first ride, and I enjoyed it much. It was made of two pieces of wood, like shafts, with a piece of canvas fastened to each, upon which I sat. There was also a small piece of wood tied to the shafts with a cord, which made a kind of stirrup to put my feet on. I was very proud of my bearers, as they had carried Radama II. They sang, and ran along at a nice trot, which kept me laughing almost till I got to my destination. When they came to a sandy place, they cried out that it burned, and ran along quickly, until they got out of it. I felt it needful at times to be careful, as there was danger of being thrown upon the ground; but my bearers were as sure-footed as mules.

Nov. 25—Numbers of people called to visit us this morning, and we were obliged to talk with them for hours. This will help us much in the acquisition of the language, as we must listen to them, and answer all their inquiries. The Governor, having much business with his officers, was unable to visit us till late in the day; but he sent his wife to us in the morning, and she remained the greater part of the day, and saw that our dinner was properly cooked. In the afternoon the Governor came, with his officers, soldiers, and band. They called us out, and presented us with a fat little ox, in the name of Rasoherina Mpanjaka, for which we gave them our hearty *velomas*, "thanks."

The Governor, his wife, and four officers, dined with us, and His Excellency, at my suggestion, said grace, in Malagasy, in a most solemn and impressive manner.

We are not yet certain of being permitted to remain here, as the Hovas are very jealous of foreigners, especially Frenchmen. They are to hold a "kabary" on the subject to-morrow. May their conclusion be the right one!

Nov. 26—The officers, or "Manamboniahitra," as they are called, were engaged all day in debating the question, "Whether the two Missionaries should remain here, or at Hiarana, until the messengers which are being sent should return from Antananarivo?" We know not yet to what conclusion they have come; but we are inclined to think that we shall be permitted to remain where we are. We know that the Governor and one or two officers are our staunch friends; but if even one should obstinately refuse to sanction our remaining here, the chances are against us. The Governor sent a messenger to us this morning, requesting that, when he and the officers came, we should ask their permission to remain here for the present. I asked the officer, or aide-de-camp, what I should say to them, and wrote down with a pencil all that he told me; and when they came I read it out to them. They seemed perfectly satisfied, and nodded assent to every word, and when I had concluded, they shook hands with Mr. Maundrell and me, and went off to finish their deliberations. I am now under the impression that the best thing we could have done would have been to go to the capital first, and get permission from the queen to go wherever we pleased. It would have saved us from much present annoyance, and perhaps future also, for aught we know. We may have difficulty in getting ground to build houses, schools, and churches, when we want them, and unless a very satisfactory answer comes from the capital, one of us may have to go there yet.

The Governor, to show his respect for us, treated us to a Malagasy dance. In the afternoon he, and all his officers and guard, came, accompanied by nearly a hundred women, and almost the same number of men. They were all dressed in their holiday attire; and the different colours of their lambas had a very pleasing effect. They danced on the level ground opposite our house. In the first dance there were twenty women, in four rows of five each. They hardly moved their bodies, and only their feet very slightly: the chief motion was made by their hands. I had some difficulty in suppressing my laughter, but I succeeded, however. In the next dance there were twenty men and twenty women: they each had a pocket-handkerchief, with which they coupled themselves by one holding the end of that of the other, and with which they manœuvred in a very nice way. After this there were several other dances of a somewhat similar kind. Though I am, on the whole, opposed to dancing, yet I saw nothing objectionable in the spectacle which I have seen to-day.

In the evening we had a great dinner given to us; and as we are not permitted at present to enter the battery, it was served up in our house, or, I should say, in the house which the Governor has kindly lent us, until such time as he hears from the capital, when we hope to be permitted to build one for ourselves; and then we shall ask him to give us our present house for a school. As the dinner was a *fac-simile* of the one given to us at Hairana, it needs no description.

Nov. 27: *Lord's-day*—Almost as soon as we opened our door this morning the people came flocking in to us. One man, who came late last night to be taught reading, was about the first here this morning. I told him, if he came to me daily I should teach him; but, as this was Sunday, I could not begin to-day. He wished me to read to him. I complied with his request; but before I had finished reading about a dozen men were crowded around me, to whom I spoke for some time. One man I found was able to read well, and I therefore promised him a prayer-book.

We had no regular church service to-day; and I question whether we shall be able to have one for some time to come, as the Governor is afraid to take any decisive step until he hears from Queen Rasoherina.

The Governor came to us at about two o'clock, and remained with us till seven in the evening. The greater part of this time we sang hymns and chants, the string band leading us. Occasionally Mr. Maundrell electrified the natives by his performances on the harmonium. The only part of the church service which we had to-day was the Litany, to which the Governor, and all who were able to read, responded. His Excellency expressed his admiration of this part of our service.

We had a very long conversation with him on Acts xv. 29. He wished to know why Christians were to "abstain from things strangled, and from blood," especially the latter. We endeavoured to explain it to him by references to other parts of the Scriptures, especially 1 Cor. x., and also by telling him something of the characteristics of the ancient idolatries. It was a difficult business to explain all this in Malagasy; but I believe we succeeded in satisfying him. In speaking of the "Pilgrim's Progress," he told us that that book was the means of leading him to Christ. I was much pleased at hearing this, as I am much indebted to the same book for my own conversion to God.

Before we separated the Governor proposed that we should have prayer. I requested him to pray, and told him that I should conclude with the Lord's Prayer. He knelt down, and prayed in a most solemn manner before all his soldiers and attendants.

Nov. 28—The Manamboninahitra came to us this morning, and informed us that we might remain here until the messengers returned from the capital. As the greater part of our baggage is at Hiarana, Mr. Maundrell went down to see it packed, and will return to-morrow. I visited to-day most of the houses on one side of the town, and the people were pleased with the visit of the *Vazáha*, "European." I read and spoke to them a good deal, and came home very tired. After dinner the Governor's wife came, and brought me some little insects, which, she said, were good for eating. I had them cooked at once, and found them very nice. I did not much like their ugly appearance; but, when I tasted them, I forgot all about that.

She asked me to teach her to read, which I promised to do with pleasure. When she left, knowing that I was alone, she sent her minstrels to keep me company, and they played to me for about an hour, when I told them they might go. The Lord seems to be making our way plainer than it has been hitherto, although we shall not be able to do as much as we should like till the messengers return from Antananarivo.

Nov. 29—Visited many houses, and conversed much with the people to-day. I had a long visit myself also from the Governor and his wife. He showed me the letter which he had written to the Queen, requesting her permission to allow us to live here, and go wherever we please to preach the Gospel, and teach the people. It was signed by himself, the Manamboninahitra, and the chief judge. I gave the chief judge, whose name is Fojia, a New Testament some time ago, and I find that he reads it daily. Several of those who came to us to-day were much pleased when I told them that Matthew x. 28, "Fear not them which kill the body," &c., was a great comfort to the persecuted Christians in the days of Ranavalona. They read and repeated it often enough to have it by heart. One man drew my particular attention to Romans viii. from the 31st verse to the end. He appeared to think much of these precious verses. I was reminded at the same time of the words of an old Christian woman about this same chapter. "Oh," she said, "I love the 8th chapter of the Romans, for it begins with no condemnation, and ends with no separation."

Nov. 30—Had a most wonderful visit from the Governor and his wife to-day. They came before breakfast at 9 A.M., and did not leave till 8 o'clock P.M. I gave the Governor's wife her first lesson, which lasted for about three hours. I also had a good deal of conversation with the Governor himself, and with those who came to visit us. The Governor himself once knew a little English, but he has forgotten it; and he will much appreciate any lessons that we may be able to give him in that language. I stole out in the afternoon for about an hour, and visited a number of houses, and tried to teach the people a few simple truths, such as are taught to infant-school children at home. May the Lord open the hearts of this people to receive his own word!

Dec. 1—Visited for about four or five hours to-day the houses of the Sakalavas. They appear to be really a fine race, and many of them are anxious to learn. It is my earnest desire that this people should know the Gospel. They are perhaps the most numerous tribe in the whole country—almost twice as numerous as the Hovas. They are fine, tall, well-made fellows, and very brave. They might be called the Saxons of Madagascar, while the Hovas might be properly termed the Normans. If several of the Sakalavas were really converted and sent among their own people, blessed results might follow. I shall always keep this prominently in my mind while I am here. I hope to master the Sakalava dialect, and then itinerate amongst them. In all the houses which I visited to-day I received a hearty welcome: the people thanked me for my visit, and wished me to come to them again. The Governor's wife had her lesson to-day. She is a very good pupil. I believe she will be able to read in about a month, and, if so, I shall try and get her to teach some other women. She has not much to do during the day, and I think she could not be better employed than in teaching her own country women.

Dec. 2—The messengers from the Governor start for Antananarivo shortly. I sent three letters to inform some of those in authority there that we intend commencing Missionary operations in this place. I sent one to each of the ambassadors who went to England, and who saw me at Mauritius on their way thither. I also sent one to Mr. Ellis, as he is likely to be asked who or what we are. As I have seen long since, we shall be crippled in our work until we get news from the Queen of Madagascar.

I visited the bazaar to-day, and read and spoke to about twenty people for three-quarters of an hour. They listened most attentively the whole time. I read to them a little Malagasy catechism, on some of the most simple truths of Christianity. I promised to visit them again and again, and was told I should be most welcome.

Dec. 4: *Lord's-day*—Had a very happy time at home to-day. The Governor and his wife visited us at a very early hour, and remained with us the whole of the day. As we shall not be able to have a regular service for three or four months, we must content ourselves by doing all the good we can under our present circumstances. This may be a good preparation for our future work, as we shall get well acquainted with our Malagasy prayer-book before we are called upon to use it in a regular full service. We shall make all who are able to read acquainted with the responses, and then, when we have a church, we shall have a small congregation prepared to respond. By visiting the people, and encouraging them to visit us, we get a good insight into their character. This will enable us to manage the different races, and break down any prejudices that may exist among them.

The Governor wished to-day to have Luke xvi. 9, "Make to yourselves friends of the mammon of unrighteousness," &c., explained to him. Both Mr. Maundrell and I gave him our opinions upon it, and he appeared to think that we were right. He seems very anxious at times to have knotty points discussed: I believe he does it solely to get information.

We had six or eight persons in our house the greater part of to-day. We began our little service by my giving out a hymn, after which I read the first lesson for the day—Isaiah v. Mr. Maundrell then prayed the Litany, and those who had books, and were able to read, responded. This being finished, hymn-singing commenced, which was continued till I was quite exhausted. I think the Malagasy could sing from six o'clock in the morning till the same hour in the evening, and be almost as fresh at the conclusion as when they commenced. They have good ears for music, and excellent voices.

Dec. 5—The messengers to the capital did not leave till this morning. The Queen's messenger, Ranjiany, called to say good bye before he started. I gave him the Proverbs of Solomon in his own tongue, and when I read him one or two of them he almost jumped with delight, saying, "That is good and true." He left, well satisfied with his book, which he intends studying on his way to Antananarivo. The Governor's wife, whose name is Reniketaka, came as early as seven o'clock this morning for her lesson. I had her again in the afternoon. She seems most anxious to learn, and I am only too glad to teach her.

The Governor's attention having been directed to-day to Acts xvi. 26, he told us an anecdote about himself. Once, when he was compelled to drink the "tangena," his judges were all assembled around him. He had just finished the drink, and laid down the cup, when the house rolled and shook, almost like a ship in a storm. His persecutors were terrified, and trembled like the jailer of Philippi. The "tangena" ordeal failed to convict him, and he was permitted to return to his own house. After dark, numbers of Christian friends came to visit him, and remained with him, reading, singing, and praying, until cock-crowing, when they stole to their respective houses.

Ranavalona has been likened, by a Malagasy whom I shall not name, to "Bloody Mary" of England, and I think the likeness is striking: certainly the effects of Mary's and Ranavalona's persecutions have been somewhat similar. The blood of our English martyrs has been the seed of England's Protestantism, while from the blood of the Malagasy martyrs thousands have sprung up who love their Saviour and their Bibles. "The noble army of martyrs praise thee, O God."

Dec. 6—Visited for about four hours to-day, and tried to explain some simple truths to the people. Most appeared to listen attentively, but some "cared for none of these things." I find that I have a great deal to learn yet. I know something of the Hova language, but little or nothing of Sakalava, or Betsimasaraka. The Hovas here are in the minority, and we are debarred, for the present, from doing much with them, as they nearly all live in the *rova*, or "citadel," as we should call it, which we are not permitted to enter. The Queen's reply to the Governor's letter will, I trust, be the key which will open its gates to us. In the mean time I intend to look after the Sakalavas and Betsimasarakas, and make myself acquainted with their language. I had some difficulty to-day in trying to explain a few truths to some women. These people seem neither to understand nor to like the Hova dialect. It is rather too much to expect that people will sit or stand listening to a man prating away in a strange language. The Hovas generally listen attentively, because they understand what I am saying. Lord, loose my tongue, that I may be able to speak thy truth to this people.

Dec. 7—Started this morning for Hiarana. After breakfast I visited several houses, and was teaching a woman the Lord's-prayer, when a person came to the door and said that a ship was coming. I ran out and looked, but saw nothing, as the trees were in the way. Suddenly a ship turned the corner, and walked—I had almost said—into the bay, like a thing of life. I almost at once recognised her as the "King Radama." She was anchored in about five minutes, and in five minutes more I was on board. I found several letters; some from my dear parents or relatives, and some from dear friends in Mauritius. I was very pleased with the valuable and handsome present which the Bishop of Mauritius sent to the Governor of Vohimare, and am sure he will prize it much. Captain Rosalie also brings the Governor a little pony.

Dec. 8—Engaged a great part of to-day in sending luggage up to Amboanio.

Dec. 9—After sending off some more of our baggage, I went up to Amboanio with it, intending to remain there and write my letters; but I found that the Governor had earnestly requested Mr. Maundrell and me to accompany him to Hiarana to-morrow morning.

Dec. 10—The Governor called early this morning and breakfasted with us. He pressed me so earnestly to accompany him to Hiarana, that I did not think it prudent to decline. I presented him with the watch, in the name of the Bishop of Mauritius, and some good people in England who love Madagascar, and wish all its people well. I translated the bishop's letter, which was not difficult, as he wrote it in a style which he knew would be easily translated into Malagasy. The Governor was delighted, and wished us to write out the translation of the letter. He thanked the Bishop and us about a dozen times, and then shook hands with us most warmly.

The presentation finished, we started for Hiarana. As the Governor and the others preferred walking, and as Mr. Maundrell and I went in filanzanas, we were at the rendezvous before them.

Before I started I threw my great coat upon the filanzana, as I expected we would would have a shower of rain, and was about to sit down upon it, when the men called out that there was a scorpion on it. It was soon taken off and killed, and we proceeded on our journey. When we had travelled for about three hours, my bearers sat down to rest under a tree, and I took off my hat to enjoy the cool breeze in the shade. Imagine my astonishment when I found another scorpion quietly sticking to the inside lining of my hat. I wondered that it did not fall upon my head with three hours' jolting, but the Lord mercifully preserved me. My bearers were frightened when they saw it, and cried out to me not to touch it with my hand, which I had not the slightest notion of doing. One of them took it out with a piece of wood and killed it. When I told the Governor, he quoted the passage, "they shall tread upon scorpions," &c.

We got a very fair insight to-day into the manner in which a Malagasy Governor travels from one town to another. The people left Amboanio in their old dresses, carrying bundles and boxes on their backs, until they got to a place about a quarter of a mile from their destination. Here they sat down and had a drink of something, water, or cocoa-milk, or what they seemed to relish most, a little rum, or "toaka," as they call it. After this they went into the houses about, and changed their garments, which they did in an incredibly short space of time. Then they "filed off," the Hova women taking the lead, with their white lambas. After these came the Governor's wife, then some soldiers, and then His Excellency, who was followed up by the Sakalava and Betsimasaraka women, singing and clapping their hands. To-day Mr. Maundrell and I had the honour, if I might call it so, of heading the procession. We pushed on rather quickly on our filananzas, and as soon as we got to our own house we turned in, and left the processionists to wend their way to the Governor's house. The sun was very hot to-day, and I had a good scorching, although I was under a thick umbrella.

Dec. 11: *Lord's-day*—We had a nice little service to-day in our house at Hiarana. The Governor, his wife, and about a dozen Malagasy, including the Romish catechist, composed the congregation.

I left Hiarana in the afternoon, for Amboanio, to prepare letters, &c., before the ship left.

EXPLORATION EAST OF THE JORDAN, BY THE REV. JOHN ZELLER.

OUR Missionary at Nazareth, the Rev. John Zeller, has recently forwarded to us letters detailing various efforts for the spread of the Gospel in different directions; amongst others, an interesting discussion with a Druse Sheikh, and a new attempt at exploration beyond the Jordan.

Mr. Zeller's sympathies have been much drawn out towards the numerous Bedouin tribes, whose homes are in the once populous, but now desolated and neglected lands which lie eastward of the Jordan. These tentative efforts are of importance: they are preparing the way for some more settled and duly-organized plan, with a view to the introduction of Christian truth amongst these wanderers of the desert. Hitherto they have been regarded as so wild and prejudiced, that to attempt any thing of Christian effort on their behalf has been looked upon as a hopeless undertaking. By degrees, however, as they come to know our Missionaries, to receive them as their guests on occasional visits, and impart to them Arab hospitality, and as our Missionaries come to understand them better, we shall find a more ready access than we had anticipated, and the Bedouins of the desert will begin to understand the simplicity and suitableness of the Gospel message. Mr. Zeller writes—

In August I went with Seraphim Bontaji, catechist of the Bishop of Jerusalem, to Yerka, a Druse village splendidly situated on the top of a hill to the north of Acca, overlooking the plain of Acca and the sea. We went there to the house of the Sheikh Said Monaddy, who received us with hospitality and evident joy. He is a man of rare intelligence, and perfect in his manners. His house is a model of an oriental household, with its remnants of truly patriarchal customs and virtues. After having rested a little in a cool and spacious hall, from our ride up the hill under a scorching morning sun, we began to converse about grammar, history, and geography, for he takes a great interest in these things, and then we came to speak about religious subjects. Among other questions, I asked him, "Do you really believe that there are, among the initiated of the Druses [Okâl], people who strive for holiness, and who obtain peace for their souls through their religion?" His answer was, "I am persuaded that all of them enjoy perfect peace of conscience, for they are convinced that their religion is the only true one. In respect to purity of heart, I must confess I have seen many Druses who really strive for holiness, who fast, who are humble and kind in the highest degree, and never say an angry or bitter word." I said, "How is it possible that the initiated Druses should have perfect confidence in their religion, as it can not be hidden from those, who only look even a little into their books, that the same contain evident falsehoods? For instance; the striking deceit practised in the spelling of the words كذب and صدق [lie and truth]. [The Druses write these words wrongly كدب and سدق.] The orthography of these words has been absolutely settled in Arabic literature, by the Korân and other old books written before the books of the Druses, and by common consent of all learned men. How does it now come that the middle letter of the word كذب [mendacium] is written by the Druses with *dal* [د] instead of *thal* [ذ], and the first letter of صدق [veritas] with *sin* [س] instead of *sad* [ص]? The books of the Druses, in order to deceive their disciples by their interpretation, have spelt these words wrongly, namely, كذب with *dal* [د] and صدق with *sin* [س], in order to prove that the same contain a certain symbolical number. The word كذب, *kethib* [lie], indicates, in their religion, the devil and his agents; the word صدق *sedcum* [truth], symbolizes the true religion and its agents. The devil and his agents make, according to the Druse doctrine, twenty-six persons, therefore they change the *thal* into *dal*, for thus they make out the number of twenty-six. If they had spelt it rightly it would make a higher number than they require; namely, according to the value of the letters, the ك [k] amounts to 20, the ذ [th] to 700, the ب [b] to 2. The whole is therefore equal to 722. This is not the number the Druses require; they therefore have changed one letter for another, in order to prove the symbolical character of these words, and thus they have made out the number of 26. For the ك is 20, the د 4, and the ب 2. In the same manner, and for the same purpose, they have changed the orthography of صدق, 'the truth.'"

The Druse Sheikh answered, "What you say is perfectly correct. I myself had my doubts about this subject, and asked several of the initiated Druses about it, but never obtained a satisfactory answer."

"In that case," said I, "you must confess, that if you have doubts, the peace of your mind cannot be real, but must be illusory. With regard to purity of heart, I must say, that true purity is only taught in the Gospel, whilst other books, whatever religion they may pretend to teach, teach only a shadow of sanctity produced by the observance of certain outward laws, ceremonies, and works. We find, therefore, many who fast, pray, practise humility, and speak honestly; but if we scrutinize the depth of their souls we find them full of worldly lusts, thoughts, and desires.

"How can an initiated Druse really obtain sanctification of heart, when we see that the Druse religion permits and prescribes deceit and falsehood, in religion and worldly matters, freely to be practised against all unbelievers for it is known that in the first chapter of the book called 'The Seven Parts,' the Druses are ordered to be truthful to their brethren only, and deception towards others is permitted to them, if such deceit is profitable. Likewise, if a stranger should have obtained a knowledge of their religion, and should question them about their doctrines, they are allowed to deny every thing. Is it, under such circumstances, possible that the heart can become really pure, if the same is taught to hate and deceive their enemies? Can such doctrine come from God, who has created all, and lets his sun shine upon the good and the bad? How different is this from the laws of the Bible, which teaches us that lying is a sin in itself against every one, and in every case; and that hatred is a crime, even if committed against our enemies; and which distinctly declares that liars have no portion in the kingdom of God, but receive utter damnation; which also says that we have rather to choose death than to obtain any worldly advantage by a denial of our faith. The Gospel teaches us to love our enemies, and to bless those who curse us, not to return injury for injury, but by returning good for evil to heap coals of burning fire upon the heads of our adversaries. These precepts alone can teach us what kind of purity the holy God demands; and as God in his dealings with sinful men shows us so much longsuffering, kindness, and love, it is evident that the true religion must make the same claims on its disciples."

In the afternoon we went to a hill east of Yerka, covered with beautiful vineyards, and met on our way a Moslem Sheikh from Acca, whose father had been Mufti, and who is the Imâm of one of the mosques there. The Sheikh Said invited him to come with us to his vineyard, and so he accompanied us. In this vineyard are some large old fir-trees: in the branches of the biggest of them we found a little arbour, affording sufficient room for the whole company. The view from here over the country before us, and over the sea, drew forth our admiration, and we entered into conversation about geography and astronomy. But the Sheikh said he could not believe all our assertions about the movement of planets, especially not the motion of the earth and its consequences; and if I could prove it to him he would leave his religion and become a Christian, because all this was against the Korán and Mohammedan tradition. Of course he could not at once be convinced by the proofs I gave him; but it was very gratifying to see how greatly he interested himself about these subjects.

In the evening, at dinner, we asked the Imâm about the object of his journey, and he told us that he had come from Safed, where he had bought a mare, which he considered to be of peculiar value; upon which Seraphin said, "We men trouble ourselves so much to obtain always the best things of this world, though they are transient, whilst we do not care for obtaining eternal and lasting goods. From the first objects men can never obtain enough, from the last we ask but little: indeed our human nature is in opposition against those spiritual and divine things. But we have to strive against such worldliness, and to be satisfied with what God gives us of earthly things."

The Imâm said, "It is true, self-denial is not to be found in this world, even not with those who pretend to teach the same. I myself, when I address the people in the mosque on Fridays, teach them self-denial, but do not practise it. Is it possible that we should do ourselves what we demand from others?"

The Sheikh said, "With regard to Seraphin, I can testify that he practises self-denial, for he left the wealth of his father's house, and is content with little for religion's sake."

Upon which Seraphin answered, "I confess that my heart is deceitful and inclined to evil as others: however, the self-denial I practise is not performed by my strength, but by the grace of God, by which I have obtained the knowledge of the way of truth, which forces us to deny ourselves."

The Imâm—"What way of truth is this?"

Seraphin—"It is the Gospel."

The Imâm—"Many Christian doctrines are quite to my taste; but not what Christianity says about the crucifixion of Christ, whilst they teach that He was God."

Seraphin—"This doctrine is really against our nature, and against credibility; however, if we learn the reasons why this was so, we are obliged to confess that it is nevertheless the truth."

After dinner we went to the top of the house, where there was a fine arbour, as every house has one, for conversation at night and place for sleeping. There we continued the conversation about the necessity of the incarnation of the Word of God in Jesus, and his death for us. We tried to show that sin, since the fall of Adam, is an evil of indelible character, as committed against an eternal, unchangeable God, and therefore has caused endless condemnation in accordance with the justice of the eternal God. Thus came upon Adam and his seed the judgment of death and eternal punishment, not only on account of Adam's sin, but on account of the inherent corruption of human nature. But as God's mercy wishes the salvation of humankind, and God's justice is condemnation, what can reconcile between justice and mercy to save man? Are repentance, sacrifices, good works, enough to obtain this object? By no means, for all these works are works of a terminable character, and are in themselves imperfect, and therefore insufficient to satisfy the eternal justice of God, so that all these works are unable to balance the weight of the sin of human kind. Even if we suppose that it would be possible for any one of the Prophets, or the righteous men, to atone for sin by sacrificing himself, we would deceive ourselves; first, because such a man could not be exempted from the judgment passed over all the race of Adam; secondly, because the creature cannot give an atonement for an offence committed against the majesty of the Creator; neither can this be done through the highest angel, as they are all created, and as there is no equality between them and the eternal majesty of God. For these reasons the Word of God was made flesh, that, by becoming one with us, Christ might be our representative, and thus give to his work the dignity of an eternal, indelible character. Thus it was possible that the Word of God should, in our stead, bear the shame, the suffering, and the death which we deserved, and thus redemption and atonement was obtained."

The Imâm answered, "Even if we concede this, what does it prove? for this *Word*, is it itself God?"

We answered, "Yes, it is."

And the Imâm asked, "How is it possible for God, that He should leave heaven and be on earth? Does this coming down mean that heaven was left without his presence?"

We answered, "No," but it is Christian doctrine that He came down from heaven upon the earth, not absolutely, but relatively, for there are many books which, in speaking of the nature of God, have to use expressions of a relative meaning, and even the Korân itself uses, in many instances, similar expressions. Thus the words do not mean that God had left heaven and came down upon our earth, as if He had been limited absolutely to a certain spot; for we believe not only that God is present in every place, but also that every place exists in Him and through Him."

He said, "Very good; but how is it possible that God should be united to man?"

Seraphin answered, "In order to indicate such a possibility, we are told in the Bible, as it is also acknowledged by you, that God was present in the fiery bush on Mount Horeb. If that was possible for God, as you believe, that He should be present in the bush in a mysterious manner, how should it not be possible for Him to be present as man? And if the Bible tells us that God was thus present, why should it be impossible for us to say that God was in Jesus in a mysterious manner, as your own books testify that it was the Word of God and his Spirit who was thus present?"

At last the Imâm said, "This explanation is very good, but it is difficult to understand and difficult to believe." He then stood up and went to his place to sleep. Then we prayed that these words might not have been spoken in vain, and that the work of Christ, once wrought on Calvary for the salvation of mankind, might have its effect on the Mohammedans and idolatrous Christians of this land.

Tour to Jebel Ajtûn, March 1864.

The land of Jebel Ajtûn, with its steep and rugged mountain side towards the Jordan, and its fine hills and valleys covered with splendid oak forests, has for many years been daily before mine eyes, and often excited the wish to examine these mostly unknown regions, and to see whether the Gospel of peace might be proclaimed among a wild population, constantly at war among themselves and with everybody else, rebellious against the Turkish Government, and, as circumstances prompt them, either friendly with the Bedouins or fighting against them, whilst the latter are accustomed to treat the peasantry as their vassels. This mountainous country is principally in the hands of two rival clans: the head of the one is the Sheikh Joseph Shreide, residing at Tibueh, possessing the northern half of Jebel Ajtûn, called El Kûra; the other half, properly called Jebel Ajtûn, is under the authority of Hassan Barakat, in Kefreujy, and the Adwân. On account of these divisions, the utter absence of any government, and the invasion of all possible Bedouin tribes, travelling is connected either with great risks or with great expenses, for lately travellers paid enormous sums to the Adwân to escort them through their country. Having been urged by the Rev. H. Tristram to accompany him, I resolved to join his party, and on March the 11th we started towards the east. Our first encampment was with Agyh Aga, east of Mount Tabor, who provided us with an escort and a letter of introduction to his friend, the Sheikh Joseph Shreide. In the evening I went to some of the tents. In one of them, belonging to the Sheikh of the Sakker, I found a large number of Bedouins, some of them of much reputation, and much too proud to speak or to stir. After other conversation, one of them asked me about my religious opinions; and when I had explained them to him, he said, "Tell us, do you think the Korán to be the word of God or not?"

I answered, "There are many religions, and each of them claims to be the true one: the Jews, the Christians, the Druses, the Hindus, believe each that their religion alone contains the truth. How can we know which of them is truly inspired?"

All said, "Speak, thou knowest better."

I continued, "I consider that religion the best which gives unto us a perfect atonement for sin, and thus reconciles us with one God. The Korán imposes alms, fasts, prayer, and pilgrimage, as necessary works, but such works are not sufficient to atone for sin; and the Korán contains so many contradictions, that it is difficult to believe in its inspiration. For instance, it says that the Tora, the Psalter, and the Gospel were sent down from heaven, and yet it requires the persecution of Jews and Christians who believe in these books. Further, Mohammed gave the law that a Moslem should only have four wives, and afterwards, when he himself had taken more, he received a revelation that the prophet of God was exempted from that law, and might have as many wives as he liked. Mohammed, at the beginning, exhorted his disciples to patience and forbearance towards their enemies, and afterwards he himself preached war and persecution."

This was certainly the utmost they were capable of enduring. I therefore left them. Next day we pitched our tents near a Bedouin encampment at Um Keis (Gadara), where I had a conversation with some Bedouins, who asked for medicine. When I inquired from them why the peasants, whom I had found last year comfortably settled in the splendid rock-hewn tombs, had left the place to the last man, the Bedouins replied, "On account of the burden of the Government." But when I asked the peasants at Tayibeh for the cause of the desertion of Um Keis by the villagers, they said, "On account of the burden of the Bedouins." The people of Tayibeh were, some years ago, for several weeks besieged in their village by a host of Bedouins from the Weled Ali and Beni Sachee; they lost, however, only four men, the Bedouins twelve. Their crops were of course totally destroyed.

From Tayibeh we proceeded to Tibneh, but unfortunately the Sheikh Joseph Shreide, to whom we had an introduction, was absent: his brother, however, received us very kindly. We staid there over Sunday, and I had much conversation with some Christian families, who had come to see me. These Christians are scarcely to be distinguished from Mohammedans, as they adopt their habits and expressions as much as possible, for the Moslem Sheikhs are very fanatical, and have absolute power over them. They deeply bemoan their condition, and feel their degradation, but they see no hope of changing their circumstances, as they are perfectly without knowledge and without spiritual guidance. The words of Christ our Saviour seemed to them like sounds from another world, which can have no reference to them in their condition. These poor Christians even begged me by no means to speak to the Sheikh about the oppression they were suffering, as he would not fail to revenge himself if he suspected that they dared to complain about him.

Sheikh Diah, the brother of Joseph Shreide, procured guides for us, and wrote a letter of introduction to the Sheikhs of Soof, near Jerash. March the 14th we set out towards the south. After having passed several hills and valleys, covered with luxurious vineyards, whose owners were busy in ploughing, we entered the primeval oak forests of Bashan. The beauty of the forest, affording a delicious shade against the burning rays of the sun, greatly delighted us, and we only wished to stay in this beautiful country, filled with game and swarming with wild pigeon: suddenly, however, our thoughts were turned in another direction, by the report of two guns in the distance. Our guides became alarmed, and brought one of our party, who had gone in pursuit of gazelles, nearly by force back to the road. My dragoman had ridden to the top of a hill, to look out for the supposed enemies, and soon afterwards reported that we had to prepare ourselves for a probable attack of robbers, as he had seen passing in the valley before us twelve horsemen, driving a herd of goats before them at full gallop. A few minutes afterwards we heard the war-cry of the shepherds, and several of them passed us, firing their guns, and running after the robbers.

Towards evening we arrived in Soof, in the hope of being out of danger, but this proved otherwise. My letter of introduction was of no avail, as the Sheikh was not at home, and the people of the village showed their evil disposition by gathering in large numbers around the tents, and picking up quarrels with our muleteers and servants. They declared that we should not be allowed to go to Jerash without the permission of Goblân, a Sheikh of the Adwân. Thus we spent a very uneasy night, scarcely able to avoid an attack. As one of our party was suffering from fever, we had to decide upon a hasty retreat; but when the people of Soof learned our intentions they declared that we first had to pay a ransom, and when this was refused, one of the inhabitants took hold of a mule, and led it away, and drew his knife against the muleteer who tried to prevent him. The whole village was gathered around us, preparing their arms, and telling us that we could not go without paying the money. All my reasoning with the villagers was of no avail, and our guides from Tibueh were threatened to be killed first in case we should attempt to use force. At last, however, the Sheikhs were satisfied with a sum of 14*l*. On our way back we came on some Bedouins, driving away three oxen, which they evidently had just then stolen, and we saw here and there little bands of robbers, lurking behind the trees of the forest like beasts of prey, but we reached the west side of the Jordan without further accident. Some weeks afterwards I happened to find Goblân and some other Sheikhs of the Adwân in Jerusalem, and made him disgorge the black mail taken from us, and they, on their part, did not fail to make themselves paid by their partners and vassals, the robbers of Soof.

This shows sufficiently the difficulties in connexion with Missionary excursions to the east of the Jordan. Only by paying very large sums of money to the Adwân and other Bedouin tribes is it at present possible to travel in those regions.

Recent Intelligence.

INDIA.

HYDRABAD—SINDH.

In this Mission field, hitherto slow to receive impressions, there appear to be openings for usefulness in the direction of zenana work, which is referred to in the following paragraph, from a Sindh Missionary—

"The Ameer's ladies and their household are willing to be taught the Scriptures, if ladies are to be found who will go to them. My monitors have told me they would gladly have their wives put under instruction if I could send them anybody. There are excellent openings for zenana work."

MASULIPATAM.

Our readers will recollect the hurricane, and irruption of the sea, with which this town was visited in November last, and the sorrow which our Mission sustained in the loss of many precious lives: more particularly the case of the ordained native, the Rev. A. Bushanam, who lost on that fearful night his wife and child, was deeply affecting. The following letter has been just received from him—

March 10, 1865—I have to convey to you, in deep affliction and sorrow, according to flesh and blood, the Lord's dealings with me on the night of 1st November 1864. That was the memorable night which I shall not forget in all my life. Though we had heard nearly twenty days before that a part of Calcutta was washed away by the sea, yet we did not experience any material change in the weather on our own coast, even one or two days before the first. This made us not to suspect any such terrible calamity and loss of life. The morning was cool; a gentle breeze was blowing, first from the north-easterly direction, and in the afternoon it blew a little stronger, and the sky was more cloudy. But towards the evening we perceived that, by the force of the wind, the weak branches of some weak trees only were falling off. This was nothing at this season to what we have been accustomed to see. And at seven P.M. my dear wife and children, and myself, took our usual supper, which was their last meal on earth; and not being able, on account of a strong north-easterly wind, to sleep in our usual bed-room, we removed our cots into the hall. But Raghavayya, a relative of mine, and my servants, were in my bed-room I had deserted. Not being aware of the danger, I was tempted to sleep a little while, but my poor wife was sitting on her cot, not being able to sleep. And about half-past ten o'clock in the night my relative, who was sleeping in the other room, came running to me, and said that salt water was coming into the room. Immediately I got up, and went to call the servants, who were fast asleep. In the mean time dear Ratam Ganam, who occupied the other side of the house, came out also, and confirmed what Raghavayya had said: and then we did not know what plan to pursue. We said—not knowing the large quantity of water that had already come into the compound—that we would surely perish if we were to stop in this old house, but let us go to Mr. Noble's house, which is at some yards distance. We ventured to open, with great difficulty, one of our doors; but my wife, in her fright, not knowing what to do, took the little boy while sleeping into her arms, and came rushing to the door, and delivered the child to our maty, and stepped out with him and with the other two servants, to go to Mr. Noble's, while I was just at the door to help dear Ratam Ganam and his children to come out. And when I went out I found none, and the sea-water in our verandah about waist-deep already. Being sadly disappointed, I returned into the house, and got upon one of our cots, and then upon a book-shelf, tore the *chaudini*, and got up upon one of the large beams that lie under the roof. My hand trembles and my heart faints to describe the scene. I expected every moment the roof to come down: the house shook most fearfully. I thought every moment that I should join my beloved wife and child in the courts above. But God had mercy and pity on me, and spared my life. I did not know till the next morning what had become of dear Ratnam Garu, his wife and children, and other servants, except my mother's brother, Raghavayya, who had got up, like myself, upon one of the beams of the roof. In the morning, when we came down, we found all except my dear wife, child, and a servant girl. All the outhouses in the compound were levelled to the ground, and some of the walls of the bungalow itself came down: the roof was standing on pillars, which were built with chunam. So we made efforts to go to Mr. Noble's, in the midst of pouring rain and in waist deep of sea water. We reached the house in great anxiety, not knowing what had become of Mr. Noble and his dear children in Christ. We found them all safe, and they received us all very kindly, and supplied us with dry clothes, &c., which they could get. Mr. Noble's escape was very providential. He attempted twice to come out, but God did not suffer his honoured servant to be swept away by the sea water. All those who attempted to come out on that night were either drowned or escaped death by holding to the branches of trees. In this way the most of them that perished were children and women. But, on the other hand, many were also hurried into eternity by stopping in their houses: the roofs came down, and they perished. In one house both the husband and wife, and one infant in the middle, were lying on a cot: the roof came down, and they were supposed to have perished by the fall of it. But in the morning the relatives of the deceased removed the roof, and found the husband and wife dead, but the child in the middle alive. And in another house, a very respectable woman was sitting and nursing a little baby: one little boy was standing on her right-hand side and another child on the left, and the husband was at her back. They were all found dead by the fall of the roof. Such were the many scenes at Masulipatam: each family has to tell its tale of woe or miraculous escape. When, one or two days after the flood, we went out in search of food and water, we found all orders of men, women, and children, lying dead in the open streets, perfectly naked. The sight was most touching and heartrending.

I have told you before how we all deserted our house, and went to Mr. Noble's on the following morning: we had nothing to eat but wet rice, boiled with rain water. We spent the day most miserably. Towards the evening we came to know the loss which Mr. Sharkey had sustained, and the loss of our dear young excellent Christian brother, Mallayya Gam and his newly-married wife. It was not yet quite four months since he was married. God's ways are very mysterious, and we cannot understand them. And on the next morning, that was, the third day after the storm, I ventured to come to my house, when I found some of my furniture was gone out of the house, and some boxes with clothes, &c., brass vessels, and my wife's clothes, &c., were floating in water. With tears and sighs I gathered them all, and was only able to leave them in one of the corners of the house. The boxes being very heavy, I could not carry them to Mr. Noble's. My servants all deserted me. I left the things in the house, and went again to Mr. Noble's. Dear Mr. Noble had no proper food the previous day, and had not even rain water this morning to wash his mouth with, so he was obliged to use salt water. A few minutes after he had done this, he told me he was fainting, and asked me whether I could not go into the town, and get him some boiled rice, or any eatables. I at once ran into the pettah, and got him some boiled rice and doll, and after he had taken this he said he was feeling a little stronger. And I was once more obliged to go into the town to get us some provisions for the day. After we had our meals, &c., my relative, Raghavayya, and myself, came to the house to see and to carry some of the clothes, &c., which were in my house. Not a single useful article was left in the house: all were stolen by thieves, who came to the house in the middle of the day. There was lying in one corner the pieces of my dear wife's beautiful work-box, which was given to her by our late good old Bishop Dealtry. When it was lying in the house, covered with mud and water, the thieves saw it, and broke the box into pieces, and stole all the valuable things in it. And as for my books, I have lost all.

The town of Masulipatam is in a very confused state. It is in appearance totally different from what it was. As I pass along some streets, I see nothing but a mass of ruined houses from one end of the street to the other. The distress of the town is still very great. The people are suffering from want of good water. The authorities have taken measures to let the Kristna water come into the middle of the town. There are still dead bodies lying beyond the town. No spot in the town is free from impure and destructive air; no house is scarcely free from sickness; diarrhœa is the chief complaint of all. Dear Mr. Noble was laid up for several weeks by the same complaint. His health, I am afraid, is very much shattered, but the good old father of the Mission still never thinks of going away for a change.

What shall I say for God's dealings with his unworthy servant on the night of the 1st November 1864? I can say nothing. My hand trembles and my heart faints to think of the sudden loss of my dear wife and child. But, however, they are not lost, as other heathen who perished in great numbers, but gone before. It was the Lord who did it. "We know that all things work together for good to them that love God." When I came out from heathenism I never, humanly speaking, expected that my dear partner would have been restored to me. "The Lord gave and the Lord hath taken away: blessed be the name of the Lord." "Naked came I out of my mother's womb, naked shall I return thither." My afflictions, however great they may be, cannot be greater than those of the patient Job; and one who is greater than Job, who patiently endured the cross, has taught us how to suffer. He hath done what is right; He never makes a mistake: all will end in good. My dear wife has not left me without leaving behind her a cheering hope. She is gone to her happy home, where no sorrow, no trouble, no anxieties or distractions can molest her rest and happiness. If I call to my remembrance the sweet consistent character of my wife's Christian life, the love with which she had loved her Saviour, and the sweet and touching prayers which she offered when we both knelt down before our common Lord and Saviour, I have every reason to believe that my dear departed ones are now perfectly happy in heaven with our dear Saviour. Truly I cannot wish them to be in a better place, or in better hands. But according to flesh and blood in our present state, the departure of our dearest and nearest relatives causes us the greatest sorrow and the deepest affliction. But blessed be God for all the consolations He grants us, even in the midst of our fiery trials!

NORTH-WEST AMERICA.

The details of Mission work in the distant Youcon were placed before the friends of Missions in a recent Number of the "Church Missionary Record." Since then it is with deep sorrow we have been made acquainted with the failing health of our devoted young

Missionary, the Rev. R. McDonald. This is one of the mysterious dispensations which run concurrently with the history and development of Missionary work,—the failure of health on the part of valuable European agents, and that not unfrequently at the moment when, according to our view of the case, they can be least spared. At such times it is our part to remember that Mission work is the Lord's; that which He oversees and directs, and that He will not fail to overrule all for the furtherance of his Gospel. One important lesson has been learned in this school of affliction, the necessity that much pains should be bestowed on the development of a native agency.

To the distant Youcon post the Rev. R. Phair, who, since his arrival from England, has been stationed at Islington, has been appointed. He volunteered for this work on hearing of Mr. McDonald's illness, and his request has been acceded to. His proffered aid is indeed most opportune. So soon as the Romish priests ascertained that ill health would compel Mr. McDonald to return to Red River this summer, they declared their intention of forthwith occupying the Youcon, should it be left vacant. The notification of Mr. Phair's appointment is dated March 14th, and he was then on the point of starting for the Youcon. We trust therefore that he will arrive before Mr. McDonald leaves.

With reference to the Sioux Indians (of which tribe we purpose shortly to give some account), and of the recent visit of Little Crow's band to Red River, Archdeacon Cockran observes—

"The American war with the Sioux has perfectly paralyzed all our benevolent efforts here among the Saulteaux. The Sioux have visited us in such numbers as to frighten off all the native-Indian population. In August we were visited by 350 lodges of Sioux, about 1500 souls. The two parties made peace, but they have no confidence in each other, consequently the weakest side is always unhappy and anxious. We have had more Sioux about us this winter than Saulteaux. I have two of them for servants, who behave exceedingly well. I could have filled my schools with Sioux children, but the Americans have succeeded in filling the minds of our people with prejudice against them, so that at present I dare not show them all the kindness which I feel towards them. The Sioux are a brave people, and they are still loyal to the English. I saw a band of thirty warriors unfurl the Union Jack which their forefathers fought under in 1814. We have had sixty-three Sioux tented among us through the winter: they have conducted themselves very peaceably; and they inform me that 2000 of them intend to visit us in the spring. Should this be true they will starve us out. We could not feed such a number for a week."

From the Fairford station the Rev. A. Cowley reports—"Our good old chief Papamas, otherwise Walter Webb Woodhouse, died last night from what was supposed to be a stroke of paralysis. Ten days since he was brought home from his hunting-grounds by a train of my own dogs. His speech and understanding were a good deal impaired from his arrival to his death; but he once told Luke Caldwell, who visited him, that he was still 'holding on to the good way;' and he also told George Bruce, who has visited him night and day, that all he could do was 'to trust in the mercy of God.'

DEATH OF THE REV. J. TAYLOR, OF THE EAST-AFRICA MISSION.

We have experienced a severe loss on the east coast of Africa. European Missionaries are difficult to be obtained—increasingly so. Indeed if it were not for the aid afforded by native Christians, Missionary operations would be in a great measure arrested. When therefore a promising European Missionary, after careful training, has been sent out, we rejoice in the prospect of the help that, by the blessing of God, he will be enabled to render. And yet how often are our expectations blighted! for scarcely has the new Missionary reached his field of labour than sickness befalls him, and he dies.

The Rev. J. Rebmann has now for many years been the sole Missionary on the dark and dreary coast of East Africa. He and Mrs. Rebmann have borne with intrepidity the trials of their isolated position, and we admire and marvel at the way in which they have been upheld. We have long anxiously desired to send him a fellow-labourer, and at length succeeded in doing so, the Rev. J. Taylor having reached East Africa some few months back. But he is no more. He was on his way to the Mauritius to meet the lady to whom he was to be married, when he was attacked by sudden illness, and died at Zanzibar. The particulars are communicated in the following letter from Bishop Tozer to the Secretaries, dated March 9, 1865.

When writing to you, a short time since, an account of my very interesting visit to your Mission station at Kisuludini, I little thought that I should so quickly have to write again, for the sorrowful purpose of acquainting you with the death of one of its devoted clergy. My dear young friend, Mr. Taylor, has been taken from us, under very sudden and painful circumstances. We have been daily expecting his arrival here, *en route* for Mauritius, and I was looking forward with pleasure to having him as my guest for a few weeks, and of renewing an acquaintance, the memory of which is still full of interest; but it was ordered otherwise.

The particulars of his illness and death are as follows—He had left Mombas in a Bombay dhow which had touched there, and was on his way to Zanzibar, when, about noon, only the day before yesterday (March 7th), he was suddenly taken ill, and so rapid was the progress of the attack, that he lost consciousness during the course of the afternoon. In this state, from which he never rallied, he was landed at half-past seven in the evening, and brought at once to the English consulate. Dr. Sewart, of Zanzibar, and the physician who is attached to Baron Von den Decken's expedition, was in immediate attendance, and never left our friend until the very last. Indeed, the kindness and attention of both these gentlemen deserve one's warmest admiration. I feel sure that every thing was done which their united professional skill could suggest, yet nothing seemed able to effect any change, or even to restore, for a single moment, the sufferer's consciousness.

A short half hour before his death, which took place a few minutes before one o'clock, I offered up the commendatory prayer from the visitation service, and committed him to the care and protection of the Father of mercies and the God of all comfort.

It was thought best to bury him at sunrise, and at six o'clock we carried him across the harbour to the English cemetery on French Island, where a deep grave had been prepared. Many, unknown to him in life, stood around his tomb, while my chaplain, Dr. Steere, and I, shared between us the burial service of our church. Our sorrow was great, but, thank God, we had a deeper feeling, one of firm, trusting confidence that our brother was with the Lord.

I have already written to Mr. Rebmann and to the Bishop of Mauritius, and to the young lady, who is, we believe, even now on her way from England, expecting to become the partner of our departed friend's hopes and joys.

A sun-stroke, in all probability, was the immediate cause of death, but the medical men suspect that latent inflammation, or some derangement of the stomach, intensified its effect.

On first hearing of this sad event, you may be disposed to doubt the wisdom of filling up the vacant post. You will, not unnaturally, connect the loss of Mr. Taylor with others which occur in the chronicles of the East-Africa Mission, and you will call to mind the very recent death of Mr. Butterworth, the Wesleyan Missionary. But while admitting that all Europeans may encounter much risk and danger in coming here, it is well to bear in mind that that which just happened here is by no means peculiar to East Africa, or even to tropical countries. Sun-strokes occasionally prove fatal even in England. I trust, therefore, that your Committee will make another venture of faith, and send, at this critical moment, another Missionary to Kisuludini. The very existence of the Wanika Mission seems now to depend on Mr. Rebmann's most valuable life; and were he to be removed, I know of no one capable of taking up and carrying on his work. Indeed I feel this so strongly, that I have written and urged him to send me down one or two of his most promising young men for training and Christian instruction, with a prospective eye to their ordination. In a case of spiritual life or death, we need not be very exacting in our qualifications for the ministry.

THE ANTHROPOLOGICAL SOCIETY AND CHRISTIAN MISSIONS.

We have observed certain animated discussions, which have taken place at sittings of the Anthropological Society, in which Christian Missions amongst barbarous races have been very freely commented upon. On a recent occasion the subject was introduced in a paper read by Mr. Winwood Reade, in which, expressing himself very strongly against the results of Missionary labours in equatorial Africa, he asserted that the attempts to evangelize the negroes had proved "a wretched bubble." He was followed by other speakers, amongst others, by Captain Burton and Dr. Colenso. The latter gentleman considered that Mr. Reade had done good service by drawing attention to the efforts made by Missionaries to convert negroes, and the results, though he did not agree with him on some points. What the points of divergence may be he has promised to explain in a paper to be read at some future meeting of the Society, and to which, when it appears, we promise our best attention. Captain Burton, however, far exceeded Mr. Reade. He did not confine himself to equatorial Africa, but, taking an extensive view of Missionary efforts in various parts of the world, pronounced them to have completely failed in effecting any improvement amongst the savage nations whom it had been their object to convert. Especially Abbeokuta, and the Mission work there, occupied a prominent position in the encouraging picture which he thus sketched. It is first described as "a nearly Christian city," and then pronounced to be "a den of abominations." If it were indeed a nearly Christian city, it would not be a den of abominations. It is because it is not so that vices prevail in it, which give to Captain Burton the opportunity of designating it a den of abominations, although we apprehend that it is not in a worse condition than other crowded resorts of human beings who are without the restraining influence of Christianity. Is Captain Burton justified in designating Abbeokuta "a nearly Christian city?" We appeal to his work entitled, "Abbeokuta, &c.," and the statements which are there given. In page 170 of the first volume he thus speaks of the amount of population—

"Mr. T. B. Freeman, in 1842, estimated it to contain 45,000 souls; in 1858, Mr. Bowen gave it 80,000; more modern travellers have raised the number to 100,000; and looking at the extent and the thickness of the population, I should not wonder if, when the soldiers return from the Ibadan war, it was found to contain 150,000 souls, nearly equal to the entire population of redoubted Dahomey."

Captain Burton also gives us the Christian statistics, so as to afford us the opportunity of ascertaining what proportion the professing Christians bear to the aggregate of population. At p. 246 of his first volume he says—"The number of converts registered is about 1500: the communicants may amount to 800."

Our readers will judge for themselves whether Abbeokuta can with truth be described as "nearly a Christian city," or whether the abominations of Abbeokuta can fairly be imputed to her Christianity.

Our readers must not be surprised at the condemnatory language which these gentlemen use respecting Christian Missions. Their principles are such that it is impossible they could do otherwise. According to the views which they entertain, Christian Missions, especially among the negroes of Africa, must be a great mistake indeed. The fact is, these gentlemen belong to a new school, the principles of which are so disparaging to Christianity, that, upon the whole, we are disposed to think that even heathen Abbeokuta has stronger claims to be regarded as Christian than this new philosophy, which, for the improvement of mankind in the nineteenth century, gives forth its lucubrations at the meetings of the Anthropological Society. The gentlemen to whom we have referred, and who were the chief speakers on the occasion, are all authors. Dr. Colenso is such, his writings having obtained considerable notoriety; so is Mr. Winwood Reade; so is Captain Burton. Their operations, therefore, are not mysteries. They are not, like the secret rites of the heathen, concealed within the gloomy precincts of some grove, where none but the initiated are privileged to enter. The vestibules of the new academy are open to all, and the page of the new inspiration is spread wide for all to read. We therefore violate no confidence, we are guilty of no intrusion, in examining and exposing this new theory, which has been boldly set forth to the dishonour of the Lord Jesus Christ, and in grievous disparagement of that alone saving faith which He rendered efficacious by the shedding of his own blood.

We first turn to the pages of Mr. Winwood Reade, his work being entitled, "Savage Africa." He has been at various points on the western coast of Africa—the Senegal, Sierra Leone, Liberia, Dahomey, Yoruba, the Cameroons, the Gorilla country, the Congo. He appears to be a close observer of the physique of the African races. His descriptions are not reserved enough for us to touch upon them; nor, indeed, have we to do with his tastes, but with his principles, and that merely for the purpose of showing that with such principles he is disqualified from forming an impartial and equitable opinion on the results of Christian Missions, and that the judgments to which he does give expression are of no value. We turn, therefore, to the last chapter, that on the Redemption of Africa.

His first statement is one with which we entirely coincide, and only regret that, finding ourselves at the same starting-point with the writer, we should be so soon constrained to part company with him. He informs us that there is "a religion," "the religion of God;" that "it is the same religion which, under different names and forms, has civilized the Hebrews through Moses, and the western world through Jesus Christ." In this we fully coincide. True religion is not devised by man; it is not the product of his conceptions; it is by revelation of God. That revelation has been progressive in its character. It commenced at the fall, and, gradually expanding, as man was able to receive it, in Christianity attained its consummation. The revelation of God has culminated in Christianity, which claims now to be recognised as the one religion of God.

But ideas of this kind are far too narrow for the gentlemen of the new philosophy. Christianity must not be regarded as the alone exposition of the religion of God. There are other modifications of it. The forms in which it is clothed widely differ; but "the divine element is always preserved unchanged." Christianity is only one of its many forms; Mohammedanism is another. Mohammedanism, as well as Christianity, is the true religion of God; it is "the same religion which, under different names and forms, has civilized the Hebrews through Moses, and the western world through Jesus Christ," and which, under the form of Mohammedanism, is to redeem Africa. "Mohammed, a servant of God, redeemed the eastern world: his followers are redeeming Africa."

Christian Missions are an interference with that which is properly the office of Mohammedans, and therefore have, of necessity, proved to be a failure. Two examples are selected of the futility of Christian Missions in Western Africa. The first is that of the Jesuits in Congo; and this is regarded by Mr. Reade as conclusive, and for the following reasons—"The Catholic religion is, of all Christian creeds, the most likely to succeed among savages. It impresses the senses by music, by perfumes, by stately rites; and with its charms, its relics, and its images, it affords that which is indispensable to the lower classes of intellect—some external objects which they can venerate, and which may constantly remind them of their Creator.

"But how can the Protestant creed, which is at once so naked and so sublime, be understood by uneducated Africans? How convey to them abstract truths, when their language cannot express to them abstract ideas?"

It is evident that the writer does not know in what consists the true force of Christianity. The Gospel of Christ is the power of God unto salvation to every one that believeth; and when that Gospel is faithfully taught, God's power works through it to the conversion even of races so savage as the Bakele, the Mpongwe, and the Fans. This is the important point which such objectors as those we are now dealing with entirely overlook, and overlook because they do not understand it. When Romish Missionaries, such as those who attempted to proselyte the people of Congo, put aside the truth, they lost the power, and the appeals which music, &c., made to the senses failed to reach the heart.

The American Missions in equatorial Africa are selected as the second proof of the futility of Christian Missions in that country. Mr. Reade does full justice to the character and abilities of these good men, but he adds—"in spite of their lives, pure and laborious as those of the ancient fathers, in spite of their unceasing efforts, they have made no palpable progress in converting the Africans." These Missions, however, are of recent origin: all new Missions are at first slow in the progress which they make. There are preliminary difficulties to be overcome: the language has to be acquired, and reduced to the service of Christianity. Time must be given that the ear and understanding of the native may adjust themselves to the new sounds and ideas which are presented to them; but we believe as much has been done as could reasonably be expected within a brief period, and under circumstances such as we have described. Certainly it is premature to pronounce these Missions a failure. Ten years more must elapse before a judgment can be formed respecting them, and by that time they will have expanded into successful Missions.

But it is evident that in so deciding, Mr. Reade is arguing from his principles, not from a patient investigation of actual results. There is, in his opinion, a great stumbling-block introduced by Christianity, which prevents the success of Christian Missions, but which Mohammedanism, by its superior action, at once evades—"Polygamy is the great stumbling-block." Marriage he regards as a purely secular question, the details of which ought to be arranged as may be found expedient. Polygamy he considers to be "as great a benefit to Africa, as in Europe it would be an evil." It is "an institution which has a most salutary effect in redeeming Africa."

Now we differ in toto from Mr. Winwood Reade. We are persuaded that polygamy, whether prevailing in Africa or in Europe, is most disastrous in its effects, nor would Christianity merit to be called a remedial dispensation, if it did not provide for the elimination of this as well as of other evils which degrade and depress man. In the pages of Mr. Reade are to be found ample evidences of the miserable consequences which flow from this so-called "civil institution." They will be found detailed in his chapter on the "Land of the Amazons," but they are not such as to permit their transfer to the pages of this periodical.

Our readers now understand Mr. Reade's principles, and they will not be surprised at the conclusion to which he comes, and the advice he tenders to us. African Mohammedans, in his opinion, are "practical Christians." And yet in the pages of "Savage Africa" we find descriptions given of African Mohammedans, as to their national customs and habits, which are intensely revolting. We mention, as an example, the details introduced respecting the Foulah, Fuli, or Pulo nation. Are the bizarre statements, which are there obtruded on the public eye, to be regarded as specimens of practical Christianity?

Nevertheless, such being, according to Mr. Reade's standard, the ameliorating influence which Mohammedanism exercises upon the African, we are exhorted to "abandon our absurd projects of converting Mussulmans." Let us rather "aid the Mohammedans in their great work—the Redemption of Africa." "The interior of Africa is in the hands of the Mussulman. We have only to gain them as our allies, to obtain the *entrée* to its mysteries and treasures."

The paper read by Mr. W. Reade at the meeting of the Anthropological Society, is simply a *resumê* of the principles enunciated in his book. But entertaining the views he does on the subjects of Mohammedanism and polygamy, we cannot be surprised if Christian Missions and their results are worthless in his eyes.

We now turn very briefly to Captain Burton's book on "Abbeokuta and the Cameroon Mountains." In the first volume he stands forward as an earnest advocate for polygamy, as preferable to the "one-wife system;" nor, like Mr. W. Reade, would he limit this admission to Africa, but, as it appears, would render it of universal application. In his opinion, Christianity does not inculcate "the monogamic sentiment." It is only the Christian bishop that is forbidden a plurality of wives, and then "the apostolic limitation of the bishop's household was soon applied to the whole ministry," and eventually the laity were involved in the meshes of the restriction, so that in the "West penalties were attached to the practice."

Now our Missionaries in Abbeokuta have acted upon the principle laid down by the apostle—"Let every man have his own wife, and let every woman have her own husband." The language of the original is emphatic—*ἕκαστος τὴν ἑαυτοῦ γυναῖκα ἐχέτω, και ἑκάστη τὸν ἴδιον ἄνδρα ἐχέτω.* (1 Cor. vii. 2).

The words "*τὴν εαυτοῦ*" and "*τὸν ἴδιον,*" express the unity of the marriage relation, both expressions excluding all community, in which polygamy consists.

Of course the fidelity of Missionaries in this respect condemns the whole Missionary procedure in the eyes of the gallant captain. "Polygamy," as he observes, "is the foundation-stone of Yoruban society," and with this the Missionaries have unnecessarily interfered.—"I would assure these and other Missionaries that had less objection been made to polygamy on their part, the heathen would have found far fewer obstacles to conversion. Those who hold it their duty to save souls should seriously consider whether they are justified in placing such stumbling-blocks upon the path of improvement."

And if, in order to facilitate its progress and gain converts more rapidly, Christianity was to accommodate itself in this respect to the sensuality of man, and, like Mohammedanism, bribe him to a nominal profession by catering to his passions, how could it ever become the regenerator of society?

Captain Burton's theories, unlike those of Mr. Winwoode Reade, are not limited to savage Africa. They are more ambitious in their character, and are urged upon the consideration of Europe as deserving of attention. Are the Christians of England prepared to adopt them? Shall they abandon the monogamistic character of their institutions, and permit the Christian law of one wife to be relaxed into the Mohammedan indulgence of four? Are the noble-minded ladies of England prepared to be degraded to a level with the females of Mohammedan countries, no longer to be the help-meets, the equals, the companions of their husbands, aiding them by counsel and by prayer, but their inferiors, lowered in their own self-esteem, united in a relationship adjusted on the most inequitable principles, which requires of them the surrender of all, while they are to be contented to receive in return, not all, but only a part; a relationship, the unity of which being destroyed by the inequality of the arrangement, can never be otherwise than a source of disunion and discomfort? And what is to become of our English homes, and the children growing up under the fostering care of father and mother, united each to the other in holy wedlock? Shall Jacob's tent, with its Leah and its Rachel, the children of the one wife arrayed against the children of the other, and all the attendant exasperations and contentions, usurp the place of the Christian home? Shall English gentlemen be contented to exchange the holy elevation and cheerfulness of a Christian household, where there is mutual confidence, hearts open as the daylight to each other, for the reserve and distrust and evil passions which are harboured within the precincts of a Mussulman harem? No! Such theories may find a home in Mussulman and

Mormon lands, but the moral tone of England is too healthfully bracing to permit their naturalization. Especially we call on the ladies of England, who owe so much to Christianity, to spurn the books which give utterance to propositions so lax and subversive of all healthful influences, and refuse them admission within the precincts of those English homes, which they would despoil of their chief ornament.

But that gentlemen so philo-Mohammedan and polygamistic in their tendencies should disparage Missions, which, as purely Christian Missions, are antagonistic to Mohammedanism as a spurious faith, and subversive of polygamy as a degrading custom, is not surprising. Does it shake our confidence in Christian Missions to find that in the meetings of the Anthropological Society they are assailed. What should we think of our Missions if they met with the approval of these gentlemen? Could we regard them any longer as deserving of the name of Christian Missions?

A pamphlet, purporting to be the address which Bishop Colenso undertook to deliver on Christian Missions and their Results, has been received, and we hope to review it in our next Number.

THE AFFGHAN MISSIONARIES IN KAFIRISTAN.

Amongst the many documents which have passed through our hands, and which, through the pages of this periodical, we have presented to British Christians, during the sixteen years of its existence, we remember none more calculated to arrest attention than the narrative which we now publish. It has been compiled from the Pushtoo diary of the two Affghan Christians, who, at the risk of their lives, penetrated into Kafiristan, and there taught and preached Jesus Christ to its benighted inhabitants. The points of interest are numerous; the series of dangers to which they exposed themselves in passing through the midst of fanatical Mohammedans of various tribes, who, had they only known them to be Christians, would without mercy have put them to death; the constant danger they were in of being discovered and betrayed by some of the many youths who, having been to Peshawur for education, knew them well; the uncertainty they were under as to the reception they would meet with at the hands of the Kafirs, when they recollected the deadly feud which for ages had existed between them and the Mohammedan Affghans, and recollected that, although no longer Mohammedans, they were yet Affghans; the dreadful butchery of several Mohammedans which took place immediately on their entering Kafiristan; and then their being moved to all this by none other than Christian motives;—who, after reading such a document, can fail to acknowledge the genuineness and vigour of native Christianity? Are these men inferior to us in courage, self-denial, and ready endurance of whatever may betide in the fulfilment of a great Christian duty? Nay, may we not learn from them? Do they not stand forth as an example? Have they not been animated by the same spirit which prompted Paul to say—"None of these things move me, neither do I count my life dear to myself, if so be I might run my course with joy, and the ministry which I have received of the Lord Jesus, to testify the Gospel of the grace of God."

And these Kafirs, so marvellously preserved in their mountain fastnesses amidst the fierce ascendancy of Mohammedanism, around which, like an angry sea, it has fretted against the barriers of their home, and yet never has been able to force an entrance,—have they not been spared for an object? Hating Islamism, from which they have suffered ages of cruel wrong, they are favourably disposed towards Christianity, and earnestly desire instruction. What if it please God that, in these mountain-tops, the standard of Christianity should be raised, until from this, as from a centre, it moves forward to reconquer the lands over which the fanaticism of the Arabian prophet has so long tyrannized?

In the summer of 1859, as a Missionary in Peshawur was returning alone, and somewhat discouraged, from preaching in the bazaar, he was accosted by a young man from Eusufzie, making many inquiries about the Christian religion, and requesting permission to visit him in his house. He was an Affghan police soldier, by name Fazl Huq, of good abilities and education, the son of a well-known and influential Mullah, of the village of Adeena. The New Testament was placed in his hands, and after instruction, and a delay of some months, he was baptized. No sooner had he become a Christian than he insisted on being independent of the Mission, and earning his own livelihood; "for," said he, "if I remain with you, the people will say I became a Christian for temporal advantages." There were difficulties in his remaining as a Christian in the police, and he therefore enlisted into the corps of guides, the finest native regiment in India, which had earned laurels in every frontier campaign, and lately had returned with great distinction from the siege of Delhi. There was already in that regiment one native Christian, a well-known Khuttak soldier, Dildwur Khan, who had been promoted for his bravery at Delhi to the high rank of subadar. By nature a fighting-man, in argument as well as in the field, Dilawur Khan had been fighting all his life; first against the Sikh infidels, and then in the Christians' ranks; and he had wished to fight us Christians, too, in religious matters, and had gone to the Mullahs to furnish himself with weapons with which to demolish Christianity. Instead of arguments, he met with only abuse, for thinking and talking on such subjects at all; but just at this crisis of his religious life he received a copy of the Mizan-ul-Huqq from Colonel Wheler, in the streets of Peshawur. Whichever way he fought, silenced he would not be; so Mullah after Mullah was visited again, to answer the Christian's charges, but they only called him an infidel for his pains. He then visited the Missionary, Dr. Pfander, who, with patience and great kindness, gave him all the information he sought; and after the siege of Delhi he was baptized by the Rev. T. H. Fitzpatrick, in 1858. From that time to the present his spare moments have been generally spent in attacking Mohammedanism before every one he meets, Mullah or layman, with all his powers of dry wit and quiet sarcasm. It could be wished that he had more of Christ's own spirit, which seems to be largely imparted to some other Affghan converts, but his talents lie in arguing and fighting; and although he is not building up Christianity, he is doing a great work in loosening the strong gripe with which Mohammedanism holds fast the people's minds.

It was in a great measure through his protection that Fazl Huq was able to remain in a Mohammedan regiment, and in his own Mohammedan country, in spite of all opposition, for five whole years; for Dilawur Khan, in peaceful argument as well as in war, always keeps his pistols primed, and his sword loose in his belt, for he knows that the Akhun of Swat has more than once sent men to take his life. Fazl Huq here proved himself to be a good soldier, and won the favourable opinion of his superiors. From the first day that he embraced Christianity he made the determination to let no day pass without carefully reading the word of God with prayer; and it was this, with God's blessing, that kept him straight, when away so long from the means of grace, and with very few Christian helps. He boldly confessed his faith, and both Dilawur Khan, and he, and others too, are known through the whole country, and are hated as much as they are known, as renegades from the faith, who have apostatized from their fathers' religion, and embraced the Christians' creed.

His old officers, however, gradually left the regiment, and the enmity on the part of the native officers and soldiers, which dared not show itself in Colonel Lumsden's time, appeared so strong that he could no longer hold his ground; and this spring he took his discharge from the regiment. It was then that the strong desire took possession of his mind to visit Kafiristan, and teach the Kafirs the word of life. There were some Kafirs in his regiment, whom Colonel Lumsden had brought from their own country, and persuaded to take service in his corps. Fazl Huq had had much intercourse with them, for they, like himself, were infidels; and he had taught some of them to read the Pushtoo Gospel, and had spoken often to them of Christ's religion. They had no settled faith of their own, and received all they heard; and urged him to go to their own country to tell their own people what he had taught them. Two of them had returned on leave to their mountain home, and from thence they sent him another message, telling him to come. The desire fixed itself deeply in his mind, and indeed nothing could turn him from his purpose, made after much thought and prayer. He knew the difficulties of the undertaking, for he was a Pathan himself, and during the late frontier campaign he had wandered alone, far beyond the heights of Umballah, through Boneir, the home of our bravest foes; for he was a Christian, and could be trusted to bring information from the midst of the enemy's land, at a time when implicit confidence could not generally be placed in Mohammedans. He knew the dangers he would meet with, for he had been discovered there to be a Christian, and had barely escaped with life. Another Christian convert, Nurullah, also from Eusufzie, who had himself been a Mullah and a Hafiz (who knows the whole Arabic Korân by heart), agreed to accompany him. They were supplied with medicines from the Medical Mission Fund, and also with many little presents for the people.

Kafiristan is a large mountainous country, north of Lughman, above Jelalabad, and stretching onwards to a considerable distance in the very centre of the Hindu Koosh, bounded on all sides by hills so high that it is almost inaccessible. Some of its snow-clad mountains may be seen on clear days from Peshawur. Its inhabitants were formerly supposed to be the descendants of Alexander's Greeks, but they are now thought to be those of the original inhabitants of the plains, who were gradually pushed forwards into the hills. Guarded in their strong castle, with its high mountain walls, they have never yet been conquered, though repeatedly assailed by Mohammedan armies on all sides. They have an inveterate hatred of the Mohammedans, and are always at war with them. In person they are fair, and their beautiful women are found as slaves in most parts of Affghanistan. In their native country they are wild and barbarous in the extreme.

On the 8th September the two Affghans left Peshawur. They were obliged to go as simple travellers, for there is a wide belt of Mohammedanism between Peshawur and Kafiristan, inhabited by some of the most fanatic tribes, where travelling is dangerous at all times, but where it is ordinarily death to be known to be a Christian. They could only travel, therefore, as other Affghans did; but when once arrived in Kafiristan, they hoped to appear in their proper character as Christian teachers. They had arranged in Peshawur with the leader of a caravan to conduct them to Jelalabad, but he had been told that they were Christians, and he declined any connexion with them whatever. They determined, therefore, on another route, and struck out boldly to the north, instead of the west, through Swat and Bajour, on a road not much frequented even by natives, and altogether unknown to Europeans. Only very few of the places visited are mentioned even in the latest Indian maps. They left Peshawur quietly, and arrived the same night at a village called Kangra, where, however, they were again discovered by a pupil of Fazl Huq's father, who abused them as Christians, and threatened to expose them. Fortunately he could do no more, for they were still on British ground. To avoid further difficulties, they left the village, as if to return to Peshawur, but, making a circuit, arrived the following afternoon at Sanderai. The next march was to Baransderai, beyond which the road was dangerous, as all the border land is, and they had to travel by night with three hired men, as guides and guards, to take them to Shahr. They here left the English territory, and entered that of Swat. On the following day they proceeded alone, with their baggage on their shoulders, and had walked but a few miles when two men confronted them, whom Nurullah knew, one of them having been a pupil in our Peshawur Mission School. They turned into the rice-fields to the left, and succeeded in avoiding observation, but they had to wade ankle deep in water to the Swat river, which they forded with difficulty, by the help of a kind countryman, who carried their clothes, and assisted them across. He would take nothing for his trouble, for he did it, he said, for the sake of God. After a long march of more than twelve hours, they reached Bar Badwan, where a hospitable potter took them in, and gave them food.

On the 12th of September they arrived at Kalumanai, after passing through Wuchuna. The road was considered dangerous, but they obtained two armed men for a guard. The following day they left Swat behind them, and entered Bajour, after crossing the Malagi river, which they did in a cradle drawn over the torrent by means of a rope bridge. They halted at Walai, and, being much fatigued, fell asleep under a tree, where they had taken up their quarters; but they were soon awoke by another disciple of Fazl Huq's father, who wanted to know what he, a Christian, was doing there. They tried to pacify him with friendly words, and gave him a present of a small Birmingham looking-glass; but he demanded ashrafees and pearls as the price of not instantly giving information that they were Christians, and having them put to death. He was at last conciliated with nine rupees, and, finding that he was ill with dysentery, they gave him medicine, which relieved him, and he then took them to his uncle's house, and gave them food.

The next march was to Mean Killai (or Mean Shahr) through Shobana. They here found forty armed Hindustanees, with their two leaders, Abdool Majid and Abdool Karim, who had fought against us at Umballah. When they heard that travellers had come in from Peshawur, several of them came to ask whether the Sahibs were preparing for further expeditions; and, after some conversation, they entertained them as their guests. Three nights had to be spent here, for the inward road was so dangerous that no one would accompany them. At last, seven men, with matchlocks, were procured, to go as far as Badan; but on arriving there no one would take them in, or give them either shelter or food, even for money. They sat down by the way-side; but after a little time they overheard a man telling another that his wife was ill. They asked what her sickness was, and sent her medicine by her husband, praying earnestly that it might be blessed to her recovery. They daily had much need for prayer; and daily they asked in faith for God's guidance and protection, and for the supply of all their wants, which, somehow or other, were all daily accorded. The woman's pain abated, and the grateful husband brought loaves and beds, and hospitably entertained them, and procured four guards on the following morning for the onward march to Ghakhai. Of these four men, they remarked that two were armed with Minié rifles, taken at Umballah, and two with matchlocks. They here left Bajour, and entered Koonur, after crossing over the Hindooraj, an exceedingly high mountain, clothed with forest on its north-west side. The first village in Koonur was Marawurm, where they were only two marches from the Nashi or Katar tribe of Kafirs, a party of whom had attacked the village two nights before, and had killed a man and a woman. They found the people all around, and keeping nightly guard in expectation of their return. They seized on our travellers, telling them either to keep watch with them, or leave their village. They sat down with them, and the following conversation with a Mullah soon afterwards occurred. "Where do you come from?" "From Eusufzie." "From what village?" "Adeena." "Do you know Mullah Pasanai" (Fazl Huq's own father)? "Yes." "Did you ever see his son, Fazl Huq (himself), whom I knew as a child, when I was the Mullah's disciple?" "Yes." "How are they all; are they well?" "Yes, they are all quite well." "Then come in," said the Mullah, "and have something to eat, for you have brought me good news." He made the people let them go, after payment of a few pice, and got them some food from the Hindu Baniya.

The next march to Pushit was a particularly dangerous one, but eight armed men were procured to escort them. On the road they met a man, Wuseek—whose brother Shafik was in the Guides—in a part of the road where they could not avoid him. They knew one another, and embraced, falling on each others' necks in proper Affghan fashion. Without giving him time to collect his thoughts, they put a bold face on the matter, and told him almost all, throwing themselves on his honour, but hinting, moreover, that his own brother was in English territory, so that of course he would be their friend. He kept their secret, took them to his house, entertained them hospitably, and washed their clothes.

Four Sowars, who were going on their road, were their escort to Koonur, a large village, with a good bazaar, and many Hindu shops. They here crossed the Koonur river on inflated skins, and went on through Kudalai and Patan to Nurghul. On the road they passed by the ruins of a large old Kafir town. At Nurghul they again found the people expecting an attack from Kafirs. Nothing could be obtained to eat, but here again their medicines came to their aid when in difficulties. A man was ill with fever: they gave him an emetic, and then quinine, which cured him, and he then brought out both bread and cheese. They here bound five skins together, and, seated on their raft, descended the stream to Tangai, and then went on to Bariabad in Ningrahar, where five students and sepoys from Eusufzie, who knew them well, were seen sitting in a mosque, as they entered the village. They retired without observation, and, meeting a man outside the village with camels and covered kajawas, such as are used by veiled women on their journeys, they bargained with him to take them, concealed as women, to Jelalabad, giving as their reason that they had enemies in the neighbourhood whom they wished to avoid. They have often spoken since of this narrow escape, feeling that they were then in very great danger of life indeed.

The first part of their journey to Jelalabad was thus safely accomplished. They had travelled on unfrequented roads some 150 miles, in order to avoid the direct road through the Khyber pass, which, although only about seventy miles from Peshawur, was felt to be impracticable for them as Christians. They had met with many dangers, but God had delivered them out of them all. They did not, however, think it safe for them to remain long at Jelalabad, and so, after one good dinner of meat and melons and grapes—great luxuries to them after the hardships they had encountered—they entered at once on their further journey, which led them first to Charbagh, through Nazarabad, after passing by many large caves overhanging the river, which are supposed to have been built by the Kafirs of former days.

They were here obliged altogether to disguise themselves, for it was near here that two former guide-soldiers lived, who, they knew, would lose no opportunity of doing them harm. The one was Majid, once a Havildar, whom the writer had known in 1856, when he employed him to bring down the son of a Kafir chief on a visit to him in Peshawur. Since then he had misconducted himself, and, after a year's imprisonment and expulsion from his corps, he had considered the absence of the regiment on the Umballah campaign to be a good opportunity for plundering some of the regimental hospital stores, and he went off with them, leaving a message behind him that his intention was to become physician to the Ameer of Cabul. Madin was another discharged soldier of the same corps, who, one day meeting in his village four Kafir soldiers of his own regiment, who were returning on leave to their country, robbed them in open day of all they had, and sent them on empty-handed to their homes. Such are many of the Affghans; bold, unscrupulous, reckless of life, whether of others or their own, clever, fertile in resource, by nature rogues who fear neither God nor man, though they pray five times a day, and would, some of them, sooner die than break their appointed fasts. How to avoid these men, and pass through their villages unseen, was a question requiring deliberation. At last they agreed to travel in women's attire, and cover their faces with burkas. Three guides were hired to defend and conduct them, and they hired a private apartment at Mulayan for them, as for women, and cooked their food; but, to their dismay, having brought them to the village, they refused to take them further, and it was no pleasant prospect for them to be found there at all, much less in this disguise. Our Affghan Christian travellers gave themselves to prayer, and, for a consideration, three guides at last agreed to accompany them to the next village, Niyazi, where they assumed their own proper dress. They were now in a country on the banks of the Mungo river, where every man's house is a fort, and every village a castle; and they proceeded onwards by successive marches to Rajai, Kotala, Adar, and thence to Kajgara, the village of another guide-sepoy, Shahbuddeen, who was their friend. They gave him a Peshawur turban, and cured his little daughter, who lay sick with fever, and he accompanied them to Niliar, the last Mohammedan village on their way. Here dwelt Abdullah the Sahibzada, who had visited the writer in 1856 with Majid and the son of the Kafir chief. He is a Sayad, and a great man in that neighbourhood, being the principal channel of communication between the Kafirs and Mohammedans. He frankly told them that if they entered Kafiristan they would both be killed. They said they had friends there, and gave him presents to induce him to accompany them, with seven guards, to Malel. The road was exceeding steep, so that they could only climb the hill by clinging to the rocks with hands and naked feet.

Half way to Malel was Munli, the rendezvous of the Kafirs, where they brought their walnuts and fruit, and bartered them to the Mohammedans for salt. Fifty Kafirs were then there on this errand. Abdullah told them not to fear, and the Kafirs came forward to greet them, putting out both their hands with the palms extended in an horizontal direction, and, after enfolding theirs', they waved them backwards and forwards with the cry of welcome—"Modaji, shabase," ("Do not be tired; we are glad to see you.") They were armed with bows and arrows and knives. Our travellers inquired for Ghara, the Kafir sepoy, who had invited them to their country, and heard that he had come to a funeral to a village some little distance off. They wrote a line in Pushtoo to tell him to come at once, for Ghara had been taught by Fazl Huq to read; and they gave a Kafir seven yards of their turban to take it, money being there of no use, and perfectly unknown. They then all went on to Malel, from which place the Sahibzada and Shahbuddeen returned, being afraid to proceed further, and our travellers were left alone with Kafirs. They had now, at least, attained the object of their journey, and saw the people face to face whom they had endured danger and hardship in endeavouring to reach. How would they be received? They knew that death was the fate of every Affghan Mohammedan in Kafiristan, and they were in the dress of Affghans. Their friends had not yet arrived, and they had no present helper but God. One of them was in great alarm, but the other cheered him with words of faith and hope, and they were much comforted in their earnest prayers. Being in want of food, they bartered four more yards of the turban for bread and cheese, when, fortunately, they saw a woman with sore eyes. They gave her medicine, and she recovered, and immediately the whole village brought out their sick to be healed. Six men out of eleven were cured of fever with quinine, and the people became most friendly. They had then time to look about them. The mountain-tops were bare and bleak, but their sides were covered with forest-trees, especially fir; there were also the walnut, mulberry, and amluk-trees. The fields were artificial, built up in small terraces with stones: there being hardly any earth, they make mould with sand and dung. The houses were, many of them, five stories high with flat roofs and wooden doors, the people ascending from one story to the next on single sloping beams with rough steps cut in them. The fires were lighted in the centre of the rooms, and they all sat round them, leaving the smoke to escape as it could. At meals they sat sometimes on the ground, but often on low stools with tables, on which they placed their food. There were also beds in the houses, but they lie generally altogether on a coarse carpet on the floor, the end of which they throw over them. The women were not concealed, and were quite fair, and extremely pretty, with dark brown hair and eyes. They mixed with the men, and even talked with their visitors. Their dress consisted of tight trousers, black below the knee and white above, with a shirt over the body which reached almost to the knees, but was loosely bound up round the waist. Their hair was wound together, and confined by a little woollen cap on the top of the head. The whole neck was covered with necklaces of berries and beads. Their feet are generally bare, but sometimes they wear boots. Both men and women wear brass or iron bracelets, ornamented with serpent's heads, and also brass and iron necklaces. The women have long heavy earrings of beads, twined round the ear, but supported by a string attached to the cap above. The men wear woollen trousers, tied up with a girdle round the waist, with goat-skin coats wrapped round the body, and long sleeves of the same material pulled on aftewards, the hair being next the skin. The head is generally either bare, or covered with the bark of trees. They shave their heads, leaving a round patch of long hair in the centre. Sometimes they shave also both beard and whiskers, and sometimes only the beard; but when the beard is worn, it is never allowed to grow long.

The women do all the work, and cook, and grind corn, and bring wood and water. They also plough the so-called fields, one woman guiding the plough and another drawing it in front. The men are ashamed to do any work, and only feed the flocks, and fight, and meet together in counsel. Cattle are very scarce, but goats are abundant.

In three days Ghara arrived. He had run the whole way, fearing they would be killed. He expected, he said, that the Missionary was with them, but no English Missionary had ventured (though more than one had often wished) to take that road. He received them with the greatest cordiality, begging them to go on to his village, and undertaking to defend them with his life.

The next morning they all departed on the road to Titani, which was very mountainous, almost entirely over rock, which sometimes was as steep as stairs. Two yards of the turban were still left, which they sold for eight cakes of bread. The night was spent on the top of a house five stories high.

A fearful initiation into their work now lay before them, exhibiting to them Kafir ferocity in its worst features. The next march was to Nikera, on the tops of the mountains. They here found twenty-eight armed Mussulmans, who had been invited by the Kafirs over from Mungoo. It was many years since a number of Kafirs had been slain in their village, and they thought the fact forgiven or forgotten, and believed themselves to be quite safe when they came armed, and in such numbers, to accept the Kafirs' hospitality. Their hosts feasted them bountifully, and, after removing all suspicion from their minds, had persuaded them to leave their arms in the huts assigned to them. It was at this time that our travellers arrived, and had much conversation with these Mungoo men, two of whom were Mullahs, and six students from Koonur, when suddenly their friend Ghara called out to them in Hindustanee to come away. "What for?" they asked. "Because they were going to dance." "Then we, too, will stop and see it." "But there will be a scene (tamasha), and you must come away." All this was in Hindustanee, which none but they understood. They withdrew quietly, and sat down on a rock above. The Kafirs brought a drum and pipes, and began to sing and dance, throwing their hands and feet about, the women looking on. Then suddenly, without one moment's warning, each Kafir knife was unsheathed, and seen poised high above his head, and, with a loud whistle, four or five Kafirs rushed on each Mohammedan, stabbing him in every part. The whole was over in a moment, and all had sunk down dead, covered with many wounds. They then beheaded them, and threw them all down into the rivulet below. Our travellers were speechless with horror, when Ghara again told them not to fear, for not one hair of them should be touched. They pointed to the dead bodies below, and gasped out that they, too, one short quarter of an hour before, had been the Kafirs' guests. He told them the reason of such dreadful vengeance. The blood feud was still unremoved, and the Kafirs had never forgotten their own brethren murdered long before. He told them, however, never to leave him. Three days after, the Kafirs sent to Mungoo to tell them to send men for the property of the slain: for Kafirs never plunder, they only kill the Mussulman. Some people went from Malel, and brought back their muskets and daggers (which the Kafirs so much valued, but could not take) and also their heads or hands.

From Nikera they passed over Walimund, the highest mountain in the neighbourhood, where last year's snow lay still unmelted in the hollows, to Begura, and thence the next day to Ghara's own village, Shaiderlain. They were here visited by many friends. Kachu, the Guide sepoy, came, with his two pretty wives; and Karuk, Shashi, Badshah, Wuskari, and Balo, all of whom had, at one time or another, taken service in the Guide corps. They brought their wives and children, with food and grapes, showing all hospitality to the strangers, and receiving presents from them in return. Missionary work had begun long before, for Ghara and his friends had always joined them in their morning and evening devotions, and there had been much conversation on religion at different times. But now it was carried on in earnest for the space of some twenty days. All day long, from morning to night, they were talking with the people, and answering questions, and were joined by them in their services; and at night they wrote their journal, giving, in Pushtoo, a full account of all they saw and heard, with names of persons, places, and things. This journal was written with lime-juice; and, on their return, appeared only blank pages of white paper, but, when heated over the fire, the letters gradually darkened, and assumed their proper shape. Ghara and Kachu, and their wives, were the most interested, but all listened, and all applauded, as Ghara translated into their own language the words they spoke. At times the whole village, men, women, and children, were assembled together.

The journal contains an interesting account of many of their customs. Men never marry in their own village, for all the women of the same village are considered as sisters; and they never marry without the free consent of both man and woman. When a man has made his choice, he asks his father to obtain a certain girl for him. The father sends a goat and three rams to the girl's father's house. Nothing is spoken, but the goats are bound inside the house. If the girl's father kills the goat, and keeps the rams, and sends the bearer home without them, the betrothal is completed. If he sends back the goats, the girl has refused. When once betrothed, the man can visit the girl quietly in the hills, but he neither talks with her in public (as he does with other women), nor brings her presents. When the wedding-day arrives, the bridegroom's father sends two men to the father of the bride, with goats, and vessels, and pans, and a spit and a candlestick, or rather a torch stick (for they do not here burn oil, but pine-wood), and, if he can afford it, a gun also. The two men remain there two nights, during which dancing and feasting are going on in both villages, men and women apart; the men, they say, seem to spend their life in dancing and playing. The bride's father then gives her clothes (black ones are considered the prettiest), and the two men conduct the bride, accompanied by several women, who carry grain with them, to the bridegroom's house. When the bride once crosses the threshold, no further ceremonies take place: she is at once his wife. The women remain with her for two days, and then return, after receiving four goats. The newly-married wife may not revisit her father's house for five years. She may then go and see her father and mother for a month or two, and, when she returns, the women again carry grain with her. Afterwards they may visit as they choose.

Adultery is never known in Kafiristan, but many men have more than one wife. The breach of the seventh commandment in any form is not for a moment endured. They believe the vengeance of their gods falls on the whole village for it. If there is a time of drought, or any misfortune befals a village, the unmarried women are suspected, for not even does suspicion ever reach the home of one who is married. An old man or a woman is deputed to discover the culprit. She is made, on pain of death, to disclose her lover. The property of both man and woman is then at once plundered, and the houses of both are burned to the ground; and, pelted and hooted by both boys and girls, they are expelled for ever from the village, and sent away to the Mussulmans. The very road on which they go is esteemed impure, for the people follow them, and sacrifice a goat at the nearest stream they cross. The god is then appeased, and it need hardly be said that this crime, so venial in Christian civilized lands, is here very rare indeed.

No thefts in Kafiristan are ever known. If a man drops a knife on the mountains, many may pass by it, but no one takes it up to appropriate it. No burglary is known. Houses are left quite unprotected. If corn falls in the leading, the owner is found out, and it is returned to him. If they kill a man, they send his weapons back to his home.

They never, however, do kill a man of their own village. If any two men have a quarrel, they meet in the presence of the village, duly take off their upper clothes, and lay down their weapons. They then have it out in wrestling, embracing each other, both before they begin, and after all is over. If either of them takes up even a stick, the whole village interferes. No one was ever known to kill or even wound a man of his own village.

If two villages fight together, they then use their weapons. Tribes are very often at war with each other, and they kill all who come in their way who do not belong to their own tribe.

It is this killing men (and women too) which alone leads to high honours amongst the Kafirs. They have no king, and there are only two ranks of nobility or distinction amongst them; the one that of the Bahadur, and the other that of the Surunwali or Soninwali. Neither of them are hereditary, and neither are attainable except by killing four men. When a man has killed his four men he must, to become a Bahadur, feed all comers for two days with two hundred goats, six oxen, and many hundred pounds weight of corn, and rice, and cheese, together with an enormous quantity of wine. To become afterwards a Surunwali, he must wait three years, during the whole of which time he has to give eighty feasts, at periods varying from a week to ten days from each other, for the Kafirs are far too intelligent to have them altogether. The proper amount of food to be given at each feast is appointed. The smallest number of goats killed at any time is twenty; but on the sixth feast they kill 150; and on the 9th one living goat is given to every comer, besides bread and cheese, and ghee and wine. On receiving his new dignity, a particular large drum, called mundoo, which is never beaten except on very special occasions, is sounded, and there is much dancing of both men and women. He is no longer required then to kill any more people, unless he does so from choice. In order to show how many people they have killed, each man erects a high pole on the outskirts of his village, with a rude figure of a man on the top of it. For every man he kills he bores a hole in it, and knocks in a peg. If he kills a woman, he bores only a hole, without any peg. A Bahadur or Surunwali always occupies the highest place at feasts, and receives a double portion.

The following is one of their most common songs. A father, in the village of Shino, is supposed to have sold his son to the Mohammedans: when the boy was grown he kills fourteen Mussulman men and effects his escape to his home, and the mother, in proud delight, sings as follows—

Parolé bélé bató warméláwe
Badal lowe bele amá bato lausousáwe
Urá pras sagor aman bato warmiláwe
Awár paras dandako partus tatakotáwe
Pa sheristán gangare sutá.

Well done, my lad, well hast thou fought;
My old blood was drying up for grief for thee,
When thy father sold my high-spirited boy.
And thou hast killed fourteen men, and come home again,
With the bells tinkling on thy feet!

At burials the custom is to bathe the corpse, and dress it in new or newly-washed clothes. The people stand around, weeping and dancing, and beating a small drum, and playing pipes. They then make a coffin on the day of death, and one man lifts up the corpse on his shoulders, and another man the coffin, which is a large one, three spans broad and three spans high, and they carry them both to some cave in the hills, where the corpse is put into the coffin, which is then closed with wooden pegs, and left with great stones on it. If one of the same family dies within three years they open the coffin, and put the body in it. If it is more than three years they make a new coffin. No ceremony is used, and nothing is spoken, only both men and women cry. When persons are dying, women sit near them, but nothing is said. If the deceased was a Bahadur or a Surunwali, the body is kept for three days, and they feed all who come, and weep, and dance, and beat the large drum, mundoo. On the third day they carry him, with his bow and arrows and knife; and for five years they keep the day of his death by beating the drum, mundoo, and giving alms and feasts. The mundoo is also beaten for a Surunwali's descendant for five generations; and if a Surunwali's son becomes himself a Surunwali it is beaten for ten generations; and if his grandson, too, becomes one, it is then done for fifteen generations.

A widow or widower may not marry again for three years, during which time they neither anoint or wash their head, or put antimony on their eyes, or wear good clothes, or eat ghee. The men, too, do not shave their heads.

In religious matters they have no temples nor Mullahs, nor books, nor observances. They believe there is only one God, but who, or what, or where He is, or with what He is pleased, they say they do not know. They have three idols, who they believe to be their intercessors with God. The one is of wood, roughly carved into the shape of a man, with silver eyes. It is called Pulispanu, and is erected in the village of Muzghal. It is resorted to on all public occasions, as when there is no rain, or too much rain, or great sickness in the land. Each Kafir brings a goat, and sacrifices it, sprinkling the blood over it. They then cook it, and either eat it there or take it to their houses. It is thought great disrespect to the idol for any woman to come near to it: they therefore bake bread and partake of the sacrifice at a distance from it. They never salaam to the idol, or prostrate themselves before it, but merely ask it to give them what they want. They have otherwise no fixed worship or posture of worship of any kind, and no great times or holidays.

The other two idols are merely common stones. The one is called Adrakpanu, in the village of Girdalares; and the other Matikapanu, in the Shaiderlam. They are used for family and personal matters, and they ask them for good harvests and for children, &c.

There are no fowls in the country: the people do not eat them, nor fish, nor eggs. They eat partridges, and different kinds of stags, including barasinghas and uriyal. There are plenty of crows, parrots, manas, sparrows, vultures, hawks, and eagles; and leopards, bears, and wolves, but no jackals. There are no horses or ponies, or donkeys, or camels, and very few cattle, or buffaloes, or dogs; but there are cats, mice, rats, lizards, scorpions, and snakes. They have a strange superstition about snakes, which they never kill, as they think some great injury will happen to them for doing so. Goat flesh is the common food of the country, which they cook in great pieces in large vessels. They eat the blood, and, indeed, most of the entrails, and almost every thing but the skin and bone. They drink wine in large quantities, and very nasty it is, if what was brought down to Peshawur may be taken as a specimen. No one was ever seen by our travellers to be intoxicated. Their drinking vessels are of earthenware, curiously worked, and occasionally of silver. They eat with their hands. The water is said to be particularly good, and the people often live to a great age, remaining strong and well almost up to the day of death. Goitures are only occasionally seen. The men are somewhat dark, but the women are said to be as fair as Europeans, and very beautiful, with red cheeks. The men hardly ever wash either themselves or their clothes: both they and their clothes are said to be often first washed on the day of the man's death. Our Affghan travellers saw no fleas; but lice are common, and there are terrible musquitos that inflict great wounds that swell and bleed. The foot of one of the travellers was still bound up on his arrival in Peshawur, from a musquito sting that had been given him a month before.

As in all uncivilized lands, fairy tales are plentiful; and the people speak with implicit confidence of some tanks high up on a certain mountain-top, filled with treasures, but which cannot be reached because the fairies guard them. They tell, too, of a wonderful tree on another hill, watched over by peculiarly large snakes, the wood of which has the property of attracting every one to the person who possesses it. When talking, they shout with all their might. Some of them had an almost superstitious faith in the powers possessed by our travellers. A girl, Marimari, one day brought her little brother, who was crying from a bad attack of toothache, asking them to pray for him. They did so, and stroked his face. The girl thought he was cured, and led him away, and on the child beginning again to cry, she slapped his face for crying, she said, after he had been healed. Whether it was nature or the blow, the child was healed, and his recovery being attributed to their prayers, they all brought their implements, a gun or plough, or bow and arrow, to be blessed. There were, however, some who clung to their own religion, and asked for miracles, such, they said, as Christ Himself had wrought, to prove the truth of Christianity. They were, however, in numbers, only very few: the large majority listened to them with respect and attention, appearing to receive and believe all that was said.

The snows, were, however, beginning to fall, and winter was approaching; and our native Missionaries had to decide between spending the winter there or returning home. For many reasons it appeared right for them to return. Ghara, and many Kafirs, accompanied them for four days' journey on their way from Shaiderlam to Begura, Nakera, Zitani, and thence to Malel, where they sent them safely out of Kafiristan, through the Sahibzada Abdullah. They travelled by the old road to Jelalabad, and thence by water on a raft down the Cabul river, to Peshawur, after two narrow escapes from the Imâm of a well-known mosque in Peshawur, whom they with difficulty avoided; and from a student who recognised them, but was persuaded to keep their secret. They arrived in Peshawur on the 10th of November, after an absence of rather more than two months, bringing with them a bow and arrow, a knife, a leathern bottle of their wine, boots, girdles, and different parts of the Kafir dress.

The following are the translations of two Pushtoo letters, sent by the Kafirs to a Missionary and his wife—

"We were very much delighted when Fazl Huq and Nurullah arrived; but we had hoped that you would yourself have come with them. We were made very happy by the stay they made with us; but when snow began to fall we sent them away for fear that they would be troubled with the cold. But if the winter had not been approaching, we would not willingly have let them go. But they have promised to return next summer to us, and tell us much more about Christ's religion. Be kind to us, therefore, and send them again next summer, and as long as we live there shall be no danger of their death in Kafiristan; and we will attend to all their wants, so that they may be comfortable; and we will do any thing for you, too, that we can. Then send them back again, that we may receive much benefit in learning their religion; and we will all soon accept the Christian religion. We hope you will always pray for us; and if they do not come we shall be much disappointed. Kunchuk, and Ghara, and Baro, and Shashi, and Karuk, and Badshah (who all sent this letter), send you salaams with both hands; and when they come back, send us a small copper vessel to mix our food in."

The letter to the Missionary's wife was thus—

"We are well, and we arrived safely back to our own country, and we often pray for you and the children. It was a great kindness in you to think of us, and to send us men to teach us about religion. It will be another kindness if you will send them back again; and as long as we live there shall be no fear of their death. We will be attentive to all their wants; and we would be very happy to be able to do any thing for you. There is a man here who has been ill for three years with a bullet in his foot: send him some medicine; and, for the sake of God, send us some medicines, for there are no doctors or medicine here. Shagu, Gharas' wife, and Maramari, her sister's daughter, and Kunchuk's two wives, send you salaams." (This letter was from Ghara and Kunchuk alone.)

We have given the above narrative as related in their own journal, written on the spot. No doubt the Kafirs, from whom most of the information comes, have somewhat exaggerated their own virtues, and the travellers were too short a time in the country to see much of the opposite side of the picture, and detect the weak points of their too great self-praise.

We may learn from the narrative, however, first, how important a position Peshawur holds, with reference to Missionary work amongst the surrounding tribes. The young men crowd to it for education, and return as Mullahs to their own villages. Wherever our travellers went, there were students or others who had direct connexion with Peshawur. The Peshawur Mullahs are celebrated, and pupils come to them even from Cabul, Balkh, and Bokhara. Students never go from Peshawur for education to the latter places, but many come from thence, and hundreds come from all the hill tribes around.

So we observe, secondly, the great importance of Medical Missions amongst these mountain clans. The bearer of medicine is respected, and protection is at once given him, together with food and shelter, whilst other travellers are neglected, or often plundered. With medicines in his hand, a man can visit them in comparative safety, for these simple tribes are not so foolish as the learned Akhun of Swat, who, suffering under a painful complaint, declines all remedies; for, says he, God gave him his disease, and God, in his own good time, may take it away. Our travellers had only very ordinary medicines, and they had only two hours' instruction, from the wife of one of the Missionaries, who made them write down what to do.

We learn, thirdly, to sympathize with our native brethren, who have become Christians from amongst Mohammedan Affghans. We see here how Mohammedans hate them. Outside our own territory it is often death to be discovered. Inside it, they are subjected to trials which, in England, people have no conception of. Yet God has given them brave hearts, a strong will, and a fixed determination. They cannot sit still idle, and it is not in their nature to fear danger or opposition, which they are so much accustomed to. Let us help them, then, with our prayers and efforts. It may be that their fearless courage and enterprise will make them good pioneers and heralds of the cross in Central Asia, where no Englishman's foot can tread. Let our Missionary Societies at home look well to the Affghans. It may be that a few good Affghan Christians may do more to disseminate the truth than hundreds of the tamer races who live in India below them.

JOURNAL OF A MISSIONARY TOUR UNDERTAKEN BY THE REV. R. H. WEAKLEY AND THE REV. J. F. WOLTERS, APRIL 1864.

IN the present state of Turkey, and the uncertainty which exists as to the intentions of its rulers with reference to Protestant Missionaries and the spread of scriptural Christianity throughout that empire, it is desirable to place before our readers all the information we can command. The following notes of itinerancy into the interior of Asia Minor, the route extending to Philadelphia, Laodicea, and Hierapolis, will be found to embrace many points of interest.

April 8—After having been commended to the care and guidance of our heavenly Father, we we ready to start at eight o'clock A.M. Our party is larger than it was last October. We take with us our Mission servant, who is to help in the sale of Scriptures. We go forth with the earnest prayer that our journey may be prospered by Him whose the work is in which we are engaged. Without the blessing of our God we go forth in vain. Oh for an open door, and grace to enter thereby. With such thoughts and desires we rode across the hills to the north of Boujah. A steep descent on the other side brought us into the plain of Bournabat. Crossing this too, we got among hills again, and reached the pass of Kavakli-deri about eleven A.M. On resuming our journey after a short halt, we were soon overtaken by rain, which we had previously noticed to fall on the tops of the surrounding mountains. The Tmolus on our right, and Sipylus on our left, were enveloped in clouds and mist, their bases alone being visible, though every now and then some lofty peaks of the former would appear through a break in the clouds. Once we caught a glimpse of the Boz-dagh (Ice-mountain), the highest part of the Tmolus, its snowy top gleaming in the sunshine—a striking contrast to the dark masses of cloud beneath. I could not help thinking of the promises of God which remain bright and sure, even though we may lose sight of them for a time by reason of the difficulties and the darkness which surround our path.

At two P.M. we made another halt at a lonely coffee-house, where we enjoyed our meal, for we had begun to feel weary and chilly because of the rain. Here we found a poor negro suffering from dropsy. He was lying on a mat before a miserable fire; but much as we pitied him, we could do nothing to relieve his pain. Mr. Weakley then had some conversation with one of the Albanian guards at the coffee-house.

Having still a considerable way before us, we were soon in the saddle again. The rain ceased after a while, and riding became pleasanter. It was not until seven P.M. that we reached Cassaba, having been longer on the road than is usual. We found Montesanto and his family well, and gladly availed ourselves of their kind hospitality, truly thankful, I trust, for the mercies which we had received during the day.

April 9—Soon after breakfast we despatched our Mission servant, Belisarius, to see whether he could sell any books; ourselves intending to visit the old Sheikh Buchukzade. Just before setting out, Belisarius returned with joyful countenance. He had already sold a Turkish New Testament, and was now coming to fetch a copy of Genesis and Psalms in Turkish, which had been asked for. We looked upon this as a token for good, and took courage. If only we succeed in selling Scriptures we feel that we shall have accomplished something.

The old Sheikh was very pleased to see us. He was reading extracts from the Mesnevi, I believe a mystic poem written by Hazreti Mevlana of Konieh, and this gave us an opportunity of coming to the point at once. The Sheikh began by reading a passage from his book, setting forth the necessity of being fitted for heaven. We asked, "How is this fitness to be obtained?" "By doing good," was the answer. "Well, but what becomes of a man's past sins?" Mr. Weakley asked. "Oh, they are all blotted out by repentance." "Can this be the case? Will a man's ceasing to increase a debt cancel a debt previously contracted? Surely we need an intercessor; one who will make an atonement for us, and pay off all our debt." The Sheikh objected to this by denying that sin is a debt. "Sin is appointed to man by God's decree: good and evil deeds are like beads strung on a string, and man cannot help committing them." When pressed, he allowed that man is responsible for his actions, and went on to talk about the four books which are from God, and therefore true, viz. the Tewrat (Law), Zebur (Psalms), Ingil (Gospel), and Korán. Mr. Weakley said the Korán could not be the word of God, because it contradicts the Old and New Testaments; denying, *e.g.*, the fact of Christ's death upon the cross. This evidently disconcerted the old man. His answer was, "I do not know: I only speak what we are taught in the Korán." After a short pause the Sheikh re-opened the attack by accusing us of worshipping three gods. Mr. Weakley produced the Miftah-ul-Asrar—a copy of which we had in our pockets—and told the Sheikh that here he would find the whole subject fully discussed. He took the book, and at once commenced reading, but we asked him to keep it, and read it at his leisure. Brother Weakley urged the necessity of examining the credentials of our Scriptures as well as the claims of the Korán. The answer was, "Others have done this before us. Are all those numerous learned Mussulmans of by-gone days wrong?" "They might be. Were not the heathen philosophers in error?"

The Sheikh then read to us a passage from his book, the meaning of which, as far as I could make out, was the following:—The heavens do not actually exist as we see them, but there is an alternate creation and destruction of the heavenly bodies going on, with such amazing rapidity, that, to our eye, they appear invariably the same; just as a stick when lighted at one end, and moved rapidly in a circle, leaves the impression of a continuous circle of fire.

After having spent about two hours in this way, we rose to go, but the Sheikh would not hear of it, and, pulling Mr. Weakley by the coat to a seat near him, he resumed the discussion by reading a part of the Miftah, making remarks as he went on. He would have no objection to call Christ the Son of God, if by this expression we understood merely a title of honour, as men in general, and especially the pious, may be called the sons of God. After again urging upon him the necessity of searching carefully for the truth, in dependence upon, and praying for, the help of God, we left, accompanied with every good wish, and the request to renew our visit whenever we should return to Cassaba.

On reaching our lodgings we were glad to find that Belasarius had disposed of several copies of Holy Scripture. In the afternoon he succeeded equally well.

While sitting at the book-store which Montesanto keeps, a Greek merchant came in, and, after some remarks about cotton prospects, and the risk there is from several causes in doing business in that article, I took occasion to press upon him the duty of preparing in this life for eternity, so that we may receive an inheritance which fadeth not away. My words seemed to fall upon "thorny ground." Afterwards Montesanto related the following incident, which I put down as illustrative of the Greek church in some of these places. At Parsa, a village not far from Cassaba, and which we visited last autumn, there is a chapel dedicated to St. Nicholas, but no resident priest. The other day was the festival of the Annunciation. No arrangements having been made for a service, the pictures, on the eve of that day, had a battle, and it was discovered on the following morning that the picture of St. Nicholas had suffered some mishap. A priest was sent for in all haste from Cassaba, who pacified the pictures by holding a service in honour of the Virgin Mary.

We have just heard that a band of robbers, Zeïbecks as they are called, has been taken, and several men killed. This will intimidate any evil-disposed persons during the next few weeks.

April 10: *Lord's-day*—Held a short service this morning with Montesanto and his family. Mr. Weakley had intended to hold a service in Turkish in the afternoon, but Gallust (our guide, an Armenian) and his assistant did not come. They are kept away by fear, most likely. We had some profitable talk with Montesanto, and were glad of a rest preparatory to resuming our journey on the morrow.

April 11—Left Cassaba at half-past seven o'clock this morning for Salikly. The morning was beautiful, and the air pure and transparent after the recent rains. The Tmolus, with the lower range of hills which run parallel to it, repeatedly commanded our admiration. These hills, being composed of a gravelly soil, are worn into fantastic shapes by the action of water, aided, perhaps, by earthquakes. Here you see what might be mistaken for the ruins of a castle, with its battlements and turrets. There you see sharp points standing out against the blue sky, with precipices and ravines in abundance. All this was clearly defined, the atmosphere was so transparent. We went on our way rejoicing, and hoping to be able to do something for our heavenly Master in the various places which we propose to visit. At one of the coffee-houses on the road I inquired after a Greek to whom I had given some tracts last October, but found that he was at Cassaba. At another I had a few words with the bahal, or keeper of a small grocer's shop. "Have you ever read the New Testament?" In answer to this question, I was shown a Greco-Turkish book, containing stories about the patriarchs and saints, in rhyme. On being told that this is not the New Testament, he said he had a copy of the latter at home. I pointed him briefly to Christ, for we were obliged to move on. About noon the Acropolis of Sardis came in sight, and, after another hour, we were resting under the shade of some willows not far from the ruins. There was not much time to spare. The hot sun, black clouds rising over the mountains, and gusts of wind raising the dust, portended rain. We were on the road as soon as the horses had rested sufficiently, and reached Salikly just in time to escape a heavy shower.

Belisarius is determined to sell as many Scriptures as possible. The rain had hardly ceased before he was ready with his bag of books. Several men came to our room for Greco-Turkish Scriptures. One Turk took a copy of the New Testament to look at, and, seating himself at the gate of the khan, began reading aloud to an audience of six or seven Turks. He afterwards exchanged this copy for one of the Gospels printed in Constantinople.

Two Albanians came to have a chat with us. They have only recently come to Salikly, and are very much afraid of the fever and ague, for which this place is notorious. We told them of one or two simple remedies, for which they were extremely thankful. An attempt to interest them in higher matters failed.

April 12—We saw a little more of Salikly this morning than we did last October. It is a miserable place, although a great thoroughfare for travellers. The houses, built, as is usual, of sun-burnt bricks, are wretched in the extreme. Pools of water and deep mud everywhere. This may be partly owing to last night's rain. The clouds were still heavy when we started. The peaks of Tmolus had received a fresh layer of snow, and the air was raw and chilly. My teeth chattered with cold, until the rising sun dispersed the mists, and raised the temperature. We still kept along the northern foot of Tmolus, which sends down numerous rapid streams or torrents. These we had to ford. Here and there we espied a village prettily situated among the hills on our right. To the left, the wide and fertile plain of the Hermus stretched for several miles, until bounded by mountains on the north. The greater part of the plain appears to be under cultivation, and here and there we noticed men ploughing in their primitive style. Our first halting-place was Menamik Café, not far from a Turkish village. We found no one who could read. About noon we spent an hour at Deri Café, near Derikin, a considerable Turkish village. Here we had some talk with a Mussulman guard, but found him so ignorant and stupid that we were really puzzled to know how to speak to him about the Gospel.

Arrived at Allah-shehr (Philadelphia) about four P.M. We had caught sight of the minarets about an hour before. The view was one that I shall not soon forget. The white minarets and sun-lit landscape in the foreground contrasted beautifully with the purple mountains behind, on which rested black clouds. A majestic snow-capped peak rose to our right, and to the left, as heretofore, extended the wide plain, bounded on the opposite side by other ranges of mountains.

Our sale of Scriptures succeeds better than we had expected, *i.e.* among the Christians. Turks do not buy quite so readily, though here, too, we have no reason to be discouraged. We had hardly been half an hour in the khan before our room was filled, mostly with Greeks, who were eager to purchase the New Testament. A few Mussulmans also gladly accepted copies of the Sermon on the Mount, and one or two other tracts. Presently an Imâm (priest) came in to see our Turkish books. He looked at several, and then said, "You must not sell these books to Mussulmans." When asked why, he said, "There is something here about Isâ (Jesus) which is not suited to Mohammedans, seeing that the Ingil has been abrogated." On opening a copy of the Gospels, his eye fell on the words "Son of God." "This is for Giaours," he exclaimed: "do not offer such books to Moslems, lest you bring trouble upon yourselves. We do not need the Injîl; the Korân contains all the Old and New Testaments." Brother Weakley tried to reason with him, but it was of no use. It was like casting pearls before swine. At this moment another Turk came in to ask for a book. The Imâm showed him the expression, "Son of God," and frightened him away immediately. We then had a visit from three Greeks, one a doctor, such as they are in these places. He said that the Imâm who had just left was notorious as a bigot, but, although entertaining exalted notions of his own sanctity, has no very great influence over his co-religionists. There exists, on the whole, a friendly feeling between the Christians and Mohammedans in this place. The former number about 350 families, the latter 800. Philadelphia is the seat of a Greek Bishop. The doctor was anxious to hear political news. Having been satisfied, we spoke about the differences between the Protestant churches and the Greek. The doctor thought the difference is very small. I said it was very great, and instanced the doctrine of justification by faith. In the Greek church it is justification by works as well as faith.

April 13—Went out this morning to see the ruins. Great portions of the city walls —large masses of brick masonry—are still standing. In some cases these large masses are balanced upon a thin edge, the action of the weather, combined, it may be, with other causes, having worn away the parts near the base. The marvel is that the slightest shock of an earthquake, or some storm, has not brought these blocks down long ago. Philadelphia is placed on three hills, or spurs, which run out from the range of mountains behind. The streets are tolerably clean for a Turkish town. At a little distance from it are three mineral springs. One of them is warm, and is much resorted to on account of its supposed healing properties.

On returning to our room we were visited by a young Egyptian doctor, Emin Effendi. He invited us to his shop, where he not only dispenses physic, but also deals in various useful articles. Here, while Mr. Weakley conversed with him I had some talk with the Greek doctor and a friend of his who had accompanied us. We discussed the different way in which Greeks and Romanists treat the Holy Scriptures, the ignorance of the way of salvation prevalent among the Greeks, &c. We were disturbed by the entrance of Emin Effendi's father, a fine old man—seventy-eight years of age, as he informed us—whose intellectual features were in marked contrast with those of the Turks in general. After having inquired of his son who we were, he turned to us, and asked whether we did not believe that Jesus lives in heaven after his resurrection. We said, "Yes." "These stupid Greeks," he replied, "believe that the body of Jesus is still in Jerusalem, and that is why they go there on pilgrimage."

In the afternoon two Greeks came in, one of them being in the Bishop's service. They had just been conversing with Belisarius, and wanted to know what I thought of the mediation of saints, and of praying to them. My reply was, 1. "What saith the Scripture? 'There is one God, and one Mediator between God and men, the man Christ Jesus.' 'Come unto *me*, all ye that labour.' 2. If saints can hear prayers, they must be omnipresent and omniscient; for two or more persons may be addressing the same saint in places far distant from each other: but God only is omnipresent and omniscient." They seemed to be struck with this view of the case, but said, "It may be so: our church, however, believes in saints, and in their intercession." After these men had left us I went to see the Greek schools, three in number. An elementary school for boys, another for girls, and a Hellenic, or higher school, for boys more advanced. I found them all in a poor condition, especially the elementary school for boys. The blame, as is usual, is laid on the Turks, on their bad and oppressive government. The teacher of the Hellenic school is a priest. He was tolerably friendly so long as I confined myself to general matters, but as soon as I touched upon religion he became reserved. However, he accepted a copy of my father's Greek sermons. On my return to the khan, I found the bigoted Imâm of yesterday hovering about, evidently watching lest any of the "faithful" should take our books. Later on, we had another visit from Emin Effendi, who was this time accompanied by a dervish. The latter was rather a hindrance, through his incoherent talk. His appearance was wild, his person filthy. Yet such men are treated with great outward respect, even by the higher class of Turks. Emin Effendi impresses us favourably. He wants books on botany, medicine, &c., but such books are rare in Arabic and Turkish. He tells us that he possesses our Scriptures, and that he sometimes reads them. On a second visit such a man might be influenced still more. We trust that our intercourse on this occasion may have left some impression upon his mind and heart.

Still later we had a visit from a young soldier, who had served in the Montenegrin war. Belisarius had left a copy of the New Testament with him in the afternoon, and towards evening we saw him reading this to several Turks who occupied the same room with himself. At first he said he wanted to buy as many Turkish Scriptures as we could spare, but when he came to our room he purchased one copy of the New Testament, and seven parts, together with a few tracts. These he proposes to take to Kula, his native town, for distribution among his friends. He sat with us a considerable time, narrating incidents which took place during the Montenegrin war. We could not talk much about what is nearest to our hearts, but feel thankful that he possesses, and is likely to read, the word of God. "It is a good thing to read the Injil" was a remark he made in the course of conversation. We had thought of going to Kula, but were prevented by the state of the roads, our horses not being very good. But now we have been the means of introducing a few copies of the word of God in Kula by another way, and we are very thankful. We cannot help feeling that we are now only preparing the way for future work. It is a cheering sign, that not only many of the Greeks seek to obtain the word of God, but that even the Mussulmans do not, on the whole, offer more violent opposition. We were glad to learn that men like the Imâm are not very numerous.

April 14—Left Philadelphia at half-past seven A.M. for Ainégul. Soon after leaving Philadelphia our course took a more southerly direction, still, however, keeping parallel to the Tmolus, the snow-capped peaks of which we could not sufficiently admire. The plain which we have hitherto skirted now becomes narrower, and near Ainégul it appears to be completely shut in by mountains. Ainégul is a large Turkish village: there are but very few Greeks. Its inhabitants we found in a very degraded state: very few are able to read. Whilst walking through the bazaar, we were stared at as if we had been wild beasts. We had some talk with a Zabtieh (guard) who had been in the Crimean war. He praised every thing English, and spoke in disparaging terms of his own countrymen. By way of directing his thoughts to something better, we told him about Missionaries going to heathen countries to preach the Gospel.

April 15—To-day we saw enough of romantic scenery. Leaving Ainégul, we still proceed in an easterly direction; the valley becomes more and more contracted. At length there is a sharp turn to the south, and the valley is narrowed to a ravine. Through this runs a mountain torrent, feeling its way between great boulders and trunks of fallen trees. The hills are scantily wooded, indeed their sides are so steep in many places that it would be impossible for a tree to obtain a hold. The road winds along this ravine, sometimes along the bed of the stream, at others at a considerable height above it, along the sides of the rocks. Then the hills become lower and less steep, and, receding, leave a small space of open country. Here, on a declivity, lies a small village, Derbent. After a short rest, we proceed on our way. Again we wind along the bottom of a ravine, though neither so narrow or deep as the other. The hills are also better wooded. We presently emerge upon a plateau, and, looking back, catch a parting glimpse of Tmolus. Before us the scene is still more beautiful. We are at the head of a valley which widens gradually as it recedes from us. We descend into the valley; forests of pines and other trees surround us; the more distant hills fade into purple; and there, straight before us, though still far away, rises the broad mass of Baba-dagh—Mount Cadmus—covered with snow. How manifold, how glorious are thy works, O God!

Arrived at the lower end of the valley, we espy on our right the large Turkish village Bulladan, nestled high up, amidst rocks, and trees, and shrubs. Again we climb a small ascent, and a new surprise awaits us. We are still at a considerable elevation. Before us lies a great part of the Mæander, apparently well cultivated: several villages may be recognised by the trees growing near them. Towards the right, across the plain, Mount Cadmus is seen. Straight before us another range of mountains, with Hierapolis, the white incrustations of which are distinctly visible. We keep close to the side of the hills which we have just crossed, until we reach the plain below; then, crossing the Mæander by a wooden bridge, over which, for safety's sake, we lead horses, we arrive at Seraï-kioi, a little before sunset. Seraï-kioi is a miserable village, and very dirty; the khan wretched in the extreme. But we are thankful for the few comforts we do enjoy.

April 15—Market-day at Seraï-kioi. Long before daylight our slumbers were disturbed by a chorus of braying donkeys and neighing horses in the yard below. A wet morning. Belasarius succeeded in disposing of a few books, but the rain prevented his doing more. We had proposed starting about ten A.M., but waited till noon, in the hope that it would clear up. We were disappointed, however, and at length started in the rain, preferring to move on, rather than remain in this damp, miserable place, where there was very little prospect of doing any good. We had a very short stage to-day, only four hours, but a very trying one. It rained incessantly. Deep, soft mud everywhere: the horses could hardly get on. Halted for a few minutes at a coffee-house, quite new, and uncommonly clean. Several Turks were assembled, but they were very rude, and unwilling to exchange words with us. The prospect on every side was hidden by the clouds, which seemed to rest upon the ground. On drawing near to Denizli the rain abated, and the clouds lifted a little. The effect was grand. We were surrounded on three sides by high mountains. Their bases only were visible, painted with indigo. Their tops seemed lost in the clouds. At length we espied the roofs of the houses of Denizli, and soon after we were glad to be under the shelter of a tolerably good khan.

April 18—Visited Hierapolis and Laodicea, the former about three hours', the latter one hour's ride from Denizli. The whole population of Denizli appears to have turned out to destroy locusts, great damage being apprehended from their ravages. Our road to Hierapolis lies in a northerly direction across the plain of the Lycus, a muddy stream, which we cross by a ricketty wooden bridge. The incrustations of Hierapolis have, when viewed from afar, the appearance of chalk cliffs. As we drew nearer, they assumed larger proportions, the more recent formations being of a dazzling whiteness. I cannot attempt a minute description of this remarkable place, especially as, on account of limited time, we did not see all that is to be seen. I can only just put down a few particulars which struck me most. The general appearance of the incrustations, when viewed in the vicinity, is that of a great waterfall suddenly petrified. We ascend along one side of the cliff by a rough path, leading our horses. On gaining the top, we find ourselves upon a triangular plateau of considerable size, a sort of ledge projecting from the side of the mountain. This is the site of Hierapolis, called by the Turks Pambuk-kalessy (Cotton-castle). The surface of the plateau is broken by numerous ridges of incrustations, showing where the water used to flow in channels. We proceed along the top of one of these ridges, and reach the ruins of a large building, supposed to have been a public bath. Over against this, on the mountain side, are the ruins of an amphitheatre. The seats are almost entire. We noticed several blocks of stone covered with carvings. A little further down are the remains of an ancient church. Half-way between the bath and the theatre are the warm springs, which cause the incrustations before alluded to. It appeared to me probable that a considerable part of the plateau covers a subterranean lake. One's footsteps produce a hollow sound, as if one were walking over a cavern. A basin about twenty-five feet in diameter forms the principal spring. It must have been built over in olden times, as there are fragments of marble pillars, &c., lying about on the rocky bottom. On one side of the basin there is a deep chasm, so deep, that though the water is remarkably transparent, we could not see the bottom. The water itself is moderately warm, of a greenish hue where deep, and very clear. It flows in channels formed for the purpose in various directions, and leaves behind those incrustations which are the most remarkable feature in the place. We have not much time to spare, and are soon in the saddle again. At noon we halted at a Turkish farm, and had some conversation with its owner. He told us in all earnest that many locusts had been destroyed by the Imâms reading verses of the Korán over them. The locusts have committed great ravages for some years past. This year the Government has ordered steps to be taken for their destruction. Every individual is required to bring in a certain quantity. Accordingly, in some places the whole population nearly has turned out. They form themselves into parties; a sheet or carpet is spread out, and into this the locusts, which at this season can only hop short distances, are swept by means of brooms or branches. They are gathered into bags, weighed, and afterwards buried. The Turks are very much opposed to to this wholesale destruction of animal life. It goes against their ideas of fate. At Cassaba we were told that the Mohammedans say, "Oh, it is all very well to collect these locusts; but those who do so do not know that after them comes an old man with a white beard (Mohammed) who sows them broad-cast."

But to return from this digression. Leaving the farm, we proceeded to Laodicea. The desolate aspect of the place is almost oppressive. There are extensive ruins, but we could not stay to explore. How signally has the threatening, Rev. iii. 16, been fulfilled!

On our return to the khan, we were pleased to find that Belasarius had sold several books, and had discovered that there are two or three Protestant Armenians in the place. One of them came to see us, and attended our evening prayers. Belisarius also met with a Persian, who, some years ago, was in Smyrna, and there met Dr. Pfander and my father.

April 19– The young Protestant Armenian who was with us last night called to introduce his elder brother, also a Protestant, with whom we were much pleased. He was very anxious to know how the work among the Armenians in Constantinople is progressing; and expressed his delight when he was told that several Mohammedans had been baptized. Before parting we joined in prayer.

Soon afterwards the Persian came to see us. His pronunciation of Turkish was so peculiar that it was with difficulty I understood what he said. He professes to have read the New Testament as well as the Mizan-ul-Haqq, and to believe in Christ as the Son of God. When asked why he did not, in that case, make an open confession of his faith, he made some remarks, not very intelligible, but the drift of which appeared to be this—The truth or falsehood of Christianity or Mohammedanism is not the chief thing. There are other more important truths which philosophy reveals: we must leave these outward unimportant matters, and proceed to higher things.

Towards evening I went out to see the suburbs. Denizli proper is a very small place, consisting almost entirely of the bazaar. It is surrounded by a wall, and access is obtained by several gates, which are closed at sunset. The inhabitants live at some distance from the bazaar, their houses lying scattered amidst fields and gardens. This is our furthest point. To-morrow (D.V.) we turn our faces homeward.

April 20—Started at about half-past six A.M., in the direction of Nazli. Our rest was much disturbed last night. A small shock of an earthquake startled us about midnight: this was succeeded by several others, one or two of which were also severe, but not like the first. They drove sleep from our eyes, though we felt safe in committing ourselves to the divine care.

Part of our way this morning lay along the route we travelled on Saturday, but how different the prospect! Then every thing was hidden by fog and rain: now all is radiant in the sunshine. At Seraï-kioi we enter upon new ground, our road lying down the valley of the Mæander, which gradually becomes narrower. We pass a hot spring, emitting a sulphurous smell. The water boils up fiercely, and a considerable space of the ground seems to be undermined and impregnated with the hot fluid. At the narrowest part of the valley the Mæander approaches the mountains on the south, and here we cross to the northern bank by a wooden bridge. Our halting-place for this evening is Ortakji-kioi, a Turkish village perched on the southern side of Mount Messogis. We ride up to it through pleasant fields and fig-orchards. As there is no khan we went to the konak, or house of the chief man in the village. This was a rude mud-cottage, one corner being portioned off to serve as a stable for horses. Food was provided for us soon after our arrival, and again in the evening. At the latter meal we were joined by one of the principal men in the village, and had to manage as best we could without knives or forks. Water was then passed round: we performed our ablutions, and, reclining on cushions placed along the walls, waited for coffee to be served. One of the attendants placed a small quantity of unroasted coffee near our host, and, after a few minutes, proceeded to roast it. This was done in our presence in a small iron pan. It was then pounded in a wooden mortar, according to a certain rythm, produced by striking the pestle against the sides of the mortar. The coffee was then boiled, and served round in small cups. Several visitors dropped in, amongst them the Agha, or head-man, and the Imâm. The conversation at first was upon general subjects. They said the English were their friends, and then they inquired about the American war. After their curiosity had been satisfied on this point, Belisarius showed them a copy of the Sermon on the Mount in Turkish, and we were surprised to see how well it was received. First of all the Agha, who has only recently commenced learning to read, tried his skill in spelling out the words of our blessed Saviour; but as this was slow work, he passed it on to the Imâm, or Khojah, the literary oracle of the village, with the request that he would read aloud. We were amused, and yet deeply pained by the blundering efforts of this man. Still, as there were one or two individuals besides who were able to read a little, we left four copies of the Sermon on the Mount, as well as one copy of Dr. Schauffler's new translation of the Gospels and Acts. Three Greeks being present—the only ones in the village—I told them we had Scriptures for sale. They objected that our New Testament differs from their's. I denied this, and asked for proof. They immediately quoted John i. 1, *ὁ λόγος ἦν πρὸς τὸν Θεὸν*, which, in the Modern Greek translation is rendered, *ἦν παρὰ τῷ Θεῷ*. Having explained to them that the idiom of the Modern Greek required the change, which, however, does not alter the sense, they said that the Bishop of Heliopolis (Aidin) had threatened to excommunicate all who should receive any of our books. The younger of the three men seemed inclined to purchase a New Testament, but was restrained by his elder companions. A trifling incident showed us the growing independence of the Christians. In the course of conversation one of the Turks used the word "Giaour," when the young Greek mentioned above immediately said, "Don't you know that the Sultan has forbidden the use of that word?"

April 21—We were up betimes. After leaving a nicely-bound copy of the four Gospels and Acts for the Agha, we took leave of our hosts, thanks being the only remuneration usual in such cases, and proceeded on our way. Our road still lay down the valley of the Mæander. The plain here widens again, but we keep close to Mount Messogis on the north. On our left the river winds its tortuous way through the sandy soil, whilst beyond are other mountains connected with Cadmus. The nearer we come to Nazli, the more beautiful the country becomes. Rich fields and shady fig-plantations are interspersed with vineyards. The road we travel along is shaded by fine trees, and reminds one of a road through an English park. Every now and then we obtain a glimpse of the Messogis, skirted by a range of hills, similar to those which skirt the Tmolus on its northern side, and broken like those into the most picturesque forms. One's heart is lifted up to God in thankfulness and joy at the sight of these beauties of nature, and yet there is a sad burden which weighs one down continually, and that is the deplorable spiritual state of the inhabitants of so fair a country. When will this moral wilderness be turned into a garden of the Lord?

At half-past two P.M. we reached Nazli, just in time to escape a thunderstorm which had been threatening us for some time previously, and which prevented our going out that afternoon.

April 22—Whilst Belisarius went out with books, we took a walk through the town, and then visited Mr. Forbes, a Scotch gentleman engaged in the liquorice trade. We were very kindly received, and taken round to see a few antiquities. Mr. Forbes speaks highly of the common Turk. He is honest, and, though slow, steady and enduring. But place him in any Government position and he is open to corruption. Few are able to read, and attempts made in former years to circulate the New Testament among them have failed.

Belisarius sold but few books. He gave away, however, a good many copies of the Sermon on the Mount. A Greek, to whom Belisarius had offered a copy of the New Testament, said he must first show the book to the priest. The result was that it was returned.

We had only just returned to our room when a Greek priest, a doctor, and another person, came to the door, and, in an imperious way, asked to see the books which were being sold. On being invited to come in, they did so, and we were soon engaged in talking about the one thing needful. The doctor, like all other Greeks who are a little enlightened, maintained that the spiritual condition of Turks as well as Greeks would be improved by a better Government. Allowing that an enlightened Government may do much to improve the condition of a people, I tried to show that more was wanted, even the Holy Spirit, to regenerate, and vivify, and lead to Jesus, the Saviour of the world. After looking over our books, they arose to go away. "Don't you like these books?" I asked. "Yes," was the hesitating and embarrassed reply of the priest. I have little doubt that they came as spies, and perhaps they thought that their appearance would intimidate our Colporteur.

April 23—Left at half-past six for Aidin. It was a lovely morning, and we still rode on through gardens of figs and vines. We reached Aidin early in the afternoon, and despatched Belisarius to look for the Protestant Armenian pastor, placed here by the Missionaries of the American Board. On inquiring about the Turks, we were told by the pastor that it would not be safe for us to make any attempts to reach them just at this time. There is a considerable amount of hostile feeling abroad. The cause is this. Some time ago the Christian population of Aidin, stirred up, to some extent, by the few resident Protestants, petioned the Government to remove the market-day from Sunday, on which day it had always hitherto been held, to some other day in the week. The petition was favourably received, and Tuesday was fixed as the new market-day. With this the Mussulmans were highly displeased. "Why should the Giaours have their own way?" Through intrigue they succeeded in having the Sunday also recognised as market-day. At the same time they themselves kept away from the week-day market, and prevailed upon the Mussulmans in the villages around to do the same, in some cases stopping them on the road, and threatening them if they did not return. The consequence was that the Christians were unable to transact any business, and as they expressed their determination not to give in, an unpleasant feeling prevailed. We were surprised to learn that all—Greeks, Armenians, Romanists, as well as Protestants—were taking the matter very much to heart. The Greek Bishop has recently preached on this subject, and exhorted his people to a better observance of the Lord's-day. The Protestants speak well of this Bishop. He is friendly towards them, and often preaches tolerable sermons. In the evening, Baron Boghas, the native pastor, took us to see the Bishop. His appearance is venerable. He was seated at the upper end of a large room, three sides of which were taken up by divans. As soon as we entered, the Bishop arose and received us very courteously. Coffee and pipes having been handed round, I remarked that we were glad to hear that the Bishop valued the ordinance of preaching. "Yes," was the answer, "I do what I can: I preach morality just as it is suited to these people." "Is not doctrine necessary too? How can you have morality without sound doctrine?" "Oh, our people are well instructed: they have no need to be taught doctrine." This exaggeration struck me. "Were there not thousands," I asked, "who trust in outward observances for their salvation?" No, the Bishop could not be moved from his previous statement. We then passed on to speak about the Scriptures. The Bishop is very much opposed to the Modern-Greek translation of the New Testament. It was easy to show the futility of his objections, but it would never have done for the Bishop to acknowledge a defeat, especially as there were some Greeks present. At length he broke out into the triumphant exclamation, "Never, never can the Greek church allow the word of God, which has been delivered to her in her pure and magnificent language, to be translated into the language of shoemakers and grocers." After this we thought it was better to put an end to the discussion, and we parted upon the best of terms, the Bishop shaking us warmly by the hand, and expressing his regret if he should have given us pain by any thing he might have said in warmth.

April 24: *Lord's-day*—Spent the morning in our rooms, where we were visited by the Protestants. In the afternoon we attended the service of the native pastor. He preached in Turkish on the words—"I know in whom I have believed." Afterwards I gave a short address in Greek on Matt. v. 13—16, "Ye are the salt of the earth," &c. Amongst others, a Greek, who holds the office of Kiatil (clerk or secretary) in the Konak, was present. With him we left copies of the Mizan, the Miftah, and the Rafi. We had intended to have made a longer stay in Aidin, but, under present circumstances, we can do little or nothing, and have decided to leave (D.V.) to-morrow morning.

April 25—We are now in Sokia, a small

but thriving place. It is divided into two parts by a broad watercourse, one side being almost exclusively Christian, the other Mussulman. The latter are. for the most part, refugees, who, during the Greek war of indedependence, were obliged to flee from the Morea and some of the islands. Most of them understand Greek. There are here two factories for the preparation of liquorice, belonging to English gentlemen. We are thankful that we have arrived so far in safety. At one of the coffee-houses we heard that, only a day or two ago, a band of robbers attacked a party or Yarucks (Turcomans), taking from them all they possessed.

The habitations of these Yarucks are worthy of notice. They frequently consist of nothing more than a cloth of black goat's hair stretched across some poles, the sloping sides being turned towards the wind. Those we saw today are formed of wicker-work, the interstices being filled up with mud. They cannot be very warm in winter, but have the advantage of allowing free ventilation in summer.

Here we are staying in the comfortable house of an English gentleman, a pleasant change after the rough life we have lately led.

April 26—Mr. Clarke, our hospitable host, related a curious instance of the superstition of the people. On account of the ravages of the locusts, the Greeks of Sokia determined to have the skull of St. Thomas brought over from Patmos, where it is in the safe keeping of one of the monasteries. The presence of the ἅγιον κάρα, as it is called, is considered the most efficient means of driving away or destroying locusts. Accordingly the ἅγιον κάρα was brought, with all due pomp, under the care of several monks. Persons who had fields sown with cotton-seed paid considerable sums of money to have the relic brought on their estates. Others, who had hesitated to sow cotton-seed, did so at once, in the full assurance that the locusts would do no injury. Even Turks put faith in the efficacy of this skull, and hesitate not to have it borne in procession across their fields. Of course all this while the monks reap a rich harvest.

Belisarius has been able to do but little. In the bazaar he was laughed at, though he managed to sell some books. We find the people less accessible the nearer we approach Smyrna. Contact with Europeans, or with those who have come under the influence of Europeans, seems to rob them of their simplicity, to make them more anxious for this world's good things, and less careful about spiritual matters.

April 27—Scala-nova. We have had a short stage to-day. The road very rough over hills, whence we had a beautiful view of the sea and Samos. We are neither of us very well. Belisarius has had indifferent success with his sales. A couple of Turkish Testaments, however, have been disposed of, besides some Greek books, and this makes us thankful. We do pray that the seed thus scattered may not remain without results; nor will it, we are sure. "Cast thy bread upon the waters, for thou shalt find it after many days."

April 28—Through divine mercy we have reached Boujah in safety, having availed ourselves of the railway from Ephesus. We have been protected from robbers and other dangers; but what we are most thankful for is, that we have been permitted to sell a considerable number of copies of God's holy word, and also, here and there, to speak a word for our heavenly Master. May God give his blessing!

THE SIOUX, OR DAKOTAHS.

The territory of Minnesota extends from the Mississippi and St. Croix Rivers and from Lake Superior on the east, to the Missouri and White Earth Rivers on the west, a distance of more than 400 miles; and from the Iowa line on the south to the British frontier on the north, also about 400 miles apart. It is a portion of the world of which we ought to know something, lying as it does in such close proximity to our own Red-River district, the sources of the Red River, which flows northward into Lake Winnepeg, being found amidst the elevated prairies and lakes of the Minnesota territory.

Such, indeed, is the elevated position of the territory, that it is the great water-shed of this part of the American continent, from whence the rivers, which have their sources within its limits, flow north and south. The Rivière à Jaques, which flows south into the Missouri, and the Minnesota, which flows eastward into the Mississippi, have their fountain-heads not far from those of the Shayenne, a tributary of the Red River of the north; nay, the Mississippi itself has its birth-place amidst those numerous lakes in its north-eastern portion from whence the Red River of the north has also its parentage.

Various elevated ridges, though not of a mountain character, traverse the territory. The plateau called the Couteau des Prairies is one of these singular terraces, extending 200 miles, with a breadth of from 20 to 40 miles, its average elevation being 1500 feet, while in some places it rises nearly 2000 feet above the sea level.

The general aspect of the country is that of a fine rolling prairie, interspersed with numerous lakes of fresh water, whose banks are clothed with a rich growth of woodland. The land is about equally divided between oak openings and prairies, the whole being well watered by numerous rivers, navigable for steamers.

Here of old extended the hunting-grounds of the Ojibways, or Chippeways, and of the Dakotah, or Sioux, the one to the east, and the other west of the Mississippi; and here, long before America was searched out by the inquisitive eyes of the white man, many a deed was enacted of sanguinary character; and when the white man came he did not bring peace with him.

Christianity gave the white man civilization, and thus he became possessed of energy. As a navigator he crossed the seas, and discovered new lands, and, as the population increased at home, he went forth from Europe to colonize. He should have brought with him the Christianity to which he had been so much indebted. But in this, his great duty, he was defective. He brought with him his vices, and the means of gratifying them. He taught these to the heathen tribes; but as to his religion, he had either corrupted it, so that, except in name and form, it differed nothing from heathenism, or he disregarded it, neither practising it himself or teaching it to others. Thus, among the Indians of America, the arrival of the white man exasperated all pre-existing evils, and the Indian was not only armed against his fellow, but against himself.

When the Sioux and Chippeways lived in amity, a Sioux chief married a Chippeway wife, and lived in the Chippeway territory. But the hatchet was dug up, and war broke out. He was a chief, and had to join his tribe. He left his wife behind him, for it would not have been safe to take her among the Sioux; but he took his children with him, for it would not have been safe to leave them among the Chippeways. The wife, after his departure, married a Chippeway warrior, and there were sons by this second marriage, who grew up as Chippeway braves, while the former children grew up as Sioux warriors. One of the Chippeway half-brothers, on one occasion, went to make his fall hunts on the middle ground towards the Sioux territory, taking with him nearly all his near relatives. Early one morning, as the young men were preparing for the chase, they were startled by the report of several shots directed towards the lodge, and, before they could arm, another volley inflicted wounds. The Chippeway chief immediately sallied out with his young men, and, pronouncing his name aloud in the Sioux language, demanded if his brothers were among the assailants. The firing immediately ceased; a pause ensued, and a tall figure in a war dress, with a profusion of feathers on his head, stepped forward: it was the Sioux half-brother. The pipe of peace was smoked, and the hunting party, which, far out-numbered as it was, would have been massacred, returned home uninjured. Yet one of the children, a son of the Chipewyan chief, who had been present on that occasion, grew up a great Chippeway warrior, and led his tribe to many a fierce affray with the Sioux. One battle-scene was the falls of St. Croix, embracing the summit land between Lake Superior and the Upper Missisipi. The streams flowing each way interlock, and the natives ascend them in light canoes, which they carry over the portages, and so descend on the opposite side. The Chippeway chief, with his warriors, reached the waters of the St. Croix, which he descended, until, on the lower side of the portage of the great falls of St. Croix, a large body of Sioux and Foxes was discovered. On the narrow neck of rock they met and fought, and many fell; until at length, overpowered by numbers, the Sioux and their allies fled. Such were these tribes—"their feet swift to shed blood."

The first attempts at Missions in these regions were from the direction of Canada and the French Canadians, and were connected with the Church of Rome. Marquette, accompanied by Alloez, had visited the south shore of Lake Superior in 1668, and made a map of the region, which was published in the *Lettres Edifiantes*. Having established the Mission of St. Ignace at Michilimackinac about 1669 or 1670, he entered the Upper Mississippi about three years afterwards from the Winconsin.

Upwards, however, of a century and a half after these dates, no morning had risen on these regions, and they continued to be wrapped in the same gloom of ignorance and barbarism which had brooded over them for ages. In 1834 the Sioux were without a written language. Then the American Missionaries entered in, and a genuine work commenced, at first painfully laborious. Days and years of plodding were spent by them in "picking up a word here and there, in writing and re-writing, correcting and re-correcting, learning the meaning of a word to-day and forgetting it to-morrow." But progress was made. "A strictly phonetic mode of writing the language was adopted, in which each character represented had a single sound." The language was found to be in many respects defective. For many and important ideas it had no corresponding words; for instance—roving in their habits, without any fixed abode around which their affections could entwine themselves—they had no word answering exactly to our English "home." Still it claimed to be regarded as a noble language, "fully adequate to all the felt wants of the nation, and capable of being enlarged, cultivated, and enriched by the introduction of foreign stores of thought. Nothing can be found more full than the Dakotah verb. The affixes and reduplications, and pronouns and prepositions, all come in to make of it a stately pile of thought. A single paradigim presents more than a thousand variations."

Gradually the Book of Genesis, and a part of the Psalms, the Gospel by Luke, and the Acts of the Apostles, the Epistles of Paul, and the Revelation of John, were prepared for the press.

In prosecuting their labours at stations, which, in order that they might better approach the wild tribes of the Dakotahs, were placed beyond the settled districts, the Missionaries have had to pass through times, not only of alarm, but of actual danger. Such a crisis occurred in 1857, when a band of these people massacred forty white persons at Spirit Lake, carrying away with them into captivity two white women, who were afterwards recovered by the efforts of the Christian Dakotahs. Yet at a time when a conflict between a small guard of United-States' soldiers and a large body of hostile Indians was imminent, the Missionaries remained at their post, occupying a house, which, with many windows and without shutters, was wholly indefensible, but committing themselves to Him who neither slumbers nor sleeps.

These threatening appearances were, however, happily averted, and the Mission progressed slowly, yet satisfactorily, until the year 1862. At that time the heathen Dakotahs became dissatisfied. The annuities guaranteed to them, in lieu of lands which they had ceded, remained unpaid. They had suffered injuries, in some cases of an atrocious character, at the hands of traders, and could find no redress, there being no proper and effective police to protect the innocent and punish the guilty. Many of them hated Christianity and its attendant civilization, and desired to arrest its progress, that the old customs might have undisputed ascendancy. They knew how the civil war absorbed the resources of the Federal Government, and believed that the time had come to strike a blow. There is no doubt that they had suffered great wrongs, and, after the Indian fashion, they resolved to profit by this opportunity to avenge themselves.

In the summer of that year there were Missionaries in occupation of two points—

Yellow Medicine and Hazlewood—and at each of these places little flocks of converted natives had been gathered. The storm burst suddenly. On August 18th an attack was made on the Lower Agency, distant thirty-three miles: the soldiers sent up from Fort Ridgely on the Minnesota were assaulted promptly and fearlessly, and one half of their number having fallen, the survivors were obliged to shut themselves up within the fort. The Indians, for the time, were undisputed masters of the frontier settlements, and massacred the whites as they had opportunity. It was a moment of extreme danger to the Missionaries, but the Christian Indians came forward to help them, and, when they found that they were not strong enough to defend the Mission homes, counselled them to fly, and helped them so to do, first to an island on the Minnesota, and then direct into the heart of the prairies, where they remained, until reinforcements coming up the river afforded the prospect of security.

About 600 or 700 whites fell in this massacre, amidst the horrors of which, although they were themselves but a little band, the Christian Sioux succeeded, during the first week, in saving the lives of 100 whites.

The conflict between the soldiers and Indians was now resumed, and at Wood Lake the Dakotahs, being defeated, became discouraged, their chief, Little Crow, with a part of his followers, flying westward toward the Missouri River, while others in considerable numbers surrendered to the American General Sibley.

A military commission was appointed to try the prisoners, and the result was, that of 393 individuals thus dealt with, 302 were sentenced to be hung, and amongst them were three Christian Dakotahs. The belief was entertained that the civilized, and even some of the Christian Indians, had participated in the massacre, but this was not the case. Some of the heathen had put on the clothes of the first whites they had slain, in order that they might approach others without being suspected, and these men had been mistaken for civilized Indians. Again, when Little Crow ascended the Minnesota from the Lower Agency to Yellow Medicine, many of the Agency Indians had been compelled to accompany him from fear. At the battle of Wood Lake some of these unhostile Indians escaped from the warriors, bringing with them several white captives whom they had delivered; yet of these very many were tried and condemned.

To these condemned Indians, the Missionary, after some difficulty, was permitted access, and laboured diligently to prepare them for the end which awaited them, an effort in which he was much aided by the Christians who were among them. These men got together for worship, the others crowding around them as close as they could, that they might hear. Encouraged by this, the Christians began to preach to the heathen, one of them in particular, an elder of the native church, who had saved his Missionary's life, speaking in a manner highly appropriate and edifying. Eventually, of the number who had been condemned, thirty-eight suffered the extreme penalty of the law. The majority, who had been so unexpectedly spared, seemed greatly moved, listening eagerly to the instruction they received, and declaring their earnest desire to become Christians; so that 274 of them were baptized on the same Sunday, February 9, 1863. Others were subsequently added, until they numbered upwards of 300.

But besides those Indians who had been selected for trial, there was a large body of Indians who had not been tried, some 1600 in number, consisting chiefly of women and children. These, accompanied by one of the Missionaries, had been removed to Fort Snelling, on the Mississippi, opposite St. Paul, where they were confined on a low, flat spot, with pools of stagnant water, in extent about three acres, enclosed by a board fence, twelve or fourteen feet high, and having but one gate, where a guard was placed. Of this prison-house the Missionary wrote—"It is a very sad place now: the wailing never ceases: from five to ten die daily." But here also, amidst the pressure of deep tribulation, the Gospel message was welcomed. God spoke of mercy, although man did not. The garret of a large warehouse was used as a place of worship, and here, seated on the floor, and packed away under the sides of the roof, assembled to hear from 300 to 500 persons. The word was in power, and many, convinced of the truth of Christianity, and of their own need of the salvation which it promises, eagerly embraced it and were baptized, to the number of 140.

In May 1863 the United-States' Government came to a decision respecting these remnants of the once great Dakotah nation whom they held in bonds. Like other remnants of decayed tribes, they were to go far west. Thirteen hundred Dakotahs and 1800 Winnebagoes were to be taken up the Missouri River, 100 miles beyond Fort Randall. "Last Monday," writes one of the Missionaries recording the event, "an order came to Fort Snelling for 750 to embark on the steamer 'Davenport' for Fort Randall. On Tuesday evening, 530, with whom I remained, were ordered on board this steamer. The last person was counted on just at dusk, after which we shoved off. As darkness shut in the skies, these Indians looked out upon their native hills, as they said, for the last time. We were, however, hardly under way, when, from all the different parts of the boat where they were collected, we heard hymns of praise ascending to Jehovah; not loud, but soft and sweet, like the murmur of many waters. Then one of them engaged in prayer, after which another hymn was sung. So they continued, till all were composed, and, drawing their blankets over them, each fell asleep. The next morning, before 'sun-up,' they were again paying their devotions to God. So they have continued, every evening and morning since; and these services were commenced by themselves, without any suggestion from any one else. The people along the route wonder to see them so peaceable and quiet."

This has been throughout the policy of the United States, to remove the tribes from the precincts of the Old States far to the west. There is a table published by Schoolcraft on this subject. He gives the names of twenty-seven different tribes thus expatriated. The estimated quantity of land acquired from these tribes during the period between March 1829 and September 1838 amounts to 109,879,937 acres; the probable value of which to the United States is estimated at 137,349,946 dollars; while the probable expense of carrying into effect the various treaties is set down at 70,059,505, of which twenty millions and a half of dollars were in money, the remainder being the estimated value of thirty millions of acres of land granted to the emigrating tribes—that is, wilderness, unoccupied land, which did not belong to any one; in which the white man had no more right of proprietorship than the Indian, and for which no charge can with justice be made, in order to balance accounts with the emigrating tribes; so that, in fact, the United-States' Government, by the removal of these various tribes of Indians, obtained nearly one hundred and ten millions of acres, worth nearly one hundred and thirty-eight millions of dollars, for twenty millions and a half of dollars.

The territory to which the Sioux have been exiled possesses but few attractions, and offers a poor substitute for the prairies, and woods, and lakes of Minnesota.

"Hardly yet the middle of summer," writes, under date of July 8, one of the Missionaries who had accompanied them, "and all these great plains are without a speck of green! Only in the lowest valleys, by the side of the river, is there any living grass; and that is fast being dried up by the burning rays of the sun, which, in this climate, know not a drop of cooling rain for weeks! It is even too dry to allow the dew to wet the face of the ground The little corn that we planted in the lowest spots, after we arrived, if it sprouted at all, only came up to wither and die. Sore as this prospect is, the Indians had better bear it now, as the feeling against them is such, that, if one dares to protest in the humblest manner, he is regarded as insolent, hostile, and dangerous."

Nothing, indeed, can be conceived more calamitous than the condition to which these people have been reduced. The corn which they planted in 1863 did not come up until

August, and the potatoes never came up. Early in January it became quite clear, that, if all remained at Fort Thompson till spring, many must starve. They were advised, therefore, as many as could do so, to scatter off, wheresoever there was any prospect of their picking up a living.

About 200 went down the river, to the neighbourhood of Fort Randall, where, partly from the white settlers in that vicinity, partly from the soldiers, but chiefly from the Yankton Indians who are settled near there, they succeeded in either begging or working for enough to keep them alive. There were only about half a dozen men among these. I have had a talk with one of those who has just returned, and who is a member of the church. He says the church members always met for worship on the Sabbath, and what pleased them most was, that many of the Yanktons were interested in the services, and would fill the house full whenever they had a meeting. They had great reverence for the worship of God, always kneeling in prayer, and trying to behave just as the Christians did. One blind man, in particular, often sent for him to go and have a meeting at his house; and many children would come to hear his little girl spell, and get her to teach them their letters. But they had no books. They said they wished some one would come and settle among them, and teach them. There are something over 2000 of these Indians—a branch of the Sioux nation. They plant to some extent, but live principally by the buffalo chase. They have a large number of horses, with which they make two or three hunts in a year, bringing in great packs of robes and dried meats.

Soon after these Indians started below, a young man who had been out trapping brought in word that there were large herds of buffalo on the plains, about 100 miles north of this. It was a doubtful undertaking, in the middle of winter, to venture out on those prairies, where one has to travel for two or three days without wood, to hunt buffalo; and these Indians were in poor plight for such an undertaking, being without horses to carry their baggage and chase the herds, and themselves very thinly clad. But they must do something. Government could give them nothing but some soup from day to day, which did not satisfy their appetites. All the men who were here determined to go, and most of them took their families.

There were probably fifty men and six or seven times as many women and children. I determined to go out and spend some time with them, and I am glad I did so, though it was a hard trip. I helped to show the Indians that they could travel over these wide prairies and keep the Sabbath; that they could kill buffalo without making charms; that they could live by the chase and worship God. By being altogether in their company from day to day, whether travelling or hunting, by eating with them and lodging in their tents for so long a time, I acquired a familiarity with their habits and language which may be of much service to me hereafter. I gratified my curiosity by seeing vast herds of buffalo, enough to supply New-York meat-market for the winter. I secured a knowledge of the country, which I was very desirous to obtain, especially of the head of the Minnesota Coteau, which I believe to be the best location for Indians in Minnesota or Dakotah.

Such, then, is the condition to which this remnant of the Dakotahs has been reduced. "In justice to this stricken and afflicted people, it should be said that they have shown not only a willingness, but also a strong desire to work; but there has been almost nothing which they could do. Especially has this proved to be the case with the women; and three-fourths of the families have no adult males with them. All the efforts made by the Indians, even with the aid furnished by the Government, have not sufficed for their comfortable support. Starvation has hung over them during the entire year, so that it has become exceedingly wearisome to see that dark cloud so near us, with no prospect of a brighter day."*

The removal policy of the United States appears to have succeeded with the principal Apalachian tribes, the Creeks, Cherokees, Choctaws, and Chickasaws. They had made some proficiency in arts and agriculture, and, when they left their ancient homes east of the Mississippi, it was to exchange them for ample and fertile areas west of that stream, where, up to the period of the great disruption, and the commencement of the civil war,

* American Board Report for 1864.

they had greatly increased in wealth and population. But as regards the tribes who, farther north, have been subjected to the same experiment, the removal policy has proved to be a melancholy failure.

"In their new homes they have been disappointed in the permanent and abundant supplies of game furnished by the forests and prairies of the west. When they removed far towards the setting sun, and abandoned the wigwams and graves of their fathers, we told them they would get beyond the reach of the vices and oppressions of bad white men, and that the Great Spirit they reverenced would supply them with the deer, bear, elk, and buffalo. Their tastes and habits made them yield a willing ear to the stories which we told them of this promised land. Their hearts saddened, doubtless, when they turned and gazed for the last time on their native heath; yet they were cheered with the hope of a bright future, to be realized in the stillness of that wild to which they were treading their way.

"The policy, when adopted towards the Indians, seemed wise and humane. Its authors never anticipated the rapid progress of the extension of our settlements and population westward. It was supposed that the Mississippi, for many long years, would mark the western confines of the Union, and present a barrier to western expansion not to be overcome. Soon, however, the illusion was dissipated, for the sturdy pioneer leaped the rolling flood of the father of waters, and began to fell and conquer the forests on the western slopes of its great valleys. In a few brief years a tier of states was formed over the waters, and then it was confidently believed that the broad plains and prairies, mountains and valleys, westward as far as the Pacific, would only be trod by the wild beasts of the forests and his natural enemy, the red hunter. A few more years, however, demonstrated the impotency of the most sanguine imagination to fix limits to our march westward. The acquisition and settlement of California and Oregon has created the necessity of converting much of the Indian wilderness into a great highway and thoroughfare. Not less than 75,000 of our citizens annually traverse the Indian country on their journeyings to and from the Pacific coast. The red man is no longer permitted to roam the wilderness free from the baleful presence of the hated pale-face: he sees the buffalo driven further and further from his lands, his lodges, and his wigwams. He finds that the annual slaughter of this noble animal for his own subsistence, for that of the white caravans that dot and enliven the plains, and for the robes to supply the wants of civilized and savage life, amounts to upwards 400,000."†

This famine is at the heels of the expatriated Indian. "The rapid destruction of the buffalo is exhausting the only larder from whence they draw their support; the broad prairie yields them nothing but game, which is now only taken by labour, toil, and privation, and, when found, the quantity is so meagre as rather to tantalize than appease the dreadful gnawings of hunger.

"Some of the tribes on the frontier of Missouri, when they leave their lodges in the spring and fall, to enter upon the precarious hunt for food, traverse several hundred miles of foodless desert before reaching the harvest-field—the herds of buffalo."

What remains for the Indian? He must till the ground or die? But what shall change his nature, and bend the obstinacy with which he clings to the old and pernicious habits of his fathers? Christianity is the potent spell. It has wrought, farther north, such wondrous changes. In the dreary wildernesses of North-west America the Indian, when brought under its divine influence, ceases to be a nomade, builds for himself a home, and cultivates the earth.

But let them have, not the *mauvaises terres* of Nebraska, but land which, when tilled, will respond to the labour bestowed on it.

† "Schoolcraft on the Condition and Progress of the Indian tribes."

We stated at the beginning of this article, that, after the battle of Wood Lake, the chief, Little Crow, with a portion of his followers, fled, as it was supposed, towards the Missouri River.

It would appear, however, that on the American side of the frontier there was no rest for him. He entered, therefore, the British territory, and, towards the end of the year 1863, was found at the Red-River Settlement.

Now the Sioux have been for generations the hereditary implacable foes of the Chippeways, the Indian nation from whence our converts at the Red River have been principally gathered, and they have ever been regarded as the most dreaded invaders of the prairies north of the boundary. Moreover, on the present occasion it might be supposed, that, infuriated by severe losses, Little Crow would spare neither Indian nor white man. The extensive settlement at the Red River was, in fact, at his mercy, if he were disposed to repeat the massacre of Minnesota. The population is considerable—some 6000—but the homes of the people are scattered along the banks of the river for a distance of twenty miles. Before, then, the men capable of bearing arms could have been concentrated the blow might have been struck. That the apprehensions of evil were considerable will appear from the following notices which we find in the journals of Archdeacon Hunter.

Nov. 23, 1863—Heard to-day of the arrival of eighteen Sioux Indians at the upper part of the settlement. They run great risk in approaching the settlement, as some 400 American troops are now stationed at Pembina, who will not spare them if they cross their path. Poor, unhappy creatures, they are reduced to a miserable state, and, within the American lines, every man's hand is against them.

Visit to the Sioux.

Dec. 15—Visited the Sioux encampment near Sturgeon Creek, consisting of about seventy tents, containing 500 souls, men, women, and children. They reached the settlement in a very destitute condition, both naked and starving, after losing some thirty of their party by the way from fatigue and starvation. This is Little Crow's band, the principal perpetrators of the massacre, and now vengeance seems to have overtaken them, and they are suffering fearfully, we must add deservedly, for the wrongs and crimes and untold agonies then inflicted. They are crowding to the houses of the settlers in search of food, and some of them have travelled down the settlement as far as our residence. They enter our houses armed, and some of the men are very forbidding in their aspect. Many of them can speak English, but are not forward to do so, but rather conceal it. How much they need the Gospel, with its humanizing, civilizing, and, above all, its christianizing effects, to subdue the cruelty of their nature, and lead them to Him who is meek and lowly of heart, that they might find rest unto their souls.

Departure of the Sioux.

Dec. 25—Heard from Judge Black the pleasing intelligence that the authorities had at last succeeded in persuading the Sioux to leave the settlement. The judge writes—"I could not call on my way down from the Upper Fort this morning; but although it is possible you may have heard already the news of our deliverance from the presence of the Sioux, I yet cannot help giving you a line, with a reliable intelligence of the good riddance we have got of these dangerous Indians. Yesterday they were all off but one family, and that small remnant it was hoped would move off to-day. In wishing you and all around you a happy Christmas, I feel that this event is fitted to make the season much happier than it otherwise could have been. A dark and threatening cloud has been removed from us—darker than any that I ever remember hovering over the season; and surely we may well regard the peaceable departure of people who have filled the settlement with consternation and anxiety as the crowning mercy of the year."

The Sioux had received no injury from the British settlers, and they did them no wrong. So far as the settlement was capable of doing so, their wants were supplied, and they left in peace. The Indian is as he is dealt with. Kindness subdues him; injustice exasperates him. No tongue can describe, no imagination conceive, the wrongs which the Red Indians of America have suffered at the hands of the white men who coveted their lands; and, lo! the lands where the life of the native owner was so piti essly taken, and his blood so freely shed, is now saturated with the blood of the white men themselves. They have rooted out the aboriginal possessors, and the land is their own, and now they fiercely contend with one another, and human life is shed with a lavish prodigality previously unknown in the history of our race.

Verily there is a God that judgeth the earth!

Recent Intelligence.

MADAGASCAR.

THE Bishop of Mauritius, in reference to the Madagascar Missionaries and their work, in a letter dated April 24, 1865, says—

I think it better to write to you at once my impressions about our brethren at Vohimare. To my own mind the accounts we have just received are of a most favourable character. The internal evidence of the worth and weight of character of these true men, of their simplicity, and real and earnest longing desire for the spiritual good of the people, and of the affectionate and faithful manner in which they are discharging their duty, gaining access and using it rightly, and giving themselves to prayer in the ministry of the word,—all these are most instructive and encouraging. Then the stamp of genuine Missionary work; the charm of the varied interesting scenes and incidents occurring day after day; the history and character of their Governor; and the process through which his scribe has been led to baptism;—all this made me read every line of their journals with a zest sustained to the last. That my friend Raniandreaniprizenana, whose long name has caused his letter to be shown so often that it is now in shreds, should, in that journey to Vohimare as Governor three years ago, have been led to prepare, by his instructions and exhortations, a youth who was just ready for our Missionaries' further instruction, having received as a parting admonition from his former Governor and teacher, Luke xii. 4, 5, and that this youth should be their first baptized convert, is indeed matter of thankful interest. The accounts of leading men of the Sakalava tribe, the visit of the second Governor of Ambohitsera, the opportunity of sending Bible portions by the Arab merchants, and the fact of their having each a separate preaching-place, with ten miles interval between them, every Sunday, makes me feel quite at ease on the subject of the population. A better centre they could scarcely have.

As soon as Mr. Ansorgé returns to Mauritius I hope the itinerating will go on with spirit. Kushlli has made one journey which had a great variety of interesting incidents in it. He has done his work admirably. His tact in seizing the attention of unwilling persons is very great. In one of the Indian villages they came to in their journey the people were very unwilling to receive them; but he began to tell them of the last days of four men who were executed some time ago, and they soon gathered round him, when he had a good opportunity, and used it well. What a prospect would open out to us if the gifts of the ministry were poured out on the natives of lands where we have converts! Have we sufficiently expected those gifts, or honoured the Holy Spirit by whom they are dispensed? I very much doubt it.

NEW ZEALAND.

THE following brief extracts, from the Bishop of Waiapu's letters, will show that, amidst the storms which have visited New Zealand, and wrought so much devastation on its infant Christianity, the root still remains in the ground, retaining its vitality, and, after a time, when the clouds are dispersed and calmer weather supervenes, will send forth new branches—

Dec. 20, 1864—This is the dark side of the subject, but the night is far spent, and the day is at hand. We know that the end will soon come when all false religions shall give way to the Gospel, and we have only to wait awhile, and Christ will take to Himself his great power, and will reign. In this diocese we have been encompassed with difficulties, but our work goes on. The enemy comes in like a flood, but the Spirit of God lifts up a standard against him. I may refer you to our third synod, which was held on the 2nd of March, for signs of vitality. True, we had no natives present from the disturbed parts of the country, but there was much to be thankful for. There was an evidence that there are numbers who regard religion as a reality, and that the desire increases for clergymen to reside among them. At Waiapu we have three excellent men, the Revs. Rota Waitoa, Raniera Kawhia, and Mohi Turei. They are living in a disturbed district, but they hold their ground, and their influence acts powerfully, and many of those who had been among the disaffected have come over to the quiet party. At Tokomaru we have the Rev. Matiaha Pahewa, a good and useful man. At Wairoa the Rev. Tamehana Huata has now the sole charge of an important district, and is faithful to his trust. A sixth, the Rev. Hare Tawhaa, we find of great service at Tauranga. He, together with Mohi Turei, were admitted to deacons' orders on the 25th of September. On Sunday last, the 18th of December, another of our teachers, Wetene Moeke, was ordained deacon. He will reside at Table Cape, taking a part of Mr. Hamlin's district. We have one other native deacon, the Rev. Ihara Te Ahu, living at Maketu.

The collections for the Endowment Fund are still going on. During this year of trouble and excitement the sum of 491*l*. has been given for this object from seven different districts, which is a sufficient indication of a right feeling among the natives. While, therefore, the enemy is doing his utmost to hinder the Gospel, and to draw away the people after lying vanities, God is manifesting his power in the behalf of his people, and He gives us the assurance that he is directing all things towards the accomplishment of his purposes, the final result of which will be the establishment of his kingdom.

Feb. 7, 1865—I returned a few days ago from Waiapu, where I had been to hold the meeting of the diocesan synod. In these times of trouble it was a great encouragement to be able to have such a meeting, in a district, too, which has been much disturbed by hostile feeling against the Government. We assembled at Te Kawakawa, which is the centre village of the parish of the Rev. Rota Waitoa, and arrangements had been made for the hospitable entertainment of the whole synod upon Rota's premises, an additional raupo house having been erected for the occasion. There were, however, seven clergymen, including my son and Mr. Clarke, and thirteen synodsmen, but all were from the eastern coast. Neither Archdeacon Brown, nor Mr. Volkner, nor Mr. Spencer, were able to leave their homes. Indeed, that part of the country is still so much disturbed that travellers are not allowed to pass along the coast.

The business of our synod was not important in itself. There was no onward progress to be recorded, but still these meetings are a means of strengthening the faith, and encouraging the hope, of those who desire to hold stedfast in a right course, and are particularly beneficial to our native clergymen.

I have previously spoken of a deputation having been sent to Turanga from Opotiki, to invite the natives to rise up and join a hostile expedition against Maketu. We found at Waiapu other messengers, who had gone for the like purpose; but, by a remarkable providence, the principal person of this embassy was struck down by fever, and died; and the Waiapu natives, though there is still a strong party supporting the cause of the Maori king, were not inclined to respond to the invitation, but only sent a party of sixteen to conduct the surviving messenger back.

THE CATASTROPHE AT OPITIKI.

Some weeks past, a telegram from Sidney conveyed to this country the startling intelligence that one of the Missionaries of the Church Missionary Society, the Rev. C. S. Vœlkner, had been barbarously murdered by the Pai Marire, at Opitiki, on the East Coast, the place where for several years he had been stationed, endeavouring by every means in his power to promote the well-being of the native race. It was stated also that his own flock, carried away by the fanatical delusions of the new sect, had offered no resistance to this cruel act, and that, in fact, he had been butchered in their presence.

We had then received no letters from New Zealand containing the slightest reference to such an event; and we waited in the hope that the report might prove groundless, the more so, as during the long and dark period of New-Zealand cannibalism, no Christian Missionary had ever suffered serious injury at the hands of a native.

It is with deep regret, then, that we find it all too true, and more horrible than we could have expected. The details will be found in the extracts of letters, which we append.

Deeply do we lament over this catastrophe, one in every point of view so afflictive For our faithful Missionary we mourn, whose earnest labours on behalf of the Maori race had, as far as this world is concerned, so painful a termination. We feel our own great disappointment as a Missionary Society, which for half a century has been unselfishly and zealously endeavouring to raise from the depths of barbarism the Maori race. We are regretful for that people, whose position, already sufficiently critical, has been now rendered tenfold more so by this savage act of the Hauhaus, and the heartless ingratitude of poor Volkner's people, who stood by, and suffered, without the slightest attempt at resistance, the murder to be perpetrated. We candidly acknowledge that, whatever unfavourable opinion we entertained respecting the Ngatiruanui of the West Coast, we never could have conceived it possible that the people of the East Coast would have so readily yielded themselves to the wild impulse of a repulsive fanaticism, and that to such an extent as to turn against their own Missionaries and compel them to flee. And yet, while admitting all this, we must earnestly protest againt the action of some amongst ourselves, who, ignorant of the genius of Christianity, would take advantage of this event to advocate alike the abandonment of Christian Missions, and the withdrawal of all sympathy from the Maori, because, in their opinion, the former are worthless and the latter irreclaimable.

We observe in the "Times" of January 7th, an article written in this spirit. Referring to the atrocity at Opotiki, it observes, "Here is the measure of the depth to which this much talked of Christianity has penetrated."

But surely nothing can be more remote from sound argument than from an extreme case of this kind to attempt to draw general conclusions as to the effect of Christianity upon an entire race.

In the case of the Maoris it is manifestly unjust to do so; for let it be remembered, that if in one part of the island fanatical Maoris have expressed their hatred of Christianity and English rule, by the murder of a Missionary, in another part of the island an influential chief, at the head of his tribe, has fought in defence of Christianity and its Missionaries, and in maintenance of English sovereignty, proving his loyalty by laying down his life in the conflict. Surely the devotion of John Williams to the cause of Christian order and civilization should plead as powerfully on behalf of the Maori as the atrocities of the Pai Marire against him. If the "Times," pointing to the death of Volkner, exclaims—"Behold the measure of the depth to which this much talked of Christianity has penetrated," we for our part would modify that conclusion by referring to the battle on the Wanganui river, where, in defence of English interests, Christian

Maoris met and defeated a persistent body of their own relatives and friends, who were intent on the destruction of the town of Wanganui. We protest, therefore, against the injustice which, while it describes in the most vivid colouring the evil deeds of bad natives, ignores the noble acts of good and Christian natives, and then proceeds to pass a sentence of condemnation on the entire race.

But while we refuse to commit ourselves to extreme conclusions, we at the same time admit that, in the presence of so dread a catastrophe, it is our bounden duty to reconsider the conclusions to which we have come respecting the evangelization of the Maoris, lest, perhaps, we may have ascribed to Christianity a more decided ascendancy over that people than it has actually attained; and whether, with this new and sad experience before us, it may not be necessary so to modify our views, as that they may coincide with the sober reality of facts. Now, we have never regarded the New-Zealand Mission as a completed work; nay, for many years we have observed it with much anxiety as a work, the progress of which towards maturity has been retarded by many and untoward circumstances. Had the Church Missionary Society regarded this Mission as a completed work, she would, several years ago, have withdrawn her Missionaries from this field; and in fact she was so moved to do, and that by individuals whose personal character, position, and experience in the native character and circumstances of the country, necessarily invested with great weight the advice which they gave. Several years ago the Bishop of New Zealand, and the present Governor, Sir George Grey, when in England together, visited the Committee of the Church Missionary Society, and in the strongest manner urged their conviction, that the time had come when the Church Missionary Society ought to withdraw its Missionaries, for that the work had so far advanced, that it might with safety and propriety be transferred to the church establishment, precisely in the same way as on a former occasion the Society had dealt with its West-India Missions; that not only indeed might this be done with safety, but that it ought to be done in presence of the vast destitution of the heathen world, which summoned us, after apostolic example, to go forward to the places where Christ had not yet been named. It was just at the moment when Sir George Grey was retiring from his first governorship that this advice was tendered, and his successful administration, and the interest which he had shown in the welfare of the native race, gave to it the weight of almost irresistible authority. The subject was a momentous one, and it was examined and sifted by the Parent Committee in a series of very animated discussions. At length, after long and prayerful and anxious deliberation, the Committee decided that the time was not come when it could withdraw itself from that island Mission, and, transferring its Missionaries to the church establishment, retire from the field. It was felt that the Mission was yet like a Himalayan river before it has emerged from the mountainous region where it had its birth; that the plain country had not yet been reached where a smooth and even course might be expected; that critical circumstances and unexpected difficulties might supervene, in which the Society, if still in the field, and retaining the position of influence which had been acquired by many years of patient labour, might tender wise counsel and yield important aid. It was content, indeed, to modify its action by withdrawing the grants which had been hitherto made to the educational department, devolving on the native Christians the duty of maintaining their own schools, which from the large sums they were then receiving from the sale of their lands they were able to do. But even for this an equivalent was obtained in the designation of one of its own Missionaries to the episcopate, and that for the purpose of correcting a great defect under which the New-Zealand Mission laboured; an evidence of immaturity so unanswerable, that so long as it remained, it were impossible that the Church Missionary Society could think of withdrawing from the field—the almost entire absence of a native ministry. Bishop Williams was consecrated for the express purpose of training up suitable agents for ordination, and so expediting that euthanasia of the Mission which alone would justify the withdrawal of the Church Missionary Society.

The apprehensions entertained by the Committee have been verified, and the decision to which they came is now shown to have been a wise one. Difficulties have supervened more severe than could have been anticipated. The native Christianity of New Zealand, as yet in an immature and feeble state, has been subjected to a fiery ordeal. Conflicting interests on land questions brought the colonist and the settler into collision. No one, with any regard to truth, can assert that in these complications the native received fair and equitable treatment. But it is now useless to refer to these matters. We have gone over them again and again, until the subject is wearisome both to ourselves and our readers. Suffice it to say that a portion of the race, becoming exasperated, committed themselves to acts of war, and brought upon themselves the whole force of British power. After a stout resistance they have been crushed, and now in the season of adversity, where Christianity was weak and superficial, it has entirely given way, and some of the tribes have returned to their old and sanguinary superstitions, which, disinterred from the grave where they lay mouldering, and dignified with a new name, have been raised on high as a rallying-point for the Maori, and the signal of uncompromising hostility to Christianity and England.

They have cast off their Christianity, because, thoroughly alienated, and disliking every thing English, they disliked the religion they have received from us. Such a result we ought to have been prepared for. They were well disposed at one time to English rule, and to fraternization with the English colonist. They became the victims, as is admitted now by the colonial authorities themselves, of an unjust war. They found that Christianity had not taught England to be just in her administrative action towards inferior races; that might was counted as right, and, if resisted, then the resistance was denounced as rebellion; and now from England, and the Christianity of England, this section of the native race is utterly averted. There is nothing new in this. The same series of events occurred in Ireland; and there, too, land feuds, wars between the natives and the intruding race, in which the more powerful prevailed, and then confiscations on a wide scale, laid the foundations of a deep-rooted disaffection to the English power and the English faith, which from generation to generation has been perpetuated to this day. This is the reason why scriptural Christianity makes such slow progress in the sister country: it is because it is regarded as English. A powerful nation can of course deal harshly with inferior races, but she must accept the consequences, in the turbulence of a disaffected people, and their reluctancy to the yoke. We regard the Pai Marire as a banner of disaffection to English rule, and to Christianity as identified with that rule.

What is to be done under these circumstances? Extermination is the cry with some. Of course this, if carried out, cuts the Gordian knot of the existing difficulty. "The savage can never be socially amalgamated with the white man, but must disappear before him." So says the "Times." We deny the impossibility, provided only that the native be dealt with according to those just principles which Christianity inculcates. This has not been done; and now there is a difficulty as to how the Maori shall be disposed of. But the difficulty is one which we have originated ourselves. To confess however, our own faults, is not pleasant: a more easy way is to disburthen ourselves of them by imputing them to the native. We load him with the conjoint weight of European and native faults, and then, pronouncing him irreclaimable, doom him to extermination. But does God approve of this procedure? Has He given authority to Englishmen to tread down native races and appropriate their land? What! He who hath "made of one blood all nations of men for to dwell on all the face of the earth, and hath determined the times before appointed, and the bounds of their habitation?" No!

there is no such authority. If we cannot colonize a land without exterminating the native race, let us abstain from it. The land will cost more than it is worth. It will cost a load of guilt, a debt which must be paid off in national judgments and disasters. The Spaniards have dyed their hands red in the blood of native races; the Portuguese too; nor have the Dutch been free from the same crime. But the Anglo-Saxon race has also participated in this dread procedure. Witness the aborigines of North America; the blacks of Australia; and now the Maoris of New Zealand, are they to be added to the doomed list?

But our Missionary efforts, it is alleged, have proved a failure. This startling atrocity has dissipated the dream of native evangelization; and now the well-intentioned but deluded philanthropists, who interposed on behalf of the Maori, and prayed that he might be permitted to live on his own land, are to be put aside, and their interference no longer suffered.

Let us consider. What does this atrocity demand from us? An abandonment of effort? Nay, a renewal of effort. Our work is not done: this is now undeniable. Then on the very foundation of this atrocity let us begin to build anew. A Missionary has been put to death amidst circumstances of the most revolting character. Is New Zealand then to be given up? That is not the genius of Christianity. There was a scene once occurred, one the traces of which are indelible. It was an act of the most malignant cruelty committed against the great Benefactor of the human race. Missionaries, after all, are but men. They have their faults and imperfections. They are sometimes injudicious in their proceedings, and are liable to be misunderstood. But in Him of whom we speak there was a total absence of all these accidents. Never was there such an expression of perfect love, and never was there one upon earth on whom was poured forth such a flood of concentrated malignity. Around him raged the surges of human hatred. "Crucify Him! crucify Him!" was the doom which they awarded him; and they crucified Him—one of themselves; of their own race—their friend, who had gone forth amongst them, doing good, and healing all that were oppressed with the devil; nay, their divine instructor, their Saviour, their Lord, who would have gathered them even as a hen gathereth her chickens under her wings, and they would not. Never was there greater exultation manifested than when they saw him uplifted on the cross. But was the divine mission therefore withdrawn, and the earth abandoned to its fate because Christ had been crucified? Nay, this very deed inaugurated new and unprecedented efforts, and the death of the Redeemer became the foundation on which was raised that superstructure of a progressive Christianity, which is yet, in our own day, advancing to its consummation. That his good should be overcome of evil is not God's way; nay, the contrary is his principle—to "overcome evil with good." His glory is concerned in this, that his good prove itself stronger than human evil. It has been so of old. It must be so now, unless, to our shame, we would proclaim to the world, that, whilst we retain the name, we have lost the animating spirit and excellence of Christianity.

Volkner has died—the first Missionary that ever suffered mortal ill at the hands of a New Zealander. Then let us build over his grave new efforts for the evangelization of the Maori race. He suffered patiently. Like his great Master, he uttered no complaint; he broke out into no revilings. Meekly, lamb-like, he laid down his life. His was a martyr's death. We doubt whether Christianity ever achieved a national victory, the foundation of which was not laid in the martyrdom of some of the first evangelists. The seed dies that it may rise again. "Verily, verily, I say unto you, except a corn of wheat fall into the ground and die, it abideth alone; but, if it die, it bringeth forth much fruit." That was true of the parent seed; and it is also true of those who, under the direction of the once crucified but now enthroned Saviour, are engaged in reproducing his Gospel through the world. Like Volkner, at some special crisis, one or another may be called upon to lay down their lives; but when it is so, their death will infuse into the work a new vitality, and Christianity spring up more vigorously than it did before.

And so we entertain the hope that these atrocities will eventuate a great reaction in New Zealand. The "Times" states that the new fanaticism seems to have aroused nearly the whole native population of the province of Auckland. Yet it is only a short time since that it detailed the rough handling which the Pai Marire, in effecting their journey across the island to the eastern tribes, where they have wrought so much mischief, received, at the hands of the Arawas, the leaders of the party, and, amongst others, the chief prophet having been captured and handed over to the authorities. This we are persuaded of, that, notwithstanding all the disastrous influences of a protracted war, there exists in the Auckland province a large body of Maoris who value Christianity, and are not prepared to surrender it at the dictates of the Pai Marire. But however this be, our duty is plain, and if a great wrong has been perpetrated, we must not rest until there has been educed from it as great a good.

CONSTANTINOPLE.

In the earlier part of 1864 Missionary proceedings in this city had assumed an interesting and encouraging aspect. A spirit of inquiry had been awakened amongst the Greek population, and this, in some measure, had extended itself to the Turks. Many from amongst this people were anxious to obtain information, and came to the Missionaries for this purpose. To facilitate such communications, rooms had been hired in a khan, an ancient building, with a court-yard, and containing a small number of rooms, opening upon galleries which ran round each storey. On the third gallery two rooms were hired, one for receiving visitors, and to this room persons of diverse nationalities—Turks, Greeks, Armenians—as they felt disposed, came of their own accord. There was no preaching outside the room; neither did the khan stand in any public thoroughfare but was approachable only by a narrow dirty alley.

As Turkish inquirers, in intercourse with the Missionaries, became increasingly interested, so that they felt anxious to examine into the comparative merits of Islamism and Christianity, Dr. Pfander's book, the Mizan-ul-haqq, was placed in their hands, a treatise which, from its profound and calm tone, is eminently fitted to convince Mohammedans that Christianity, in its doctrines and precepts, and in its influence upon the human character, well deserves the most serious consideration. Of necessity such a work is, to a certain extent, controversial, because Mohammedanism, in its original structure, is an aggression upon Christianity, which therefore requires to be vindicated from various misrepresentations. It was with this object, many years ago, the Mizan-ul-haqq was written in the Persian language, having been subsequently rendered into the Hindustanee for the use of Mussulmans in India, by whom it has been extensively read, and more recently into the Turkish. To those at Constantinople who were desirous of having such a book, it was sold; but this was done privately: there was no public sale, nor was colportage used on its behalf.

The Hatti-sheriff of 1856 fully justified such proceedings. It conceded religious liberty, the free exercise of all religions within the Sultan's dominions, and guaranteed that none should be hindered in the exercise of the religion he professed. A Turk, then, if so disposed, was free to embrace and profess Protestant Christianity, and, according to the provisions of the Hatti-sheriff, he was entitled to state protection in so doing, so that he should not be molested. And if free to decide upon a question of such importance, and to register his convictions by an open profession of Christianity, then surely he was free in all the preliminary matters,—free to inquire, and, for the solution of his doubts, at liberty to approach any Protestant Missionary who might be accessible to him, that he might ask and receive instruction.

The Missionaries were in Turkey, in obedience to their Lord's command, "Go and teach all nations." They are under an obligation to enter in at every door which his providence had opened, and to remain there until forcibly excluded. As regards a residence in Turkey, they were precluded by no law, and, while there, it was their duty to do the best they could in order to make Christianity known. Of course their endeavour would be to fulfil this duty as quietly as possible, avoiding all needless irritation; and such, in fact, has been the action of our Missionaries at Constantinople. There have been no extravagant proceedings; no "going about preaching publicly against Mohammedanism" on the part either of Missionaries or their converts; no "irritable plan of conversion." Missionaries only did that which was absolutely necessary, if their presence in Turkey was to be of any utility whatever; and if this were not permissible, there was no use in their being there.

The Turkish authorities appeared for a season to have accepted these movements as the natural and necessary result of the Hatti-sheriff of 1856. "American Missionaries preached the Gospel in every province of the empire. They gathered converts from every church—Catholic, Greek, and Armenian; from the latter a large number. They published books explaining and enforcing evangelical truth in opposition to all other churches. In all this they demanded and received the protection of the Government. When their converts were persecuted by their former co-religionists, the Turkish authorities always protected them." So likewise, when Missionaries addressed themselves directly to the Turks, and sought to evangelize them and communicate to them Christian instruction, the Government at first seemed as though it did not disapprove of their proceedings; for in one instance, which occurred about six years ago, when a Turk and his wife embraced Christianity at Bebek, Aali Pasha visited the house of the American Missionary, and examined these persons, to see if any force had been used in their conversion to Christianity. On that occasion he declared himself perfectly satisfied, and assured them officially that they had as good a right to become Christians as a Christian had to become a Mussulman.

These appearances were, however, deceptive. There were those who viewed with a jealous eye the progress which Christianity was making. If they did not act before, it was simply because they lacked opportunity. The benefits conferred on Turkey by the Christian powers were fresh in people's minds, and the liberal tendencies of the late Sultan rendered hopeless all attempts at a retrograde movement. But time brought its changes. What was not deemed practicable in 1858 was resolved upon in 1864. The thunderbolt fell as in an instant. The book-store of the British and Foreign Bible Society, established for many years in Constantinople, and the private rooms of the different Protestant Missionary Societies—Propagation of the Gospel, Church Missionary Society, and American Board—were suddenly seized, the officials expelled, and the doors, after having been locked and sealed, guarded by an armed police, which refused all access to the premises for two days; while several Moslem converts, quiet, inoffensive persons, were laid hold upon by armed men, violently dragged through the streets, and cast into the common prison.

These violent measures were attempted to be justified by the plea that the proceedings of the Missionaries had so inflamed the popular mind, as to render the authorities apprehensive of an outbreak; but that any grounds existed for such an apprehension to this day remains unproved. Constantinople at the time was in perfect tranquillity, and the only disturbers of the public peace were the authorities themselves.

Supposing, however, that the apprehension was well founded, and that there did exist an underground swell amidst the population of the city, yet surely it was the duty of the Grand Vizier to submit, in the first instance, the proceedings of the Missionaries to the British authorities, in order that, by calm and impartial investigation, it might be ascertained whether they were in any measure blameable, and, if not, that, whatever might ensue, due protection might be afforded them. But to deal with parties against whom nothing had been proved as though they were criminals, and offer them up as a propitiary victim to popular indignation, seems to be a strange mode of preserving the public peace, and incompatible, not only with religious freedom, but with any freedom whatsoever.

Now in a country circumstanced as Turkey is, where so much depends on the private views and feelings of a few individuals, who may chance to be at the head of affairs, and in positions of influence, occasional attempts to escape from concessions made to freedom of conscience are to be expected. Protestants in Turkey are especially liable to be so dealt with, not only because the scriptural Christianity which they profess is the common foe of all false religions, but because they are as yet, in that empire, few and feeble. But at every previous crisis they had something to fall back upon. Her Britannic Majesty's late Ambassadors, Lord Stratford de Redcliffe and Lord Cowley, recognised Protestantism as possessing the right of free action; and, so long as its course continued to be wise and temperate, entitled not only not to be molested, but to be protected by the State; and if at any time there was a reluctancy to acknowledge these rights, the British Embassy invariably befriended the Protestant interests with the same earnestness which the French and Russian Ambassadors never fail to exhibit on behalf of their co-religionists. Had the same policy been adhered to, the Turkish authorities never would have adventured upon such extreme measures. But the views which prevailed at the Embassy were not such as they had been. The Ambassador considered that the Missionaries had acted unwisely; that they had been too aggressive in their proceedings, and had themselves caused the difficulties which had supervened. The course which they ought to have pursued, according to his judgment, is thus stated in a letter addressed by him to the Secretary of the Committee of the Evangelical Society, Constantinople—

I venture, indeed, myself to say, without impugning the duty of propagating Christianity in the abstract, or conveying any censure upon you for the manner in which you regard that duty, that, under the circumstances which we have to consider, it becomes a question whether Protestants may not do more towards Christianizing the Mussulmans by practising quietly and simply the tenets of their own faith, and leaving others to do the same, gaining in this manner general goodwill, and allowing, in the mean time, the tide of civilization, which is connected with Christianity, to mount, slowly if you will, and imperceptibly, until it gradually overflows the at present semi-civilized East, than by any more violent or provocative action, any lectures or lessons against Mohammedanism, any employment of salaried converts, to spread Christianity. Remember that things "may be lawful, and yet not always expedient."

Christianity, in short, was to divest itself of all aggressive action. It was to content itself with a silent testimony, and be as a dumb man, who speaks not by words, but by signs. This is irreconcileable with the genius of Christianity. The council of the Jews commanded Peter and John not to speak at all, "nor teach in the name of Jesus;" and their answer was, "We cannot but speak the things which we have seen and heard." Christianity seeks not to coerce, but to win and persuade; but, if this is to be done, it must have liberty to speak; and if Missionaries may not speak, it is best they should withdraw.

It would be tedious to go through the long correspondence which ensued on these subjects. It will be found in a Blue Book published this year. But the result of it is important, and our readers will be anxious to know what is the precise position, at the present time, of Protestant Missionaries in the Ottoman dominions. Have they freedom in their work, and are they secured against further molestation?

On the important subject of the distribution of the sacred Scriptures in the various languages spoken throughout the Ottoman empire, the British and Foreign Bible Society is for the present left free and unfettered in its action. The Turkish authorities wished to limit the sale of the Scriptures to shops or private houses, and disputed the right of colportage.

In favour of the maintenance of this right the Committee of the Bible Society assert that the practice has been for many years permitted without obstruction; that the Society never distributed Bibles gratuitously, but always sells them; that many millions of the subjects of the Sultan are Christians, and are entitled, according to the provisions of the Hatti-humayoun, to the free profession and exercise of their religion; that in many parts of the empire, such as Bosnia and Bulgaria, it would be impossible to set up shops for the sale of books; that, in fact, the common, the established, and most efficacious method of distributing Bibles by the Society is the method of colportage, or hawking; that in this way the Bible is eagerly sought after and extensively spread, and that no disorder or disturbance of the peace has accompanied the sale; that the Turks, far from feeling any aversion or repugnance to the practice, consider the Old and New Testaments as books containing the records of divine revelations prior to the age of Mohammed; that Turks who do not choose to buy the Bible kiss the book with reverence, and return it to the person offering it for sale.

Finally, they allege that this mode of distribution is a lawful, peaceable, and harmless method of spreading among Christians and Turks alike a knowledge of the Christian religion.

These arguments appeared to Earl Russell "conformable to treaty, to the profession of the Turkish Government, as proclaimed in the Hatti-humayoun, and to the privileges of British subjects in the Ottoman dominions." The British Ambassador, therefore, was instructed to urge the Turkish Government "to allow the free distribution of the Bible by means of travellers, or hawkers, employed by the Bible Society or other British subjects, as an essential and indispensable part of religious liberty guaranteed by the Hatti-humayoun, and confirmed by the practice of many years."

The Ambassador (Blue Book, No. 30, p. 34) states the result of his communication with Aali Pasha on these points. "I urged the request of the petitioners in every possible way, without obtaining a positive assent or dissent." "The impression left on my mind is, that the Porte will never grant the request in such a manner as to accord a positive and irrevocable right." A verbal assurance that "there is no intention to interfere with the colporteurs if they conduct themselves quietly," appears to be the utmost which the Turkish authorities were disposed to grant in answer to a direct application on the part of the British Government.

With respect to Missionaries and their labours, the Porte was willing to concede to Protestantism a *locus standi* within the empire, provided it was satisfied to divest itself of all aggressive action. "The Ottoman Government," observes Sir H. L. Bulwer, in his letter of August 1, "is willing to allow Protestants and all Christians to exercise their own religion in the Ottoman dominions in churches, or quietly at home, but it will not allow any attempts, public or private, to assail the Mussulman religion. It will allow Mussulmans to become Christians, but it will not allow them, any more than it will other Christians, to go about speaking publicly against Mohammedanism. It says its policy is to protect all religions, and not to allow persons of one religion to attack another."

Assuredly the Hatti-sheriff of 1856 must be regarded as a fictitious document, if this were all that it intended to grant in the direction of religious liberty. But such, we are persuaded, was not the intention at the time when it was promulgated, as assuredly such was not the sense in which it was understood by the representatives of the Western Powers. Can it be imagined for a moment, that at a time so critical, when the safety of Turkey depended on the fidelity with which those Powers adhered to their engagements, such a deception would have been permitted? for what did it amount to? Precisely this—as if one who had long imprisoned a bird within a cage were to resolve thus—"Prisoner, you shall be free: I shall throw wide open the cage door; but first of all I must clip your wings, and deprive you of the power of flight: you shall be nominally free, but practically just as much within my power as before."

British Christians were not silent at such a moment. The Committees of the various Religious Societies who were directly interested in the question memorialized the Foreign Office. The Church Missionary Society contended that the Hatti-sheriff of 1856 "guaranteed to the Mohammedan convert the exercise of all legitimate means of informing his conscience by resort to Christian Missionaries; and that it guarantees to those Missionaries the reasonable and peaceable exercise of their office. It would have been a mockery to guarantee to the inquirer immunity after he had actually embraced the Christian faith, whilst the "temporal arm" might interfere to prevent all reasonable means of his becoming acquainted with the claims of the Christian religion." They prayed, therefore, that their Missionaries "should not be under any such restrictions as are inconsistent with the concessions of 1856, and claimed, on behalf of Turkish converts and inquirers, that they should have the full liberty of conscience and exemption from all molestation, to which the Porte pledged itself in the diplomatic agreement entered into with the British Government in 1856."

The decision of the Foreign Office on these controverted points is contained in a despatch dated December 15th, 1864. It recognises the fact that the Hatti-humayoun had been violated, and wrong done; and therefore, while indisposed to seek redress for the past, Earl Russell proceeds to say—"I must ask assurances for the future; and if, in reply, I am to be told that the reference to the Hatti-humayoun, in the treaty of 1856, and the promises made to Lord Stratford de Redcliffe, have no practical value, and that neither Missionaries nor converts can derive any protection from those documents, I am convinced the feelings of the English nation towards Turkey will be very seriously affected, and their disposition to defend the integrity of the Turkish empire much abated."

The reply of Aali Pasha to this communication is important, as in this document, if anywhere, we may expect to find an avowal of the future policy of the Ottoman Porte in relation to Protestant Missionaries in Turkey. It is contained in a despatch to M. Musurus, the Turkish Ambassador in London.

It reiterates the charges made against the Missionaries—"My former communications have made you acquainted with the conduct of certain Protestant Missionaries, and the measures which the Sublime Porte was obliged to adopt." The Turkish minister then refers to the Hatti-humayoun of 1856, "as establishing the free exercise of all forms of religion existing in the empire," and to the obligation imposed in consequence on the Turkish authorities of "watching indiscriminately over the safety of all religious interests, and guaranteeing each creed against the aggression of the others, by giving to all an entire liberty in their religious manifestations."

There is therefore no ambiguity as to the position which the Turkish authorities would assign to scriptural Christianity. It may exist in the Turkish empire if it settles down into a truce with the various creeds around, and refrains from reproducing itself. The light may be in the midst of darkness, provided that it does not enlighten that darkness. But where, then, is the "entire liberty in all its religious manifestations" which the Hatti-humayoun is supposed to have established?

The incompatibility of such an enforced reserve with the enjoyment of any thing which deserves the name of religious liberty had been pointed out by the British Secretary of State in more than one of his despatches, and to such expostulations Aali Pasha thus refers—"Lord Russell has stated repeatedly, in his speech, the difficulties which arise in the application of the principle which is in question. His lordship declares that he cannot form a conception of the liberty of religious creeds without the freedom of recording, in the ardour of conversion, the arguments through which those creeds have been adopted. The noble lord goes so far as to allow the attack, in a private manner, of a religion which is considered erroneous, but he sees offence in the act of publicly attacking and reproaching that religion."

Assuredly Christianity could not exist with a less amount of liberty than this—that, however in public reserve be enforced, the tongue be loosed in private, and men be there free to converse on subjects of all others the most important. Is this minimum of free action at once and unreservedly conceded? We shall quote the words of the Turkish minister—

Doubtless, the liberty of opinion leads to that of recording it. Nevertheless, we believe that it is forbidden to employ other methods than that of persuasion. So far this mode of making known religious convictions is, we consider, justified on the principle of liberty of opinion. But his lordship, who condemns the aggressive expression of religious convictions when they are made in broad daylight, will not dispute that there is a great step between a spontaneous and tolerant manifestation of convictions and a systematic propagandism which makes use of powerful means, and acts with the settled purpose of effecting the subversion of other religions; which draws all its energy from the intolerance and the hatred of those religions; which speculates not only on the ignorance of the masses and the weakness of faith, but even upon political views, and, above all, upon motives of interest; which insults and, reproaches, instead of respecting the opinions of others, and fears not to have recourse to corruption when it cannot obtain its object by persuasion. It would be vain to affect in practice all the consideration which the Missionaries have too much neglected. Such a system would be none the less the contradiction of the principle of religious liberty, for by its very existence it attacks that liberty in others, and that respect for the convictions of others, without which religious tolerance would be but an empty form.

Persuasion, then, provided it avoid publicity, and confine itself to corners, is conceded. But whether in public or in private, Protestant Missionaries have never used any other method. It would not answer their purpose so to do. Converts, except on conviction, are worse than nothing. Coercion and bribery yield a fictitious material. Protestant Missionaries repudiate such a system; yet they are accused of a "systematic propagandism, which speculates upon political views, and, above all, upon motives of interest; which insults and reproaches, instead of respecting the opinions of others, and fears not to have recourse to corruption when it cannot obtain its object by persuasion." Assuredly these are procedures of which Protestant Missionaries know nothing. Such appliances scriptural Christianity eschews. They would not facilitate its progress; nay, they would prove as embarassing as Saul's armour to David, when he said, "I cannot go with these."

This, then, if we understand these state papers correctly, is the maximum of free action, which the Turkish minister permits to Protestant Missionaries, they may use persuasion, provided that in doing so they avoid publicity. But is such an arrangement practicable? Who shall discriminate between what is public and what is private? Does the Turkish minister offer any pledge, concede any promise that the persuasive action of Christianity shall not be confounded with a dangerous propagandism? None whatever. Christianity must not be openly placed in juxta-position with Islamism, so that the truth of the one shall exhibit the erroneousness of the other. "The established religion of the country must be respected." "Can it be supposed," observes the Turkish minister, in the "ardour of his convictions," contending against "the pretensions of the Missionaries," "that whilst condemning religious persecutions, the Sublime Porte has consented to permit offence and insult to any creed whatever? that at the same time she was proclaiming liberty to all non-Mussulman creeds, she had given them arms against Islamism?"

Such, then, is the decision of the Turkish authorities: they are opposed to propagandism, that is, to the Missionary action of Christianity. That it should commend itself to the acceptance of many as the alone true faith, however mildly and persuasively this may be done, is, in their view, a propagandism which cannot be tolerated, and which the Hatti-humayoun never was intended to sanction.

The answer of the British Secretary of State is brief. Waiving further discussion as useless, he falls back upon the clause of the Hatti-humayoun, to which the Turkish authorities have affixed so narrow an interpretation, and so closes the controversy.

I gather from this despatch that the Sultan will observe inviolably the sixth article of the Hatti-humayoun of his late brother, which is in these terms—

"Seeing that all religions are and will be freely practised in my States, no subject in my empire will be troubled in the exercise of the religion he professes, or be in any manner disturbed on this account. No one will be compelled to change his religion."

I understand further, from the termination of the despatch, that the free sale and circulation of the Bible continue and will continue to be authorized in the Turkish empire.

If these two declarations are maintained and acted upon, I am quite willing to close the controversy.

In a future paper we shall review the aspect of Missionary affairs in the Turkish empire since the close of this correspondence in January last.

JOHN WILLIAMS, OF PUTIKI, WANGANUI.

The war in New Zealand was transferred, about the beginning of the present year, from the Waikato country to the Taranaki and Wanganui districts on the west coast.

The country from Cape Egmont to the Houranga stream, within a few miles of Wanganui, extending over ninety-seven miles of coast, and comprising nearly 1,300,000 acres, is claimed by the Ngatiruanui and Taranaki tribes, together somewhat more than 2000 in number. These people have been throughout the most bitterly hostile to the Europeans. They commenced hostilities by the murder, on the south of New Plymouth, of unarmed settlers and boys; and when the war with the Ngatiawa of William King was terminated by an arrangement, these two tribes, on account of their bad conduct, were excluded from its operation, and reserved to be separately dealt with so soon as the war in Waikato had ended.

Is there any possibility of accounting for the embittered spirit of this people? We place before our readers the following narrative—

In April 1834 the bark "Harriet," J. Guard, master, bound for Cloudy Bay, was wrecked at Taranaki, near to the spot where the English settlement now stands. For six days the shipwrecked mariners were treated as friends; but from some unexplained cause a quarrel arose, in which twelve sailors and twenty-five natives were slain, and Mr. Guard, two children, and ten seamen were made prisoners. Guard and several sailors were allowed to depart, on promising to return with powder as a ransom for the others.

In consequence of Guard's personal representations, the Government of New South Wales sent His Majesty's ship "Alligator," Captain Lambert, and a company of the 50th Regiment, to rescue the prisoners. On the arrival of the force at Taranaki, the captured sailors were delivered up, and the two interpreters who were sent on shore promised that a payment should be made when the woman and children were released. The soldiers were then landed, and as they formed in battle array on the beach, two unarmed and unattended natives came down to meet them. One introduced himself as the chief who had got the woman and children, rubbed noses with Guard, in token of ancient friendship, and told him that Mrs. Guard and the children were well, and that they would be surrendered on the natives receiving the promised payment. The officer in charge of the boat, attributing evil motives to this man, seized him, dragged him into the boat, and stabbed him with a bayonet.

A few days afterwards Mrs. Guard and one child were released, and the wounded chief was restored to his friends. The other child was subsequently brought down to the strand on the shoulder of the chief who had fed it, and he requested to be allowed to take the child on board ship in order to receive the promised ransom. When told none would be given, he turned away; but before getting many yards he was shot, and the infant was taken from the agonizing clutch of the dying man, to whom it clung as to a friend. The *dead man's head was then cut off, and kicked about the sand;* and Mrs. Guard afterwards identified it as *the head of their best friend.* In consequence of a shot discharged, by whom and at whom none knew, the ship's guns and the soldiers commenced firing, and after destroying two villages and several canoes, and killing many natives, the troops re-embarked, and the expedition returned to Sydney.

The Government of New South Wales then urged on His Majesty's Government the necessity of supporting the British Resident with an armed force, as that officer was placed in a position neither creditable to himself nor to the English he represented.

It would have been well for the honour of the English name had the Government of New South Wales been, like the Resident in New Zealand, powerless; for the Taranaki campaign resembled the operations of insulted buccaneers more than an expedition of His Majesty's forces. A Committee of the British Parliament expressed its disapprobation of this affair; pointed out that the New Zealanders fulfilled, while the English broke, their original contract; and stated that this opinion was drawn even from the one-sided evidence of the culpable parties, the chief witness being an old convict, who said a musket-ball for every New Zealander was the best mode of civilizing the country.*

The Ngatiruanuis never forgot the way in which their people had been slaughtered by the commander of H.M.S. "Alligator" in 1834, having kept, as mementoes of their treatment, some of the shot which had been thrown at them. Eventually, when estrangements arose between the natives and settlers, they became the staunchest supporters, first of the anti-land-selling league, and then of the king movement.

In April 1863, Sir George Grey, convinced, on investigation, that the colonial authorities had no right whatever to retain possession of the Waitara block, which had been wrested from William King, resolved on surrendering it to the natives. But there was another block of land to the south of New Plymouth, that of Tataraimaka, the property of the Government by purchase, but which the natives held as a pledge until the Waitara was given up. In presence of the irritation which prevailed the utmost caution was requisite, and common sense would have suggested not to touch the Tataraimaka block until the Waitara had, by public proclamation, been surrendered. Unhappily this course was not adopted. Tataraimaka was occupied before the natives were made aware of the intention to surrender Waitara, and, resolved on retaliation, the Maoris struck the first blow by cutting off two officers, two sergeants, and four men of the 57th regiment. This was done the very day month after the occupation of the Tataraimaka block, the Ngatiruanui being the perpetrators.

A month subsequently the natives were defeated by General Cameron at the Tataraimaka block, and dispersed; and immediately afterwards, the troops, with the exception of a small force left for the defence of New Plymouth, were transferred to Auckland, and the Waikato country became the seat of war, the garrison of New Plymouth acting on the defensive, and contenting itself with repelling the natives in their attempts to approach the town.

So matters remained until April 1864, when a reconnoitring party, under the command of Captain Lloyd, of the 57th Regiment, fell into a strong native ambuscade, and, being completely surprised, suffered severely, Captain Lloyd and six of his party being slain. On this occasion the Ngatiruanui, casting off all pretence to be regarded as

* Thomson's "New Zealand," pp. 272—274.

Christian and civilized men, appeared in their true colours as unreclaimed barbarians. They cut off the heads of Captain Lloyd and of five others, and carried them away.

Emboldened by their success, they ventured, at the end of April, to attack the posts, which defended New Plymouth, a movement which brought upon them a severe repulse, several of the Ngatiruanui and Taranaki natives having been found among the slain.

Hating the foreigner, they have now, in their aversion to him, cast off the religion which they had professedly received from him.

Strange to say, the new superstition, which is designated the "Pai Marire," has identified itself with the head of Captain Lloyd, which appears to be regarded as the symbol and centre of the system.

Under the direction of a native, called Te Ua, who arrogated to himself the office of high priest, and professed to be inspired by the angel Gabriel, this head was exhumed and cured after the old native fashion, that, being carried through the length and breadth of the land, it might henceforth be the medium of communication with Jehovah. The following are the tenets of the new religion—

The followers shall be called "Pai Marire."

The angel Gabriel with his legions will protect them from their enemies.

The Virgin Mary will constantly be present with them.

The religion of England as taught by the Scriptures is false.

The Scriptures must all be burnt.

All days are alike sacred, and no notice must be taken of the Christian Sabbath.

Men and women must live together promiscuously, so that their children may be as the sand of the sea for multitude.

The priests have superhuman power, and can obtain for their followers complete victories, by uttering vigorously the word "Hau."

The people who adopt this religion will shortly drive the whole European population out of New Zealand. This is only prevented now by the head not having completed its circuit of the whole land.

Legions of angels await the bidding of the priests to aid the Maoris in exterminating the Europeans.

Immediately the Europeans are destroyed and driven away men will be sent from heaven to teach the Maoris all the arts and sciences now known by Europeans.

The priests have the power to teach the Maoris the English language in one lesson, provided certain stipulations are carefully observed, namely, the people to assemble at a certain time, in a certain position, near a flagstaff of a certain height, bearing a flag of certain colours.

The following more detailed account has been furnished by a New-Zealand resident—

On the occasion of the fight at Ahuahu, Captain Lloyd's blood was drunk by the natives that killed him, and after having finished their orgies they cut off his head, and buried it. Next night the Archangel Gabriel is said to have appeared to those who had partaken of the blood, and desired them to disinter the head, and dry it in the old Maori fashion, in order that the Captain's spirit, speaking through the head, might become the medium of communication between the Almighty and mankind, and be carried through the island as a banner under which a crusade against the Pakehas was to be preached. This was accordingly done, and the head is asserted to have spoken and propounded the new creed, as well as appointed its chief priests.* The following are the principal articles of the new faith—Its professors were to be called "Pai Marire" (good and peaceable), and the word "hau," pronounced short, like the barking of a dog, was to be their sacred watchword, the rapid utterance of which would ward off all danger, even to the extent of causing edged weapons to glance from their bodies in battle, and bullets aimed at them to change their course, and rise into the air. The proselytes were to be initiated by drinking water in which the head had been dipped, or which had been poured over the head, and took an oath to destroy every white person without any distinction of age or sex, till all are killed or driven from the land. The professors of the new faith were to be under the special protection of the Virgin Mary, who would be personally present among them; and they were to be assisted in their task of driving out the Pakeha by the Archangel Gabriel and hosts of angels, and as soon as the task was completed, these heavenly messengers were to teach them all arts and sciences known to Europeans. The professors would be enabled

* These people are adepts at ventriloquism.

to learn English or any other foreign language perfectly in one lesson by observing certain forms, namely, standing for a given time in a certain position, under a flag of a peculiar colour and pattern, hoisted on a flagstaff of certain dimensions. The priests claimed to have acquired this power, and Matene lately, when at Waitotara, got possession of a piece of newspaper in which some article purchased in town had been wrapped, and pretended to read it aloud in English, and afterwards translate it; and performed the cheat so adroitly, that one of the Waitotara assessors present, a very intelligent native, who from his boyhood has had intercourse with Europeans, was deceived into becoming a convert, and has since been deprived of his office in consequence. All the European creeds were to be regarded as false, and done away with. All Bibles and other books relating to them were to be destroyed; the observance of the Sabbath was to cease, all days being regarded as holy; and marriage and its obligations were to be dispensed with, in order that the race of believers might increase the faster, and become as the sand of the sea in multitude. The fact that the extraordinary powers promised have not been conferred was accounted for by its being necessary that the head should first visit the whole island.

Thus these fanatics were urged to attempt the expulsion and destruction of the European race, which their prophets assured them could be easily accomplished. They accordingly divided themselves into two parties, one of which marching northward towards Taranaki, made a desperate attack on a redoubt occupied by a small party of the 57th, poor Captain Lloyd's regiment, under the command of Captain Shortt. Although this officer had only seventy-five men under his command, he repulsed the enemy, with the loss of nearly one hundred killed and wounded, while on his side only one man was wounded.

The other party moved in the direction of the Wanganui river, where, at Pipiriki, about eighty miles from the mouth of the river, they hoped to find sympathizers, and thus, having strengthened themselves, to attack and destroy the town of Wanganui.

The Wanganui river has its sources on the north-west side of the Tongariro mountains, and after a course of 200 miles, during which its volume is increased by the accession of several tributaries, flows into the sea on the western coast to the south of the Taranaki district, the town of Wanganui being situated four miles from the sea, on the western bank of the river. Opposite the town, on the east bank, is the old Church Missionary station of Putiki.

On May the 3rd of last year, as our catechist, Mr. Booth, was proceeding from Wanganui to Pipiriki, he was met by Hemi Hape, the native assessor, and learned from him that the natives up the river were in a state of great excitement in consequence of the arrival from the coast of a party who had brought with them the head of Captain Lloyd. This news was confirmed as he went further up the stream, and he was advised by the native teacher of a pa not far from Pipiriki not to go on, as Matene, one of the leaders of the new superstition, had threatened to take his life. Mr. Booth, however, for various reasons, thought it his duty to go on.

Next morning we had another warning, but I still thought it my duty to go: accordingly, after breakfast, we proceeded on our journey. When within about three miles of Pipiriki we met Hamarama, the brother of Pehi Turoa, and the old fighting chief of Wanganui. He allowed the canoes to approach each other without making a salute. When we got near enough he made signs with his hand, as if warning me off. When the canoes were opposite each other all the men in his canoe commenced barking like dogs, and continued doing so until they had got some distance away from us. When we got within sight of Pipiriki the rapid was so bad that we had to get out and draw up our canoe. It was usual on such occasions for the natives of the place to come to our assistance. At this time they stood on the bank looking on, and although we failed in our attempt to get the canoe up the rapid, they still stood passively looking on. When at last we got to the landing, the man who had brought the head with this party, and a great number of the Pipiriki natives who had joined him, made the most violent demonstrations, barking, howling, and flourishing their tomahawks, and this they kept up for some time. I kept my seat in the canoe. Young Hori Patene, with about four or five others, came and sat down by the water-side, and cried over us. When Hori had done crying, he told me that he was unable to protect me; that I had better return. I agreed to this, and asked him to go with me across the river, and to my brother's place (which is about a mile distant from the Pipiriki pa), to fetch the remainder of our children, with my brother and his wife and child. During our absense we heard a great noise by the river-side, and when we got down again we found that the natives had come across the river armed, threatened Mrs. Booth, and had forcibly taken the canoe, which, when they had taken to the Pipiriki side of the river, they speedily emptied of its contents, consisting of our and the children's clothing, and stores for my brother. I demanded to be sent away at once, but two men came across to say that we should not be allowed to go. Soon after this, three others came, and commenced their invocations to the Angel Gabriel, by whom they suppose themselves to be inspired (this karakia consists of a barking similar to the barking of a dog, making motion with the hands at the same time). They continued this for some time, and then took forcible possession of a half-caste child, who has been staying in our family nearly four years. I struggled to keep the child, but was not able to do so. A messenger then came across to say that we were not to be allowed to go away from Pipiriki: we must stay there. They wanted me to make a promise to this effect, which I refused to do, saying that they had first expelled me from the place, afterwards taken away my goods, clothes, &c., then taken away the child; and I was sure that the only purpose for which they were detaining us was that they might take our lives. Hori Patene and Haimona said that there was nothing to be afraid of now. The demonstration had been made before me merely to show their determined hostility to the Governor, because I was of the same skin, and not because of personal ill-feeling towards me. We then went across to the Pipiriki side, myself, wife, and children, my brother, wife and child; but we refused to get out of the canoe. We asked for some blankets out of one of our bags to cover us on our way down. They did not cease their efforts to make us promise to stay. We continued there in the rain until the afternoon, when Epiha Patapa, king native, came down from Ohinomutu (Pehi Turoa's residence), having heard the noise. When he had learnt what it was all about, he said to me, "Friend, continue to stay until to-morrow, when Pehi and I will come down." On this word I consented, and we all went up to the Mission house. The men still continued to ask us to consent to stay, and said that they would set Pehi's word at defiance if he did not agree to what they proposed. With some difficulty we got rid of them, then locked ourselves in the house. In the mean time our blankets were brought up, but the boxes containing our stores and my brother's stores were kept in the pa. As soon as it was dark they commenced barking and making the most dreadful noises we ever heard, seemingly exciting each other on, and at the same time marching round a flagstaff, and this they kept up until midnight.

On the following morning (Sunday), after breakfast and prayers, a native came to ask for my brother, saying he wanted to buy something. We told him to remember that this was the Sabbath-day, and of course no business could be done. He said that Matene had done away with the Sabbath; there was no Sabbath now; every day was alike: that if my brother did not consent to sell his things they would take them. We told him that we were determined to honour God before man, and take the risk; that we also wished to be left quiet, that we might worship God in peace. About the middle of the day a woman came to say that Pehi had gone past; that he had left no word for me. We continued all day with the doors locked, and felt much comfort from reading the services of the church, especially the Psalms for that day (8th). At nightfall they commenced the noises which we had heard on the previous night, in which they continued until near midnight. On the following morning Hori Patene came up to say to my brother that they had broken open his packages, making a mock auction of the contents, giving three or four shillings for a blanket worth a pound (20*s.*), shirts 1*s.* each, and so on in proportion. He gave him the money which he had received (about 15*l.*); then, turning to me, said, "They have also broken open your boxes, and taken out whatever they considered valuable; and now my word to you is to get a few things ready, and go as quickly as you can. If we cannot get you away I feel sure there will be murder." With this he burst into tears. In a few minutes we had our things ready. Then a man came up to say that the angel had just said that we were not to be allowed to go; that we must stay quietly where we were. They wanted me to consent to this, and I told them, "All I can do is to stay as your prisoner." One man after another came up with the same message, and we began to feel it would be impossible to get away, Hori's efforts on our behalf being quite without avail. When all hope seemed gone, we went into the house, and read the 68th Psalm, and prayed very earnestly that it might please God to make a way for us to escape. This was about eleven A.M. After we had prayed, I said, "There seems to be no chance of our getting away just now. We had better give the poor children some breakfast." I was going into the kitchen for that purpose when Hori ran up, and said, "It is all right: you may go." We took what we could lay our hands on just in the moment, but on leaving the house we overheard them saying to each other, "Let them get on to the canoe and get off; then we will bring the canoe on shore and tomahawk them." Hori and Haimona (old Hori's brother), with Porokoru and their wives, helped us down to the canoe. They told us to make haste and take our seats. They were crying as though their hearts would break. I asked Hori to come on our canoe until we had passed the pa, for fear the natives, being so excited, should fire on us. Hori said, "You will be safer if we will walk on the river-side opposite to the canoe until you get well away. Make haste, and get down to Rauana, where there are Government natives, and there have some food; then go as quickly as you can to town: do not stay there, but take your passage in the first steamer, as the place will be attacked at once, and I am afraid you will lose your lives."*

These Pai Marire natives now decided to attack the town of Wanganui. Before Mr. Booth left, two war canoes were being prepared to bring down the war party, and messengers had been sent to Taranaki and Waitotara, so that the coast natives might co-operate with them in the attack.

The European force at Wanganui was at this moment very feeble, and active efforts were made to bring up reinforcements. But before this could be accomplished the affair was decided. The friendly natives of Putiki and other places on the lower part of the river resolved to prevent the Gabrielites from carrying out their intention. Having in vain endeavoured to dissuade them from their purpose, they determined to act. They took possession of the island of Moutoa, almost midway in the river, about 300 yards long and twenty wide, raised some twelve or fifteen feet above the level of the river, thinly covered with manukau scrub and fern, and presenting certain irregularities of ground which afforded considerable shelter. Here, divided into three parties, they awaited the enemy. On Saturday, May 14th, Matene, the prophet, and his followers, landed, in seven canoes, on the shingles of the island. So soon as they had formed, which they were permitted to do without interruption, they forthwith commenced their incantations, shouting "Hau, hau!" (Up, up!) and using gestures not unlike the passes made by mesmerists. This continued for two hours, the advanced parties not being more than twenty yards distant from each other. At length the conflict commenced, and volleys were exchanged. The advanced party of the friendly natives suffering severely, three of the leading chiefs being shot down, gave way, carrying the reserve with them; but at the extremity of the island they were rallied by the chief, Haimoni Heroti, who, shouting, "I will go no further," with twenty men, who gathered round him, checked the pursuers, and a hand-to-hand conflict ensued. At length the rebels, having lost several of their leaders, broke and fled, being hotly pursued till they reached the river's bank. Here, with the exception of a few who escaped in a canoe, the survivors took to the river, and were most of them shot down. Matene, the prophet, although badly wounded in swimming, succeeded in gaining the bank, but was almost immediately tomahawked by a native policeman, Te Moro, who lost no time in swimming after him.

Of the friendly natives fourteen men were slain; amongst them, Hemi Hape, the assessor, and the warden, Kereti Hiwitahe. On the side of the aggressors not less than eighty fell, ten of whom were chiefs. Forty prisoners were taken, men, women, and children, and brought down to Wanganui. In this conflict the friendly natives proved that they did indeed deserve that name, for, as they said themselves, "We have fought for the Queen and for the protection of the Pakehas. We have killed in the battle of

* "Blue Book." Statement of Mr. Booth, made at Wanganui, May 12, 1864.

Moutoa many of our nearest relatives and friends;" and by this timely interposition the town of Wanganui in all probability was saved. The superintendent of Wellington notwithstanding all his efforts, did not succeed in reaching Wanganui with reinforcements until the afternoon of the day subsequent to that on which the battle was fought. He "found the whole population, European and Maori, in a state of great excitement in consequence of the news which had arrived early that morning that the rebels (composed chiefly of the adherents of the new religious sect, or fanatics, as they are appropriately termed) had been defeated by the friendly natives. As to the details of the battle the most contradictory statements were afloat. The settlers were enthusiastic in their praises of their native allies, and the Maoris, elated beyond measure with the success their friends and relatives up the river had achieved, were prepared at once to clear the Wanganui river of all kingites, and at the same time to march to Taranaki, sweeping all before them. Some hundred natives were preparing to reinforce their friends up the river. Having ascertained that our native allies were really short of ammunition and guns, and that it was more than probable that the Waikatos, Taranakis, and Ngatiruanuis, and other tribes, would at once muster in force to avenge the defeat and death of so many of their relatives and chiefs in the battle of Moutoa, he determined to furnish the friendly natives with arms, ammunition, and food, and to proceed himself up the river with the reinforcement, taking with him Dr. Fletcher to attend the wounded, and Mr. Booth as his interpreter."

Dr. Featherstone accordingly left Wanganui on Tuesday, May 17th, in a canoe, manned by a crew of some fifteen men, under the guidance of Hoani Wiremu (John Williams).

The main body, under Hori Kingi, Mawai, and other Putiki chiefs, had started some two or three hours, amidst the cheers of the Wanganui settlers, who had loaded the canoes with provisions of various kinds. Few who witnessed that scene will forget the heartiness with which the Maoris responded to the hip, hip, hurra, hurra, hurra, of the settlers. And yet, while these Maoris were going again to engage in a contest in which they had little or no concern, to risk their lives a second time almost solely in defence of the Europeans, there were some few settlers who grudged them the arms and ammunition the Government had supplied them with, and deplored the infatuation of the Government in trusting them, or, as they expressed it, in arming savages against their own race. It was dusk before we reached Raorikea (Laodicea), where we found Hori Kingi and his people engaged in a tangi which lasted nearly the whole night. We pitched our tent on the opposite bank of the river.

Besides conveying supplies to the friendly natives, and so strengthening their position as to enable them to repel any new attempt which might be made by hostile natives to force the river, there was a further object contemplated—to ascertain the intentions of Pehi.

This chief had for some time aided the insurgents in the Taranaki district, and afterwards, from some cause or other, he withdrew from them, and retired into his own territory on the Wanganui river above Pipiriki. Here he occupied a dubious position, siding neither with one party or the other, his sympathies being no doubt with the king's party, yet unwilling to commit himself by an open avowal, until, by some decided success, they had made good their ground. His conduct was the more inexcusable, inasmuch as, in 1862, both he and his brother, Hori Patene, had pledged themselves not to allow the peace of the Wanganui river to be disturbed; and yet in the recent conflict with Matene and his fanatics he had given no help. He was reminded that hitherto he had stood on "the outside," and had rendered no active support to the Government; but that the time had now arrived when he must needs declare himself. Pehi, however, would give no pledge of better conduct for the time to come. He wished that the prisoners taken at the battle of Moutoa should be delivered up to him, and when he found that the superintendent was determined not only not to accede to his request, but to take them down with him to Wanganui, he got up in a state of considerable excitement and said, "If you take the prisoners, I follow you down the river quickly;" and, in tracing the course of events, we shall find that he was true to his word.

The battle at Te Ranga, on the 21st June 1864, in which so many of their chiefs fell, and, amongst others, the renowned Rawiri, broke the power of the Waikatos, and this they themselves appeared to feel, when, immediately after, 133 natives, including several chiefs of high rank, came in, and laid down their arms. And now, Waikato having disappointed their expectations, the eyes of all disaffected natives were directed towards Taranaki, for there they felt the conflict must be decided: it was their last stronghold, the chosen place where the new superstition had set up its standard, and, if unsuccessful there, nothing remained but submission. The Governor was equally convinced that Taranaki must now become the battle-field. But to maintain the position which had been gained in the Auckland province so large a draught of men was required, that the force available for service in the western districts was not such as the urgency of the case required. Still there appeared to be no alternative. There the natives were in open rebellion, continually aggressing upon the outposts of the New-Plymouth garrison, and threatening the town of Wanganui. Accordingly, towards the end of 1864, General Cameron transferred his head-quarters to Wanganui, and commenced a series of operations with a view to the complete occupation of the country between Wanganui and the Patea. The hostile natives were not slow to meet him.

On January 25th his camp at Makumaru, near Wanganui, was suddenly attacked by a body of natives 600 strong. The outlying pickets on the right and front of the camp were simultaneously driven in, the enemy, under cover of the high fern and flax bushes, having approached, without being perceived, until close upon the sentries. The attack was pushed with resolution, nor were the insurgents repulsed until they had not only incurred severe loss themselves, but had inflicted much loss on the British, the return of casualties, particularly in the 50th regiment, being heavy. This engagement sufficed to convince General Cameron that the insurgent natives had succeeded in concentrating a large force in the western districts, and were likely to offer a most determined resistance to his advance through a difficult country. He felt that the force at his disposal was wholly insufficient for operations of a decisive character, no less than two-thirds of its strength being employed in the protection of the different settlements or in the occupation of land taken from the rebels. He applied, therefore, for a reinforcement of 2000 men to be sent out from England, and "for a still larger reinforcement if, in addition to the occupation of the country between Wanganui and the Patea, the road between Taranaki and Wanganui is to be opened, and more land to be confiscated and occupied north of the Waitara, which I understand to be the plan of the Colonial Government, approved by your Excellency."

In the mean time, so urgent was the necessity for an immediate augmentation of the orce, that he had withdrawn the whole of the detachment from Wellington, and 250 men from Taranaki, besides calling upon the militia and volunteers in Wanganui to garrison two posts on the frontier. He had thus succeeded in advancing along the coast to the distance of thirty-six miles from Wanganui. The country in his rear, however, was only imperfectly subdued: many of the pas in which disaffected natives had entrenched themselves had been passed by, and their occupants, finding themselves unmolested, prowled about with the view of getting plunder or cutting off the settlers they might meet with.

And now Pehi threw off the mask, and, abandoning his pretended neutrality, declared his intention of attacking and destroying Wanganui. The troops left to defend the town were comparatively few, but the friendly natives again interposed. As they had blocked the passage of the river to Matene and his fanatics, they resolved to do the same in relation to Pehi and his followers; and accordingly 400 of them, under the command of Hoani Wiremu (John Williams), the Putiki chief, and head catechist of the Church Mission, were placed in a favourable position for this purpose.

This was not the first time that John Williams had been so engaged, risking his life in defence of the Pakeha against the anger of his fellow-countrymen. Some nineteen years before, during the time of Rangihaeata's wars, Wanganui, then a very infantile settlement, with a population of not more than 200, was endangered by a disaffected chief called Mamaku, who, with his people, had come down the river, full of hostile purposes; but the Putiki natives barred the way, and Mamaku retired, threatening to return soon with a larger force. "This coat," he said, "is small; but I shall return at Christmas with a warmer one."

The first blow struck was on the lone homestead of a settler in the immediate vicinity of Wanganui. A band of Maoris attacked his house. The man, thinking it was only his life that was sought after, escaped from a window, leaving his family undefended. When the wife saw that the natives continued to assault the house, although aware that he had escaped, fearing for the lives of her children, she put them out of a back window, following herself with one of the youngest. She was seen, pursued, and struck down with a wood-axe, together with three of her children: the others escaped by running into a swamp, and concealing themselves amongst the flags. The marauders plundered the house, set it on fire, and then fled up the river.

When tidings of this cruel deed reached Wanganui, there was a great sensation, and on the next morning many of the settlers and officers visited the place where it had been committed. Strange to say, the eldest daughter, although fearfully gashed, was found living, the cold of the night having staunched her blood, and saved her life.

John Williams and the Putiki chiefs now held a meeting, and it was resolved to pursue the murderers.

Hoani Wiremu, taking several determined young men with him, set off without loss of time, selecting a light and swift canoe. They paddled up the river, justly supposing the murderers would hasten by that way into the interior: they called at every place to inquire, and were not mistaken. On reaching Ikunikau, they told a feigned tale to the natives of the place, who immediately manned a large canoe, and continued the pursuit. At last the murderers were perceived. The Putiki natives laid down in the canoe, lest, being recognised, the object of their journey should be suspected. On coming alongside, they jumped up and seized them; a struggle ensued, and the canoe was capsized: they however retained their grasp, and secured five of the murderers, one having previously left their company. Having bound their prisoners, they hastened their return. On reaching Waipakura, Maketu wanted them to stay there for the night, but when they declined doing so, he fired at them. They proceeded on their way, and safely delivered up their charge to the military; not having been more than twenty-four hours from the time of their starting, during which they had paddled seventy miles. No time was lost in trying the prisoners by court-martial: the trial commenced on the 24th April (25th was the Sabbath), and on the 26th they were condemned and executed, the boy only being spared, as it was proved he did not assist in the barbarous deed; but he actually entreated to be hung with his companions.

These youths being connected with the Ngatiruaka, caused that tribe to rise in arms. They were joined by the Ngatihaua, under Mamaku, and by the Patutokotoko, and thus approached the town in considerable strength.

In the first skirmish they obtained possession of a part of the town, which they not only plundered, but coolly remained in to feast on the ducks and fowls they found there, cooking some dozens of them. The military and inhabitants took shelter every night in two stockades and three of the strongest houses, two of which were surrounded with trenches. The town then presented a singular appearance, its entire population being thus shut up in these few fortified spots, all herding together, and, from their contracted quarters, much sickness and death ensued.

Throughout this critical time Hoani Wiremu and his people rendered most valuable aid, until at length, after two months, the besieging force grew wearied of the war, and, breaking up their camp, returned to their own homes.

The name of John Williams, as that not only of a loyal chief, but of a zealous catechist and a good Christian man, is interwoven with the records of the Wanganui Mission from its earliest period.

The seed of the Gospel was first borne to this part of the island by some of those young natives who, during the successful wars of the Ngapuhi chief, Hongi, had been brought as prisoners to the Bay-of-Islands district, and there received Christian instruction in the Mission schools. Subsequently, when on the death of Hongi the power of the Ngapuhi was broken, and they who had been detained so long in bondage were set free, they returned to their old homes, and communicated to their heathen relatives the first rudiments of Christian truth. When, therefore, Archdeacon Henry Williams, in December 1839, reached Putiki Waranui, the site of our present Mission station, the natives flocked about him with great eagerness, and, on his putting questions to them, he was pleased to find that they could answer very many. He was the first Missionary who had penetrated to this portion of the coast. So interesting did the aspect of things appear to be, that, on his return to the Bay of Islands, the Rev. W. Mason was appointed to occupy this new sphere of action, and reached Putiki Waranui in June 1840. Two years subsequently we find the name of John Williams introduced into his journals as one of the natives in whom he had special confidence, and who was wont to accompany him on his journeys. On Mr. Mason's untimely death he proved to be the same to his successor, Mr. Taylor, a stedfast, reliable Christian man; always ready to use his influence with his countrymen for good. Such has been the course which, through God's good help, he has been enabled to pursue for twenty-five years, until at length he ended it by laying down his life in defence of Christianity and civilization.

In the recent conflicts on the Wanganui, when the friendly natives barred the river road to the advance of Pehi and his men, John Williams was in command, occupying the most advanced post, and was exposed to much danger. Various attempts were made to cut him off. First a small party of four placed themselves in ambush for this purpose, but were themselves captured, and, after having being well treated, were liberated on the following morning. The next night another party, intent on the same object, was captured in the vicinity of the post: these also were allowed to return, John Williams declaring that the first shot must be fired by the enemy. This Christian forbearance did not avail to turn Pehi and his people from their purpose, and they moved forward to attack. It is not our province to enter into the particulars of the conflict. A pa, the main position of the enemy, was defended by seven redoubts. Several of these were carried, and at length the pa itself was assailed. The conflict was severe, and many of Pehi's people fell. At length a flag of truce was hoisted, and Pehi and about eighty of his people surrendered themselves as prisoners. But the victory cost us dearly. When advancing on a pa, John Williams was shot in the right breast.

He did not fall, but, although the bullet had entered deeply, and rested within him, he still could walk away erect as when he was first stricken. People thought the ball was a spent one, and the wound not mortal; but when his hurt was examined by the doctors, they could see that the injury was fatal, and that he was suffering the intensest agony.

Mr. Taylor, in a letter dated March 8th, pays the following tribute to the memory of his friend—

This was on the 23rd of February. He was brought down to Putiki. I was called up about three A.M., and I took him over to the colonial hospital, where he died on the following morning, and on the 27th he was buried. Nearly all the authorities, military as well as civil, followed him to the grave, and the British ensign formed his pall. Colonel Logan, the officer in command, took a grand flag, which was to be presented to the natives by the ladies of Wanganui, and laid it on his coffin. It was then borne before it in procession to the church. At the grave a party of the militia fired three volleys.

John Williams was indeed a Christian warrior: though he fought in defence of the European community, he did not forget his dependence on God. When he went up the river, he wrote down to me, stating that he had established prayer-meetings in every place, to supplicate the divine blessing on their arms, and he wished us to do the same. He also wrote to Abraham, my head teacher, and to the women, to pray for their husbands and relatives, and all attended daily, morning and evening, with the greatest regularity.

In the removal of John Williams, the entire community has experienced a great loss. He has always been the friend of the European, and the directing mind of the Maori, and I fear there is no one capable of supplying his place. One proof of the esteem he was held in by the Europeans was given at his funeral, by some of the settlers relieving the bearers of his coffin, and carrying it up the steep ascent to the cemetery, on their shoulders. He made Hakarais acquainted with all his plans and intentions, and by carrying them out the enemy was repulsed, and Hepa taken. Indeed it has surprised our countrymen that in so short a time, and with so small a force, he should have accomplished what General Cameron has not yet done, though commanding as many thousands as John did hundreds. But John put his trust in the God of battles, and kept his commandments. The Governor has arrived, and he seems to be much concerned for John's death, and has promised to educate his two sons.

I trust we shall have peace up the Wanganui, and if the Governor is equally successful, we shall have great cause for thankfulness. Our great comfort is in knowing that "the Lord reigneth."

I send a copy of poor John's last letter, written two days before his fatal wound was received—

"*Hiruharema, Feb.* 20, 1865.

"RESPECTED MR. TAYLOR,—Health to you and all your children, to Mr. Baird and Abraham. Respected Sir, your letter has reached us. Your word is good, very good, to all our hearts. Strive constantly in prayer to God for us, that He may preserve us from the deceitful and hostile men who are striving to destroy and cast down the dwelling-place of the Spirit of God. Do you strive day and night. But we too have urged the teachers of every pa to pray to God that He may go in the midst of us. This is all from your loving son.

MADAGASCAR.

WE publish another journal received from our Missionaries in Madagascar. They are beginning to understand more clearly the spiritual condition of the people amongst whom they have been placed, and they find them, as the heathen are everywhere, grievously demoralized under the influence of idolatry. It is the same as it was in olden time—"the people sat down to eat and drink, and rose up to play." Superstitious rites and festivals are used as opportunities to excite and indulge evil passions. No one can read the details which they give without feeling convinced how vitiated the people are, and what need they have of the Gospel in its renewing and sanctifying power.

And as the Gospel is needed, so already has it begun to tell. A first-fruits has been yielded in the conversion and baptism of the Governor's scribe. Let there be much prayer on behalf of this Mission; for our Missionaries, that they may stand perfect and complete in all the will of God; and for their work, that it may be largely blessed.

Dec. 17, 1864—Hiarana. Mr. Campbell departed yesterday for Amboanio. Captain Rosalie sailed this morning at six o'clock. The Governor and his whole suite left immediately afterward, and I have remained at Hiarana, which small village has again resumed its perfect quiet.

Dec. 18: *Lord's-day*—Spent the most of the morning in preparing a short address for the mid-day service. At eleven o'clock A.M. Boto, who joined Mr. Campbell and me previous to our first departure from Mauritius, and who was with us in our subsequent tribulations at Johanna and the Seychelles, began to call the people together for the meeting. At twelve o'clock about twenty-five had assembled. We commenced by singing. I read a portion of the morning prayers and the Litany, and then I spoke to the people on the first portion of the fourth chapter of St. John's Gospel; of the gift of eternal life and its importance compared with the trifles of this world. Though those present were chiefly Sakalavas or Betsimasarakas, they appeared, as far as I was able to judge, to understand and appreciate what was said. Osini, the chief Sakalava of the village, was present. He is rather an aged man, but reads very well, and appears to be anxiously seeking after the truth. I have heard a curious circumstance relative to this man. Many months ago, when no ship had visited Vohemare for a long time, Osini, accompanied by many of the inhabitants of the village, went to the entrance of the harbour, and there, looking towards Mauritius, offered up a prayer that some vessel might speedily arrive. At the same time he threw a dollar into the sea, as an offering to God.

Dec. 19—Came from Hiarana in the morning. Arrived at Amboanio at half-past nine A.M., and found Mr. Campbell teaching the Governor's wife. The Governor himself came soon afterward, and kept Mr. Campbell and me engaged with him the whole day. Two letters arrived to-day from Antananarivo. They are frequently from six weeks to two months in coming.

Dec. 30—Mr. Campbell and I have spent the whole day in arranging our luggage. Hitherto it has been in a most higgledy-piggledy state, but at present our one-roomed house is in first-rate order. Close to the sides of the house, all round, are placed our boxes, drawers, &c. &c. At the further end of the house from the door are placed our small portable beds, while our only respectable and English-looking furniture consists of a small table, a few chairs, and a harmonium, and our only picture a portrait of our good Bishop.

With the case of the harmonium we have made a book-shelf, which affords a resting-place for a few necessary books of study and reading. Few as they are, there was doubtless never such a library in Amboanio before.

Dec. 22—During my visits to the people this evening I called on Rainibiby and his wife, the latter of whom has been suffering extremely from sore eyes, a complaint to which many of the people here are subject. I found Rainibiby and his wife and child removed to a very small house, and the former consulting the Sikidy on behalf of the two latter. This he did by means of small seeds, which, when he moved them from one position to another, were made to divine, in a manner I have not been able to ascertain, the proper course to be taken for the recovery of his wife and child. The man was astonished at the exhibition of his folly in believing that the seeds of trees and plants are able to hear and answer his prayers. After a long conversation with him, I read the fourth chapter of John. 1—24, and prayed.

Dec. 25: *Christmas-day*—This has been one of the happiest days I ever spent. Happy has been the contemplation of the first coming of our Saviour; happy has been the thought of his future coming in power and great glory, and happy has been the thought that this day helps to strengthen the bond of union that unites in one spirit the scattered members of Christ's church—that many have been the prayers and best wishes the one for the other; happy too, indeed, has been the work in which Mr. Campbell and I have been engaged here. In the morning, at eight o'clock A.M., the Governor, Mr. Campbell, and I celebrated the holy communion of the body and blood of our adorable Saviour. This Mr. Campbell and I had not been privileged to do from the time we left Mauritius, July 3rd, and the Governor not for many years. After this short service, the Governor retired, but at twelve o'clock he came again, followed by a large number of officers and friends, and all of them dressed in their best clothes, presenting the most pleasing sight that I have witnessed since I arrived. About sixty entered, and then commenced a most interesting service. Mr. Campbell and I read the whole morning service, and then the Governor spoke to the people from the ninth chapter of St. John; explained to them the nature of the day that we were commemorating; and told them, that unless they left their idols, and sought the only true God, they were still ignorant of the blessings of the coming of Christ in the flesh. His words were simple, and to the point. After the service, the remainder of the afternoon was spent in singing and conversation. At half-past five P.M. sixteen of our friends—thirteen men and three women—joined us at our Christmas dinner. We were all very happy. The poor were not forgotten. The Governor and his wife interested themselves on their behalf, and collected subscriptions for them from many.

Jan. 1, 1865: *Lord's-day*—The usual attendants at our Amboanio service came early this morning, and were with me nearly the whole day. They consist of the Governor, his wife, Ratsiza, the Governor's scribe, a few officers, and two women, viz. Raketaka and Rasoanoro. All, except the Governor and his wife, who breakfasted with us, retired to their homes for a short time at half-past nine A.M. They came again at twelve o'clock, when our morning service commenced. During the afternoon there was singing and reading of the Scriptures. At half-past four P.M. Ratsiza desired that we should pray the Litany again, but I told him and the others present that there is a proper form of prayer for the evening, which we accordingly used. Most of the persons present can read, and are beginning to follow in the responses.

Jan. 3—Studied the language during the heat of the day, and visited the people during the cool of the evening. This Mr. Campbell and I do most days, and we find it the best way of acquiring the language, for what we learn in study and reading is made use of, and stamped upon the memory in conversation. I have been much struck to-day, as on many previous occasions, at the numerous cutaneous and other diseases which are afflicting this poor people, and especially the Hovas. Go where I will, enter whatever house I will, there some phase of poor suffering humanity presents itself to my view, and with this comes the conviction that, in most cases, what I observe is the result of the most immoral living.

Jan. 4 — The Governor arrived for breakfast. The Governor came for an English lesson. Many years ago he had mastered a considerable portion of English, but has forgotten the most of it. He is exceedingly pleased when he has overcome some slight difficulty, or has mastered a new word; so much so that his look of joy and inward satisfaction more than compensates for the trials of one's Mission life. How much more the fact that the Missionary imparts the joy consequent on the reception in the heart of the knowledge of a crucified, risen, and coming Saviour!

Jan. 7—To-day Mr. Campbell and I have witnessed the sacrifice of an ox. It was brought to the middle of the Sakalava town, and there thrown down, and made fast by the legs. Rasoanoro, a Sakalava woman, who has attended many of our meetings, placed one small vase of incense on the ground, a little distance in front of the ox, and another a little distance behind it. She then poured some water over the ox from a bottle. After this, Rafojia, the chief of the Sakalavas in this part of Madagascar, kneeling down, prayed to *Yanahary* ("God"), and to the *razana* (the "ancestors"), on behalf of a sick child, for whose recovery the ox was being offered up. When Rafojia had finished, an old Sakalava woman also invoked *Yanahary* and the *razana*, and then the ox was slain by an Arab. When the ceremony was finished, Rasoanoro and many others listened to me attentively while I told them that God is the only hearer and answerer of prayer. Oh that they may soon learn to worship Him in spirit and in truth!

Jan. 8: *Lord's-day*—On our way to Hiarana yesterday I saw the remains of another bullock that had been offered up in sacrifice by the Sakalavas; and when I arrived here I found that Osini, the chief of the Sakalavas of Hiarana, had also offered up a bullock on behalf of a woman in childbed. This ignorance and superstition led me to choose St. Paul's speech at Athens (Acts xvii. 22—31) for my subject at this morning's service. Between fifty and sixty people were present, and chiefly Sakalavas. I was delighted to see such a large number. My heart was moved towards them, and I was greatly enabled to declare unto them their folly, the character of the "unknown God," and the blessings of the one perfect sacrifice of Christ.

Osini was not present in the morning, but he came in the evening, when I dwelt upon the errors of praying to the ancestors. He and many others confessed that it is wrong.

During a conversation with Kalo, a Betsimasaraka, she told me that she had been taught to believe that the falling stars are wicked men, who, when they die, go to the gates of heaven, but are driven from the presence of God; and that the earthquakes are the attempts of those who are bound in chains to escape. These are not the traditions of the Malagasy, but notions which Kalo has learned from either Creoles or Indians with whom she formerly lived as wife.

Jan. 9—Returned early to Amboanio. The Governor and others have been with us the whole day.

Jan. 10—While visiting to-day I found that most of the people, whether Hovas or Sakalavas, were engaged in dressing their hair, in preparation for a great festival of the Sakalavas which will take place to-morrow. Most of the women here, and many of the Sakalava men, bestow more time and labour upon their hair than any people I know, and each tribe has a different way of plaiting and wearing it. The Hova men, being soldiers, keep their hair cut short over the whole of the head, except a small portion above the forehead. They have no whiskers, but wear a moustache. Most of the Betsimasaraka and Sakalava men wear the hair plaited, but the plaits of the Sakalavas are smaller and more numerous than those of the other tribe. The customs, too, of the women of different tribes, as regards their hair, are so various, that, to say nothing of their different features and complexions, the way in which a woman's hair is plaited is almost a certain indication of the tribe to which she belongs.

To-day, in nearly every house I visited, I saw one woman plaiting either the hair of another woman or that of her husband, and not unfrequently the one whose hair was being plaited was lying asleep on the floor of the house.

Jan. 11—During the whole of last night there was much beating of drums, dancing, singing, and drinking, in all parts of the Sakalava and Borizany towns; and as our house is situated between the two, it was with some difficulty that Mr. Campbell and I were able to sleep. To-day has taken place the Sakalava festival which is called, in their own tongue, *Manansana Savatra*, which means literally, "The lifting up of the circumcised." It has been held in honour of nine Sakalava youths who were circumcised a year ago.

The Sakalavas have no rejoicing at the time of the performance of the rite of circumcision as the Hovas have. The rite is performed privately by the father. On the following year the youth is publicly shown to the world, and a great rejoicing takes place on his behalf. After this he is no longer considered a child, but is looked upon as a man, and eligible for any of the offices of the *fanompoana*, or "Government service." It was the rejoicing on behalf of nine youths of the most influential Sakalavas in Amboanio that Mr. Campbell and I have witnessed today. The Governor sent to us early to inform us that he would wish us to accompany him to the festival. Rafojia also, the chief of the Sakalavas, and father of one of the nine youths, wished us much to honour him and his countrymen by our presence. We accordingly consented to comply with their pressing invitations, especially as the reason of their joy appeared so lawful. We met the Governor at the bottom of the street that leads to the Rova, or Hova town, and, having greeted him, joined his procession to go to the booth that Rafojia had erected near his house. Under this booth we sat, amidst Hova officers, soldiers, and women, and a large number of Sakalavas. All parties were dressed in their best clothes, and most of the women had silver chains round their necks, some of which were very large and handsome. The son of Rafojia wore the largest of any. It was given to Rafojia by the Queen, Rasoherina, when he went to the capital to acknowledge her as the Queen of Madagascar.

Innocent, however, as the cause and object of the rejoicing might have been, it was soon evident that Mr. Campbell and I were in the midst of heathenism, superstition, and sin. One lot of Sakalava women was singing and dancing, and knocking long slender sticks together over their heads, close to Rafojia's house. Another lot of men and women, chiefly Sakalavas, went a little distance into the field, and lugged to the meeting-place, near the booth, two stems of trees. As they brought them along they danced, and shouted, and ran, and gesticulated as if they had been mad. One man ran in amongst the riot and sprinkled them with water, while Rasoanoro scattered rice upon them. When they had succeeded in reaching the booth, the men planted the largest stem in the earth, having first painted it at the top, while Rasoanoro and other chief Sakalava women began to make crowns for the nine lads before mentioned. These were made of rufia-wood, in the form of a sugar loaf, and covered with a lamba, a part of which hung from the top of the crown down the lads' backs.

At this time (two o'clock P.M.), I returned home. The Governor, however, soon sent for me to see the sacrifice of three bullocks. These were made fast by the legs, and lay in a row in front of the pole that had been previously planted in the ground. Then, after Fojia had prayed to Yanahary and the razana on behalf of the Queen, nobles, officers, the nine lads, and the "Vazaha" *i.e.* the English and French, each of the fathers of the nine lads took his child on his back and began to dance round the bullocks, sometimes stepping over their necks. They each bore a musket charged with powder only, which they fired at the head of one of the bullocks; and one of them, taking a spear, stabbed one of the bullocks in the side—an act for which I afterwards reproved him, telling him that it is not right to cause any animal unnecessary pain. As soon as the dancing was finished the bullocks were killed, and then Mr. Campbell and I returned home. During the day we had many opportunities of speaking to Fojia and many others of the folly and sin of praying to any one except God, through our Lord Jesus Christ. All listened with marked respect and attention, which greatly astonished me. Thank God for the open door we have; but, alas! how sunk in ignorance and sin are all the people!

Jan. 12—Went to Fojia's booth early this morning. I found him and many other influential Sakalavas sitting under it, and conversing together. The pole that was brought from the field yesterday was close by, and I observed that it was smeared with blood, and that the humps upon the backs of the three bullocks which were killed yesterday were placed on the top of it. On making inquiries, I was told that all this was done in the way of offering a sacrifice to God, not, however, for past guilt, but to avert future calamities, and to obtain present and future blessings. I accordingly spoke faithfully to Fojia and others of their error, and of Him who is the full, perfect, and sufficient sacrifice both for past sins and for the obtaining of future blessings. I spoke to them, also, of the sin of praying to their ancestors. Fojia acknowledged that it was not right, and that he wished not to have done so yesterday, but was obliged on that occasion to fall in with the wishes of the people.

Tried to visit the people in the evening, but found most of them either intoxicated or too much excited to hear with profit what I had to say.

Jan. 13—The "tsitialaingia" arrived here to-day from the capital. The word is composed of *tsi* "not," *tia*, "to love," and *laingia*, "falsehood;" meaning, literally, "not loving falsehood," or "lying." The tsitialaingia is a silver spear, with the name of the reigning sovereign and the word "tsitialaingia" engraved upon it, and is carried by the messengers of the Government as a badge of official authority. At the death of each sovereign those belonging to the Governors of the provinces are returned to the capital, and new ones are sent in their place, invested, as it were, with new power. In cases of trial for grievous offences, the tsitialaingia is carried by the judge to the house of the prisoner, who is judged before it. In the time of King Radama II. the Malagasy police supplied its place, which was certainly a better arrangement than the present.

Many important letters also arrived to-day from Antananarivo, and amongst them one forbidding the importation of slaves by the Arabs. This measure is simply carrying out the terms of the treaty concluded between the English Government and Radama I.; and though it prevents the external slave-trade, it in no way suppresses the internal, which is constantly being carried on to a large extent by both Hovas, Sakalavas, and Bestimasarakas. The greater portion of the population here, of all parties, are slaves, who have been either bought or taken captive in war.

Jan. 14—Most of the people have been drinking rum or toaka to-day. (The latter spirit is made by the Malagasy themselves from the sugar-cane.) Fighting has consequently ensued. As I was returning home this evening I witnessed, to my great sorrow, a fight between Rasoanoro, whom I have mentioned above, and Raketaka, one of the most hopeful women, as I thought, of Hiarana.

Jan. 15: *Lord's-day*—Two new comers from the capital came with the Governor to the morning service. They have given me a most encouraging account of the work at Antananarivo. The chapels there are crowded.

Jan. 19—The Governor told Mr. Campbell and me to-day that the man who was tried yesterday before the tsitialaingia was fined seventy-five dollars.

Much drinking and fighting to-day.

Rasoanoro called at evening prayers, and I spoke faithfully to her of her sin on Saturday last. Oh that the Spirit of God may change her heart!

Jan. 20—Radosy called. He is very friendly, but, alas! like many others here, given up to drinking and immorality, the two sins which are the curse of this people. He is a brother, by the rite of *Fatidra*, to Ratsiza, the Governor's scribe, but in no way his brother in spirit: the one is a child of darkness, the other a child of the light. *Fatidra* is the name of a ceremony at which any two persons may enter into a mutual and solemn pledge of friendship. The ceremony is performed by each party partaking of a small piece of liver dipped in the blood of the other party. The fathers of the Governor and Rainifiringia, who went to England last year, entered into this bond of friendship. And when the Governor and Rainifiringia were together last year at Tamatave, they did the same.

This ceremony, however, from what I have heard, is not worthy of encouragement. Christianity is the only bond of real and pure friendship. The blood of Christ purges the consciences of his people from dead works to serve the living God, and unites them together in one holy brotherhood.

Jan. 23—The Governor, his wife, and other friends, have been here all day, singing and learning English and Malagasy. At the breakfast-table the Governor related to us a very curious custom of the Malagasy. It appears that when a bullock is killed by any person whatever, its body must be given to the sovereign and nobles; and if any person neglects to do this he is fined sixty dollars. Again, one of the legs of a fowl belongs to the elder member of the family. If others take it, they are fined a dollar.

This evening, soon after the departure of our friends, as Mr. Campbell and I were sitting quietly alone, we heard some strange Malagasy singing in the distance—strange, because so much unlike the general Malagasy singing here. It gradually approached nearer to our house, and we were astonished on hearing words of our hymns repeated by the singers. They entered the house, and turned out to be Ratsiza, Rasoanoro, and others, who attend our services. They sang several hymns, in a most enthusiastic manner, and remained to evening prayers. We enjoyed it amazingly.

Jan. 26—Several persons called early in the morning for medicines. They formerly came at various times of the day, till we made them understand that they would please us much by calling at a given time. We fixed upon eight o'clock A.M., the hour for morning prayers. Those, therefore, who come for medicines for the body, are told of Him who is the Physician of souls.

Jan. 27—Found this evening, as I have on former occasions, how delightful it is, when speaking to Sakalavas of the sin of offering sacrifices to God, to lead them to the consideration of the death of Christ, the one "full, perfect, and sufficient sacrifice, oblation, and satisfaction for the sins of the whole world." This blessed and comforting doctrine I set before several Sakalavas this evening. At the end of my discourse, one of them thought it *fady*, "unlawful," to take my hand. The others were pleased with what I said.

Jan. 29: *Lord's-day*—Hiarana. The rain which has fallen of late has enabled the people to plant their rice. Many of them are in the fields, working on their small lots of land. The service this morning was consequently thinly attended. In the afternoon I called on Fojia, who came here yesterday. He was reading his Prayer-book, and was anxious to know what the strange Malagasy words Keriobirug, Serafima, Maritiry, and Anjely meant. They are as puzzling to the Malagasy as the *pons asinorum* is to boys learning Euclid.

I conversed much with Fojia on the nature of Christ's sacrifice, and the sin of offering any other to God. He told me that he believed the people of Vohemarina will not do what is contrary to God's word when once they have learned that word.

In the evening I had another thinly-attended service. Fojia, as well as Osini, the chief of the Sakalavas at Hiarana, were present. I do hope that God is influencing the hearts of these two men for the furtherance of his work among the Sakalavas.

Jan. 30—When I arrived at Manambery this morning a man was driving a herd of bullocks through the river. As they entered the water, I asked if there were any crocodiles in it. I had scarcely received a reply to my question, when one laid hold of a bullock by one of its fore legs, pulled it under water, and was taking it away down the river. The bullock struggled hard to keep its head above water, while some Sakalavas, armed with spears, entered a canoe, rescued it, brought it ashore, and, finding that its leg was broken, they killed it. From this may be seen the danger of crossing the rivers of Madagascar.

Feb. 1—Studied till eight o'clock A.M., when Mr. Campbell conducted family prayers. He took a few of the first verses of the last chapter of St. John's Gospel, and gave one of the best expositions of Scripture in Malagasy that I have heard him give at all. Thus it is very satisfactory to feel that my brother Missionary is making progress in the language and able to speak intelligently to the people. At twelve o'clock we had our weekly prayer-meeting on behalf of our own work and that of our brethren at Tamatave and Mauritius. At three o'clock P.M. those who are able to read came to practise singing.

The Malagasy flag has been flying to-day in honour of the arrival of Ramanansoa. This man is bitterly opposed to Christianity. When invited to dine with the Governor, some time ago, and on the Governor's saying grace, he left the table.

Feb. 2—The Arab who arrived here the other day from Antomboka is a very interesting and hopeful character. He has been associated with the Romish priests at Nossibé, and is able to repeat the Lord's Prayer in French. Mr. Campbell has given him some Malagasy Testaments and Psalms, to be given by him to those who are able to read at Antomboka. In this way those young men whom I saw at Hiarana on my arrival here may at last receive the word of life, which they took from me at that time, but returned to me again with tears, saying that they feared their father.

Feb. 4—All parties are busy in making every possible preparation for the coming Fandroana, *i.e.* the feast of the Malagasy new year, which takes place at the beginning of the month of March. Every woman, whether Hova, Sakalava, or Betsimasaraka, is obliged to make one mat, of a certain length and breadth, for the Governor. At the same time they are all busy making mats for their own houses. These mats, when clean and properly laid down, give the Malagasy houses a very comfortable and respectable appearance.

Feb. 5: *Lord's-day*—Had our usual services to-day. The Governor, whom I had not seen all the week, came to breakfast. He has suffered for several days past from fever, and is looking thin and weak. Poor man, I am afraid he has a very difficult position to fulfil, and receives but very little sympathy from any of his officers. There he lives in the midst of the Rova, where Satan's seat is, surrounded by unbelief, ignorance, superstition, idolatry, and blind opposition to the truth. He disclosed to me the fact that Ramanansoa (see journal of Feb. 1), who professed such friendship for us when he called the other day, is doing all in his power to prevent our settling at Amboanio, and that he held a habary last evening with Radosy, the second commander, the three idol-keepers, and many other influential men, for the purpose of speaking to the Governor on the subject. The Governor was made acquainted with their deliberations by a friend, and was consequently troubled in mind the whole of the night. After conversing a little on this matter, we read together the 2nd and 3rd Psalms, and were greatly comforted in the thought that the Lord of all flesh is our hope and confidence.

Feb. 6—The second commander of Angoney, who arrived yesterday on a friendly visit to the Governor, called on us to-day. He had on a beautifully clean dress and lamba. Ramanansoa accompanied him, and professed the greatest friendship.

Feb. 9—Heard from the Governor the result of the three habarys, which were held respectively on Saturday, Monday, and yesterday by the enemies of the truth, for the purpose of expelling Mr. Campbell and me from Amboanio, and of confining us to Hiarana. The Governor and a few others fought hard against them, reminded them that it was by their consent we came to Amboanio, showed them their folly and duplicity, and told them they ought to remember the good England has done to Madagascar; that Missionaries have only one object in coming to their country—the present and eternal welfare of the people; and finally he ended all dispute by saying that he would not consent to any of their measures, but quietly await the Queen's message. What a source of thankfulness to God! what a monument of the power of his grace we have in the Governor! Nothing is plainer than that the Lord has placed him here for the defence of his truth.

The second commander of Angoney called for medicines this morning. I asked him to take some copies of the New Testament and Psalms with him for those people at Angoncy who are able to read, which he did, with a copy of the Prayer-book. Thus the word of God is preceding us to surrounding towns and districts not yet visited by the Missionary. From what we have heard of Angoney I am led to think that it may be a good centre for Missionary operations. It is healthy, with nearly as many* inhabitants as Amboanio, and what is of great importance, it is only about two days' march from Maranaset, a district as thickly populated as Tamatave.

The rain has come at last. Nearly every day since our arrival here there have been dark thunder-clouds, which make their appearance above the mountains to the north-west, but very seldom reach as far as Amboanio. I am of opinion that the wind, blowing from the south-east or north-east, brings with it quantities of moisture, which is taken up from the Indian Ocean, and, on reaching the mountains in the interior of Madagascar, is formed into clouds.

Feb. 11—The Governor and his wife came and informed us fully of the battle he fought with our enemies. They have been defeated in their wicked attempt to remove us to Hiarana; and finding that Mr. Campbell and I go everywhere among the people here, and that we intend going to the regions beyond as soon as convenient, they have become on a sudden so solicitous of our welfare, and equally desirous of fulfilling to the utmost one of the laws of the Queen, which commands them to protect the Missionaries, that they intend coming in a body to beseech us not to venture out alone, or go far from Amboanio, lest we may be killed by robbers, or stabbed by an evil-disposed Sakalava.

In the midst of this opposition it is very comforting to witness the love that some of our friends have for the word of God. Fojia is daily reading the New Testament, or the Prayer-book, and this he does publicly, sitting at his door or window in the sight of all who pass by, that all the Sakalavas may know that he is not afraid. I was at his house this evening, and he told me that the idol-keeper visited him the other day, and said to him, "You pray to Andriamanitra according to the books of the white people. I shall report you to the 'Andriana' (the sovereign and nobles), and have your head cut off." Fojia knows too much of the feelings of the Madagascar Government to fear such a threat, and he quietly said to the poor idol-keeper, who had been drinking rum, "You are drunk: please to mind your own business."

Feb. 12: *Lord's-day*—As I have felt a little unwell during the past week Mr. Campbell has very kindly gone to Hiarana in my place. Had rather a large attendance at the morning service. The wind was very violent at the time. I was afraid the house would be blown from over our heads.

Feb. 15—This has been the hottest day, I believe, we have had. Hitherto the thermometer has been from 86° to 88° in the shade at noon: to-day it reached 92°.

Feb. 19: *Lord's-day*—Came to Hiarana this morning. All the people are still busy preparing for the approaching "Fandroana." Only twenty persons came to the morning service, and about twenty-five to that of the evening. They were chiefly Sakalavas.

Feb. 22—Ramanansoa and Radosy brought us a goose this morning. They entered while Mr. Campbell was giving his exposition at morning prayers. As he was engaged, it devolved upon me to keep our unexpected and noisy visitors in order, which was no easy

* Some say more. We shall be able to speak definitely after that part of the country has been visited by one or both of us.

task. Mr. Campbell continued his exposition amidst the cry of the goose and the suppressed salutations from Ramanansoa, who hoped to have been heedless to Mr. Campbell's remarks by holding a conversation with me. With some difficulty I quieted him every time he attempted to speak, so that he was obliged to hear the plain statements of the word of God.

Feb. 23—Went to Hiarana in the morning to visit the "Vistula," a small schooner from Seychelles, commanded by Captain Huteau, a creole of Mahé. He went to Angoney for a cargo of rice, but found on his arrival there that the "Clifford," from Mauritius, had forestalled him. He then attempted to enter Sambavana, but was unable, and is come here to take a cargo of bullocks. He has kindly promised to take letters from us to Seychelles and England.

After my return to Amboanio, I went out to speak to the people, and met with the idol-keeper. He listened while I said a few words about the power and works of God, but the moment I opened my Testament to point out to him the sin of idolatry he walked away.

Feb. 24—For several days past the people from the surrounding villages have come up to be present at the "Fandroana." Amboanio is full, and though much drunkenness prevails, Mr. Campbell and I have many precious opportunities of preaching the Gospel of Christ to congregations of twenty to forty persons, whom we get together in the streets, or who come to the morning and evening prayers. Most of those who hear us are Sakalavas. They are a fine, strong, and hardworking race of men, and, if converted to Christianity, they will prove an inestimable blessing to Madagascar.

Feb. 25—This is the first day of the Malagasy new year of 1865. All their houses (and our's too) have been decorated by new mats, called *Tsihy mandrosa, i.e.* "invitation mats"—mats on which they invite their friends to sit and feast with them. All cooking utensils have been thoroughly cleansed, and every person is dressed in a new or nicely washed lamba, or European suit. The flag was hoisted at the Rova early in the morning. The cannons were fired this afternoon, and men, women, and children are either singing, playing, or drinking.

The bathing of the people I was not able to see, as it took place inside the Rova. From what I have heard, it appears that they either sprinkle warm water upon their heads, or have it thrown upon them by another person, while they repeat the words, "Saruba, Saruba, Andriamanitra Andriananahary; arivo tratra ny taoma," the first part of which is a Malagasy form of benediction, and the latter equivalent to the exaggerated wish, "May I live a thousand years."

Feb. 26: *Lord's-day*—This has been a strange day, as a brief account of its proceedings will show. At half-past seven A.M. took place the baptism of Ratsiza. He is a native of Amboanio, and has never left the district. The account of his conversion is so interesting that I must not omit it. A Hova man of Angoney was his first teacher, who taught him to read, and preached the truth to him. The people had not then heard of the release of the Christians by Radama II., and Ratsiza and his friend often retired to the sea-side to read, sing, and pray in secret.

His second teacher was Raindreperenina, who is now at Tamatave, a dear friend of good old Symeon of Moka, Mauritius, and who, when at Tamatave, on his way to the north of Madagascar, about two years ago, wrote to Mauritius for books for the people of Vohemare. On his arrival here he preached the Gospel of Christ to the people of Amboanio, and sanctified his teaching by a holy and consistent life. He became a great blessing to Ratsiza, who was his almost only Christian friend. On his departure he took Ratsiza out of the town to admonish him for the last time. They wept and prayed together, and Raindreperenina gave Luke xii. 4, 5, to Ratsiza as his parting words. From that time till now, Ratsiza, as the Governor says, whose scribe he is, has shone as a light in a dark place. He is about twenty-five years of age, and his past and present conduct leads us to hope that he will be a most efficient preacher of the Gospel to his fellow-countrymen, either as a layman, or, if released from the "fanompoana," as an ordained minister. The baptismal ceremony was performed by Mr. Campbell, in the presence of the Governor and about twenty-five of our friends. We all enjoyed it much. The rest of the day has abounded with folly, worldliness, and iniquity. Many Hova and other visitors called, either out of curiosity, or to ask for something. The latter they are very fond of, and unless we denied them we should preserve nothing.

At two P.M. the chief Hova and Sakalava women went in procession to the sea-side, to play, sing, and drink rum. Each has tried to outdo the other in dress. They returned about five P.M., when most of them were nearly or wholly drunk. The same horrid scene of drunkenness presents itself in every part of Amboanio. The Governor told me that he was nearly intoxicated yesterday from the smell of rum. Oh that the word of God may soon teach the people better!

March 3—Every day since last Sunday has caused me much pain, in consequence of the abominable drunkenness that has prevailed. The houses, too, of the people are so foul with the stench of beef, which they present the one to the other at this season, that it has been impossible to visit. In the midst of this sin, as many as twenty to twenty-five persons have continued to attend our morning and evening prayers. To-day the Governor has invited those who attend our services regularly to a dinner at his own house in the Rova. As many as twenty-two were present, and it greatly rejoiced our hearts to witness the striking contrast between their return home and that of the heathen dinner parties. They who attended the latter returned invariably drunk, singing heathenish songs, while the Christian party returned this evening singing one of the songs of Zion.

March 4—The Governor, his wife, and twenty-two of his officers, dined with us this day at twelve o'clock, to celebrate the Malagasy new year.

March 5: *Lord's-day*—The twelve o'clock service was better attended than usual: eighteen persons were present.

Rafaralahovony and his brother, sons of the late Governor of Vohemare, who have a fair knowledge of God's word, have promised to renounce drinking rum. By God's blessing, they will be a great blessing to us.

March 8—While Mr. Campbell and I were engaged at our twelve o'clock prayer-meeting, a letter arrived for us from our brother Missionary, the Rev. J. Holding, Tamatave. It was written on March 8th last, and has come a distance of nearly 500 miles. Mr. Holding has opened up the work as far north as Fenerrivo. May the Lord continue to bless him!

March 12: *Lord's-day*—Came to Hiarana yesterday evening, and found the people glad in the hope of meeting together to-day. About forty persons came to the mid-day service. It was exceedingly hot at the time, scarcely a breath of wind, and the sun shining in its full strength. The second service took place at four o'clock P.M. Subject in the morning, Rom. vi. 23: in the afternoon, Acts x. 15, for the Sakalavas.

In the evening, after I had dined, they came for a third time. After we had sung several hymns, the mosquitos came in such swarms that the whole congregation was engaged in smacking their naked legs and faces. I could hardly hear my own voice. In consequence of the number of mosquitos flying round, and the light being nearly extinguished, I was compelled to dismiss the people.

March 14—As I was going to visit a poor sick woman this evening, I witnessed a Malagasy fight between two men. They fought with their legs. About 100 persons were watching with pleasure. At first I was told that they were playing, but on perceiving that it was a very rough kind of play, I interfered, and cried to several influential men in the crowd to stop them. Immediately, all who before stimulated the combatants, separated them.

Recent Intelligence.

NEW ZEALAND.

THE despatches from New Zealand, communicating details of the late most unhappy and unexpected occurrences in New Zealand, have been published by the Parent Committee, in a pamphlet entitled "The Murder of the Rev. C. S. Volkner." It extends to thirty-two pages, and contains, besides the remarks of the Parent Committee, the diaries of Mr. S. A. Levy, and the Rev. T. S. Grace, as well as the journals and letters of the Bishop of Waiapu.

This pamphlet reached the editor of this periodical on the 17th of July. At this advanced period of the month it would be impossible to reproduce its contents in the pages of our present Number. All we can do is to present the following summary of what has occurred, referring such of our readers as may desire immediate and fuller information to the Society's pamphlet.

The Pai Marire, or, as it is popularly called, the Hauhau fanaticism, from the yelping with which its ceremonies are accompanied, has developed itself with an alarming rapidity, and has assumed the most horrible features. News was received of the murder of the Rev. Carl Sylvius Volkner, once a Lutheran clergyman, but who, having been ordained in the Episcopal Church, has been labouring as one of her Missionaries for several years at Opotiki, on the eastern coast of the northern island. This gentleman had lately taken his wife to Auckland, and, in company with the Rev. T. S. Grace, Church Missionary at Taupo arrived at Opotiki on the 1st of March, in a small schooner, the "Eclipse," commanded by a jew, named Levy, who was in the habit of trading there, his brother being a resident storekeeper. The natives were found to be in a considerable state of excitement, in consequence of the appearance of a party of Taranaki Hauhaus a few days previously, having with them the preserved head of Mr. Hewitt who was murdered at Wanganui two months since), another of a soldier of the 70th Regiment, killed at Taranaki, and a captured soldier of the 57th, named John Brown, who, according to his own account, had been a prisoner for eighteen months, together with a comrade named Louis Baker.

The whole settlement had in a few days renounced Christianity, and become converts to the new religion, and, in their new-born zeal, ransacked Mr. Volkner's house, sold his goods by auction on the Sunday, and had compelled Father Grange, the resident Roman-Catholic priest, to save his life by flight. The "Eclipse" had no sooner entered the river than she was seized, the crew and passengers being ordered on shore, and confined in a native "wharre." Captain Levy, being a Jew, was unmolested, the Hauhaus laying claim to be in some way allied to the ancient people of God. The cargo of the vessel was next brought on shore, and partially distributed, that belonging to the two Levys being handed over to them. On the following morning a fall and tackle were procured from the schooner and made fast to a tree, when Mr. Volkner was led out in the presence of several hundred natives. The Taranaki fanatics then stripped him of his outer garments, his own congregation standing by and offering no resistance. At two o'clock, the hour fixed for his execution, they bound a handkerchief over his eyes, allowed him a few minutes for prayer, and then, amid taunting yells and derisive shouts of laughter, he was hoisted up by a "tiu," or fanatical priest, named Kereopa. This Kereopa was a brother of a young chief taken prisoner by the loyal natives at Maketu, near Tauranga, last year, and shot by the wife of Beckham, the only friendly chief who lost his life in that engagement. Scarcely was life extinct when Mr. Volkner's body was cut down, taken to an enclosure near the church, in which he had laboured with much earnestness, and decapitated. The details of what followed are most revolting; but, without morbidly dwelling on them, it is absolutely necessary to say that the brains were extracted, the eyes torn out and eaten, and the blood licked by an eager crowd of men, women, and children. Having been otherwise mutilated, the body was first thrown to the dogs, and then, to quiet their fighting, it was thrown into a cesspool. The few settler residents were now pinioned and placed in confinement with Mr. Grace and the "Eclipse's" crew. Captain Levy and his brother were also pinioned, but let loose again, and allowed to attend a night meeting in the Roman-Catholic chapel, where Mr. Volkner's head was exhibited, and placed in the pulpit to excite the natives while going through their fanatical ceremonies. The pinioning of the two Levys was a fortunate affair, since it led to the bands of others being loosened, as a sort of compensation for the evil that had been inflicted on two of what they regard as a sort of sacred race. Mr. Grace alone was not allowed to walk at liberty, but considered a prisoner at large. At a meeting which took place on Sunday the 5th (one portion of the new creed being that all days are alike) it was decided to accept Hori Tupaea as a ransom for that gentleman. This Hori Tupaea is a Hauhau priest, taken prisoner some weeks previously by the friendly natives of Tauranga, but who had been already liberated by the Governor. Captain Levy was intrusted with a letter to the Government proposing a ransom; but as the Taranaki Hauhaus were starting southward, to where Bishop Williams was residing, the "Eclipse" was to be detained a few days until they returned. While waiting their return the Levys obtained possession of Mr. Volkner's remains, and decently buried them in the ground attached to the church in which he had for years laboured and rejoiced with much Christian hopefulness.

While these latter events had been transpiring, the news of Mr. Volkner's murder and Mr. Grace's detention travelled from pa to pa, eventually reaching the camp at Tauranga. Colonel Greer, in command there, decided to take no steps in the matter on his own responsibility, but sent the news on to Auckland. The Governor and General being both at Wanganui, Commodore Wiseman did not feel altogether at liberty to act without express orders, but at last he sent Her Majesty's despatch steamer "Eclipse" to Tauranga, Bishop Selwyn being allowed a passage in her. On arriving at Tauranga they found that fears were entertained for the safety of the Bishop of Waiapu (Williams), who lives with a few settlers at his Mission station, about fifty miles south of Opotiki. The "Eclipse" accordingly proceeded to Turanga, not far from which anchorage Bishop Williams resides. Turanga must not be confounded with Tauranga. The former, where Bishop Williams lives, is in the Bay of Poverty, near Napier; while the latter, where the Gate Pah repulse was sustained, is in the Bay of Plenty, near Auckland. The fears were not groundless, the murderers having already arrived with the preserved heads and soldier prisoners at a neighbouring settlement; but as the Turanga natives were eager to turn them back, the "Eclipse" sailed for Opotiki in search of Mr. Grace, under the impression that the Turanga party, accompanied by Bishop Williams and the Rev. E. B. Clarke, would succeed in their object. This anticipation, however, was not realized. The fanatics very speedily succeeded in so far bringing over the Bishop's allies as to induce them to fraternize, and his lordship's influence, becoming daily less and less, was at last insufficient to warrant his continuing on the station. After having been compelled to keep constantly on the watch both day and night, he and the few settlers took refuge in a couple of coasting vessels early this month, and are now in Auckland. Archdeacon W. L. Williams and the Rev. S. Williams, with three or four others, have, however, at the risk of their lives, remained behind to watch proceedings, and endeavour to prevent the wanton destruction of the Mission property, which now almost wholly represents the labour of many years.

On the 16th of March Her Majesty's ship "Eclipse" steamed in sight of Opotiki, and the two Levys paddled off to her under the pretext of delivering the letter mentioned above. Captain Freemantle was desirous of landing some of his blue-jackets, but neither the force nor the money-ransom offered by Bishop Selwyn was deemed likely to effect the rescue of Mr. Grace, and Captain Levy, after procuring a boat from his schooner at the mouth of the river, returned with a couple of his men to the shore, hoping to induce some of the principal natives to come off to the steamer. While pulling up the river Mr. Grace was seen, and, on his stating that all the natives were engaged indoors attending a meeting about the steamer's arrival, and that there were only a couple of women left to watch him, he was taken into the boat, covered over, and pulled out to sea with the greatest promptitude. The women gave the alarm, and the meeting broke up, but the boat had too good a start, and the side of Her Majesty's ship "Eclipse" was reached in safety. The little schooner "Eclipse" was now the object of intended vengeance, but while the natives were preparing to seize her, Lieutenant Nelson and a party of the steamer's crew had towed her over the bar in safety. Next day Captain Freemantle and Bishop Selwyn met the natives on shore, with a view to arrange for the safety of the few settlers who, strange to say, still determined to remain there. This done, the two "Eclipses" made the best of their way to Auckland.

Such is a brief outline of events which fill columns of the local journals. Elsewhere the Hauhau fanaticism is on the increase, and threatens to pervade Maoridom. Much uneasiness is necessarily created wherever it makes its appearance, and the conviction that no atrocity is too great to be committed tends to create panic; so that while the English public may prepare itself for further mischief, it must give but a limited credence to the reports which the northern journals by this mail promulgate. Governor Grey left Wellington on the 8th instant for Opotiki and the north, to inquire into the circumstances, and organize some means of checking the danger. He takes with him a young half-caste gentleman, long in the public service; and it is proposed that he shall raise a Maori force 200 or 300 strong, and endeavour to put down with a high hand the pretensions of the fanatical party. What other steps are taken must depend entirely on the temper of the natives, which, it is to be feared, is none of the best.

We are constrained to say that a smoke out of the bottomless pit has overspread New Zealand, and that for the moment Satan triumphs; but this triumphing will be but short. The very rush of the Pai Marire delusion proves it to be a whirlwind, which, although fearfully desolating, will not last long. As Bishop Williams remarks—"The Pai Marire is a deep-laid snare of the devil, whom God will bruise under our feet shortly."

The new delusion is, however, spreading with fearful rapidity through the island. Kingism, and widely-extended disaffection to the English rule, have prepared the way for it. It is "the counterpart of Kingism, embracing besides every thing that is subversive of morality. Wherever Kingism has taken deep root, Pai Marire has become its parasite." To use again the words of Bishop Williams—

A few sacred words are blasphemously mixed up with a large amount of nonsense. There is no attempt at system, no doctrine, no deliverance from sin, no salvation; but these forms are put together, and are repeated for the present with an amount of earnestness which works wonderfully upon the feelings. There is also the practice of, I fancy, a mesmeric influence, or of electro biology, which, upon weak and superstitious minds, leads to a belief of something supernatural. They have trifled with things sacred, and God seems to have sent among them strong delusion that they should believe a lie. But it is not here only that these extravagances are rife. When you have in Protestant England, and among those who have been instructed with great care, a disposition to fall into the abominable superstition of Popery, we need not wonder at what happens in New Zealand. The great moving principle of Pai Marire is, that it is a scheme which promises a successful termination of the war with which we are afflicted; and it is mixed up with an amount of abomination, which is meant to draw out the vilest passions of our sinful nature. Happily the time is short. He who said, "Lo, I come quickly," is nigh at hand. He has given us the sign of his coming, and we may almost, now in the time of trouble, lift up our heads: our deliverance is nigh.

After the arrival of Mr. Grace at Auckland, a meeting of the Missionaries was held, to express their thanks to God for his deliverance, and their deep sympathy with the widow of Mr. Volkner, when the following minutes were adopted—

Present, — Archdeacon Kissling; Rev. T. Chapman; Rev. C. Baker; Rev. B. Y. Ashwell; Rev. T. S. Grace; Rev. R. Burrows, Secretary.

After reading the Scriptures and uniting in prayer, the following extract from a sermon preached by Bishop Patteson, at St. Mary's church, and copied with his permission, was read to the Conference.

"A dark and dreadful crime has been committed in the land. Innocent blood has been shed—the blood of one esteemed and honoured for his works' sake among all men; to many of us endeared by closer bonds of private friendship and most true affection.

"We know — and we thank God that we do know—how good he was, how simple-minded, how guileless; a man of prayer, full of faith and good works that he did, meekly following his Saviour in pureness of heart (for to him such grace was given), walking humbly with his God. We who can ill afford to spare him from among us, who dwell with loving affection upon the intercourse we so lately were permitted to have with him, thank God from our hearts that not one cloud rests upon the brightness of his example; that he has been taken from us, we most surely trust, to dwell with Christ in paradise, and has left behind him the fragrance of a holy life. It is not for him we sorrow now. What better thing can we desire for ourselves, or our friends, than that we and they shall be taken in the midst of the discharge of our duties from the many cares and sorrows of this world, if only by the grace of God we may be prepared for the life of that world which knows no cares, which feels no sorrows? Indeed these are no conventional words. We must not seek to anticipate the season of rest. It is a blessed thing to work in the Lord's vineyard: it is cowardly and ungenerous to wish to shorten our time of service in the army of Christ. But oh, the thought that a time will come, if our faith fail not, when we shall feel the burden of anxieties, and trials, and disappointments, and bereavements taken away, and the continued warfare against sin all ended, and for ever,—the thought of this cannot surely be given us for naught. It must not make us less diligent now; it must not withdraw us from our appointed task; but it stands written as a word of consolation and encouragement for all, 'There remaineth therefore a rest to the people of God.' 'Blessed are the dead which die in the Lord: they rest from their labours.'"

Resolved—That the foregoing extract fully conveys the feelings and sentiments of this Conference; and they can find no more appropriate language to describe the character and labours of their departed brother, who suffered a cruel and painful death for the Gospel's sake.

Resolved—That this Conference desire to express their deep sympathy with Mrs. Volkner, and at the same time to thank God for that grace vouchsafed unto her, by which she has been enabled to bear her trial with Christian fortitude, and humble submission to the Divine will.

Resolved—That this Conference also desire to record their humble thanks to Almighty God for the providential deliverance of their brother, the Rev. T. S. Grace, now present with them, from imminent danger; and they request Mr. Grace to forward to the Parent Committee, by this mail, a copy of his journal during his captivity.

We shall give to these despatches our most earnest consideration, and endeavour to present in our next Number the lessons which these events are fitted to convey.

THE THEORY OF DEVELOPMENT.

THE "Social Science Review" for June contains an address delivered by Bishop Colenso, "On Missions in Natal and Zululand." We are therefore at liberty to regard it as an authentic document, published with his approval, and containing a true exposition of his opinions.

What those opinions are we propose to consider. We feel ourselves under an obligation so to do, because they are the opinions, not of an isolated individual, but of a school to which he has attached himself—a school of philosophy, falsely so called—which is pertinaciously occupied in devising and propagating diverse theories irreconcileable with the explicit declarations of Holy Writ, and calculated, if not to unsettle the faith, at least to disturb the minds of many.

The task we have to discharge is a painful one, yet it is needful, and may be salutary. It may serve to convey a useful lesson—one much needed at the present day—the danger of tampering with those inspired writings which God has given to guide us to the knowledge of Himself, and of his merciful will respecting us.

Holy Scripture possesses in Dr. Colenso's eyes no infallibility. Irreverently has he dealt with it. Disregarding the unanswerable weight of testimony which exists as to the genuineness, authenticity, and consequent inspiration of these books, he has occupied himself in searching out difficulties, and parading them before the public mind. His objections are verbose and puerile. If from the heaps of tedious and worthless matter could be extracted all the truth which they contain, the whole, when balanced against the evidences which can be accumulated in support of the inspiration of the Scriptures, would be found to bear to them about the same proportion which a molehill does to a mountain mass.

His sophistries, however, have injured many, and, amongst these, they have done most injury to himself. In abnegating the infallibility of the Scriptures he has cast off his moorings, and has drifted down the stream, much more rapidly than he is aware of, towards the final issue—the great maelström of open infidelity, and avowed rejection of the Christian faith.

We shall not weary our readers by imposing upon them the wearisome task of accompanying us through the details of the Bishop's address on Missions in Zululand. As a matter of duty, not of choice, we have been constrained to its perusal. The task reminded us of a peregrination through an Irish bog, wide-spread as far as the horizon, a few hills looming in the distance, scarcely breaking the monotony of the scene; the pathway requiring great caution, as ever and anon a dangerous quagmire approached it, deceitfully hidden by a thin scraw, on which, if you attempted to lean, it would be to find yourself plunged into a miry slough, from which, if you emerged at all, it would be only after much effort and grievous defilement. Certainly they are dreary places these wastes of infidelity. They are dangerous enterprises these, to leave the sure ground of what God has said, and climb with a presumptuous spirit the perilous heights of speculation. We lament the misdirected energy which prompts young men to imperil the lives, given them of God for higher purposes, on those alpine heights, where even the chamois does not venture. So enthusiastic have men grown on these ascents, that at last they ventured to attempt the Matterhorn, a tower of rock rising some 4000 or 5000 feet from an elevated plateau or ridge, itself 10,000 feet in height, the summit of this tower being a level space of no great extent, the highest point being rather nearer the western than the eastern declivity. In fact, the Matterhorn is "a tower without a stair." "Mount Cervin," observes one writer, "is assuredly a different sort of affair from Mont Blanc or Mont Rosa, or any other of the thousand and one summits which nature has kindly opened to man, by leaving one side of them a sloping plain of snow, easy of ascent, till the brink of the precipice is reached, which descends on the other side. The square massive lines of terraced crags, which fence the Matterhorn, stand up on all sides nearly destitute of snow, and where the snow lies thinly on the rocks it soon melts, and is hardened again into smooth glassy ice, which covers the granite slabs like a coat of varnish, and bids defiance to the axe. Every step of the way lies between two precipices and toppling crags, which may at any moment bring down on climbers the most formidable of Alpine dangers—a fire of falling stones." Truly these dreary summits, where all "seems strangely rigid and motionless, are out of keeping with the beating heart and moving limbs, the life and activity of man;" and when the foot slips, and the dexterity of the practised climber is found unequal to the preservation of life amidst such dangers; when the rope, the last resource breaks; when the doomed victims roll helplessly down the steep which slopes to the edge of a precipice so sheer and dread, that the very thought of it is painful, and over the brink the fatal plunge is made, the stones and ice feel no pity and extend no help. But the heights of infidelity, those towering summits, up which men venture, prompted by the love of notoriety, and the desire of being distinguished, if not in any other way, at least by the singularity of their opinions, —are not these more perilous? What a precipice do they not overhang? It is very well for such men, who, denying God's truth themselves, are diligently occupied in perverting others to the same scepticism, to persuade themselves that there is no precipice, no such dread result as eternal punishment, and thus say one to another as they climb, "Wold immer achtung," "no fear;" but unless, by God's mercy, they are brought to repentance, the final issue must come, and the dread plunge be made over the brink of an abyss, compared with which the walls of the Matterhorn are as nothing. The body is crushed and broken in the one: the soul is lost eternally in the other.

Nor do these men endanger only themselves. According to their influence and position they have attached others to them, and bound them in the same cords. Bishop Colenso—if the statements in a pamphlet, purporting to contain an address of his "on the efforts of Missionaries among savages," be reliable—admits that on one occasion he stopped a Missionary when telling the Zulus that they were all involved in Adam's sin and its consequences, and in danger of eternal perdition—"by nature the children of wrath, even as others." "Of course I told them not to believe this;" and thus, unless the rope break, there is danger lest the guide and the disciples perish together.

But as to the principles avowed in the address, this is one of them—"The human race, instead of sinking from a higher to a lower condition, by reason of the fall, as is generally supposed, has been rising gradually from a lower to a higher."

From what depths we may have ascended the bishop is not as yet sure; he has not yet quite to his satisfaction sounded the abyss; but he is engaged in doing so, as our readers will perceive by the following quotation—

> There are some good people, I know, who are very much disgusted, if they are not dismayed and distressed, at the very suggestion of the bare possibility of their having had any such a parentage, and who look with horror upon the gorilla and chimpanzee—those near approximations, anatomically considered, to the human form—as having any, the slightest possible claim to be regarded in the light of our ancestors. Though I am not with Mr. D'Israeli on the side of the angels, yet I confess I am not on the side of the apes; or rather, I should say, I do not feel competent at present to pronounce any decisive judgment on this question.

We fear, however, that little doubt can be entertained as to the decision to which he will eventually come. The bishop is in a condition of progress; we cannot say on the ascending scale, rising from the lower to the higher. In his religious history he presents, very unhappily, an exemplification of the opposite principle, sinking from the higher to the lower. As yet, however, he is not prepared to accept unhesitatingly the progenitorship of apes; the plummet has not sunk quite so low. He appears to think that man, in his primeval state, was, after all, a man—not a chimpanzee or a gorilla—but "a companion of beasts which have now disappeared for long ages, and that for thousands and ten thousands of years before the usual date assigned by traditionary views to the creation." Through this long lapse of ages "his intellect was gradually sharpened by necessity to invent contrivances for the relief of his own wants. Thus he learnt to provide himself, first with food, then with houses, cities, government, laws; next with letters, carved on stone or written on parchment; then with the compass and printing-press; and, alas that it must be said! with 'the villanous saltpetre' and the cannon-ball; and so onward, as the ages rolled, till at last we are living in the age of steam, photography, and the electric telegraph. In one word, it is joyous and refreshing to know that we are not laboriously toiling to recover some of that almost infinite extent of ground which Adam lost for us by his one act of sin: it is hopeful to be assured, by the plainest evidences of scientific research, that all our present advances in art and science are the just results of the proper development of the great human family, as part of their great Creator's scheme from the first; and to know that every fresh fact, brought to light by a course of honest and persevering inquiry, is a fresh blessing bestowed upon the race from the Father of lights—a fresh conquest, either in the domain of the present or the territories of the bygone past, which the mind, that guides and governs all, has permitted and enabled us to achieve, with the powers entrusted to us."

We have quoted the passage *in extenso*, because, culminative and weighty as it is designed to be, it lacks congruity; for if all these steps of progress be "the first results of the proper development of the great human family," how did the "villanous saltpetre" and the "cannon-ball" intrude themselves? If the saltpetre be among the first results, how comes it to be villanous; or, if villanous, how was it permitted to mar the fair process of development? In short, according to this theory, how did sin find entrance into the world? The proper development of the great human family "has been," we are informed, "the great Creator's scheme from the first." Is sin, then, a part of the designed process, a link in the golden series of predestined results; or, if it be an evil of man's introduction, how is this to be reconciled with the assertion, that he has not "fallen from a higher to a lower condition," but has been gradually rising "from a lower to a higher?"

But again, how can this theory be reconciled with the actual condition of the world? Man is not ignored of God: he is cared for by Him who "maketh his sun to rise on the evil and on the good, and sendeth his rain on the just and on the unjust;" and yet on him and on his portion rest unmistakeably the evidences of the divine displeasure. Suffering abounds. "Man is born to trouble as the sparks fly upwards." So saith the Scripture, and what Scripture affirms, experience verifies. Death awaits man, and that not merely when he has attained old age, and his nature might be supposed to break down beneath the weight of its own infirmities, but it comes prematurely, suddenly, upon the tender babe, on opening youth, and manhood in its prime; and thus "our bones lie scattered at the grave's mouth, as when one cutteth and cleaveth wood upon the earth."

Why should this be? for man has always been progressing, "rising gradually from a lower to a higher state;" from a condition so low that he was once "a companion of beasts," to the "age of steam, photography, and the electric telegraph." Man, then, has made marvellous progress: he has improved to the utmost the resources of his nature. Whence, then, the suffering? Let the disciples of the new school grapple with facts, and explain to us how their new theory is to be reconciled with our every-day's experience. With the Scripture principle, that man has fallen from a higher condition to a lower, all is reconcilable. The mystery of our existence is at once solved. Man has displeased God, therefore he is in suffering. Yet is he not cast off, but continues to be an object of the divine concernment, because, although fallen, he may be recovered. He is therefore placed under corrective dispensations, that, thus humiliated, he may the more readily appreciate and thankfully receive the salvation which God has provided for him.

But again, the facts which connect with languages refuse to harmonize with the principles of the subversive school. Certainly, if a nation is in a progressive state, its language may be expected to advance with it. Bishop Colenso speaks of degraded tribes of human beings as specimens of man as yet undeveloped. According to his theory, they have never been in a better condition: low as their state is, it is, nevertheless, as yet their highest stage of attainment. Surely, then, it may be expected that their language will be found in the same embryo state, imperfectly fashioned, and with no further capacity than what may suffice to express the few wants of a savage life.

But does experience coincide with this? On the contrary, it makes us acquainted with the remarkable fact, that the languages of rude and savage people are often most elaborate in structure, and capable of reduction to a most perfect system of grammatical rules. Yet of this the people themselves are entirely ignorant.

A Missionary enters some new field of labour, and locates himself amongst a savage race only recently discovered. To acquaint himself with the language is one of his first necessities, and he commences the work of lingual exploration. But it is as when the stock-keeper in Australia struck the quartz rock, and the rich gold stood revealed. The richness of grammatical forms astonishes, and at first confuses him, and no little perseverance and exertion are required to ascertain their often strange peculiarities and fine differences. The language is, confessedly, in a more advanced state than the people. The people are rude; their language richly grammatical. They are unconsciously using for the ordinary purposes of a rude life a beautiful machinery of words. It is as though their household utensils were made of gold, and they knew not their value, and dealt with them as though they were common earthenware.

Let it be remembered, however, that, according to the principles of the new school, neither in their own persons, or in that of their progenitors, were these tribes ever in a more advanced state than they are at present, for they have been rising gradually from a lower state to a higher. When, then, or how, did they acquire their language?

The problem can only be solved on the principles laid down in Genesis xi. 7. But the universal deluge and its adjuncts are not portions of Bishop Colenso's Bible. These he has discarded to make way for his new theory; and we now call upon him to explain in what way the sceptical principle to which he has committed himself can be adjusted to lingual experiences and facts.

But we pass on to another of those novelties which are set forth in this "address on Missions to the Zulus," and which sound so strange and startling, and that the more so because enunciated by the lips of a Christian Bishop.

The common parentage of the human family, and the unity of all the races upon earth in one progenitor, Adam, is the next point assailed in the address we are reviewing. In this antagonism Dr. Colenso is not alone: there are many associated with him. Our attention has been especially directed to a book entitled "Adam and the Adamite," in which the same theory, with much ingenuity, is advocated. Unlike Bishop Colenso, the writer does not despise and reject, as undeserving of serious consideration, the Scripture narratives respecting the creation of Adam and the Noachian deluge. These he admits to be true. But the common parentage of the human race is his stumbling-block. He does not deny its possibility, but, in admitting it, he imagines this formidable difficulty, that the time required for the development from one source of races so diverse in complexion, physiognomy, language, as the tribes of man, must be far more extensive than the Mosaic chronology could afford to allow. Dr. Colenso is of the same opinion. He, too, thinks it highly probable that we are not all sprung from the same parentage, unless, indeed, sufficient time for that development be allowed, namely, the lapse of millions on millions of years.

We have to congratulate ourselves that this school of philosophy has not yet ruled it an impossibility that the negro or the Hottentot should have sprung from Adam. We do not, indeed, see how, with any degree of consistency, they could so decide, for surely the difference between a Bushman and a Caucasian is not so great as that which exists between a monkey and a man. The most degraded man can speak; but even the best educated of monkeys can only jabber. Bring Christianity to bear upon the most degraded of men, and it illuminates them so that they acknowledge God and their responsibility to Him; but a monkey can never be brought into any communication with the unseen world: yet these gentlemen absorb, without an effort, the greater difficulty, while they stagger at the less: a monkey may develop into a man, but that a savage man could ever have deteriorated from Adam, is ruled by them to be next to an impossibility. How is it that they strain at a gnat and swallow a camel? Because to admit the descent of inferior races from Adam would be to overthrow the ambitious theory of development, by which they hope, having risen from a depth so profound, to ascend so high that "they shall be as gods." To admit, therefore, that men have deteriorated in their descent from Adam, is exceedingly distasteful to them; or if, indeed, they are constrained to admit the possibility of a common parentage, for this concession they must have an equivalent: their sceptical spirit must be gratified by an irreverent rejection of scriptural chronology as untrue, and the substitution of millions of years for the 6000 of human existence.

Now the author of "Adam and the Adamite" is not prepared for this. He would retain the chronology, but surrender the common parentage. "No culture," in his opinion, "will transform a negro into a Caucasian, and no degradation will convert the Caucasian into a negro." The races, therefore, he fancies, must have had different parentages, Adam being the progenitor of the Adamite, or superior race, and of none other, and it is only of this race that the Bible is a record. "The Bible is the history of a particular race, the Adamite: his creation, fall, restoration to Paradise, are the theme of holy writ from Alpha to Omega." (p. 285.)

The Bible, then, is an imperfect record. It relates only the origin of one race, although at the time when that creation took place, about 6000 years ago, the earth was peopled by other human tribes of low condition. Therefore the author of "Adam and the Adamite" publishes in this, the nineteenth century, a supplement to the Bible, which, filling up the void of the scriptural narrative, shall at once harmonize philosophy and revelation, and terminate the discussions of the present day.

Let us consider more particularly the Adamite theory.

We are told, then, that the unity of mankind, and the unity of mankind in Adam, are two different propositions: the progenitor may not be one, and yet the races are to be regarded as one.

But if there be races of mankind which have not a common progenitorship in Adam, of necessity they are excluded from the beneficial action of the Gospel. The effects of Christ's death extend no further than the effects of Adam's sin. "As in Adam all die, even so in Christ shall all be made alive." And such was the teaching of the Old Testament. The Goel was alike kinsman and Redeemer: none but a kinsman could be a Redeemer. Christ was the seed (if one must employ, for distinctness' sake, the nonsensical phraseology of the new school) of the Adamite woman, and He is only in a position to redeem those who, with Him, are partakers of the same parentage.

And yet these collateral races are affected by the same disease of sin as that by which the Adamites are vitiated, and need a physician. This is a matter of fact which even the scepticism of our new philosophers, who, although they have cast off the principles of Christianity, still retain its name, is constrained to admit. Before the Adamite was in existence (such is the new theory) there were races of men on earth. They were the contemporaries of "the mammoth, the woolly rhinoceros, the cave lions, &c." "Climates have changed," "tides have ebbed and flowed," lands have been submerged, and others have appeared in their stead—"all these phenomena proclaim the long lapse of ages throughout which our planet has been the abode of races of men who never reached a higher social position than that indicated by their stone and bone implements which survived them." The inferior races preceded the advent of the superior, and "the Mongol and the negro were inhabitants of the earth before the birth of the first of the Caucasians." But how came sin amongst these races? for that they are vitiated with it, and that to a great extent, is undoubted. Moreover, it is with them, as with the Adamite, a hereditary taint; it descends from father to child; it is in the blood of the race; it must have come from the first parentage, otherwise the race could not have been universally affected by it. How, then, is this reconcilable with the Scripture declaration—"By *one man* sin entered into the world, and death by sin, and so death passed upon all men, for that all have sinned?" for, according to this new speculation, sin entered in, not by one man, but by many.

"Moreover, "generation after generation of these primeval natives lived and passed away" before the Adamite, the superior man, appeared upon the earth. Either, then, sin was in the world before Adam, or human death was in the world before sin. Either alternative contradicts the word of God, which expressly tells us that "by *one man's* disobedience sin entered into the world, and *death by sin*, and so death passed upon all men, for that all have sinned."

In his avoidance of one error, the writer of the "Adamite" has fallen into another just as anti-scriptural, and, while professing a great reverence for Scripture, inflicts upon it a grievous wrong. We can have no more sympathy with him than we have with those who would set aside the chronology of Scripture.

This, however, is the enterprise to which the gentlemen of the development theory address themselves, the chronology of Scripture being, in their judgment, the weak point of the citadel. They wish especially to get rid of the limits assigned by revelation to years of human history, and so remove the origin of man to a point removed from us by millions of years. This vastness of time is a favourite refuge with these new philosophers, when they meet, as they often do, with insuperable difficulties in their speculations. But "no length of time will suffice to cause that which is absurd in principle to cease to be absurd, though it is by these enormous drafts on time that men bewilder themselves." Every absurdity must have a beginning, and the difficulty lies there, whether the initiative moment be near to us by a few thousand years, or remote from us by millions of years. If the man was once an ape, there must have been a moment when, to use Dr. Colenso's words, the *barrier* was passed which separated the monkey from the man. That is an impassable barrier, and whether it be comparatively near or far off, it remains the same. Speculators place it afar off, in the hope of removing it from the domain of common sense, and inducing men to think that an impossibility is possible. In truth, the idea is so degrading and repulsive, that we cannot be surprised if its inventors are ashamed of it, and consign it to the remote distance of millions of years.

Let it be observed, moreover, that so attached are men of this school to long and vague periods, that not only do they invent them to veil impossibilities, but very unnecessarily introduce them to account for changes which true philosophy proves to have been accomplished within very limited periods. The "Christian Observer," in its review of "Wainwright's Christian Certainty," deals powerfully and satisfactorily with this point, and to that periodical [*Vide* Number for August 1865] we would refer our readers, confining ourselves to the notice of that remarkable upheaving on the western coast of Crete, discovered by Captain Spratt, R.N., when officially engaged in the survey of that island, and made known to the public in his recently-published work, "Travels and Researches in Crete." These upheavings, which have taken place since the commencement of the Christian era, attain a maximum of twenty-six feet, obliterating ports which were known to have existed, and changing islands into peninsulas. Thus Lissos and Suia, coast-cities, had each an harbour, yet "at neither is there now any place to shelter a boat, unless hauled ashore." Phalaserna, the most western city of Crete, according to Strabo, possessed an artificial port: this is now filled up, and far removed from the sea. Off the south-west cape of Crete once lay three islands: of these only one exists now, and that separated from the mainland by a narrow and shallow channel. These changes, according to the new school, could not have been effected except during a lapse of thousands of years; the fact being that they have all occurred subsequently to every historical record of the cities on the western coast of Crete, while at the same time they are of a character so decided as to render it difficult to reconcile modern features with ancient descriptions.

Before we part company with "Adam and the Adamite," let us inquire whether the writer of this book is of such sound judgment, that to him may be entrusted the difficult task of reconciling the apparent discrepancies of Scripture and science? We say *apparent* discrepancies, because revelation does not refuse to harmonize with true science, but only with that which assumes to be such.

Let the interpretation which he has put on Gen. vi. 4 decide the question—"And it came to pass, when the Adamites began to multiply on the face of the earth, and daughters were born unto them, that the sons of God saw the daughters of men that they were fair, and they took them wives of all that they chose." The daughters of the Adamites are the female descendants of Adam, according to this rendering. But who are the sons of God? That is the dilemma to which the writer is reduced by limiting the expression, "daughters of men" to the "daughters of the Adamites;" for it would not consist with his theory to apply the high expression, "sons of God," to the inferior cognate races. So by the sons of God we are to understand, kind readers, "the fallen angels, who thus mingled their blood with the race of Adam." The only difficulty in so understanding the passage is, that the angels, being spirits, had no blood to mingle.

But the enormity to the adoption of which the writer is forced in this passage shows how baseless is the attempt to limit the universality of the word Adam, so that it shall only include a part, and not the whole of the human race.

We have been engaged in examining the "theory of development." Let our readers understand it: it is one utterly irreconcilable with Scripture, so that revelation and the new philosophy can never harmonize. Let us add, that not only is it irreconcilable with Scripture, but contrary to fact. There is in God's terrestrial works "a persistence of type" which refuses to reconcile itself with the theory of development.

On this interesting subject we would again refer our readers to Captain Spratt's work, and more particularly to the chapter in the second volume on the "Development Theory." It will there be seen that proofs of the unsoundness of the development theory have been brought up from the depths of the ocean.

Fifteen miles to the south of the south-west extreme of Crete lies an ocean depth of 1950 fathoms, or nearly 12,000 feet. Not far off rise in the centre of the island the white mountains, to the height of 8000 feet, showing a difference of level between the bed of the Mediterranean and the top of the white mountains of nearly 20,000 feet, in a distance of about twenty-five miles. In the surface zone of these deep waters, and, indeed, throughout the Mediterranean, is found swarming in abundance that interesting pteropod, the criseis. As from year to year, and age to age, they have died, their glassy shells have sunk down into the depths below, and they are found in hundreds in every cup of mud brought up from the bottom of these seas. They are also found fossil in the marls of Crete. The living and dead have been compared, and the persistence of type is undeniable. The past and the present are the same, nor during the lapse of ages has there been development.

Passing from delicate organisms to great organisms, the same may be shown of the mammoth. "The whole range of the mammalia, fossil and recent, cannot furnish a species which has a wider geographical distribution, and has at the same time passed through a longer term of time, and through more extreme changes of climatal conditions than the mammoth. Yet persistency of type is evidenced in its "most important and characteristic organ, *the tooth*, even including the little pigmy species recently found fossil in Malta, and the Siberian or pre-glacial mammoth."

From these and other interesting exemplifications it is shown that "the inherent elasticity of every species is strictly circumscribed."

Captain Spratt introduces the opinions of the late Edward Forbes on these points, as embodied in lectures given at the Royal Institution a few years before his death. We introduce them because they are so brief and decisive.

"Is man a member of the last organic province in time? for, if so, he need not have been the last member, and species might have appeared after him.

"Argument on this point—The members of the present animal and vegetable population of the world are members of a centre in time, which had its point of creative maximum anterior to man's coming."

"Man's appearance a unique geological fact. Man not a member of the last centre of creation, but a unique being, and concentrated act of creation, equivalent to an entire province in himself."

"That the creation of man was a final act, and the great purpose to which previous creations tended."

"That such a view accords with the dignity of position and moral and social stand taken by man in the world."

Such are the convictions of a real philosopher, and to these we add, still quoting from Captain Spratt's book, the recent statement of an eminent anatomist, M. Gratiolet, who, after a patient dissection of some of the pithecoid apes in reference to man's place in nature, declares—"The facts upon which I insist, permit me to affirm, with a conviction founded on a personal and attentive study of all at present known, demonstrate that anatomy gives no grounds for the idea, so violently defended now-a-days, of a close relationship between man and ape. One may invoke in vain some animal skulls, evident monstrosities found by chance, such as that of Neanderthal, and here and there similar forms may be found: they belong to idiots."

One more point remains to be noticed, and then we have done: it is one which connects with Missionary action, and in which, therefore, we have a special interest.

Both the writer of "Adam and the Adamite" and Dr. Colenso are of opinion that the cognate races, human, yet not Adamite, have a claim on us for the communication to them of that salvation which was wrought out by the "seed of the woman." Dr. Colenso says—

"Whenever we meet with the power of speech, with reason and conscience, with tender human affections, we must confess that the owner of such gifts is a friend and a brother. . . . . We are bound to teach him, as God shall give us opportunity for so doing, what we ourselves have learned. . . . . Most of all, we are bound to impart that highest knowledge, that knowledge of God Himself, in which consists eternal life," &c.

And what shall we tell them?—that they are disconnected with Adam? How, then, can we prove to them their connexion with Christ? The uncertainty of the grounds on which we approach them will at once confirm that natural indisposition to the Gospel message, which, as experience proves, never fails to show itself in the first instance; and they will then say to us, as they have often said, even under advantageous circumstances, "Go; you mistake. Your message is for the white man, not for us. It may suit him, not us. Go, then: the Redeemer you speak of was not of our race: we owe Him no regard, and desire not to hear of Him." Such undoubtedly would be the result. This new fable about races, this ethnological folly, destroys all sympathy between Christ and the inferior races, which, in the preference shown to the Adamite, must necessarily feel themselves humiliated and disowned.

EVENTS IN NEW ZEALAND EXPLAINED AND INTERPRETED.

SELDOM, if ever, in the annals of Missionary history, has a scene been enacted of such painful features as that which recently occurred at Opotiki. Missionaries have often been persecuted by such portions of the people whom they had come to evangelize as disliked their teaching, and hated them for the truth's sake; but at such times the Christian flock has gathered round them, endeavoured to shield them from injury, and often suffered in their defence.

It was so on a recent occasion with the Christian Sioux. When their heathen countrymen, in a moment of ungovernable fury, rose up to massacre the whites, they befriended the Missionaries, and conducted them and a large body of the settlers to a place of safety.

At Opotiki it was otherwise. When the Hauhaus led forth the Missionary Volkner with the intention of murdering him, no one interfered; no hand was stretched out to rescue him; no tongue pleaded that he might be spared. His flock was there, the people for whom he had prayed and laboured. Within sight of the church where he had been wont to assemble them, to tell of God's love in Christ Jesus, they saw him ignominiously dealt with as a malefactor, and yet not only did they refuse all sympathy, but so filled with savage cruelty was every heart, that when, on his head being cut off, the fanatics rushed forward, eager to taste his blood, many rubbing it on their faces, "some of his old friends took part in all this."

We throw a veil over further details: they are too revolting. But the Missionary died a Christian's death. So surprised, so suddenly overtaken by death in such a form, and from a quarter so wholly unexpected, he quailed not. Very affecting are the details of the eventful day on which he suffered, as related by his companion in tribulation, the Rev. T. S. Grace. When the last attempt had been made, but in vain, to obtain release by a money-ransom, they had prayer with their fellow-captives, and read together Psalm x., "Why standest thou afar off, O Lord? Why hidest thou thyself in times of trouble?" It is even so. God sees his own people in sorrow, yet He does not rescue them: He sees the wicked prospering, yet He smites not. This state of things is but temporary. Yet a little while, and He shall "judge the fatherless and the oppressed, that the man of earth may no more oppress." About one o'clock "we had prayer and reading for the last time, the portion read being Psalm xiv., the words of which so exactly described the rampant ungodliness of the natives—'The Lord looked down from heaven upon the children of men, to see if there were any that did understand, and seek after God. They are all gone aside, they are altogether become filthy: there is none that doeth good, no, not one.'" "My poor dear friend," observes Mr. Grace, "offered up a most earnest prayer. During the morning I could not help noticing the calmness of his manner, and the beautiful smile that was on his face."

He was now led forth alone, none of his fellow-prisoners, not even Mr. Grace, being permitted to accompany him. They took his coat and waistcoat from him, and led him beneath a willow-tree. If doubt had previously rested on his mind as to their intentions, there could be none now. He asked for his Prayer-book, which was in his coat-pocket: they brought it. He knelt down and prayed. He then *shook hands with his murderer.* Forgiven of God, he had learned to forgive even those who rendered him evil for good. He then said, "I am ready." That was the triumph of Christianity. They who had become his enemies might take his life, but they could not take from him his hope, his peace. When this mad excitement is over, and the Maoris reflect, they will acknowledge respecting him that he was indeed a man of God. When the period of tribulation has passed away, the surviving tribes will not fail to erect, on the spot where he suffered, a memorial of the gentle, loving Missionary, whom their fellow-countrymen, in a moment of wild fanaticism, had savagely put to death.

But what moved the people of Opotiki? A mad delusion had seized them, and they acted as though they had been possessed. A fortnight before Mr. Volkner's murder there arrived at Opotiki a messenger to say that the Pai Marire, from Taranaki, were at hand. At their head was Patara. This man, orignally of Waikato, is well known at Wellington as a notoriously bad character: with him was associated Kereopa, a pretended prophet, who carried about with him a soldier's head, which by the aid of ventriloquism he used for his own purposes. They were coming, it was said, to obtain men who should fight the soldiers at Taranaki, and to instruct the people of Opotiki in the new religion. The tidings excited not regret, but joy. The people of Opotiki were at once on the alert. Great were the preparations. Some were erecting tents, others putting up flags, carrying wood, &c. As the Pai Marire drew near, the women, 257 in number, who had formed in double line for their reception, opened, and Patara passed through them amidst the greatest rejoicings and welcomes. A review followed, the Opotiki natives going through their war manœuvres, and the Pai Marire flags being hoisted on a very high flag-staff near the church. A Jewish merchant, Levy by name, recognised one Hebrew letter on the flag-staffs. Then came the feast after the old Maori fashion—dead oxen, potatoes, and water-melons. When it was evening, Kereopa, placing himself in front of the skull, addressed the people, maligning the Missionaries, by whom he declared they had been robbed of lands, money, and blood; and then, conducting them into the church, initiated them into the new religion, the Taranakis running round the new proselytes, shouting, and going through many old-fashioned forms of incantation, until the people seemed to be possessed, falling on the ground in a state of stupidity, and some of them remaining without meat or drink for four or five days. These orgies continued through the whole night, the people remaining in the two churches. We can only compare the process to Luke xi. 24—"When the unclean spirit is gone out of a man, he walketh through dry places, seeking rest; and finding none, he saith, I will return unto my house, whence I came out. And when he cometh he findeth it swept and garnished. Then goeth he and taketh to him seven other spirits more wicked than himself, and they enter in and dwell there; and the last state of that man is worse than the first." Aroused to a savage furor, the natives were now prepared for the tragedy that was to follow, and Volkner was murdered—an act which will ever remain a blot on the Whakatowhea nation.

The Pai Marire is a revival of old superstitions under a new name. The curing of heads is unmistakeable. "In olden times the heads of fallen chiefs were carefully preserved from decay by an ingenious process, and deposited within their ancestors' houses, to be brought forth on future occasions to excite men to revenge their deaths. The bloody heads of the enemy were stuck round the fences of the village, for the purpose of being insulted. The people were roused to desperation by the excitement of oratory and the war-dance, until they became frenzied, and rushed to the bloody conflict in fits of temporary madness. On the battle-field the dead were decapitated, the brains, tongue, and eyes scooped out, and their cavities filled with fern or flax." The features of identity are complete. The Pai Marire have cast off their profession of Christianity, and relapsed into their old heathenism, under a new name, and with some slight modifications.

The hold which Christianity had on this lapsed portion of the Maori race must have been very slight. Undoubtedly it could have been only superficial, and when the gilding was removed by the friction of unexpected trials, the old savage stood revealed.

The Maori race came over to a profession of Christianity in a mass. Nothing could exceed the rapidity with which they renounced heathenism, and placed themselves under the instruction of the Missionaries, with a desire to be taught and become Christians. It needed, then, that they should have been dealt with as the Tamils in Tinnevelly have been dealt with—subjected to a systematic, persevering, and minute process of Christian instruction, until a sound foundation of Christian knowledge had been laid in their minds, and feeling and excitement had been improved into sterling and influential principle.

And so it has been in those localities of New Zealand where a European Missionary has permanently resided, and has been uninterrupted in his work. But this has not been the case everywhere. At one time there were not enough of clergymen in full orders to administer the necessary ordinances. Opotiki, in particular, suffered under great disadvantages. The Rev. James Hamlin, on visiting this district in 1850, observes —"I am sorry to say the priests have gained considerable advantage here, from the weak state in which this district has *always been left*. *No ordained minister* having been placed here, our people have been, and still are, put to great inconvenience for the administration of baptism and the Lord's Supper, and are thus become a reproach to their Popish neighbours. They are consequently much discouraged; and some of them have joined the Romanists. I hear, indeed, that the Rev. C. Davies has been appointed to Whakatane (a neighbouring station) by the Bishop; but as he is only in deacons' orders, this will not facilitate the administration of the sacrament of the Lord's Supper.

In his reports for 1852, 1853, 1854, Mr. Davies laments over the greediness for worldly wealth which exibited itself among the Opotiki people, so that they had grown lax in the service of God: this unhealthy state resulted in a war, of which the place next beyond Opotiki was the scene, and in which several of the combatants lost their lives.

Mr. Davies having been obliged to withdraw from ill-health, *Opotiki was left for five years without a Missionary*, with a Romish priest living in the midst of 500 natives, the native teachers, to whose care the spiritual interests of the Protestant natives were confided, not being energetic men.

Indeed the whole of the Eastern District appears to have laboured under similar disadvantages. The Bishop of Waiapu, when Archdeacon W. Williams, in his report for 1858, observes—"It becomes a matter of serious importance to inquire how suitable provision is to be made for these native districts, particularly in the prospect of but a limited provision on the part of the Society. When the supply of Missionaries was most effective, that supply was but scanty as compared with the parochial system in England. The deficiency was met, in the only way practicable, by native teachers. But those teachers were not regularly prepared for their work. They were such natives as seemed to be best informed in the different villages to which they belonged. They were very imperfectly taught, and could not therefore teach much; and, in the majority of cases, they have grown weary of their work, and have resigned their posts to others not better qualified than themselves. It may be asked, Why have we not made provision earlier for this necessity? I will speak for the Eastern District. I came to it in the year 1849, and for *some years I occupied it alone*, having to travel continually north and south."

Whether at home or abroad, Christian congregations, if they are to be preserved from strange opinions, must be well instructed. For this great object the Christian ministry was especially appointed, as Paul informs us in Ephes. iv. 14—"that we henceforth be no more children, tossed to and fro, and carried about with every weight of doctrine, by the sleight of men and cunning craftiness, whereby they lie in wait to deceive," &c. But if the ministry be scanty, and below the proper standard, and the congregations be left in an immature and childish state, then we are not to be surprised if mischief ensues, and the tares spring up among the wheat. So it proved to be in this Eastern District. In 1857, many natives were carried away by a belief in an audible intercourse with the spirits of their departed friends. To such an extent was this carried, that on one occasion all the villages of an extensive district were excluded from the Lord's Supper. Inasmuch as any direction given by any medium of those supposed spirits was most implicitly followed out, as though it were a direct revelation from God Himself, several superstitious practices were revived. But what was, if possible, still more alarming, as showing the unsound state of the Christian community, the native teachers, with few exceptions, were among the most zealous followers of the "spirits."* Let it be borne in mind that we are describing, not a state of things which has long since passed away, but one which existed only *seven* years ago.

But we can bring these investigations still nearer to us as to date. In April and May 1861, the Rev. E. B. Clarke visited portions of the Eastern District, amongst other places, Opotiki. What was its condition four years ago? The following is an extract from the notes of this tour—"*Opotiki.*—Alas! I am tempted to begin my account of this place with the word 'Ichabod,' for of it I may truly write 'the glory is departed.' Once an orderly, industrious, and thriving people, they are now the very reverse. Spirits and their runanga are their ruin. Their runanga, or native council, is most oppressive, and is, in fact, their old tana, or robbing system, in another form. They eagerly seize upon any pretext for the exercise of their power, and are most extortionate in their decisions." Mr. Clarke next refers to the prevalence of another evil—the use of spirits. "The natives, as well as the traders, are in the habit of bringing large quantities from Auckland. One hundred pounds' worth have been known to have been bought by them, taken up to their cultivations inland, and retailed at exorbitant prices. Men, women, and children are frequently seen in a state of intoxication. As usual, other crimes follow." Then follows a paragraph, to which we would specially direct the attention of our readers—"I have heard of several instances of the natives of this place having had recourse to the old *harakia Maori.* Their instigator is an old woman from Whakatane. She tells her followers that they are not to give up their former ways, as the Missionaries teach them to do; but, on the contrary, they are to persevere in them. She says that her principles are not opposed to Christianity. She also exorcises the 'harakia'—evil spirits—who are supposed to be the sources of human suffering, by administering to her patients a decoction of native herbs." On the occasion of Mr. Clarke's visit, the communicants had dwindled down from sixty-four in the previous year to twenty-six. Of these people Mr. Clarke, in conclusion, says—"They are indeed as sheep without a shepherd; and if there be one place in New Zealand which needs the prayers of the Lord's people, that place is Opotiki."†

It was not until the autumn of 1861 that Mr. Volkner became resident at Opotiki. He had not been with the people for a long previous period, so as to have had time and opportunity to have acquired influence over them before troublous times came. The troubles had already commenced. The act of incendiarism in connexion with the Waitara block, which kindled a conflagration so fierce and wide-spread as that which has since involved the northern island of New Zealand, had been perpetrated on March 5th, 1860.

On his arrival at Opotiki, Mr. Volkner addressed himself to the improvement of this neglected and unsettled people, and, for a time, every thing seemed to progress favourably. A new church was commenced, at which the natives laboured diligently, at the same time contributing liberally to its cost. Village schools were opened, and the people gathered in, that they might learn to read and write. But now the war-feeling, which had hitherto been confined to the western and Waikato districts, began to spread

* See "Church Missionary Record" for 1858, pp. 363, 364.

† See "Church Missionary Record" for 1861, pp. 387, 388.

eastward, and a general distrust as to the intentions of the Government pervaded the native race. Messengers arrived from the seat of war, moving the Opotiki people to join therein. At first Mr. Volkner's efforts to restrain them appeared to be successful; but the hope was soon disappointed. In a letter dated May 30th, 1864, he thus states the facts—

On Christmas-day we had a feast. The Protestant party had hoisted the Queen's flag, and all rejoiced. About dusk I went home to tea, leaving them all in a state of happiness. In about half an hour I returned to bring the feast to a close, and to get synodsmen elected. But how was I disappointed when I found them all in a ferment, and talking about it being their duty to go to Waikato to help the people there in fighting. When I spoke about electing synodsmen, they replied, "Do not speak to us about that: our eyes and our thoughts are turned to Waikato." On inquiring what had caused this sudden change in their thoughts, I was told that the Roman-Catholic priest had brought a letter from the rebel party at Waikato. I did not believe he had done so, and went to him with the man who had told me. When I asked the priest whether he had brought the letter, he hesitated a little, and then answered in the affirmative; and, in going out with me, he told me the contents of it, which were that all the Maoris in the Bay of Plenty and the East Coast were to come at once and drive the Europeans away, of whom the writer spoke in an offensive way. From that moment the people, step by step, became more deeply involved in the war, and, in spite of the Governor's kindness in writing to them, and in many other ways, and of all my efforts, they would not be convinced that the home Parliament had not given instruction to the Colonial Government here to destroy all the natives who fight them, take the island, and make slaves of those who remain quiet.

I have not been able to trace the source from whence this report comes; but it does not sound at all as if of Maori origin. On January 30th a meeting was held, in which all the tribes of the Bay of Plenty were represented. They decided in favour of the King movement. On February 1st they started for Waikato. They were stopped on their way by the Arawa, which led to a collision of these tribes, in which six persons were killed.

When the tidings of Mr. Volkner's murder reached this country, that portion of the daily press which, for reasons best known to the writers themselves, takes pleasure in disparaging Missionary effort, immediately laid hold upon them, as affording a favourable and unexpected opportunity for prosecuting their work of depreciation; and forthwith articles were penned, which proclaimed with a loud voice the worthlessness of the efforts carried on by weak-minded, although well-intentioned persons, to ameliorate, by such means as they employed, the condition of barbarous races. "Behold," exclaimed the leading journal of the day, "the measure of the depth to which this much-talked-of Christianity has penetrated." But is this correct? Has this Christianity been much talked of, much vaunted? Has it been described as a deep-laid and well-consolidated structure which might bid defiance to the tempest? Have the Opotiki natives been set forth as favourable specimens of Maori Christianity, by whose conduct might be proved its reality and power of endurance? Who has so described them? Certainly not the Church Missionary Society. The extracts given in this article, which speak so unfavourably of the principles and conduct of the Opotiki people, are to be found in the published Reports of the Society. In those yearly accounts they have been spoken of as an ill-instructed, unsettled people, now carried away by the love of gain, now yielding themselves to the influence of old superstitions.

Other portions of the New-Zealand work are of the same kind. First impressions were not followed up with that pertinacity and minuteness which were necessary to render them permanent and influential. The European Missionaries were not sufficiently numerous to meet the requisitions of that new state of things which arose, when, on the cessation of native wars, the Maoris, dispersing themselves over their extensive lands, cultivated with a view to the European markets, without, however, any settled homesteads, and shifting about from place to place. Several of them were only in deacons' orders. The native agency employed to help them was itself uninstructed, and inadequate to its duties. The development of an efficient native ministry was very slow; the withdrawal of the Church Missionary Society from the work of education was not supplemented by adequate efforts on the part either of the Government or the natives themselves. The first converts died, and were gathered in to their rest; but their children grew up no better instructed than their fathers, and without their spirituality. A portion of Maori Christianity was such as we have described, superficial, and ill-fitted to endure the severity of the ordeal to which it has been subjected. It has been otherwise where European Missionaries have been long stationed; where, through their indefatigable exertions, the people have been well instructed; where schools have been well worked; where godly influence has been acquired over the native mind, and old superstitions rooted out. So it has been at Wanganui, for thirty years the station of the Rev. R. Taylor. Our last Number brings out the men of Opotiki and the men of Wanganui in memorable contrast; the one, carried away by the impulse of a wild fanaticism, murdered their Missionary; the others indignantly repudiated the new creed; and when its bloodthirsty followers proposed to carry out at Wanganui deeds of blood similar to those which had been enacted at Opotiki, they fought and defeated them. So is it also at Otaki, the station for thirty years of the Venerable Archdeacon Hadfield. His people, too, at this crisis, have rendered invaluable services to the cause of Christianity and evangelization.

In the letters from New Zealand, which will be found under the head of Recent Intelligence, it will be seen that, after the murder of Mr. Volkner, the Pai Marire entered the districts more immediately under the superintendence of Bishop Williams. The people of Turanga at first appeared to be fixed in their resolution of withstanding them, and the bishop was requested to remain quiet where he was, as in that district the Pai Marire should have no power. But when they did come in considerable strength, making an imposing display of their karakia, the natives, who had promised adherence to the cause of Christianity, melted away so rapidly, and the aspect of affairs seemed so uncertain, that the bishop, with the ladies and children of the Missionaries' families, embarked for Auckland, leaving behind his son, Archdeacon Leonard Williams, with the Rev. S. Williams, and one of his nephews, to watch the course of events.

Just at this crisis arrived a party of influential natives from Otaki. Amongst them were Wi Tako and Matene Te Whiwhi, both influential chiefs and decided Christians. How timely has been the visit of these chiefs to the Turanga district, and how useful they have proved, will best appear from the following letter received from Archdeacon W. L. Williams, and dated April 22nd—

Just at that time a party of chiefs had arrived from Otaki and Ahuriri, including Wi Tako and Matene Te Whiwhi, having been invited a short time since by the Turanga chiefs; but they were so disgusted to find that the Hauhau religion was being received with so much favour that they talked of returning home immediately. They agreed afterwards, however, to go to Whakato, where they would meet most of the principal men of the district. I was unable to be present at the meetings, which took place on the 7th and 8th instant; but, from the reports of them which I received, there seemed to be little prospect of matters taking a favourable turn. Most of the speakers seemed altogether to repudiate the notion of their having done any thing wrong in entertaining the murderers of Mr. Volkner. The Rev. S. Williams, who had accompanied Wi Tako and his party from Napier, was present, and he and the Maori visitors spoke very strongly, urging the Turanga people to show their detestation of the proceedings of the Hauhau by at least compelling them to leave the district.

Patara is a relative of Wi Tako's, but, at the same time, he is a man of notoriously bad character; and Wi Tako, by exposing him, did much towards weakening the influence which he was fast acquiring over the Turanga people.

In accordance with an invitation which they received from some of the Waerenga-a-Hika people, who had not joined the Hauhau, the southern chiefs were to have come here on the 10th; but, in accepting the invitation, Wi Tako had intimated that if his kinsman Patara was to be present they need not be expected. The Teitanga-a-Mahaki Hauhau determined to bring Patara with them, relying on his effrontery for the support of their cause against the attacks which might be made upon it; and accordingly, about noon, they arrived in the pa (many of them armed), bringing with them Patara and the Urewera. Soon after their arrival the whole party were harangued by several of the chiefs in very violent language, some of the speakers threatening that all strangers and all sympathizers with the Government should be driven into the sea. These threats were understood to have reference to myself and the pupils in our schools, and also to a few Uawa people who were then here, and who are adherents of the Government. Under these circumstances I was recommended by my Maori friends to move out of the way; but, before I had started, I was told that the whole of this warlike party had returned again to Taureka, in consequence of some difference between them and the Waerenga-a-Hika people.

Most of the Teitanga-a-Mahaki came back on the two following days to meet the visitors, leaving Patara and his immediate followers behind them. The Hauhau were drawn out at these meetings, and induced to state quietly the reasons which had moved them to adopt the new religion. Their arguments were very satisfactorily refuted by our Otaki and Ahuriri friends; and the refutation was the better received as coming from Maoris, we having frequently been told by those who take up extravagant views that we oppose them because we are English, and not Maori.

In the evening of the second day Henare Ruru, one of the Hauhau of this place, stood up and exposed the absurdity of the doctrines, and the wickedness of the practices of the new religion; and on the following morning he openly recanted, and urged me to stay quietly at Waerenga-a-Hika; saying, at the same time, that if he had not been beguiled into meddling with the Hauhau he would have strenuously opposed the Bishop's leaving. He assured me, moreover, that if any one should come to do me harm he was prepared to lay down his life in my defence. He was then urged by Wi Tako and others to go immediately, and to use his influence with the Teitanga-a-Mahaki to induce them to follow his example. This he undertook to do; and we promised to wait till Monday, the 17th, before deciding upon any movement, so as to give him an opportunity of bringing the subject before the people.

On the afternoon of the 13th Wi Tako fell in with Patara, at the house of a settler, and reproved him sharply in the presence of some of the Teitanga-a Mahaki whom he had deluded. Patara was absolutely confounded, not having a word to say in his own defence.

On Saturday, the 15th, it was decided that a deputation of the Rongowhakaata tribe, accompanied by several of the Otaki and Ahuriri chiefs, should remonstrate again with the Teitanga-a-Mahaki, with a view to induce them to retrace their steps. This decision was strengthened by the arrival from Auckland, on the same day, of Rutene and Rawiri, the two chiefs who had gone away in H.M.S. "Eclipse" a month before to try to effect the deliverance of Mr. Grace.

On Sunday Patara and his party left Taureka for the Bay of Plenty (Kereopa having already left for Opotiki on the 5th), and on Tuesday, the 18th, the deputation came, and the Rev. S. Williams and I accompanied them to Taureka. They were supported by Rawiri, who spoke of the egregious failure of the Hauhau at Opotiki in the attempt to draw H.M.S. "Eclipse" on shore, and of the rough treatment which he and his companion experienced at the hands of the Opotiki natives in consequence of the escape of Mr. Grace. There were not many people to meet us, but Horomona, the principal man of the village, was there, and he spoke very moderately, and in such a way as to encourage us to hope that their attachment to their new religion is not very deeply rooted.

On the following day we went to Patutahi, the other stronghold of the party. There were more people present here, but the tone of the most influential speakers was the same as that exhibited at Taureka. It was evident that a great change had come over them, for the Patutahi people were among the most violent in their language at Waerenga-a-Hika on the 10th. Patara, however, was with them; but, since that time, he has left them somewhat ignominiously, feeling, doubtless, that the presence of Wi Tako and others who were able to expose the falsehood of his assertions, and to show the real object of his fair speeches, was fatal to his success.

Finding now that matters have begun to wear a more promising aspect, I have concluded, with the advice of the Rev. S. Williams and our Maori friends, to remain quietly at this place for the present, and to endeavour to get our establishment into working order again. I hope soon to be rejoined by the Rev. E. B. Clarke, and I think that he and I together may be able to hold our ground for some time longer—at all events, till we get another alarm.

The Rev. S. Williams, with the Otaki and Ahuriri chiefs, are now leaving us, having done the district very good service during the three weeks that they have been with us.

Some of the Turanga chiefs are to accompany them, in order to have some communication with the Government. One or more of these wish to join the Government decidedly, but whether any thing will come of their wish at present is doubtful.

Though I have concluded to stay here, I must admit that I am not without fears of our being disturbed again. It may be before very long; for, in the event of active measures being taken by the Government at Opotiki, it may become necessary for all the Turanga people to choose which side they will take. In such an emergency, they would probably be split into two hostile parties, and we might then, perhaps, find it necessary to break up our whole establishment. These anticipations, however, may not, after all, be realized; and as we cannot but feel that the kind providence of our heavenly Father has been watching over us throughout the trying events of the past few weeks, so we have every encouragement to trust in Him for the future.

Now it is from these well-worked parts of the Mission, where Christian truth is really understood and felt, and where it has taken strong hold upon the native mind, that, under God, we look for help at such a time this: all else in New Zealand seems involved in dire confusion. Affairs there, civil and military, present such a tangled net, that in our present Number we shall not venture into these complications. But we look for a healthful reaction amongst the better portion of the natives. The proceedings of the Otaki chiefs in the Eastern District are full of hope; and further encouragement is afforded by the following address to the Governor from the leading chiefs of Wellington and Hawke's Bay—

Pakowhai, March 20, 1865.

From the whole meeting at Pakowhai assembled on the occasion of the arrival of parties of the Ngatitoa, Te Atiawa, and Ngatirauhawa, and from the chiefs of Heretaunga.

To the Governor—

SIR,—This is a letter to express to you our vexation at the wicked doings of the Hauhau which are being perpetrated in this island. We had already expressed our displeasure at its being carried about and taught in our villages, and we told them to take it back to the land from whence it came and carry it on there. But now that we have heard of the murder of the Rev. Mr. Volkner at Opotiki, we are overwhelmed with vexation and horror, for now at last has the most frightful kind of murder been perpetrated in New Zealand. There were plenty of armed men with whom they might have fought if they wanted to show their bravery, instead of which they turn upon a defenceless and innocent man—upon their own father, like a miserable coward turning his weapon against his own father who had nourished him.

Those murderers, by travelling through the country of other tribes, have saved themselves, and have obtained time to spread about their doctrines; for had they come this way we should have seized them, and with our own hands handed them over to you. But as they have not yet come, we have laid down the above rule for our conduct with regard to those bearers of Pakeha's heads through our places, and if they resist us we will not spare them: we will kill them.

Sir, we wish to express to you and the people our unmeasured distress at the doings of our country. Not satisfied with fighting with men, they actually attempt to fight against God, and are working downwards again to the deeds of the darkest times. But do not suppose that this wicked course is general, for there are many tribes who still stand aloof from such wickedness, and may God preserve and keep them! That is all. From your friends—Karaitiana (Ngatikahungunu): Wi Tako (Ngatiawa, West Coast); Renata (Ngatikahungunu); Matene (Ngatitoa, West Coast); Henare (Poraughau); Wi Parata (Ngatirauhawa, West Coast); and others.

We desire, also, to refer our readers very particularly to the following letter from the Rev. T. S. Grace, the late Mr. Volkner's companion in tribulation, and who so very nearly shared his fate—

Auckland, May 5, 1865.

You will be glad to hear that the Pai Marire superstition has received a check at Turanga. I had a conversation with two natives from there this morning, from which it appears evident, that though the Turanga people were willing, for political purposes, to join the fanatics, yet they found the murder more than they could defend or excuse. I believe the tide of this dreadful superstition has now turned, and that it will recede, or at least take a less objectional form.

When at Opotiki, during the worst days of my stay there, I was strangely impressed with the feeling that dear Volkner's blood had not been shed in vain. Had this outrage not been perpetrated, there cannot be a reasonable doubt but that Turanga would have followed Opotiki, and that the Taranaki party would have marched triumphant round the East Cape, and carried all before them, in which case the northern part of the island would have followed. But this dreadful murder has made it self-evident, even to the natives themselves, that the Pai Marire superstition is the work of the devil.

If the enemies of Missions at home are like those we have here, they will, no doubt, make the most of this murder to show the failure of our work. If the natives are such a blood-thirsty race of cannibals as they are now said to be, what must have been the amount of the restraining influence of the Gospel for the last fifty years, so as to enable hundreds, yea, thousands of settlers to live in perfect safety in their midst, though entirely at their mercy? The causes which have led to the present state of things, for which we Missionaries suffer both from natives and Europeans, are entirely political, and have been caused by the war. From the natives we are suffering because of the supposed assistance we have given to Government, which they believe intends to take their island from them.

From the whole subject, as placed before us, we would deduce two lessons. There is an admonition conveyed to all Missionary Societies to take heed that the work they take in hand be thoroughly wrought out; that the foundations of the native churches be well laid on the Rock, and the whole structure not carried up too rapidly, nor yet at the same time unwisely delayed, but built perseveringly and surely. So soon as Christian congregations have been got together, let educational institutions be organized; schools for the children; training institutions for the development of a native agency, schoolmasters, catechists, native ministers. The more effectively this is done, the sooner will the maturity of a self-supporting native church be attained. To deal liberally in respect to such organizations is the best economy.

At home and abroad all work done for the Lord needs to be of this character, especially at the present time. There is abroad an energetic influence for evil, subtle and penetrative, seeking for what is unsound to fasten upon, and where it exists, sure to find it out whether it be in individuals or churches. Its action is like that of an epidemic which lays hold of predisposed constitutions. It is variable, and with facility adapts itself to the disposition and tendencies of men. In Europe it comes to the philosophical mind under the guise of science, falsely so called; to minds anxious on religious subjects, yet ignorant and uninstructed, it presents itself under a different aspect, and suggesting forms and ceremonies as especially deserving of attention, diverts men from the great realities of Christian truth. Availing itself of some moment of discouragement, when with the profession of Christianity which he has embraced, there are mingled tribulations, it commends to the recently-converted native the old times and the old customs, and, if the heart be not right with God, causes him to retrograde.

We are reminded in all this of one verse from holy writ—"Woe to the inhabiters of the earth and of the sea; for the devil is come down unto you, having great wrath, because he knoweth that he hath but a short time." A forward movement on the part of Gospel truth has ever been followed by such a season.

The exhortation, therefore, of the apostle is peculiarly appropriate—"Be ye stedfast, unmoveable, always abounding in the work of the Lord, forasmuch as ye know that your labour is not in vain in the Lord."

INDIA—ITS PROGRESS.

The following paper on this subject well deserves the attention of our readers. It was drawn up by one of our native pastors, the Rev. W. T. Satthianadhan, who is engaged in Missionary labours at Madras, in answer to certain questions of an important character, proposed to him by the Honorary Clerical Secretary of the Parent Society.

We shall first present the questions *seriatim*. It will be seen that they are precisely such questions as the friends of India, who are interested in her true progress, would desire to see ably answered, and this we think has been done by Mr. Satthianadhan. It is desirable that we should see India as it is from the stand-point of a native mind alike intelligent and Christian.

The queries which, it will be remembered, have more especial reference to Madras, are as follows—

1. Is there among the higher classes any thing of the same desire for superior English education, and for literary and scientific English cultivation, as there is in Calcutta?

2. Are they becoming Anglicised in their habits?

3. Do they seem in any way freed from the claims of Hinduism, and at all more favourably disposed towards Christianity?

4. Is there any increasing acquaintance with the Gospel, or respect for it among the middling and lower classes?

5. Any spread of female education, any breaking down of caste prejudices?

6. Are the native Christians becoming bolder, more independent, more feeling themselves to be a distinct body?

7. Among the native Protestants is there much sectarian animosity or denominational jealousy; or do they feel themselves to be one body in Christ; and is there any prospect of the rise (in the good sense of the words) of an Indian Catholic Church?

To these Mr. Satthianadhan replies as follows—

May 26, 1865—Your letter is a very important one, and requires a good deal of thought and observation. I look to God for help, and earnestly trust that He will enable me to answer your questions in such a manner as to convey not only clear but correct impressions of things, and stir you up to more prayers on behalf of our benighted country, and of the church planted in it. I will now proceed to answer your queries in the order in which they occur in your letter.

1. "Is there among the higher classes any thing of the same desire for superior English education, and for literary and scientific English cultivation, as there is in Calcutta?"

The Hindu community in Madras may be divided into two bodies, viz. the wealthier classes and the middle and poorer classes. To the former belong the trading classes, chiefly the Komaties, Beri Chetties, and Guzarati Soucaris. These people are not eager for English education. They are actually rolling in wealth, and do not therefore feel the need of superior education in English. If they attain the three R's they are contented; or should any of them deviate from this rule, and aspire after a higher standard of education, it is only with a view to fill intelligently their calling in life, and to acquire facility for intercourse with European merchants. These people are still untouched by the Gospel. The middle and lower classes, on the other hand, have a great thirst for English education. Among these classes education makes rapid strides. An idea may be formed of it by a reference to the results of the Madras University. This was founded in 1857, and it has accomplished a great deal during the nine years of its existence. The number of matriculated students in the year 1857 was 20, whereas this year their number is no less than 225. In the year 1858 there were two B.A.'s; this year they number 11. To sum up: there are 657 matriculated students, 56 B.A.'s, 13 B.L.'s, and one M.D.

This thirst for English education on the part of the middle classes is increasing every day. The moment a school is opened, and the matriculation standard set up, young people flock to it in great numbers. The attainment of a University degree seems to be their sole object of life. I am not speaking of the Mohammedan population. Compared with the Hindus, they are a dull race, and display no taste for English education. But the Hindus are all for English, and they strain every nerve to attain it, even to the neglect of their own mother tongue. Some of them have taken a high place in the world of letters. Gopaul Row, a Brahmin of Combaconum, and the second master in the provincial school of that town, was one of the first B.A.'s, and, though a self-taught man, could not be approached by any of his companions, although most of them, if not all, were the *alumni* of the Presidency College. Of the eleven persons who took the degree of B.A. this year, one stands out foremost. His name is Ranganadham Mudali, first a pupil of the Pacheiyappan's Institution, and afterwards a student of the Madras Presidency College. He was the only one who was admitted into the first class, and, as such, carried off the valuable gold medal awarded by His Highness the enlightened Prince of Travancore, who liberally offers it to every one who takes the first-class B.A. Although English education is thus making rapid progress through the Presidency, yet it cannot stand in competition with Bengal. Baboo Keshub Chunder Sen, the late Secretary of the Brahmo Somaj, who visited Madras a few months ago, in an English lecture delivered in the hall of the Calcutta Bethune Society, makes the following observations—"In education and intelligence I believe the Bengalees are superior to both the Madrasses and Bombayites. They are remarkable for the quickness of their understanding, their penetration, and the general acuteness of their intellectual powers. This hardly admits of a doubt; and many Europeans have cheerfully borne testimony to this fact. The magnificent results which have attended the educational efforts of our University contribute also an incontestable evidence, and have all along challenged admiration. There are many in Bombay who have expressed wonder at the long list of B.A.'s and M.A.'s, and other graduates, who every year receive honours from the Calcutta University; and they are really at a loss to make out by what mysterious agency we manage to manufacture so many degree-holders annually. The fact is, the Bengalee mind is possessed of a high order of intellectual powers."

There is no gainsaying this statement of the Baboo. As a confirmation of this, I may mention, that though there are fifty-six B.A.'s, Madras University can boast of no M.A.'s, while in the sister University in Calcutta there are, I believe, several who have attained this enviable distinction. There are various causes to account for this difference, the chief of which is poverty. The people being poor, compared with their richer brethren of Calcutta, they quit the school before they acquire that amount of knowledge which is necessary for the attainment of this maiden honour. For example, Ranganadham Mudali, above alluded to as having won his bachelor laurels, and become an admiration to many, has taken up a teacher's post at the Presidency College, and is thus debarred from prosecuting his studies with the same exclusive attention as before. This is only an illustration of the general state of things.

2. "Are they becoming at all Anglicised in their habits?"

There is a great tendency on the part of the educated classes to adopt English manners and customs. Indeed, I may say that this tendency runs through the whole community. It is apparent in the erection of their houses, furniture, dress, and even food. The native houses were miserable buildings, with pent-up roofs, hardly admitting the air; but the style of their houses is far superior at present, exhibiting not only marks of architectural skill, but also showing a knowledge of the laws of health. Not only do they build fine, open, airy houses, but they also get them well furnished. There is no native house of any importance in Madras which has not tables, chairs, sofas, globe lights, &c. Nay, some houses have even pankahs. In their dress, too, this change is perceptible. Educated young men do not ride, or take a drive in the evenings, without wearing shoes and stockings. Some of them take their wives with them for a morning or evening drive. Some of the lowest classes, I mean the Pariahs, adopt the European dress, and rank themselves among the East Indians. This they do from motives of expediency or policy. As by birth they take a low place in the scale of society, they are treated with contempt by the higher classes. In order to avoid this, they assume European dress, and assimilate themselves to East Indians. Hence the East-Indian population is fast rising in numbers. The orthodox Hindus, however, do not thus denationalize themselves by putting on European costume entirely: they take a medium, combining the national dress with a portion of the European garb, at least when they are out of doors. This change affects their food too. On special occasions they have grand dinner parties, which more or less partake of the character of English entertainments. Almost all the dishes seen on European tables are seen on theirs, including the use of spirits. But this only occurs occasionally, and among a few of the so-called enlightened of the native community. Though there is this tendency on the part of the educated classes to imitate Europeans, and though, in some respects, they have adopted their manners, yet their progress in this is not so great or striking as it is in Bengal and Bombay, especially to outsiders. I may here introduce another extract from the Baboo's lecture. "Let us," says he, "next turn our attention to Madras. From the picture I have given you of this Presidency, it may be at once inferred that, being eminently bigoted and orthodox, she will not easily forego the ancient order of things. Under the influences of liberal education, she will advance with her other sisters in the path of civilization: however slow her progress may be, she will in time give up her prejudices, and obnoxious social institutions; but she will at the same time guard her nationality with unscrupulous care against the ravages of foreign fashions. Her conservatism will contribute a safeguard against denationalization. Bengal is in danger of being denationalized. Bombay is more so. In both these places I apprehend the tide of outlandish fashions may, in its sweeping course, destroy many of the good and useful institutions of Hindu society, and deprive us of many of its advantages and excellencies. Madras seems destined to hold out always her warning and protest against this process of denationalization, and thus help India in making national advancement, so that she may enjoy the priceless benefits of western civilization with all the simplicity of her primitive manners and the purity of her national institutions. It is certainly desirable that the great fabric of India's social aggrandizement should be upreared on the firm basis of her nationality; and that in being reformed we may not be converted into a different race or people altogether. Let us conscientiously throw aside all moral and social evils, whatever is impure in our domestic and social economy; but let us not extinguish our nationality, and seek meretricious prosperity with a mere patchwork of foreign customs and exotic manners. In this important work I hope Madras will greatly help us by carefully preserving whatever is good and pure in our social system."

3. "Do they seem in any way freed from the chains of Hinduism, and at all more favourably disposed towards Christianity?"

Hinduism, abstractedly considered, has very little hold upon the people. As a general rule, they see and acknowledge the inconsistencies and absurdities of their system. "Hinduism is sick unto death," according to the opinion of a Hindu; but what keeps it up and infuses a kind of life into it is the monster system of caste. Let the latter disappear, and we may be sure the former will die with it. In proportion as caste rules over the people, in the same proportion Hinduism rules over them. Caste, which is the bane of India, is more rampant here than it is in the sister Presidencies. Let Baboo Chunder speak again. "In comparison with Calcutta, Madras seemed to me to be the very fort of orthodoxy. Caste prejudices rule over the people with a despotic sway. The *photas*, or sacred paint, which the Madrassees wear on their forehead, the educated as well as the uneducated, denote the two grand religious sections into which they are divided—the Vaishnavas and the Saivas. Their kudumi, or *teeki* (the tuft of hair on the head), also strikes us as an unmistakeable evidence of their inveterate orthodoxy. They attach great importance to this hair-lock; hence, for some time, I continued to be 'the observed of all observers,' on account of my head being innocent of it. Equally singular is their custom of leaving their shoes at the gate when entering gentlemen's houses or public offices, a custom to which the people adhere with religious strictness. The Brahmins of Madras are certainly less fortunate than their brethren of Bengal, as they are not only compelled to live exclusively on vegetable diet, but are strictly enjoined not to see the face of a Sudra during dinner, lest the defiling sight of that inferior sect may contaminate the purity of their character. The Sudras of Madras, however, enjoy greater license in matters of diet than those of Bengal. They are allowed to take, not only mutton, but fowl and onion."

But with the spread of education and European ideas and thoughts, the decline of caste, as well as Hinduism, is perceptible. This, I think, is the place for noticing the Veda Somajam, which was lately established by the educated Hindus of Madras, in imitation of the Brahmo Somaj of Calcutta. Its aims and objects may be gathered from its covenants, which are as follows—

1. "I shall worship, through love of Him, and the performance of the work He loveth, the Supreme Being, the Creator, Preserver, the Destroyer, the Giver of Salvation, the Omniscient, the Omnipotent, the Blissful, the Good, the Formless, the One only without a second; and none of the created objects—subject to the following conditions.

2. "I shall labour to compose and gradually bring into practice a ritual agreeable to the spirit of pure Theism, and free from the superstitions and absurdities which at present characterize Hindu ceremonies.

3. "In the mean time, I shall observe the ceremonies now in use, but only in cases where ceremonies are indispensable, as in marriages and funerals; or where their omission will do more violence to the feelings of Hindu community than is consistent with the proper interests of the Veda Somaj, as in Sradhas. And I shall go through such ceremonies, where they are not conformable to pure Theism, as mere matters of routine, destitute of all religious significance, as the lifeless remains of a superstition which has passed away.

4. "This sacrifice, and this only, shall I make to existing prejudices. But I shall never endeavour to deceive any one as to my religious opinions, and never stoop to equivocation or hypocrisy in order to avoid unpopularity.

5. "I shall discard all sectarian views and

animosities, and never offer any encouragement to them.

6. "I shall, as a first step, gradually give up all distinctions, and amalgamate the different branches of the same caste.

7. "Rigidly as I shall adhere to all these rules, I shall be perfectly tolerant to the views of strangers, and never intentionally give offence to their feelings.

8. "I shall never violate the duties and virtues of humanity—justice, veracity, temperance, and chastity.

9. "I shall never hold, or attend, or pay for, nautches, or otherwise hold out encouragement for prostitution.

10. "I shall encourage and promote, to the best of my power, the re-marriage of widows, and discourage early marriages.

11. "I shall never be guilty of bigamy or polygamy.

12. "I shall grant my aid towards the issue, in the vernaculars, of elementary Prayer-books and religious tracts, and also of a monthly journal, whose chief object shall be to improve the social and moral condition of the community.

13. "I shall advance the cause of general and female education and enlightenment, and particularly in my own family circle.

14. "I shall study the Sanskrit language and its literature (especially theological), and promote the cultivation of it by means not calculated to promote superstition."

"To-day, being the —— day of the month of ——— of the Kalyabda ——, I hereby embrace the faith of the Veda Somaj, and in witness whereof I set my hand to this."

Though we may say from all this that the Hindus are generally becoming freed from the fetters of heathenism, yet I do not think they are favourably disposed towards Christianity. Young Madras tries to set up a religion of its own, as young Bengal has done. Theism is its chief feature. Intuition is made the standard of judgment. The idea of an atonement does not enter into their system. Their religious instincts and aspirations being thus satisfied with a semblance of religion, their carnal mind, which is enmity against God, revolts from truth. Hence their opposition to Christianity.

4. "Is there any increasing acquaintance with the Gospel, or respect for it among the middling and lower classes?"

There is a great and increasing acquaintance with the Gospel on the part of the educated natives and the middling and lower classes. The multiplication of Christian schools, the circulation of Christian books and tracts, and the public and open-air preaching of the Missionaries, have all contributed to produce this result. We cannot address a crowd without meeting with objections founded on a knowledge of Christianity. Only the other day, while I was preaching to a large audience from the steps of the Memorial Hall, one of them asked me the following question—"Well, you say that God was not the author of evil. How, then, is it stated in Genesis that God planted in the midst of the garden the tree of knowledge of good and evil, and that the eating of that fruit had produced evil, which shows clearly that the tree contained the germs and principles of evil?" Another man said, "We find in Scripture that circumcision was enjoined on the Jews as a perpetual ordinance, and that even Jesus Christ was circumcised. Why, then, do you Christians transgress this divine law by a studied neglect of it?" A third individual said, "You say that God has no form, and that He is a spirit: how can this be true in the face of that statement in Genesis, 'Let us make man in our own image," &c. Frequently we hear people quoting the very chapter and text from a certain book, and making it the ground of their objection. I have often preached to the people in Tinnevelly, but have not observed so much intelligence and knowledge of Christianity as I find possessed by the people here.

While there is this increasing acquaintance with Christianity, I cannot say that there is much respect for it among the middling and lower classes. Very often there is a spirit of apathy and levity among them. They speak flippantly, and turn the most serious matters into ridicule, or into topics for most trivial conversation. Some of them go a step further: they take a hostile attitude, and destroy the tracts they have purchased. Occasionally some show even greater violence than this. A few weeks ago, while the catechist Samuel and I were preaching at the Elephant Gate to a large concourse of people, some of them became very boisterous, and even threatened to ill-treat us, but by God's help we returned home in safety. All this shows a want of respect for Christianity on the part of the people; still I think there is much cause for encouragement and gratitude. When I contrast the present state of public feeling in respect to our holy religion with what it was about nine years ago, there is every reason to thank God and take courage. Nine years since, while I was in Madras studying, I remember preaching to the heathen occasionally, and the opposition I then met with was something awful. The people would not receive Christian books and tracts even when we gave them gratis; but now many people buy them readily, and read them carefully. We never give away a single tract gratis. Some of them listen most attentively, and argue very fairly and rationally on the subjects which we bring for their consideration and reception.

5. "Any spread of female education, any breaking down of caste prejudices?"

I may safely affirm that female education is spreading, chiefly through the agency of Missionary Societies. Of all the religious bodies, the Church Missionary Society takes a most prominent part in disseminating knowledge among the girls of a lower grade, both Christians and heathen, while the Free Church Mission takes a similar part in extending this blessing to the high-caste girls, chiefly heathen. There is a Society called the Native-Female Education Society, composed of European ladies of rank, who are interested in the spread of female education. This Society co-operates with the Church Missionary Society, and is eminently successful in conferring the boon upon a large number of poor children. There are two central schools, one in Black Town and the other at Chindatrepettah, in connexion with this Society, where there are about 230 children receiving a sound elementary education. The number of girls belonging to poorer classes, chiefly Pariahs, both Christian and heathen, receiving Christian education in schools belonging to all Societies, may be estimated at 800, and the number of high-caste heathen girls in all schools is about 650, of whom about 420 girls belong to the Free-Church Mission. Our Society had no caste-girl school whatever till last year, when my wife, impelled by a desire to do good to her heathen countrywomen, began one of her own accord on a small scale. This is the only school to which our Society can point throughout South India for the education of high-caste girls, if, perhaps, we except a similar school at Chindatrepettah, under the management of the Native-Female Education Ladies' Committee. This is a school started about a year since by Mrs. Winslow, the wife of the late Dr. Winslow, an American Missionary of happy memory in Madras, and was transferred to the Ladies' Committee on Mrs. Winslow leaving India about six months ago.

While the Missionary Societies are thus endeavouring to promote female education, the Hindus are not altogether indifferent about it. Time was when they were perfectly apathetic in the matter, but now the most enlightened of them manifest a desire to educate their female as well as male children. To quote the Baboo again—"In the midst of so much orthodoxy," he says, "it is cheering to notice the progress which female education is making in Madras, while the comparative liberty which the females enjoy there is something really astonishing. These signs of enlightenment are not, however, the results of English education, nor the upshot of western civilization: they are, on the contrary, the established usages of the country, and indicate the primitive character of Hindu society."

I concur in the views expressed by the Baboo in regard to the spread of female education in Madras, though I do not agree with him in saying that it is not the result of the labours of European Christians. There are thirteen schools in the city of Madras, established by the Hindus themselves for the education of their female children. The number of girls receiving education in these schools is about 400. This speaks well for the Hindus of Madras, and is an indubitable proof of enlightenment on their part. I do not mean to say that it is as it ought to be. There are still mighty obstacles in the way of female education, arising from inveterate prejudice, caste, and custom, on the part of the majority of people, chiefly women; but what I do say is, that a day of better things is beginning to dawn, and I believe that, before long, the Hindus will feel it their duty to spread female education to the extent of their power. Even in the Mofussil there are signs of improvement in this respect. At Madura, a town noted for its orthodoxy, bigotry, and conservatism, there is a school opened by native officials for the education of females; and it is in reference to this that my brother, Joseph Cornelius, writes as follows in his journal—"Among other things I witnessed in Madura, my attention was particularly drawn to a Hindu female school, altogether conducted by Hindus, with two schoolmistresses from Madras, and a schoolmaster. I was asked to examine the girls. They are taught reading, geography, sewing, arithmetic, &c. This augurs well for India. It will not be long before her daughters are delivered from the thraldom in which they have been hitherto lying. When knowledge prevails, ignorance, the mother of superstition, will fly away. From such facts India's friends may well take courage."

I must now proceed to answer your inquiry regarding caste. The spirit of caste is gradually wearing away, while the form is kept up with great pretensions. Among the educated classes there are many who care very little about caste, and who show a great desire to break its fetters, and yet they retain its form for the sake of conformity with the usages of the country. Purushotam Mudali, who lately visited England, and who conceived the extravagant notion of building a heathen temple in the metropolis of Great Britain, is a type of this class. I have little doubt but that he detests caste from the bottom of his heart, seeing the many evils which it entails on those who are under its influence; but still he does not renounce it *in toto*, simply because he thinks that, if he did so, he would not command the respect of his orthodox countrymen. There are many of his stamp among the educated natives in Madras. They disregard the performance of many of the religious duties belonging to their respective castes, and endeavour to promote the re-marriage of widows, and discourage the early marriages of their children. They sometimes have social meetings, at which they partake of food promiscuouly, although they belong to different castes. They sometimes invite even some respectable native Christians to such gatherings. I do not say that the Madrassees are so far advanced in this as their bolder brethren at Calcutta. Compared with Bengal, Madras is still the "benighted Presidency," not only as regards learning and wealth, but also in respect to civilization and social improvement. Still I have reason to believe that the tide of change and advancement has set in here, and that it will, ere long, sweep away the barriers which stand in the way of India's reformation.

I am, however, grieved to say that the Government is not so helpful as it might be in bringing about this state of things. True, it is doing a noble work in educating the people, and thus indirectly helping forward the country's reformation; but by a strange and mistaken policy, it has put its ban upon the Bible. "Every thing but the best thing" seems to be its motto. Education is given in all branches of western science, but the divine science of the Bible has no place whatever in its curriculum. Not only is the Bible thus studiously excluded from the Government system of education, but it seems that no allusion, however remote, can be made to it, and no attack, however feeble, can be made on caste by any individual, in a public manner, with impunity. Mr. Richards, one of the Government Chaplains, and a Fellow of the Madras University, in his address to the graduates who took the degree of B.A. the other day, made a passing allusion to the Bible and caste; and yet the address, though an able and an excellent one, has been condemned by a majority of Fellows in the Senate, all of whom are high in position, and the usual rule has been set aside in refusing to request its publication. Perhaps the insertion of those passages in Mr. Richards' address may not be out of place here. He says—

"Your almost sole benefactor hitherto is the Government; and now what are the ends of Government herein? You have doubtless sufficiently studied the British character to know that there is at the heart of the British nation, in spite of all that may sometimes seem to belie it, a genuine, simple, earnest desire to benefit the races of men with whom the providence of God has brought us in contact, to raise and improve their condition as best we may. You have also been taught clearly to perceive what are the obstacles to improvement on the part of your fellow-countrymen, that they are evils for which education is the only remedy,—ignorance, prejudice, blind submission to custom, and that fearful system of caste which darkens the whole land, holding the masses in the most abject thraldom, and crushing every upward tendency of their nature. I believe the British Government hoped, in giving you a large and liberal education, to enlist your hearty services in making war on these gigantic evils."

In reference to the Bible, he makes the following observations in the last paragraph of the address—

"Gentlemen,—I have just one word more to say. I have intimated that it was the discovery of the records of a former civilization which quickened Europe into intellectual life; but there was one record which contributed more to this grand result than all the rest put together, and that was the Bible. The same dead and forgotten language, in which lay buried treasures of Grecian art and literature, had also entombed the originals of the Bible, and it was its translation into the mother tongues of England and Germany that, beyond all other causes, tended not only to the development of those languages, but the formation of the English mind and the German mind. Hence western civilization in its best aspects; hence also western science; for it was the knowledge of the Bible which set free the human mind, emancipating it from the long thraldom of a false philosophy, and started it upon its new career of discovery. Why should I hesitate to speak to you about the Bible? It is the greatest fact in the world's history. I hesitate not, indeed, to avow my entire concurrence with the policy which determined that it was not to enter into the course of instruction provided in the institutions of Government; but, at the same time, I avow my opinion, that this has been to your loss. Gentlemen, I am constrained to remind to you that there has been just one defect in your education—an unavoidable defect, I admit, under the circumstances of the case—it is, that no provision has been made for the development of the higher and nobler part of your being. Be assured that, after all, literature can do but little, physical science can do less, to satisfy the cravings of your higher nature. I can only express my most earnest and ardent hope that, through some other agency, you may have the want supplied."

What is in all this, I ask, which could give offence to a Christian Government or a University chiefly composed of Christian gentlemen? I think that Mr. Richards' allusion to the Bible was very meagre, and his statement, that the Government is right in excluding it is not what I am prepared to admit; and yet the whole address was unceremoniously thrown away, because it contained a few commonplace remarks on the Bible and caste. The policy of Government seems to me to be suicidal. It promotes education on every hand, but "knowledge is power." Like a two-edged sword, it may cut either way. Knowledge unrestrained by moral or religious principle is more likely to become potent for evil than for good. It may lead them to rebel against the lawful Government, and to the commission of such atrocities and brutalities as a Nana alone is capable of perpetrating. But the Government, by a strange infatuation, does not see its own interests and advantages. The knowledge of the Bible will arm the people for war against superstition, custom, and caste, which tend to the prostration of India's mind, and the thraldom of ages to which she has been subject. Even the Hindus see and acknowledge this in terms more decided than Mr. Richards', especially in reference to caste, which, like the deadly Upas, spreads its noxious and blighting influence far and wide over this benighted land, and renders it a waste moral wilderness, where "all life dies, and death itself lives." I beg to introduce a passage from the writings of a learned and an enlightened Hindu, which will show how even the Hindus deplore the evils of caste, and how they devoutly wish for that time when this hydra-headed system of caste shall be swept away from India—

"Though not myself a Christian, in marshalling arguments against the institution of castes, I cannot well overlook the beautiful doctrines of that revelation, which makes no distinction but between the virtuous and the vicious, recognises no uncleanness but that of the heart, and invites the poorest and the proudest to one common heaven. The heaven of the Hindus, like their earth, is made for Brahmins alone, and, before the soul can wing its flight thither, it must, as a general rule, have passed its Brahminical birth. But the religion of the Gospel inculcates doctrines of a different character. Is thy soul athirst for God? Dost thou pant after Him as the hart panteth after the water-brooks? Have the words of the law been a lamp unto thy feet, and a light unto thy path? If so, be of good cheer, whoever thou art, it matters not if thou art Jew or Gentile—the gates of heaven shall be open to let thee in. Christianity everywhere recognises the equality of mankind. The rich and the poor meet together, it says, for the Lord is the maker of them all; and it tells us to be as brothers to each other, to love our neighbours as we love ourselves, and to do to others as we would be done by. How does all this contrast with the injunctions of caste, which declare to the Brahmin that he is God's vicegerent upon earth, and that he must not pollute himself by coming into too close contact with his neighbours; and to the Sudra that servitude is his portion through life, and that he must invariably look up to the higher classes with reverence and fear." Let this speak for itself.

6. "Are the native Christians becoming bolder, more independent, more feeling themselves to be a distinct body?"

I may answer this question by a "Yes." In thought and feeling they are much more decided and independent than before, but in action they are not so. The majority are poor, consequently they have no social status. They are hardly recognised by Government, nor owned by the Hindus. Their poverty, their fewness in number, and their ignorance are some of the causes why they occupy such a low place in the scale of society. True, there are some Christians who fill respectable positions in Government, such as native judges, collectors, surgeons, &c., but unfortunately these are men who do not present a bold front, nor act as centres of influence and light to their heathen countrymen. However high they may be for official fitness, they do not shine as Christians. Being surrounded by influences hostile to Christianity and the growth of personal piety, their course is marked by declension in spirituality, and even by a want of honesty and integrity in the discharge of their duties. Their temptation is to imitate their fellow-heathen officials, and sacrifice truth and moral probity. There are a few honourable exceptions, but this, I think, is the general rule.

Add to this the influence of caste, to which so many are still subject. I grieve to think that there are a great many who boast more of their caste than of their Christianity. The Jaffna Christians, of whom there are some in Madras in high situations under Government, are emphatically so. Most of them are able men, the graduates of the University, and well versed in mathematics, physics, metaphysics, &c., but they are ignorant of the A B C of Christianity. Some of them are avowed heathen, and none of them are Christians beyond the bare name and profession. The native Christians belonging to the Leipsic Lutheran Mission are also of this description. It is a melancholy fact, that while the other Societies are waging war against caste, and are striving to uproot it from the church, the Lutheran Society tolerates and fosters it. All caste Christians find an asylum in this caste-tolerating Society, as it may be called. The consequences are obvious. There is no bond of union between these Christians and others who have no caste, or renounced it. No wonder, then, that such Christians fail to manifest a real concern for the salvation of their countrymen, or any feelings of patriotism or philanthropy so essential for the spontaneous outgoings of a loving heart, or for any bold action on the side of humanity and truth. These remarks are applicable only to caste-keeping Christians and others whose religion is not of a high order. There are some Christians in connexion with every Society who have a real desire to benefit their countrymen, and extend the Redeemer's kingdom in this dark land.

7. "Among the native Protestants, is there much sectarian animosity or denominational jealousy, or do they feel themselves to be one body in Christ; and is there any prospect of the rise (in the good sense of the words) of an Indian Catholic church?"

I am very happy to be able to state that among the native Christians there is no such thing as sectarian animosity or denominational jealousy. The Lord has graciously preserved his infant church in India from this evil; for I consider it an evil, inasmuch as it has an injurious effect upon others. There is too much of this spirit among many European Christians, which unfortunately tends to mar that union, sympathy, and co-operation which ought to exist among the disciples of the Lord Jesus. However faulty the character of the native Christians may be in other respects, in this matter I may thankfully mention they are free from blame. Most of them being converts to Christianity, their sympathies and views run in the same direction. I think a good deal of sectarian spirit is the result of education and early association, but the education which the native Christians receive, being of a general character, this result is absent. Consequently they feel to be one body in Christ, and manifest a common interest in the cause of their common Master and Redeemer. Of course I am now speaking only of real native Christians. This is the place for me to introduce a brief account of the Satthia Veda Somajam, or the true Veda Society. This is an Association formed by the leading native Christians of Madras, belonging to almost all religious Societies, whose object is to "help forward the religious, moral, and social progress of the Hindus, by means of lectures, discussions, and occasional tracts, in English and the vernaculars, based on sound Bible principles." This was got up principally with a view to counteract the influence of the Veda Somajam, already alluded to, and to place the truths of Christianity before the mind of the educated natives. Several leading European gentlemen take a real interest in the Somajam, of whom the Lord Bishop and his able and excellent chaplain, Mr. Smith, and the venerable the Archdeacon, are the most prominent. They have delivered lectures on behalf of this Somajam, adapted to the mind of the educated Hindus. Mr. Smith has delivered a course of lectures on the Bible, and conducted the "Satthia Dwajam," or "Banner of Truth," the organ of the Somajam, in an efficient and admirable manner, but he leaves for England next month, and it will be a loss to the Somajam, and, indeed, to the whole country. All this will show that there is a real union among native Christians of different Societies, and that they endeavour to exercise an influence for good among their countrymen. This is certainly a hopeful sign; but nevertheless I am not in a position to give an affirmative answer to your question regarding the Indian Catholic church. My feeling is that the prospect is yet far distant in the future. Neither the numerical strength nor the social importance of the native Christians is such as to warrant a speedy realization of this desired object. The native Christians, as a rule, are still in a state of pupilage and dependence. Those elements are wanting in their education which will advance them socially and intellectually among their countrymen, and ultimately end in their freedom and independence.

The Hindus are making rapid progress in intellectual attainments, and if the native Christians do not keep pace with them, they will be left in the back-ground. I think that friend is right, to whom Mr. Thomas alludes in his report, as having made the following remark—"If you keep back your people from a knowledge of English, they will be found, some years hence, infinitely distanced by their fellow-countrymen in knowledge, status, and influence." This has always been my view of the case. India is in a transition state. Western science and western civilization affect the whole current of public thought and feeling. Inveterate prejudices are removed, time-honoured institutions fall before the march of intellect and civilization. Every thing indicates progress and improvement. If the native Christians do not, by their knowledge and attainments, rise to the exigencies of the age, they will not only sink in the estimation of their heathen countrymen, but will also fail to exercise that moral influence over them which, as Christians, they ought to do. You will think that I am a strong advocate for English education. And so I am. I feel persuaded that nothing short of a thorough sound English education, combined with a complete knowledge of the vernacular, will answer the objects contemplated by the church. At present there is not a superior educational institution in the Madras Presidency: the Government schools and colleges impart superior secular education; but I mean an institution which combines this education with a sound biblical instruction, similar, perhaps, to the college which has just been opened by our Society at Calcutta. Such an institution will answer two important purposes: it will be the means of giving a liberal education to native Christians, which is a great *desideratum*, and scriptural education to the Hindus. Such an education to Hindus is a crying want of India. The secular education they receive from Government re-acts injuriously, not only on their own minds, but on the country in general, and unless counteracted by a Christian institution of superior pretentions, it may ultimately lead to dangerous results.

I fear my letter has run to a great and tedious length, and must therefore draw it to a close. On taking a calm and dispassionate view of the subject of the letter, I think that the one word by which it may be characterized is *progress* — progress in material prosperity, progress in railway and telegraphic communications, progress in intellectual attainments, and progress in Christian institutions. The view that may be taken of all this may be different in different cases. The statesman may be satisfied with improvements in the administration of the country; the philosopher may be satisfied with the progress of arts and sciences; the patriot may be satisfied with the outward freedom and prosperity of his country; but the Christian views every thing from a peculiar stand-point and in the light of eternity. He sees in the progress of knowledge a fulfilment of prophecy. "Many shall run to and fro, and knowledge shall be increased." He rejoices in every change which tends to the elevation of his race; he hails every improvement and every upward and onward movement; but never will he be satisfied until he sees his dear Redeemer's kingdom stretch from pole to pole, and until all the nations of the earth are brought to know Him, and crown Him Lord of all. This is the consummation that he is devoutly wishing for, praying for, labouring for. May the Lord pour down his Holy Spirit upon his church and the heathen world, and make his arm bare in the sight of nations, so that they may all know Him, from the least to the greatest, and find pardon, peace, light, and life in Him!

No one, we think, can rise from the perusal of this paper without feeling persuaded that the present condition of India is one of the deepest interest. The development of that great country under western influences is decisive and rapid; and the convictions which we gather from this document are strengthened by the fact, that it is not from Calcutta, where the process of assimilation is strongest, but from Madras, where it is weakest, that the survey has been made. Material improvements are progressing. The great Trunk Road from Calcutta to the north-west, and the use of horses instead of bearers, were welcomed as evidences of advancing civilization; but now the railway, with its inflexible regulations, has come into action, and caste is found to be an incumbrance and discomfort. Native intellect, roused up from the torpor of ages, is thoroughly awake, and, with remarkable acuteness, is applying itself to the acquisition of western knowledge. What need is there not of Christianity to regulate the national movement, and teach men how to use aright the new powers they have attained? The danger is, lest secular knowledge so far outstrips the onward movement of Christianity as to work mischief before overtaken by the higher influence; and the danger is increased by the fact, that while Government applies all its power to the acceleration of the one, it stands aloof from the efforts which are promotive of the other. There is the more need, then, for private enterprises of the true Christian character. Christianity has gained a footing in India, that country of strong prejudices and ancient superstitions. It has won the attention of the natives, and, commending itself to their esteem, is being increasingly and respectfully regarded. The present moment is opportune for work

—a time not to slacken but to intensify our efforts. Yet at such a crisis pecuniary means are wanting, and the Church Missionary Society, its Indian fund exhausted, and its ordinary income unequal to the existing expenditure, is compelled to stay the extension of its operations.

That, if we had the means, the men would not be wanting, is evident from the paper which we have just submitted to our readers. Addressing ourselves on a point like this to influenced Christians exclusively, we must remind them that the gifts which are needful to qualify a church for usefulness, are not produced by the force of intellect, but the gifts of the administrating Spirit, in answer to prayer and the diligent use of appointed means. "There are diversities of gifts, but the same Spirit. And there are differences of administrations, but the same Lord. And there are diversities of operations, but it is the same God which worketh in all." When, in the midst of a heathen nation, a Christian church has been raised up, He who formed it will not fail to furnish it with all the gifts and appliances which may be needful to render it, in the midst of that nation, an evangelizing church.

Only let us not hinder its growth by undue caution, and render it weak and dependent by affording it no scope for the exercise of its powers. Complete the organization of the native churches, and, by the blessing of God, they will do their work. Give them not only the native pastorate, but the native episcopate. As the proper juncture arrives, let them be set free, as the native church in Western Africa has been set free, and we shall soon see them in healthful evangelizing action.

Recent Intelligence.

NEW ZEALAND.

The following extracts from various letters and journals will place before our readers the details of intelligence from this distracted Mission.

First, we introduce some from the correspondence of the Bishop of Waiapu, in which he describes the proceedings of the Pai Marire after Mr. Volkner's death, and the position in which he found himself—

Turanga, March 25, 1865.

The accompanying notes will give you some idea of our present position. Our three families all sleep under my roof, and the house is guarded through the night by men under arms. The cause for apprehension is the near position of Mr. Volkner's murderers; and so long as they are in the neighbourhood, we shall feel it necessary to watch. But a sad feature of this case is, that the natives who ought to be rallying around us are those who are led away by these fanatics. We are, therefore, left to ourselves, and, with two exceptions, there are only the men belonging to the school who are with us. It might be supposed that perhaps there had been a long-existing alienation of these natives from among us, but the contrary is the case: there has existed a most friendly feeling. I believe, too, that the Whakatohea had a very kindly regard for poor Mr. Volkner up to the time of the arrival of these Pai Marire. This fanatical delusion is clearly a device of Satan. The form which they have prepared for worship is a most miserable attempt—a few sacred words, which are blasphemously mixed up with a large amount of nonsense. There is no attempt at system, no doctrine, no deliverance from sin, no salvation; but these forms are put together, and are repeated for the present with an amount of earnestness which works wonderfully upon the feelings. There is also the practice of, I fancy, a mesmeric influence, or of electro-biology, which, upon weak and superstitious minds, leads to a belief of something supernatural. They have trifled with things sacred, and God seems to have sent among them strong delusion that they should believe a lie. But it is not here only that these extravagances are rife. When you have in Protestant England, and among those who have been instructed with great care, a disposition to fall into the abominable superstition of Popery, we need not wonder at what happens in New Zealand. The great moving principle of Pai Marire is, that it is a scheme which promises a successful termination of the war with which we are afflicted; and it is mixed up with an amount of abomination which is meant to draw out the vilest passions of our sinful nature. Happily the time is short. He who said, "Lo, I come quickly," is nigh at hand. He has given us the sign of his coming, and we may almost, now in the time of trouble, lift up our heads; our deliverance is nigh.

Journal of proceedings relative to the Taranaki fanatics who visited Opotiki.

March 1—Harawhira Te Nahu came early to my house to say that a messenger had come from Opotiki, bringing letters from Mohi Tamate, a Turanga native, and from Henare Parekura: two of these were for me, and stated that Pai Marire, from Taranaki were at Opotiki; that Mr. Grace's house at Taupo, and Mr. Volkner's at Opotiki, had been plundered, and all the property sold by auction; also that these natives were on their way to this place for the purpose of making Hirini Te Kani king. There was some excitement through the day, and in the evening the runanga met at Pohoo Mahaki. There was a good assemblage, but the people from Waikato were not present, owing to the want of early information. The character of the speaking was very good; all against the proceedings of these people. Manihera, the messenger, was called upon to give his statement, and confirmed all that the letters contained, and intimates that all the Whakatohea had joined this delusion. Addressing me, he said, "We received our Christianity from you formerly, and now we give it you back again, having found some better way, by which we may be able to keep possession of our country." As he had made no mention of what they proposed to do with the white people, I said, "Now don't be afraid of speaking openly before me. Whether it is good or bad, let us hear what you think of doing with the Pakeha." He replied, "The orders of Horopapera are, that all the Pakeha shall be killed, whether they are clergymen or laymen." "Very good," I said; "we now have a clear understanding of the matter."

March 6—It was near ten o'clock at night when Wi Pere came to tell me that Aperahama Tutoko had just arrived from Opotiki, and stated that "Mr. Volkner and Mr. Grace had arrived at Opotiki; that Mr. Volkner, and one hundred persons from on board the vessel, had been killed; and that the Tiu of Horopapera were on their way to this place, bringing with them the head of Mr. Volkner, and also that Mr. Grace was being brought as a prisoner with another white man." Messengers were despatched immediately to Whakato and to Turanganui, to call the people together. It was also said that Aperahama had a special charge from Mohi Tamatia of this place, who is at Opotiki, to tell Horomona secretly what had happened, and recommend that all the white inhabitants should get out of the way for the time, until these Tiu are off the ground.

March 7—At nine o'clock I was talking with two of our friends from the coast, who came last night, when a party of twelve, nearly all leading men from Whakato, came up to the back of the house. While they were there having breakfast, others were collecting rapidly on the lawn in front, and soon there was a large assemblage. They were come to give expression to their feelings, and to take counsel. The first speaker was

Paraone Te Hinake.—His opinion was, that the strangers should not be allowed to come nearer than Taureka, which is about two miles off. That if they were persons we could approve of, we should treat them with hospitality; but that now they should return from thence to Opotiki.

Rev. Hare Tawhaa said if these people had gone to Waiapu, or to Lokomaru, they would have found natives of like mind with themselves; but that they had no business at Turanga.

Renatu Te Atopaki.—"If we reject this new superstition, these our Pakehas, and ourselves, will be safe; but if we trifle with it, and give it any countenance, we shall then destroy them and ourselves."

Kerehona Pirraka.—"The object of these people is evident: they have been trying for a long period to induce Turanga to take up the quarrel with the Pakeha; but having failed, they wish now to persuade us to join them in murder, and to elect Kirini as king, in order that we may be involved in one common trouble."

Anaru Matete.—"There is no reason for the bishop to move: let him and all the Pakeha remain quiet. We will, in the mean time, go up to Taureka, and hear further particulars from this messenger."

Tamiti Ta Rangi.—"Let the bishop remain quiet where he is; and as for the proposal to elect a king, we will not hear of it: it would only be a cause of evil."

Whiteriki Oikau, a person of inferior importance, spoke of the great power of the Tiu, and that, though there were 500 here to protect me, it would be of no avail against the thirty Tiu.

This sentiment met with no favour from the meeting: they looked upon him as a man under a delusion. There were a few others who volunteered their advice that I should move out of the way. To this I replied that we had abundant proof that Tius are subject to all the casualties of flesh and blood, like other people; that, some months ago, a party of one hundred, under one of their leaders, went to Wanganui to cut off the white people; that they were met by Wanganui natives, and were all killed; and that, a few weeks ago, at Waitotara, some of the same parties rushed madly on the soldiers, believing themselves to be invulnerable, when seventy-seven of their number were killed. I added, that the assurance of the natives of this place was quite sufficient to remove any grounds of uneasiness on my part.

March 11—After three days of suspense, during which we had serious misgivings whether these fanatics would come at all into this district, and consequently whether Mr. Grace might not be left indefinitely to their tender mercies, news was brought at sunset that this party is at Waikohu, up the valley, and that they may be here to-morrow. Messengers were at once sent off to bring the natives together. Raharuhi was hesitating about bringing the people upon Sunday; but I wrote decidedly to them to leave at daybreak. It is reported that Mr. Grace is left behind.

March 12: *Lord's-day*—I went out at daybreak, but all was very quiet; but presently a woman came into the yard for water, who told me that a number of the older people had come up in the night, and that the body of the natives were to leave at daylight. Went after breakfast to Te Pohoo Mahaki, to see those who had arrived, and settled that we would wait till the rest of the people had come up. At about half-past eight a cloud of dust announced their near approach, and presently about 250 armed men marched up in the greatest order. It was a new sight for Turanga, which had not been seen for five-and-twenty years—men under arms, and that, too, on the Sabbath-day. Preparations had been made for our friends, and, with the help of 200 lbs. of bread from the school, they were soon refreshed. We then had service under the trees, and all was as quiet as though there had been no excitement. On the 11th of March, last year, our friend Volkner arrived from Opotiki, to attend the Synod. He came through the forest by the same road which his murderers have now traversed. He interested us much by his lively account of the natives at Opotiki, and of the painful excitement through which he had passed on occasion of their determining to go off to Waikato to join Tamihana. Now, at our English service, I had the painful circumstances of his cruel death to allude to. But he has joined the company of those who, having come out of great tribulation, have washed their robes, and made them white in the blood of the Lamb, and are now before the throne of God. Heard in the evening that this party is to be at Taureka to breakfast, which is distant about two miles.

March 14—The whole body of our natives, perhaps about 600, went to Taureka. It was understood that, when they had an interview, the chief Hirini was to require their return from this place. After the usual ceremony of speaking had been gone through, the meeting was broken up in confusion, and, by a preconcerted plan, these fanatics were invited to go to other villages, to be there treated with hospitality. I was also told that the tribe Te Whanau Kai are intending to receive this new abomination, and that there is a general disposition to fraternize with these wretches. I wrote a very strong letter to the runanga, and my son wrote another, which I committed to Tamihana Rutapa, one of the leading men. I told them that if they follow out this course, and unite themselves with murderers, I will at once leave them. Went to the runanga's house, which is close by, and found the people much cast down by the aspect of affairs. Poor old Raharuhi said, "You will not go: I will send these people away myself."

March 16—These fanatics having said much about their power to work miracles, and, among other things, being able to draw ships on shore, a native went to them this morning and gave them a fair challenge to drag on shore a steamer now at anchor. This led to a thorough discomfiture of the party, and they decamped in great anger to the village they slept at the preceding night, where they have met with more favour. It is said they wait there until they are joined by a party of their friends, who are daily expected by way of Wairoa.

April 1—These Pai Marire are still here, and have done an immense amount of evil. They have worked upon the minds of many weak natives, and some of those in whom we placed the greatest confidence have been led away.

The Government have most kindly responded to our call. First H.M.S. "Eclipse" came with Bishop Selwyn. Then the steamer "Lady Bird" followed, to render any assistance that might be required. But at that time there was a better prospect.

We then concluded that the children and the females should be sent away, so as to leave those who remain less embarrassed.

This was about to have been done to-day, by a sailing vessel belonging to this place. In the mean time the Government have sent the steamer "St. Kilda," and the party will go off in her to Napier. There will then remain Mrs. Williams and myself, my son Leonard, and Mr. and Mrs. Clarke, and two of my daughters. If then there should be a sudden alarm from a distance, we shall be in a position to move from our present residence to a part of the bay where natives can be relied on.

In the mean time the Lord of Hosts is with us, the God of Jacob is our refuge. He will, I doubt not, overrule all that is now passing to the furtherance of the Gospel.

This Pai Marire is a deeply-laid scheme of the devil, whom God will bruise under our feet shortly.

The object they had in coming over to this side of the island is this—They have been beaten in Waikato; they had before them the prospect of being beaten between Taranaki and Wanganui; and they were anxious to look out for a convenient retreat. They fancy they can find this here, and they talk of coming back with 600 men shortly; but should they do so, they will find themselves met by stout opposition from the Government. The natives are much to be pitied; but they have allowed themselves to be brought under this delusion in the face of the clearest warning.

April 5 -- Napier. On the 1st, we were under serious apprehension. These fanatics were living within two miles of us, under the countenance of the natives. The murderer of Mr. Volkner had made no scruple to avow his wishes respecting myself. The principal natives, who had stood up boldly in opposition at first, were now being drawn under the evil influence. Patara, a most designing, artful man, who professed to disapprove of the murder, but was most undoubtedly privy to, and approving the whole transaction, had contrived to insinuate himself into the good opinion of those leading men; and a few days ago he called at the stores of some of the settlers, under the escort of those chiefs, professedly for the purpose of assuring them that there was no reason for apprehension on their part; but on this occasion he made use of most insulting language, which amounted to a threat to treat them with violence on the return of these fanatics. This he did in the presence of the chief, and therefore with their sanction. This proceeding was sufficient to alarm the settlers generally, and several families were leaving on the 1st. On the 2nd, which was Sunday, we received a further intimation, which arose out of the arrival of a party from Otaki, who had been long expected as visitors here. The chief man of the party is Wi Tako, a man well disposed to the Government, and taking a strong view against these Pai Marire. He reprobated strongly the vacillating policy of the Tauranga natives. This expression aroused the worst feelings of the fanitics, and they prepared at once to act on the defensive, and threatened to make a general raid upon the white inhabitants. The friendly natives advised that we should at once remove out of the way. I was prepared to leave our home, and go and occupy our old station, among natives more to be depended upon, and there to watch proceedings. It was finally concluded that all the females should be removed, and that only my son Leonard, with Mr. Samuel Williams, and one of my nephews, should remain and watch the course of events. On the afternoon of the next day, the 3rd, I left in the steamer "St. Kilda," which had been kindly sent by the Government to look after the refugees. Our party consisted of nineteen, including Mr. and Mrs. E. Clarke. The prospect for the natives is very gloomy. If they persist in following the blind course which they now have taken up, they must come into collision with the Government. A meeting was to have been held yesterday, and I hope that the influence of the chief Wi Tako may induce them to retrace their steps. It is a sad conclusion, after twenty-five years of labour, to be obliged then to leave; but God has his own design to accomplish, and we know that the end will be his glory. We start for Auckland on Friday.

We add to these an account of the proceedings in the Turanga district, written by the Rev. S. Williams, and addressed to the Superintendent of Hawke's Bay—

Turanga, April 20, 1865.

SIR,—I have the honour to inform you that the Hau-hau, which, up to the 31st ult., were fast gaining ground, and, only a week since, were making use of very insolent and defiant language, have, to say the least, received a most decided check.

Their arguments have been thoroughly confuted, and the falsehood of their statements with reference to the success of their party, as well as their unfounded claim to supernatural power, have been completely exposed.

Kereopa had been so well received that he was expected at Makaraka, in company with some of the Turanga chiefs, to have his likeness taken, when the news of our arrival induced him to keep in the back ground; and after threatening to gratify his cannibal appetite upon Wi Tako, as well as upon the clergy, he left the district on the 5th inst., much discouraged and alarmed. Patara, who found it convenient to disclaim any connexion with the Opotiki murder, and pretended to condemn Kereopa's proceedings, was using every means in his power to establish himself in the district, and to push his way to the Ngatiparou at Waiapu and the Kauakaua.

The Taitanga-a-Mahaki Hau-hau were determined, in defiance of all that was said in opposition, to bring Patara forward at the Waerengaahika runanga; but, upon reaching the spot on the 10th inst., and finding that the friendly natives would not meet him, they made use of most violent threats against all strangers and sympathizers with the Government, and then retired. Most of them, however, returned on the following morning, without Patara and the rest of the Taranaki party; and, at the termination of the meeting, it was evident that what had been said had made a most decided impression, for there was a marked change in their tone and manner. Several of them have since left the Hau-hau, among whom is Henare Ruru, one of their most influential men, and who has openly denounced their proceedings. The manner in which they ran from Whakato when challenged to draw the "Lady Bird" on shore; their failure in attempting to get the "Eclipse" ashore at Opotiki; as well as the failure of the Urewera and Wairoa party in attempting to draw the "St. Kilda" ashore at Whareongeongo, have been constantly cast in their teeth in not very complimentary language. Patara evidently found the ground breaking from under him, and he left Taureka on Sunday last for the Bay of Plenty.

At the Whakato runanga the constant cry of the natives was, "Stop the war, or every corner of the island will soon be in arms." The reply was, "How can you speak of peace when you have been encouraging people in your district who are not only Hau-haus, but murderers of innocent Europeans? Had you apprehended these murderers upon their reaching this place, and handed them up to the authorities, you would have distinguished yourselves, and might have obtained a hearing." The residents again said, "Stop the war, and the Hau-hau may soon die out. It is only supported by sympathy for the people who are being slain, and for the land which is being taken from them. As for the murder, let the Governor arrange that at Opotiki." To this it was replied, "You are putting the cart before the horse. First give up the murderers and put down the Hau-hau, and then talk of peace."

The extraordinary amount of suspicion which was exhibited by many towards every thing that had been said or done by the English, and as to their ultimate intentions with regard to the native race, was most painful to witness; but the testimony borne by the Otaki and Ahuriri chiefs to the truth of the statement, that it was not the wish of the English to exterminate the Maoris and deprive them of their land, but that, on the contrary, a very kindly feeling had all along been manifested towards them (murderers excluded), and that the Government would rejoice at the prospect of peace if it could be secured on a satisfactory basis, appeared to have a very great effect in restoring confidence and allaying irritation of feeling. After considerable discussion, it was arranged that if the Hau-hau were expelled from the district, a general meeting should be called at Ahuriri, as being the most central spot, to which the leaders of the tribes now in arms against the Government should be invited to discuss the terms of peace.

I cannot speak too highly of the valuable assistance which has been rendered by Wi Tako, Matene te Whiwhi, and their party, who came up with me in the "St. Kilda," in checking the advance of the Hau-hau, and in keeping the peace of the district during the recent crisis; for there is little doubt that, but for their presence, and the exertions they have made, Kereopa and Patara would by this time have had the whole district under their command.

Since the departure of the Taranaki, party I have visited Taureka and Oatutahi, the head-quarters of the Hau-hau, in company with Archdeacon W. L. Williams and some of the friendly chiefs, where we were treated with great civility. The people generally appeared ashamed of their late conduct; and from the way in which the principal men expressed themselves, I am led to the conclusion that their attachment to the Hau-hau religion is not very deeply rooted, but that, on the contrary, its influence is already declining. From these considerations I am encouraged to hope that there need be no apprehension of any immediate disturbance in this district.

It is only just to state that there were some of the Taitanga-a-Mahaki tribe who were deeply grieved at the conduct of their own people, and who would, I believe, have been ready, if it had been necessary, to risk their own lives in defence of the bishop and his family.

In conclusion, I would remark that the fact of the bishop having left the district, as he did under such trying circumstances, had a most salutary effect in inducing the natives to reconsider the position in which they were placing themselves, and was a powerful lever in the hands of those who were trying to expel the murderers from the district, and to put down the Hau-hau.

The following suggestions are from the pen of one of our correspondents—

Auckland, May 5, 1865.

The political aspect of the country is deplorable. The real cause of nearly all our troubles appears to be our having had a constitutional Government at least thirty years too soon. It looks very doubtful whether any thing but an absolute Government will be able to extricate us from our present difficulties. The natives have lost all confidence, and are worked up to desperation, while Europeans appear equally desperate and most unreasonable. Our basis of Government, since 1854, has been, in a great measure, unsound and unjust, and we are now reaping the consequence of our doings.

The prospect before the natives appears to be extermination. If this be the case, can any thing be done to prevent it? I feel that something may even yet be done. The first step should be an *absolute Government*, which many, even here, are beginning to feel will have to be resorted to.

Next, if the home Government would determine to try separation, and give up the idea of amalgamation, and determine that certain native districts should be proclaimed, in which no land should be sold to Europeans, and in which no Europeans or traders would be allowed to settle, there would still be hope, and every reason to believe that we should save and civilize and christianize a large remnant of this race.

The first district thus proclaimed might take in the whole of the Waiapu diocese, with a little more. I would carry the boundary-line from where it now starts to the north-east of Tauranga to a mountainous range on the west side of Taupo, a principal point of which is called Titiraupinga; from thence along the summit of the range to Ruapaha; and then, turning eastward, strike the north bank of the Mohaka river at Tarawera; and from thence follow the east bank of the river to the sea. If Tauranga should fall into the hands of Europeans, I would commence the line half-way between Tauranga and Maketu.

There might also be two other smaller native districts, one from the heads of the Wanganui, down the west side of the river to Pipiriki, and from thence to Mount Egmont, and another to the north of Wellington. One also in the north of the island. I quite believe that if the natives now living in the first-named district felt sure that their lands would not be touched, but be secured to them and their children, they would at once draw off from the war; and it should be remembered that they comprise full one half of the native inhabitants of this island, and are so compactly situated, and in such an inaccessible country, that it will take many years and a vast amount of blood and treasure to exterminate them.

Could these districts be proclaimed, natives living out of them might be encouraged to sell their lands and buy into the native districts, and so live amongst their countrymen. Those who would prefer to live amongst the Europeans would for a certainty die out in a few years. For the purposes of trade the natives are quite able to sail their own vessels, and so take their produce to the towns, and procure what they want in the way of European supplies. An absolute Government would also be able to make arrangements for the protection of natives trading in the towns, and effectually to prevent contraband traffic in spirits, arms, &c.

The impossibility of the two races living together struck me very forcibly after I had been a short time here. On my journey to Taupo in January last, I met with a highly respectable gentleman, who has travelled much amongst aborigines, and spent many years amongst the Indians of America. The result of all his observations and experience is, that he lays it down as a settled point, that it is quite impossible for the civilized and the uncivilized man to live together, and that separation is the only hope for aborigines. This he considers has been done in America with some success.

There is no doubt but that the natives of this country are the finest race of aborigines that have been met with in modern times; and though in the case of Mr. Volkner's murder they have been verily guilty, yet they ought not to be judged too severely. They were in a state of desperation at the time; they were thirsting for revenge for their own chief, murdered on our side near Matata, which we have allowed to pass over for more than a year without taking any notice of.

There has been a good deal of clamour here for the Governor to take immediate steps at Opotiki to avenge the murder. His Excellency has very wisely not given way. Had he done so, in all probability the whole of the eastern coast, from the Wairoa to Maketu, would now be in arms, and the murderers further from our reach than ever. As it is, there is a change at Turanga for the better, and there is a report that the natives themselves have made Kereopa a prisoner.

MISSIONARY RESULTS.

Fifty years have elapsed since the sword was sheathed upon the plains of Waterloo. Since then there has been a pause in the wild commotions of the world. It seems as though the four angels, standing on the four corners of the earth, have been holding the four winds of the earth, and thus, although there have been partial outbreaks, there has been no universal war. During this period of comparative peace, another angel has been flying in the midst of heaven, having "the everlasting Gospel to preach unto them that dwell in the earth, and to every nation, and kindred, and tongue, and people."

Throughout this half century the Church Missionary Society has been engaged in the active prosecution of that great duty which the Lord Jesus bequeathed to his professing church when He said, "Go ye into all the world, and preach the Gospel to every creature;" a responsibility which is laid on every one who possesses Christian privileges, and for the due discharge of which he will have to account.

There has been a large expenditure of life and means. Missionary after Missionary has gone forth, and many of them, succumbing to the influence of unhealthy climates, and borne down by the pressure of the work, have laid down their lives in the distant Mission fields of China, India, or of Africa. Yearly sums have been collected from willing contributors in all ranks of society, for the Lord has his people amongst rich and poor, and they who had experienced themselves the preciousness of the Gospel message commiserated their fellow-men who were without it, and gave according to their power, and beyond their power, that its sound might go forth into all the earth, and its words to the ends of the world.

At the termination, then, of so long a period, after so much of prayer and effort, it is assuredly not unsuitable to inquire what has been done? It is very true, if there were no results which could be specified, and it seemed as though we had laboured in vain and spent our strength for nought, still it would be our duty to go on. But inasmuch as the Lord has promised that his word shall not return to Him void, but shall accomplish that which He pleases, and prosper in that whereto He sends it, if, at the end of fifty years, no results could be produced, it might well be questioned whether there was not something faulty in our work, something seriously defective in our mode of operation.

But, besides this, it is no unusual thing to find Missionary efforts decried as vain and ineffectual proceedings. In monthly serials, and throughout a portion of the daily press, such assertions are being very frequently made; and the popular fallacies which prevail upon this subject are thus encouraged and strengthened. The writer of a sentimental story interrupts its progress that he may point a shaft against the enthusiasts who are expending on foreign enterprises the money which might be so much better employed at home in relieving the indigent, and in the instruction of the ignorant. Such critics overlook the fact, that Missionary efforts are the fulfilment of a great duty, and are done in obedience to a divine command. Moreover, it very frequently happens, that the persons who thus criticise are wholly incapable of forming an impartial judgment on the subject, inasmuch as of the actual results they know nothing, nor have they ever thought it worth their while to investigate such details. They dislike the whole movement, and forthwith condemn it. It may seem strange that an effort of such pure benevolence should be so distasted by many; but it is an expression of Christian vitality; a proof that the Gospel has lost nothing of its power; that it is still the same truth which went forth of old conquering and to conquer; and there are many who, when they hear of conversions in distant lands, are reluctantly compelled to acknowledge that there is in Christianity a power of which they as yet know nothing, and in that consciousness they feel self-condemned.

There is another class of persons on whose account this question needs to be thoroughly sifted and placed upon a proper footing. They are such as wish well to Missions but know little of them, and altogether misapprehend the results which may be looked for. They are of opinion that to evangelize to a profession of Christianity large masses of the heathen is the work which the European Missionary may be expected to accomplish; and when, on examination of what is being actually done, they discover how few are the foreign Missionaries, how sparsely scattered over the heathen world, how limited the results are which have been attained, they are amazed, and very reluctantly find themselves constrained to acknowledge that nothing, or next to nothing, has been effected.

Conclusions of so unfavourable a character exercise at home an injurious influence, and many, who at first felt well-disposed towards the Missionary work, are chilled and discouraged, and feel disposed to abandon it. They say, After all, what has been done? A tiny spot here and there has been reclaimed from the waste and fashioned into a garden, where, by artificial means, the plants are kept alive; but beyond lie the vast wildernesses, and, at this rate of progress, when shall they be changed? The nations of heathendom rise before us as of old, like chains of rugged mountains whose crags and precipices bid defiance to the feeble efforts put forth by man to subdue them to his use. Here and there, indeed, at their base, or on some elongated spur, less intractable than the central mass, traces of incipient effort may be seen, but they are so feeble, so diminutive, as to stamp the enterprise with utter hopelessness.

How would the world have fared had the early heralds of God's merciful purposes to man been thus desponding and fainthearted? How, then, should Christianity ever have reached the once barbarous island of Britain, and chased away before its morning light the gloomy mists of Druidical superstition?

In the present aspect of Christian Missions there is no ground for discouragement, but the reverse. They have accomplished all that could be rightfully expected of them. Only let it be understood what the measure of this is. Let us not first entertain extravagant expectations, and then condemn Missions because they come short of them. Let us first ascertain what a foreign agency, such as that which we send out, may fairly be expected to accomplish, and then, when we have provided ourselves with an equitable rule, let us proceed to measure the work.

The foreign agency, then, is merely initiative. It is not its province to evangelize upon a large scale, but, from the midst of the heathen, to raise up that by which the more extended work shall be done.

The true function of the European Missionary is to prepare the leaven, and introduce it into the mass.

Let it be remembered that the leaven is homogeneous with the mass on which it is designed to act. It is a portion of that mass, a fragment broken off from it. This, separated from the rest, is subjected to a peculiar process, in virtue of which it becomes endued with new properties of a pungent and penetrative character. When this is done, it is deposited in the mass. In quantity it may be very small—so small that, when put into the lump, it disappears and seems lost. Yet, if genuine, although hidden, it will be felt. Diffusing its peculiar properties, it will permeate the mass, and, becoming influential, assimilate the whole to itself, so that the whole lump shall be leavened.

This aptly illustrates the work of a European Missionary, where, on some distant shore, he prosecutes his arduous enterprise. He has been there some years, long enough to acquire the language, and render himself intelligible to the natives. He has obtained some influence, and many have gathered around him, some of whom have felt the power of the truth, and have become true converts to Christianity; while others, in different stages of progress, are more or less hopeful. These first converts are few, when compared with the multitudes around; yet do they constitute the portion which has been broken off from the mass, in order that it may be prepared to act as leaven. If it be limited in extent, it comes the more readily and entirely under his influence. To the alteration of this he addresses himself, leavening it with Christian truth, until it becomes so enriched with real converts, and with so true a work of grace, as to be changed into a Christian leaven, possessed of new properties, and capable of imparting those qualities to the heathen when brought into contact with them. He then places the leaven in the lump, and assigns to the new Christians the evangelization of their own people as their proper work. The further prosecution of the work in that locality is not his function. His duty is to go forward to new places, where nothing has as yet been done, to prepare new leaven, and fulfil the same preparatory work. It is true, he will be careful to maintain communication with the native church which he has left behind, and so aid it in various ways that it may not deteriorate, but rather increase in pungency and power. As the careful housewife looks to see whether the leaven is at work and the dough rising, so will he remember and revisit and pray over his old flock. Nor is the housewife disappointed if the results she looks for be not instantaneously produced; if every thing looks unchanged, and the leaven seems to be lost. She is not impatient. She knows that time must be afforded; that the leaven is hidden, but not lost. And so it must be with us. We must not be impatient, nor, by injudicious tampering, retard the work, but commit it to the Lord.

Are such views correct? How shall they be proved to be such? Is there any standard of appeal; any authoritative document to which we can refer? The Acts of the Apostles is such a record: it is an inspired history of the Missionary proceedings of the early church. Paul and his companions were foreign Missionaries. They introduced the Gospel into provinces and nations where formerly it had no existence. Did they act on the principles which we have stated? Let us consider.

The first Missionary itinerancy was from Antioch, on a spot lying somewhat in advance of the old Jewish platform, and looking forth on vast regions yet in darkness. Paul and Barnabas went forth to the arduous undertaking like Jonathan and his armour-bearer. Before them lay the stronghold of heathenism. They were only two, but they said, "It may be that the Lord will work for us; for there is no restraint to the Lord to save by many or by few." With such holy resolution, armed with the sword of the Spirit, which is the word of God, went forth the two evangelists. They preached Christ, and wherever they went there were some who felt the converting power of that wondrous theme. At Antioch in Pisidia there were "many" whom Paul "persuaded to continue in the grace of God." At Iconium "a great multitude of the Jews, and also of the Greeks, believed." At Lystra and Derbe there were fruits. Paul did not stay with any of these young converts, inexperienced as they were, and surrounded by trials. Like his great Master, he had to preach the Gospel to other cities also. But after a time, he came back to see whether they had stood fast—"they returned again to Lystra, and to Iconium, and Antioch, confirming the souls of the disciples, and exhorting them to continue in the faith, and that we must through much tribulation enter into the kingdom of God;" and then, when he had proved the work, and found it to be a reality, he proceeded to organize the converts, to mould them into a church, and fit them for usefulness—"they ordained them elders in every church." Thus, over the platform of Asia Minor, at the great centres of population, he raised up points of light; and having done so, he went forward to new places, leaving these native congregations behind to prosecute the work, each in the area of which it was the centre—"And when they had ordained them elders in every church, and had prayed, with fasting, they commended them to the Lord in whom they believed."

Thus, so far as Asia Minor was concerned, the leaven was prepared, and put into the mass; and now Paul was not permitted to remain any longer in that region. There were, indeed, districts of that province into which he had not yet penetrated, and thither he was anxious to go. But He, under whose guidance he was, considered that the initiative had been sufficiently accomplished, and that the leaven would do its appointed work without any further action on the part of the foreign Missionaries; and so they were constrained to go forward. "Now when they had gone throughout Phrygia and the region of Galatia, and were forbidden of the Holy Ghost to preach the word in Asia (proconsular Asia), after they were come to Mysia they assayed to go into Bithynia; but the Spirit suffered them not." At Troas the mystery was solved. There, in a vision of the night, the man of Macedonia stood and prayed Paul, saying, "Come over, and help us." A new region was thrown open to these first evangelists, the vastness of the European continent, and, as in Asia Minor, so in Macedonia and Greece, at the various centres of population—Philippi, Thessalonica, Corinth, &c.—churches were raised up, until throughout these lands the same results which had followed his labours in Asia Minor had been attained, and the apostle could say, "From Jerusalem, and round about unto Illyricum, I have fully preached the Gospel of Christ."

And now he considered that throughout Eastern Europe his special work was done, and he began to look farther west for a new sphere of effort. Writing to the Romans, he says—"Having no more place in these parts, and having a great desire these many years to come unto you; whensoever I take my journey into Spain, I will come to you." "Having no more place in these parts:" not surely that all in those parts had been brought to a profession of Christianity, but that he had put the leaven into the lump. He had done this here and there in a variety of places. He had accomplished his proper work, and, in that sense, "had no more place in these parts." He had raised up native churches over the wide extent of the regions he had traversed, and he now left it to them to complete the work. But as he went forward he remembered them, maintained intercourse with them, nourished them with words of faith and sound doctrine, reminded them of the duties they had to discharge, and commended them when they were diligent and faithful. Writing from Rome to the Philippians, he admonishes them to be "blameless and harmless, the sons of God, without rebuke, in the midst of a crooked and perverse nation, among whom ye shine as lights in the world, holding forth the words of life." To the Colossians he says—"Walk in wisdom toward them that are without, redeeming the time. Let your speech be always with grace, seasoned with salt, that ye may know how ye ought to answer every man." The Thessalonians he commends, because they were already in the active communication to others of the truth which they had received, and were as leaven in the midst of the lump.—"From you sounded out the word of the Lord, not only in Macedonia and Achaia, but also in every place your faith to godward is spread abroad." No doubt it was this which exposed these early churches to so much of persecution, that they were aggressive churches, and bore their testimony fearlessly for the Lord's truth, and against the delusions of the prevailing heathenism. Had they been disposed to do so, they might have compromised, and the world have consented not to molest them, provided they kept their Christianity to themselves, and did not obtrude it upon others. But the night was dark, and souls were perishing, and, as beacon-lights, these early churches stood forth, discharging with fidelity the high office entrusted to them, and guiding distressed sinners to the haven where they might cast anchor, and find rest.

Not only did they take up the work which lay more immediately around them, but they co-operated with the apostles in their more distant labours. Paul had expressed his hope to the Corinthian church, "that when your faith is increased we shall be enlarged by you according to our rule abundantly to preach the Gospel in the regions beyond you." Thus, when a prisoner at Rome, he appeals to the sympathy of the Ephesians, "praying always with all prayer and supplication in the spirit, and watching thereunto with all perseverance and supplication for all saints; and for me that utterance may be given unto me, that I may open my mouth boldly, to make known the mystery of the Gospel, for which I am an ambassador in bonds, that therein I may speak boldly as I ought to speak." Thus the Philippians aided him with material help, and so kept him from absolute want. Nothing can be more touching than the passage in which he refers to this; and as they helped him in his Missionary work, he told them of what he had been enabled to accomplish—"all the saints salute you, chiefly they of Cæsar's household."

Furthermore, when these Christian churches had leavened the mass which lay immediately around them, and universalized the profession of Christianity throughout their own lands, they became the centres of a more distant evangelization, and sent out their messengers, as foreign Missionaries, to localities where they were strangers. And so Gaius is commended of John because of his sympathy with and Christian kindness towards the devoted men who had left their homes that they might penetrate into heathen lands, and lay the foundations of a new work—"Beloved, thou doest faithfully whatsoever thou doest to the brethren and to strangers, which have borne witness of thy charity before the church, whom, if thou bring forward on their journey after a godly sort, thou shalt do well, because that for his name's sake they went forth, taking nothing of the Gentiles. We therefore ought to receive such, that we might be fellow-helpers to the truth." (3 John 5—8.)

Such, then, were the principles on which Missionary action was prosecuted in the early days of Christianity. The functions of the foreign Missionary, and the native churches, whom he was instrumental in raising up, were quite distinct. The one commenced the work on a small scale; the other extended it to large masses of the heathen. The one was the hand which prepared the leaven; the other was the leaven which leavened the whole lump.

Having now a clear perception of the results which may be expected to follow the labours of a foreign Missionary, we shall be in a better position to consider in another paper whether the Missionary efforts of our own day have been effectual, or, as some say, a failure.

MISSIONARY PROCEEDINGS IN CASHMERE.

The great trigonometrical survey of Cashmere, carried out by Captain Montgomerie, of the Bengal Engineers, has made us intimately acquainted with the details of this beautiful valley. A map has been completed, on the scale of half an inch to the mile, embracing 8100 square miles of country, including the valley and surrounding mountains, with no less than 4606 villages, &c.

The hardships endured by the surveying party in carrying out this great work have been very great. "The character of a trigonometrical survey demands that the stations shall be fixed on the highest summits;" and on these, in order to obtain an adequate number of good observations, several days must be passed. In the Punjal range, which separates the valley from the plains, points were visited upwards of 13,000 feet, and nearly 15,000 feet in elevation. To the north of Cashmere a summit was reached upwards of 16,000 feet in height. Moreover, most of the stations had to be visited so early in the season, that the snow was still heavy at 11,000 feet; and on these cold heights, in consequence of clouds and storms, the party had to remain pitched on the snow for upwards of a week at a time. "Space sufficient even for the very small camp could never be got quite close to the stations on the peaks. During the day this did not matter; but at night, though the distance might not be more than 200 yards, it was rather a difficult matter to get back from the observatory tent, after the surveyor had finished taking observations, to the camps. Soon after sunset the surface of the snow becomes as slippery as glass, affording by no means a satisfactory footing on a ridge, with either a precipitous slope or a precipice on either side."

The difficulty of obtaining supplies and firewood at such elevations may be imagined; yet, "great as the hardships entailed on the European officers undoubtedly were, they were slight compared with those endured by the native establishment with the utmost cheerfulness. The signallers and headmen were mostly natives of Hindustan, to whom extreme cold is a condition of positive suffering; yet these men were loyal and contented, as they have been in all survey parties over India during the mutiny."

We think it good to refer to these arduous enterprises, so successfully accomplished by resolute men. We admire their pluck and perseverance, their devotedness to the discharge of their assigned duties, their submission to authority, their cordial co-operation among themselves. Let Missionaries, engaged in a far higher enterprise, imitate such examples, and be careful that, in the discharge of their duties, they be characterized by the same high qualifications; for shall earthly governments command such exemplary services, while that which is rendered to Him who shall be "King over all the earth" is permitted to be of an inferior stamp? Missionaries who are employed in surveying unknown lands for Christ, preparatory to his enthronement over the nations, ought to surpass other men in self-renunciation and devotion to their work; and in many instances it has been so. The noblest characters which the world has ever produced are to be found in the ranks of Missionaries.

Let us now look down on the valley itself, although "the grandeur and beauty of Cashmerian scenery cannot be described, but must be seen to be fully understood or appreciated. "The high masses of mountains, many covered with snow, which surround the valley on every side, the lakes and streams, the variety and luxuriance of the foliage, and the mildness of the climate, are, together, not to be met with in any other part of India.

"The town of Cashmere, or Sirinagar, is quite an easteren Venice, the place being intersected with canals in every direction, and the houses built out from the water. The lake adjoining, with its pretty little island of Chinars, and its numberless floating gardens, is like a mirror reflecting the surrounding mountains on its surface, so as quite to give the idea, when passing over in a boat, that one is skimming over the peaks and crags in an aerial machine. At the bottom of these mountains, on the borders of the lake, are the famous gardens of Shalimar and Nishat. Streams from the mountains are made to run through them, forming cascades and canals, the Chinar trees casting their shade over them, and the walks lining the sides."

The flat portion of the valley, elevated about 5200 feet above the sea, is about 89 miles long, with an average breadth of 16¾ miles. It is drained by the Jhelum river, formed by the confluence of various tributaries, which have their sources in the mountain ranges around the southern portion of the valley. From Islamabad it flows northwards in snake-like curves along the valley, expanding occasionally into beautiful lakes, the largest of which is the great Wulur lake, about 21 miles north-west of the city of Sirinagar. Eventually its waters find their way out of the valley by the Burrumulla pass, one of the grandest of defiles. "The great chain of the Himalaya is cleft in two by a chasm upwards of 7000 feet in depth; the bottom is very narrow, and is wholly occupied by the river. Near Uri it is but 70 feet across, with almost perpendicular sides. Through this natural sluice passes the whole volume of the Jhelum river with the most astonishing velocity."

Here, in this lovely valley, from age to age, various dynasties have lived and reigned

Hindu princes followed one another in long succession. "The most ancient Hindu history extant—the Raju Frangrini—is a history of the kings of Cashmere." "From this we learn, that, at a period when half Europe was in a state of semi-barbarism, the Hindu had attained to much excellence in many of the arts, architecture, sculpture, &c." During the earlier period of these Hindu kings, Buddhism was the religion of the valley. This eventually was superseded by Brahminism, Ramagupta, king of Cashmere, having, in the tenth century, destroyed the Buddhist images and burnt the monasteries. In the neighbouring country of Ladak, however, which constitutes part of the present Maharajah's dominions, Buddhism retains its ascendancy.

At length the Mohammedans came: attracted by the beauty of the valley, and, full of iconoclastic zeal, they soon possessed themselves of it, a race of independent kings of that creed ruling there from A.D. 1341 to A.D. 1586, when, reduced by the Emperor Akbar, it became an integral part of the empire of Delhi.

By the Mogul princes it was used as a sensual paradise, whither they might retreat from the hot plains of India, and there, divesting themselves for a time of the cares of government, abandon themselves to pleasure. Akbar beautified it with palaces and gardens, and his son and successor, Jehangir, who, with his empress, Noor Mahal, loved to retreat into its most secluded and beautiful recesses, built many palaces and summer-houses, and completed the construction of the celebrated Shalimar gardens.

The hand of the Mogul, enervated by voluptuousness, at length became unequal to sustain the ponderous sceptre of his ancestors. The mountain gem of Cashmere was grasped, first by the Affghans in A.D. 1753, and then by the Sikhs, under Runjeet Singh, in 1819. That was a year of disaster to the valley. An earthquake came and destroyed 1200 persons; it was followed by a pestilence, which carried off 100,000 more; while gaunt famine, following in its steps, wrought up to such a height the miseries of the people, that numbers fled to Hindustan and the Punjab; and the population was reduced from 800,000 in 1819, to 200,000 in 1833.

The Cashmerians, in form and feature, are amongst the finest specimens of the Indian race; but they have lost all manly tone, and, in their present degraded condition, are effeminate and servile. The uprightness which ought to characterize the man, the self-respect which is woman's true ornament, are alike wanting.

"The dress of both men, women, and children, is pretty much the same. It is a long woollen gown, generally grey, like an English night-gown, reaching nearly to the ankles, with a single tuck below the knees. It formerly was the dress only of the women; but, on account of their cowardice, the men were obliged, by some former ruler, to put on the woman's dress, and they still retain it. The Mohammedans button on this gown at an opening on the right side of the neck, and the Hindus on the left, which is exactly the reverse of what is customary in India. The women fasten it in the centre. The men also throw a thick woollen cloth over their shoulders, and, of course, wear a turban. The women are not concealed, like the Mohammedan women of India: they wear a veil over the head, but the face is exposed. The girls wear no veil, but only a little round cap on the head, and their hair hangs down beneath it all over their shoulders in numberless little plaits, which are united together behind, and lengthened by long tassels tied to them. This head-dress is very becoming. The features of both men and women are often very striking: many of them are as fair as Europeans, and the beauty of the Cashmere women is proverbial. The children are often remarkably handsome, intelligent, and seem as if they could learn any thing. The majority of the people, however, have a coarse expression, the consequence of their degraded state for many past generations. The Cashmerees appear to talk all day long without cessation or weariness. They are very excitable and quarrelsome, and, when angry, they pour forth torrents of abuse.

"The persons and dress of the common people are generally filthy, and covered with vermin; and woe to the unfortunate traveller who allows them to spread a cloth for him to sit on. An English person can hadly sit on the edge of their shops, or come in contact with their dress in any way, without suffering."

Such is the description given by our Missionary, the Rev. Robert Clarke, of the condition of the people. "The glorious beauty, which is on the head of the fat valley," has been indeed a fading flower, and Cashmere, once the earthly paradise of mighty kings, is now degraded, and stricken in the dust. "Very different," observes Mr. Clarke, "is Cashmere now to what it was when Jehangir and Noor Mahal made it their favourite residence for thirteen summers, and became so enamoured of this little kingdom, that Jehangir often declared that he would rather be deprived of every other province of his mighty empire than of Cashmere; or when, 200 years ago, the Emperor Aurungzebe, as Bernier relates,* left Delhi on his way to Cashmere with 25,000 cavalry, 70 large cannons drawn each by 20 yoke of oxen, and 50 small guns, together with elephants, and horses, and birds of prey, dogs and leopards, nilghaus and lions, rhinoceroses, buffaloes, and tamed antelopes, in his train; when two months were required for him to travel from Delhi to Lahore with his camp of three or four hundred thousand people, of whom, in order to prevent a famine, only one in every four was permitted to enter Cashmere. The Jhelum at Sirinagar was then lined with beautiful residences, with gardens attached to them. The Hurree Purwat was crowned with handsome houses and gardens, and surmounted by a mosque and hermitage, and the whole hill, now bare and barren, was crowned with a large quantity of fine trees, from the verdure of which the hill received the name of Hurree Purwat, or the green mountain. The declivities of the mountains beyond the lake were then also covered with houses and flower-gardens. Then was the time of Cashmere's earthly glory, when art and wealth combined with nature to render the country, as Bernier calls it, unequalled in the whole world by any country of the same extent. Now, however, is the time of her desolation: her palaces are in ruins; her city is composed of tottering, bending structures and dirty streets; her country is impoverished; her lake a marsh; her people"—just what we might conclude they would be with so much to debase and nothing to correct or improve. Is it surprising if the features of human character, as sketched by various travellers, are painful in the extreme? Place any portion of the human family in the same circumstances, and there will follow the same results.

But in the good providence of God the light of Christian truth entered the Punjab, and a new centre of effort was formed at Peshawur. Amidst the various objects of interest, Cashmere was not forgotten. Men who knew the value of Christianity as the great remedy for sin, perceived and commiserated the lost condition of the people of the valley. The reigning corruption appeared more loathsome when contrasted with the beauty of the scenery. To introduce some light into the midst of its darkness, so as to raise the tone of morals, and rebuke vice, was rendered necessary by the painful fact, that Cashmere had become the Capua of some Englishmen, who, far from home, had cast off the restraints of Christian education, and abandoned themselves to the indulgence of their lusts. It is said that its pleasures contributed not a little to the downfall of the Mogul dynasty. Such demoralizing influences need to be averted from ourselves. Let the marsh, then, be reclaimed, and so cease to send forth pestiferous exhalations.

Compassion for the Cashmerees, regard for ourselves, the remembrance of the Lord's command, the sense of responsibility—all moved to action. A meeting was held at Peshawur, collections made, a Committee formed. Since then, Cashmere has been visited every summer by a Missionary of the Church Missionary Society, and efforts

* Bernier was the French physician who accompanied Aurungzebe in 1664.

have been made to instruct the people in the truths of that Gospel, which every man needs, and which God has commanded that every man should have.

Cashmere, it will be remembered, on the subjugation of the Sikh power by the British, was ceded in independent possession to the late Maharajah Gholab Sing, his son, the Maharajah Rumbeer Sing, being the present ruler.

During the summer of 1863 the Missionaries in Cashmere were the Rev. W. Smith, of Benares, and the Rev. R. Clark. When Mr. Smith left the valley in the middle of October, Mr. Clark remained behind him, in the hope that he might be permitted to continue there throughout the winter, but in every possible way he was discouraged and obstructed. A few inquirers had gathered round him: some of them were arrested and subjected to great indignity, being beaten by the soldiers, spat upon, &c., without any other charge being brought against them than that they were inquirers. Men were placed on the bridge before the Missionary's house, with orders to watch every native who should enter the door, and arrest him on his leaving. Warnings were sent to Mr. Clark not to attempt preaching in a certain part of the city, for that if he did he would be set upon and beaten. A young convert of nineteen years of age was forcibly taken from the Missionary's house. Finally, in November, Mr. Clark was obliged to leave, and to return to the Punjab.

In the spring of 1864, Mr. Clark returned to Cashmere. Before leaving the Punjab he had taken the precaution of hiring a house in Sirinagar, from the proprietor, Ghulam Hussan, of Umritsur, paying 300 rupees in advance. How he was received on his arrival is related in the following paragraph—

On our arrival near the city (Sirinagar) on Friday evening, the 15th of April, I sent some of our servants onwards in advance, to give notice that we were coming, in order that the house might be ready for our reception. An hour afterwards they returned, stating that they had been stopped by some 400 men, who had collected on the bridge and before the house, and who were determined not to allow us to enter, and had driven them back with threats and stones. Our arrival was evidently generally expected. I had myself, when sitting within the boat after dark, heard a man from the shore call to the boatmen to ask if I were the Padre Sahib. Instead, therefore, of going on, I gave orders to halt at the entrance of the city for the night (although the rain was pouring down in torrents), and determined to go on next morning to the Hurree Singh ka Bagh, where the houses of the English visitors are, rather than be the cause of any disturbance, or excite opposition unnecessarily on the part of the natives. However, as we were going to bed, Shah Munir, one of our native Christians, (a Malik and Zemindar from Eusufzie who had accompanied us from Peshawur,) returned from the city, where he had been for some business of his own, and he told me that he had been at the house after my servants left; that he had found every thing perfectly quiet, and had heard from the people that I was expected, and that every preparation had been made to receive me. I therefore again changed our plans, and this morning we arrived here at the house. The outer gate was open, and the gardener went off at once for the keys of the inner rooms. Every thing was evidently prepared for us; even the garden, which was sown last year with barley, was laid out neatly in beds.

Whilst waiting for the keys, Mons. Gosselin, the shawl merchant, whose house is just across the river, heard of our arrival, and at once kindly came over to see us. After some conversation, he asked why we had not gone into the house. I replied that the gardener had gone for the keys. "But Mrs. Clark," he said, "cannot wait out here in the rain. The bungalow is your's, and should have been open to receive you." He told the man to bring him a hammer. A little hatchet was the nearest tool available, and he told his servant to knock off the native padlock. We all came in, and began to get the things out of the boat.

Before this could be accomplished, a man called Shekh Aziz arrived, and asked why we had gone into *his* house. We told him that we had never heard of him before; that we had taken the house from Ghulam Hussan of Umritsur, who was the owner of it, and had paid 300 rupees in advance for rent, and had his written agreement in due form making it over to us. He then gave us, or rather Ghulam Hussan, the lie direct, declaring that he himself, and not Ghulam Hussan, was the owner of the house, and that he did not wish to let us rent it. I simply referred him to Ghulam Hussan, and told him to write to Umritsur, and that if there was any difference between him and Ghulam Hussan, his course was to apply in the ordinary manner for justice; and that, as far as we were concerned, the English Resident would be here in a few days, when he could at once find out whether we had any legal claim to the house or not.

He went away, and in an hour or two the house was literally besieged with men and boys. They stood by hundreds on the bridge, and lined the river on both sides, shouting, and one man striking a gong to collect the people. Not a chuprasse, or police officer, or soldier, or official of any kind, appeared. The tumult quickly increased, and no efforts of any kind were made to stop it. The people began to throw stones, and some of them broke down the wall of the compound, and began to get in by the stable. Our servants became greatly alarmed, for they threatened to burn the house. The number present was computed to be between 1000 and 1500.

In the midst of all, my surprise was very great to see M. Gosselin crossing over the bridge from the opposite side, alone, with a hunting whip in his hand, which, however, he never used. They all fled before him like sheep; but at last, returning, they surrounded him, shouting and gesticulating, and throwing their hands wildly about over his head. My first thought was to go out and join him, as I had great fears for his safety; but I felt that my doing so would only increase the disturbance. I feared they would crowd and press around him, and as the bridge had no protection on the sides, I knew that the least push would precipitate him into the swollen river below. He told me afterwards that his fear was that the bridge would give way from the weight of so great a crowd, as one actually did last year, when many people were killed in its fall. However, on he went, and I sent three men to him to urge him to come in, and not to expose himself in such a way.

The native Christians were all with me, and it was suggested that we should together, in prayer, ask for God's protection. I read a few verses, Acts iv. 18 to the end of the chapter, and we then commended ourselves to Him who had sent us here to make his Gospel known. Not till we had concluded did M. Gosselin return, and we then found that he had been to the chief Moulwie near, to request him to stop the uproar. The man professed his inability to do so; and M. Gosselin told us that the matter was becoming serious: that it was far worse than he had imagined, for the mob had been let loose, and some of them were much excited.

Mr. Clark now resolved to go in person to the Wuzeer, and appeal to him for protection. Opening the river door, he got into a boat, and was rowed to the palace. It was not until after long delay and much difficulty that he succeeded in obtaining an interview with the Wuzeer. "His manner," observes Mr. Clarke, "was kind enough, as he assured me that whatever was the cause of the disturbance, a Governor's first duty was to put it down, and that he had done so, a messenger having been sent to the Kotwal with instructions to disperse the mob."

It was evident, however, that the occupation by the Missionary of a house within the city was distasteful to the authorities, and that they would be very glad if, by some means or other, they could induce him to leave it.

Affairs remained quiet for a few days, when, on a trivial pretext, another disturbance arose, the Wuzeer at this time being absent from Sirinagar, and no longer within reach of any appeal which might be addressed to him for protection.

Affairs began to be again very serious, and for a few moments we almost doubted whether it would not be necessary, after all, for us to leave the house until the Resident arrived. There was, in M. Gosselin's opinion, a very fair chance of the house being really attacked, and perhaps even burnt, and a possibility that we might lose every thing, and run considerable risk of personal safety. Mrs. Clark was referred to as to what she wished to be done, and she decided the matter by declaring that we would not go; that we were in the path of duty; that she was not afraid for herself or her children, but was confident that God would protect us; and that at every risk we ought to remain. M. Gosselin then turned to me and asked if that was my opinion too. I replied that I could not feel comfortable at leaving, for I felt it would be shrinking from a difficulty, instead of trusting to God to bear us through it.

At this crisis they were again indebted to M. Gosselin for prompt aid. Accompanied by two European gentlemen, he hastened off to the palace, and seeking out the Wuzeer's deputy, Lala Shankar Dass, told him, that if the Government declined to interfere on behalf of the Missionary and his family, they would stand by them, and that the responsibility of whatever might occur would then rest with the authorities. This decided them to act.

Orders were sent to the Kotwal to allow of no gathering of the people whatever; and very soon the Kotwal himself appeared at our house, and left with us one of his own men to send him word of the slightest appearance of uproar. Thus has M. Gosselin, a French gentleman, and a Roman Catholic, been the means, under God, of again preserving us.

In July Mr. Clarke was joined by the Rev. W. Handcock from Peshawur, whose health had rendered it necessary that he should leave the plains during the hot season. From his journals we extract the following brief notices of Missionary proceedings in the valley during the period of his stay, from July 1st to September 30th, 1864—

July 2, 1864—The difficulties of Mission work in Cashmere arise not merely from the natural repugnance of a people to receive a new creed, but also from the determined opposition of the authorities to the teaching or preaching of the Gospel of Christ. This hostility, from the rulers of the country, has manifested itself in the various departments of labour in which the Missionary has been employed. Not to mention the disgraceful manner in which the Rev. Robert Clark and his family were treated by the mob on their arrival in April last, which conduct appears to have been encouraged by the Government officials themselves, I need only to state the fact of an individual having been imprisoned on becoming an inquirer into the truth of Christianity.

Nevertheless, the word of life must not be withheld from those who are perishing for lack of knowledge. With the object of setting forth this good news we went to the bazaar this morning. Numbers gathered round and listened; but the crowd on two occasions was dispersed, once by a frivolous hearer, and again by some bigoted Mohammedans, who addressed the people, and urged that Christians ought not to be listened to.

July 30—On the afternoon of this day the Cashmere inquirer, Mohammed Hussan, was baptized. This is the first baptism that has taken place since the commencement of the Cashmere Mission. On that account it is most interesting, as being, we trust, the first-fruits of the harvest that is to follow. Mohammed Hussan is a young man of respectable family, and a Syud. During his course as an inquirer he has undergone many reproaches and persecutions. By his own family he has been cast off, as unfit to associate with them; and by the Cashmere Government he has, on two occasions, been imprisoned. When he was last in charge, it was only through the interference of the British Agent that he could be released. The treatment which he underwent, when in prison, was of a most cruel kind. Indeed he was placed in a dungeon, and fettered in the same manner as those who were guilty of murder and of the gravest offences. And when, by the influence of Mr. Cooper, C.B., the order was given for his release, he had been lying on the ground for three days, and unable to rise. From this position he had been prevented from moving by reason of a ponderous log of wood that had been fastened, in a most painful manner, to one of his legs. We cannot but thank God for the grace vouchsafed to this young man during these seasons of trial, and for the strength given, by which he was enabled to witness a good confession for Christ. The time, too, that has elapsed between his release from prison and his baptism, has afforded an additional evidence of the Spirit's work in his heart; for, during this interval, his Christian deportment has been highly satisfactory, and his diligence in studying the word of God most exemplary.

Such being the promising character of this young convert, Mr. Clark, under whose instruction he has more particularly been, did not hesitate to baptize him. May God give him grace to keep the holy vow which he has this day made!

During the present summer there have been in the valley the Rev. W. Handcock and a medical Missionary, Dr. Elmslie. The work progresses, notwithstanding the opposition which it meets with, not from the people, but from the officials. The medical department is rendering valuable help, disarming prejudice, and facilitating the work of Christian instruction. In a letter, dated June 11th of the present year, Mr. Handcock thus sums up the chief points of intelligence—

In my last I alluded to the difficulty we found in obtaining food in the city of Sirinagar, and expressed a hope that, on the arrival of the bishop, matters would take a turn. It was not so, however, for the Maharajah's official positively refused to allow the shopkeepers to supply the native Christians with me with the usual meal of which bread is made, although every one else was supplied. The result was that we were obliged to go into the villages, where we have obtained every thing.

Dr. Elmslie has fared better, being, from the first, regularly supplied with provisions. His work, also, is prospering. Two days ago he had as many as forty patients, all of whom were addressed on the precious truths of salvation by Christ before their varied bodily ailments were attended to.

I am thankful to say that here in the villages the people are very willing to listen to the word of life; and yesterday our hearts were gladdened by the accesion of an inquirer, who is a young Mohammedan, named Sumadu, and who is a bookbinder by trade. Last year he first heard of the Gospel of our blessed Saviour, and was then so far convinced, that he wished to accompany Mr. Clark on his leaving the valley. Indeed, he did accompany the Missionary party for some distance down the river; but two of the Government officials, having heard of this inquirer, took the Maharajah's boats, and went in pursuit, and very soon overtook him. The soldiers then violently beat him, and, having pinioned his hands behind him, led him off to prison. On being brought into the principal court, he was asked if he had accompanied the Missionary party of his own freewill. His answer was in the affirmative; and he further stated that he had gone to hear about the Christian religion. He was then sent back to prison, and four days afterwards he was sentenced to be *publicly whipped*. This shameful treatment accordingly took place in the presence of a great crowd of witnesses. Meanwhile news was forwarded about this young man to Jummoo, and an order was sent back from the chief Government, that he should be imprisoned for three months. He was therefore put in chains, and kept confined until the term was expired. His two brothers then, at the order of Government, pledged themselves, in writing, to employ every means in their power to prevent his going in future to the Missionaries.

The man, however, is evidently in earnest, and has, in the face of the bitterest persecution, by the grace of God, come to us.

It would be a great blessing if the Maharajah would sanction a law that no one should be persecuted on account of his religion, at least not by the Government itself. May the Lord hasten the day when this shall be the case!

A FRAGMENT OF MISSIONARY WORK FROM KURRACHEE.

In the centre of our Kurrachee bazaar is a book-shop. It has no great attraction, either in external appearance or in its glitter of handsomely-bound books. But the word of God is there in several languages, and an experienced Christian teacher is always present to comment upon and expound its blessed truths. During every day thousands of people pass to and fro by the shop. Many pass on without deigning to notice the humble shop of the Christians, or, if they do, to turn away with undisguised expressions of contempt. Some, however, do turn aside to ask what books are sold, and not a few have carried away with them portions of the Bible, or Christian books. Early in the year 1864 a man, in the dress of a Mohammedan pilgrim, entered the little shop, and after asking for Mohammedan books, began a conversation with the Christian teacher sitting there. He seemed pleased to hear of the Lord Jesus Christ, and said He was a great prophet, and was spoken of with great respect in the Korán. Not much was said at that interview, and the man soon left. The following day he returned, and seemed to listen with some interest to the teacher's explanation of the Christian religion. These visits were repeated, and each time the man seemed more and more impressed with the truths he had heard. During this time he had, like all the Mohammedan pilgrims, been living within the outer courts of the mosque. So pleased was the teacher with his earnestness, that he induced him to leave the mosque and live with him in the Mission compound. Never shall I forget the joy of the old man when telling me of the eagerness with which his young friend drank in the words of Christ. It was worth years of labour to see these joyous fruits of Christianity. In due time the inquirer came under regular instruction, and then I learned his history. He told me his father was living, and was a Zemindar of the town of Bussi, in the Rajah of Pattialah's territory. Being the son of a Syud, a descendant of Ali, he was, from his earliest years, instructed in Persian and Arabic literature; and that he is well acquainted with both we have ample proof.

He continued to reside with his parents till the commencement of the mutiny, when he left them, to live with an uncle at Jujur, near Delhi. When there, he heard of the dreadful massacres of our countrymen by both Hindus and Mohammedans. The former he had been taught to despise from his infancy; but his heart was filled with sorrow when told that his own people, the Mohammedans, were amongst the murderers. His faith at this time received a terrible shock, for he discovered that the religion of the Korán was propagated by the power of the sword. From Jujur he removed with his relatives to Mussurie, where he met a Christian teacher, but had only passing conversation with him, though he mentioned that he often thought over what he did hear. After a time he set out on the usual pilgrimage to Mecca. On this journey he met with few troubles, except those incident to pilgrims. His mind was full of reverential feelings, and though doubts would obtrude themselves, he hoped they would all disappear when he should have seen and conversed with the Mullahs of Mecca. After long and wearying journeys he reached the city he so ardently looked for, and gazed, he said, long and with the greatest reverence on the Caaba. After the usual purifications he was admitted, with his fellow-pilgrims, within the sacred precincts, and soon stood before the Ajar Aswar. This is the famous black stone supposed by the Mohammedans to have descended from heaven. His companions bent before the sacred stone, and, with the most profound adoration, kissed it. Much as he wished to act with his fellows, he stated that he could not follow their example, for he thought it idolatry, and, watching his opportunity, secretly left the place. Near Mecca is a hill, to which all the pilgrims resort to complete their haj, or pilgrimage. It is called Jubul Arafat, and every true Mussulman who visits it, and makes the accustomed offering, is declared by the resident Cazi to be a Haji, and is ever afterwards acknowledged as such by all Mohammedans. Through all these ceremonies our inquirer passed, but felt no satisfaction. His mind was ill at ease, though he did not know why. And thus he left, by way of Medina, for home. In his route lay the plains of Kerbelah, the burial-place of the sons of Ali Husain and Hassan. It is the most celebrated of all the cemeteries of the East, and is held in great reverence by all the Sheeahs. There, if anywhere, he thought his faith in the religion of his fathers would be revived. There lay his forefathers, some members of his own family, and there he himself wished, as a true Mohammedan, to be laid; but the feeling was only transient. He saw Kerbelah, and left it disappointed. He had tried now many means to recover his former attachment to Mohammedanism; but there was nothing to satisfy his inquiring mind. He passed on to Bagdad, and, after travelling through Persia, came on to Kurrachee. As a Haji, he was at first received with joy, and was openly acknowledged as a Syud. Great, however, was their anger when they saw him with our Christians. They mobbed him and pelted him with stones, but he stood firm, and replied calmly to their threats and abuse. After the usual probation and examination he was admitted by baptism into the Christian church. This step greatly irritated the Mohammedans. Again they set upon him, beating and stoning him in the open bazaar. The ringleaders of this disturbance were arrested, but, on a deputation of most respectable Mohammedans waiting upon me to ask pardon, the case was not proceeded with. After a short stay with us, he left for the north-west, thinking that there he could be more useful, and be amongst his own people. Months and months passed, and we heard not a word of him. We thought he had gone back to his former faith, though I ever clung to the hope that he was true, but, being young, might be drawn aside for a time. I could not believe that the days spent teaching him could have been in vain, or that all the knowledge of our religion he had so eagerly learnt, as well as his earnestness in prayer, could have been hypocrisy. Many were the prayers we offered up to the Lord for him, and we believe these prayers have been answered. A letter has been sent by him to me, not asking for any thing, not breathing an unjust word against any one, but solely to assure me that his faith in Christ is unshaken; that he daily rejoices that he has embraced Christianity; and that he hopes, by God's grace, to remain faithful as long as he lives. He is living with his family, his religion is recognised, and he is allowed to speak about it. We do therefore thank God that He has been graciously pleased to watch over, and keep stedfast in the faith, this young Christian. Who knows what the result may be? Possibly the spread of the Christian faith in a province from which the Gospel has hitherto been excluded.

WELCOME COMMUNICATIONS FROM JAMAICA.

Many years ago the Church Missionary Society, compassionating the degraded condition of the slave population in the West-India islands, put forth efforts with a view to their improvement. So early as the year 1826 a sum of 200*l.* was placed at the disposal of the Bishop of Jamaica for the establishment of schools in that island, a catechist being, at the same time, provided for the Blue-Mountain valley district, containing a population of 5500 persons. Schools in Antigua were also brought into operation.

The condition of British slaves in the islands, at that period, was indeed most piteous and degrading; nor need any stronger proof be adduced of this than a reference to Lord Bathurst's proposition for "the abolishing of the driving-whip, the regulation and record of punishments, and the abolition of female flogging." At that time a slave, being regarded as his master's property, was made answerable for his master's debts. He was therefore liable to be seized on by the sheriff's officer, forcibly separated from his wife and children, and sold by public auction.

Can we wonder that the consignment of many thousands of Africans to a condition of so great degradation, in which, deprived of all the rights and privileges belonging to them as men, they were let to live physically, that they might work, while on the intellectual and immortal life a sentence of death was passed, should enkindle the eloquence of such a man as Wilberforce, when he pleaded before the British public the cause of the oppressed slave in thrilling accents such as these—"Should England proceed as she has hitherto done—making free with the rights and liberties of those whom Providence has placed under her protection—the time of retribution cannot be far distant; for she cannot expect, in that case, that a great and just God will continue to her her own abused blessings, which she has so long enjoyed with so little gratitude."

As the heart of the nation became stirred, and the conviction that the evils of the slave system could not be permitted any longer increased in force, until, like the tide coming forward in its strength, it spoke in a voice of thunder, warning all opponents that they must give way, the Society enlarged its operations, in the hope of preparing the negroes for the hour of freedom, and facilitating their critical transition from a state of long and deep oppression to one of political emancipation.

Facts, indeed, ought to have convinced the planters that such a measure could no longer be delayed. The insurrections which ever and anon took place, explosions inseparable from the high-pressure state of things, the destruction of property, &c.,

warned them, as they would not drive the slave to desperation, to strike the fetters from his limbs, and set him free. The change, no doubt, was a great one, and the question naturally arose, When they have liberty, how will they use it? The true answer should have been, Evangelize them, give them Christian instruction, and then you may set them free without injury to yourselves: in lieu of fetters on the limbs, give them Christian principle in the heart, and all shall be well. Instead of this wise procedure, an insensate cry was raised against Missionaries, as promoters of sedition, and as the cause of all these disturbances. To counteract the injurious influence of such a misconstruction, the Jamaica Committee of the Church Missionary Society, appealing to the friends of negro education in the mother country, strongly urged them to "use their best endeavours that a prejudice so unworthy, which would ascribe to the instruction of slaves those lamentable events, which instruction has the strongest tendency to hinder," might be obviated.

It was well for the West-India planters that amidst evil report and good report, the Missionaries persevered. The jubilee trumpet sounded, and the freedom of the slave throughout the British dominions was proclaimed. The day of emancipation, August 1, 1834, instead of being a day of terror, was one of devout worship and peaceful commemoration. The religious celebration of the day had been enjoined by most of the authorities. Proclamations were issued by several of the Governors inviting the people, in their churches and chapels, to return their humble and grateful thanks to Almighty God for the happy termination of the system of slavery; an invitation which was heartily responded to. Well might the late Sir T. Fowell Buxton say of that great act of emancipation, "It has cost us twenty millions, but it has saved the colonies." From what did it save them? Let the present wrecked condition of the Southern portion of the United States answer that question. They are, indeed, like a gallant ship, which, when it first left harbour, seemed as though it could not fail to accomplish a prosperous voyage. The storms met it; and long and bravely did it struggle with the adverse elements. Often, as it shipped tremendous seas, did it shake itself free from the superincumbent load, and rise again triumphantly to its work. At length, and in an unexpected moment, it succumbed. There was a weakness within; the slave institution, instead of being cast adrift, was pertinaciously retained; and the great Confederacy, so aspiring, so haughty, so assured of victory, lies helpless and dismasted among the breakers.

At the time of the American disruption, England, in her efforts to cripple and put down the shipment of slaves from the African coast to Cuba and elsewhere, was grievously hindered by the action of the United States. Southern influences swayed unduly the action of the great Republic. In his correspondence with the English authorities the American Secretary of State claimed that the stars and stripes should protect every vessel over which they floated, and exempt her from the right of search, although we knew that there were slaves on board. That obstruction is at an end, and reunited America has emancipated the slave, and treats slave-dealers as pirates. But through what an ordeal of sorrow has this position been attained—what fearful conflicts—what a loss of human life! From some such terrible convulsions the Slave-emancipation Act preserved the mother country and her West-India islands. To use again the words of Sir Fowell Buxton, "It has cost us twenty millions, but I trust it has saved us from the anger of the Deity, who could not but have looked on us in wrath and indignation, had not this evil been removed."

At this critical period in the history of the islands, this transition state, fraught with so many dangers, the Church Missionary Society helped to its power, and beyond its power. In August 1839, there were no less than twenty-two stations occupied by the Society, and these, moreover, precisely in the localities where help was most needed.

It has ever been a principle of the Society, as far as practicable, not to interfere with other men's labours. Before entering upon ground where it has not been before, the question has always been asked, Are there other Missionaries already there? do they teach and preach Jesus Christ? It is true they may not be Church-of-England Missionaries, they may be Presbyterians, Independents. But if they teach what saves the soul, the differences which exist in other respects do not, in the judgment of the Church Missionary Society, justify interference. A man is not saved by being an Episcopalian, or a Presbyterian, or an Independent, but by believing in Jesus Christ. The question is, do the existing Missionaries teach and preach Jesus Christ as the Way, the Truth, and the Life? then does the Church Missionary Society prefer to move in another direction; nor will it enter a field so pre-occupied, except on some special necessity. Unless this principle be acted upon, how shall the heathen world be fairly dealt with, or an initiative agency be sent forth in some degree commensurate with its great necessities? Clearly, if the Episcopalian lays it down as a rule that the preaching of Christ crucified is ineffectual unless carried out in connexion with Episcopacy, the Presbyterian, the Congregationalist, &c., will think themselves necessitated to adopt the same rule; and so, crowding together into the same contracted field of labour, they will jar and clash, to the great injury of our common Protestantism, and the undisguised exultation of the Church of Rome.

That the Church Missionary Society is that which it professes to be—Church of England and Episcopalian in its principles—cannot now be gainsayed. Its Missions, as they mature and develop, open out in the form of Episcopalian churches. They do so naturally, and without an effort, because the training has been throughout in that direction. No Church-of-England Society surpasses the Church Missionary Society in its solicitude to lead onward the native churches which it has been instrumental in raising up, to the maturity of the native episcopate; and that because it believes that, in doing so, it best provides for their stability and future usefulness. But it is not prepared to shut up Christianity within the limits of Episcopalian churches, and deal with other Christian communities as though Christian truth, when taught by them, has no saving power.

Acting according to its convictions in this respect, the Church Missionary Society formed its stations in unoccupied and remote parts of Jamaica, where no house for the Missionary could be rented. Buildings became requisite, and these proved to be expensive. Yet, although the cost of the Mission proved to be much greater than had been anticipated, there was a rich recompense in the happy results which followed. Large congregations were gathered. The decencies of human life became respected, and the degrading habits of former days were abandoned. Christian ordinances came to be valued and frequented; many were confirmed; others became communicants; schools were well attended; and affecting proofs were afforded of the readiness of the negro to assist in the expenses of the Mission.

The Society, however, found itself unable to carry on the work. During the year ending May 1839, its total of receipts had been 72,000*l.*; its expenditure amounted to 91,453*l.*: of this sum no less than 19,193*l.* had been expended on the West-Indies' Mission. Cotemporaneously there had been a large augmentation of the ecclesiastical establishments of the West-India islands. The duty of the Society therefore was plain —to adopt measures with a view to the transfer of as many of the stations as possible to the general ecclesiastical establishments, and thus gradually to relinquish the Mission.

Both Missionaries and people deeply regretted their severance from the Society. The Missionary at Birnam Wood expressed his feelings thus, in a letter dated December 5, 1842—

"I cannot find it in my heart to leave you altogether. I allow the change to take place in form; but I shall always work and pray for your success. My appointment as island curate came unsolicited, and partly unexpected, and therefore I receive it thankfully as a favour from God. I feel some reluctance in giving up my Missionary name; but since you consider such a change desirable, and I am allowed to remain in my sphere of labour, I still consider myself a Missionary indeed.

"I send my first year's subscription of one guinea, which I intend to continue as a thank-offering. I hope, moreover, to send you in future a yearly collection from my congregation; but other calls make it impossible at present."

The severance undoubtedly was a painful one, and the more so because several of the lesser stations were left, either totally without spiritual instruction, or, at least, less efficiently provided for than before. Thus, at Church Hill, which was to be left without a teacher, the catechist being transferred elsewhere, the singing on the last Lord's-day but one was drowned with sobs and crying. All the week the poor people were bringing their little farewell presents of yams, fowls, preserves, &c.; while on the last Lord's-day the congregation was large, the place crammed, the interest great, and the tears, sobs, and cries overpowering. On the evening before the Missionary and his family left a meeting was held. The people seemed broken down with sorrow, weeping long and loud. Quietly and slowly they came up to shake hands, and say "Good-bye." The women, with tears, exclaimed, "Oh, massa! oh, missis! what do we do now? We heart break!" While the men, almost choked with feeling, feebly, yet forcibly, uttered, "Good-bye!" Amidst many tokens of affection did they embark, scarcely daring to look back at the weeping company behind, whose eyes were intently fixed upon them, and whose hearts, there was every reason to believe, were lifted up in earnest wishes for their safety. "In a few minutes, the vessel being under weigh, we lost sight of a field where we had spent two and a-half years of interesting labour, leaving a hopeful people without a guide."

There is no doubt that it was a painful crisis, and we earnestly hope and pray that the Church Missionary Society may never be subjected to a like experience. It was about this time (1843) that Bishop Spencer entered upon the see of Jamaica, and feelingly does he describe the scenes which met his eye.—"It would give me great satisfaction to hear that the improved funds of the Church Missionary Society would induce that excellent Institution to resume some of their abandoned stations on this still thirsty land. Closed chapels, dilapidated school-houses, scattered congregations, and thousands of Maroon wanderers, all emancipated slaves, deprived of all means of Christian worship or instruction, notwithstanding the liberal provisions of the late Clergy Act, present me with an unhappy picture on my arrival in this colony, and show the disastrous consequences of your abandonment of a field which your Missionaries and catechists were so well qualified to occupy."

But although the funds did improve, the men were not available. Old Missions required to be reinforced; new fields of untouched heathenism—China, for instance—claimed help at the hands of the Society. In the very next Report the Committee declared, that if sixteen additional Missionaries were at that moment available, they could be instantly absorbed by the pressing necessities of the Missions, and that exclusive of any addition to the China Mission. They therefore appealed to the Universities and the younger clergy of the church to meet the immediate wants of the Society, and urged upon the friends of the Society generally the employment of earnest prayer, as the most efficacious means of obtaining a supply of men.

Thus the Society was literally compelled to a surrender of the West-Indies' Mission. The limited nature of the supplies received from home left it no option, and how shall it be with us at the close of the current year? The financial position of the Society is critical. Unless there be a decided increase on the income of the last year, the existing expenditure cannot be sustained. Old, experienced Missionaries are falling fast. Bühler, of the Yoruba Mission, whose letters we have so often read with such deep interest, has entered into his rest; and Rogers, the indefatigable itinerator in the Bombay Mission, is no more with us. Truly we may say, that if sixteen well-qualified men were to offer themselves at this moment, they could all, if pecuniary means were available, at once be disposed of. But where are the men? Let them only offer themselves, and the means will not be wanting. If the men offer themselves, the churches will be ashamed to withhold the money.

Many years have passed since the West-Indies' Mission was given up, during which the islands have passed through many changes. Many of the coloured people, leaving their old homes, emigrated to the mountains, often at a distance from the means of grace, and there cultivated the land on their own account. Every inhabitant of Jamaica who retains the enjoyment of bodily and mental health, by the exercise of a very moderate industry, can obtain all that is necessary for a life of independence. The wages, therefore, of the labour-market had for the free negro no attractions, and thus it became necessary, that, in 1858, Acts should be passed, enabling the employers of labour on plantations to obtain contract labourers by emigration from India and other countries. Thus the free negro of Jamaica found himself, not only freed from all compulsory labour, but freed from the necessity of working for wages, and placed in the position of an independent man, working his own land for his own supply. It is not surprising that, intoxicated for a time by the advantages of his new position, he should have declined in his respect for Christian ordinances, and such appears to have been the case in Jamaica in 1859, when not one-third of the population were in the habit of attending public worship.

Since then, however, there has been improvement. In 1860, there came upon the Jamaica population one of those extraordinary movements which are so remarkably fitted to arouse lifeless congregations from their sleep, and, if the people be wisely dealt with at such times, to place them in a more hopeful position than they were in previously. Important results followed. Concubinage, which had been lamentably prevalent, was abandoned by numbers, who came to be joined together in the holy state of matrimony, and noisy quarrelling in a great measure ceased, so that people lived in peace and quietude. Young people became more disposed to attend religious meetings than formerly, and the excitement, as it passed away, left behind it a deep-seated conviction as to the necessity of faith in Jesus, and of preparedness for his coming.

Amidst these fluctuations we could have no reason to suppose that the Church Missionary Society and its former labours could still be remembered in the island. The flux and reflux of events could scarcely have failed to obliterate all such reminiscences. It was therefore an event the more grateful, because entirely unexpected, to receive from Jamaica the following letters—

The Cottage, Gordon Town, P. O.,
Jamaica,
23rd May, 1865.

Reverend and dear Sir—As the Secretary of the Jamaica Church-of-England Home and Foreign Missionary Society, I have the pleasing duty of forwarding to you, by direction of our Committee, a bill of exchange for 80*l*., payable ninety days after sight, which sum it is requested may be placed to the credit of the Church Missionary Society for the use of its African Missions.

Our Society was established in 1861 by the Lord Bishop of Kingston, and its progress hitherto has been most encouraging. I forward a copy of the first Report, in order that you may see the objects of the Society's work. The special grant which has now been made to the Church Missionary Society, and which, we trust, may become an annual contribution, perhaps of increasing value, has arisen from the fact that several of the stations in this island, which were originally Church Missionary property, kept up by having ministers paid by the Church Missionary funds, feel a desire to show their gratitude for, and appreciation of, benefits bestowed on them in years gone by.

Moreover, the desire for the salvation of the heathen world by Missionary labours, spreading the knowledge of the one true God and Jesus Christ, whom He has sent, is, under the blessing of God, rapidly gaining ground among my clerical brethren; and this appears to be about the first opportunity that some of them and their congregations have had of sending their mite to support the efforts of that Society to which they owe so much.

Permit me to suggest, that the transmission to me, for distribution among some of my brethren, of a few of the Church Missionary Society's Reports and publications, may be of much benefit to the Society.

The contribution of 80*l.*, though sent as a grant from our Jamaica Missionary Society, I may tell you was sent in for this special purpose by four clergymen.

Rev. D. B. Panton, M.A. . .	£50
Rev. H. H. Isaacs, B.A. . .	15
Rev. G. T. Braine, B.A. . .	10
Rev. A. Findlay . . .	5
	£80

Messrs. Panton and Isaacs have churches and congregations which were formerly supported by the Church Missionary funds. Mr. Findlay was originally a teacher, sent out here and supported by the Church Missionary Society; and Mr. Braine has his sympathies warmly interested in that Society's behalf.

Pardon me if I am tedious, but I think you may like to have this information, and I think you will allow—when I tell you that this 80*l.* is, with very few exceptions, the voluntary contributions of black, and coloured people chiefly black—that the people of Jamaica are not unmindful of past favours bestowed on them.

I enclose a letter from the Rev. D. B. Panton, which I think will be gladly received by you.

Our fourth Report is in course of preparation; when printed I shall have the pleasure of sending some copies to you. Our good bishop, the Lord Bishop of Kingston, is at present in England, having taken his family home a few weeks ago, and you may possibly see something of his lordship, as he is deeply interested in the Missionary work.

I am, Rev. and dear Sir,

Yours faithfully,

(Signed) G. B. Brooks,

Bishop's Secretary, and Secretary to the Jamaica Church-of-England Home and Foreign Missionary Society.

The Rev. H. Venn, &c., B. D.

Birnam Wood, from which the next letter is dated, had been one of the Society's stations—

Birnam Wood, Parish St. George, Jamaica,
May 23, 1865.

Dear Sir,—With feelings of the greatest pleasure I have transmitted, through the Jamaica Home and Foreign Missionary Society, the sum of 50*l.*, as a contribution for Africa from the congregation of St. James' church, Birnam Wood, to the Church Missionary Society. It cannot but be gratifying to you to receive a thank-offering from one of that Society's stations, established in Jamaica thirty years ago, and to know that the members of the station generally hold in very grateful remembrance the generosity of the Society to them in past days.

The revival of Mission-work in the established Church in Jamaica is, under God, due to the Bishop of Kingston, who has brought its necessity very urgently before his clergy. The Lord's blessing has attended the effort, and I am one of many clerical brethren who feel that it is not only our duty to stir up the people of our charge to take an interest in that which is essentially the work of Jesus Christ our Lord; but that it is an exceeding great privilege to aid in a work which brings so rich a blessing to the pastor's own soul.

The money sent is a free-will offering. It comes from cheerful givers. Of the 50*l.* 46*l.* 10*s.* is the willing tribute of black and of a few coloured people. As an instance of the spirit in which the money was given, I may relate that one man, a black man, whose face I had not seen for two years, and whose very existence I had forgotten, came to me with 2*s.* 6*d.* in his hand, and on his lips this tale—"Minister, things have not been going on well with me these two years. I have been quarrelling with my neighbours. I have spent the little I had got by the sale of my coffee, in going to law. I had given up coming to church, and I had partly flung myself away; but when I heard of the good work that was going on up at Birnam Wood, I said, 'My wife, this wont do. The church members are getting a blessing by helping the Missionaries; but we are getting no blessing: a curse is upon us. Times used to be different. We must make the old times come back. We must pick up ourselves, and give something to the Missionaries.' My wife said, 'There is nothing in the house, not a sixpence.' But I told her 'There's yams in the field.' So, minister, we dug some yams, went to market yesterday, and sold them for 2*s*. 6*d*. Here, Sir, is the money." Another man gave 3*s*., but returned a few days after with 2*s*., saying that he felt he had not done enough for the Lord; that even the 5*s*. was too little, but that next year he hoped to do better.

Whilst thus forwarding our contributions, we thank God for this opportunity of supporting a Society, which has for its object the extension of Christ's kingdom throughout the world, and from which we ourselves have received in times past so many benefits.

The Rev. H. H. Isaacs, of Woodford, forwards, through the same channel, the sum of 15*l*., contributed by the congregation of another but considerably smaller station. Mr. Isaacs desires me to express on his behalf the great pleasure which it gives him to work in support of the Society, with the principles of which he so entirely agrees, and whose former exertions on their behalf are still remembered with gratitude by the people of Woodford.

He unites with me in earnestly requesting from you all means of information relating to Missions which can be supplied by the Church Missionary Society's Reports, &c., as without such means we cannot expect to sustain the freshly-awakened interest of our people in the cause of Missions.

(Signed) D. B. PANTON.

This is gratifying to us, and, what is better still, full of encouragement as to the Church of England congregations in Jamaica. There is no stronger proof of spiritual death in a congregation than indifference as to the great duty of Christian Missions. And when that duty is so felt as to constrain to effort and self-sacrifice, there is no stronger evidence of spiritual life. Moreover, as all such efforts spring from life, they re-act beneficially on the root from whence they are derived, and strengthen it. We joyfully welcome, then, these new helpers in the evangelization of Africa, once the children of the Society, now its willing co-operators. We may well impart intelligence to those who willingly give of their means to the work. In fact, it is now their work, and even if we wished to do so, we have no right to withhold from them that which is their own. We are persuaded that news from the Missions, regularly communicated month by month, will greatly increase interest, and, in benefiting the people, benefit the Society.

A VISIT TO THE PROPAGANDA COLLEGE IN ROME, BY THE REV. J. LONG.

HAVING spent six weeks in Rome during the winter of 1864, and having witnessed the wonderful activity of the Jesuits and other Roman ecclesiastics in the cause of Ultra Montanism, I was anxious to know something also of what Rome was doing in Missions among the heathen. I had read with much interest, in India, the accounts of the self-denying labours of Père Andrada and other Italian Missionaries in the wilds of Thibet, and among the Buddhists of Central Asia, as well as of the indefatigable exertions of the Jesuits at the Court of Akber and Shah Jehan.

I found the ecclesiastics connected with the Missions in Rome very polite, and willing to afford information: they, in fact, pride themselves on their Missionary zeal as one of the marks of a true church, and are very fond of contrasting what they consider the superior zeal and self-sacrifice of their Missionaries with that of Protestant Societies—certainly in this point, *fas est ab hoste doceri.**

I paid repeated visits to the Collegio della Propaganda Fide in the Piazza de Spagna. It was founded in 1622 by Pope Gregory XV. with the express object of training, as Missionaries to heretical or infidel countries, young foreigners, who should return to their native land to spread the Romish faith. Rome has always adopted the maxim, a diamond can best cut a diamond; and this college, very different from some Protestant Missionary Societies, has preferred training native agents to the costly machinery of foreigners. The external success has shown it was a wise step. The number of pupils now amounts to about 120 from all countries. I met two students from

* The Propaganda has a cardinal as Secretary, and the business of its Missions is managed by a Committee composed of ten or twelve cardinals: a report is given in every Sunday to the Pope.

India there, who, in common with the pupils of the English, Irish, Scotch, and German Colleges, attend the lectures on theology and science of the Jesuit fathers. At the Collegio Romano I heard some of these lectures, and it was a striking sight to observe more than 400 youths in their picturesque gowns, blue, red, white, according to their respective nationalities, taking notes of the lectures. The professor delivers all his lectures in Latin, which is the *lingua franca* of the Roman colleges. There is special instruction delivered in the learned languages of the East. I was acquainted with one professor in the Collegio Romano who was sent to Syria to complete his studies in Arabic: he is now adding Sanskrit to his acquisitions.

The policy of Rome is "unity amid diversity." During the Epiphany week, which may be called the Missionary week in Rome, a Missionary sermon is preached every day—on one day in English, another in French, another in German, another in Italian. I heard two delivered in English—one by the President of the English College in Rome, the other by a Capuchin friar; in both, the audience, as is so often the case in Rome, was composed chiefly of English travellers, who, however, did not seem to contribute a large sum; but Rome's chief reliance is in the untiring zeal of her collectors, who are fully organized.

In rituals, Rome shows her malleability. While in England a parish is often thrown into endless confusion by a young clergyman's slavery to the letter of every rubric, Rome allows a wide range: though in Europe she insists on the Latin ritual, she permits Eastern churches to celebrate the offices in the Oriental languages. I attended one of the services in the Propaganda chapel during Epiphany week, in which service was performed at five different altars in Syriac, Chaldee, Greek, Slavonic, and Armenian. The priests, dressed in the oriental ecclesiastical dress and with the flowing beard, presented a very venerable and dignified appearance. The Abbé Bertrand gives full information on this subject of the use of oriental liturgies.*

The library of the Propaganda contains 30,000 volumes, chiefly on theology and canon law, very few are on Missions. There are, however, some valuable manuscripts on Indian languages, and one contains a report of the Synod of Diamper, which decreed the burning of the manuscript documents of the Syrian churches, and whose proceedings are worth being known.

* Histoire des Missions de Madura.

Attached to the college is the printing-press. well supplied with oriental types. Many works of great typographical beauty have issued from this. But Lyons has taken the lead of Rome in Missionary publications. I visited the Propaganda printing-press at Lyons, and was surprised at the great activity and ability exhibited in the publication of the "Annales de le Propagation de la Foi," which are issued simultaneously every second month, in five or six of the leading languages of Europe. They have a circulation of 220,000 copies, viz. French, 142,000; English, 20,000; German, 20,500; Spanish, 1950; Flemish, 6000; Italian, 25,000; Portuguese, 2500; Dutch, 2000; Polish, 500. The expense of the "Annals" and other Missionary publications amounts to 217,000 francs annually.*

I was present in the chapel of the Propaganda at the annual festival of languages in the Epiphany week. It lasts two days, amid a crowded assemblage of cardinals, monsignors, and visitors from all nations, admitted by ticket—when the pupils recite speeches and poetry in their respective languages, relating to the work of Missions as the result of Christ's manifestation to the Gentiles. The visitor is supplied with an Italian translation of what is recited. The performance is varied by some choice music. The day I was present thirty-two different languages were spoken: among these was the Hindustani. This, and other scenes in Rome, showed the wonderful power the Papacy has of attracting within the sphere of her influence all nationalities, and giving scope to every kind of talent.

It is a curious fact, that while at Rome the old trunk of the papacy is rotten at the core, yet it is sending out vigorous branches and offshoots abroad: the Papacy has more moral vigour in Paris than she has at Rome;† while

* The modern efforts in connexion with the Propaganda began in 1816, in the labours of two females to collect subscriptions among the workmen of Lyons for Missions in America, and weekly sou subscriptions were received. The first four years 4000 francs annually were collected, but the next year it rose to 105,000 francs, and now it has reached 4,000,000 francs: in 1822 it was fully organized at the Propaganda, with Lyons, its cradle, as its centre.

† The "Annals de le Propagation de la Foi" give many details of the zeal exhibited in collecting for Missions—by knife-grinders in the Alps, girls of the working-class at Leghorn, poor villagers in Ireland, the operatives of Amiens, poor soldiers, the inmates even of hospitals, and the fishermen of New Caledonia;—while more than 500 Romish females have, within the last twenty years, gone out from Europe to engage in

in Italy her numbers are rapidly lessening, in England they are increasing, and in India there are twelve Italian Bishops, and a host of Italian Missionaries. Out of 2000 Jesuit Missionaries now in the field, 490 are from Italy. The Pope's Chamberlain told me they were strengthening their forces at Calcutta and Bombay. The dissolution of the monasteries in Italy will supply many candidates for foreign work.*

But Rome is being counterchecked in a quarter where she least expected it—in the movement now increasing rapidly among Italian priests and laymen in favour of a reform in the Italian church, similar to that of the English church, in favour of Catholicity in opposition to the *modern* claims of the Papacy, and though the movement *at present* aims only at *disciplinary* reform, yet the following points, warmly advocated, must lead *further*, and involve doctrinal changes, viz. the abolition of celibacy, the free circulation of the Bible, the liturgy in the vernacular, and the restoration of their rights in the election of bishops to the clergy and people. I met at Naples the leader in this movement, which comprises more than 800 priests, and has the cordial support of the leading journals in Italy.

I visited at Naples a Missionary college, founded a century ago by the celebrated Jesuit Missionary to China, Father Ripa, for the training of Chinese youths for the Mission work in Europe. It contains now twelve pupils. The numbers formerly were greater, but experience has taught Rome, that while it is expedient to have a few natives trained in Europe, yet the danger of denationalizing them counteracts in various respects the benefits they would derive from a residence in Europe.

At Paris there is a flourishing Romish Missionary College in the Rue de Bec, which has sent out a great number of labourers into the field, and who, in the spirit of self-sacrifice and identification with native society, set a noble example, worthy of a purer creed. Some of the Missionaries and Bishops have won the crown of martyrdom in China and Cochin China within the last ten years. A room in this College, called La Salle de Martyrs, is set apart for exhibiting some of their relics and the instruments of torture by which they met their death.

---

female education in India and China, where they labour with great zeal and self-denial *for life*. Two sisters from Trent, in Italy, have lately gone to the Kishnagurh Romish Mission in North India.

* In 1863, France contributed to the Romish Mission 3,307,000 francs; Italy only 420,000 francs, or one-seventh. France has 90,000 females in orders as Sœurs de Charité, &c.; Rome has very few belonging to the active class, but plenty of the so-called contemplative. In France, much of the money is raised by subscriptions of one sou weekly: there is a collector to each ten persons, and another head collector to each of these ten collectors, or 100 subscribers: there is a chief collector for 100 collectors, who transmits the amount to the Councils, one of which is at Lyons, the other at Paris, composed of ecclesiastics and laymen, who distribute the amount among the different Missions: they render their services gratuitously. Each collector circulates a copy of the "Annals" among his ten subscribers. After being read, it remains with him: 180,000 copies are circulated every two months among subscribers.

HEADMEN IN INDIA AND HEADMEN IN RUSSIA.

It is the growing conviction, both of Missionaries of all Societies in India and of Mission Societies in England, that the time is come when it is "expedient that native converts should be trained, at as early a stage as possible, upon a system of *self-government*, and of contributing to the support of their own native teachers." The usage that has prevailed hitherto was one in which the Missionary was the pastor of the natives, and, practically, dictator in every thing: he did almost every thing *for* them and little *by* them; but experience has taught Missionaries the evils of this in the following particulars—

In respect of the Missionary: his hands soon become so full that his time and energy are wholly occupied by the converts, and he extends his personal labours to the heathen in a continually decreasing ratio. His work also involves more or less of secularity and account-keeping. The character of a simple Missionary is complicated with that of the director and paymaster of the Mission.

In respect of the converts: they naturally imbibe the notion that all is to be done *for* them — they are *dependents* upon a foreign Mission, rather than *members* of a native church. There may be the individual spiritual life, but there is no *corporate* life: though the converts may amount to thousands in number they are *powerless as a body*. The principles of self-support, self-government, and self-extension are wanting, on which depend the breath of life in a native church.

In respect of the Missionary Society: the system entails a vast and increasing expense in its oldest Missions; so that instead of advancing to "the regions beyond," it is detained upon old ground: it is involved in disputes about native salaries, pensions, repairs of buildings, &c.: and as the generation baptized in infancy rise up under this system, the Society has found itself in the false position of ministering to a population of nominal Christians, who, in many instances, give no assistance to the progress of the Gospel.*

The following admirable recommendations are given for working out this principle—

That the converts should be encouraged to form themselves, for mutual support and encouragement, into "*Christian Companies.*" (Acts iv. 23.) In Africa the term "company" has already been adopted for their native Associations. The members of such companies should not be too numerous, or too scattered, to prevent their meeting together in familiar religious conference.

One of each company should be selected, or approved of, by the Missionary, as an elder or "*Christian headman,*" to call together and preside over the companies, and to report to the Missionary upon the moral and religious condition of his company, and upon the efforts made by the members for extending the knowledge of Christ's truth. Each Christian company should be encouraged to hold *weekly meetings* under its headman, with the occasional presence of the Missionary, for united counsel and action, for reading the Scriptures and prayer, and for making contributions to the Church Fund, if it only be a handful of rice, or more, as God shall prosper them.

Monthly Meetings of the Christian headmen should be held under the Missionary, or some one whom he may appoint, at which meetings the headmen should report upon their respective companies, hand over the contributions, receive from the Missionary spiritual counsel and encouragement, and commend their common work, in united prayer, to the great Shepherd and Bishop of souls.

The FIRST STEP in the organization of the native church will be taken when any company, or one or more neighbouring companies unitedly, shall be formed into a *congregation, having a schoolmaster or native teacher located amongst them, whose salary is paid out of the Native Church Fund.*

A SECOND STEP in the organization of the native church will be taken when one or more congregations are formed into *a native pastorate, under an ordained native, paid by the Native Church Fund.*

The Christian headmen of the companies comprised within a native pastorate should cease to attend the monthly meetings of headmen under the Missionary, and should meet under their native pastor.

As long as the Native Church Fund is under the management of the Missionary Society, the native pastors, paid out of that fund, must remain under the general superintendence of some Missionary of the Society, who shall be at liberty to minister occasionally in their churches, and to preside jointly with the native pastors at the meetings of headmen and other congregational meetings; the relation between the native pastor and the Missionary being somewhat analogous to that of curates with a non-resident incumbent.

A THIRD STEP in the organization of the native church will be taken when a sufficient number of native pastorates having been formed, *a District Conference* shall be established, consisting of pastors and lay delegates from each of their congregations, and the European Missionaries of such district. District Conferences should meet periodically for consulting upon the native-church affairs, as distinguished from the action of the Society.

When any considerable district has been thus provided for by an organized native church, foreign agency will have no further place in the work, and that district will have been fully prepared for a *native episcopate.*†

But events are marching on rapidly: "the large number of native Christians in South India, the maturity of many of them in Christian attainments, and the liberal contributions which they make for religious and benevolent objects, suggest the inquiry whether they should not only be placed in an independent position, but have their organization completed by a native bishop being placed at their head, to have exclusive authority

* "Minute on the Organization of Native Churches," 1861, p. 1.

† Ibid., p. 3.

over all the native agents who might be transferred to him, supported by the native church, the European agents remaining under the authority of the English bishop, who would have the native one as his suffragan." One of the most experienced Indian Missionaries in South India suggests on this subject—

While the native bishop would be entirely independent of the European clergy, they would be able to assist him, and strengthen his hands in a variety of ways, until the time arrived to withdraw altogether. The native church would by this means be materially strengthened, and experience would be gained by the bishop, native clergy, and catechists, in self-government and management of their own affairs. A great increase would, I am persuaded, soon appear in the number of ordained agents; not men who aspire to European views and habits, but men who would be *veritable native pastors*, in charge of one or two congregations, with moderate salaries, not necessarily very much above what the catechists receive now, but enough to keep them respectably in a relative position to their flocks.

One very great advantage of trying this plan while the Missionaries are still carrying on their operations in the same field, would be, that we should avoid the sudden transition of the church into native hands, and the possible breaking down of the bishop and his clergy if left to themselves without any previous preparation and aid.

At a native meeting held lately in the Tinnevelly district, attended by 140 headmen of congregations, besides native clergy and catechists, the people responded heartily to this proposal.

This plan of a coadjutor native bishop for native churches has met with the cordial concurrence of the Bishop of Calcutta and of the Church Missionary Committee, and will, we hope, ere long, be a reality.

While the Indian Government has long been working out the plan of training natives for self-government politically—while Hindus are now members of all the legislative councils of India, and sit as judges in the highest courts of judicature—it is of vital importance that the Christian church should not lag behind in this great object of preparing for an independent position; and that, as we have native judges and native members of council, so we should have native bishops. Surely when Africa has a negro bishop, the Aryan race of India is entitled to a native one.

This proposal of village Christian headmen is quite in accordance with the old village institutions of the Hindus, which have maintained their ground in India from the day when the Brahmins entered the valley of the Ganges; each village had a portion of ground attached to it, committed to the management of the inhabitants. Colonel Sykes, in his admirable treatise on the "Landed tenures of the Dekhan," and Briggs on the "Land Tax of India," show that, before the period of the Moslem invasion, the villages had a constitution for their internal government, each village having a *Patel*, or chief, assisted by a village accountant; he was held in great esteem, even under the Mohammedan Government: the office was an object of ambition to chiefs: it was hereditary; free lands and other emoluments were attached to it; the hereditary lands of extinct families became their property, or that of the village community.* The Patel was responsible to Government for the village revenues, which formed a definite sum fixed by the Government, but the details were settled by the Patel, who, for his trouble, had a right to a portion of grain from each cultivator. Cases have occurred in which women held the office of Patel. The Patel superintended the police of the village, regulated its internal economy, and presided in all the village councils: he had the power to fine, imprison, and seize all offenders. A number of villages constituted a circle, with an officer over them: eighty-six villages formed themselves into a district, at the head of

* Many of the headmen could not write, and the signature of an agriculturist was the figure of a plough, of a tradesman a pair of scales, of a silversmith a hammer, of a policeman a sword, of the village astrologer an almanac, of a washerman the mallet.

which was a *desmukh*, who was responsible for the revenue, on the collection of which he had a per-centage: he superintended the cultivation and police of the district, and carried into effect the orders of Government, serving as a link between the village headmen and the Government. Unfortunately the English Government has, in too many cases, allowed these men to be superseded by a bureaucracy, and by ill-paid, venal employés, whose only aim was to fleece the peasants.

The Hindus have had this training for self-government, not only by village councils, but also by various *Sabhas*, or assemblies, of which there were fifteen different kinds, composed of all classes, from the village merchant to the village barber. Their *Panchayat*, or jury composed of five, has existed in India from time immemorial, and has been recognised by the English Government as one of great importance. In 1811 they granted the jury system, in an improved form, to Ceylon, and in 1827 to Madras, now it is extended to all India.†

Nor has this beautiful and successful system of self-government been confined to India. Baillie, in his "Land Tax of India," writes, "In Persia, and the country about the Oxus, the cultivators are represented as being pretty much in the same way as they are still found in India: they are congregated in mouzas or villages, to which the lands that they cultivate are in some manner attached, and which, in some instances, appear to have peculiar customs of their own, so that the system of village communities, which is usually considered an institution peculiarly Hindu, was a phase of society common to India, with the countries bordering it on the north-west."

Each village in Russia forms a commune, *mir*, or little world, a republic in miniature, which elects its own chief (*starosta*, *i.e.* elder) by universal suffrage, for three years or annually; but if the commune is dissatisfied with him, it can remove him. He has to submit an annual account of the expenditure to the commune, which elects the receivers of taxes, votes the communal budget, divides the land, apportions the taxes, and selects the persons to be recruits in the army: family disputes or litigation about property are decided by its arbitration. All its decisions are made publicly and verbally, as few of the peasants can read. In some localities where the majority of the men are absent engaged in distant labour, the women constitute the communal assemblies, decide on the division of the land, the taxes, and recruiting, and discharge all the duties except those of the village chiefs. A number of these headmen reunite in a district (*volosta*) to vote on the election of a district chief, the district budget, and to decide on disputes between the different communities forming a kind of federal administration.

The bureaucratic despotism of Russia interfered in practice with the working of this in various cases; still it has effected an immense amount of good in preserving among the peasantry the elements of self-government; and this year has witnessed, in Russia, peasants, elected to the local parliaments, discharging satisfactorily and calmly, in unison with the nobles, the duties devolving on them, and forming a broad basis for constitutional government in Russia, the advent of which is near at hand. The new institutions of Russia, as well as her noble work of self-emancipation, rest on this principle of village headmen elected by the community, which has for ages preserved the seeds of national life in Russia amid the distractions arising from Polish or Tartar invasion, and it is destined to achieve greater things yet. The most eminent statesmen of India have equally regarded the village commune as of vital importance for training the Hindus for self-government, and saving the European from that system of "meddling and muddling" which has been so mischievous in India both in Government and Missions.

† See Ram Raz on "Trial by Jury," Journal of the Asiatic Society, Vol. iii. pp. 244—257.

MINUTE ON THE MORE COMPLETE ORGANIZATION OF THE NATIVE CHURCH IN SOUTH INDIA.

The large number of native Christians in South India, the maturity of many of them in Christian attainments, and the liberal contributions which they make for religious and benevolent objects, suggest the inquiry, whether the time is not come when the older congregations should be placed upon a self-supporting system, and become independent of the Society. The more intelligent native Christians, also, feel that they ought to relieve the Society from the support of native pastors, and take the charge upon themselves; whilst many of the most experienced Missionaries think that such a change of system would probably cherish the more rapid growth of the native church, and set them at liberty to devote themselves to the evangelization of the heathen. The subject has, during the last year, been brought under the special consideration of the Committee by the Senior Missionary in Tinnevelly, the Rev. J. Thomas, who has laboured for thirty years in that province, and gathered large numbers from amongst the heathen. He has been latterly in charge of congregations numbering 12,000 converts, and has had the superintendence of several native ministers. The following are extracts of his letter upon the subject—

Extracts of letter from Rev. J. Thomas, to Rev. H. Venn, dated Mengnanapuram, June 21, 1864.

Ever since I left England, the question, "What can be done for the best interests of the native church in Tinnevelly?" has occupied my thoughts continually. Perhaps you will feel disposed to say, "Do precisely as we have suggested in our printed minute on the subject." Admirable as these suggestions are, they cannot be acted upon without some modification, especially in the older Missions of the Society; at the same time, to carry out their spirit, and adopt them literally, as far as possibly may be, is my earnest desire.

My thoughts have been much directed to the kind of superintendence which should be exercised over those agents who are paid by a native church fund. It appeared to me that, so long as the European Missionary of the district superintended and paid both kinds of agents, it would be difficult to convey to the minds of our people generally a correct idea of the distinction between a native church fund and a Missionary fund. And, supposing that all the congregations supported by native contributions were transferred to one European Missionary to superintend, in the character of rural dean, archdeacon, or commissary of the Bishop of Madras, in all probability many objections would be raised against such a measure, and it would only be preparing the way for the appointment of an European bishop; a measure which, I think, would not be the most favourable for the development of the native church.

The next question which presented itself was, "Is the time arrived for the appointment of a native bishop, who should have authority alike over Edeiyenkudy in the south, and Panneivellei in the north of Tinnevelly?" This assumes that European clergymen, as well as natives, would be placed under his authority and superintendence, a measure which has universally been considered as a very formidable objection, if not an insuperable one, to such a scheme.

It then occurred to me that it might be possible to have a native bishop in Tinnevelly at once, who should have exclusive authority over all the native agents who might be transferred to him, supported by the native church, while the European agents of foreign Societies, in the character of Missionaries, and as ministers of the English church, might still continue, as long as they are required in the province, under the authority and superintendence of the Bishop of Madras.

I do not think it wise to anticipate or suggest objections to this scheme; all I would ask in mooting the question, is a candid consideration of such objections before the scheme is discarded *in limine* as anomalous and impracticable.

My proposal is this, that a native bishop should be appointed at once, to whom should be transferred the self-supporting congregations and spiritual agents. I should be prepared to hand over to him, at once, fifteen or twenty of my best congregations, and make the utmost endeavour every year to increase the number as contributions increased. Other districts might be willing and able to double this number, and there would be at once, not a mere nucleus of a native church, but a goodly number of congregations to be superintended, which would form by no means an insignificant episcopate.

As far as I have mentioned the subject to our own Missionaries, and I did so at our Conference in April last, and to some of the Society for the Propagation of the Gospel brethren also, no hostile opinion has been expressed by any one, but all seemed prepared to look upon it as likely to solve the great difficulty connected with this question.

While the native bishop would be entirely independent of the European clergy, they would be able to assist him, and strengthen his hands in a variety of ways, until the time arrived to withdraw altogether. The native church would by this means be materially strengthened, and experience would be gained by the bishop, native clergy, and catechists, in self-government and management of their own affairs. A great increase would, I am persuaded, soon appear in the number of ordained agents; not men who aspire to European views and habits, but men who would be *veritable native pastors*, in charge of one or two congregations, with moderate salaries, not necessarily very much above what the catechists receive now, but enough to keep them respectably in a relative position to their flocks. Our catechists now maintain themselves comfortably on 8 rupees. They are, to all intents and purposes, the native pastors, and mere ordination would not necessarily involve any very heavy additional expense, so that a moderate increase above 8 rupees would be a very suitable provision, *nor would this be hopelessly beyond the resources of the native church*, as is the case with regard to those who have been ordained already.

One very great advantage of trying this plan, while the Missionaries are still carrying on their operations in the same field, would be, that we should avoid the sudden transition of the church into native hands, and the possible breaking down of the bishop and his clergy if left to themselves without any previous preparation and aid.

If this plan in the main should be considered feasible, the subordinate points can be dealt with afterwards.

We have had recently three very important and interesting meetings in these districts. The one at Mengnanapuram, which was held this day fortnight, was attended by 140 headmen of the congregations, besides native clergy and catechists. I entered at length into the whole question, and the people responded heartily, and several of them spoke with great propriety, for the character of the meeting was that of a Committee, where every member was at liberty to say what he pleased, and not a formal public meeting. When every one who wished to give expression to his opinion had done so, I proposed for their adoption a series of resolutions to the effect, "That it is the duty of Christians to support their own teachers, and to take measures for extending the kingdom of Christ among the heathen; the duty of headmen in particular to exert themselves, not only in giving, but in urging the people under their influence to support liberally the scheme now initiated." It was also agreed that from the 25th of this month fourteen congregations should be supplied with catechists, to be paid out of the Native Church Fund.

I told them what my views and wishes were with regard to a native bishop, and the desirableness of having a *distinct native Tamil church*. They received the announcement with joyful approbation; and one of them, the most intelligent and influential, exclaimed that he hoped he might yet be permitted to see that blessed consummation. This meeting was a most important one, and I felt thankful that I had come out from England this third time, if it were only to be present on the occasion. I have now briefly sketched out what I conscientiously believe to be the best method of dealing with the church in Tinnevelly, and I am prepared to exercise whatever influence I possess among the people, after nearly twenty-eight years' connexion with them, to promote, foster, and strengthen this measure.

Similar meetings to that held here were held at Satthankullam and Asirvadapuram, which I fully proposed attending; but, in consequence of absolute prostration of strength, I was unable to do so, and my son and the native clergymen attended both places, and he speaks of the result as indeed not quite so enthusiastic as at Mengnanapuram, though I am disposed to think that the people of Asirvadapuram were not a whit behind those of this district.

The two main inquiries which arise out of the proposition of Mr. Thomas are—as to the sufficiency of funds for the support of a native pastorate, and as to the supply of men competent for the pastoral office.

With respect to funds, there is little to fear. The 30,000 native Christians of Tinnevelly already raise more than 1600*l.* a year for religious and charitable purposes. There have also been "Native Pastorate" endowments commenced in twenty-one different districts in South India, which amount in the aggregate to 3300*l.* As Christianity gradually spreads among the wealthier classes of society, the supply of funds will become more abundant; but even at present more than 100 native pastors might be supported by the contributions of the people.

With respect to the supply of suitable men, the following Minute of a Conference of Missionaries, held in Tinnevelly, in January 1865, will show that the statement of Mr. Thomas is confirmed by the judgment of the rest of the Missionary body—

It appeared to the brethren every way desirable that spiritual and devoted men should, as opportunity offers, be ordained as pastors to the congregations in which they are now respectively labouring as catechists; their pay at the present rate being supplied by the Native Church Self-sustaining Fund, and subsidized by an equal amount on the part of the Church Missionary Society. Where men of character, piety, maturity of age, and judgment, can be found, we think that their being thus set apart as ordained ministers of the congregations in which they are now acting as catechists would have a wide and beneficial influence for good.

A copy of the letter of Mr. Thomas having been submitted to the Bishop of Calcutta, his lordship made, in reply, the following important remarks and suggestions upon the scheme—

Extract from a letter of the Bishop of Calcutta to the Rev. Henry Venn, dated February 8, 1865.

As it is getting near post time, I am hardly able to enter at length upon Mr. Thomas's important letter. But would not one way of meeting his views, and removing my objections, be to consecrate a native as coadjutor to the Bishop of Madras, with such work as the diocesan bishop assigns to him? And it might be agreed that he should receive a salary from the Church Missionary Society, or from the Church Missionary Society and the Society for Propagation of the Gospel together, on condition that he ordinarily resides in Tinnevelly, and takes the charge of such native congregations as are handed over to him. Then he might also be employed in travelling at intervals about other parts of the diocese, and confirming the Tamil congregations more frequently than can be done now. He should be consecrated by the Metropolitan and two of his suffragans, and not removable without the Metropolitan's consent. In this way the geographical difficulty would be obviated, my serious objection to separating Europeans and natives into different churches would be removed, the general influence and supervision of the Bishop of Madras would be retained for Tinnevelly, and the native bishop's position to the English Missionaries residing near him would be less ambiguous than on any other plan. Doubtless the question of discipline in connexion with such a bishop must be carefully considered, as we learn to our cost from the mass of troublesome technicalities now before the Privy Council, and I have no doubt that an Act of Parliament would be necessary. It seems to me that power might be given to the Metropolitan, on the application of any diocesan bishop, with the sanction of the Crown, to consecrate such a coadjutor to the diocese of the bishop making the application, Government not being charged with his salary. In this way I might myself hope some day to have both a Bengalee and Hindustanee coadjutor. It seems to me that some such plan as this would be at once most ecclesiastically correct and practically useful.

There are two recent precedents of the appointment of coadjutor bishops by the Crown without Acts of Parliament. In 1836 Dr. Mountain was consecrated by the Archbishop of Canterbury, under letters patent, by the title of Bishop of Montreal, to be a coadjutor to the Bishop of Quebec. In 1856 Archdeacon Courtenay was in the same way appointed and consecrated coadjutor to the Bishop of Jamaica. The letters patent thus limit the exercise of the episcopal functions—"Provided nevertheless, and it is our royal will and pleasure, that the said Reginald Courtenay shall not have, use, or exercise any jurisdiction, power, or authority within the said diocese of Jamaica, save and except such jurisdiction, power, and authority as shall be thought requisite, reasonable, and convenient by the said Bishop of Jamaica, and as shall be licensed and limited to him by a commission or commissions, under the hand and seal of the said Bishop of Jamaica."—*See Parl. Paper, "Church Affairs of Jamaica," 20th May*, 1856.

H. VENN,
R. LONG,
C. C. FENN,
M. DAWES, } *Secretaries.*

CHURCH MISSIONARY HOUSE,
July 10, 1865.

ITINERATING IN AFFGHANISTAN.

The valley of Peshawur, to which the following remarks relate, occupies the north-east corner of Affghanistan. Its extent is about sixty-five miles in length, with a breadth of about fifty, whilst its Affghan population somewhat exceeds 500,000. The soil, for the most part, is very fertile, and produces abundant crops of wheat, rice, maize, and sugar-cane.

It is now ten years since the Missionary first came amongst the people of this valley, and during this period about fifty souls have been gathered out from its heathen and Mohammedan inhabitants, and led to confess the faith of Christ crucified. But it is not only in the number of those who have been already turned from the false religions of their forefathers that we observe an indication of God's signal blessing resting upon this Mission; we see it also in a marked manner in the favourable change that is gradually coming over the public mind. Indeed, when it is remembered that within the last year or two the head British official of the district positively forbade the Missionary to itinerate amongst the Affghans of the Peshawur valley, on account of their religious fanaticism, the following notices of a journey just made through this very district will appear in a more favourable light.

The Missionary party consisted of the Rev. Thomas Wade, three converts, and myself. Of the native Christians who accompanied us, two were Affghans, a brief account of whom may prove interesting, as they are from the neighbourhood in which the itineration took place. Their respective names are Fazl i Haq and Yacub. The former is the son of a learned and wealthy Mussulman, and is a young Affghan of energy and devotion to his Master's cause. In the five years that he has been a Christian he has had much to suffer for his faith, having been cast off by his father, and rejected with scorn by many of his former Mohammedan friends. Yacub, the other Affghan, is a Syud, or, in other words, belongs to the family of Mohammed. He is somewhat past the meridian of life, a great portion of which he has entirely devoted to study. In his character he differs widely from his determined brother Affghan, being of a quieter temperament, but manifesting a steady zeal for the advancement of our Saviour's kingdom.

On the 24th of March 1865, we started from the city of Peshawur. Our baggage, consisting of a tent, a table, and a few other necessaries, was placed on camels, which are the usual beasts of burden in this part of Asia. Leaving the city by the Lahore gate, we passed close by the palm-trees on which it is said that Avitabile used to suspend the heads of offending Affghans, and found ourselves on the famous Trunk Road. This road, after running 1600 miles, terminates at Peshawur, the point of our Indian empire nearest to Central Asia. The valley looked very beautiful, being covered with rich green fields. In the midst of these rose village walls, and here and there a watch-tower, which bespoke the predatory character of the Affghan tribes. The mountains which surround the valley had a most imposing appearance: the Khyber Pass, of historical celebrity, looked dark and threatening, whilst the snowy ridges beyond, some of which rise to 12,000 and 14,000 feet, had a most sublime aspect. As we passed along the road we could not help contrasting the perfect beauty of God's creation, as here exhibited, with the marred and deformed character with which Satan has imbued the inhabitants of these regions. Our little company halted at the village of Pubbi, where we had determined to remain for the night. At the approach of evening the Christians, and as many as liked to come, assembled for divine service. After a portion of Scripture had been read and explained, Mr. Wade led us in prayer as we thanked God for the mercies of the journey, and committed ourselves into his hands for the night.

On the following morning, as a storm was pending, we determined to press on to Nowshera; so, after a short address to a crowd in the village on the salvation which the Gospel offers, we passed on. About noon we arrived at our destination, which is a small Affghan town in which the Mission has lately opened a commodious school. In the course of the afternoon Mr. Wade visited this establishment for conferring a Christian education, free of expense, on those who like to avail themselves of it. He found about thirty boys and young men in attendance. The next day being Sunday, we rested from travelling; and, as opportunity was afforded, we had intercourse with the natives. In two places preaching was successfully attempted. The subject of one of the discourses was the Prodigal Son, and this in particular engaged a number of willing hearers.

Leaving Nowshera, we crossed the Cabul river by the bridge of boats, and came to the low range of brown hills which run along the opposite bank. These formed a pleasing contrast to the valley adjoining the river, which was covered with green corn-fields. The ground over which we were passing was the scene of Runjeet Singh's victory over the Affghans in 1824. An old Affghan, who was himself engaged in the battle, told us the story of it. It appears to have been a dreadful conflict, as, in the course of the few days that the fighting continued, no less than 50,000 Affghans either fell by the sword, or, in seeking to cross the river close by, found a watery grave. A few hours marching brought us to Hoti Murdan, which is a British outpost where the regiment of Guides is stationed. We had scarcely pitched our tent before several native friends came to visit us, one of whom was Dilawur Khan, the Christian officer. The next morning our hearts were cheered by visits from a great many natives who came from the village and neighbourhood. With them conversation was held, and, on their leaving us, we gave those who were able to read some publication in their native tongue. Towards evening the number of visitors gradually increased, so much so, that, although we were all engaged in speaking, we could no longer attempt to have conversation with each one separately. Preaching, therefore, was resolved on. Mr. Wade, one of the Christians, and I, addressed the assembled crowd, and endeavoured to set before them the way of salvation by Christ. When quite wearied, we gave the people permission to go away, and those, who could read, took with them copies of the Gospels or of some other publication. Indeed, on this day more than a hundred books, of one description or another, must have been disposed of.

Dnring our stay at this encouraging sphere of labour, Mr. Wade and I visited some Buddhist ruins, called Takht i Bhaie. From these remains it is evident that there was at one time a flourishing Buddhist colony here, of which there is now no other trace left than piles of old buildings. From these and other ruins Dr. Bellew and Major Johnstone, who are staying here on duty, have collected many interesting relics. Whilst we were thus examining the Buddhist temples and houses, the day had so far advanced, that we found it necessary to take shelter from the hot rays of the sun in an adjoining Affghan village. On proceeding towards it, some of the principal men met us, and invited us into their "hoojras," or great chambers. These hoojras are to be found in every district. Indeed each headman feels himself bound by every tie of honour to support one. That which we entered was a fair specimen of those we had seen in many other villages. It was about twenty-four yards long, by four in width, and some eight feet in height. The walls and the flat roof were composed of mud, the latter being supported by poles, placed across, over which, also, was a layer of twigs. The doorway was the only means for the admission of light and for the exit of smoke. The furniture consisted of a number of low bedsteads, on each of which was a rug and a pillow. On these we seated ourselves, and were presently surrounded by the chief men. They then besieged us with offers of hospitality; and we felt ourselves constrained to accept of some milk, eggs, and other food that was brought us. The Affghans, like the Arabs, are very attentive to strangers who place themselves under their protection. And, as a rule, they feel themselves compelled to entertain all travellers who may be passing through their territories. When the heat of the sun had somewhat subsided, we returned to our tent, being thankful for the timely shelter and refreshment afforded. On our arrival, there were again visitors waiting for us. Indeed, so great was the desire of the people to have conversation with us, that we were obliged to make a few days' halt.

Setting out from this interesting field of labour, where a Missionary might, with every prospect of success, be permanently stationed, we came to Hoporegurrie, in Eusufzaie. This village contains about three thousand inhabitants. Here, as in most parts of Affghanistan, the people are followers of two living Mohammedan saints, part adhering to the Mullah of Kotah, and part to the Akoond of Swat. Between these sects there exists great enmity, and, to such an extent is this opposition occasionally carried, that the civil power has to be called in to suppress it. The more influential of the two reputed saints, however, is the Akoond of Swat. It was his influence, it will be remembered, during the Umbeylah war, that enabled the enemy to gain so many advantages over the British troops. He is now about seventy years of age, and, as he advances in years, he becomes more popular. He is supposed to work miracles, and by many is looked upon as almost divine. People from far and near go to obtain his blessing. Indeed, he is said to have more than a thousand visitors continually at the village where he lives. These, according to the popular report, he entertains in a miraculous manner, the notion being that money is found every morning beneath the small carpet on which he prays. But the truth is, that all who visit him take with them a "nazr," or gift, in order to propitiate his favour. And though he refuses to accept these gifts with his own hands, yet those who are his immediate attendants take all the money that is brought, and are thereby enabled to provide for the wants of so numerous a party. It appears that the Akoond has no pretensions to learning, but that his popularity is rather due to the austerity of his life and his strict attention to the performance of the five daily Mohammedan prayers. Seeing that no single individual in Affghanistan has so much power over the minds of the people, a few points in his history are worth mentioning. He was born in the district of Surkamur, Eusufzaie, and till thirty years of age followed the occupation of herdman. At this period of his life he left the service of his master, and went to the village of Shah Dang. Here, as he was walking past the tomb of a Mohammedan saint, it is said that he paused and began to ponder about the vanity of the world. Before he had left the spot he had made up his mind to renounce the pleasures of the world, and lead a life of self-denial. With these resolutions, he threw down on the grave the few remaining coppers that he possessed and commenced the life of a religious devotee, A few years later we find him living in solitude, on a small island, near Torbela, on the river Indus. His asceticism, in this retired spot, appears to have brought him into note. Indeed, on leaving the island, his fame was evidently established. Since that time his power has gone on increasing. He nominated the King of Swat, and his choice was accepted by the people. And the late Dost Mohammed, and his son, Shere Ali Khan, the present sovereign of Cabul, have not thought him unworthy of sending messengers to crave his blessing, the former when he started for the siege of Herat, and the latter when he ascended his father's throne.

As we passed from village to village, we endeavoured, both by conversation and by distributing books, to spread the message of the Gospel. In one place, where we received visits from several villagers, an intelligent man mentioned a circumstance to us which showed the dread that some of the learned Mohammedans, who obtain their living out of the people, have of the New Testament. This man had a copy given him by a Missionary in Peshawur. He took the book home and showed it to a learned man, who forthwith took possession of the volume, and destroyed it. This conduct may possibly be traced to a report current amongst the Affghans, that every man who reads the New Testament becomes a Christian.

At Nowakilli we did not meet with the usual good treatment that we had met with at other places. This town is just on the border of the British territory, and almost within gunshot of the Umbeylah, the scene of the war that took place little more than twelve months ago. Here the more bigoted Mussulmans refused us permission to draw water from the wells, saying that those would be polluted which Christians used. This opposition, happily, lasted only for a time, for one or two leading men used their influence, and obtained for us what we required. Notwithstanding every precaution that was taken, an expert young Affghan robber succeeded in loosing a pony from the stand, close to the tent, and, mounting the same, made off with it at full speed. As Nowakilli had been visited in the September of 1864, and a few books left, inquiry was made if they had been read; and it was encouraging to find that at least in one case, the only one we had the opportunity of investigating, the Mizan-ul-Haqq had been perused.

Maneyra was our next halting-place. Here we met with a native village magistrate, whose acquaintance had been made on a previous visit. He gave us a hearty welcome, but was somewhat alarmed at our travelling without the guard of soldiers, which it is customary for Europeans to take when travelling amongst the Affghan tribe. This native gentleman had occasionally looked into the New Testament that had been given him, but without, it is to be feared, the degree of interest with which such a work should be set about. During our stay here it was gratifying to find that one book given, on the Mohammedan controversy, was taken to the house of a learned man, where its perusal was commenced.

The last place we visited before passing out of Affghan territory was Hoond. At this large village we were entertained by the Khan of the district, who had pressed us to be his guests. The news of our visit to Hoti Murdan, and the demand for religious books at that place, had preceded us to these distant villagers, who also begged us to leave some with them, a request with which we were too happy to comply.

And now, in reviewing this itineration amongst the Affghans, we cannot but lift up our hearts to God in thankfulness for the many mercies which He vouchsafed to us, in preserving us from the hand of violence, and in giving us, generally, a favourable reception among the fanatical tribes of this region. One illustration will suffice to indicate the change that is coming over the Affghans, and that God is now owning the labours of those Missionaries who have gone before, some of whom have entered into their rest. When first the Mission was established, a native agent spent six weeks in the adjoining district of Huzara, in endeavouring to sell Christian books amongst the Affghans. On his return, it was found that the sales altogether amounted only to a few pence, and these had been received, not from an Affghan, but from a Hindu.

Recent Intelligence.

PESHAWUR.

This important Mission has been greatly tried by the sickness and death of valuable European Missionaries, and thus it has for some time been insufficiently occupied. Yet a spot more rich in opportunities for important and extensive work cannot be found, for here the Affghans are to be met with, several of whom have already become converts to Christianity, and who, when they become such, openly avow it, and fearlessly advocate it. We ask for a reinforcement for Peshawur. The officials of the Government do not shrink from Peshawur, when assigned to it as their post. Are the motives which prompt to spiritual service unequal to the same self-sacrifice? It seems to us, however, that Cashmere should now be inseparably linked with the Peshawur Mission, and that it should be used as a sanatarium where the Peshawur Missionary may go and work during the summer months, and recover health for the resumption of his Peshawur duties.

Meanwhile God is blessing his own word, and souls are being won to Christ. The following is a letter from the Rev. J. Stevenson—

We are blessed with three candidates for baptism, who, we hope, will be admitted into the church shortly; in fact, I think I might say four. One is a poor African boy, who is now in very respectable service. He was stolen away from his parents and his country before he knew any thing of either, and was brought here *viâ* Arabia. He has manifested much desire to learn the Christian religion, and his faith in Christ seems sincere, and, from close observation on all hands, he seems to be leading a very consistent life. Another case is a young Mohammedan, who was somewhat shaken in his creed by the bandmaster of a Sikh regiment. He also has been for some time under instruction, and has manifested the same consistency of life and the same steady desire and seeming faith. God alone can read the heart. Another is a soldier of a native regiment here. He, the other day, before the whole regiment, avowed himself a Christian, and it is needless to remark he is suffering a most fiery persecution, so much so, that all manner of plots are being laid against him by his unprincipled heathen countrymen, and, indeed, in a place where life is thought so little of as it is in Peshawur, his cannot be considered safe. The last case is a very interesting one, and one full of romance too. A young man, whose name is Amir Baksh, came down from Charikai (the other side of Cabul), being dissatisfied with his own religion, to learn ours. His appearance is any thing but prepossessing: his long matted hair, the large piercing eyes, the thin, somewhat tall and bony figure, stamp him at once as proceeding from the hills. Many of the natives viewed him with great suspicion, thinking he had come down for some mischief. However, as he professed a wish to learn, we could not turn him away upon mere suspicion, and therefore took him into the Missionary compound, where he has been learning ever since. He told us he did not want to live at Peshawur, but wished only to learn our religion, and then, if we could give him some books, he would return, and teach his countrymen. He has manifested the greatest purity of life, and either he is a very spiritually-minded man or a great hypocrite. We cannot, however, suppose he is the latter, as he gives every proof of being a true Christian. He says he is new born, and has the light of God in his soul. To a question yesterday, as to whether he prayed regularly, and what he prayed for, he said, "I pray daily. The first thing I do is to confess what a great sinner I am, and then ask God to pardon me for Christ's sake." I was very pleased with the answer. I could have wished he could have remained with us longer, but the climate of Peshawur is killing him: he looks wretched; so he has asked to go back, and will take some books for his own and others' instruction. He says he will come down again, and bring others with him. I am sure we shall follow him with our prayers that he may be successful; that in such a remarkable manner God may open up a country to his Gospel which has hitherto been closed against it, and, I fear, will be for some time to come. He is very intelligent, and in every way fitted, I think, for the arduous task he has designed for himself. May God speed his way, and may our hearts be rejoiced by hearing, by some means or other, that the Gospel is making its way even in Cabul.

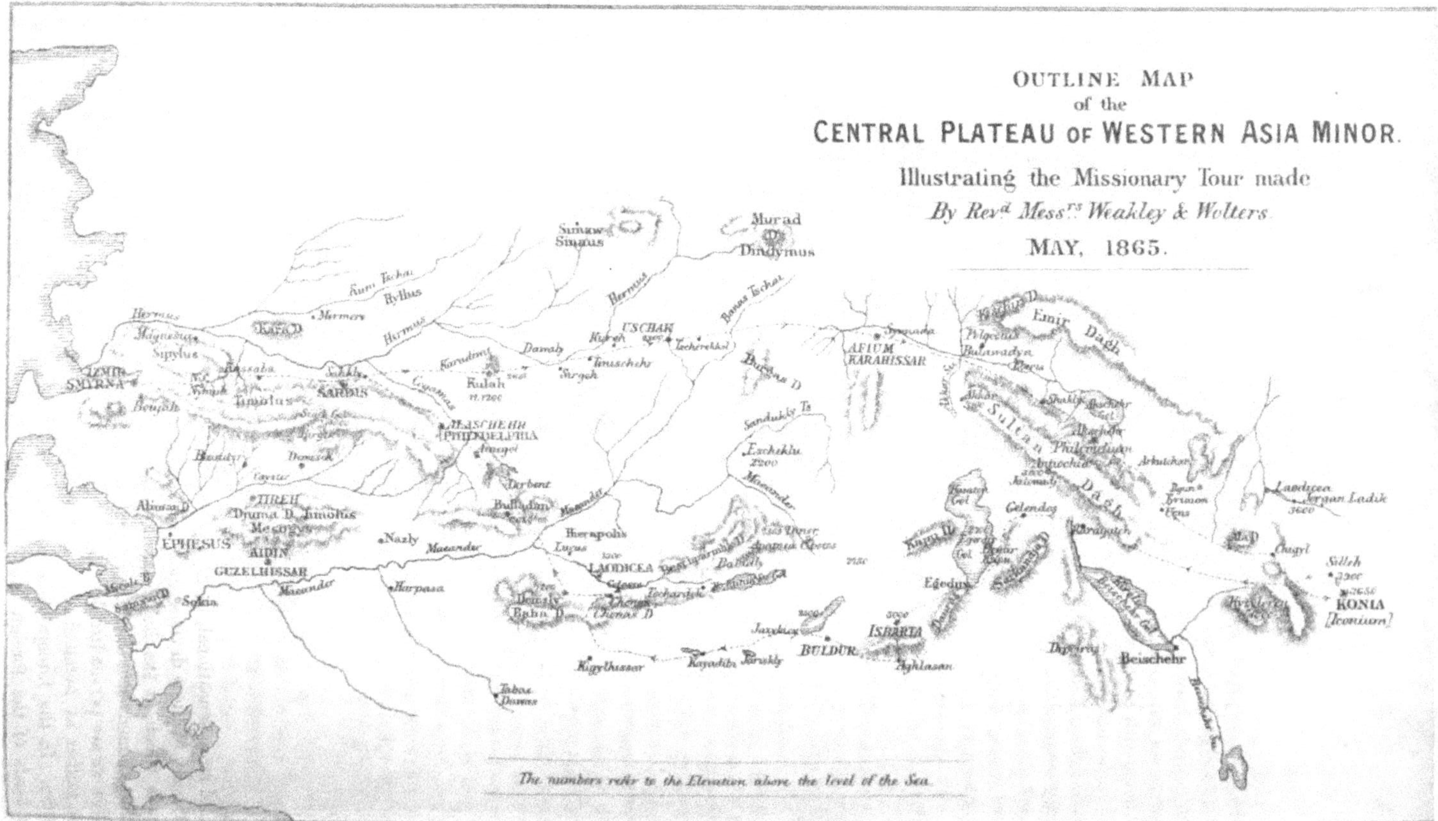

W Penny Lith. Lincolns Inn Fields

MISSIONARY RESULTS.

In a previous paper we explained what the results are which European Missionaries may be expected to accomplish. It has become necessary so to do, not only because on this subject there exists so much misunderstanding, but because such misunderstandings exercise an injurious influence on the cause of Missions. If the European be expected to accomplish that which lies entirely beyond his province, then, when such results are not forthcoming, friends are discouraged. Then enemies exult, and say, "Do you not see how these boasted Missions of your's are confessedly a failure? Much time has been consumed, valuable means have been expended, and yet, after all, what has been done? You expected large results, the ingathering of a glorious harvest, and, lo! instead of this, there is produced something so small, that it is absolutely contemptible. Why then persist?"

Such disparagements produce their effect, and that, too, even on some who have hitherto aided the Missionary enterprise. It does not go so far as to touch the great duty, and lead to its abandonment, so that there shall be no more Missionary work. That it must be done because the Lord has commanded it, is a conviction too firmly established in the conscience to be so easily surrendered. It is not so much as regards the principle that an injurious influence is exercised, but rather as to the mode of operation hitherto pursued, and the way in which the work has been prosecuted. On points such as these misgivings have arisen. Men who, under misconception, have been led to think that the results which Missionary effort has yielded are worthless, because of their small extent, conclude that a better way may be devised for the fulfilment of the great Missionary duty than that which has been hitherto acted upon. Nor is this idea confined to the work of foreign Missions. As regards home work, as well as foreign, there is a conviction widely spread abroad that the evangelical principle is deficient in power; that, having been tried, the effects which it has yielded are unsatisfactory. No one can read the proceedings at the various Church Congresses without perceiving that this is the conclusion to which that wayward thing, the human mind, is hurrying at the present moment. It is not that men are indisposed to work. The leaden sleep of former days has passed away; it is gone like the ice which had placed the ocean in chains, when, invaded by the increasing power of the sun, it relaxes its hold and breaks up. There is, then, for a time, a rough and stormy period, and the fragments, driven to and fro, come into fierce collision with each other, until, under the influence of some powerful currents, they are swept onward in one direction. So the spiritual stagnation has broken up. These new men, whose energies have been recently aroused, look around, and, despising the slow progress which, according to their ideas, has been made, in their inexperience conceive that it is reserved for them to accomplish great things. Hence they are full of new projects. Amidst the noisy excitement which prevails, there is scarcely room for the old evangelical principle to make itself heard. It has had its day; it has been tried, and found wanting; it is not suited to the age; something is needed more sensational, even though it be the monastic vow and the friar's garb. In fact, many of these devices are of a retrograde character, and savour of the old superstitions which, at the Reformation, our forefathers abjured. But the current at the present moment sets in strongly in this direction, and men are borne away by it.

Now we are persuaded that the evangelical principle is very grievously maligned, and that, neither at home or abroad, is justice done to the results of which it has been productive. In the foreign field undoubtedly it has worked well. It has hitherto been in the hands of the foreign Missionary, and is now being transferred to the custody of native churches, as a faithful and valuable deposit, which they are to transact with, in order to the enlightenment and salvation of their heathen countrymen. Happily it is too late for the new school to arrest the action of the evangelical principle in the field of Missions. The new churches raised up from amongst the heathen have caught—if indeed it is to be so regarded—the infection. In fact they were born with it. It is to this, under God, they owe their existence. By the evangelical principle they were begotten; in this they have been raised; by this they have grown from an helpless and dependent state to one of vigorous and independent action. Let the men of the new school, who despise the evangelical principle, and the mode in which, agreeably to that principle, Missionary operations have been conducted, go and try whether they can, by their novelties, produce like results. They would change every thing. Instead of the Gospel in its integrity, they would send forth the Church in its entirety. They would initiate a system in which there should be more form and less spirituality; more to affect the eye, less to affect the heart. Let them bring down their theories into the arena of practice, and see what they will be worth. If, at home, the popular mind accepts the new nostrums, the nation will deteriorate. If, in the Mission field, the old mode of action is to be supplanted by the new, Missions will deteriorate. If men must needs make the essay, let them do so, but until they have proved, by actual results, the value of their new procedures, let them at least be modest—"Let not him that girdeth on his harness boast himself as he that putteth it off."

As regards the Mission field, there is no excuse for this crusade. All that could be wished for has been accomplished; and this we are prepared to prove. At home, the Evangelical principle has not had the same measure of free action. It has been always opposed by numbers, who discredited it because they had never felt its power. By those who occupy the seats of power and influence it has been rarely encouraged, often rebuked, or, if not rebuked, yet distrusted, and reluctantly tolerated. Yet at home it has done much, far more than men are aware of. What it has done will soon be known, if the men of the new school succeed in banishing it from the pulpits, and substituting in its place an elaborate ceremonialism. But this is not our province. Our duty lies in the Mission field, and if we can show that Evangelical Missions have been unjustly disparaged and unfairly dealt with; that, misapprehensions being rectified, they have done their work; then, so far, this is an argument in favour of the working of the Evangelical principle at home, for it is difficult to conceive that a principle which has worked well in the field of foreign Missions, should be at home so worthless and undeserving of support as some assert it to be.

The objection, most pertinaciously urged against Evangelical Missions at the present moment, is the limited extent of the results. But this is precisely that which a right perception of the subject would lead us to expect, and therefore, so far from shaking our confidence, it confirms us in our conviction of their reality. Results on an extended scale are not to be expected from the foreign Missionary. It never was intended that he should evangelize great masses, or accomplish extraordinary national movements. On the contrary, the effects to be wrought out by him were purposely designed to be apparently feeble, in dimensions small, and little calculated to attract attention.

Are they indeed worthless because thus small? Is not the seed the germ of the forest tree, and yet is it not small? Is not the leaven, when put into the mass, so small that it disappears and is hidden, and yet is there not in it a concentrated energy, so that the little dominates over the much, and, by its superior influence, subdues to itself the mass which had absorbed it? Has the philosophy of the present day accepted this as an axiom, that small beginnings are incapable of expanding into great results? Can any thing be more contrary to fact and the experiences of every-day life? "Behold how great a fire a little fuel kindleth." And if this be a principle which pervades nature, why should the explanatory force which it carries with it be excluded from the philosophy of Missions? There is between nature and grace a wonderful analogy, so much so, that the phenomena of the one are continually made use of in Scripture to illustrate the other. If Evangelical Missions are to be put upon their trial, let them at least have fair dealing. Let not their opponents place themselves in the position of an unjust judge, who, having conceived a strong prejudice against an accused party, resolves beforehand on his condemnation, and refuses to entertain the evidences of his innocence. Let it only be admitted, that principles which are undeniable as having force in the order of natural things, may also have place in the kingdom of grace, and then the objections urged against Missionary efforts, because the results which they have as yet yielded are so small in bulk, fall at once to the ground; for these small beginnings do often marvellously and unexpectedly open out into consequences of astounding magnitude. It is so in nature, and it was foretold it should be so in the workings of grace. That which smote the image of Nebuchadnezzar's dream was but a stone. It lay within a small compass, yet because of that it was the more manageable. While thus small, it did its work. It was not as though the mighty avalanche of some loosened mass fell upon and crushed the image, but the stone, aimed at a particular part, smote the image on the feet, and when it had done its work of destruction, then the stone that smote the image became a great mountain, and filled the whole earth."

The Saviour Himself recognises the same principle—the small beginning, and yet its expansion into great results. He borrows it from natural things, and uses it to illustrate the laws which should govern the development of his kingdom—"Another parable put He forth to them, saying, The kingdom of heaven is like to a grain of mustard-seed, which a man took and sowed in his field, which indeed is the least of all seeds; but when it is grown it is the greatest among herbs, and becometh a tree, so that the birds of the air come and lodge in the branches thereof." "Another parable spake He unto them: The kingdom of heaven is like unto leaven, which a woman took and hid in three measures of meal, till the whole was leavened." In both illustrations there is the small beginning, and yet from this originate results which arrest attention by their magnitude.

The foreign Missionary sows the seed; he prepares the leaven, and places it in the lump. His work is small in compass, so small, that it seems lost amidst the dense masses of prevailing heathenism; and men despise it as a thing of nought, and lose sight of it as they do of the buried seed, or the hidden leaven; but that it should be thus humiliated is a part of the singular process through which it has to pass; and, when least expected, it will appear again, like the seed when it springs, or the leaven when it has leavened the mass.

And if we look into the Mission field, we shall find that the position of the European Missionaries is precisely this—they are busily occupied in their own initiative work; they are preparing the leaven in diverse places, in order that it may be introduced into the contiguous mass. In some instances they have done more than this: the leaven, having been prepared, has been introduced into the lump, and already there are evidences to show that it is working.

In Africa a portion was broken off from the great mass of population. In Africa there are diverse nationalities, and the fragment was homogeneous with the parent mass, so that the individuals composing it were of diverse races, and spoke diverse languages.

This was placed in the hands of the European Missionaries, that they might prepare it as leaven. To this task they addressed themselves, and at what cost of health and life need not now be stated. The records are before the church. They were prospered in their work. Sierra Leone is now a land of Christian profession like our own, and, like our congregations at home, the native church there, amidst much that is evil and fictitious, includes very many real Christians. There is much gold in the quartz.

This is the leaven. It is now being put into the lump. Along the banks of the Niger the process is going on. Amongst the heathen Ibos, at Onitsha, were introduced a few Christian men of the same race, part of the leaven prepared at Sierra Leone. The quantity was small, but in quality it was genuine. It wrought. There is now there a Christian congregation, consisting of 135 converts, with 48 communicants, and the work is spreading. At the Confluence, higher up, there is a confluence of nations, and we have placed there a leaven made up of Christian men of the same races. "Gbebe," observes Bishop Crowther, "being a place forming a nucleus of languages, such as Igbira, Nupe, Hausa, Eki, Yagba, Igara, Kakanda, and Gbari, it requires the knowledge of two or three of those to be most useful here; but Igbira is the native language of the people, which must be learnt by the resident teachers here, the others being introduced by mere sojourners from other places through the unsettled state of their country from war when they came to sojourn here. Onitsha possesses this one great advantage over Gbebe, that the Christian teachers have to deal with a people of one language only, while at Gbebe they have to do with about half-a-dozen."

When introduced into the lump the leaven was left. From various circumstances, communications with Lagos and Sierra Leone being interrupted, the work was isolated for months, nor could any one from without approach to ascertain whether the leaven was doing its work: when, however, the station was revisited, it was found that the leaven had wrought effectually. Men and women had turned from their idols; they had embraced Christianity; they desired baptism. On a recent occasion, at the Confluence, Bishop Crowther administered the Lord's Supper to a company of twenty-five converts, and afterwards baptized ten adults and seven children of converts. A few of the converts were from among the Mohammedans, but the greater part were from the heathen tribes of the Igbiras and Bunnus. Well might the bishop say—"The Gospel is fermenting among the measures of meal in which it has been hid."

The process has been marvellously accelerated by the appointment of the native episcopate. Of European bishops there have been several on the coast, but they have fallen rapidly. The European episcopate can with difficulty retain its hold on the coast; it could never pass up and down the Niger, and carry on, from station to station, the work of superintendence. The leaven, by the appointment of the native bishop, has been set free to work.

Again, India, like Africa, consists of various nationalities, and from these also a leaven has been prepared. The mode of operation has not been the same as in Africa. The representative specimens of races have not been gathered from out of their own localities, brought into one place, and there put into the hands of the European Missionary. This process has not been requisite in India, because, being under British influence, the whole land is accessible to the European Missionary; nor does climate interfere in the same degree that it does in Africa.

The initiative agents, therefore, have gone into the localities of the different races, learned their languages, and on the spot prepared the leaven. Thus, for instance, the Missionaries of the Church Missionary Society have made converts or raised up congregations from amongst Tamils, the Malayalim speaking people, Telugus, Bengalees, the Urdu-speaking people of the north-west, Punjabis, Affghans, the people of Sindh.

In some cases, as in the case of the Affghans, the leaven prepared is very small in quantity, but especially quick, pungent, and penetrative. In exemplification of this we refer to the narrative of an Affghan Mission to Kafiristan, recently published in the pages of this periodical.

Amongst the Tamils the leaven is comparatively large in quantity, there being no less than 33,000 Christian Tamils under the charge of the Missionaries of the Church Missionary Society, besides those which connect with the Society for the Propagation of the Gospel. There is among these thousands a genuine element, although mixed with others that are less valuable. The people are well instructed: they have been brought up, not in a formal ritualism, but in the knowledge of the word of God. They have been taught, not through the eye by ceremonies, but, through the understanding, by sound doctrine. They can read—do read—their Tamil Bibles. They can give a reason for the hope that is in them.

The congregations have yielded an efficient native pastorate. The people value their Christian ordinances. Like the Sierra-Leone church, they prove that they do so by contributing liberally to their support. They are anxious for the evangelization of their heathen countrymen, and are putting forth corresponding efforts.

Let the following testimony as to the state of these Tamil Christians be duly weighed. It is that of the Rev. J. Thomas, the senior Missionary, who thus speaks of them on his return from a health-visit to Europe—

> The number of Christians under my care is 10,751. They are orderly for the most part, and I think the signs of stability in general are more visible than ever, and the instances of true piety more numerous. I do not for a moment doubt but that this people would retain their religion if the English raj, and, with it, all the Missionaries, were providentially withdrawn from the country. Their stability arises very much, I think, from their knowledge of God's holy word, and the very great extent to which the power of reading that word has been afforded by means of our village vernacular schools. It is not a mere ritual formality that our Christians have been trained in, but in a knowledge of, and supreme regard to, the divine oracles, which they are taught to reverence as God's revelation, containing all that man need know, and more than he could know in any other way. And here it would be unjust not to acknowledge the invaluable aid which we have derived from the Bible Society in supplying the people liberally with the Scriptures in every form, adapted as well to our schools as to our reading population, and for distribution among the heathen, &c. The people have made that acknowledgment, not in word only, but by a donation this year of fifty rupees to the funds of that noble institution. I may mention, in proof of the stability to which I have referred, the efforts made by almost every congregation some time ago to raise a separate fund in each village for the support of their own teachers, when it was thought possible that the Church Missionary Society would be compelled to withdraw from the Mission some part of its annual aid. Of course the native church is altogether inadequate to pay the present staff of agents: still it was felt, that if the withdrawal of aid were unavoidable, the people, by uniting together in localities where the congregations are contiguous to each other, would be able to maintain a catechist.

Have the European Missionaries done nothing? Have they not prepared a valuable leaven, which is fitted to influence, and that powerfully, the heathen masses? Only let force and concentrativeness be given to the native church in Tinnevelly, by the appointment of a native bishop, and, by the blessing of God, we shall see it rising up to a measure of Christian influence and evangelistic labour, which shall put to silence the gainsayers in this land of England.

Again, in Travancore a leaven has been prepared. The population there is strangely composed of various castes and races—Brahmins, Nairs, Soodras, mountain tribes, slaves, besides the Syrian Christians. From amongst these various sections there has been gathered together a body of native Christians, more than 9000 in number. The adaptation of the leaven to the lump is at once evident. If the population to be influenced is mingled, the leaven is of the same character. In this respect it resembles the Christian leaven at Sierra Leone, and stands in the same relation to the population of Travancore, which that prepared at Sierra Leone does to the nations and languages of Africa. There is something admirable and exquisite in the similarity of arrangement under circumstances so different. There presides undoubtedly over the widely-extended Mission work a divine superintendence. The earthly agent sees little more than the contracted sphere of present and personal duty. He is often under discouragement; and so feeble does his work seem to be, when compared with the urgent necessities of the heathen, that he cannot realize how it can tell with any thing of beneficial influence on the future. Yet these apparently feeble efforts are links in the great chain of events by which God is working out his own great purposes.

One quotation may be introduced, in order to show that the Christian population of Travancore does possess the energy of leaven. It is from the report of the native pastor, the Rev. K. Koshi—

I have much cause for thankfulness that the leading men in this congregation are Christians of approved character, using their united influence for good, and striving, according to their ability and opportunities, to make the truth known amongst their friends and neighbours. In my visiting tours I have sometimes had to pass by a house or shop without giving the intended call, for fear of disturbing the conversation or reading that I could overhear was going on within, either with Syrians or heathen, or both, as it may be. Is not this a gratifying proof that there is leaven hid in the meal? May it ever go on doing its silent work until the whole lump is leavened!

There are some practical lessons which may be drawn with advantage from this subject, but we reserve them for another Number.

GOD'S HUSBANDRY.—HOW BEST TO SECURE A FULLER HARVEST.

Men are by nature estranged from God, barren in the production of good, exuberant in the production of evil. It is not God's purpose that they should remain so. If the proprietor of large estates perceives that one outlying portion of his property yields him no return, that the productive powers of which it is possessed are all wasted upon the growth of thorns and briers, he commands that it should be reclaimed, and the work of husbandry commences. So it is as regards God's dealings with men: the divine husbandry is going forward amongst them. His judgments and afflictive dispensations go before to break up the hard earth, and disturb the ease, and self-complacency, and self-righteousness of the human heart, so that, instead of carelessness and indifference, there should be, on man's part, a readiness to attend; and then the sower goes forth to sow the divine seed in the furrows of humanity.

This seed has been most carefully prepared, and at a most costly price. It is necessary, in order to successful cultivation, that the seed should be adapted to the soil into which it is to be cast. The divine seed is the word, and this word is sown by being proclaimed, published, preached. "Preach the word," was Paul's admonition to Timothy. It is said that there is in every seed a heart, and that the seat of vitality is there. This heart is wrapped about with farinaceous lobes, and when the seed strikes, these lobes resolve into a fine dust, which becomes the first material on which the infant germ feeds. In the divine seed there is a heart, and that heart is Christ wrapped up in the lobes of sound doctrine. Paul teaches this in his Epistle to the Romans. He is explaining that Christ is not far off, but near to the sinner, that he may lay hold upon Him in order to justification—"Say not in thine heart who shall ascend into heaven (that is to bring down Christ from above); or who shall descend into the deep (that is to bring up Christ again from the dead). But what saith it? The word is nigh thee,"—and therefore Christ is nigh, for it is in this word, so nigh as to be "in thy mouth and in thy heart," that Christ is presented to the sinner that faith may lay hold on Him. It is this the sinner needs—one to save from urgent, imminent danger; one who can render present and powerful help; and Christ is that mighty one on whom our help is laid. His personal acts commend Him to the acceptance of the sinner, for the sinner knows well that for his sin there must be suffering. The displeasure of God against sin has been felt by him in his inmost soul. Of this he is convinced, that between himself and God there must be somewhat interposed which shall avert from him that high displeasure. It is in this respect the atonement of Christ especially commends itself to him, and in this consists the adaptation of the seed to that sinful and ruined humanity in which it is intended to be sown. Christ, apart from his work of substitution and atonement, does not meet the sinner's want. As an example, He is useless except on the foundation of his atonement. It is in the belief of this, that, obtaining full and undelayed remission of all past sins, the man enters into a state of acceptance before God, and therein finds the motives and the strength which enable him to a new life of obedience. He who would be liberated from the power of sin must first be freed from the guilt of sin; for so long as sin holds the conscience under guilt it will hold the life under its power. The blood of Christ must be put between us and our sins, otherwise our sins will interpose between us and our God, and shut us out from Him. When the Israelites were on the same side of the Red Sea as Pharaoh they were in dismay—"they were sore afraid; and they said unto Moses, Because there were no graves in Egypt hast thou taken us away to die in the wilderness?" But so soon as the Red Sea was interposed between them and their enemies, they sang the song of praise to Him who had saved them that day out of the hand of the Egyptians. So let the blood of Christ be interposed between us and those past sins, which, pursuing after us, would drag us back into captivity, and we also shall sing a new song, even praise unto our God.

In this, then, consists the special adaptation of the Gospel message to the necessities of the sinner; and this blessed truth of a way of escape, immediate and effectual, through Him whom God hath set forth to be a propitiation through faith in his blood, is to be made known to men through the medium of sound doctrine. Christ crucified is to be presented, not in pictures to the senses, but through scriptural teaching to the understanding. This was the apostolic mode. It was by "speech and by preaching" that Paul "declared the testimony of God"—"whom we preach," as he reminds the Ephesians, "warning every man, and teaching every man in all wisdom." The idea of elaborating a ritual which shall so picture forth Christ to the senses as to dispense, in a great measure, with the necessity of preaching, is a delusion. Rome has long tried this mode. She left pure teaching, and adopted symbolism in its stead, and the effect has been deadening and destructive. It is through the incorruptible seed of the word that the Spirit regenerates, and if this be slighted and disregarded, there can be no spiritual results: the man may be formalized, but he will not be converted to God. Let, then, the preaching of Christ crucified be esteemed the great business of the minister at home and the Missionary abroad; and as for the forms in which Christian worship should be clothed, let the principle laid down by the Church of England in that prefatory chapter to her Prayer-book entitled "Of Ceremonies," &c., be adhered to—"Some ceremonies are put away, because the multitude of them hath so increased in these latter days, that the burden of them was intolerable; whereof St. Augustine in his time complained, that they were grown to such a number, that the estate of Christian people was in a worse case concerning that matter than were the Jews. And he counselled that such yoke and burden should be taken away, as time would serve quietly to do it. But what would St. Augustine have said, if he had seen the ceremonies of late days used among us; whereunto the multitude used in his time was not to be compared? Thus our excessive multitude of ceremonies was so great, and many of them so dark, that they did more confound and darken, than declare and set forth Christ's benefits to us."

And the old Reformers, who so sedulously laboured to cut away this unscriptural redundancy of form, which, instead of setting forth, overshadowed and concealed the great object of faith, and desired that congregations should content themselves "only with those ceremonies which do serve to a decent order and godly discipline," what would they say now, if only they were to see the crimson-vested thurifers, and the censers, and the incense floating in clouds, while the priests group themselves with artistic effect around what it pleases them to call an altar, during the singing of the Magnificat. Is it indeed true that the simplicity of our Protestant worship is thus painfully invaded? Then is this to "confound and darken, rather than declare and set forth Christ's benefits unto us."

We claim for the Church Missionary Society, that, in the selection of its Missionaries, it has ever had special regard to the sowing of the seed. Its anxiety has ever been that they should be men determined, by the grace of God, to sow none but the pure seed of God's word, as He Himself has provided it.

Well, now, this seed has been sown, not, indeed, universally, but very extensively, over the field of this world. In our own days considerable additions have been made to the old cultivations, and large portions of the heathen desert have been sown with the Gospel seed. Let it be remembered, that wherever this has been done, the results have not been in any case all that could be desired. The growth upon the fields which are under divine husbandry is not such as would content the man who ploughs and sows to gather in a material harvest. The good seed does not fail: it yields its results: but the produce thus yielded does not find itself in exclusive possession of the field. Its claims are disputed, its growth interfered with: "When the blade was sprung up and brought forth fruit, then appeared the tares also." Tares are in appearance like the genuine wheat plant, more especially in the infancy of the crop, when the blade is yet tender; although, however similar in appearance, yet yielding a grain which, if used as food, is deleterious, they are essentially different. It is not merely the parable of the tares and wheat that conveys this lesson of a mingled crop, but many others unite with it in so describing the condition of the professing church during the period which lies between the two advents. And practically we find it so to be: congregations at home and congregations abroad are identical in this respect. Wherever the good seed has been sown, there are some raised up who are Christ's in reality; while others are intermingled with them who have the name of Christian, and nothing more.

Why, then, should that be charged as a fault on the results of Christian Missions which equally prevails at home? There is, it is alleged, so much that is superficial, so many who are content with a name to live whilst they are dead. Undoubtedly it is so. In every group of converts there are those in whom there is indeed nothing of open opposition; so far from it, that they very readily conform to all outward arrangements; but in whom spirituality is wanting, and concerning whom there is reason to fear that they are as yet strangers to the experimental working of Christian truth upon the heart and life. But is it not so at home, and can it be expected that those infant churches, which have so recently emerged from all the darkness and evil of heathenism, should already, at this brief period of their growth, have surpassed in their attainments the old mother church? Nor are we to be surprised if betimes, on the part of such professors, there is open backsliding, and if, when tribulation or persecution ariseth because of the word, they be offended? It has been so in New Zealand. There have been tares among the wheat, and, under adverse circumstances, they have broken out into open opposition. Perhaps if a similar strain were put on congregations at home, and a perseverance in their profession and attendance upon ordinances involved loss of property, liberty, and endangered life, like apostasies might occur.

Let it be observed that this spoiling of the crop is the work of an enemy. His object is to raise up those who shall in all respects resemble true Christians, except in this, that Christ is not honoured by the surrender of the heart. The more like they are to true Christians in other respects, provided there be this reserve, the better they answer his purpose, for they encourage other men to think that they also may be Christians without being devoted. Moreover, it gratifies his personal enmity to the Lord Jesus, that even amongst those who bear the Saviour's name there should be many who love Him not. He hopes thus to lower the tone and standard of Christianity in the world, and to diminish its usefulness. He has various ways of accomplishing his object. He sows the seed of a deteriorated Christianity. Through his agents he so alters its doctrine as to destroy its efficacy. It is as though a medicine, powerfully counteractive of a prevailing epidemic, be tampered with, until its original virtue is gone, and all that it does, when administered, is to modify the action of the disease, so that it is less alarming in its symptoms, yet equally destructive. Sin is the virulent disease of human nature; the Gospel is the sure specific. Just in proportion as its original simplicity is departed from, does it lose its power, until at length, its efficacy being destroyed, it can no longer regenerate. Under such teaching the sin of our nature remains unsubdued: all that is done is so to modify its action as that it may consist with the name and appearance of religion.

There are many who prefer a diluted Gospel, and thus, by a secret process carried on within their own hearts, assist the enemy in the attainment of his object. The Gospel in its purity is too strong for them. It asks more than they are prepared to grant. They do not mean to be openly irreligious, yet they are fully intent on self-gratification. They would compromise, therefore, after the manner of the Laodiceans. They did not like the extremes of hot or cold; they tempered them together until the admixture became lukewarm. In contributing to the formation of this, each extreme lost something. The hot element lost something of its heat; the cold lost something of its chill. So there are many who blend together religion and the world; so much of religion as consists with the enjoyment of the world; so much of the world as consists with the appearance and profession of religion. In this admixture each of the ingredients loses something. Religion loses its earnestness, and is reduced to a form; the enjoyment of the world must be restrained within the bounds of decency. No open sin on the one hand, no heart surrender on the other; and so the temperature is attained which is preferred by many, and that is lukewarmness.

In these various ways the enemy works. Sometimes the doctrine is corrupted; in other places where the truth is preached the natural mind rises up in opposition to it, and, by a secret process within, neutralizes its virtue. But thus it is that the crop is of a mingled nature, and tares and wheat must grow together to the harvest.

Now let us suppose the case of a husbandman who has many fields under cultivation. He adopts the most approved of process; he selects the best seed; he spares no cost. And yet he finds that, with all his diligence, his crops fall short of the desired standard, and that his fields yield him far less than he is justified in expecting. He goes from one field to another, yet he finds in every case that it is invariably the same. What is to be done under such circumstances? It is indispensable to him that he should have larger results, and yet his fields will yield no more. What, then, is to be done? If he has the opportunity, let him extend the boundaries of his farm, and bring more land under cultivation. Suppose his farm lies at the foot of one of our Cumberland mountains, some of whose projecting spurs lie within his boundaries; and as yet he has only cultivated the lowlands; but now he begins to climb the hills, and subdue the neglected slopes to his use. Or suppose that the farm lies on the edge of one of the vast Irish bogs, stretching out as far as eye can see. But there are portions where the slane has been at work, and the peat has been cut away for firing, until the gravel sub-soil has seen the light; and these recovered spots he has neglected, but now he proceeds to utilize them, that his year's produce may be increased. Or realize another scene—the back-wood settler in one of our Canadian provinces, and the log-house, the home of the expatriated man, where his wife and children find a shelter, and around which lies the area of cleared ground; and yet the produce is not enough for the maintenance of those who are so near and dear to him: what then does he do? He girds himself for fresh labour, and proceeds to deprive the land of more of its forest clothing, that he may dig, and sow, and have more food.

And so with us, the servants of that great Lord, "who is the Saviour of all men, specially of those that believe." We desire a richer, fuller harvest, a larger ingathering of souls. We desire it for the Lord's glory, in compassion to the souls of our fellow-men. How then shall we obtain an increase? Pray for the Spirit! Undoubtedly that is indispensable, for the power is with Him: "Except the Lord build the house, they labour in vain that build it; except the Lord keep the city, the watchman waketh but in vain." But we are now speaking of the means to be used, not of the power. What means, then, shall be used in order that the harvest of souls may be increased? "Stay at home," some wise man says; "cultivate more diligently the fields you already have." But we shall never obtain otherwise than a mingled crop. Concentrate upon one assigned spot all the available agencies in the world; abandon your Mission stations and transfer all your Missionaries to the home field; the tares will yet spring up together with the wheat. The increase of results will not keep pace with the increased expenditure. You will find no compensation at home for the disregard of other fields, and this unpitying neglect of the outlying portions of the world. In no one parish, in no one congregation, will you attain the maximum of universal conversion. Nay, instead of home being benefited by this monopoly of effort, it will suffer injury; the spiritual results will be less instead of greater; and you will, too late, discover that there is no surer way of inflicting serious injury on the cause of true religion at home, than by holding back your hands from the great work of foreign Missions.

Such council, therefore, is only worthy of rejection. We must not stop; we may not stay. From year to year we must enlarge our boundaries. The Church or Society which thus decides—this must be the utmost limit; we can go further—from that moment will begin to be impoverished and to decline. Proceed to inclose the Mission fields already under cultivation within a ring fence, and say, beyond this we may not pass; on these chosen spots we shall concentrate our efforts, nor desist from their cultivation until they become as the garden of the Lord; from that moment will the dews of blessing be diminished, and the trees of righteousness begin to droop. Let this hedge of separation be removed, and the wide wilderness appearing to view be permitted by its desolation to claim some pity at our hands, and then, as we go on to master new languages, and to gladden new nations with the Gospel sound, we shall so enrich home, that it shall yield the full measure of which, under present circumstances, it is capable, while for the tares which shall still mingle with the wheat we shall find compensation in the increase which the new fields shall yield us.

MISSIONARY ACTION OF THE TAMIL CHURCH.

After the article on Missionary Results, which will be found in the present Number, had been sent to the press, some papers arrived from India which very remarkably confirm the views therein expressed, namely, that the native churches and congregations raised up by the European Missionary from amongst the heathen are designed of God to reproduce Christianity amongst their countrymen on a far more extended scale than we have yet seen; and that their smallness as to numbers no more incapacitates them from doing so, than the smallness of the leaven unfits it for being influential on the mass. However few in number, if only they be genuine, they possess the necessary qualifications for usefulness, and will be sure to work.

Amongst others of these *primitiæ* from amongst the heathen, special reference was made to the Tamilian church. That church was spoken of as a Christian reality; not, indeed, as though all its members were spiritual persons, but that there was enough of true spirituality to invest it with reproductive power. The truth of such assertions might perhaps be questioned. It is therefore well that we are enabled to substantiate them, and to prove by facts that the Christian Tamils are already and actually fulfilling the functions of leaven, and that not merely on their native soil of Tinnevelly, but in another land. We refer to the Tamil Cooly Mission, the ninth report of which has just reached us.

It may be well to refresh the memory of our readers by a brief *resumé* of its history.

It originated in the visit to that island, in the year 1854 55, of one of the Secretaries of the Parent Society, the Rev. William Knight, now Rector of High Ham, Somerset. He was invited by some of the coffee-planters to visit their large settlements of coolies from South India, and to devise, if possible, some means whereby their moral and religious welfare might be promoted. Mr. Knight had just before been in the midst of the Tamil Mission work in Tinnevelly, and he saw at once how effectually the influence of the native Christians in Tinnevelly might be brought to bear upon the heathen coolies in Ceylon. They were both Tamils. The one needed Christianity, the other had it to give. An appeal was made to the Tinnevelly Christians whether some from amongst them would not offer themselves for Missionary work amongst their heathen countrymen in Ceylon. It was similar to the appeal made to the Christian negroes of Sierra Leone to volunteer for Missionary work along the banks of the Niger, and it was with the same alacrity responded to. A handful of Tamil leaven was put into the heathen mass in Ceylon, and now, at the expiration of nine years, we are enabled to see how it is working.

First, then, as to the number of native agents employed, and their qualifications—

The number of agents employed has continued to be on the average, throughout the year, twelve catechists, one schoolmaster, and one colporteur. To this list may be added a catechist labouring in the Ratnapoora district, in connexion with the Cooly Mission, though not supported by its funds. Besides these agents actively engaged in the Mission field, there are two catechists absent on leave in Tinnevelly, and it is expected that they will re-enter upon their duties in a month from this time. The general conduct of the catechists during the past year has been such as to give much satisfaction. They are generally men who have had the advantage of a careful education, and a long training in the Missionary field of Tinnevelly. The superintendent reports that a contented, prayerful, and earnest spirit prevails among them.

These agents, after the example of the mother church in Tinnevelly, are divided into stationary and itinerant. In Tinnevelly, some of the European Missionaries are stationary and others itinerant, the native agents being assigned, some to one, some to the other department of the Mission. We entertain the hope that the Tinnevelly church, and other native churches after its example, will always sustain the itinerant agency, so long at least as there remains a heathen element to be evangelized.

Within the limits of the districts assigned to the stationary catechists are to be found the little groups of converts which constitute the rudiments of future congregations, and some interesting notices of this portion of the work will be found in the following paragraph—

In the last annual report allusion was made to the advisability of increasing the number of the stationary catechists. The full supply of native agents, the large number of professing Christians in certain districts, and the watchful care which would be exercised by warm friends of the Mission, led the Committee to feel that the time had arrived when the plan must be carried out to a certain extent. The apparent results of this movement during the past year have been highly encouraging. For all practical purposes these so-called stationary catechists are itinerants. Every morning sees them carrying the message of the Gospel to a different estate, until the cycle of estates is completed. The valley of Kallibokka may be taken as an example. There are twenty-three estates in the district visited by this catechist. Each estate is visited twice a month. The catechist is allowed, on nearly every estate, to preach to the people for a short time at morning muster. But the Committee attach great importance to the visiting of the lines. There are great opportunities here of teaching the sick, or of holding conversations with those who are not working. The catechist is generally engaged in this work from seven o'clock till ten. In the afternoon another estate is visited, and if it be not convenient for the catechist to preach to the people, his duty is to spend some time in conversing with the people in the lines. In the case of the Kallibokka catechist, the Sunday work is laborious and interesting. From fifty to eighty Christian worshippers meet for divine service, and there are inviting opportunities of preaching to the heathen. Such is a fair description of the work of the stationary catechist, the only difference being, that where the Christians are not numerous, as in the neighbourhood of Matella, Gampola, and Navelapittia, the catechist is employed in preaching in the bazaar. There now six of these catechists at work. The impression thus far perceptible from the labours of these men differs in the different districts. In Kallibokka, Maturatta, and Matelle, there have been many cases in which the awakening and renewing power of God's Spirit has been manifested, and there has been an apparent breaking down of heathenism on several estates. On one estate, where there has been a well-sustained plan of visiting the lines, and of preaching to the people, the manager declares the people have ceased to offer to Muniande, and what is perhaps still more worthy of notice, seven men have come forward for baptism. On another estate in the same neighbourhood, two men sought to be baptized. They learnt with dilgence the Creed, the Lord's Prayer, the ten commandments, and the simple doctrines of the Gospel, as is the custom with all candidates. They persevered in the prescribed course of instruction with a steady, earnest determination, and were in due time baptized in the presence of the coolies on the estate. There was a peculiar solemnity about the service, and a considerable effect was produced by the head Cangany rising up after the concluding prayer, and saying to all the people, with much apparent emotion—"There shall be no more offerings to the devil on this estate."

During the past year, fifty-four men and women have come forward as candidates for baptism. Of these, thirty-eight have been received into the visible church of Christ by this ordinance, after careful instruction. Thus it has pleased God to give a considerable increase, and it is interesting to observe that the largest number of inquirers have come forward in those districts where the people, through the stationary catechists, have received line upon line, and precept upon precept. The work of each stationary catechist is brought under the eye of the superintendent every six weeks, by his visiting the district, and by the catechist coming into Kandy.

The next paragraph refers to the itineration and its results. One instance given is deeply interesting, as showing the reflex action of Christianity; how, like a sunbeam, emitted from Tinnevelly and lighting up Ceylon, it is again thrown back on South India, and brings with it to the country from whence it originated a rich reward.

The six catechists who have been employed in the wider fields of labour have been enabled diligently to make known in every direction the glad tidings of salvation. Their labours, it is humbly believed, have been greatly blessed, not only among the heathen, but also among the professed native Christian coolies scattered in the remote districts.

On one of the distant estates, six men from North Tinnevelly heard the catechist preach with a kind of wondering interest. These men had listened to the same message of the Gospel from this very catechist five years before, in their own village. This fact arrested their attention, and drew them favourably towards the teacher. They expressed their surprise that he should have come so far to make known this Vedam. The catechist said that this Vedam was the only true one, that it was necessary to all men, and that the King of the whole earth, and the Creator of all things, had given a command to his servants to go and preach the glad tidings to all men. They listened with lively interest to the message of the Gospel, and it pleased God to carry home the word with power, for they diligently sought, from that day, to understand the way of salvation, and, after four months careful instruction, five of them were received into the church by baptism.

It would be easy to mention many similar cases in which we may reasonably believe we can see the presence and blessing of God resting upon our work.

The Committee are fully aware of the wisdom of speaking with moderation when looking at apparent results among the Tamil people. We are not in a position to balance apparent failures with apparent successes. We see not the links which connect one event with another. In the report of last year it was mentioned that one of our Tamil Christians, who had been brought under the influence of the Gospel through the instrumentality of the Cooly Mission, had contributed the large sum of 100*l.* for the building of a church in his own village near Trichinopoly. The sequel deserves notice. The Committee of the Society for the Propagation of the Gospel, being made aquainted with this man's donation, sanctioned a grant of 100*l.* towards the same object, and thus a handsome church is being built. But a further result followed. The people in an adjoining village, seeing what had been done by one who, a few years before, was a heathen, resolved to possess a place of worship as permanent and beautiful as their neighbours. They therefore raised among themselves 100*l.*, and having obtained the same help from the Parent Society, they also will rejoice in a suitable and substantial church, in which they can meet to worship the true God. These two churches will be, throughout the district of Trichinopoly, silent witnesses of Ceylon. Men will observe that temporal and spiritual good may be obtained in this island.

It appears that there are now on the coffee estates and in Kandy 1006 professed Christians of whom 609 are baptized and 131 communicants. Like all other Christian congregations, they are a mixed body, consisting of tares and wheat. On this subject the Report speaks very truthfully—

The Cooly Mission Report would be incomplete without one or two remarks upon the professed Christian coolies. St. Paul was obliged to say of some even under his own ministry—"There are some of whom I have told you often, and now tell you even weeping, that they are the enemies of the cross of Christ, whose end is destruction, whose God is their belly, and whose glory is in their shame, who mind earthly things." As it was in the favoured church at Philippi, so it is on the estates, in the bazaars, and in the households of Ceylon. It is often thrown in the teeth of the Mission. How unjustly so, we may well ask any candid man to consider. It is true there are many who have the name of Christ, and yet they walk not according to his teaching. There may even be the form of godliness, but there is none of its power. But among the professed Tamil Christians there are often features which should not be overlooked while we form a judgment of their Christianity. Some have received a Christian education, but misconduct may have obliged them to try their fortunes in Ceylon; some are ignorant, and away from social influences, and they fall into evil habits. Such is the case with some, but they do not form the rule, but the exception. The Gospel possesses a divine power to change the heart when it is truly received, either by the European or the Tamil, and we rejoice to know that there are a large number of Tamil Christians who show, by a good conversation, the reality of their faith in Christ.

Besides the means of communicating a knowledge of Christian truth already referred to, there are three other instrumentalities employed—a Missionary colporteur, the germ of a more extensive system; street preaching; and schools.

The labours of the Mission colporteur have been attended with encouraging success. With the permission of the authorities, a small book-stall was placed in a much frequented part of the bazaar. Here the sale of English, Tamil, and Singhalese Scriptures was well sustained. There has been a great demand for elementary educational books.

It is a proof of the spirit of inquiry and the thirst for knowledge among the people when so large a sale of copies of the Scriptures and elementary educational books can be effected in Kandy and its neighbourhood. The rate of sale diminished only by the difficulty of obtaining a supply of the books in demand. The work done by the colporteur may be said to be two-fold. He has sold useful books to the value of 38*l.*, and he has had large opportunities of making known the Gospel to the circle of readers or inquirers who might generally be seen surrounding his box or table of books.

A systematic plan of street-preaching in Kandy has been kept up during the past year. The present year, it is hoped, will see the plan extended to Gampola, Navalapittia, and Matelle. On Sunday, after mid-day service, the word of God is preached in three different places in the bazaar. The object on these occasions is to bring the Gospel before the large number of Tamil coolies who come into the town on that day. On Thursday evening there is a well-sustained plan of preaching among the Tamil-speaking Mohammedans and Chetties. Controversy is neither sought nor avoided. Among the Mohammedans and Malays there has been often warm opposition, and occasionally threatened violence. The seed thus sown has not been unproductive. God has given testimony to the word of his grace, and several have visited the superintendent and catechists in the manner and spirit of Nicodemus inquiring "How can these things be?"

With the exception of the personal allowance of the superintending Missionary, this Mission is entirely dependent for its maintenance on local funds. That was the original principle on which it was commenced, namely, "that a local fund should be raised and maintained, for the purpose of providing and maintaining catechists, supporting schools, and defraying all other expenses of the Mission." This resolution, we rejoice to say, has been successfully carried out. The planters have liberally contributed, many of them, in letters addressed to the Local Committee, expressing their deep conviction of the good which has been done to the coolies on their estates, and assuring them of their sympathy and hearty co-operation.

But the native Christians, also, are alive to the duty of communicating the Gospel to their countrymen, and, desiring to take part in that Missionary work from which they have themselves derived so much benefit, come forward cheerfully to do what they can. The Report says—

The Christians in Kallibokka contribute a part of the salary of the catechist in that valley. They have contributed 10*l.* for the purchase of a handsome communion service, which is now on its way to Kandy, being sent out by the Rev. S. Hobbs. But perhaps the most encouraging proof of the influence of the Mission among the coolies will be seen by reference to the subjoined list of native contributors to the proposed Tamil church in the Kandy bazaar. More than 113*l.* has been contributed voluntarily by the Canganies and coolies, and a few other Tamils, during the past year, towards the erection of the proposed new church. In one case a Tamil Christian put 2*l.* into the hands of the superintendent, saying, "I do not give this to please you, but for Christ's sake." In another case a heathen Cangany, after being present at a service during which two men received baptism, gave the catechist a five-rupee note, saying, "Your religion is a good one, and I wish to help it: please take this."

We wish very sincerely that our readers could see the list of native contributors, to which the Report refers, without the necessity of transferring it to our pages. But the fact is, that the names occupy no less than six pages of the Report, at the rate of fifty contributors to a page, and therefore, deeply interesting as they are—and there is not one of these names on which we would not ask a blessing—we have no space which we could appropriate to their use, and we must content ourselves with introducing the final paragraph.

The Committee of the Tamil Cooly Mission desire particularly to draw the attention of their friends to the fact, that no effort has been made during the past year to obtain subscriptions from Europeans for the proposed church. It was thought desirable that the Tamil people should give a substantial proof of their zeal and sincerity by first contributing utmost of their power. The above list of voluntary contributions will show to the satisfaction of every unprejudiced mind that the Tamil people are willing to do all they can. No doubt further subscriptions will be given by them when the building is in progress of construction, but in the mean time the Committee confidently appeal to their friends for assistance.

We may conclude with the following sentence, which presents an admirable summary of the Mission—"The coolies in Ceylon receive the benefit; the native Christians in Tinnevelly supply the catechists; the planters in Ceylon liberally provide the salaries; the Church Missionary Society is honoured by the management and superintendence of the whole work."

MISSIONARY PROSPECTS IN TURKEY.

The distinctiveness of Turkey, as a nation, might have been preserved. True, indeed, its condition had become one of extreme decadence, and the well-known illustration of the sick man accurately described what that condition was. Sick, undoubtedly, it had become, even unto death—sick of Mohammedanism. That false religion has poisoned the blood of the body politic, so that, from the sole of the foot even to the head, there was no soundness. One remedy, however, was available, which might have arrested the progress of the disease, nor, extreme as the case had become, was it too late for its administration. Moreover, an opportunity for doing so appeared to be afforded. The Hatti-Sheriff of 1856 had proclaimed liberty of conscience, and promised to the Turk, as well as to the Ryot, freedom to embrace and, without molestation, profess whatever religion had established itself in his convictions; and if the Turk was free to inquire and profess, it became the bounden duty of the Christian Missionary not to be absent at such a crisis, but to be on the spot, so as to afford to the inquiring Mohammedan the opportunity of obtaining information. The door into Turkey, as a Mission field, had opened, and it was the duty of the Christian Missionary to enter in. It was impossible for him to do otherwise, for wherever a door is opened, God has commanded that the Gospel should be introduced. Christian Missionaries therefore entered in; they did so at the command of Him who is King of kings and Lord of lords, and whose are the kingdoms of the earth, although they do not yet acknowledge Him. They brought with them the divine remedy. They commenced to administer it, at first on a small scale; and some few of the Turkish population, under the awakening influence of Christian truth, had become convinced of the falsehood of Mohammedanism, and had renounced it. But now the Turkish authorities took the alarm. There are, it is true, few events of sufficient force to arouse Turkish officials out of that indolence which fatalism engenders; we doubt almost whether any thing would have sufficed to do so short of the conviction that active aggressive Christianity, something very different from the dead formalism of the Greek church, had entered into the land, and was actually at work. But this did. In the season of national adversity, when the vessel of the state was in danger of being shipwrecked, they were ready to promise any thing, even that they would befriend Christianity. But it was an engagement which they never intended to fulfil; indeed, they never expected to be called upon to fulfil it. It looked well on paper, that Turkey had recognised the principle of religious toleration. It bespoke sympathy; it satisfied the claimants of the day. But they never imagined that genuine Missionary effort would be commenced in Turkey; or, if it did, they never thought that it could convert Turks. But so soon as this unexpected result did take place, the fanatical party at once took the alarm, and bigoted members of the royal family were forthwith enlisted on their side. A powerful pressure was brought to bear upon the ministry and the decision was come to that the Christian movement must be stopped. There was in Constantinople no Lord Stratford de Redcliffe to interfere by firm remonstrance, and save Turkey from the most ruinous course she could adopt.

The language of the Hatti-Sheriff was examined. It was resolved to put the narrowest interpretation possible upon it. A Turk might be a Christian provided he kept his Christianity to himself; and a Missionary might reside within the dominions of the Sublime Porte, provided he was careful never to utter any thing which might suggest a doubt as to the truth of Mohammedanism. All religions were to recognise each other as children of the same family, and settle down into a system of mutual forbearance. Protestant Christianity had exceeded these bounds: it must be rebuked and repressed. Resolutions of this kind were not to remain a *brutum fulmen*. They were vigorously acted upon. Turkish fanaticism showed that it was not dead. It broke through all engagements, and acted with unbecoming violence. The details are too recent to be forgotten. It is unnecessary to repeat them.

An opportunity, then, has been afforded. The great panacea was introduced: it wrought efficaciously, and showed, if not interfered with, what it was capable of effecting. It was stupidly rejected, and the process of inquiry was stopped. Since then the Missionaries have done nothing.

Has Turkey prospered in consequence? Have there been no evidences of the divine displeasure? The cholera came and scourged the outlying dependencies. It broke out at Mecca, and decimated the pilgrims. Egypt suffered fearfully. The cloud of pestilence then came and settled upon Constantinople, and the angel of death went forth to smite. The victims fell by tens of thousands. What had the Turkish Government to offer to its suffering people instead of that Christianity which it had forbidden them to approach? The panic-stricken crowds were commanded to take holiday, and to be festive. Bands of music perambulated the streets; fireworks were let off; and so within the homes of the people there was wailing, and, without, din and discord. What a strange sympathy this—what a mockery of the people's sufferings. We regret to find from the following letter, written by one of our Missionaries, that the terrible infliction failed to awaken amongst the population a sense of religious need, and induced no inquiries after Christianity.

I received your letter, dated July 25th, and should have written at once, had it not been that, in this terrible time of pestilence, my own household has not escaped sickness, although, through great mercy, we have been spared the disease in its virulent form. The cholera, too, is generally decreasing, although the mortality is very great, far beyond the published official returns. The scourge has been terrible, and the panic universal. We pray that the people may hear the rod, but, as yet, the only effect it has produced among the natives seems to be a terrible increase of selfishness, and, in very many instances, the most reckless ungodliness. Our own work seems as entirely at a stand still as it was immediately after the persecution of last year. No inquiring Turk has visited our Mission-room, neither do any of the few who used to come to my house in a friendly way ever see me now. Of late we have made some effort to reach those men who were imprisoned last year. Our catechist, Mr. Ghazaros, was directed to seek them out at their homes, to learn their condition, and to endeavour to induce them to attend a service on the Lord's-day, which we were anxious to open for them: the result of this effort was very discouraging. Those whom Mr. Ghazaros saw were still living in their old residences in one of the Mohammedan quarters of the city, but in such fear, that they only ventured to see one another at long intervals, and, at all other times, scrupulously avoided even a casual meeting in the street.

If the Lord permit, when the epidemic has passed we shall try once more to gather them for instruction and prayer in a little house we have taken in Galata, where they will be less likely to be molested than in the room we have just relinquished in the khan. In the mean time the hostility of Aali Pasha to Protestants, and especially Protestant Missionaries, is more clearly pronounced than ever. We know this from the character of his proceedings with regard to the Protestant (native) community's civil affairs, as well as from the character of his intercourse with the Protestant embassies upon the subject. This, together with his late official declaration to the Ambassador, that he would not allow the publication of any religious books in the Turkish language, goes far to show that, as yet, a Christian Turk is not a recognised individual among the subjects of the Sultan, and that directly aggressive Mission work among the Turks will not be tolerated. There seems but little hope at present of our being able to do any thing in the capital in the way of civilization. We can only wait until it shall please the Lord, in his good providence, to open the door. It can hardly be, humanly speaking, that the present state of things can last, and any change that may take place cannot well obstruct work still further. Not many days ago the chief of the Protestant community died of cholera, after a few hours' illness. This man has been a chief cause of the weakness of that community. This event will bring about some change which will deeply interest us. As it is, the treasury is nearly always empty; officials and employés, the military and the navy, with some few exceptions, are long in arrears of pay, and the producing population, as we had many opportunities of observing, are taxed beyond their power, and are universally discontented. And should the contemplated conversion of the home debt into foreign stock take place, the dependence of Turkey upon foreign Governments will be materially increased; and as the payments of interest must be punctually performed, the already too heavy taxation of the agriculturist will have to be made heavier still.

With so many elements of probable and possible change about us, our eyes wait upon the Lord our God, until He make our path plain. In regard to the inhabitants of the capital, it may be said that ignorance is the mother of devotion, and that education, so far as it goes, leads only to infidelity. Men of devotional sympathies attach themselves to one or other of the numerous sects of Dervishes which abound everywhere, making their choice according to the reputation of the Sheikh for occult spiritual power. Mysticism, and the supposed near contact with the unseen and all-pervading spirit, meet, and temporarily satisfy their cravings after something inexpressible and intangible by carnal sense. On the other hand, the French education of others (and the education of neo-Turks is almost wholly French) leads them to consider their highest good to consist in the gratification of the senses, and the casting aside of all restraints of religion whatever, with a vast affectation of philosophy. Among those who are learned, and have not been touched by European influence, there are many who are thorough infidels. The only Turk who has visited our rooms of late is an Atheist, in long robes and a green turban. "God!" said he the other day to me, "what is God? Is he a worm? (alluding to the doctrine of spontaneous generation). I can neither see Him nor hear Him: the air fans my cheek, but I know nothing of God." Still among the middle and lower classes, and notably in the interior, there is a large residue of those whom we may call sincere and pious Mussulmans. More than once have my dear brother Wolters and myself been led to say, during our late journey, "If the Lord shall bless our labours to these people, what beautiful Christian characters we should find here! What simplicity! what devotion!"

Scarcely had the cholera abated its ravages, than the fire came, and, destroying 5000 houses, left homeless a vast body of the people, thus to the horrors of pestilence adding the sufferings of poverty. The Turkish Government has now its hands full, and it is only to be hoped that it will exhibit the same energy in aiding the people that it did in repressing Christianity. Perhaps, had it acted a more honest part as regards the Hatti-Sheriff of 1856, it might have fared otherwise. But it has sown the wind, and it must reap the whirlwind. There are now in Turkey all the marks of a falling empire, nor, if Turkish officialism continue to interpose between the mercy of God and the need of man, can it be desired that such an obstruction should be perpetuated.

Undoubtedly, as, for the present, the door of Constantinople is closed, it behoves us to look elsewhere for opportunities of usefulness. Our Missionaries cannot wait. "If they persecute you in one city, flee ye to another." Time is short; souls are perishing: they must go where they can teach and preach Jesus Christ. Under such circumstances the following letter, from our experienced Missionary, the Rev. J. T. Wolters, of Smyrna, dated September 7, 1865, is well worthy of perusal—

I take the liberty of addressing you at this time on the present aspect and future prospects of the Asia-Minor Missions, with an especial view to the adoption of such means as may, under the blessing of God, be most efficient in promoting the great object which the Society, and we who are your humble labourers in the Gospel of our Lord Jesus Christ in the land of darkness, have at heart, namely, the making known of the blessed Gospel to its benighted inhabitants, and especially the Turks, praying daily that it may please the Lord to bless our feeble efforts, to the glory of his name in the salvation of immortal souls.

Allow me, therefore, to solicit the kind

attention of the Committee to the following statements—

1. With regard to the present aspect of the Mission, I may again say what I have expressed in my letter of July last, although we cannot call it bright, in regard especially to the difficulties we meet with in our endeavours to bring the claims of the Gospel before the Turks, yet, on the whole, we think it is not altogether dark and discouraging. I will now only say, on the present occasion, that after the troubles of last year and the efforts of the enemies of the truth, not only to hinder, but if possible to destroy our work, the Lord has comforted our hearts, and cheered us by the conviction that He has still a work for us to do in this land, and that our recent troubles will be overruled for the furtherance of the Gospel in this great empire.

There can, therefore, be no question as to the continuance of our Mission, not only at Constantinople, but also here at Smyrna. This latter place, it appears to us, as first in rank after the capital, claims our special attention with a view to a Turkish Mission. Its intercourse with, and influence on, the chief places of Asia Minor, chiefly inhabited by Mussulmans, is great. Light springing up here must reflect some rays on the dark interior, which must more or less influence the town of Smyrna. From all the chief places in the interior people come here, on account of business, and return to their respective places with goods bought, and sometimes with a copy or copies of the holy Scriptures, accompanied by words of the Missionaries or their native agents.

But in order to cultivate our intercourse with the interior, itinerancy should be practised as much as possible in the favourable seasons. Places should be visited again and again, and the precious seed of the Gospel sown wherever and whenever it is possible. The journeys of Mr. Weakley and my son have been hitherto more of an exploratory character. They have returned, however, with the conviction deeply impressed on their minds that there is a field to be cultivated in the interior, which ought not to be left as it now is, bearing only the fruits which a false religion and a corrupt Christianity can produce. By frequent intercourse with the people in the interior, friendship will be established, prejudices removed, and opportunities afforded of making known the truth. Some of the people with whom acquaintances have been formed will eventually come to Smyrna and visit us, and bring, perhaps, others of our friends and fellow-travellers, who for the first time will hear a good word from our lips.

The last journey of our Missionaries to Koniah, in the spring of this year, has been particularly interesting. At some places, especially Kulah, they were very kindly received, and their message was listened to with great attention; and, more than this, they were invited to visit them again, and instruct them in scriptural truth. There seems to be a growing desire among the people in the interior to receive the holy Scriptures as the rule of Christian faith and practice. But the journals of Mr. Weakley and my son will best show this.

But it may be said, the people who received our travellers so readily were Christians, and especially Greeks, while with the Turks they had, as it appears from their journals, comparatively little intercourse; and is not our Mission especially and prominently directed to the Mussulmans? Yes; and we do not wish to lose sight of this point for a moment. But the important question arises, "How shall we bring the Gospel to bear upon the Mussulmans as long as it cannot be preached publicly, in the streets, in the bazaar, and wherever there is a concourse of people who will listen to us?" To attempt such a mode of proceeding would soon prove fatal, and, instead of furthering our work, would perhaps throw it back for years. Under Mohammedan rule, this public method of preaching the Gospel is impracticable. As one of the elder Missionaries in Turkey, and after more than thirty years' experience among Mussulmans and Eastern Christians, I may be allowed to express my decided opinion, that in order to bring the claims of the Gospel before the Mussulmans, we must endeavour to influence the Christians who live amongst them. Every unenlightened, superstitious, and ignorant Christian, who by his life denies the power of godliness which the Gospel affords, is a hindrance and a stumbling-block in the way of the Missionary who desires to make the Gospel known to the Mussulman; while, on the other hand, every truly converted Christian in a Mohammedan country, who makes the word of God the rule of his faith and practice, is a light in the darkness, and a helper to the evangelical Missionary, though he (the native Christian) be not officially so by being employed in the Mission. There is also another consideration bearing on this subject. A European agent can have but a very limited intercourse with the Mussulman, who looks upon him quite as a stranger, while an Eastern Christian finds it easy to talk with a Mohammedan, having intercourse with and access to him continually.

By these remarks I have prepared the way for the introduction of the chief subject of this letter, namely, to ask the Committee to allow us to respond to the call of the Christians in the interior, especially at Kulah, by exerting ourselves for the purpose of instructing them in scriptural Christianity. Our object is, not to establish a new Mission for Eastern Christians, but simply to cultivate intercourse with them, and to afford them Christian instruction whenever they are ready to receive it, as appears to be the case at Kulah; and all this to be a stepping-stone to approach the Turks more easily. Looking upon the thousands of Mussulmans around, it grieves us deeply that we cannot reach them with the preaching of the Gospel as we most earnestly desire. When, therefore, the Lord seems to show us a way by which we may reach them, *i.e.* by bringing the light of truth to the Christians in the interior, should we not gladly avail ourselves of such a means at once? The success which our American brethren have had among the Armenians is indeed encouraging and cheering. The efforts hitherto made among the Greeks have, it is true, not met with much success; but it must not be forgotten that the Greeks in the interior, and especially those of Kulah, are a different and more independent set of people than the Greeks at Smyrna and other towns bordering on the sea-shore. They are, generally speaking, more inclined to religious inquiry, reading, and reflection, than here and at Constantinople, where they exhibit a cunning, worldly, and—if I may use the expression—vainly-proud character, boasting of their nationality and orthodox church.

I may remark, also, under this head, that to influence the Greeks in Anatolia, with a view to reach the Turks, requires no separate agency, as it would do at Constantinople, where there is a difference of language. In the interior the Greeks speak the Turkish language, and we may hope, that if meetings for prayer and exposition of the word of God were here and there held, well-inclined Turks may come and hear.

We now give to our readers the Rev. R. Weakley's narrative of the Missionary tour into the interior of Asia Minor, accomplished by him and Mr. Wolters, prefacing it by the following passage from one of his letters, in which he describes the general impression left upon his mind by the reception which he and his brother Missionary met with.

On the 6th of the month I despatched my journal, addressed to yourself, which I trust has arrived safely.

The impression received by my dear brother and myself during the journey was, that in a time of straitness and discouragement, the Lord had providentially opened a field of labour for us in the interior. The greater part of the ground has not been visited by Missionaries of modern days: every town we have visited is in constant communication with Smyrna, which is the emporium of the whole tract of country. The population of the towns is five-sixths Mussulman, and the villages are wholly Turkish. The Christians nearly everywhere received us with much pleasure, and took an interest in our work, while in Kulah and Koniah they most anxiously entreated us to stay and instruct them; and, besides all this, we found an unexpected demand for the word of God. But we have found in this, as in former journeys, that without some intermediary, except under special circumstances, the Turks of the interior were hardly accessible. In the capital the intercourse between all classes of the community, Frank and native, is so general, that direct intercourse between the Missionary and the Mohammedan population is possible, and, under an assurance of liberty and security, easy. In the interior it is far otherwise. The Christians, however, and notably the Greeks, have constantly business transactions with Mussulmans, and, in very many instances, are on very friendly terms with individual Turks; besides which they are gradually and surely gaining position and influence. When there, we found these people so anxious to possess the word of God, so impatient of the religious darkness in which they had long been sitting, so desirous of our instruction, and so interested in our work, we could not but feel that the Lord had opened a door for us in answer to much prayer, and given us the very means of gaining a footing in the interior, and access to the Turks. We have reason to believe that this interest among the Greeks in scriptural Christianity is sincere, and has proceeded from those who have in times past obtained Scriptures from our Smyrna Mission, and carefully read them. In Kulah, where we were received with much respect and evident pleasure, the wealthy chiefs of the community were the first to welcome us, while those in humbler circumstances were not backward in bidding us stay.

Our standing, as ministers of the Church of England, having episcopal ordination and using a scriptural liturgy, gave us a weight and influence which we should not otherwise have had; for although the minds of our Greek friends are thoroughly disturbed upon such questions as the intercession of saints, the nature and number of the sacraments, the adoration of the Virgin Mary, &c., their ideas of church order remain the same.

The natural function of our Smyrna station seems to be itinerancy. It is the emporium of all, or nearly all, the vast tract of country that stretches away eastward as far as the Halys or Kizil Ermak. It is, to use the expressive simile of the natives, the pulley of Asia Minor. Thither, about August in each year, all the merchants and traders of the towns resort to sell or barter their various produce, and at other seasons the flux and reflux of travellers never entirely ceases. . . . . I really think that this is at present the only *active* work which can be carried on in Turkey without the interference of the present Government. Though the news of last year's persecution has been widely spread everywhere, it has produced no effects antagonistic to our work; indeed, on several occasions we saw, on the contrary, that the minds of many had become familiarized by it to the idea of a Mohammedan renouncing his creed for Christianity. The idea also occurred to us more than once, that the poverty and discontent of the people, on account of the oppressive taxation, had, in some degree, softened their behaviour towards Christians, and rendered them more accessible. The friendship and sympathy of the Greeks were, and would be again, a cover and help to the work; and as the sale and circulation of the word of God has the largest guarantee of freedom, there is hardly a point in which the Turkish Government could openly interfere with this Missionary plan. The whole scheme, too, having its centre and rendezvous in Smyrna, would bring a new influence to bear upon what has hitherto been a hard, and apparently sterile field, and might, under the divine blessing, awaken some interest there.

ITINERATION IN ASIA MINOR.

HAVING, through the merciful kindness of our heavenly Father, been brought safely through a severe and dangerous illness, I left Constantinople on the 22nd of March, intending, if it should be his will, to recruit my strength in the milder and less changeable climate of Smyrna for a season, and afterwards to carry out the project of a long journey into the interior which had for some time past been made the subject of much prayer and thought by Mr. Wolters, jun., and myself.

April 21—After making the necessary preparations, and taking with us a heavy boxload of Scriptures—about one-fourth of which were Turkish—together with a few small books and tracts of Christian instruction and devotion, we started about eleven A.M. for Nyf (Nymphæum), intending merely to rest there for the night, and then pass rapidly on, as we hoped to dispose of the whole of our books in places which are more distant and less visited. We arrived about four P.M., and there met M. Renan, who was on his return to Smyrna, after a short tour in the interior. The evening was spent in walking about the place and the ruins of the old castle which overlooks the town: we found, however, no opportunity of having serious conversation with any one. The Turks we saw were mostly day-labourers, very poor and very ignorant: the Greeks, which form the chief part of the population, are better off, and appear to have most of the trade in their hands. Nyf is a small place, in a situation of great natural beauty, and surrounded by a well-watered and richly-fertile country.

Cassaba.

April 22—On the morrow we rode on to Cassaba, stopping only for a few minutes at a way-side coffee-shop, the only inmates of which were two or three very rough Albanians. At midday we arrived at our destination, somewhat fatigued by a wearisome ride through rough and marshy cross-country and the numerous fords of a rapid river. We spent the evening in conversation with our agent, who resides here, on his work and prospects, and learnt much that was encouraging. Notwithstanding the general shyness which has been shown by the Turks since the events of last year, he is frequently visited by Mohammedans from the surrounding villages when they come to the market, which is held twice in the week, and occasionally by the merchants, who are constantly passing through Cassaba on their way to and from Smyrna. Besides this, he has made friends in the place itself, and is generally respected (as we had opportunity of observing) by all sections of the community.

Cassaba, or, more properly, Durghudly, is a flourishing town of about 15,000 inhabitants, chiefly Turkish, and will probably be connected with Smyrna within a year by a railway which is now in progress, and by which its importance will be largely increased.

April 23: *First Sunday after Easter*—Brother Wolters held divine service in Greek, and afterwards we joined with Montesanto and our servant in the communion of the Lord's Supper. It had been our intention to visit one or two Turks in the afternoon, but our visit was anticipated by one of them, a wealthy and intelligent man, who, hearing of our arrival, sent his servant to beg that we would call and converse with him. Accordingly we went, and were warmly welcomed. After the usual salutations and the coffee, he began to ask about the Constantinople difficulties, saying that the matter had been much talked of in Cassaba, and that he wished very much to know the truth concerning it. I endeavoured to explain at length the circumstances of the case, and how, according to the opinion of most persons, it was a clear violation of the religious liberty which had been proclaimed by the Government. With reference to the last statement, he said that he certainly understood it so; and, taking a large book (the title of which I did not ask), he read some passages from the imperial edicts, in Turkish, which declare that every subject of the Sultan is at liberty to change his religion, and shall not be molested in the exercise of it, and that no compulsion should be used in any case. "Now," said he, "the terms exclude no class of His Majesty's subjects; and although our Ulema dispute with me, and say that the declaration refers only to the question of Christians embracing Islam, I take my stand upon what is here written, and assert that Mussulmans have an equal right and liberty to adopt the Christian faith if they choose to do so." He then asked a variety of questions, and we got very soon upon the subject of personal religion. He had been giving directions about the sowing of his fields to a man who wished to do the work by contract, when, turning to me, he spoke of the vicissitudes and difficulties of life, and of the weariness which he, in common with so many others, oftentimes felt. Upon which I remarked that bitter was always mingled with the sweet of the world, and that sin, and sin only, was that which had produced the bitter. He agreed, but said that we know not the sweet but by the bitter, and that just as God had created every thing in pairs in the beginning, so also good, and evil its counterfoil, were ever found side by side. This at once led to the discussion of the nature of sin as being rebellion against a just and holy God, who is of purer eyes than to behold iniquity, and can by no means clear the guilty; and as consisting not only in outward acts but in inward thoughts and desires. I supported this explanation with passages of Scripture, and then asked him how he hoped for deliverance. "We can only entreat for mercy," he said, "and the prophets help us." "How so?" "They are the beloved of God, and He hears them." "They were but men," I replied, "and so come under the description of the holy word, 'There is none that doeth good, and sinneth not;' and, although faultless in what they delivered as God's word, were but sinners, and faulty in their personal behaviour and service. Besides, supposing them to be faultless, their obedience sufficed but for themselves, and could not suffice to make up the deficiencies of others. Supposing you, a rich man, owed me the whole of your property, could you help another man in that respect who was indebted to me to the entire amount of his?" "No, certainly." "Yet we all owe to God obedience and service, in all our time, our property, our relations, our business, our thoughts, or words, and works; and this being so, no man can redeem his brother, or give to God a ransom for him, nor can one become a mediator between God and man." Here he looked surprised and interested, but simply remarked, "I see." "Now," said I, "we come to the great point on which Mussulmans disagree with Christians—Christ, not merely man, for that would not suffice, but having the divine nature; God's Son—a title not to be carnally understood, but to be received as that by which God has been pleased to reveal to us a relation in the divine unity, as when He said, 'This is my beloved Son, hear Him'—Christ is the Mediator and Saviour. And Christ says in the Gospel, 'Come unto me, all ye who labour and are heavy-laden.'" After entering a little fully into the Gospel plan, I said, "What can give one greater happiness and comfort than to be certain of forgiveness and the favour of God?" "Nothing," he replied. "Well, the Gospel offers us this certainty, and although all suffer alike the ills of life, yet a true Christian enjoys an inner happiness which they cannot affect." He then asked some questions, and we took our leave after he had expressed the hope that we should not forget to visit him again. We wished to call upon one or two more, but the sun was setting, so we returned to our lodging, with the resolution that, should the Lord prosper our way, we would remain one or two days in Cassaba on our return. Our servant sold several copies of sacred Scripture here.

April 24—Started for Salykly. The clouds which capped the mountains descended after we had been two or three hours on the road, and deluged the valley with rain, which continued to fall undiminished until we reached the khan. For some distance the water had so covered the road that our only guide was an opening in a mound some distance before us, through which we had to pass. We were recognised, and welcomed in the khan, and the best room was made ready for us, but we saw no one with whom we could converse.

Our indefatigable servant, however, managed to sell four copies of sacred Scripture in the pouring rain.

Kulah.

April 25—The weather having cleared, we started for Kulah. The plain was full of water and mud as far as the Cogamus, and some little distance beyond, where we rested for a few minutes after passing the ford. The rising ground then commenced, a series of low and well-cultivated hills gradually increasing in height until we reached the foot of a long and difficult ravine, which led us up to a small plain high up in the mountain, where we halted for a couple of hours to refresh ourselves and the horses. Thence, still ascending, we pushed on to Kulah, being refreshed and delighted on our way by the vast panorama of mountain scenery to the north and east, which our elevated position enabled us to enjoy. Kulah is situated in a narrow plain of considerable elevation, shut in on the south and open towards the north. The space on the southern side, between the town and the hills, is laid out in enclosures, where the vine and madder are cultivated; but the northern side, which, at some distance from Kulah, opens out into the valley of the Hermus, is entirely filled by that indescribable and terrible chaos of lava and ashes, which Strabo calls the κατακεκαυμένη χώρα, and which extends as far as Adala, eight hours' journey distant. In Kulah we were very kindly received into the house of one of the most wealthy Greek residents, and treated with great respect. As soon as our object became known—which it did the next day—we found very many persons among the Christians who were not only willing but most anxious to converse with us on the subject of religion. In the schools we found enlightened teachers and good attendance. The chief master visited us several times during the two days we stayed, and asked many questions; indeed, our conversations with him and several others, which were wholly on the doctrines of the Gospel, lasted on each occasion till midnight, and were of a deeply-interesting character. Besides this, we were asked several times by different persons to come frequently, and to stay some days at a time, so that they might be at liberty on the Lord's-day to hear the Scriptures expounded, and to join in prayers which they could understand. They would gladly provide a place for us to do so. The thirst for scriptural instruction is general in the community, and appears to have been awakened by the reading of the Græco-Turkish Bible by a few serious men among them. There is also an earnest desire with some to benefit their Mussulman neighbours, with whom they are generally on friendly terms. "We shall be glad to learn how to speak with them," they said to us.

Our intercourse with the Mussulmans was very limited, but very friendly, and did not go much beyond conversation on matters indifferent. Two or three came to our room in the khan, looked at our books, and talked awhile. The books were good, they said, but they could not be persuaded to buy them. In the bazaar the Turks wished much to see the holy Gospel in their own language. Some sat reading for awhile, and then returned the copy, saying they could not take it then. Others were offended at finding the name "Father" attributed to God, and abruptly closed the conversation. Others, again, freely discussed with our servant; and one frankly told him that he would read the New Testament attentively, and that, if it commended itself to his conscience as better than the Korán, he would adopt the Christian faith.

Nearly eighty copies of sacred Scripture were sold here, a very few of which were taken by the Mussulmans. Books of prayer were very much in demand, also the Book of Common Prayer and Reference Bibles. The two latter have never yet been printed in Græco-Turkish.

We are informed that the Turks know perfectly well what happened in Constantinople last year, but that the most prominent piece of news they received was to the effect that several thousand Turks in the capital were ready to embrace Christianity, and that very many had done so—a rumour which, in various proportions as to extent, was rife in the capital itself at that time. The Mussulmans of Kulah had manifested no signs of displeasure at the news, nor made any disturbance. An expression of surprise, and the remark, "If these things are done where the Sultan sits and reigns, what can we say?" was all. Our friends had read in the native newspapers many things of an exaggerated character, which they asked us about, and which we were very glad to explain. Aali Pasha's letter to the Ottoman Ambassador in London had been printed lately, by command, in most of the native newspapers, in their different languages, and thus the misrepresentations made at the first have been perpetuated. Kulah contains about 2000 houses, of which 400 are Greek, the rest Mussulman, eleven mosques, two or three convents of Dervishes, and two churches. All the Greeks speak Turkish, and but very few know Greek. The inhabitants are chiefly factors and merchants, who travel about in Asia Minor during a great part of the year, buying up produce of various kinds.

which they take down to Smyrna. The place itself has no trade. There is but little land in the neighbourhood capable of cultivation, and the only manufacture carried on is that of a few fine carpets, which are made by the women at home. The ruddy complexion and robust frames of the women and children strike one as quite a remarkable characteristic of the people. When we had left, our servant told us that many more people wished to see us the evening before for religious conversation, but that they felt ashamed to come to the house in which we were staying. This place affords us an opening for usefulness, which it would be for the general interests of our holy work not to neglect. We have felt constrained to promise them another visit in the autumn.

April 28—Rode on from Kulah after a warm farewell from our friends, and a visit from the elder of the two priests. Our road ran through deep ravines, and over rocky steeps, gradually severe, and twice in the course of the day we crossed the Hermus, once by a bridge. Towards evening we passed through a semi-ruined village called Yeni-Shedr, two or three mosque-like minarets indicating what had once been the size of the place. Shortly afterwards we reached the farmstead where we were to pass the night. Here we were guests, and had a good deal of conversation with our hosts, who are natives of Kulah. We were told very much about the oppressive taxation, which has been much increased of late, and from which the Turks seem to be the greatest sufferers.

Ushak.

April 29—After taking a bath in the Hermus, which is here very rapid and full of sand, we rode on to Ushak, on the way passing by another semi-deserted village. At Ushak, after we had taken a room in the khan, and arranged our things, we were received into the house of a Greek merchant, to whom we had a letter of introduction, and a number of persons came to call upon us. It was impossible, however, to induce religious conversation. Money, merchandize, profit, loss—these were the all-absorbing topics, a most marked contrast to what we had met with in Kulah. A Turkish gentleman came in upon some business he had with a person present, who farms some of the taxes in the district, and, during his short stay, called for and drank several glasses of raki. I tried to draw his attention to the evils of intemperance, by telling him of the interest which many good people in England take in the reclamation of drunkards, and how, on this account, a great number of persons had agreed to abstain from strong drink altogether, and to persuade as many as they could to follow their example. He said it was good not to drink raki, and that such efforts were praiseworthy; he also tried to excuse his drinking so much, but while saying "I beg you will pardon me," did not cease asking our host to order more for him. He was evidently ashamed, but, having begun, seemed to have no control over his appetite, so that when he left, after half an hour's conversation, he appeared quite silly from the effects of what he had drunk. We were told that the habit of raki drinking was very prevalent among the Turks of Ushak. The town, which is almost entirely built of unburnt brick, and has a very dirty and poor appearance, contains between 2000 and 3000 houses, of which 100 are Greek and 50 Armenian. The finest wheat is grown in this neighbourhood, which is a rich plain, and nearly half the women of the town are employed in making carpets. The Turkish women make the thick rich carpets which are so well known in Europe, while the Christians manufacture a durable and handsome carpet, with a smooth surface, much used by the people themselves. We are informed that the earnings of these poor women amount to only one piastre (2¼*d.*) a day. Of late years the people have become much impoverished, and the possibility of having railway communication with Smyrna is looked upon as a ray of hope, and furnishes matter for conversation and speculation to all. Thus, when we alighted a number of Turks flocked immediately around us to learn who we were; and when one or two tried to lift our boxes of books, which were very heavy, they concluded at once that they contained money—which, in the interior, is almost wholly copper—and that we had come to commence railway works forthwith. In a little while this was bruited about in the bazaar, soon, however, to be corrected by the appearance of our man with his bag of books.

April 30: *Lord's-day* — We succeeded, by candidly stating our views concerning the Lord's-day, in obtaining a little time of retirement for reading the word and praying. Our host had thought to do us honour by taking us to see the town and what antiquities it possessed. Some little time later several persons came in, and one asked for information about the difficulties we met with in Constantinople last year. They had heard many rumours, and seen several notices in the newspapers, but wished to know the truth. We had thus an opportunity of speaking of the progress of the Gospel among the Turks, and of denying the foolish assertions that money was our chief agent in the work, and that we had stirred up the people by publicly preaching against Mohammed. The latter accusation they did not believe, nor does it seem to have gained credit anywhere except in certain quarters in Constantinople, so utterly improbable, and—in connexion with the safety of the persons so acting—so impossible does it appear to every one. A gentleman who was present said that he was in Constantinople about the time when these things took place, and could say, from his own personal knowledge, that there were many Turks there who were reading the New Testament. He mentioned especially one person, a fellow-townsman of his (Kutahyah), an Imam resident in Constantinople, whom he saw while there, who taught a number of persons secretly from the Gospel. He gave me the man's name and address, so that I might find him out on my return. Most of the afternoon we spent with our servant in the khan, with whom we had prayers. Previous to our going down thither, a few hairs of Mohammed's beard were brought into the town on the back of a camel, with great pomp and solemnity. Most of the inhabitants had gone out to meet the relic, which is a present from the Government at Constanstinople to the town of Ushak. In the evening we had an opportunity of speaking a few words for our Master to two or three persons. One of them acknowledged sadly his godless state. "We are so swallowed up," said he, "with business, merchandize, and money, that we never go to church, or keep a fast: we find no time either to think or to pray." A visitor told us that the people (Christians) were very much alarmed at our presence: they had rather one of their number should become a Mohammedan than a Protestant.

May 1—Visited the Greek school, and found the master prepared with a perfect storm of opposition to us as Protestants, and our work as Missionaries. He held a long controversy with Mr. Wolters in an acrimonious spirit, but always shrunk from appeals to the word. From thence we went to the room in the khan, where I had the opportunity of conversing with two or three people. Besides these, several Turks came in for a few minutes, but would neither stay nor purchase Scriptures. A Softa, who had bought a New Testament and a copy of Genesis and Psalms, brought them back, saying that he had shown them to his Hoja, who told him that they were not the true books, and that he should return them. After a few words with him, I found he was terribly ignorant. Controversy with such a man would only make disturbance, so the money was restored, and he went off in good humour. The Turks generally seemed very ignorant and very bigoted, and the gift which came yesterday, together with the near approach of the Bairam, has not tended to make them any more disposed to tolerate conversation, or to buy our books.

On our return to the house, we had a visit from the owner of the farm where we lodged on Friday night. He was exceedingly friendly, and offered to introduce us to several Turks in the neighbourhood of his farm when we should next visit him. He wishes our work God speed.

In the evening our host, and a gentleman who was staying there, asked us some questions about our liturgy, and especially about the degrees of relationship which were prohibited in marriage. On being informed, they expressed much surprise at the liberty which the Scriptures and the Church of England allowed, and told us that the restrictions laid upon them by the Greek Church were felt by the people to be a great burden, and particularly in Asia Minor, where the Christian communities are comparatively small. It occurs not unfrequently—as at this moment in Ushak—that a young man is entirely debarred from marrying in his own town, because of some remote relationship which he may have with nearly the whole community.

We gave our kind host a New Testament, which, with one other copy, were the only books we could dispose of in Ushak. But although the people are very ignorant and rough, neither we nor our servant met with any insult.

Route to Kara Hissar.

May 2—Left Ushak for Kara Hissar, two days' journey. Our road lay through beautiful uplands, apparently very fertile, but only half cultivated. Here for the first time we saw women ploughing. The villagers, however, for the first few hours were more numerous than usual. About midday we halted at Islam Keuy—a poor village on the east bank of the Banas, a tributary of the Meander—having the Murad Dagh (Dindymus) on our left, and the Ahar Dagh on our right hand, both being capped with snow. After resting awhile, we passed on through a pleasant valley, in which is a celebrated warm spring, much frequented by the sick and superstitious, both Christian and Turk, who tie numerous pieces of dirty rag to the bush close by,* as they do, indeed, at the tombs of their saints and every other holy place. At ten hours from Ushak we arrived, in heavy rain, at a farm, where we were most comfortably lodged in the travellers' room, and soon had a large blazing log fire to dry and warm ourselves by. After a plentiful meal, provided by the owner of the farm, that person, known by the title of the Mollah Effendi, came in, and, lighting his narghillé, sat down to converse with us. He asked many questions about England, and the way in which our

* The same superstitious custom prevails in Ireland.

Government was conducted, and thus we sat until ten P.M., conversing about the nature of our institutions, and the liberty and security which was enjoyed in our country; and, above all, we dwelt upon the moral tone which prevailed, and which was the result of the influence, acknowledged or not, of the word of God, that holy book being constantly taught in our schools, read publicly in our churches, and privately by individuals, in a language that all could understand. He seemed very much interested by this statement; and when I told him that we had with us some copies of the New Testament in Turkish, and that, if he would accept and read it, we would give him one, he said he would be delighted to have it. Anticipating the usual surprise which a Mohammedan feels on finding the holy Scriptures to consist in great part of narrative—their idea of revelation being that it is ever in the form of direct utterances from heaven, and so is said to descend, or to be sent down—I explained that he would find in the New Testament a record of the words and acts of Jesus, and the teaching of the Apostles, all being written for our instruction, &c.

May 3—In the morning very early he came in again, and reminded me that I had not given him the book. A copy of the new translation of the Gospels and Acts, lately printed, was in readiness for him, and he received it with evident pleasure. We then had some more conversation. During the night the rain had changed to snow, and the wind was intensely cold. Our kind host invited us to remain another day, but we thought it best to push on to Kara Hissar, since, if the snow should continue to fall, we might have difficulty in finding the road, or even be compelled to remain where we were, in a lone farm, with poor accommodation for the horses; and if, on the other hand, it should clear up, and we waited till it did so, we should not have time to reach our destination, which was a long day's journey distant. So, taking our guide with us to the next village on the main road, we started; but when we got out of the hollow in which the farm lay, we found ourselves exposed to the fury of the mountain blast and blinding snow, which stunned and bewildered both horses and men. The poor beasts dreaded the rude shocks, and turned their tails to receive them, while the intense cold made the hands and feet of their riders unconscious of stirrup and rein. Thus, after about two hours and a half of painful struggling to get on, we were driven to take shelter in a little Turkish village, where a warm room and blazing pine logs, which the people kindled for us, brought life again to our benumbed feet and hands and battered heads. Here a great many rough Turks, some of whom were of larger stature than is usually met with, came in to bid us welcome, and to drink coffee with us. We had some pleasant conversation with them, but could not introduce our message. When talking with a number of ignorant Turks, one is obliged to wait for something to drop from them which gives an easy opening for speaking upon religious subjects, otherwise our object is likely to be defeated by their suspicious fanaticism, or by all leaving us. The state of the crops, wheat, barley, and opium, and the depredations which the cattle of the Turkomans make in their fields, and their general poverty, form the principal topics of conversation. The compulsory settlement of the Turkomans or Yurouks is a boon much desired by the farmers, especially by those in the highlands (Yaïlah), which are their summer camping places. These nomads have usually much cattle—sheep, goats, horned cattle, camels, horses, asses and mules—and as these do not all feed together, and are often numerous, they cannot be properly tended. The population of the camp, even if willing to do so, is never sufficient to prepare their produce for sale, weave their carpets, attend the markets, perform their domestic duties, and, at the same time, watch the cattle, which, in consequence, make sad ravages on the crops, for which redress is very rarely given. Indeed, the people generally choose the lesser evil of patiently enduring their losses, rather than run the risk of a quarrel with neighbours who have it in their power to be very troublesome.

Kara Hissar.

May 4—Weather intensely cold, but the snow had ceased. Notwithstanding the request of the Agha, that we should consider the room as our own, and stay till the weather moderated, we thought best to get on as soon as possible to Afium Kara Hissar. We were glad, however, to have a hard gallop occasionally, to warm the horses and quicken our own circulation. At length we reached the beautiful level plain on the edge of which Kara Hissar is situated, and which, from the absence of prominent enclosures and the occasional protrusion of masses of rock from the smooth surface, bears much resemblance to a vast lake, dotted here and there with small rocky islands. The town itself takes its name from a remarkably isolated mass of rock, which rises to a great height, and is nearly perpendicular, being crowned with the ruins of an ancient castle, and having the houses about its base. Kara Hissar signifies the black castle, Afium being prefixed to distinguish it from another Kara Hissar at no great distance off. Opium is the chief article of produce and commerce, of which large quantities are sent down to Smyrna every year for exportation. An oil is expressed from the seeds of the poppy, which is used universally instead of fat or olive oil in cookery, the smell of which is very disagreeable. The people say that the use of this oil produces the baldness which is so prevalent in Kara Hissar; but while in Koniah we found, on inquiry, that the same defect existed, although the poppy oil is but little, if at all, used there. The town is large and busy, containing between 5000 and 6000 houses, of which 400 are Christian (all Armenian). There are from thirty to forty mosques, one of which is of an ancient date, and very richly endowed, and, as a gentleman remarked to us, not a single school for the Mussulmans; meaning, no doubt, nothing better worthy of the name than those wretched establishments in which children are taught to read, write, and do a little necessary arithmetic, as well as to repeat a few passages from the Korán, the meaning of which is equally unknown to the teacher and the taught. One cannot be surprised at meeting with gross ignorance where the instruction of the young is so neglected. Many Dervishes reside in Kara Hissar, and have several tékés, or convents, some of which are largely endowed. A gentleman, to whom we had a letter of introduction, hearing that we were in the khan, came and carried us to his house, where we could appreciate many comforts after our experience of the last two days.

May 5—Went about the town, and passed through the bazaars, which are extensive. The whole place was in a bustle, as the Mussulmans were making preparations for the Corbam Bairan, a feast of three days, commencing on the morrow. In this they commemorate the offering of Ishmael (?) by Abraham, and every one who can afford to do so buys a sheep or goat, sacrifices it, and then feasts with his family and friends on its flesh. Sometimes the rich provide a number, the flesh of which is distributed to the needy; and it is not unfrequent that, in fulfilment of a vow made in reference to the success of some enterprise, a recovery from dangerous sickness, or a deliverance from impending danger, a sheep or sheep are sacrificed at the tomb of some reputed saint, and either given to the Dervishes or divided among a number of beggars. We then called to pay our respects to the Caimakam (deputy governor), who talked with us freely for some time, and told us of the vast improvements he had begun and was about to carry out in his province, &c. &c. We also saw another official of rank, but did not stay with him, as he was very busy. In the evening several persons came to see us, and much inquiry was made about the Stamboul business of last year. All had heard that there had been a wonderful movement among the Turks in favour of Christianity, and that the Government had interfered to put a stop to it.

May 6—Yesterday all was bustle; to-day every shop and stall is shut up, the feast has commenced, and the Turks are making holiday, while the Christians have left their businesses, partly because there is nothing for them to do, and partly because they fear the Turks, who do not scruple to ill-treat them now and then on such occasions. There was no hope of our doing any thing among the Turks, but we found a number of Armenians, in our room in the khan, buying Scriptures, and conversing earnestly with our servant on religious subjects. In the afternoon we had some conversation with an exiled Pasha, a very intelligent and handsome man. We learnt from other persons that he had been deprived of all his property, and that, since his residence in Kara Hissar, he had been obliged to part with all the valuables he brought with him, and then with every thing he had, until he had nothing left but the clothes he wore, so that he might obtain necessary food for himself and his two motherless children. He had attempted to open a little school where he might teach a few children French and other things, but the authorities promptly put a stop to it. His circumstances are such that he is often without food, and then he finds a welcome and sympathy at the table of Christians. He held a responsible position under Reschid Pasha's government, and still receives occasional help and sympathy in a private way from some of his old associates and friends. We then called at the houses of two or three well-to-do Armenians, and found that we were less disliked on account of our religion than on account of our stedfast refusal to drink raki with them. What a sad life some of these rich people live! money-getting and raki-drinking absorb the chief of their thoughts and the greater part of their time. However, thank God, our presence has awakened inquiry among some of the Armenians, and a good number of sacred Scriptures and selections of prayers in Armeno-Turkish have been sold. A number of persons wished to see us on the morrow, the time and place we left for them to arrange. All speak Turkish, and are ignorant of Armenian.

May 7: *Lord's-day*—We attended, by invitation, the examination of the Armenian schoolchildren, which took place in the church. We stayed only an hour. There were 300 or 400 people present. One of the boys delivered an oration, which, with the exception of a sprinkling of Armenian terms for law, Gospel, church, &c. &c., was in very good Turkish, and delivered with a great deal of spirit. Some little time after, we went to the khan, and found five or six Armenians, who asked many questions relative to passages of Scripture, and the doctrines of the Gospel. These people told us that they all, and many more, were very anxious for some one to reside among them and teach them the Gospel. The chief schoolmaster came in, and entered heartily into the conversation: he appeared to have read the sacred Scriptures attentively, and could quote readily and appositely. The conversation was prolonged for some time, and, when all had left, we returned to the house, with our servant, and had prayers in Greek. We learnt from him that he had been kept up till near midnight by Armenians, who came to the khan to converse about religion, and who were all anxious that we should either stay with them for a while, or send some one to remain with them. Long after sunset we were sitting and conversing with our host, when a messenger with a lantern came to invite us to a house where several persons were assembled who wished to converse with us. We went, and found five or six persons waiting for us, one of whom opened the conversation by saying that, some years ago, a few copies of the word of God were brought to Kara Hissar: these books had been read with deep attention by many of their community (Armenian), who found that some of the tenets, which formerly they held in their ignorance, were wrong, and did not scruple to express their convictions. They were then persecuted by the richer and more powerful Armenians on account of their new opinions, and were stigmatized with the epithet of Protestants. The thing then slnmbered for a while, in consequence of the opposition met with. Last year, however, hearing of the progress of Christian work in Constantinople, and the rumours of many Turks embracing, and many more being ready to embrace, Christianity, they thought it a favourable time to express their convictions openly, and to petition the Governor to obtain for them the permission to constitute themselves a Protestant community, and the privileges which belong to such a community. Their old enemies then obtained the help of the Turks, who made common cause with them in persecuting the petitioners, and put eight of them in prison for forty-five days for the crime of separating, or wishing to separate themselves from the church.

In consequence of this treatment, and seeing the power of the local government and that of the chief men of the Armenian community arrayed against them, all had remained quiet, not knowing what to do. Nearly 200 heads of houses would have separated from the Armenian church at that time, but of these by far the greater number, alarmed and depressed, had given way to despair, while the rest still held to the hope of seeing a teacher of their own to minister the word of life to them. He said, in conclusion, "Your coming among us has rekindled the hope we have long cherished. Can you not help us? Can you not give us a teacher? Tell us what we must do that we may become a recognised community, and so enjoy protection in the avowal and exercise of our conscientious convictions." We told them that we sympathized with them very heartily in the troubles they suffered on account of their wishing to follow the Gospel of our Lord Jesus Christ; but for the present there did not seem to be any other alternative but patience; for, in the first place, they had no teacher and no assembly for worship, and were thus without any visible claim to be recognised as a separate community; and that, secondly, if it were not absolutely necessary for them to have some slight evidence of unity and the beginning of organization, the present was not a fit time to make an application for enrolment in the Protestant community, since the affairs of its Chancery was in a very unsettled state; indeed, we could not, in regard to their own welfare, advise them to separate formally from the Armenian church until they could be assured of protection elsewhere. Besides all this, we thought that it would be well for them to habituate themselves to the expectation of a persecution which they would certainly, in one shape or another, have to suffer for the name of Christ, if they boldly professed to be his, and strove to follow his example. Our advice was, then, that they should patiently wait until the Lord opened a door for them; that during this time of waiting they should meet often to read the word of God, and pray together for guidance, strength, and perseverance, to endure all hardness for the sake of Him who loved them and gave Himself for them; that they should not allow themselves to doubt that those who sincerely sought the Lord would ever be forsaken by Him. They had already seen something of persecution; they had also been allowed to feel their own weakness; they must, therefore, not forget the lesson they had learnt, and be ready always to make more account of the Lord's help and presence than of the disposition of those with whom they had to do. They must *know* Him in whom they had believed. We would, however, consult about their case on our return to Smyrna; and as some of them would be coming there, in the way of business, in the autumn, we should be glad to see them there. Thus we conversed with them for some time, and, after praying together, we bade them farewell, and left, among many tokens of respect. This was the end of our stay in Kara Hissar. We heard much of the sadly impoverished state of the farmers, which goes on continually from bad to worse. The Turkish merchants and the Christians, who are most engaged in trade, do not suffer so much. We learnt also, that, not long ago, an order came from Constantinople commanding all Mussulmans to observe the stated prayers five times a-day, &c.

Route to Ak Shehr.

May 8 — Parted with our kind friends, leaving with them a New Testament and a note for the exiled Pasha, whose case had awakened our sympathy, and led us to pray and hope that, by reading the words of Jesus, he might be led in his sorrow to Him, and there find rest for his soul. We have not compassed much more than a third of our projected journey, and two-thirds of our books have been sold. The journey of this day was over level plain, a great deal of which is uncultivated, and in some parts covered with standing water. We had ridden some hours, and were skirting the mountains on the western side, when a violent thunderstorm broke suddenly upon us. Our macintoshes had been sent on with the books earlier, as it was very fine when we started. Our horses were thoroughly frightened by the crash upon crash, and we were temporarily blinded by the beating of the rain and the fierce glare of the lightning. Thus we sped at full gallop till we arrived at the village of Chai, where we found a miserable windowless lodging, the best place that could be found. However, by nailing up coverings over the four large apertures, and getting a good fire of well-burnt charcoal, we managed to dry ourselves, and pass a comfortable night. Here a Turk purchased a New Testament. We could converse with no one.

May 9 — The rain continued incessantly, but we thought it better to face it than to stay in our wretched lodging. The weather was, however, more violent than we anticipated, and so, at the end of four hours' buffeting, we were obliged to relinquish our intention of reaching Ak Shehr, and to seek shelter in the village of Ishakli. Our men, not being so well protected from the rain as ourselves, were wetted to the skin, so they lit a large fire in the stable, and hung up their dripping clothes to dry, while they crept close to the flame to get warm. Our lodging was a little dirty coffee-shop, there being neither guest-room nor khan in the place: still we were in shelter, a sufficient cause for thankfulness. About a dozen Turks were sitting smoking in the place. Our books were shown to them, but the greater number could not read, and those who could had no desire to read religious books or have religious conversation. One respectable Turk, who, like ourselves, had been driven to shelter, was very friendly. He said he was going to Koniah, and would be glad to renew our acquaintance there. Very shortly after, the rain held up a little, and he proceeded on his way. We could not go on because of the pitiable plight of our men, so we walked about the place, which is prettily situated between the Sultan Dagh on the west and the Lake of Ak Shehr on the east. This is probably the Thymbrium mentioned by Xenophon in the Anabasis. We saw, however, no ruins of earlier date than that of the lower empire, and these were merely fragments of sculpture set up in the cemetery as tombstones. A massive caravanserai, with a little mosque in the courtyard, according to the inscription over the entrance, the work of Sultan Alaed'din of Koniah, is an object of curiosity to the present inhabitants, some of whom went with us to ask what it might be. In the walls of the mosque, which is dilapidated and filthy, we observed tombstones of the period of the empire, built in with the other masonry. The country around was covered with clusters of fruit-trees, chiefly apricots, and in every respect is fertile and beautiful.

Ak Shehr.

May 10 — Started very early for Ak Shehr, which we reached about half-past ten A.M. This is a town of about 2500 houses, a small proportion of which are Christian, chiefly Armenian. It is situated at the foot of the pass, and runs up into the ravine, through which passes the road to the site of the Pisidian Antioch, now Yaloratch, six hours' distant. Many Christians came to see us in the khan, and two or three Turks. Several books were sold. The people wonderfully misunderstood the name Protestant, and were very suspicious of our motives. We stated very frankly who we were, what Protestant signified, and what our object was in thus travelling the country; but they could hardly be persuaded that we had not some ulterior object. As in other places, so here, Græco-Turkish Scriptures were in demand, but our stock of them had been exhausted some days. Mr. Wolters had a long conversation with an intelligent young Greek who came in again in the evening, and was present at our prayers. We noticed, and were informed, that there is more friendliness between the Christians and the Turks here than in most other places, but did not find the latter disposed to have intercourse with us.

In the middle of the Turkish cemetery is a noted place of pilgrimage, the tomb of Haja Nasr Ed'din Effendi, whose sayings and doings are household words among the Turks, but have nothing either of piety or morality in them. One is led to think that he was considered a saint on account of his not being quite sane. The ludicrous is perpetuated even on his tomb, which is covered with an immense green cloth cap and turban, and surrounded with earthen water-pipes, set upright, for candlesticks. At the bottom of the tomb is a small hole, whence the pilgrims carry away handfuls of earth, as having a healing virtue. Here, as at other holy places, were dirty rags in abundance, left by the sick pilgrims, who, whether Christian or Turk, will go anywhere rather than to the Good Physician. We were more than once surprised and grieved to find potsherds at the tombs of Mussulman saints, containing fragments of burnt charcoal, upon which Christians had sprinkled incense; nor is it unknown that Turks in their need have visited Christian sanctuaries. We were informed that at Ladik, a place two days' journey distant (the ancient Laodicæa Combusta), the inhabitants were all formerly Christians, and that, until within the memory of some now living, they recognised relationship with some of the Christians of Ak Shehr, and even now were exceedingly friendly with Christians. By that route it would take three days to reach Koniah, whereas by the direct road it was only two long days' journey. On this occasion we thought it best to take the shorter route, and to make more inquiries about Ladik at Koniah, trusting, if the Lord will, to pass that way another time.

May 11—Left Ak Shehr for Koniah. After crossing a somewhat undulating and partially cultivated country, we halted at midday in a little village, wholly Mussulman, as is the case in the villages, with very few exceptions. As usual, the people came in to see us and bid us welcome, and to ask who we were. They inquired what books we had, and when told that we had the New Testament, which we should be pleased to show them, they coldly refused. During the course of conversation, one of them said, in reference to their condition, with great bitterness, "We sleep three hours, work all the rest, eat a piece of bread, and thank God!" The Imam and one or two others then asked if there was war in Constantinople. I replied, "No." "Had the title Ghazi (conqueror) been yet added to the titles of the Sultan?" "Not that I was aware of; but why?" "That they might read it in the Khotbé in the mosque on Fridays. I remarked, that Sultan Aziz had subdued the Montenegrins: had they not added it on that account? "No; it must be a war with other Governments; indeed, the Jehad;" (a holy war against infidels, not his subjects.) I said that in that case I did not think it likely the Sultan would ever bear the title. All said at once, "Please God it shall be so." I explained that the Government had no longer the power to enter into conflict with Christian Governments, at which they were offended, and would talk no more. After leaving this place we soon entered the pine forest, the cool shade and sweet perfume of which were doubly grateful after our long ride in the burning sun, without a tree for shelter. At the village where we stopped for the night, the guest-room was crowded with Turks, who seemed to be a far more frank and simple people than those whom we saw at midday. They were on very friendly terms with some Greeks, who, like ourselves, were guests. The principal topic of conversation was here, as everywhere else, the ever-increasing burden of taxation, which, as the chief man said, did not leave them enough for their ordinary necessities. Indeed the depression of the people was marked on their countenances.

Koniah.

May 12—Rose very early, and proceeded on our way through a series of valleys, some of which were very beautiful, and arrived at Koniah in the gloaming, having been nearly fourteen hours on the road. The best room we could get in the khan was worse than many stables we had seen, with two small open apertures for windows. However, it was dry and private, and wonderfully exempt from unpleasant inhabitants, a comfort which we could thoroughly appreciate.

May 13—We had a succession of visitors to talk with most of the day. The conversation was throughout such as we always desire. First came in two Armenians, one of whom, a native of Cyprus, had evidently read the Scriptures carefully, for there were few things we said that he could not support with a fluently quoted passage. His companion shook his head when pressed to receive and follow the Gospel of Christ. "How can I?" said he; but his careless laugh showed that his heart and mind were pre-occupied. A younger man, also an Armenian, who came in before the others left, showed by his words and behaviour that he was no stranger to the power of the word. He is the servant of the Governor's physician, and told us afterwards that he was a native of Kharpoot, and a Protestant, his name being Bedras. He felt sadly alone, and met with much annoyance from the Armenians on account of his not going to mass, and because of his quiet observance of the Lord's-day. His master, who is a European, places much confidence in him, and has lately given him more liberty to follow out his convictions concerning the sanctity of Sunday. We then went out for a short time about midday, and called on a respectable merchant, to whom we had a letter of introduction. From thence we walked about the bazaar, where the Turk whom we saw at Ishakli called to me from his shop, and, after the usual salutations, said he intended to call upon us. After leaving him we passed through the yards of two mosques, which seemed to be the principal ones in Koniah. In one of these is the tomb of the Pir, or founder of the great sect of Meolevis. I had some talk with one of these Dervishes, who was sauntering in the cemetery beyond. He was exceedingly friendly, and spoke about a conviction which he entertained that all men would soon be of one faith. When we had got to this point he uttered two or three mysterious and, to me, unintelligible sentences, and, wishing us good-bye, went off. On our return to the khan we found Greeks looking at our books, and one or two young Armenians. We had some conversation with them, after which one of the Greek schoolmasters, an intelligent young man, came in, and talked for a while in Greek with brother Wolters. One of the Greek priests also visited us, and invited us to call upon him. We had constantly applications for Græco-Turkish Scriptures, and the disappointment which our visitors showed when told we had no more was evidently real. In the evening we were invited to visit an Italian physician, who had married in the Armenian community, and settled in Koniah. He offered us his house during our stay, and said that he was but expressing the wishes of others, as well as his own, when he asked us to stay some time in the town, and ultimately provide them with a Protestant minister. He would gladly give a room in his house to such a person, and no expense for living should be incurred by him. We understood, from what he said, that there was a great deal of discord in the Armenian community, and the wish for a Protestant teacher seems to have emanated from one party in the dispute. In reply, we said that we were unable either to stay a long time or to provide an instructor, and that we feared there was little hope at present of others supplying what they wished for; besides which, it was no part of the plan of Christian Missions to profit by the disputes which may arise in a nominal Christian community. Our object in relation to such was to urge on them the means of securing their spiritual and eternal well-being. We exhorted men to be diligent in the reading of God's holy word, and in prayer for the light and guidance of the Holy Spirit. We had no design of making a new community attached to ourselves. So we urged him to set the example in this respect, and to induce others to do the same, waiting patiently for such guidance as God, who heareth prayer, would be pleased to vouchsafe. We did not accept the proffered hospitality, as we deemed that to remain in the khan would be more convenient for our work.

We regret that the length of this document compels us to break off here, and reserve the remainder for our next Number.

Recent Intelligence.

YORUBA MISSION.

The political complications which have so long distracted this country, and so very seriously interfered with the progress of Missionary work, are, we rejoice to say, in some measure modified. Peace between the Ibadans and the people of Abbeokuta is restored. Ibadans come to Abbeokuta almost daily, by thousands, peacefully, for the purpose of trading, and the Abbeokutans are going to Ibadan in like manner. Moreover, the Ijebus, both Iremmos and Ode, are free to come to Abbeokuta unmolested.

The Ibadans have expressd their goodwill by returning many captives, and, among them, the wife of the Bashorun, and the wives of the chief Ogudpe. They were sent back without any price being paid for them, and were loaded with presents.

Thus, from Abbeokuta as a centre, the roads are open in any direction through the Yoruba country, that to Lagos excepted. This remains closed, the Governor of Lagos maintaining the blockade. We trust that it will soon be removed, and the chiefs and people of Abbeokuta on fair and reasonable terms be restored to the position which they once enjoyed, that of being recognised as the friends and allies of Great Britain, and of being admitted to free and open communication with the British settlement at Lagos.

We feel persuaded that there is every readiness on their part to accede to every fair and reasonable requirement, if, indeed, they be only informed in a straightforward manner what it is that is expected of them. Restoration of a friendly understanding between Lagos and Abbeokuta is all that is now wanting to the establishment of a universal peace throughout Yoruba.

THE NIGER MISSION.

On the 29th July Bishop Crowther sailed from Lagos for the Niger, having with him two ordained native Missionaries, with their wives; one catechist and schoolmaster, with their wives; two unmarried schoolmasters, and two colporteurs, all natives, and all for the Niger Mission. Our Missionary at Lagos, Mr. Nicholson, says—"I could not help thinking, as they sailed away, that they presented a complete answer to the Anthropological Society. All who sailed, from the bishop downward, were the fruit of European Missionary work, and now these men have become Missionaries to their countrymen."

SOUTH INDIA.—TELUGU MISSION.

Our readers will remember the interesting facts respecting Venkia, the headman of the Mala caste in the neighbourhood of Ellore, how he was led to feel the worthlessness of idols, and to seek a better faith. The last intelligence we received of him was, that, converted himself to the faith of Christ, he had become the teacher of his tribe.

The following brief extract from a letter received from our Missionary at Ellore, the Rev. N. Alexander, dated June 25, 1865, will be gladly welcomed, assuring us, as it does, that this promising movement is healthfully going forward—

I am sure you will be glad to hear that the movement amongst the Malas in the district still continues. Very lately several persons, in two separate villages, came forward and asked for religious books for themselves, and schools for their children. I have established a school in one of the villages, and a second will be commenced as soon as I can get a teacher. There are not many children in them, but they are invaluable as giving us a foothold in the village, and supplying spiritual instruction to the elders, as well as letters to the children.

I consider that most of these Malas have come over to us chiefly from a feeling that, under our protection, they will be freed from the grinding tyranny of the higher castes, and from a rising conviction that heathenism fails to satisfy the cravings and necessities of man's heart. Most of the elders are dull, very dull, very ignorant, and depraved; but in the whole lot many bright pearls will, I hope, be found to adorn the diadem of our heavenly King.

CEYLON MISSION.—JAFFNA DISTRICT.

This Mission was visited in August last by the Bishop of Colombo. On this occasion three native candidates, Messrs. Hoole, Handy, and Champion, were admitted to deacons' orders, and the native deacon, the Rev. J. Hensman, to priests' orders. They were examined in "Pearson on the Creed," and the "Evidences of Christianity," the Prayer Book, the Thirty-nine Articles, and Scripture.

Our Missionary, the Rev. C. McArthur, thus describes the ordination—

Sunday, August 13, was a most eventful day in the history of the Jaffna Church Mission; I trust a day long to be remembered. It was my happy privilege on that day to present to the bishop three native catechists for ordination as deacons, and one native deacon to be ordained as priest. The ordination was held in the Nellore church, it being more central and more roomy than any of our other churches. Both the church and the verandahs were filled with natives, Christians and heathen. Several of the Europeans from the town were also present. After the ordination 230 native communicants remained to commemorate the dying love of the Lord Jesus.

Various confirmations were also held, of an interesting character, during the time of the bishop's visit.

It is evident, then, that there has been gathered in the Jaffna district a considerable body of native Christians, from the midst of which a native pastorate is being led forth. They are in a position to commence and vigorously sustain the great work of reproducing Christianity among their countrymen. We pray God that so deep a sense of their responsibility in this respect may take possession of this Christian body, that by their zeal and diligence they may prove themselves to be indeed of the salt of the earth.

THE CALCUTTA BRAHMO SAMAJ.

We print the following brief but interesting notice from the pages of the "Calcutta Christian Intelligencer"—

"A native Correspondent has lately favoured us with an account of a recent schism in the Calcutta Brahmo Samaj, the facts of which may be interesting to our readers. A reform movement seems to have caused the split, and our Correspondent writes—

"'It was all along believed by every one, except those who were in the secret, that the Calcutta Brahmo Samaj advocated enlightened principles of reform, and that any movement that might be calculated to break caste, and its concomitant evils, would be encouraged by the Samaj. But it appears that such movements have brought about the recent schism. There were in fact two parties in the Samaj. The one was for compromise, and conducting business in a manner that might not shock the prejudices of the Hindu community at large. The other, which might be called the ultra-radical party, was for reform, not caring for any consequences that might ensue, nor for any prejudices that might be shocked. These parties were both secretly developing their principles, till some bold steps taken by the radical party made the other give vent to its opinions and feelings. An 'intermarriage,' *i.e.* a marriage between Hindus of different classes, taking place a few months ago, under the auspices of the reformed party, first touched the conservative party. Subsequently, two other bold steps, successively taken by the younger members, proved more than the older ones could bear. An article, advocating reform and radical changes in the Samaj, written by Baboo Keshub Chunder in the "Indian Mirror" newspaper, which was thought to be the recognised organ of the Brahmo Samaj, was one of these. The other was the proposal made by the reformed party to allow no one who recognised caste to take a leading part in the divine services of the Samaj. Such proceedings could hardly be tolerated by the conservative members. They also had power on their side, for amongst them were the Trustees of the Samaj, who, exercising the legal authority with which they were invested by the late Rajah Ram Mohun Roy, the founder of the institution, cleared the Samaj of the ultra-radicals.'

"Such is the account which our correspondent gives of the schism in the Samaj, and from some personal intercourse which we have had with the writer, we believe his statements to be trustworthy. But the Brahmo Samaj is itself a reforming Society. Why, then, does it cling to caste, and dread more reform? The fact seems to be that the practice of its older members does not tally with their theories. In theory they renounce idolatry and caste, but in practice they are afraid to separate themselves from their Hindu relatives in customs which in heart they despise. The reforming party, however, acting in accordance with their theory and their conscience, show an honesty of purpose and a fearlessness which cannot but give hope to the Missionary, and commend them to us all in a Christian point of view. How many an 'almost Christian' among the natives would be altogether one but for the want of the moral courage which these reforming Brahmos have begun to show! May the next step lead them to inquire boldly into the truths of Christianity, and, if they are persuaded, to profess it also boldly, without fear of man!

OUR POSITION AND ITS DUTIES.

From the moment when the Lord Jesus, having completed the great work of reconciliation, sent forth the Gospel message on its mission of love throughout the world, it has met with increasing opposition. Nor can we be surprised at this. Satan is the god of this world, and holds the nations of the earth in miserable degradation. Yet he knows that his dominion is only for a time; that it shall be wrested from him, and the kingdoms of this world become the kingdoms of the Lord and his Christ. He is well aware, also, that the preaching of the Gospel is the appointed instrumentality by which his rule shall be overthrown. Men despise it as the foolishness of preaching; so did the men of Jericho regard with profound contempt the solemn procession of the Hebrews, as, day by day, they marched around the walls of the doomed city. Not so the enemy. He knows that the energy of God works through the utterances of the Gospel, and therefore he has never ceased in his efforts to impede its action. His favourite plan has been to corrupt its doctrines, and thus destroy its efficacy, so that, changed into another gospel, it should work for him, instead of against him. But when this device is unsuccessful, and faithful men, contending earnestly for the faith once delivered to the saints, continue to teach and preach Jesus Christ, then he stirs up hindrances of various kinds, and, if it be possible, persecution. Willing agents to co-operate with him in such an enterprise have never yet been found wanting. The natural mind distastes the Gospel because it interferes with its pride, self-complacency, and self-indulgence; and, influenced by feelings such as these, men first dislike the truth, and then, as they can, seek to hinder it. Its progress, therefore, has hitherto been in the midst of difficulty. The Gospel cause has been as a ship beating up against wind and tide. Its course has been like that of the Indus river. That river has its source in the south-western slopes of the Gangri or Kailás mountain, at an estimated height of 17,000 feet. For a brief space, about 260 miles, it is a broad stream, rolling its waters through open, grassy plains. But soon its character changes. It enters a mighty gorge in the mountains, which, for sublimity, is perhaps unequalled, and, amidst much disquietude, the river has to force its way through this gloomy chasm, and so prepare itself for new and protracted conflicts. The whole length of the mountain course is upwards of 1000 miles, and the whole fall is 16,000 feet. Christianity, like the Indus, has its source on high, and its earlier history is like the mountain course of that mighty river. Nor has it yet emerged from these obstructions, so as to expand into the broad rivers and streams which shall so fertilize this barren earth, that "the wilderness and solitary place shall be glad, and the desert rejoice and blossom as the rose."

And as the opposition has thus been unceasing, so there are times and seasons when that opposition becomes more violent. A ship, from the moment when it left harbour, has had to contend with unfavourable winds; but as it approaches its destination, the weather becomes more rough, until it blows a hurricane. And so along the course of its history there have been times when the Gospel cause has appeared to be in more especial peril—when the usual opposition has wrought itself up to a more determined effort.

The present appears to be just such a moment. Satan has come down, having great wrath, and that because he has met with great discomfitures. Stroke upon stroke, wound upon wound, have been inflicted upon him. Some of his choicest strongholds have been broken down; portions of his territory, where his iron rule had been so long perpetuated, that it appeared to be invincible, have been wrested from him. Especially on the Mission field has he met with reverses. Heathen lands had been long under his yoke, and he had strongly fortified them. Subtle systems of idolatry had been devised, marvellously adapted to the evil restlessness of the human mind, which, left to itself, now yields itself to the seductions of sin, now collapses into remorse and dread. The false religions which Satan has elaborated so blunt the conscience and deaden its action, that the man sins without fear. Like the fabled upas tree, which was supposed to exhale a poison so deadly, that throughout a distance of from fifteen to eighteen miles around no life could exist, these systems are surrounded by regions of spiritual death. Under their blighting influence the knowledge of the one true God becomes entirely obliterated, and personifications of evil are worshipped in his stead.

So firmly established did Satan's sway over heathen lands appear to be, that the first evangelists were classified as insane persons, so hopeless did the undertaking seem. Abroad, idolatrous priests despised them as Goliath did David: at home, nominal Christians —who, having never felt, did not believe in the power of the Gospel—mocked them. Few as they were, there appeared to be no footing for them on the dreary shores of heathenism. The heathen did not want them: they would have discouraged them by indifference; and, when this failed, they persecuted them. But, through evil report and good report, they held on. They grappled with and overcame the difficulties of barbarous languages, and in these the Gospel found new utterances. As it spoke, and the people began to understand, it was as of old, when God said, "Let there be light, and there was light." Prejudice gave way; hard hearts were softened; consciences were quickened out of their benumbed state; and men began to ask, "What shall I do to be saved?" For fifty years the conflict has been going forward: it has been long and arduous, but the results are manifest. In various directions commanding points have been won, and Christianity, having entrenched itself there, is making preparation for an onward movement and for more extended victories. The enemy has become alarmed; the necessity of some counter-stroke is incontestable. Not only has he decided upon this, but has already evolved his new policy, and that so far with marvellous success. England is one of the grand centres from whence those aggressive efforts on his heathen principalities have emanated. A large portion of the operations which so disquiet him have their basis in this country. Here are the grand associated organizations which send forth the soldiers of the cross, and provide the means by which the conflict may be sustained. What, then, if, while the cause of Christianity is pressing onward in the van, it could be assaulted in the rear? What if the central citadel could be surprised and carried? What if the home basis on which the grand forward movements in the Mission field have rested could be wrenched away from them? What if England could be recovered? What if she could be induced to repudiate the distinctiveness of Protestantism, and yield herself once more to the seductions of a corrupt Christianity?

England!—to recover this would be to secure the victory. The Protestantism of England,—this is now the object of assault, and there is no device which can be conceived which is not being brought into requisition for its overthrow. This is the citadel that is to be carried *per fas et nefas*.

When, at the Reformation, England cast off with loathing that corrupt Christianity under whose demoralizing influences she had so grievously suffered, and embraced that scriptural truth which, dearer to them than life, her martyrs had professed and vindicated amidst the fires of Smithfield, a commanding position was lost to the enemy. That the Christianity of the Bible should not only be free to circulate throughout the range of British rule, but that it should be lifted up on high in a national church establishment, and thus be acknowledged and honoured before the nations of the earth, has always been a vexation to the enemy; and as, under the ameliorating influence of true religion, England rose to an extended dominion and high pre-eminence, what truth had gained and evil had lost became more and more apparent.

We are reminded of Gibraltar, when it was conquered from those who were at the time the enemies of England. To them its loss was a perpetual humiliation and disquietude, and as its fortifications were improved until the rock was rendered impregnable, and the importance of its position as commanding the entrance into the Mediterranean became more and more apparent, these painful sensations grew more intense, until at last it was resolved that Gibraltar should be recovered. Hence the memorable siege, when two powerful nations put forth their utmost strength to wrest it from England, and were ignominously defeated. England is the Gibraltar which, at the time of the Reformation, was won over to the cause of scriptural Christianity. It is this the enemy desires to recover. Romanism and infidelity are in combination for this purpose. They are making their approaches from different directions; but the influence which moves them to action, and the object which they have in view, are identical. They are antagonistic to each other; but in one feature they are alike —hatred to God's truth; and they are satisfied to merge their differences and unite until the common foe be overthrown, and English Protestantism be displaced from its high position. Until this be done they are as restless in spirit as Haman the son of Hammedatha the Agagite, when he said, "All this availeth me nothing so long as I see Mordecai the Jew sitting at the king's gate."

Now, if the enemy was without the walls, and all was loyalty within, the danger, although rendering precaution necessary, could cause no apprehension. But the solemn fact, that the assailants have within the citadel numerous sympathizers, renders the crisis perilous in the extreme.

Yet just at such a crisis some of our best men, in whom we had confidence, have been removed by death. Henry Venn Elliott, able, discriminating, consistent, whose lengthened ministry at Brighton had given him such influence—John Scott, of Hull, the attached friend of the Society; both of these earnest Secretaries of important local Associations—Stowell, whose noble bearing and eloquent words of holy truth cheered and encouraged to new efforts the Lord's servants; whom God had graced with such a holy consistency during the many years in which he stood forward as a standard-bearer in the Gospel cause,—these, at their Master's summons, have entered into rest. "Merciful men are taken away, none considering that the righteous is taken away from the evil to come." Hambleton, too, wise and holy, who had gathered about him the rich experiences of a lengthened and faithful ministry,—he is no longer amongst us. Younger men, also, who were winning to themselves increasing confidences—Oakley, gifted and attractive, and rising with each year into influence; Kite, holy, devoted;— these also have put off their armour.

What are we to learn from this? There is a lesson designed to be conveyed: what is it? "Put not your trust in princes, nor in the son of man, in whom is no help. His breath goeth forth, he returneth to his earth; on that very day his thoughts perish. Happy is he that hath the God of Jacob for his help, whose hope is in the Lord his God." The Lord would concentrate on Himself the reliance of his people. Help is needed, for the battle of the reformation must be fought over again in England; but it is from God Himself the help must come. He alone can gird us with strength proportionate to the crisis, so that we shall be faithful and enduring.

And if special help be needed it is precisely the moment in which, in answer to earnest prayer, we may expect that help will be vouchsafed. The enemy is coming in like a flood. Collecting his resources for one decisive effort, he threathens to bear down all before him. But if the moment be critical, there is a promise suited to the emergency—"When the enemy shall come in like a flood, the spirit of the Lord shall lift up a standard against him."

Often on a battle-field a critical moment supervenes. The enemy, having received unexpected reinforcements, prepares himself for a final effort. Massing his troops together, he bears down on the point where the line of defence seems weakest. For an instant, on the defensive side, there is a misgiving, a consciousness of reduced numbers, a sense of inability to resist. It lasts but for a moment. The very danger seems to call forth new efforts. Men, previously unknown, press forward into the front, lifting on high the standard which had fallen from the hand of some honoured leader. The well-known signal rallies many. Men are ashamed to desert the ensign under which they had so often fought and conquered. They think no more of giving way. Shoulder to shoulder, heart to heart, they stand fast. They meet and endure the shock of the enemy as the rocks which guard the shore meet the swollen tide of the storm-agitated ocean, and, like those rocks, remain stedfast and unmovable, while the enemy is broken and recoils.

Undoubtedly the enemy is coming in like a flood; then is it the time for us to expect the fulfilment of the promise. The brunt of the battle has come: there must be no compromise, no surrender. Let the Church of England cease to be evangelical, and then her usefulness, at home and abroad, is at an end. She has lost her fitness for service, her qualification for the Lord's work.

May the Spirit of the Lord uphold England's endangered Protestantism, and, by whatever hands, cause the standard of the Gospel to be lifted up more boldly, more distinctly, more extensively than at any previous period. May the importance of the crisis constrain many a man who has been hitherto timid and irresolute to decide for the Bible and its truth against the devices of the enemy! may infidelity, in its arrogance, be rebuked, and Rome, by its insidious endeavours to recover her lost supremacy over England, call forth the latent Protestantism of the country, in a protest so strong, that she may abandon the enterprise, and retire in despair.

It will be, moreover, for our encouragement to remember, that, in the present movements of the enemy, there is nothing new. In this attempt of Romanism on the citadel of English Protestantism we are reminded of the action to which she had recourse at the era of the Reformation. When defeated and humiliated in Europe, and deprived of a large portion of those territories over which she had been wont to reign, she determined on finding compensation for her losses in heathen lands, and sent forth her Jesuit Missionaries to execute her scheme. And now that, on the Mission-field, she has been humiliated; when the results which she had acquired from amongst the heathen, bulky and imposing as they appeared to be, have proved to be fictitious and destitute of permanency, and her conquests in Japan, Congo, Paraguay, have all disappeared, resembling in this respect the temporary island of Sabrina, which, in 1811, rose from the deep off the coast of St. Michael, one of the Azores, increasing until it had attained the height of about 300 feet, with the circumference of a mile, and then, after an existence of eight months, beginning gradually to disappear, so that, when a twelvemonth had expired, not a trace of it was visible; while those obtained by evangelical Missionaries, in their permanency and enduring character, remind us of the coral islands, which are lasting structures, because resting on huge masses of solid rock, formed by the persevering efforts of those industrious sea-workers, which toil and spin in the midst of the waves;—when thus put to shame upon the Mission field, she turns back again to Europe, and, taking advantage of a perilous time of great prosperity, in which wealth affords to many the opportunity of being luxurious and self-indulgent, boldly attempts the reconquest of England as that which would amply compensate for all the reverses she ever has experienced.

We cannot doubt the issue of the conflict. How is it possible we could do so, if only we call to remembrance the words which Bishop Latimer addressed to his fellow-sufferer when the fire which was to consume them was on the point of being applied—"Be of good comfort, Master Ridley, and play the man: we shall this day light such a candle, by God's grace, in England, as I trust will never be put out."

DEATHS IN THE MISSION FIELD.

Our anxieties at the present moment are for home; our encouragements are from abroad. Blessed be God for the great revival of thirty years back, and for the comparatively tranquil period which has been since enjoyed, during which evangelical Christianity has been permitted to go forth and do a great work in the distant Mission fields. At home the enemy is the assailant, and approaches in full confidence of victory; but in the Mission field scriptural Christianity is the assailant, and, having rescued many from the degrading yoke of heathenism, has reinforced herself with these, and is using them as her willing agents in reproducing Christianity among their countrymen. The native churches, alive to their responsibilities, are prepared to communicate to their countrymen the light they have received, and to occupy themselves in the illumination of the dark districts in the centres of which they have been providentially raised up. The European Missionaries, relieved to a great extent from the pastoral care of the native Christians, find themselves free to resume their proper work of evangelists, and are preparing to enter the "regions beyond." It is a moment of intense interest when the standard of the Gospel is about to move forward, and new positions are about to be taken up as a prelude to more extended conquests. If, at home, every good soldier is needed at his post, that the endangered citadel of Protestant truth may be successfully defended, equally so in the Mission field the presence of every Missionary that can be mustered is imperatively required; for, compared with the magnitude of the undertaking, they are but few in number. So far as our own Society is concerned, they were, at the time of the last Annual Meeting, one more than 200.

And yet, since then, at a time when, to human judgment, they could least be spared, we have lost several experienced and faithful men;—Peet, of Travancore; Rogers, of the Bombay Presidency; Bühler, of the Yoruba Mission;—these have died. There have been losses at home, and there have been losses in the Mission field. The lesson is the same: God would remind us of our dependence upon Him. He has gathered in these his servants to Himself. He has had a right to do so, for they were more his than ours. He lent them to us for a time, but now He desired they should be with Him, and He called them in. It is with Him to raise up suitable successors, who shall supply their place, and fill up the gaps which have been made in the Missionary ranks. Our duty is to approach the footstool of divine grace, and humbly supplicate the Lord of the harvest to send forth labourers into his harvest. Does it seem improbable that a supply shall be forthcoming?—and remembering how often we have appealed, and how feeble the response has been, are we under discouragement? Then let us remember the Lord's words to his disciples, "Have faith in God. For verily I say unto you, that whosoever shall say to this mountain, Be thou removed, and be thou cast into the sea; and shall not doubt in his heart, but shall believe that those things which he saith shall come to pass, he shall have whatsoever he saith. Therefore I say unto you, Whatsoever things ye desire, when ye pray, believe that ye receive them, and ye shall have them."

To the faithful Missionaries whose names we have mentioned, and who have fallen asleep, we desire to consecrate a portion of this, the concluding Number of the year. It is becoming that we should do so, honourable to the dead, and edifying to the living. We have some brief notices of each, records of their labours, proofs of the help vouchsafed them, when those labours had reached their end. Who can tell but that these memorials of the dead may be the means, in God's hands, of leading forth the successors who shall supply their place? It shall then be as when the dead man was cast into the sepulchre of Elisha, "and when the man was let down, and touched the bones of Elisha, he revived, and stood up on his feet."

OBITUARY OF THE REV. EDWARD ROGERS, OF THE WESTERN INDIA MISSION.

On the 18th of November 1846 the instructions of the Committee were delivered by the Hon. Clerical Secretary to the Rev. Richard Martindell Lamb, M.A. Trinity College, Cambridge, on the occasion of his departure to the Meerut station of the Calcutta and North-India Mission; and to Mr. Edward Rogers, a student from the Society's Institution, on the occasion of his departure to the Bombay and Western-India Mission.

Both these faithful men have now been removed by death from the list of the Society's Missionaries. They have been promoted from the ranks of the church militant to the glory of the church triumphant, but not until they had rendered good service.

Mr. Lamb was the first to go, killed by a fall from his horse at Mussoorie, June 1857.

Missions commenced in Meerut about 1814, "under the patronage of Captain Sherwood and his wife, who opened a chapel and school there: she paid the teacher at the rate of four rupees monthly, and four annas for each scholar, and by her writings showed the interest which she felt in India. She fitted up a room in her garden, in which she employed a native catechist to read the Hindustanee service to a congregation of forty persons. She gave him instruction in geography and history, and attended also to the religious welfare of her heathen servants; but she left Meerut in 1815 for England. Her last act there was to assemble her domestics, with the catechist, and hold a religious service with them. However, the same year she was succeeded in her sphere of usefulness by an individual who may be called the father of the Meerut Mission, the late Rev. H. Fisher.* Though he came out at rather an advanced period in life, he applied himself diligently to the study of the Urdu language, became the instrument of the conversion of many Hindus and Mussulmans, and founded a native church at Meerut, which he superintended until 1832, when he became presidency chaplain in Calcutta. The circumstances which led to his coming to India border almost on the romantic: we shall give them in his own words—

> I had just finished my morning Sabbath service at the village of G— O—, and was conversing in the churchyard with the gathering group of parishioners before returning to my home, when I perceived a stranger in the crowd, whose attention to the sermon which I had been preaching had drawn my eyes frequently towards the pew in which he had been seated. The villagers were pressing round with their affectionate inquiries after my health, &c., when the stranger addressed me with a courteous smile, saying, somewhat abruptly, "It is a blessed occupation for a minister of God to preach the μετάνοια to a sinful world." (My subject had been from the third chapter of St. John and the fifth verse.) In reply to this address, which somewhat surprised me, I observed, "Very true, and blessed are the people who know the joyful sound." "Will you go to India?" said he. "If opportunity served I should not hesitate: I have often thought of it." "Have you?" said he, "then think of it again; and when you have made up your mind, let me know: I am Dr. Buchanan." We shook hands, and I mounted my horse and rode away. You remember, my dear sisters, what followed. Some little delay arose from various causes before my final decision was made; but difficulties and impediments were overruled, and finally the way was open. I bade farewell to my English home, and relatives, and friends, and set off for London, with my family, to make all the necessary preparations for my departure.

Mr. Fisher died at Mussoorie, March 5, 1845, aged seventy-three years. He was one of that class of chaplains who came under the censure of Sir J. Malcolm, when, in his

* He entered the ministry in 1795, and was led to a knowledge of the truth subsequently, by the spiritual counsel of his excellent sister, Mrs. Stevens, who is well known for her religious writings, and the meetings she conducted for many years in Yorkshire. Mr. Fisher was eminently useful in Yorkshire, in the cottage lectures which he delivered to the poor. He took an active part in the Meerut Mission, and used to give the native catechist texts of Scripture on which to write sermons, that were corrected subsequently by himself.

"Political Sketches of India," he recommended "that chaplains should be prohibited from using their efforts to make converts.

Mr. Richards was appointed to Meerut in 1828, and was ordained in 1837. At his solicitation the same year the Begum Sumru gave 10,000 rupees for the erection of a chapel—St. Paul's—for the native Christians, and also made a grant of fifty rupees monthly towards the expense of the Mission, which was continued as long as she lived. She gave the Bishop of Calcutta 10,000*l.*, to be appropriated to the support of a native ministry, and 5000*l.* for the poor and debtors. In 1832, almshouses for Christians were built.

Mr. Richards continued his labours at Meerut until 1852, when his declining health compelled him to leave, and Meerut was left without a Missionary, the Parent Committee not having it in their power to appoint another. In 1854 the Bishop of Calcutta found nothing but the few faint embers of a fire which, a few years previously, had been burning brightly, "All is sinking into inanition—the chapel closed, the Mission-house uninhabited, the Committee desponding: I could hold no confirmation; I had no audience to address; no subscriptions were collected; no effort made."

The Parent Committee put forth appeals, and they were responded to. Mr. Lamb offered himself for Meerut, and was accepted. There was a peculiar appropriateness in his doing so, for he had been born in the neighbourhood of Meerut, and was baptized by Henry Martyn. He gave up an English incumbency for the Missionary work, for at the time when he offered himself to go forth and labour for the revival of the Meerut Mission he was Perpetual Curate of Over Darwen, Lancashire. The writer of this brief notice found him there when abroad on deputation work for the Church Missionary Society, and had much and interesting conversation with him as to the relative claims of home and foreign work. It was evident that his heart inclined much to the Mission work, and, once convinced that the door was open, and that he was free to offer himself, he did not hesitate to do so. During the ten years and a half of his Missionary life he was privileged to accomplish a great work. The Christian flock, which, at the time of his arrival, had been reduced to less than fifty, increased from year to year, rising to 100, 150, 170, until it became necessary to enlarge the church. He gave himself zealously to the work of itinerancy, and expanded the action of the Mission, establishing out-stations at Bareilly and Landour. Among the earliest of his converts was one mán, who, as the ordained native Tulsi Paul, remains a living memorial of Lamb's work. He had been his munshi, and, first as a catechist,* and now as pastor over a native flock, he shows that the stones which Lamb built into the foundation of the building were genuine.

Scarcely had he been removed by death, when, in the Meerut district, there sprung up a remarkable movement in favour of Christianity. At Mulliana and Khunker-Khera, places in the vicinity, a spirit of inquiry manifested itself; and now the native converts in the city and neigbourhood have risen from less than 300 in 1859 to more than 700 at the present time, with 300 communicants, the central station having in affiliation with it seven out-stations.

But Richard Martindell Lamb must ever be regarded as the man who, in the hands of God, raised up the Mission from its ruined state.

His name is associated with that of Edward Rogers: they received their valediction together, and how, in noticing the one, could we refuse a tribute of respect to the memory of the other? Shall the new grave be garlanded and have flowers planted upon it, while that which is some few years older, not many, is left to neglect and forgetfulness?

* See "Church Missionary Record" 1850, pp. 200, 201.

While Mr. Lamb proceeded to the North-Western Provinces of India, Mr. Rogers reached Bombay. It was a critical moment in the history of that Mission. Two years before, a Missionary, the Rev. J. Dixon, who had rendered most valuable services, especially in the translation of the sacred Scriptures and of the Common-Prayer Book into the Mahratta language, had been removed, after seventeen years of unremitting activity; while, yet more recently, a Missionary of not so many months' labour, but who, during this short period of service, had endeared himself to every one as the exemplar and promoter of love and peace and godly unity—the Rev. A. Dredge—had been called away thus early and unexpectedly.

Reaching Bombay in January 1847, he was admitted to deacons' orders by the bishop of that diocese in the next month, and proceeded then to Nasik, just then left without a Missionary in consequence of the return to Europe of the oldest labourer in the Bombay Mission field, the Rev. C. P. Farrar. Here he had associated with him the Rev. C. C. Mengé from Junir, Mr. Rogers being as yet ignorant of the vernacular, and unable alone to meet the exigencies of the station, although at that time the baptized Christians were only nineteen in number.

But the remarkable decrease of Missionaries in the field of Western India at this time rendered it impossible that two Missionaries should long remain together at a station, and the next year (1848) Mr. Rogers was transferred to Junir, to supply the place of the Rev. J. Mulheisen, who had returned to Europe.

Junir is the capital of a hilly district of the same name in the province of Aurungabad. It occupies a central point between Nasik, Poonah, and Bombay; Nasik being seventy-two miles distant to the north-west, Poonah fifty miles to the south-west, and Bombay sixty or seventy miles to the west by south, while Ahmednuggur lies east by south forty miles distant. The population is about 25,000, of whom 2000 are Brahmins. Besides the care of the infantile results which had been raised up at Junir, Mr. Rogers had to visit two out-stations, Malligaum, a town and strong fortress in the province of Kandeish, lying about seventy miles to the north-east, and Astagaum, a village twelve miles from Ahmednugger, where a few converts had been gathered by the Rev. C. W. Isenberg.

Mr. Rogers had now mastered the vernacular, and commenced forthwith those itinerant labours in which he persevered to the end of his life. In one of his earliest reports from Junir he says—"Accompanied by a native catechist, I made a Missionary tour in Kandeish. In some of the villages through which we passed the Gospel of Christ had been preached by a Missionary about ten or twelve years ago, but many had never heard the glad tidings of redemption before." What painful destitution, and it still prevails! Was ever a more glorious field for Missionary labour presented to a Christian nation than that which India presents to England? a vast field of heathenism over which, without interruption, the sower may go forth and sow. Yet how few the sowers!

Soon again was Mr. Rogers interrupted in the prosecution of his itinerant labours. Another death in the Mission summoned him to Bombay. The Rev. Thomas Jerrom, the Principal of the Money Institution, after three years and a half of Missionary service, had been suddenly called to his rest. With untiring zeal had he given himself to his work, so that, under his superintendence, not only had the number of scholars increased, but the school had been raised to a higher state of efficiency: above all, the communication of scriptural knowledge had occupied his thoughts, and earnestly had he endeavoured that the youths under his care might become wise unto salvation. To fill up for a time, until help could be procured from home, the vacancy thus caused, Mr. Rogers was called away from itinerancy to take part in educational work at Bombay. To these duties, however, his health proved unequal.

The new Mission in Sindh, being at this time without a Missionary, in consequence of the transfer of the Rev. C. C. Schreiber to Nasik, the Rev. A. Matchett and Mr. Rogers proceeded to Kurrachee; but Mr. Rogers' health continuing in an enfeebled state, he returned to England in May 1853. After an absence of two years, his health being restored, Mr. Rogers hastened back to his old sphere of labour at Malligaum. From this as a centre he carried forward his work of itinerancy, travelling from village to village, and preaching Christ amidst the vicissitudes to which that kind of work is specially subjected; now finding the people intently occupied in bowing their necks to the iron yoke of idolatry, and willingly practising the barbarous rites which it required at their hands—"A swinging machine," he observes on one occasion, "is set up within a few yards of my tent; and I should think twenty persons must have been suspended from it during the afternoon, many of whom were women. It is truly a painful sight to witness; painful to see the poor deluded victims in their sufferings; painful to notice the want of humanity manifested by the spectators"—now, when he told them of a Saviour's love, and his readiness and power to save, exposed to mockery; "Preached to a large congregation, but were often interrupted and very much insulted by the Brahmins. When we were leaving, they followed us through the streets, hooting after us, until they were stopped by the Kulkarani, a Brahmin and Government official." Then, again, there were seasons of encouragement, when they met with large and attentive audiences, and were followed to their tents by some whose hearts seemed to be in some measure moved, and who wished to inquire further.

One extract from the proceedings of 1858 we introduce, because it expresses so admirably the feelings of this good man, his compassion for the heathen, and his yearnings after them in the bowels of Jesus Christ.

Dec. 15—Pasta. This morning I walked the whole stage, and reached this place just at sunrise. The morning air was cold and bracing, the starry heavens above me clear and beautiful. In the southern heavens was visible the "Southern cross," and as the bright morning stars arose in the east, the constellation of Orion gradually sank beneath the western horizon. Many pleasing and elevating thoughts had been excited in my mind by the sight of these glorious objects, as I walked alone in the temple of God's creation. Painful indeed was the contrast, when, at the end of my walk, I found myself seated in the midst of a crowd of idolaters, in the temple of a filthy idol, which they call Mahadeva (the great god). Oh how idolatry degrades man! In vain did I point to the heavens above, and to the earth beneath, and try to awaken in the minds of my hearers the same feelings of admiration, reverence, and adoration, that had filled my own mind while contemplating the glorious works of Him who is indeed "the great God." In vain did I try to make them feel their responsibility to Him, and thus bring home to their hearts the conviction of sin, and their need of a sinless Saviour. There were those who coldly assented to the truths we spoke to them, but there was no deep response of the heart. Their "great god," being a stone, a filthy emblem, all sense of responsibility to a superior being seems well nigh to have perished, and nothing that is great, glorious, and holy, has any attraction for the Hindu mind. After preaching, I had some conversation with an old Brahmin. He believes as firmly in the existence of Mount Meru, and its concentric seas, as if he had seen them. A shopkeeper, more intelligent, said, when leaving, he would be glad to see me again.

These journeyings were alike laborious and extensive. In the early part of 1861, previous to the monsoon, Mr. Rogers and his catechist had preached in seventy-four towns and villages, some of which had been visited before; but in regard to others, the ground broken up was entirely new. Amongst other places reached was Yeolah, now a Church Missionary station, a town with a population three times greater than that of Malligaum. Here they preached in the bazaars to a large number of people, and were engaged in conversation with persons who came to the tent from morning until evening.

The Missionary who thus devotes himself to the great work of itinerant preaching is a sower of the seed, and the sowing-time is one in which faith requires to be strong, for it is all giving forth, while nothing comes back in the way of return to recompense for the outlay. "I am grieved," says Mr. Rogers, writing about four years ago, "that I have so little to say of the triumphs of Christianity over heathenism. The Gospel of Christ has been preached in the streets of Malligaum and in the villages around, and yet we see no results at all answerable to our expectations. It is painful indeed to be obliged to write, year after year, of the small success that has attended our labours, and we can only hope that hereafter the fruit of the preparatory work which we are even now doing may be seen in the conversion of many souls to God."

Mr. Rogers judged rightly of the nature of his work. It was truly preparatory work, and, because preparatory, characterized by an absence of present results, and that is a time when the workman must be content to labour for the future, receiving nothing now. He must be content to sow that, the results of which he shall not himself reap, because, tardy in its growth, its rich harvests shall be reaped by other hands. He must be prepared to find himself toiling strenuously, laboriously, and be conscious at the same time of the gradual wasting of his physical powers, and yet be unable perhaps to communicate to friends at home the glad tidings of even one soul converted to God. He must make up his mind to be regarded as an unsuccessful Missionary, and, when so misapprehended, to say—"My judgment is with the Lord, and my work with my God."

All honour be to the men who, under such disadvantages, go on with unflinching constancy, borne up by the promise, "Cast thy bread upon the waters, for thou shalt find it after certain days." Of their single-mindedness in their work there can be no stronger evidence. At home, when a man is gifted, popular, waited upon by a crowded congregation; or abroad, when he finds himself borne onward by some remarkable movement, while congratulatory letters are heaped upon him from friends in England, it is easy to go on. How shall the vessel do otherwise, when the sails are filled with prosperous gales? but it is not so easy at such times to analyze the motives by which the individual is actuated, and how much of earthly ingredients have mixed themselves with the divine element.

And these pioneers, are they not doing a grand work? How shall the superstructure be erected if the foundations be not laid? And how shall the foundations be laid if there be not labourers of this particular cast of mind, patient, yet persevering; humble, yet undaunted: men who can work without the approbation of their fellow-men, if only they have the sense of the Lord's favour in their hearts? And these little-valued, often sorrowful men, who go forth weeping, bearing precious seed, shall they not yet rejoice over the results of those labours which they carried forward amidst many tears? Yes; for it is promised—"He that goeth forth weeping, bearing precious seed, shall doubtless come again with joy, bringing his sheaves with him," and then "both he that soweth and he that reapeth shall rejoice together."

In May 1862, Mr. Rogers lost his wife, the daughter of the late Rev. T. Jerrom, of Bombay. She died of cholera, and in the subsequent December, Mrs. Jerrom died also. Mr. Rogers was with her to the last, and witnessed her peaceful departure as, entrusting herself to her Saviour's care, she said, "He does not change."

Thus the Lord was weaning him from the world, and loosening the earth from about his roots, that he might be the more easily transplanted. Deeply did he feel these bereavements. Of his wife he spoke in terms of touching affection.—"It was said that she was beloved by all who knew her, both old and young. This is true of the European community. It was still more true of the native Christians. She had learnt their language, had faithfully instructed both the aged and the young, and by all was greatly beloved. Her sudden removal distressed them exceedingly, and I shall ever remember with feelings of great thankfulness their genuine kindness and deep sympathy."

And now this good Christian and faithful Missionary has followed those whom he so loved. His Lord called him, and he has crossed over to the happy shore.

The following letter, dated August 8, 1865, from the Rev. T. K. Weatherhead, Secretary to the Corresponding Committee, closes this Obituary—

The sad intelligence of our brother Rogers' death reached you by last mail. He arrived in Bombay under the kind escort of the Rev. C. Laing, the chaplain of Malligaum, on Tuesday, the 18th of July, and on Saturday, the 22nd, he was called to the home of homes above. We have to mourn *our* loss, not *his*. In him we have lost a faithful and zealous Missionary, one who felt much the needs of our Western-India Mission, and who was raising up a class of native agents likely to be valuable, under God, as Scripture readers and catechists.

As an itinerator, Kandeish will bear a full testimony to our late brother's earnestness and energy. He was seldom to be found in his station when the season permitted him to be abroad in the districts. The large market-towns will well remember him, with his colossal umbrella, going out even when the sun was high—this umbrella, with its stick, resting on the ground, overshadowing him. I have been with him in the districts, and much enjoyed witnessing the character and boldness of his testimony, and at the same time that gentleness and kindness which bore with opposition.

As a watchman and pastor over the few God had gathered out by him, he acted as a father over his children. His visit to Thanaje, who died of cholera last year, was immediately on hearing of his attack. His tattoo was mounted, and the sick man reached, just in time to have a few parting words. This man's wife and children make up a part of his crown of rejoicing, and they were all baptized by him.

He had had several attacks of fever. Not two years ago I met him at the Nandgaum station. He was then on his way to Malligaum, suffering from fever, leaving his tents behind. His good friend, Mr. Laing, received him on that occasion, and, throughout one night, when exhaustion and weakness threatened dissolution, watched him, and fed him every half-hour, and thus, humanly speaking, preserved him. In this last attack the same exhaustion and weakness followed. At first the change to Bombay appeared to benefit him. We all entertained some hope. Even on the morning of the day he died Major Candy wrote that Mr. Rogers was better; but about midday a change took place, and he sank rapidly.

His work was done; his time come; and his Lord called him home.

OBITUARY OF THE REV. JOSEPH PEET, OF THE TRAVANCORE MISSION.

On Sunday, December 23, 1832, two students of the Church Missionary College, Islington—Mr. Joseph Peet and Mr. George Pettitt—were admitted, by the Bishop of London to priests' orders; and on the next day they received the instructions of the Committee, delivered to them by the Rev. W. Jowett, having been appointed to labour, the one in the Tinnevelly, the other in the Travancore Mission.

Mr. Pettitt, after twenty-two years valuable service in the Mission field, returned to England in 1856, and is now ably filling an important home position, as Incumbent of St. Jude's, Birmingham.

Mr. Peet died in the Mission field, after a lengthened service of no less than thirty-two years. We copy the following notice of his death from the "Cochin Western Star"—

It is our painful duty to record the death of the Rev. Joseph Peet, of Mavelicara, one of the oldest and most devoted Missionaries of the Church Missionary Society in Travancore.

Mr. Peet arrived in Travancore in 1833, and was appointed to Cottayam, where for some time he had the entire charge of the Mission, and acted as Principal of the old Syrian college; the other Missionaries of the station having been forced to proceed to Europe on account of ill-health. After a few years of incessant labour, he removed to Mavelicara in 1838, on the return of the other Missionaries, to lay the foundation of a new Mission in a wholly untried field. In the face of severe opposition and constant difficulties and hindrances arising from the prejudices and ignorance of the surrounding Hindu population, he established what has proved, under Providence, one of the most successful and flourishing Missions in North Travancore. The fierce antagonism to his project only called forth the innate force of his character, and, without departing from the benign principles of the faith he toiled to propagate, he lived to see a contented and peaceful colony of Christians, by whom he was beloved and esteemed. With the exception of a short visit to England, the whole of his time, until a recent period, was devoted to the sacred cause for which he laboured. Besides his own immediate station, he had occasionally the charge of other Mission districts, as well as the management of a small estate called Munro Island, granted to the Mission as an endowment for educational purposes by the then Regent, Ranee Parwatee, through the interest of Colonel Munro, the British Resident at the Court of Travancore.

A few significant facts of his unwearied industry may be briefly noticed. According to the registered statistics of the Mavelicara and Tiruwella districts for 1863, we find that Mr. Peet had under his superintendence twenty places of worship, scattered over thirteen stations, with congregations numbering 3435 members, amongst whom might be found converts from all classes, from the high-caste Brahmin to the lowest Pulaya. Of the nine native clergymen in connexion with Travancore and Cochin, nearly all have, for a greater or less period, been his pupils, and many a young man, in respectable and useful situations, owes his training to the kind care and attention of the departed Missionary.

We must not omit to mention, as an instance of his persevering industry, the unquestionably great service he has done towards the improvement of the language and literature of this coast by the publication of his Malayalim grammar, the first and only work of the kind extant in that language, and which is generally accepted as the standard authority. He also published various other original and translational works, which are highly appreciated by persons engaged in the work of education.

More than a year ago Mr. Peet was compelled, through failing health, to leave his Mission work for a time, and visit England, but unhappily he derived little benefit from the change. Whilst there, it is related that he called on a lady, who is herself much interested in Indian Missions, and whose late husband had toiled in the same cause on this coast, and, at that interview, expressed his very earnest desire to return immediately, without reference to his health, as his only wish was to live and die amongst his people at Mavelicara. Even so he returned in April last, and joined his flock, who appear to have been the first object of his care. He suffered much from an affection of the brain, attended with occasional fits, and on Friday, August 11th, this earnest and devoted Missionary breathed his last, and ceased from his earthly labours.

To this brief sketch of the long-life labours of our departed Missionary, and of the great results which he was privileged to bring about, we may add a few details.

When Mr. Peet had been in the Mission about six years he was led to break fresh ground, and to take up Mavelicara, as a Mission station, a commanding point in the kingdom of Travancore.

In a letter to the Corresponding Committee he thus describes this place.—

Mavelicara is a large town in the kingdom of Travancore, situated about thirty miles north-east of Quilon, in 8° 36′ north lat., and 75° 30′ east long.

This town was formerly the seat of Government, and a place of great note: it is, even now, called by the natives the "Eye of Travancore." Of its ancient greatness there are still many vestiges: besides large buildings and tanks, there are the remains of a very extensive fort, in which the arsenal was kept, and the Rajah had his palace; and, what is very uncommon in a country of India with which foreigners, till lately, have had but little internal intercourse, and at a place at which, before the recent Mission establishment, it is probable no European ever resided, there still remain the relics of large, and—considering the nature of the soil—well-constructed roads, leading to the several gates of the fort; on either side of which have been planted, in regular rows, a species of the lofty and majestic pine-tree, which, though fast going to decay, still, by their regularity and beauty, present quite a home-like appearance. and afford a most agreeable shelter from the scorching rays of the sun.

Mavelicara, together with the surrounding country, is very low and flat, and the soil, for the most part, is a fine whitish sand, which renders this place neither so agreeable nor healthy for the residence of Europeans as many other parts of Travancore, the heat, from its low situation and loose soil, being excessive in the dry season; and these, together with the rising of the rivers and heavy rain, make it damp, and unpleasantly close and sultry, in the monsoon: the range of the thermometer is now, in the midst of the cold weather, from 80 to 88. With these exceptions, Mavelicara is perhaps one of the best places in Travancore for a Mission station, as it is situated within a few miles of twenty-one Syrian churches, most of which are easy of access from it; and, according to a census taken in 1837, there is in Mavelicara and the adjacent districts a population of no less than 267,352 individuals, composed of all the principal classes and castes in the country. In Mavelicare alone the population amounts to 63,652. Among this number are some of the most rich and influential people of the land. Most of the reigning Rajah's family dwell near the Mission premises; and in consequence of this place having been the seat of royalty, a vast number of Brahmins is fed and lodged at the public expense. The Nairs here are also numerous and respectable; and the Syrians, of whom there are about 900 or 1000 families, have a richly-endowed church in that part of the town where their own people reside. In addition to these advantages, the main road from the different parts of the country to the capital, and one of the high roads from the old "Pandyan," or Company's territories, pass through Mavelicara, close by the Mission premises: in consequence of which there is almost a continual influx of people; among many of whom I have been enabled, from time to time, to scatter a few seeds of the word of life, in the hope and belief that He, who has declared that his word shall not return void, will make it accomplish the purposes for which it has been sent.

The desirableness of occupying such a place as a Mission station has been seen and felt by the Church Missionary Society for the last twenty years; but want of agents and funds have, up to the last summer, deterred them from doing more than occasionally visiting it, and establishing one or two small schools. It is, however, with heartfelt gratitude and thankfulness to the wise and beneficient Disposer of all good that I am enabled to add, that the Society has at length been so far enabled to fulfil its wishes, as that a dwelling-house for a Missionary, and a temporary place of worship, are now erected, and a Missionary has been appointed to labour in this place, in the midst of its teeming population.

A new church was opened in May 1839.

At the opening of my church, which took place on Wednesday, May 22, the brethren from Cottayam, and two from Allepie, were present. Some of our congregations from Cottayam and Mallapalli came, by previous invitation; and, in the course of the day, between one and two thousand persons of all classes crowded in to see this new thing. A little before eleven, A.M., the bell was rung, in all probability for the first time in the midst of this dense population—this chief seat of darkness and "reign" of spiritual death, to invite the people to the worship of the only living and true God in a manner agreeable to his holy will, and best calculated to advance the growth of piety in the hearts of men. We had a full service, as usually conducted in churches at home; viz. singing, morning prayer, with the litany, commandments, &c., read at the altar by two officiating ministers, sermon, and the eucharist. At the latter service, three respectable Syrians, under previous instruction, openly expressed their determination to join us, by partaking of the Lord's Supper with about twenty of our old congregation. This is the first-fruit of that great harvest which I do hope the Lord Jesus intends to gather in here.

My church is calculated to hold about 400 persons; and, if the porch were filled, 500 could be comfortably accommodated. With the aid of my dear partner, we have contrived to make it wear quite a respectable appearance. The inside, with the exception of pews, is altogether English. For a ceiling we have nice white mats; and the floor is covered with the grass mats of the country, such as find their way into gentlemen's bungalows. The pulpit and desks are stained with a lasting dark colour, and are well varnished. A vestry and bell make our church quite complete, and command the attention and respect of those who come only to sneer and scoff.

Converts began now to be gathered in, as well from among Syrians as heathen, Amongst others, the case of a Nair and his wife, baptized by the name of Cornelius and Mary, is especially interesting; but we can only refer our readers to the "Church Missionary Record" for 1840, pp. 223, 224, where they will find an account of them.

Having planted the standard of the Gospel at the very head-quarters of Travancore

Brahminism, Mr. Peet, like a valiant soldier of the cross, took his stand by it. "I am surrounded," he observes, in a letter written about the year 1843, "by untiring, crafty, potent foes, without a single, powerful friend, in this part of India, to whom I may look for advice and protection. I sometimes think my faith would entirely fail, but for the support of the Gospel, and from the heart-upholding assurance that I share the sympathy, and have an interest in the prayers, of those who love the Lord Jesus Christ in sincerity. We must, if faithful, contend with the powers of darkness, the demon of error, and the blind obduracy of souls most deadly opposed to their own best interests. We have to cast down from its elevated position, and trample under foot with indignation, the blasphemous creed which exalts the creature at the Redeemer's seat: we must. in a word, preach, without compromise, that only panacea for the world's woes, the great and saving doctrine of justification by faith."

Such was Mr. Peet. He had a strong grasp of the doctrines of grace, and his resolve was, with the help of God, to teach them. From this he swerved not. Opposition, instead of intimidating him, called forth his energies, and he wrought the more earnestly. And such he continued to the end, so that even when the body grew enfeebled, the mind retained all its vigour and earnestness of purpose.

The interest and importance of the Malevicara station increased from year to year. The town lies just on the skirt of the low rice-grounds which stretch westward to the sea. At times, during the monsoon, the country around is completely flooded by swollen mountain streams. Beginning at Mavelicara, eastward the ground rises, and hilly jungles, interspersed with patches of cultivation, overtop each other, till they reach the ghauts. In 1846 there lay amongst these hills five out-stations, while others were in process of formation to the south and north. The Mission, moreover, had begun to yield valuable help towards its own extension, and two ordained natives, the first-fruits and pledges of a native ministry—the Rev. Jacob Chandy and the Rev. George Matthan—were rendering, in this wide and populous district, efficient aid.

Instances occurrred from time to time which served to show that the Christianity introduced among the people was of an active energetic kind, and that the character of the Missionary had impressed itself upon the converts. A low-caste heathen, who had tried all the sects of Hinduism, and, besides these, Mohammedanism, Popery, Syrianism, in the hope of finding rest to his soul, obtained, at last, in the belief of the Gospel, that which he had so earnestly sought after. He desired in some way to express the gratitude he felt. He went about amongst his friends and neighbours, telling them what the Lord had done for his soul, and many of them became Christians. He wished that they should have a suitable building where they might meet to worship God. Although only a mere labourer, earning two chuckrums, or about twopence a day, he actually purchased a piece of ground for the site, at a cost of 500 chuckrums, besides paying all legal expenses, and on this a church was erected. A similar case presents itself in a woman, a convert from heathenism, a member of one of the lowest classes, but possessing good natural abilities. At the time of her conversion there was much persecution abroad against the Christians, and not only did she take patiently the spoiling of her goods, but fearlessly exerted herself in confessing Christ, and so succeeded in persuading part of her family to submit to his easy yoke. She then moved these her fellow-Christians to unite in founding a place where they might meet for Christian worship, and a neat temporary building was soon finished, covered with a mat and provided with a pulpit, the whole building, with the ground on which it stood, being the free gift of these poor people to the Gospel cause.

These notices are only fragmentary, yet are they sufficient to explain to our readers the progress of the work, and we shall now close them by a reference to one more document, a letter written by Mr. Peet in 1861, at a time when his health had greatly declined, and his physical system, worn out by long and arduous labour, seemed as though it must collapse from sheer exhaustion. At such a moment it was just what we might expect from him, that he would take a retrospective view of the work, to which he had given himself heart and soul for so many years, and this he does in the following characteristic letter—

As to the Mission—it has, through many difficulties, gone on steadily, healthily, increasing in numbers. In 1859, the native contributions were, in round numbers, 240 rupees: last year they were 404 rupees. But how collected? All the people in the Mission (that is, church members) hold monthly prayer-meetings: the whole Mission is divided according to neighbourhoods. On each occasion the Scripture is read, or expounded, as the case may be; our Litany and prayers are used; and then a collection is made, each, at the beginning of the year, stating the amount he intends to give regularly, though at times an additional sum is added. The whole amount, then, for the year 1860, collected at these prayer-meetings, exceeds 200 rupees: the rest are fees. Of heathen baptisms, the number of adults was 108; of heathen children, 46; total baptized heathen during the year being 154. Now the baptized congregations consist of 1708 souls; unbaptized, 130; total, 1838. But this by no means shows the real number of inquirers—not here stated, because irregular. The writer has congregations from heathen and some from Syrians; and when he goes especially to some of the latter congregations he usually has a larger number than is ordinarily the case, and often excellent opportunities to communicate useful knowledge, and scatter good principles, especially among the irregular hearers, thus brought, by various motives, within the reach of truth. Of these occasional hearers the writer has had from three to 150, and more; and his usual method, when the people are quite strange, is to go outside about eight in the morning, as strangers always come early, to try and call forth their special attention to some common topic likely to interest; then to ask them to come into the porch, where all sit, and the writer in the midst, when the people, having been told of the especial object of the Sabbath, are invited, in the first place, to ask questions on what they will, by which means errors are corrected and suitable lessons imparted. In this way one most profitable service is concluded before our usual service begins, and often by the first service lasting friendships are formed that give me or my people opportunities to spread the Gospel for miles around. In this way, too, the writer had many opportunities, during the mutiny, to stop the progress of it here; and numbers, having confidence in his veracity, regularly came or sent to know how matters stood.

In addition to this is to be told, to the glory of our heavenly Father, that after more than twenty years struggling, during which he obtained a tacit admission of some of his people's rights, he has, through the aid of the present Resident, and Madava Row, the Dewan, lately acquired a legal status for his people, similar to that of the Mohammedans in Hindu India, that is, as fellow-subjects they have now the equal public right of walking in the public road, and appearing in a court of justice; they have also obtained deliverance from the infamous system of compulsory labour, and can hold property in their Christian names.

It may be asked, How was all this? What was done, and what is the exact standing of the Mavelicara Mission?

The writer commenced the Mavelicara Mission in 1838, upon principles drawn up for his own guidance from the word of God, and a knowledge of Hindu notions and practices. These principles were—

1st. That he should not undertake any indirect labour that might unfit or prevent him doing the work of an evangelist; and therefore,

2dly. That he could not advocate Mission orphanages and similar establishments, these being the work of a Christian church; whereas his business is to raise that church from, in the first instance, the adult population.

3dly. From historical knowledge, years before he came to India he had learned to know, and, in India, afterwards saw, the practical evil of establishing workshops, &c. By this the first Missionaries in Bengal voluntarily placed their Mission, in Hindu estimation, on a caste level with the despised low classes and outcastes; and, not to speak of the folly of hoping to compete with Indian mechanics, those low castes would necessarily oppose, for trying to deprive them of the profits of labour.

4thly. Another principle has been, never, as a rule, to give temporary support to any adults, under the plea that embracing Christianity deprives them of the means of gaining a livelihood. It is a home-supported mistake, which at least generates a puny, stunted, slavish spirit. It creates a hot-bed race, usually requiring a constant dependence on Mission support, which failing, the people are scattered to the winds; and at best it produces an unfitness to bear, or to honour, the cross of Christ in the midst of an opposing blaspheming race.

5thly. Above all, or including all, the principle of this Mission has been to repudiate and entirely ignore caste in every form.

Well! and the results? The plan has here succeeded: the number of Christians has been shown, all of whom have rights and a status similar to that of the Mohammedans of Hindu India, though our catechumen and baptized slaves, from present peculiar circumstances, are, neither in number nor standing, included in the above account. But of the others I may add, that all gain an independent living, there not being a single Mission pauper nor dependant, of course excepting readers and schoolmasters. But all the adults, as seen above, render pecuniary assistance, and one of our churches has just paid 130 rupees and one 60 rupees for bells, and from another I hold 300 rupees for rebuilding or repairing their present church; all these amounts being partly the result of the abovenamed and similar collections.

All this is respectfully submitted to the especial consideration of those purposing to raise new Indian Missions.

OBITUARY OF THE REV. GOTTLOB FRIEDRICH BÜHLER, OF THE YORUBA MISSION.

THE following paper has been forwarded to us by the widow of our valued Missionary, the late Rev. G. F. Bühler. According to German custom, after the funeral sermon, a biographical sketch of the departed one was given in the church, the particulars having been previously obtained from the near relatives. This Mrs. Bühler has translated, and in other respects adapted for use among friends in England. We give it a place in the pages of this periodical.

Gottlob Friedrich Bühler was born, the youngest of a numerous family, at Adelberg, in Württemberg, on the 3rd of July 1829. Trained by God-fearing parents, he was sent, as soon as he was old enough, to school, and remained there until his confirmation. Soon after, he expressed the wish to devote himself to the work of education, a wish which his parents were agreed to gratify, and sent him to the Preparandi Institution of the Rev. Mr. Voget, at Bonfeld, where, for two years, he prosecuted his studies with good success. In 1845 he was received into the Training College at Nürtingen, where he also remained two years, and, after passing the examinations honourably, was appointed assistant-schoolmaster in the Government school at Dürrwangen. Here he was again stationary for two years, and was then removed to Asperg, near Stuttgart. His wish to be in the more immediate neighbourhood of his relatives was soon after unexpectedly gratified, when he was appointed to Eichstatt, near Welzheim; and although his sojourn there brought him much that he would hardly have desired for himself, it was important in deciding the character of his future life. He became acquainted with an excellent man, who promoted his welfare in many ways, and through whose influence he became tutor in the Royal Educational College at Salon, near Ludwigsburg. During his residence here, a desire, which had doubtless been long growing up within him, came to maturity—the desire to go out and preach salvation to the heathen. Possibly the example of his eldest brother, who had been sent to India by the Bâsle Missionary Society some years before, may have contributed to the growth of this desire. In the spring of 1851 our departed friend applied to be admitted into the Missionary College at Bâsle, and was received there a few months after. Here he studied for three years, and was then dismissed into the service of the Church Missionary Society in London, whither he repaired, after taking leave of his relatives and friends. The next year was spent at the Church Missionary College at Islington. After being ordained deacon in 1855, by the Lord Bishop of London, he was sent out to West Africa, and entered on his work in the Yoruba country with vigour and with enjoyment. Of his Missionary career, that part is best known to us where he was at Abbeokuta, in which town he was stationed for several years, and where, in company with other messengers of the Gospel, he laboured devotedly, preaching amongst the heathen, instructing the young, and visiting his people. His project of forming an Educational Institute, in which some of the more promising African youths might be trained to become schoolmasters and catechists in the Mission, received the sanction of the Society, and he soon had more than twenty pupils, to whom he gave daily instruction in the necessary branches of education. And while he spared no pains, and shunned no sacrifice of time and of strength to bring them through the requisite course of study, he endeared himself personally to them by his kind and friendly bearing, and by the warm interest he took in all that concerned them, so that they learned to regard him with the love and esteem of children for their father.

In 1859 the Bishop of Sierra Leone (Dr. Bowen) visited the principal Mission stations in the Yoruba country, and, during his stay at Abbeokuta, held an ordination, when our departed brother was admitted to priests' orders In the same year his failing health obliged him to visit Europe, where, after a time, he recovered strength, and in the next year returned to his work in the Yoruba country. Again he laboured with great energy, especially when, at the beginning of 1862, he was appointed to a fresh station, that of Igbein, in Abbeokuta, which had become vacant through the death of the native Missionary, the Rev. T. King. Here he found full scope for his exertions, and, in addition to his usual occupations, had to superintend the extension of the Mission premises, and the erection of a simple but commodious building for the purposes of the Institution.

In the month of March 1864 Abbeokuta was attacked by the King of Dahomey, whose cruel intentions were, however, put to nought in an almost miraculous manner by Him who is the ruler of princes. The king was obliged to withdraw his forces, and fled before them to his own territory, while many of his warriors, male and female, remained prisoners in the town they had hoped to possess. During the most anxious hours of this time of distress and danger, and while the battle was at the hottest, the Christians continued in prayer to God for deliverance; and He heard the cries of his children, and so plainly revealed his helping arm, that even the heathen were heard to say, "It is the God of the Christians who has saved us: He has heard the white people's prayers."

In the course of the same year it pleased the Lord to call our departed friend from his sphere of active exertion into his special school of discipline—that of sickness and suffering. A cold, caught while returning home during a tornado, was followed by repeated attacks of fever and ague, and, in the month of September, by a severe inflammation, from which it was feared that he could not recover. This was a time of sharp affliction, which was, however, to produce the peaceable fruit of righteousness. His life was spared, and as soon as he had recovered strength sufficiently, he repaired to Lagos, hoping much from a change of air, which was considered necessary by his medical adviser. The sojourn at Lagos did not, however, result in the desired improvement in his health: he still suffered considerably from fever, and at this period he wrote to his relatives in their far-off home—"The last few months have been the most trying ones of my whole life. I have often longed to depart, and to be with Christ." But his earthly journey was not at an end. He returned to Abbeokuta, and, at the beginning of the present year, prepared to come home to Europe, where it was hoped he might regain his health. He left Lagos on the 7th of February, and for a few days appeared to be gaining strength; but fever again came, and for three weeks he was scarcely able to leave his cabin. Arrived in England at the beginning of March, he spent some time with his relatives and friends there, and availed himself of the best medical advice, which was not without effect; so that, in the month of June, he was able to set off on his journey to Würtemberg. On the way he suffered much from pain and weakness, and, on arriving at Stuttgart, was induced to consult a celebrated German physician. As, however, in the course of a few weeks, he began to be convinced that his illness was beyond the power of medicines to cure, he resolved to hasten home to his birthplace, where some of his brothers and sisters, with his aged father, were still living. To break the journey, he was to spend a few days in the town of Schorndorf, where he had some intimate and dear friends. He reached their house on the 27th of July. The next day he was too weak to leave his bed, and from that time it became evident that he could not recover. Not all the affectionate and considerate attentions of his host and hostess, nor the anxious care of his more immediate attendants, could stay the progress of disease. In the midst of pain and suffering, nothing strengthened and refreshed him so much as a few verses from the Bible; and he frequently asked to have one of the last chapters of St. John's Gospel read to him. Sometimes he repeated a verse from some of the beautiful hymns of the Lutheran church, which he had learnt in his childhood. Every expression that fell from his lips testified that he was looking forward with calm and happy confidence to the "city without foundations, whose builder and maker is God." After three weeks of great pain and weakness, borne with submission, and even cheerfulness, the servant was called home by his Master into the heavenly rest, and fell asleep on the evening of the 14th of August, at the age of 36.

Let us praise God for all the mercy and lovingkindness which He showed to our departed friend during these thirty-six years; but especially for having privileged him to join in the great work of extending the kingdom of Christ among the heathen. May the Divine Comforter be with those who are left behind to mourn one so dear to them, and help them to give him up with resignation, yea, even with thanks and praise to Him who "doeth all things well!" May a blessing rest on all those who knew our brother in life, so that they may not only keep him in friendly and affectionate remembrance, but be encouraged by his example to persevere in fighting the good fight, and to labour earnestly, each in his sphere, to promote, whether by action or by suffering, the glory of God. Oh, may we henceforth direct our steps more unswervingly towards the heavenly city, the city of the living God, in which are "many mansions," prepared for those who love Him! Amen.

FEMALE EDUCATION IN INDIA.

A LABOURER in the Mission-field, now at home, has forwarded to us the following communication on this important subject—

The extract from the "Calcutta Christian Intelligencer," in your last Number,* respecting the Brahmo Samaj, is so full of interest, particularly when taken in connexion with the notice in the "Times of India" (August 23rd) of the establishment, in Calcutta, of a female branch of the Samaj, that I venture to draw the attention of your readers to what appears to be another most encouraging indication of the influence of "the leaven."

"The split" in the Samaj has, apparently, originated on the intermarriage question, and has led to the formation of this branch for the women. The "Times of India" says, that on August 15th an address was delivered to the first meeting, in which those present were exhorted "to cultivate their minds and souls under the shadow of the true church, looking for strength to the merciful providence of a holy God." The "Indian Mirror," the organ of the new party in the Samaj, tells us that there were thirteen ladies present, and that the sermon was on the motherhood of God.

This was in Calcutta; but in the "Hindu Patriot" of September 11th we have the notice of the formation of a new Society of men at Dacca, who pledge themselves "to promote the cause of intermarriage, widow-marriage, and female education, by all means in their power." And in the same paper is a notice of a prize of 200 rupees, which has been offered for the best drama, in Bengalee, on the condition and helplessness of Hindu females.

These, Sir, although not the efforts of Christian men, are, I believe, indications of the leaven of Christianity, which is gradually influencing the whole of the upper and educated classes of Hindus in Bengal.

To appreciate it, however, at its full value, it is necessary to remember, that for ages the condition of women generally, in Bengal at least, has been one of ignorance and degradation.

"Is woman to live and die,"* asked the Rev. K. M. Banerjea sixteen years ago, "as an irrational creature, notwithstanding her capacities for improvement? . . . . "To suffer an intelligent creature," he continues, "to degenerate to the condition of the beasts of the field is to destroy her intellect by denying its nourishment; and yet such a crime is daily perpetrated before our eyes by the Hindu and Mohammedan population, who consider their females as little better than animals of burden, and, far from providing them with means of education, count them as mere slaves, calculated to render such services as they choose to demand."

"The excellence of woman," say Babu S. C. Dutt,† "unmarried or married, or widow, throughout the country, among great and small, is rated only by the scale of servile fear and capacity of endurance and toil."

Banerjea says again,‡ "The females of Hindustan are living in a state of the utmost degradation." . . . . "Half the population of India living within the purdah as victims of ignorance, and almost debarred from the light of the sun and the free air of heaven." . . . .

When the woman is a widow, her lot is still worse. "It is not from religious prejudices and early impressions only," wrote Rajah Rammohun Roy, in 1822,§ "that Hindu widows burn themselves on the piles of their deceased husbands, but also from their witnessing the distress in which widows of the same rank in life are involved, and the insults and slights to which they are daily subjected that they become in a great measure regardless of existence after the death of their husbands."

---

* *Vide* "Church Missionary Intelligencer" for November, p. 352.

* Sermon on Female Education, 1849, p. 7.

† Miscellaneous Essays, quoted in Dr. Kay's Sermon on Woman, p. 33.

‡ Sermon, p. 12, above quoted.

§ Ancient Rights of Females, p. 8.

Or, more recently,* a native correspondent of the "Calcutta Morning Chronicle" (Nov. 30, 1850), wrote, addressing his countrymen—"My friends, are we so lost to every sense of humanity and justice, and even of common propriety and expediency, as not to reflect for one moment, during the whole round of our feasts and revelries, on the deplorable condition of our daughters and sisters?" . . . "We lounge and roll about on spring couches, whilst our daughter, our child, our own blood, lies down on the bare floor, withering away prematurely in the deepest agony of mind. It is a shame, a blasphemy, a sacrilege, and a murder."

Now and again an educated voice has been raised against this state of things. "The well-being of the millions who inhabit this magnificent country," said the Rev. K. M. Banerjea, in 1859,† "calls for the improvement of their female society. The nation can never prosper so long as ignorant mothers and wives exercise so baneful an influence on the rising and the present generations."

"Female ignorance,"‡ said Babu Nobin Kristo Bose, addressing the members of the Bethune Society, "stands in the way of any bold or enterprising attempt to deviate from the beaten track, and the influence of an affectionate mother, or a beloved wife holds him (the educated man) fast to orthodox practices and modes of life." . . . . . "Female ignorance, like some great centripetal force, retains even well-educated men within the prescribed sphere of antiquated customs and superstitious rites;" and many an earnest spirit has longed to see that dawn of day for women which we are now privileged to behold. The difficulties to contend against have been greater than most people in England appear to understand: it is therefore necessary to remind such that it is an assumed principle of Hinduism, interwoven with the social and domestic history of the nation, that women should be kept in a state of ignorance and degradation.

"In the representations of female excellence,"§ says Banerjea, "which the Hindu classical writings contain, the images are principally, if not solely, those of beauty and bodily charms. The Hindus appear never to have entertained any notion of the intellectual and moral capabilities of the sex."

It is true some few were learned, and their names stand out prominently;‖ "but the other educated females of whom we read in the Hindu classics did not, many of them, profit much by the study of letters." Their irregular conduct "produced, in process of time, a prejudice against their improvement, the effects of which are sadly visible in the present state of society."

It would appear from many passages that the compilers of books held sacred by the Hindus never contemplated the education of women. Banerjea says, in his lecture on Vedantism,* "The founder of the Vedant has declared that women and Sudras are not entitled to *hear* the holy sentences of the Vedas, and the Vedas themselves take this exclusiveness for granted." Certain it is,† "there stands the opinion and the practice, that it is no part of a girl's duty to study, and no part of a father's to persuade her to do so."

The ignorance and degradation of woman stand out prominently in the Hindu system. Take a text or two from Menu's Code, compiled 2700 years ago, and still the text-book of the old school of Hinduism.

"It is the nature of women in this world (ch. ii. v. 213) to cause the seduction of men, for which reason the wise are never unguarded in the company of females. . . . . A female, indeed, is able to draw from the right path in this life, not a fool only, but even a sage, and can lead him in subjection. . . . . Let no man, therefore, sit in a sequestered place with his nearest female relations."

Again, ch. ix. v. 15—17 — "Through their passion for men, their mutable tempers, their want of settled affection, and their perverse nature (let them be guarded in this world ever so well) they soon become alienated from their husbands; yet should their husbands be diligently careful in guarding them, though they well know the disposition with which the Lord of the creation formed them.

"Women have no business with the texts of the Vedas: this is the law fully settled: having, therefore, no evidence of law, and no knowledge of expiatory texts, sinful women must be as foul as falsehood itself: and this is a fixed rule."

Thus "bereft of the advantages of reading and observation, their thoughts seldom extend beyond the walls of the zenana, or soar above the roof under which they are secured." . . . . "Intellectual amusements and recreations are wholly unknown to them: . . . . they live in a state of moral insensibility, and do not consider themselves bound, as rational and responsible agents, to perform any thing besides their assigned work in the house."‡

* Quoted in the "Missionary," Jan. 1851, p. 55.
† Sermon, p. 8.
‡ Proceedings of Bethune Society, 1861, p. 42.
§ Prize Essay on Female Education, p. 67.
‖ Ibid, p. 21.

* Printed in the "Missionary" for January 1851, p. 51.
† Minutes of Madras Conference, p. 191.
‡ Banerjea, quoted in "Madras Minutes," p. 193.

"Secured," says Banerjea; and, as untrustworthy, they were literally secured, secluded in the inner house, and guarded by bolts and bars, and latticed windows, and able-bodied guards.

Dean Milman, in his exquisite translation of "Nala and Damayanti," has given us a picture of the past, and present too, excepting those houses into which the influence of the Gospel has extended.

He tells us how Nala asks, in wonder—

"Strictly guarded is yon palace—
How may I find entrance there?"

And how Damayanti inquires, when she saw Nala—

"How hast entered in our palace?—
How hast entered all unseen?
Watchful are our chamber wardens—
Stern the mandate of the King."

And then how Nala tells her—

"Know, O loveliest, I am Nala—
Here the messenger of gods;
Through their power, their power almighty—
I have entered here unseen."

Nor is this merely a poetical description, or an account which refers to one time or person. So closely confined women were and have been, and, I may say, are still, in some places, that they are spoken of as those who have not seen the sun.

In Dr. Muir's Sanskrit texts, Part I, pp. 89—91, there is an account of Harishchandra selling his wife into slavery to enable him to pay the fee to Viswamitra; and the words of his lament are striking, "She, my spouse, whom formerly neither air, nor sun, nor moon, nor stranger had beheld, is now gone into slavery."

In modern times, Babu Brijo Kishore Ghose, in his history of the Juggernath Temple at Orissa, says, p. 55, "It is much to be lamented that such voluptuous priests are not only supported by the respectable Hindus, but entrusted with their wives and other female relatives, who have never seen the face of a stranger."

Shama Churn Sirkar, a native pleader in Calcutta, in his Dialogues on the Manners and Customs of Hindus, says, p. 367, "Women in their private apartments wear head wrappers; they do not show their faces to their superiors, nor do they converse with them, or speak in such a way (so loud) that they should hear them." Again, "Our women never touch their superiors, and hardly even any one else; and, so far from eating with men, they do not even eat in the presence of a man."

And again, "A Hindu does not speak to his wife before his superior." (p. 377).

Mr. Murdoch has quoted, in his Indian Year Book, p. 129, a passage from the "Indian Reformer," edited by the Rev. Lal Behari De, to the same effect, viz. "In their estimation (women) a woman who has not seen the face of any other man than her husband, if such a thing be possible, is a prodigy of virtue."

Well might Dr. Kay embody in his sermon the exclamation of the native essayist when urging the re-marriage of widows among Hindus—"Woman! in India thy lot is cast in misery." (p. 24.)

With such a back-ground, exhibiting such domestic associations to contend against, it is easier to understand the difficulties which surrounded the first attempts to improve the condition of women.

Banerjea* recorded his conviction sixteen years ago that "neither the Hindus nor the Mohammedans are likely to adopt vigorous measures for female education without the counsel and help of their Christian neighbours. . . . Having for ages immemorial debarred their females from the advantages of education, there is little probability of their spontaneously returning now to a sense of duty."

And Banerjea was right.

Babu Prosonno Coomar Tagore† was the first Bengalee gentleman who engaged an European governess for his daughter, and for years he was the only one. It was not until 1855, and then through the painstaking and energetic efforts of the Rev. Messrs. Smith and Fordyce, that the first acknowledged Christian teacher,‡ Miss Toogood, was allowed to attend regularly to give instruction in a Hindu family. She was soon joined by the first pupil from the Calcutta Normal School, Miss Marr; and with these two earnest workers commenced the public movement in Bengal in favour of female education among the upper classes.

The movement has been necessarily slow in its progress, but now, stimulated and encouraged by Christian exertion, the Hindus themselves have, as we have seen, taken it up, and are seeking, apart from Christianity, to educate and enlighten their women. The elevation of woman, however, is emphatically a Christian work, and even this effort of the Brahmo Samaj must be Christian in its tendency.

"To the Gospel,"§ says Isaac Taylor, "thus

* Sermon above quoted, p. 9.
† Banerjea's Prize Essay, p. 116.
‡ Minutes of Bengal Conference, 1855, p. 152.
§ Lectures on Spiritual Christianity, p. 117.

working reformation by the noiseless operation of its ethical principles, blessing us often unawares, and even against the bent of our perverse wills—to the Gospel woman owes every thing good, for she derives from it her power to bless indeed those whom she loves, and thus to become herself happy."

There are, moreover, hundreds of the women of the upper classes in Bengal now under direct Christian instruction. Some have been baptized; others are not far from the kingdom of heaven.

But now that their husbands and brothers have taken up the work of their education, should we not rejoice, that, after so long a night, the day is breaking?

What incalculable blessings—what momentous consequences, humanly speaking, hang upon the emancipation of the women of Bengal from their state of bondage!

Is it not a reason why those who long for the salvation of India should pray more earnestly that the Lord himself may impart the life-giving spirit to the leaders of this great movement, and bring them, and the women they are endeavouring to teach, to the foot of the Cross, that they may find there pardon and peace, and, being cleansed from all their sins, may serve Him with a quiet mind.

It is, also, surely a call to renewed effort, that the Missionaries, both to men and women, throughout Bengal, may be so increased in number, that the good news of the true Teacher, who is the way, the truth, and the life, may be carried to the homes and hearts of all who are willing to hear it.

Apologizing for the length of this letter,

I remain, dear Sir,

X. Y. Z.

ITINERATION IN ASIA MINOR.

VERY reluctantly we were compelled in our last Number to interrupt the narrative of Messrs. Weakley and Wolters' itinerancy on the central plateau of Asia Minor. But the length of the document precluded the possibility of its being published in a single Number.

We left them at Koniah, the ancient Iconium, and the extreme point of their journey. The route which they pursued homeward led them by Colosse, Laodicea, Philadelphia, and Sardis. In the portion, therefore, of the narrative which we now publish, our readers will find much that is interesting.

Koniah.

After leaving the house we went to view the town of Koniah from a mound — the only elevated place in the town — upon which stood the palace, and now stands the tomb of Sultan Alaed'din. At the back of this ruin is the shell of an old Greek church, massively built, with a cupola in the centre. On knocking off some of the plaster and wash which has been roughly laid on inside, we discovered some pictures in good preservation. All the walls seem to have been painted in this manner. The Greeks have endeavoured to get their ancient edifice restored to them, but the Chelebi Effendi, the representative of an elder branch of the reigning family, and the descendant of Jellaled'din Roomi, or Mollah Hunkiar, refuses to give his consent. This person's power in Koniah is more absolute than that of the Sultan. He does what he pleases, and none dare say him nay. From the slight eminence upon which we stood we were able to form some idea of the extent of the town. It contains about 14,000 or 15,000 houses, nearly all built of unburnt brick, and having a poor aspect. The remark of a native gentleman, with whom we conversed on the subject, aptly describes the place. "Koniah," said he, "is the greatest of Turkish villages." Some five mosques, the wooden residences of the Governor and the Chelebi Effendi, and a few other houses, stand out conspicuous from the general wretchedness. Here and there inside the town are large open stagnant pools, the general receptacle of the drainage, and very offensive: a part of the ancient moat serves the same purpose. The old town is simply a desolation. In it the remains of two or three mosques exhibit a massiveness of structure and profuseness of ornament which are not seen in the more modern buildings. The elaborate stone-carving and the very ingenious arrangement of coloured bricks in these old structures are well worthy of remark. Large portions of the wall, and the ruins of a castle which once defended Koniah, are still standing, surrounded by a deep and broad ditch. The wall is massive, being built of rough masonry, faced with cut stone, among which may be seen an abundance of fragments of sculpture, both heathen and Byzantine, the materials of more ancient buildings. Here and there inscriptions may be noticed, while the symbol of the Christian faith not unseldom stands in juxtaposition with the bas-relief of some mythic deity. Among the ruins we constantly stumbled over shot and shell, which were scattered about in great abundance. They are now the playthings of the boys of Koniah. In every available place on the walls, the old mosques, and other ruined buildings, slabs bearing the name and style of Sultan Alaed'dunya ved'din, are inserted, but they appear to be of modern workmanship.

May 14: *Lord's-day*—About twenty Greeks came in to see us. They wanted Græco-Turkish and Reference Bibles. We had none left, but we told them that in any case we should not sell books to-day, as it was the κυριακή. So they sat down, and I proposed reading a passage from the New Testament to them. I chose Matt. v. 1—16, and expounded at some length. They paid great attention as I set before them sin as the root of all misery, pride, strife, and alienation from God; and the felt knowledge of sin to bewail it and hate it as the true preparation and qualification for all the blessings of the kingdom of God; that the knowledge of Christ and our debt to Him, was the source of all unselfishness and humility, the very fountain of good works; and that out of Christ each one lived for himself, while in Christ each lived for all, as He died for all; that persecution would certainly come, in one shape or other, on all who would live godly in Christ Jesus, but that such persecution was one token of real discipleship, and of being a co-heir with Christ; and that, finally, the disciples of Christ must be either a light and an influence, or nothing." They asked some serious questions, and, after I had given them a parting exhortation, left, with many expressions of regret that we could not stay a long time to teach them more perfectly the way of life, and that we could not supply them with the holy word. Other people came in until midday, one or two of whom had a long conversation with brother Wolters in Greek. About this time a zabtieh (gensd'arme) came from the Kadi to say that our servant was wanted at the court. The reason of this summons was, that yesterday an Armenian had purchased an Armeno-Turkish Bible, which he afterwards brought back, and asked for the money, which was returned without demur; he then came a second time, and wished for the book, which our servant let him have, on the express understanding, that if he brought it back again it would not be received. The young man wished the second time to return the book, but was not allowed to do so, according to agreement; upon which he made a complaint to the Kadi, and summoned our man in order to compel him to take back the Bible. Our servant explained to the judge the state of the case, and what the books were, at the same time handing to him a copy of the Turkish New Testament, and informed him by whom he was employed. The judge said that he was perfectly in the right, and demanded the reason why the book was sought to be returned. The Armenian said it was a bad book. The Kadi replied, that of course he must prove that, which the other professed to be able to do. The Kadi then turned to our servant and said, "You are perfectly right, but this man is ignorant: for my sake give him his money, and let the matter end." Our man replied, that he could not do so after what had passed: the Armenian had said in open court that the books which we sought to distribute were bad, and asserted that he could bring proof in support of the charge. If the money was returned there, it would immediately go forth that the books were bad, and that the Kadi Effendi had compelled the return of the money. Let the man bring his proofs on the morrow: it was not a question of money but of defamation. So it was agreed; the Kadi and functionaries round him joining in praise of the English, which, of course, every one present echoed. The Kadi said, among other things, "If it had not been for the English the throne of the Sultan would have been swept away long ago;" a somewhat astonishing confession in such a place and by such a person. In the afternoon several Turks came in, one of whom seemed a superior sort of man, and was treated with respect by the others. We learnt afterwards that he was a Bektashi. This person sat reading the New Testament for some time. He then asked for another copy, upon which one of those with him objected to his buying such books. His reply was curt and decisive—"Yes, I shall buy and read them: there may be wisdom in this book of which we know nothing." We allowed him to take away the books, the price to be called for on the morrow. Some other people came and went away; after which I read the evening service in Turkish with Mr. Wolters, our servant, and the young Protestant, Bedros. We felt much sympathy with this solitary one, and tried to comfort and strengthen him. It was a great source of joy to us to see that he did not hide his light. In the evening we went to the doctor's house and, upon his urgent invitation, slept there. Here we were told that the Armenian priest had preached against us and our books in the church, and had forbidden the people to come near us, or to look at our books. We were bad, designing men, and our books were false. This will account for the affair before the Kadi.

May 15—Went out with the doctor to call upon some of the chief Turks of Koniah. We first called upon a Sheikh of reputation among the Mevlevi, who is the representative of Shemsed'din Tabrizi, the bosom friend of Mevlana, and a great saint among the Turks. The Sheikh, a very venerable-looking old man, with flowing white beard, received us very kindly, and called us his children. He told us, moreover, that he was the father of all, both Christians and Mussulmans, just as Adam and Eve were the parents of all. We did not stay many minutes with him, but before we left he had the tomb of the saint opened for us to see. On the wall we noticed a representation of Zulfakar, the two-bladed sword of Ali. Going from thence, we visited the Sheikh, who resides in the cloister of the mosque which contains the tomb of the great Jellaled'din Roomi, usually called Mevlana, the founder of the sect of Mevlevis, and the person to whose care young Othmar was committed by his dying father, Ertogrul. The Sheikh, who is known as the Ashji dedeh (chief cook), a title with a mystical signification, expressed himself as very pleased to see us, and talked very freely about our Lord, who, he said, lived four years in a monastery a few miles off, and that on this account Mevlana had spent forty days there. A grave old Turk who sat beside him shook his head at the story, and I told him that it was quite new to us, and not according to the Gospel. We then talked about our having sacred Scriptures, and the Sheikh asked for a copy, which he said he would be glad to read. We promised to send him one, and after a little further conversation he told us that he would be glad to see us again when we came that way, and requested us to give his salutations to the Governor of Sparta, "who," said he, "is one of us." He then sent a dervish to open the sanctuary for us. This is a great place of pilgrimage. The mosque and tomb are more tastefully and beautifully decorated than most other places of the kind. On entering, there is an elevated waxed platform for the dancers, and beyond that a dimly-lighted compartment, in which are numerous tombs, containing the remains of the children and successors of Mevlana. His tomb is distinguishable by its size and the breadth of turban which crowns it. Here we were presented with a metal bowl of water to drink, and invited to be present at their dances on Friday. We next went to the palace of the descendant and successor of Mevlana, the great Chelebi Effendi, but he was absent. The Pasha also, we learnt, had gone to a distant part of his province (the Chichek Dagh) to settle a dispute with the Kurds; and two other persons whom we called on had not yet risen. Another dervish conversed very freely with us in his house, not the least part of his conversation being taken up with the distressed state of the people from taxation and bad government. In the khan we found more people to talk with, whom, in our own private place, we could address more freely on the great subject of our mission. A well-dressed Bektashi dervish came in, and sat for some time talking. He bade us remember a prophecy, of which the following is the substance—"Among the kings of the earth great commotions will arise, and many will fall; but England will stand. And when the Mehdi comes many Mussulmans will be destroyed, but England will recognise his mission, and be safe." We tried to talk with him about the coming of Christ, and gave him a New Testament, which he put carefully in his girdle. The difficulty—if it deserves the name—of yesterday was happily settled this morning while we were making calls. A Zabtieh came from the Kadi, having several Armeno-Turkish books which had been sold under his arm, and accompanied by two or three Armenians. When they entered the room, several Turks were reading the sacred Scriptures. The demand that the books should be taken back, and the money restored, was again made, and again firmly refused, on the ground put forward yesterday. Our servant then spoke a few words to these men about their behavour in regard to the holy Scriptures, and asked them who could believe that they were Christians when they publicly stated that the Bible was a bad book, and their priest forbad the purchase and reading of it. If the books we sold were not the true sacred Scriptures, it would be very easy to prove it by a comparison with the Bible which was in their church, but they had not done so, and thus confessed their inability to prove their heavy and unjust charge. The Armenians then became very much ashamed, and excused themselves by saying that they were ignorant, and did not understand the language of the book. "If that is the case, your money shall be returned to you immediately," was the reply; but the others said that they did not wish for the money, but would be thankful if Turkish Scriptures were given them in lieu of those they wished to return. This was done, and, besides the copies thus given in exchange, they purchased several small Turkish tracts. Up to the time of our leaving we had constant applications from the Greeks for Scriptures and Prayer-books. Just as we were about to start, we saw another Protestant, an elderly man, who had only then heard of our being in Koniah, and came at once to see us. He was living, like young Bedros, in the belief that he was alone in Koniah, and was overjoyed to see us, and to find another brother by our means. The Cypriote whom we conversed with on Saturday we discovered to be a worthless character: he is known to be a drunkard and gambler. We saw him playing at dice yesterday morning, since which time he has shunned us, and we have had no chance of speaking with him.

Sillah.

In the afternoon we left for Sillah, about an hour and a half N.W., Bedros accompanying us to the wall of the town, and reluctantly bidding us farewell. Sillah lies just off the plain on the two sides of a narrow defile: the houses are built of stone, and, from the steepness of the hill-side, looking as if they stood one upon another. The church is very large, and is said to be the first of a number of churches which the Empress Helena built when on her pilgrimage to the holy sepulchre. We were lodged for the night in the bishop's residence, which was empty, the late bishop's successor being still in Constantinople. There is a very large population of Greeks here, and many came to see us. As everywhere, so here, the demand was for Græco-Turkish Scriptures and Reference Bibles, none of the latter having yet been printed. We were greatly pleased with the frank and manly bearing of these men, and the scriptural knowledge which some of them had. One or two, who understood Greek, readily bought copies of a little Modern-Greek Testament; and, one who understood the ancient language, pleaded so earnestly for brother Wolters' little Pickering Testament, that he felt compelled to give it him. One of the schoolmasters, somewhat of a pedant, came to criticise our Modern-Greek translation, and was most amusingly perplexed when he could not find the points he was in search of. The chief schoolmaster we found to be an old acquaintance of Mr. Wolters, sen. He seemed very glad to see us, is an enlightened man, and his daughters have charge of the girls' school. The people bade us stay with them several days, but we had no books, and the only place where we could rest on the Lord's-day, or do any work, was several days' journey distant; so we said, if it should please God to allow us to visit Sillah again, we would stay longer. They told us that they were the descendants of Lacedemonian captives brought thither by the Sultans of Koniah, and alleged this as the explanation of the strange dialect of Greek which they use among themselves, and which is unintelligible to other Greeks. We learnt that the same dialect was spoken by the Greeks of Fertek, several days' journey E.N.E. The preservation of their language, whilst almost everywhere else in the interior both Armenian and Greek have succumbed perforce to the language of the conqueror, speaks much for the independent character of this people, a character which they bear very visibly still. After dark a priest came in, and conversed for a long time in Greek: his soft assent to every thing that was said formed quite a contrast to the open individuality of his flock. A gentleman to whom we had a letter of introduction told us that the road we must pass on the morrow was dangerous, and that a guard was necessary for the journey.

Route to Sparta.

May 16 — Taking our guard, a stalwart Sillahli, well mounted, and armed with a short native rifle, brace of pistols, yataghan, and with a club hanging at the saddle-bow, we pushed on, through the valleys of a somewhat hilly country, to a small village called Kizil Ouren, where we rested for more than an hour, and thence on through a pine forest and partly cultivated plain to Chukur Aghl, which was our halting-place for the night. This is a poor little village, ten hours from Sillah. The women do all the ploughing, sowing, and harvesting, and tend the cattle: of the men but few were in the village, the rest being in Smyrna as hamals (porters), compelled to go out in this way by the pressure of poverty and debt. The people cultivate only barley and wheat, and keep a few goats and sheep. The chief man told us that what they grew was barely sufficient for their own consumption. This is the only place in which we did not get enough to eat.

May 17—Dismissing our guard, we went on our way towards Sparta, the next place of any size, and in which we may hope to do something. As we drew near to the lake of Beishehr we came down into a beautiful plain, in which were several large villages, and at about the middle of which we halted at midday by the side of a copious warm spring, over which a cupola had been built. Inside the building we found a large swimming-bath, which all our party were very thankful to make use of. The water had no peculiar taste or smell, and leaves no deposit. A few yards off is a small spring of cold water. Three or four hours further on we passed near the head of the lake of Bei-shehr, an extensive and beautiful sheet of water, dotted with small islands and overshadowed on its western side by the lofty snow-clad Dipoiras, or, as the Turks call it, the Anamass Dagh. Here we saw more villages, and some well-filled orchards and gardens, but we met but few people. Still further on we passed another large basin of clear warm water, and then, after another half hour, a remarkable cold spring, which gushed from an aperture in the rock, four or five feet wide and from two to three in depth, pouring forth in continuous, rapid, silent, copious flow. A little after sunset we reached Kara Agadj, a little Turkish town of 800 or 900 houses, just as heavy rain commenced falling, our horses somewhat lame, and ourselves much fatigued with the very long day's ride. Here, before we laid down for the night, an Armenian Bible was sold to a traveller, and a little Turkish boy bought a Psalter. The latter was sent back with his book shortly after.

May 18—Wishing to reach Sparta before Sunday, we did not stay in Kara Agadj, which is wholly Mussulman, but, next morning, rode on through defiles in the mountain which separates the plain of Kara Agadj from the shores of the lake of Egherdir. While on the mountain we were overtaken by a sudden and violent storm of wind and rain, which compelled us to take refuge for a time in a little coffee-house in the defile. Getting clear of the mountain, we came down a small semicircular plain, which reaches down to the lake, and afforded us a glimpse of its beauty, if not of its extent. Near the centre of this plain is Gelendos, the village at which we rested for the night. There being no khan, we were guests in the travellers' room, of which a farmer was the owner, who treated us very kindly, and sat down with us at the meal which he provided. My dear brother suffered so much here from pains in the head and limbs that I feared he was about to be laid aside with fever: yesterday he was ill, but not in so much pain. We had medicines with us, however, and, through mercy, on the morrow he was so much better as to be able to proceed with comfort.

Two or three people came in to bid us welcome and to talk. The thing uppermost in their minds was the difficulty they have in getting on with the increased taxation, which, they say, is utterly beyond their power to endure. I was sorry that I could not turn their minds to the theme we so much wished to dwell upon.

May 19—We expect a most delightful day in riding from Gelendos to Egherdir. Shortly after starting we met a large troop of Yuruks on their way to their summer encampment. Their wealth in cattle and fine carpets was astonishing. After we had passed these people at the extremity of the plain, the whole of the journey was on the edge of the lake, and mostly on a narrow road cut in the precipitous side of the mountain, which goes down suddenly into its waters. The woods, the multitude of wild flowers and flowering shrubs, the general luxuriance of fertility, the winding shores and beautiful expanse of water, the many-tinted intervals between the white-pebbled beach at the foot, and the dazzling mass of snow on the top of the mountain opposite to us, with many other features of fresh beauty, suffered not the day to seem long, nor the eye to grow weary, as now, with hands wreathed in the horse's mane, we scrambled up the narrow ascent, and now, on foot, we carefully descended the road, too steep for man and horse to go down together, or struggled painfully through the loose and roadless shingle at the edge of the water.

Egherdir is a little semi-ruined town, part of which is built on a promontory jutting out into the lake. The place was nearly deserted when we arrived: all had gone to their vineyards and gardens. We walked about the place, but saw no one to speak with, and our man took his bag into the half-closed bazaar with no success. Two or three Greeks asked for Græco-Turkish Scriptures. Later, we found that the keeper of the khan, a grey bearded Turk, was of Greek origin, and that, although he conformed outwardly to Mussulman observances, yet in his own house with his wife he held to Greek faith and practice still. He spoke and read Greek, and was glad to receive some tracts, and a little book of prayers in that language. He told us also of a man of some substance in Sparta who was in the same case as himself: both are Sciotes. There are two islands on the lake, one of which is inhabited, a large proportion of the people being Christians. We were told that there were several ancient MSS. preserved in the island. The people have a tradition that the lake, which is about forty miles long, from three to six broad, and having six fathoms of water in its deepest part, did not always exist, and that the valley which it now fills was called Chukur Ova, *i.e.* "the plain in the hollow."

Sparta.

May 20—Rode on to Sparta, hoping to get a day or two's rest for ourselves and our jaded horses, and to do something for our Master before we leave. On the road we passed by a deserted village, its mosqueless minaret standing by what seemed to be a shelter for cattle. It is possible that the people have been absorbed by the growth of a large village at no great distance off. Sparta is situated at the foot of a high mountain, and looks over a narrow sandy plain. About the town are many gardens and orchards, which are well watered, and give the place a beautifully embowered appearance. We alighted at a quiet khan near the entrance to the town, and very soon afterwards our servant found out, and brought with him, the Sciote of whom we had been told at Egherdir. We had some little talk with him, but others coming put a stop to the conversation. However, at this time, and subsequently, we learnt that he was a very ignorant and depressed man; that while he adhered secretly to his ancient faith, the members of his family—who were all strict Mussulmans—would be his greatest enemies if he ventured to act and speak otherwise than as a Mussulman; and that, although he wished very much to have Christian Scriptures and other books, yet he dared not take one home: indeed, he feared that his visiting us would arouse suspicion, and get him into trouble; still he hoped to find an opportunity of taking a Testament before we left.

A Greek gentleman, to whom we had a letter of introduction, took us to his house: we found him to be the chief of the local Greek community, and a wealthy, active man. He treated us with great respect, and showed a great deal of sympathy with us in our work as Missionaries among the Turks, and expressed himself as being very glad indeed that something was being done for them. He told us, moreover, that one or two copies of the Mizan-ul-Haqq had been brought to Sparta by Greeks who had read the book, and handed it about among their friends, but not as yet among the Turks, for fear of disturbance. Still they were glad to know something of the controversy, and were much interested in the spread of Christianity among the Turks, to help which good work they would do what they could, and would like us to visit Sparta now and then. During the whole of our stay in this house the conversation was mainly on questions of scriptural doctrine and practice. Our host told us that he had brought Scriptures occasionally from Smyrna, which were sold to the people; and that now, with the exception of certain appointed days on which the lessons were read in Greek, the Scriptures were read in the church in Turkish, so that all might understand. Several persons came to bid us welcome, and it was late ere we laid down for the night.

May 21: *Lord's-day*—Went down to the khan and had service with our servant: no one else came. After this, our host took us to the Caimacam (deputy governor), to whom I delivered the message from the Sheikh at Mevlana's tomb. He seemed in bad health, and so weak as hardly to be able to keep up the conversation. In a very short time we took our leave, when he told us that he was much gratified with our visit. We then called upon the Bishop of Pisidia, who seemed very much occupied with secular business. After lunch, the bishop sent a messenger to say he would be very glad if we would go and sit an hour or two with him. We found him seated in the corner of the divan in a large room, at the door of which one or two priests and his archdeacon were standing. He rose as we entered, and bade us sit down beside him. The conversation, which was for the most part in Greek, turned freely upon the Gospel, and our work of trying to win Mussulmans to Christ, the state of the country, &c. When we left, the bishop greeted us very heartily, and told us how happy he had been to see us, and that he hoped to see us often. Whilst sitting with him we had an opportunity of witnessing the homage which the Greek priests pay to their bishop. Four or five of these men came into the room, and crowded up to the corner where the bishop was sitting: the latter then leaned forward and held out his hand, when each in turn crouched forward till his knuckles touched the ground, went forward, still in a bent posture, kissed the extended hand, and then crept away backwards to the door. The whole business seemed painfully servile. The rest of the evening was spent in conversation with various persons, all Greek.

May 22—Went down to the khan and conversed with a few persons, but no Turks. Græco-Turkish Scriptures were in great demand, but, alas! no supply. One or two inquiries were made for the Mizan-ul-Haqq. Several Turks in the bazaar asked that the New Testament might be left with them for an hour or two, which time they spent in reading it together: however, they did not buy the book, although they praised it. A New Testament, bought by a Turk, was sent back again: some expression had given offence. Unhappily we cannot go into the bazaar to explain difficulties: controversy would ensue in public, with no other result than disturbance. However, a respectable Greek tradesman, who said he had a great deal of intercourse with Turks, expressed a wish to buy the whole of our remaining stock of Scriptures, as he thinks he can dispose of them all in Sparta. He told us, what we have heard elsewhere, that if there were an established assurance of liberty many Turks would freely inquire, and some would at once renounce Islam.

May 23—The person mentioned yesterday came in the morning and purchased all our

Turkish and Arabic Scriptures, and the few copies of Modern Greek which remained. May the Lord bless this seed! There were left then only a few Hebrew Psalters and Pentateuchs, and an Albanian New Testament: thus the chief means of our intercourse with the people was exhausted, and there remained but little probability of our being able to do any thing until we reached those places which we had visited before, and in which we were known.

Route to Denizlee.

Our object was now to push on as quickly as possible to reach Denizlee, in order to spend the Sunday there. So we started from Sparta about midday for Buldur, *viâ* Aghlasoun, the Caimacam having furnished us with a mounted guard, as the pass over the mountains was a favourite resort of robbers. After riding for some time along the bottom of a deep ravine, often in the waters of the stream which nearly covers it, we suddenly commenced the ascent of the rocky zigzag which took us to the summit of the pass. Here we rested for a few minutes to breathe the horses at a little guard-house, and then began the descent on foot of a declivity, without exception the most difficult and dangerous we had yet seen. But the vast tossing ocean of mountains before us, bounded, far away to the south, by the mighty snow-clad Taurus, reminded us that we were among the mountains of Pisidia, and most probably on the very road by which St. Paul went up to Antioch and down to Attaleia on his first Missionary journey. Doubtless it was among these mountains that he was in perils of robbers, and suffered from weariness and painfulness. In such a place, as Missionaries, how many reflections, comparisons, and hopes filled our minds and hearts, and furnished us with solemn, pleasant themes of conversation. At the foot of the steepest part of the descent we rested at a fountain, beneath a solitary tree, and took our dinner of hard goat's flesh and bread; and then, having sent on the horses to the little village four or five miles distant, where we should sleep, we struck off to the left, to wander awhile among the ruins of Sagalassas, once ἡ πρώτη τῆς Πισιδίας, but now, with the exception of the theatre, and here and there a broken gateway, or a piece of massive wall, level with the ground. It must have been a fine city in the days of its glory, and, from its situation so high up on the side of the mountain, and the whiteness of the marble of which its large edifices were built, must have greeted the eye of the traveller from the south a full day's journey or more ere he reached its gates. One is led involuntarily, when traversing these and so many other silent and desolate witnesses of the former wealth, power, skill and population of Asia Minor, to reflect with astonishment upon the disappearance of it all. Remove the ruins of buildings and fragments of sculpture with which the whole land is sown, and who would ever dream, as he rode through the towns and villages of Asia Minor, that it had ever been great in art, or wealth, or intelligence. We arrived at the village about sundown, where we were guests, but had none of the usual visitors. This was explained in the morning by the Mudir, who came to see us before we started, and said that he thought we must have been too tired by our excursion to care about seeing any one to keep us from our beds.

May 24—Went on with another horseman, both guard and guide, to Buldur. This is a closely-built town, somewhat larger than Sparta, and near a lake of water, so brackish (we were told) that no fish could live in it. Here, for the first time since leaving Cassaba, we met with two or three Jews: at the latter place there are many. They looked at our two or three Hebrew books, but would not buy any. Without sacred Scriptures, and knowing no one, we could do nothing here during our few hours' stay.

May 25—Having obtained another man from the Caimacam to take us on to Denizlee, we started early, and, skirting the lake, passed through a village called Yasakeuy, thence across a plain but very scantily cultivated, to another lake of fresh water, in the neighbourhood of which we were overtaken by a violent storm, and obliged to ride hard to shelter in a village called Yarisly Keuy. The storm soon passed over, but the road had been so obliterated in some places, and was so sodden in others by the great rush of water, that it was with much discomfort that we managed to reach, by sunset, Kayadibi, a little place of thirty houses, very poor, and all Mussulman, where we rested for the night. From the Agha we learnt that the sandjak (subdivision of province), which is eighteen hours' journey across, contains only 900 houses.

May 26—Rode round part of the pretty lake of Kayadibi, and then through pine forest, down into a narrow and fertile plain; then another hill, and then a plain, and so on, till we reached the foot of the Cadmus, which we ascended at the pass called Kazik Bely. Hitherto each plain seemed slightly lower than the preceding one; but now from the pass we descended to a very considerable depth lower, and began to experience painfully a very different temperature. The pass looks down upon a most lovely valley, formed by spurs of the mountain, which nearly meet at their further extremities, the higher parts being clothed with dense pine forest, which runs up as far as the bare rock, patched with snow, which forms the summit of the mountain itself, while below in the depth are the walnut and other full-foliaged trees, watered by full and flowing streams. At the very bottom we arrived at Chukur It began to be dark ere we arrived, and it was some time before the inhospitable people would show us a place where we might rest.

Colossæ.

May 27—Giving instructions to our men to go on with the baggage-horse to Denizlee by the direct road down the valley, we started some time before them by a more circuitous route, in order to pass by the ruins of Colossæ. To do this we crossed the spur of the mountain to our right, and in little more than two hours of riding we arrived at Khonas, a prettily situated village on the declivity. Here the Mudir, seeing us pass by, called us to come in and rest a few minutes. He was seated, with two or three of the chief men, on a platform about seven or eight feet high, built in the middle of a yard. We ascended and sat down with him, told him who we were, and that we had come a little out of our way to see a place noted in ancient history, but still more interesting to us on account of its being mentioned in the Gospel as a place where, not many years after the ascension of our Lord, the Gospel was preached, and many turned from idolatry to faith in Christ. The Mudir hardly paid attention, and turned the conversation. He would give us a man to show us where the ruins were, and a few minutes after announced that the man was waiting to take us. So we took the hint and bade him farewell. From the village we went straight down towards the Lycus, and near the middle of the valley, on both sides of the river, we found what is left of Colossæ. A great part of the ruins—which are merely scattered blocks of stone, much worn by the weather — is on the main road which runs up the valley towards Dinair, the ancient Celenæ. The platform-topped mound on the south of the river, on which stood some large buildings, was now covered with barley, which some reapers, mostly women, were cutting. The massive stones which were once piled there now form the fence which protects the fields on each side of the road. The people of Khonas know nothing of Colossæ, and, alas! no more of Paul, Philemon, and Archippus. We noticed a very large gush of water which falls into the Lycus close by, and which, we are told, comes up out of the plain but a short distance off: it was like a full millrace. Our attention was also attracted by the hollow sound which the tramp of our horses produced, as if we were riding over empty vaults; and by the peculiar water deposits, similar in character, but not in colour, to those at Hierapolis. Little runnels had left their deposits in such abundance, that from a channel in the ground they had grown to a low wall, on the top of which the hollow still remains, though the water has ceased to flow. From thence we went on to Denizlee, a most painful ride to us, as both man and horse were suffering from the sudden change we experienced in our descent from the breezy plateau to the close burning atmosphere of the low valley.

Denizlee.

We arrived at Denizlee in the afternoon, and met with a hearty welcome from one of our Protestant friends, who is now the landlord of the principal khan, and who gave us his own furnished and carpeted room. From him we learnt that the Persian with whom we conversed last year was dead; and that some of the tracts (Sermon on the Mount) we had distributed to the Turks had been torn and burnt, but that there was a growing desire among the Armenians for scriptural knowledge: each one, however, feared the other.

May 28: *Lord's-day*—Several Greeks came in who, with our friend, his brother, and an Armenian, made a little congregation. By a great oversight we had sold every single copy of Turkish Scriptures, so that we had not one to read. We read, however, the morning and evening services in Turkish, and our servant had a little Testament in Modern Greek, so I read the Litany with them, and brother Wolters read a chapter from the Testament, and addressed them—as nearly all present knew something of the language — in Greek. All showed the deepest attention. After service we had a good deal of religious conversation, and then two respectable Turks came in, one of whom told me that last year he had heard of our being in Denizlee, and wished to see us, but that when he came to the khan we had left. When in Constantinople some time ago he had seen Mr. Williams (Selim Effendi, now deceased), and heard something of Christianity from him. He now wanted a New Testament, and instruction. He said, however, that in about twenty days he would leave for the capital, and that then we might converse at greater length and more fully. He gave me his address in Constantinople, and asked for mine. We then had some conversation on the death of Christ and the integrity of our Scriptures, which he considered as beyond controversy, in opposition to the doubts of his friend. One of the Greeks present began to make objections to parts of the Old-Testament narrative in such a carping manner, that the elder of the Turks took him to task severely, and gave so true a description of the sensual, worldly, godless life he led, and wished to lead, that he became ashamed and silent. As it happened, we had met with this Greek gentleman before, and knew something of him; but the utterance of so much that was good and true from the lips of a Turk astonished all present. Another Greek, who keeps a khan in Denizlee, was deeply attentive, and asked some interesting questions. In the afternoon we saw more people, with whom we conversed till near evening. At night we had one young man present at our prayers.

May 29—Rode down the plain, and, crossing the Meander, not far from its confluence with the Lycus, proceeded up the beautifully-wooded pass which leads into the northern valley, and rested for the night in a little village called Derbend, situated in a valley between the ascent from the Meander and the opening of the deep rocky ravine which runs down into the valley of the Cogamas, and through which probably the head of that river runs. We saw no one to converse with here.

Philadelphia.

May 30—Passed through the ravine, and, after a mid-day halt at Ainegöl, passed on to Alla Shehr (Philadelphia), which we reached just in time to escape a severe thunderstorm. Our friend, the young Arab doctor whom we saw last year, called upon us, from whom we learnt that he was a Bektashi, that there were several more of his sect in Philadelphia, and that the sect was increasing, but secretly, for fear of the other Turks, who would quietly put them out of the way if they knew what doctrines were held by them. In reply to an inquiry what their doctrines were, he said that there were some mysteries connected with their teaching, but that they held the doctrine of one God: they believed that there was no difference between the prophets and other men, and that man was a cycle, and never really died. On leaving, he invited us to call upon him. A Turk also, whom we saw last year, and who was then a Softa, came in to see us, and told us that he had lately lost his father, and had inherited his farm. With him we had some conversation upon the way of salvation. As soon, however, as brother Wolters began to speak of Christ the way, the truth, and the life, he rose hastily, and bade us good bye.

May 31—A Greek doctor and a very respectable Turk came to see us in the khan. The former conversed in Greek with brother Wolters, while I talked with the latter. He told me he had bought books of us last year at Salykly, and that he had read them; that subsequently, when in Smyrna, he wished to go to a Turkish service, and was taken with one or two friends of his, also Turks, to the American Mission chapel. That he wished to speak with us freely, and would look after us for that purpose in the evening. We then went into the bazaar to see the Arab, and sat conversing with him in his shop between the visits of his patients. He told us that he had read the New Testament, and that the Bektashis were exceedingly near of kin to Protestant Christians, an idea which I sought to disabuse his mind of, and to show him what true Christianity is. He told me also that he was our advocate with the Greeks, many of whom had looked with great suspicion upon us at the time of our last journey, and that now they had satisfied themselves that our Scriptures were genuine and uncorrupted, and had obtained more copies from Smyrna. This latter particular we knew to be the fact. After our mid-day meal we sat in the room for a while, and as no one came in, we went to call upon the Bishop of Philadelphia, who received us very cordially. Then he conversed with us very pleasantly about the work of Christ among the Turks, and several other topics of Christian interest. He did not think there was much hope of their doing any good to the Turks, although he thanked God they were not oppressed as in former days. Just as we were leaving, a messenger came to say that the Turkish gentleman whom we saw in the morning was in the khan waiting for us. When we arrived he was gone, but we found an invitation to his house, whither the messenger would conduct us. A thunderstorm was gathering, but thinking the house to be near, we went on. Our guide, in answer to our frequent interrogations as to the whereabouts of the house, answered, "It is quite near," and posted on, although we left the town, and were threading narrow lanes, where the rain came upon us in torrents, and the lightning was fearful. It was no use to think of returning, as we might be much nearer a shelter in the house than in our khan, so we persevered, until we reached a coffee-shop under some trees. Here we sat in suspense for a while, waiting for the rain to cease, and then another messenger came to conduct us to our friend's house, to reach which we had to go back again into the town. When we arrived, the whole was explained. He had wished to give us an entertainment, and had ordered musicians to go to the coffee-shop, a favourite rural resort, to await us, but the rain had come on before he could stop our going thither. I need not say we were thankful for the rain in this case. The entertainment would not have been such as we should think proper in itself or suitable to our office and work. He then gave us Turkish robes to replace our sodden coats while they were drying, and ordered two large braziers to be lighted and brought in. When he had made us thus warm and comfortable, he began to tell us his mind. He had been much influenced by reading the Mizan-ul-Haqq, which he said had really opened his eyes. Indeed, so much did he value what he had learnt from it, that he had made his eldest son, a youth of sixteen or seventeen, and also his wife read the book. The latter we understood to be as much or more affected by it than himself. He said he did not wish his children to grow up in darkness as he had done, nor be the dupes of Mohammedan teachers, who were (might God give them sorrow) blind leaders of the blind. He therefore wished to hand over to us his younger son, when he was old enough, to be educated, and would gladly go to any expense for that object. We told him that we knew where to place his son, and would be very pleased to look after him; that we wished him to consider that religion was not merely a set of opinions or doctrines, but a new life, and so on. We also gave him the address of the Smyrna Missionaries, that he might call when in town. Shortly afterwards another Turk was announced, when our friend cautioned us not to say any thing about religion before him. This was disappointing but not surprising, as we well knew how the Turks fear one another, The two, however, drank a great deal of raki together; indeed, our friend had been drinking at intervals previously, and became now too excited to talk very sensibly. Seeing we could do no good by staying longer, we rose to depart, as it was after dark; but our host detained us by force, saying that he had already been humbled by the way in which we had got wet on his account, and that we should by no means leave his house till we had eaten. So we sat down until a huge tray was brought in, laden with nearly half a sheep and sundry other viands, around which we sat on the floor. When we had finished he dismissed us, with a servant bearing nearly all the contents of the tray to provide for our wants on the road on the morrow, and, besides this, a present of a large quantity of tobacco, his own growth, which we knew nothing of till we arrived at the khan. This evening's adventure only served to confirm our impression, which has been again and again made on our minds, that, in Asia Minor, one of our chief foes, as Missionaries, will be the love of raki. Our servant told us that he had been frequently asked during the day for sacred Scriptures, both by Turks and Christians, in the bazaar, a cheering token of the influence of our visit last year.

June 1—Rode on to Salykly. On the road we were overtaken by a Greek gentleman of Smyrna, who wished to go down to Cassaba in our company. Stopping at a farm on the wayside for rest at midday, the proprietor, a Turk, called our servant aside, and talked with him about our work, and made special inquiries whether there were really any Christian Turks. He did not converse with us, nor did we learn this till after we had started. There was quite a crowd of travellers resting there. Our companion made himself exceedingly agreeable on the road, and in the evening seemed glad of the opportunity of joining us in prayer, after which, till we went to rest, he was very thoughtful and silent.

Cassaba.

June 2—On to Cassaba. The view of Sardis, always affecting, seemed still more so as we passed it from the east. From that side we see more of its greatness and more of its ruin. It has not even a name to live now: that which it seemed to have has been taken away. Our friend has been opening his mind to brother Wolters. He seems to be deeply impressed. The Lord bless him, and make him a blessing to his own people! We felt as if our toils were over, and all our dangers past, when we alighted at the house of our agent in Cassaba, who received us with great joy. The evening was spent in hearing what had been done in Cassaba. Montesanto's report was very encouraging, and our visit does not appear to have been without an influence on the people.

June 3 — Visited, with Montesanto, the house of our old friend, the Sheikh, who was not at home. Afterwards we went to see a Turkish gentleman, who was formerly Mudir of Cassaba. He was unwell, and we did not stay long with him. In the course of our conversation he remarked upon our visit to Koniah, "You can go there and everywhere: you have an open door before you now: every man, according as he thinks best, may become what he wishes: a Jew may become a Mussulman, a Turk a Christian: there is liberty for all." He himself, however, is a rigid Mohammedan, and stoutly defends his creed; he is also a dervish, as, indeed, many of the better Turks are. In the afternoon we sat for awhile in the bookshop, and then visited Ibrahim

Effendi, who was delighted to see us again. Since we left Cassaba he had obtained a copy of the Mizan, and had been reading it. A Turkish officer, and another person, were sitting by, so we conversed on general topics until they left. He then told me how much he had been interested in the book "which," said he, "has opened my eyes not a little. The author does not speak without proof; but it would make the Softas wild if it were to fall into their hands; and even the gentleman, whom you called upon this morning, would be ready to tear it up." I told him that the design of the work was to lead men to think of the way of salvation, and then to point out the way to them; and that to know ourselves, and what we really needed as sinners, was of the last importance to us. I begged him therefore to be in serious earnest about his inquiries. To all this he paid the greatest attention. He then, in the course of conversation, told us how a new dervish Sheikh had come to the town and commenced holding worship. Several Turks of his acquaintance had joined the man, and he was persuaded to go on one occasion. They sat perfectly silent and still for a very long time, until at last he became uncomfortable and vexed; so he spoke out in the meeting, "We have been sitting here a very long time and not a word has been spoken. I have learnt nothing, and my soul is vexed." They only motioned him to be silent, but he would not. "If you have any good thing, of which I am ignorant, why do you not tell me: of what profit is your silence to me?" He was told at last that if he would be initiated he would then know. I then drew his attention to the restless craving after something better which produced all these strange dervish sects. "Men cannot find what they want with the Softas and Hojas, so they go to the Sheikhs, and from one Sheikh to another, seeking rest and finding none. Each one has a fantastic theory, the fruit of his imagination, and, having no root or foundation, like the trees and houses in that picture," said I, pointing to a painting on the wall, in which were trees, houses, and other things floating about confusedly in vacuo. He laughed, and said it was quite true. I continued, "When God speaks, and we listen and obey, leaning not to our erring understanding or imagination, but to his infallible wisdom and knowledge, we have rest from doubt and security from fear." I then spoke of the Gospel and the love of God in Christ Jesus. We left soon after this, our friend begging us not to forget him, and to send to him whatever Christian books we might have. He said, when we parted, "Oh that we had a leader to bring us out of our darkness." To which I replied, that he must seek the light for himself, and be a leader to others as far as he could. God would certainly bless him.

June 4: *Lord's-day*—How glad we were of the day of rest. In the morning brother Wolters held service in Greek with the family. The remainder of the day was spent in conversation with Protestants, whose account of the state and prospects of the Cassaba out-station was very encouraging. The work in this place, like that which we have been endeavouring to commence in other towns of the interior, may, with constant attention, be developed very much, and, when supported by efficient services in Smyrna, whither residents of all parts of the country are constantly going, will form a scheme of Missionary operations which, under the guidance and blessing of the Holy Spirit, will do much to spread abroad in the vast plains and mountains of Asia Minor the light and power of the Gospel of salvation.

June 5—Started early for Boujah, which we reached in about eleven hours, safe and well. Thus, through the protection and blessing of our heavenly Father, have we accomplished a long and fatiguing journey among a people, the greater part of whom have never been visited by any Missionary, and who have the reputation of being among the most bigoted and ignorant in the empire, and through a part of the country but little traversed by Europeans, and often dangerous on account of robbers, without having met with an insult or seen a robber, and without having been retarded a single day by accident or illness. To Him be glory, thanksgiving, and praise!

June 10—Started from Smyrna by the Austrian steamer, "Archduke Maximilian," and joined my dear wife and children safe and well, through mercy, in Scutari on the 12th.

Recent Intelligence.

NORTH INDIA—AGRA.

We have just received the Twenty second Report of the Agra Church Missionary Association, and, as our duty is, we proceed to glean from it a few points which may be interesting to our readers.

There are in the Agra Mission field four congregations of native Christians; one at the city of Agra, consisting of 142 adults, besides 107 children; one at Secundra, consisting of 45 adults, besides 332 children. There is another little flock of 26 at Muttra, with 27 children; and another at Allygurh of 10 members, with four children.

Of schools, there is at Agra, St. John's College, with 270 pupils, of whom 32 are Christians, 70 Mohammedans, and 167 Hindus. At Secundra there are the Orphanages, containing 122 boys and 163 girls: there are, besides, two girls' schools at Agra, and and schools for boys at Muttra, Hatras, &c.; altogether containing a total of 747 children under Christian instruction.

Engaged in this work are four European Missionaries, two European laymen, and one European lady. But besides these are thirteen catechists and readers.

"In the important work of preaching to the heathen," observes Mr. Hœrnle, "I have been ably assisted by my two faithful and zealous catechists, Lowther and Peter Wazir. Four or five times in the week I accompanied them to fixed preaching-places in the city: they, however, used to go out also every morning except Wednesday, when they attended morning prayers in the church. Upon the whole, I can speak favourably of the bazaar preaching this year. We met frequently with large and attentive congregations, and not seldom had interesting conversations and discussions on religious subjects. According to the places we visited, the majority of our hearers were either Mussulmans or Hindus. With the former we could not always avoid controversial subjects. The preaching to the Hindus is generally less interrupted by objections. We have, however, often to refute the errors of Pantheism and the new form of Deism which is spreading in Bengal, and finds adherents also in the North-west Provinces. We have met this year with less violent, sneering opposition than in former years: objections and inquiries were generally made with civility, and attacks with a certain reserve, which, in many cases, seemed a sign of their own weakness.

"In January last I made a Missionary tour to Bhurtpore and Futtehpore Sekri. In the villages near the road we found many opportunities to preach the Gospel. In Bhurtpore, where we spent six days, we met with very much encouragement: the people were eager to hear, and great multitudes listened with attention. Twice, morning and evening, we went to the bazaar to preach. Wherever, on the first day, we went and stood, the crowd was overwhelming, so that we found it more convenient to take our preaching-place in our book-shop, which had an elevated position. We could thus be seen and heard better by the people, who assembled in great numbers, and we had also more rest, in sitting down when we had done preaching.

"I visited also, in October, the mela in Goberdhan; in November, the fair at Batesur; and in December, the mela at Baldeo. We spent thus nearly five weeks in those places, which were crowded with devout worshippers of idols. In the first place we stayed three days, and had plenty of work, for the mela was attended by an unusually large number of people, and I and my two catechists were the only preachers. In Batesur, where we remained five days, the congregations were very large and very attentive, so that it was quite a delight to preach to multitudes which were anxious to hear, and very gratifying were the expressions of many on the approval of our blessed religion, and the condemnation of idolatry. In Baldeo, which is a very bigoted place, where we had always met with much opposition and great frivolity, especially from the Brahmins connected with the temple, we found this year very favourable opportunities of preaching the Gospel. We had also an evening service in the house of the inspector of police, who is one of our former Secundra Christians. With his numerous family and our native-Christian servants we formed quite a little congregation."

W. M. Watts, Crown Court, Temple Bar.

CPSIA information can be obtained
at www.ICGtesting.com
Printed in the USA
LVHW022013120422
716028LV00006B/207

9 783752 589887